MW01248498

Salvation Is to Be Found in Her

David Sahatdjian

Design and cover by Integrative Ink

ISBN: 979-8-218-09626-7 (Hardcover)
ISBN: 979-8-218-15017-4 (Paperback)
ISBN: 979-8-218-09627-4 (eBook)

Author website:
davidsahatdjian.com

Hardcover Edition back cover photo by author:
Woodstock Music Festival, Day 3, August 17, 1969

With love for all who trudge the road
seeking the light—
and Susanna, always.

PART I

Chapter 1

On the stage in the great hall stood the poet, his bald head gleaming in the cone of light from above. What hair that showed was his grizzled goatee, his mouth an opening and closing slit encircled within it.

Was Luther hearing what he thought he heard from the open mike? Was the poet signifying self-satisfaction with his lip-smacking pauses, and seeking to win every last ounce of acclaim from the craven audience?

Poetry frightened Luther. It would always be a world outside his understanding, one requiring slide rule precision. Meter. Rhyme. Anapest. Dactyl. A high school friend mocking those who couldn't write a single line of iambic pentameter. That essay *How Does a Poem Mean?* that had been assigned back in his junior year, and which he could remember nothing of but its odd title.

After the reading a sad-faced girl named Elinore approached. Her boyfriend was having a party. She said he could come. While her face was somber, no one would ever hold this against her. Her intelligence made it permissible.

The college was atop a hill. All around were the sullen streets of Harlem, still reeling from the rioting several years before when an off-duty police officer took it upon himself to shoot a black teenager in full sight of others. Tell Luther that he hadn't seen the same some years before on One Hundred Twenty-second Street, just east of Broadway, with the Jewish Theological Seminary bearing witness, only then there had been two skinny black boys lying prone on the sidewalk as the retiree chatted casually with the white officers.

To the west and to the east were rivers only pretending to be minding their own business.

The bus inched out of the depot at the bottom of One Hundred Twenty-Ninth Street and climbed the hill in low gear. The stall continued when the driver pulled into the stop and involved himself in a lengthy and bogus examination of some papers attached to a clipboard with the door closed. From the sidewalk Luther stared up at him behind the wheel, noting not for the first time the artful ways that people had of offering their hostility to the world.

"Do you see what he's doing?" he said to a girl who, like himself, seemed to be off by herself and apart from the small group clustered around Elinore and her boyfriend. Her receptive black eyes glittered in the light of the street lamp.

"What who has done?" she asked, genuine curiosity in her voice. Just then the door of the bus swung open.

Before Luther could reply, a young man broke off from the group to place an arm around her shoulder and claim her for his own. He had a gigantic white Afro, hair even more abundant than Luther's, and frizzy, too. Luther boarded the bus and took a seat across from them. He had been lit up by the girl and her attention to him. It seemed a cruel trick that she should just be snatched away.

Harlem was housing projects and beautiful brownstones and broken dreams. It was streets on which he grew tense whenever he walked them. He had been a witness to what rage could lead people to do. There had been the riots. The fear might be unreasonable, but it was there. He relaxed as the bus turned onto Broadway, passing under the el. The Jewish Theological Seminary and Union Theological Seminary and Juilliard provided a sense of stability and safety, as did the vastness of Columbia University, even as it let you know there was another world not your own you lacked the standard of excellence required to be part of it.

Luther stared at the bus driver, seeking to distract himself from the girl. White and middle-aged and ruddy-faced, he was a reminder of a world Luther had stepped away from, the world of the Irish along Amsterdam Avenue who had been his friends through high school. Fatso Scully's father had been a bus driver. Those quart bottles of Schaefer beer clanking in the brown paper bag he carried up the tenement steps after his shift, and the evening hours he would spend getting his load on.

The party was in the same building where Luther happened to live, a rooming house just east of Broadway on One Hundred Thirteenth Street and some buildings down from a row of Columbia frat houses where livelier parties were going on. The Belvedere. A beautiful view? His window looked out on a brick wall and the filthy alleyway below.

Within the confines of the single room, and hearing the easy chatter of these people who frightened him, Luther kept to himself. He sat in a corner flipping through a shelf of record albums and pretending to read the liner notes. The capsule of speed he had swallowed earlier in the evening gave him the armor he would need to stay.

The young man with the hair began to pluck at the strings of a guitar and was soon croaking the lyrics to a slow, sad song.

"Do you mind if I look through the records with you?" asked the girl he had briefly spoken with at the bus stop. Her voice was soft and intimate. Instantly the glow was back.

Luther moved to share the space with her. Was she too trying to hide in the albums? Had her boyfriend's Woody Guthrie act driven her away? After a while she rose and placed a record on the spindle of the machine, smiled wanly at Luther, and returned to the balladeer, who had since put aside his instrument. Luther noticed a thin run in her black stocking, beginning at the inside of the knee and ending at a point unknown. Something was happening. It had something to do with him and her and no one else, he was sure.

Soon the room went dark and the small group formed in a circle on the floor. A thick candle in the center provided a wavy light in the drafty room. Luther seated himself next to the girl and sucked strongly on the plastic tip of the water pipe each time it came to him. The candle flame seemed to perform an interpretive dance to the snarled lyrics of Dylan. The hashish had boosted Luther's confidence. All that he desired was possible. He grazed the girl's knee with his own and then let his finger follow the path of the run, incrementally pursuing its course beyond the hem of her knee-length dress. Now that his touch had been accepted, or at least not physically rejected, only further advancement, not his hand resting on the area it had already secured, might be dangerous. The flame was a sort of talisman; no harm could come to him so long as his eyes were faithful to it.

Then it was *Rubber Soul.* He was Norwegian wood and he once did have a girl and he could only hope she would be one more.

It came as a jolt when the music abruptly stopped. A further shock followed. The girl had stood up. Now what he had not even considered would occur. She would expose him. In desperation he sought even more the protection of the candle's flame. From somewhere far above he heard the girl ask for directions to the bathroom. The door opened halfway. The dull yellow hallway light penetrated the darkness as the girl stepped out. He leaned back, using his elbows for support. As soon as the music resumed and the woman returned all would once more be in order.

But now the ceiling light came on. It was as if the covers had been pulled off and a spotlight was being shone on him in the middle of the night.

"If you do that again I'll break your ass." The girl's boyfriend stood over him. He held the guitar by the neck as if it were a baseball bat. From where Luther sat he looked enormous. A fight was the last thing he needed, not when he was in hash heaven. Stoned as he was, he was sure to lose and receive the beating he deserved.

Luther's eyes returned to the flame. The naked bulb shining in the overhead fixture had overwhelmed the candle's protective flame.

"You've been pawing her, you bastard," the boyfriend went on. There was self-consciousness in his voice, as if fighting words did not come naturally.

"You have no call to make me die, " Luther said.

"Fred, please. Let's stop this," Elinore said, in a plaintive voice. Violence, her entire being said, was foreign to her.

Luther stood up and grabbed his pea jacket and exited. The girl was standing, pale and frightened, in the hallway.

"I live on the second floor. Room 2B. Meet me," he said.

The room was cramped and damp. A musty smell came from the walls. He sat smoking on the narrow bed, using a Coke bottle for an ashtray. He put his right hand to his face. It was cold. Speed always made his hands cold, and his feet too. Something to do with his blood vessels constricting. Nothing he wanted to have to think about. He stared at the luminous face of the clock. Perhaps she wouldn't come. He might more reasonably expect a delegation composed of the justifiably outraged.

Ten minutes passed in the hash fog he had surrendered to before he heard the floorboards creaking under someone's weight followed by a tentative knock at the door that seemed to confirm the power of his will. She stood smiling incredulously, her camel-hair coat over her arm.

"I shouldn't say it, but I thought you were crazy. Are you crazy?"

Crazy was not knowing right from wrong, and he knew he had done wrong. "If I say yes will you leave?"

"No. It's exciting," she said, stepping inside. "Anyway, It's awful back there. Poor Fred. Everyone's trying to console him. I just had to get out."

"I caused a problem, " Luther said.

"Oh, he'll survive."

Her name was Marcia Wolf. Fred was not her boyfriend. They had just met through a dating service. When Fred had arrived at her door earlier in the evening toting his guitar, Marcia's impulse had been to send him on his way. So she said.

"Well then, it's not so bad, you're leaving him, is it? It's not like you violated the UN Charter. You can still consider yourself part of the world order," Luther said.

"They began blaming that girl Elinore for inviting you. She said she knew you from the building where she used to live down the block. She said that you were the landlady's son, and since you were also a student at CCNY, why shouldn't she invite you? Is that true about your family?"

"That is true," Luther said, flinching at the mention of family. She had come too close to home.

It wasn't every night that a girl came to his door. He had turned on a lamp, and in the dimness of its light they got undressed and fooled around. Her plumpness had been somewhat minimized by the black dress and tights she now shed. He blew on his cold hands before touching her.

She did not stay the night. He was relieved to see her go. Now he could be alone with his sleeplessness and not have to share his bed with a heavyset stranger. He thought of the man named Fred and his guitar and the injury he had done him. Marcia had left the better person behind in the other room. Fred, musical and socially integrated, had more going for him. Luther was not happy about the wound he had inflicted. You weren't supposed to do stuff like that. His thoughts grew darker with the night. He saw himself as a skeletal freak. His dismal performance on the SAT presented itself. In body and mind was he deficient, and what else was there? He held his head in his hands and curled into a fetal position. With dawn and the chirping of birds did sleep finally come.

Chapter 2

The speed he took was potent. Fifteen milligram Eskatrol, obtained from a dealer in the neighborhood. The capsules made him feel smart and able to focus on the textbooks he was required to read, like the thick sociology book. It was good to be able to focus, to not have your mind flying about here and there so that three pages later you had no idea what those pages had been about. The page he was on now was about anomie—a kind of rootlessness or separation, a deviation from the group. The theory was developed by Emile Durkheim, a Frenchman, and now Luther would be able to tell anyone just that. How much he wanted to learn, and how much there was to learn. But those numbers, those low board score numbers. Always they came back at him. Always. Always. They had permanent residence in his mind and were the dividing line between him and the Ivy League. They were his anomie. What had happened in that room with Fred and Marcia had been his anomie.

Still, he was progressing. Had he not completed his first year at Queens College and done well enough that CCNY accepted him as a transfer student? No more hours spent on subways and buses. Instead he was just two stops and a short walk away on the IRT local. Sure, he had stumbled that past fall, taking a calculus course he quickly was lost in, and so had to withdraw, leaving him with only nine credits for the semester, but he was now carrying fifteen credits in courses that spoke a language he could understand. No more trying to absorb the sine of the curve and elegant equations he had no hope of fathoming. In a way it served him right for going where he didn't belong, for holding to the belief that your strengths didn't mean anything, that it was your weaknesses you had to work on, especially if those weaknesses were in math and science, where the manly men hung out.

The building that Marcia referred to rose twelve stories over Broadway. Foreigners, many of them students, lived in single rooms. Elinore had said it right. His mother was the landlady and would have given him a room rent-free but the building was a suctioning thing that had pulled his brother back and didn't let him go and never let two of his older sisters go in the first place. So it was imperative to get away and establish who he was independent of it even if the distance was less than a block. Because he did have a family but he didn't have to say anymore than that if it worked to his detriment in the moment he was being asked.

He went to see his mother so he could draw near to her but not have to stay. He found her where he often did, in the basement laundry room amid the big equipment: the extractor and the mangle into which she and an assistant fed the sheets between the canvas-covered rollers, and the giant washing machine, the laundry sloshing around in its steel belly that rotated clockwise and then counter-clockwise to rid the load of all the dirt it could.

No speed today. He knew to be good to his body and stay away from the drug's punishing action until the time was right to do some more.

"Were you looking for me, my son?" His mother stood before him in her black gabardine skirt and rubber stockings and support shoes that looked as if they belonged on the feet of a man. A giant ring with the master keys for all the building's rooms hung from a belt around her waist. She was old now, over sixty, but she had been old, forty-three, when he was born.

"I was," he said.

"Do you not eat? You have no weight on your bones. Do you not see that your flesh is leaving you?"

"I eat," he said.

"Come and let me feed you. I will prepare you some good chicken."

It was toward evening, when she would cook for the family after a day of showing rooms and distributing the linens. The building drew the future of the world to it from India and Pakistan and South Korea and Ethiopia and Kenya and everywhere so they could get a Columbia education in engineering and the sciences and go back and build their countries to where they were supposed to be. Not that slender, graceful Ethiopians in dashikis, fierce-looking Sikhs with beards, and Hindus with red dots in the middle of their foreheads had been the plan. His mother's older sister, Auntie Eve, had once owned the building. To hear his mother tell it, bad people did Auntie Eve wrong. They took the building away from her. All Auntie Eve had now was a long-term lease to manage the property. Her vision that the building should be a way station for roving missionaries had faded, like the verse of scripture from the Book of John on the side wall overlooking Broadway, the one about God giving his only begotten son as a sacrifice so others could live.

Of one thing Luther could be sure. His mother loved Auntie Eve. She said her sister was a saint and if the world only knew all the bad things the bad men had done to her.

"Did you not hear me?" she went on, having received no response.

He could not say to her that the kitchen in the family apartment and anything that came from it were off-limits to him. True, as a child he had devoured his mother's broiled chicken and chicken a la king and lamb chops and pork chops and Birds-Eye frozen vegetables, but that was before images of cockroaches and mice and the kitchen sink with the eroded enamel had taken stronger hold, creating a physical aversion no amount of willpower could surmount.

"I have to not do that tonight," he said.

'What?" she shot back. Her impatience with his tangled syntax jarred him, accustomed as he was to her unyielding softness.

"I've eaten," he said.

She took off her glasses to wipe them and was now looking at him with eyes that were more severe and smaller than what you saw through the lenses. His mother came from a farm in Sweden. Sweden was a blue and white and yellow flag and offered certain cheeses that she favored on limpa, a Swedish rye bread. To his ear Swedish was a language softer and more musical than the guttural sound of German.

"Go to the hospital to visit your father. It would mean so much to him."

"Tonight?"

"He's calling to you right this minute. Now go to him."

"But for God's sake."

"Do not use God's name in such a way."

He gave her a quick kiss and went away. Physical displays of love and affection for his mother always brought embarrassment. The intimacy was too much. He couldn't say why.

Lights were on in all the windows of the row of frat houses along the side street east of Broadway. It was again party night for the Columbias. He could only imagine the sustained state of grace they lived in by virtue of their high IQs. At the corner of Amsterdam Avenue, he paused. Across the street the new wing of the hospital stood with blond-brick freshness. Behind it stood an older building with an ornamented façade grimed by the city's soot.

The tenements and the stores on the facing side were gone: Funelli's grocery and the other grocery owned by the two Arab brothers and the meat store and the florist shop and the liquor store. The kids were gone too. Fatso Scully and Kevin Donnelly and

Jimmy Riley and Luis and the rest. Gone not to college but to war in Vietnam.

In a semiprivate room in the old pavilion his father was sitting up, the bed raised to an obtuse angle. Luther flinched seeing his big nose and slack mouth and the glint of the metal bridge when he opened it in greeting. And there was that broad swath of baldness down the middle of his pate but abundant hair sprouting from his ears and gray tufts visible in the V-neck of his loose-fitting gown. To see his father was to see decrepitude and impending death.

"What is wrong with you that you come to me in this way, my son?"

"What way is that?"

"Why do you not get a haircut and be normal as you were when you were a boy?"

"My hair is not normal?"

"Your hair flies out all over the place. Your face is solemn. And you are disappearing into thin air," his father said.

"I am trying," Luther said.

"You were my good son. Now you are an aggravation."

Luther pushed past his father's displeasure, though his criticism was hurtful. "Are you OK? I mean, what did the doctors do?" They were questions he hadn't wanted to ask.

His father removed the sheet from his right leg. Luther tried to look away but couldn't. His father's right leg was missing below the knee. There was just an ace bandage. The revulsion started in Luther's stomach and radiated from there. When his father leaned forward and unclasped and patiently unwrapped the thick bandage, it was everything to stay in place and not run out of the room. But again Luther could not look away and shuddered at the purplish slab where his father's leg ended at the knee. While he struggled with a feeling of nausea, his father leaned forward and calmly and with seeming pride examined the surgeon's work. He would soon be fitted with a prosthesis, his father said, as he carefully rewrapped the bandage.

"God has been so good to me. Mommy has been so good to me."

Luther had slumped into a chair, amazed at his father's equanimity at losing a major part of a limb, but he realized the explanation was right there in what his father had just said. "God." That word . It reeked of dependency and thus shame. A crutch for the weak. The word "Mommy" too. A word reserved for a child's use.

Luther pictured the black wicker chair in the dining room where his father would sit and the little bookshelf behind the chair filled with religious pamphlets from A. A. Allen and Morris Cerullo and Billy Graham and other evangelical ministers his father admired. The one TV program his mother and father allowed themselves was Oral Roberts on Channel 9 from Tulsa, Oklahoma. The image lingered of the faith healer in shirtsleeves laying his hands on a woman in a wheelchair and invoking God to make her whole. God was his father's world. And "Mommy" was his world, too, saying when Luther was still a child, *"I don't know what would have happened to me if I had not met your mother."* Men were weak and women were strong and men were nothing without them, Luther had heard his father to mean.

"Why did they go and do that to you?" Luther asked.

"It is my diabetes. A cut can turn into an infection quite fast. Gangrene set in and spread up my leg. They had no choice."

"Aren't you going to miss walking around?"

"I am ready to leave this earth."

"Where do you plan to go?"

"You don't talk to me like that."

His father was from Armenia. Not really Armenia. Armenia had ceased to exist as a Near East nation. A Christian people, they had been absorbed into overwhelmingly Muslim Turkey. Luther's idea of Armenia growing up was that no one had ever heard of it and that everyone dressed in black in the nonexistent country and hung rugs on their walls and ate olives. In Armenia women were stoned to death for being fresh to their parents and the men were always getting aggravated and slept in coffins and only came out at night. Armenia was over the water in a land without civilization as we know it. The Turks came and drank their blood and feasted on their livers. The Turks had bloodied his family but he himself had escaped to wander rootless through the cities of France before immigrating to America.

"There is a war on. Others are dying so we may live. It is the filth of this country that defies the government. In Armenia they would be shot for this."

His father was referring to opposition to the war in Vietnam. He was in support of America. It could do no wrong. It had given him a life he could not have elsewhere.

"Stoned," Luther said. "Armenians don't use bullets. They use stones."

"Please. What is this nonsense that you speak?"

"Just American nonsense," Luther said, seeking to appease his father.

"There. You finally speak the truth. Treat me better than this. I am not here long," his father said.

Can you leave a place you have never been? Luther reserved the question for himself. He had given his father enough trouble, the kind he wouldn't have dared to when his father was mobile. He was not a good son to his father. He was not a son at all. His father had ruled the house with his hand, a lethal instrument the size of the head of a tennis racket, or so it had seemed. Those threats. *Don't make me get up. I just don't know what I might do. I might lose all control…Are you trying to aggravate me?...In Armenia you would be stoned for speaking back to your father in this way…*And those times he did get up. Luther's mother saying, her chest heaving, after his father had kicked Luther's older brother Luke in the face with his size thirteen wingtip shoe, *Are you crazy?* It coming to Luther after the beating that he was of one parent only, that being his mother. His father he would have nothing to do with.

Why should he love a father so temperamental that little could be asked of him and who loved God but neglected his children, except to terrify them? He was where he was with his father.

And he was not always mean toward his father in his thoughts. There was even a degree of protectiveness. He would never say that the preferred word his father was looking for was *irritate,* not aggravate. Luther knew too well what it was like to be ignorant.

Chapter 3

Marcia at twenty-one was two years older than Luther and a philosophy major at New York University downtown. Her particular focus was Kant and Schopenhauer, she said. Luther had only heard of them and imagined, like all philosophers, they had big heads that enabled room for big thoughts.

"What about you? What are you studying?" Marcia asked. They were in a coffee shop on Broadway across the street from Lincoln Center, close to where she lived.

"I failed calculus so now it's just a lot of paperback books on the south campus."

He meant the liberal arts area of the CCNY campus, math and science being reserved for the north campus.

"What does that mean?"

"It means *The Wild Duck.*"

"What?"

"Henrik Ibsen. There are austerity measures in his dialogue. Every word counts. The thrifty bastard."

Outside a cold March rain was falling. It beaded the coffee shop windows and was but a hint of nature's power, raindrops like two-ounce fishing sinkers slamming the streets and sidewalks while the buildings went on standing. Marcia had arrived protected by a beach-size umbrella, while he was drenched.

"Come over," she said.

"What's wrong with my place?" He had been noticing a faint mustache above her lip.

"How can you live in that room?"

He took the hurt in what she said and responded with a shrug.

Her father and stepmother were on a cruise ship somewhere in the Caribbean, she explained, as they walked under the protection of her umbrella. Her building was not vintage New York but more of what Luther vaguely associated with the nouveau riche: white brick and sealed windows. The doorman wore a blue wool coat down to his ankles. It came with gold epaulets. An expression of forced civility was superimposed over his natural hardness.

"Not the friendly type," Luther said as they rode the noiseless elevator up to the eleventh floor.

"What are you talking about?"

"The doorman. You have no idea."

"He's a nice guy happy to have a job. You see things that aren't there."

What he did see was a two-bedroom apartment with low ceilings buffered from street noise, deep carpeting everywhere, color-coordinated furniture and surfaces without dust.

"This is nice. But don't you feel restricted living at home?"

"I spent my first year of college out in Iowa at Grinnell. It wasn't for me. I missed the city. My father said I could come back only if I lived at home."

"Why was that?"

"I got in some trouble in high school. He didn't want me off on my own in Manhattan."

"What kind of trouble?"

"Boy trouble."

"Where's your mother?"

"She's gone."

"Gone?"

"She got sick and died. Cancer. Five years ago."

"I'm sorry," Luther said. And he was. Losing a mother. That was bad.

She lit a tightly rolled joint, needle-thin the way his fumbling fingers could never make them. They took turns toking and afterward he followed her into the bedroom.

"Do you like this?" She had been grazing his abdomen with her full lips.

He liked it fine. What he did not like was the heaviness of her body and its whiteness. An image of the polar bear at the Central Park zoo came to him. Then there was that humming noise that rose from her throat when they made love. He had never heard that before in a girl.

"I like being with you," she said.

"Why?"

"There's something comfortable about you."

"Who told you that? Fred?"

"You have nice eyes. They're sad, but they're nice."

The grass made him drowsy, and he soon passed out. When he came to, Marcia was standing over him, with a gift-wrapped box in her hand.

"I have something for you," she said.

"Oh no," he said.

"Oh no what? It's just a small gift."

He removed the bow and the wrapping carefully and opened the box, then held up the long sleeved flannel shirt.

"It's winter and you run around in nothing more than a pea jacket. Your closet has two shirts in it."

"Now it has a third. Thank you," he said, feeling more uncomfortable than he could say. Her niceness was hard to take. It was feeling like a burden.

The cafeteria in the student union building smelled of grease. He had some idea that rats, intractable in their claim, had infested the kitchen. Cooked meats and cold cuts and cheeses would be their prime targets. So far as he knew, rats were not into hot coffee. That he could allow himself to order.

The walls were covered with day-glo graffiti. Who had created the eyesores and when—not in daylight hours, surely? As he pondered the mystery, Elinore approached the table, books cradled against her chest.

"Are you a sociopath?"

"Why do you ask?" The word stung, even if he was unsure of its precise meaning.

"I feel sorry for you."

"Why?"

"Because you didn't care about anyone else's feelings."

"Are we talking about Fred, the guitarist?"

"We're talking about everyone affected by that kind of behavior, Fred being at the top of the list."

"And where are you?"

"Where am I?"

"On the list."

"Right up there."

"Why is that?"

"Because you disappointed me. And because I caught hell for inviting you in the first place."

"Do you want to come back to my room with me?"

"Why would I want to do that?"

"You could punish me or we could fool around or we could do both." He knew she wouldn't ever cross that line with him as much as he didn't know it. Somehow it was an adventure to ask. It was throwing himself into the thrilling moment of uncertainty, because you never could predict what kind of motion, destructive or otherwise, you might trigger with such an invitation.

"Why do you say things like that?"

"Because you have unfinished business with me. You invited me to the party for a reason."

"To be nice."

"How about Schopenhauer? Was Schopenhauer nice?"

"What?"

"Tell me one essential thing about his life."

"What is this idiocy?"

"Maybe you can't."

"He was into dark thoughts and had no friends and his first name was Arthur. There, I gave you three things. Now what can you tell me about Schopenhauer?"

"A great man who had no friends. I can't tell you how much hope that gives me. But I don't know about Arthur. Arnold would be better. It gets things off the ground. Arthur just lies there flat on the page."

He kept his eyes on her, on her crown of frizzy hair and kissable thin neck. "What should we do, now that we're together?"

"You should see yourself."

"See myself how?"

"I think you're afraid of people. You're also ignorant."

"I've read some books."

"Like what? You didn't even know who Schopenhauer was."

"That's not the important thing."

"What's more important than knowledge? What are you doing here if not for that?"

"The important thing is that we reach some conclusion."

"Conclusion about what?"

"About us."

"Us? What conclusion can we reach? I have a boyfriend."

"That word 'have' needs looking at."

"Can you make a life picking things apart?"

"Can you make a life holding things together?"

"You are selfish and destructive. My boyfriend has qualities you could never possess. He is studying molecular biology and has a life of promise ahead of him."

"You are a truth teller and it only makes me love you more."

"You don't know the first thing about love, for yourself or for others."

That night he looked up *sociopath.* A person antisocial in his behavior and his attitudes and without a conscience. Elinore was wrong about the last part, however correct she had been about the first two.

Momentum was building. He could sense it. Finally the tide had shifted and he did not have to go toward the world and hang around in it unknown and unconnected. Now it was truly coming toward him and all he had to do was wait and listen.

Marcia was the first to arrive a week later. "You didn't call. You made me come looking for you," she said.

"Let's back this up. Arthur is his first name."

"Arthur?"

"Arthur Schopenhauer. Though to get the whole thing off the ground it should be Arnold."

"This is all you have to tell me? Look, let's get out. Let's go to a movie."

She had her way. They saw a film with a European setting. Handsome men removed their tuxedos and beautiful women shed their evening gowns. Glasses clinked and significant looks were exchanged and sometimes they whispered instead of shouted when danger was near and the guns were drawn to replace the sex that had been there only moments before. There were fast getaways on roads with mountain views and small villages with flocks of sheep. Mostly it was the water beading on the leading woman's skin as she came sun-kissed from the ocean with her hair so wet and embracing of her scalp.

"We should do that. We should do exciting things," Luther said, at a café down the block from the theater. Waiters slashed between the tables while holding their trays high.

"My father and stepmother go to Europe," Marcia said.

"Should we kill them and flee the country with their assets? Is this where we are headed?"

"I've wanted him to die so I can live for a long, long time," Marcia said.

"What does that mean?"

"Nothing," she said, with surprising finality.

Her parents were back in town, and though Marcia said that was no deterrent to having him over for the night, the willies were the willies and he had them in a major way to think of sharing a space with her father and stepmother. Any further fooling around would have to be on the premises of his stinky domicile, whether she was thrilled or not. And so they returned to his room.

"How long have you been wearing that shirt?" she asked.

"Why?"

"Because it smells."

"It's the shirt you gave me."

"Not to die in."

"I was just breaking it in," he said, with some embarrassment.

"My friend Edeline is coming down from Massachusetts. I've told her all about you."

Edeline. He felt fear at the mention of this girl with the strange name. She was coming down to do what, to evaluate him?

"Bring her down. Bring all the inspectors general you need."

"There's no inspection. She's just a friend," Marcia said, as he placed a hand on her shoulder. "By the way, I got my period. Are you sure you want to do this?"

He did and he didn't, which meant that they did.

Some days later Luther stood on line in the lobby to pay the woman behind the grille the rent and to pick up the mail, not that he frequently received any. A withered woman she was, in body and spirit.

"I'm not here to listen to your goddamn problems. Just pay your goddamn rent," she said, railing at the older man wearing khaki duds and a blue dress shirt from the time that he was still in the workforce. She had coiled tufts of gray hair with glimpses of scalp between them.

"Yes, but…"

"Never mind the yes but stuff. Just give me the rent." The woman's face was against the grille. The man murmured something inaudible but extracted his wallet from the back pocket of his baggy pants. The street was a scary place to be. It didn't seem that far away to Luther as he stood on the line waiting his turn.

"Room 2F," Luther said, sliding the dollar bills through the window.

"You got a name?"

"Yes, I do." It was always something with her, he thought, as she flipped through the ledger book.

"You look like a skeleton. What's the matter with you anyway?"

"You should be more understanding of skeleton-ness."

She looked up from the receipt pad and put a burning eye on him. "What the hell does that mean?"

"It takes skeleton-ness to know skeleton-ness in the same way as it takes fatness to know fatness, and you have high skeleton-ness just like me."

"Get out of here."

"I see," Luther said. He kept a steady eye on her.

"You see what?" she shot back.

"I see you and you see me and that way we're both together. You know, connected." He gave her the thumbs up.

"I don't want to see you until your rent is due again," she said, handing him the receipt just as a cleaning woman wearing a white apron came to the window.

"Don't be taking no money from this bum." She looked Luther up and down as if he were the filth she thought he was.

"Has he been causing you problems, Yvette? Do we need to deal with him?"

"If it was for me, I'd take my broom and sweep him away. Because you never saw such sheets and the condition they was in to prompt my aggravation. I would throw his dirty ass out in the street. If you could only see those sheets all bloody. This man is a Mr. Piggishness. I don't clean his room no more."

It was Marcia, of course. He should have listened when she cautioned him that she had gotten her period.

A few people were standing around, as if to help the cleaning woman's commotion to gather force. Elinore and her boyfriend were among them, looking at him with the eyes of those securely situated in the social context and who knew how to gather all the support needed so that you were on the outside looking in no matter where you positioned yourself.

"You heard Yvette's report, Buster. You watch your ass now," the rent woman said. "Next," she shouted, pressing up against the grille again with the suppleness of a bat. But Elinore and her boyfriend were not focused on her smoke. They had their eyes on Luther, as if to communicate that they had his number and the power necessary to keep him isolated in the guilt that he was earning for himself.

Edeline. Marcia presented her as a friend from high school who was now attending prestigious Wellesley College, in Massachusetts. Neither Marcia nor Edeline applied the word "prestigious" but he did; he felt her high board score status wreaking terror within him. Neither the action of the pitcher after pitcher of beer he consumed or the speed capsule that he had swallowed before downing the brew could lessen that divide, could make her one with him instead of the sharp and piercing obsidian glass that she was. Intelligence equaled power and its lack meant defenselessness against that power. It meant exposure to the high risk of savage ridicule. It meant the nakedness of difference.

The booth where they sat was spacious and the padding provided softness; even so, he felt trapped as he took in the crowd packed three-deep around the horseshoe-shaped bar. Students and non-students alike looking for whatever girlie action they could find at The End on a Saturday night. He had been there alone in his skinniness in that scene and now he wasn't.

"Have you come to appraise me?" he said to Edeline.

"What?"

"Are you here to appraise my essence?"

"Your essence? What are you, a perfume?" Edeline looked to Marcia for support but met with a hapless smile and realized she was on her own. She was Marcia's opposite in flesh as well as spirit, a bone-thin girl with piercing blue eyes and straight brown hair pulled into a severe bun and a thin-lipped rat trap thing of a mouth.

"So you answer a question with a question. Even so, you provided the answer. Your appraisal has begun."

"How's this for an appraisal? I don't like you."

"Edeline. You sound like some kind of car destined for hopeless obscurity."

"You're drunk."

And yet her emphatic assertion of his condition did nothing to end their evening together. Antagonism had a power to bond as well. Or maybe Edeline—that name—sensed that she lacked the power to shake Marcia loose from him. Or could it be that her annoyance was hiding an attraction to him?

They went to his room with a half gallon of California red wine, the kind that had no cork in it. With the candle burning and the wine flowing and the three of them entering smoke heaven, it seemed that the evening was growing ever brighter with possibilities. The fact that Edeline was not facing him but sitting to one side with Marcia on the other served as a further indicator of her interest.

In the light of the candle Marcia's moon face seemed detached from her body. Even as he took in her vulnerable expression his hand reached for Edeline's knee. Adventure was calling. You couldn't know until you knocked on her door, as he was doing now.

In one smooth motion Edeline rose to her feet, snatched coat and bag, and fled. Briefly there had been the light from the hallway, but now, with the door's closing, the darkness had returned.

"You're only involved with yourself," Marcia said.

Silence descended on them. In his pot haze Luther was lost to any sense of time. They seemed to be waiting, but for what? Heavy footsteps and loud voices at some point came from the hallway. Now someone, the whole world, would be banging on the thin door. Luther turned to Marcia but she had averted her eyes. He stood up and turned the lock.

The door flew open and a small, squat man sent him across the room and to the floor, his attacker following up with a hard shoe to the forehead. Stunned, Luther crawled on all fours, the shoe finding his ribs. Above him an outraged voice that was all snarls and curses to go with the punches and kicks.

"Scum. I should kill you," the voice muttered.

Was the man a cop? There would be no end in sight if that was the case, just the apparatus of brutality that Luther would be consigned to. But cops did not call you "scum." "Scumbag," but not "scum." Luther struggled to his feet and managed to get his burly attacker in a bear hug from behind and move him out the door.

"Come near her again and I'll kill you. If I can't do it, I have people who will. Believe it," the man said.

His attacker seemed far away, as if Luther was staring through the distancing end of a pair of binoculars. Behind him, in the pale hallway light, stood Edeline and Elinore and her boyfriend, and others in the delegation of the just. His head throbbed and it hurt to breathe in.

"Give me my hat, long-haired scum," the man said, allowing himself a snicker and playing to his audience. Luther went back in the room and turned on the light. A veteran's cap lay just inside the door. He guided the hat into the hallway with his foot, as if it were a hockey puck, then gave it a final flick with his foot toward the man.

Goaded by what he saw as disrespect, the man had to be restrained from making another rush.

Luther returned to his room and locked the door, finding comfort in the darkness and the remains of the wine. Outside he heard a voice from among the gathered. Clearly, it was Marcia, sounding soft and pleading. "Oh Daddy, Daddy, please let's go."

Chapter 4

Conflict was not new to him. With the morning light came that awareness. The grade school classmate who threw him out of his parents' apartment when Luther pulled the trigger on a BB gun after being warned not to; a second classmate who caught him stealing a coin from his collection; the third classmate who ejected Luther after Luther purposely derailed his model train by throwing a switch. Or his shoplifting. Or his vandalism of the cafeteria in the John Jay building at Columbia University, and the detective's warning to his mother that the next time he would be sent to reform school. Or the time a pair of detectives brought him home, having found him wandering about the streets with a switchblade knife he compulsively clicked open. And then his expulsion in sixth grade for throwing rolls of toilet paper at the Episcopalian nuns from the second floor boys' bathroom as they walked on the sidewalk below.

Anomie. It was a role he had been given.

He struggled through the day, sore and bruised from the assault by Marcia's father. More difficult was the mental suffering, the stark awareness of his physical and intellectual inadequacy that the speed crash and the lack of sleep brought on. And fear had found him. He needed to stay on the straight and narrow if he didn't want to flunk out of school. A mediocre college that had seen better days CCNY might be, but he was lucky to be there. He had to be there. It was his only path free of the building that had ensnared his family. And there was the war.

Too strung out to roam the bars, he tried to study. I am cracking the books, he heard himself say. An odd expression. Books in need of being, at the very least, slightly abused as the price they had to pay for being explored.

Soon the sense that he was reading superseded the poli sci content he was trying to absorb and he was lost in a delirium of happiness once again that he could make sense of words, as others were able to. He had a story to tell. He was sure he did, the realization, as a child, that he could read a book, remembering the living room chair he had been sitting in able to free his mind, if only briefly, from the reality of the painful untidiness of the apartment and how he had to take a break from the reading so he could save it for later, and how there was an organ grinder in one of the illustrations and a monkey and a red brick wall and a leafy tree overhanging it and how it could break your heart to see nature and civilization existing in such harmony, as if everything you had ever known or longed for was in that one color plate.

The knocking was loud and shocking, putting an end to his reverie. Could it be Mr. Brutal Brutale, with his show-no-mercy henchmen, coming to finish what he had started? Luther was sure to break a leg if he leapt from the window, but they were sure to do much, much worse.

A voice called out. "It's me, Vera. Your sister. You know, the cause of all your joy. Open up."

He gathered himself to full attention, so he could be present for the crisis of her arrival. As he opened the door, she gasped.

"What happened?"

"I beat him up good and then killed him dead, so don't you worry. He's just a stinking corpse by now. You have my word."

"What's going on with you?" For a moment she looked earnest, but she was sure to soon return to her mirthful ways.

"I had a visitor. He didn't like me very much."

"He didn't like you very much? He didn't like you at all."

"A story for another time," Luther replied.

"Well, be like that. See if I care. Look, I have exams coming up. I need some ups. " She attended Julia Richman High School, on the East Side. She did just fine for who she was, even if she tried to rule him when she was present.

"I don't know," he said.

"You don't know what?" she said, with challenge in her voice.

"It's just..."

"Just what? Good for you but not for me?"

Reluctantly, he opened a dresser drawer, took the amber bottle from under the sock pile. Her ferocity melted into a smile. He placed two capsules in the palm of his sister's outstretched hand and cautioned that they were stronger than the Dexamyl he had previously given her.

"You could be up for for days."

"We're going out. I'm supposed to meet Pam at The End. Anyway, this room smells," she said, ignoring his words of caution.

Pam Becker. That didn't sound like a lot of fun. The younger sister of his brother's former girlfriend. A girl he could tell had no interest in him. But he could not say no.

At the corner they stopped for the light. Trolley tracks had once run up and down the avenue, but the rails were buried under the repaved roadway so no one could see what had been there before or consider what the islands in the middle of Broadway really meant in terms of stops along the trolleys' route. On the other side of the street stood the building of his origin, the façade darkened by fumes and soot and the grit of New York City and the windows with rotting sashes and no curtains and with three out of every four tenants peeing in the sinks of their single occupancy rooms. From a place on Broadway south of the building you could see on a windowless wall of the building a verse of scripture from John 3:16:

For God so loved the world that he gave his only begotten son that whosoever believeth in him should not perish but have eternal life through Jesus Christ our Lord.

The sign, in bold gothic lettering, had been commissioned by his aunt to mark his family for all time and to make a statement to the men of intellect that she had the higher calling of her knowingness to which they would have to bend down in subservience or risk the flames everlasting.

"I'm getting out of there someday soon," Vera said. "I have to."

She had a room outside the family apartment but on the same floor. The model Verushka was her hero and fat-lipped Mick Jagger was her love life in terms of the two posters she had on her wall.

"Look at me," Luther said. "I'm nineteen and a half block from home. I'm your beacon of hope." The speed worked against laughter, even if he was now only feeling its aftereffects; it was a solemn high.

He hadn't been to The End since the night with Edeline and Marcia the week before.

A man occupied a barstool just beyond their booth. The floor was further down than his skinny legs could reach. His face had a gray cast to it and cigarette smoke poured out of his nose and mouth. He wore a jacket over his white shirt and a pair of dress slacks and shoes to give himself respectability. His wide open Buster Keaton face did not try to hide the fact that everyone had gone away.

"I remember you two from when you were this high," he said, holding out a liver-spotted hand to a few feet off the floor. He had watery eyes and a slack mouth that did not entirely hold its contents. He addressed himself to Vera. "You're going places. I can see it in you. But your brother's going to be a bum. He doesn't have the necessities."

Vera merely basked in the approval that had been bestowed on her and did not seem to evince any pain at all about the denouncement laid upon her sibling.

The man was familiar to Luther. He lived in the building where there was order across the street from his family's building. The man's building was where there were clean, well furnished apartments and doormen. It was not a building with rotting sashes and lost souls in single rooms.

"So you say," Luther said.

"Did your sister beat you up, Sonny? Somebody sure wailed on you."

Luther started to get up, but he could think of nothing to say to the man and so he slumped back on the bench.

"You're what's wrong with this country with all that hair on your head. Why don't you cut it off and beef up and join the army and take it like a man?"

Luther stood back up and bent at the knees so he could go nose to nose. "You ask me questions for which I have no answers. All I can say is that I am in my time and in my place and 'California Dreaming,' not Frank Sinatra, is playing on the jukebox."

"You leave Frank Sinatra out of this," the man said, supplying more of his fire.

A bearded young man squeezed himself into the booth next to Vera. He wore a scarf and a tweed jacket and a shirt buttoned at the top. His eyes were all liquid fire and made a point of establishing their dominance.

"Who's our bruised and beaten friend?" he said, speaking as if he and Vera were one.

"This is my brother, Luther."

"So Luther, are you a midnight brawler? You don't quite have the physique for fisticuffs."

"I walked into something, or something walked into me. Something like that."

"I like that. I like that a lot," Vera's friend said, as if assuming Luther would care what he thought or didn't think. And Luther did find himself caring.

Pam soon showed up. She had brought a girlfriend, a pretty girl with curly blond hair and a serious, even severe, expression.

Vera made the introductions. The young man was named Amory Wooster and she had to add that he went to Columbia. Luther stared at him and his huge head as if he were a higher echelon being to whom he had to be in thrall because of his Ivy League status. Pam's friend was named Mona. The two were students at Music and Art High School.

"And what institution of higher learning does our friend attend?" Amory put a smiling look on Luther that left him no choice but to answer.

"The City College of New York."

"And what are you studying at the City College of New York?"

"Anomie. I'm studying anomie," Luther replied.

Amory laughed, as if he had never heard anything more uproarious.

"Luther is a study in anomie, whatever that is. Always has been," Vera said.

Amory patted his black beard. "Only in the arts are the French worthy of esteem. In all other aspects are they ghastly. And the Baudelaire of *Fleurs du Mal* is the best of them, with Celine at his most scathing right up there."

"Wow. You are so deep. You know everything there is to know. That's why you are at Columbia, I guess," Pam said. She was a round, soft girl with straight blond hair and big, expressive eyes. She was also a gusher. It was just her nature.

"What have you been doing with yourself?" Vera asked, ignoring everyone in favor of Amory.

"I'm in our drama club production of *Othello.*" He stroked his beard and began to speechify. It went on a long time, with threats and maledictions and passion in every line.

"You are totally brilliant. Who is saying that?" Pam asked.

"The Moor in the blackness of his jealousy." He held his arm up and looked at his watch. "And now I must be going. Parting is such sweet sorrow. I bid you adieu until the morrow."

The tyranny of the Columbias extended over the entire neighborhood. One false move and they put their laughing thing upon you. Luther had some Shakespeare in him, too. Hotspur riding his horse on the perpendicular and how he was the theme of honor's tongue and Benvolio saying, "Take thou some new infection to thy eye/and the rank poison of the old will die." Not like what Amory had, but he had it. A weight had been lifted with Amory's departure.

The president was looking down at them on the cantilevered TV screen. He was not crying but his face was a feat of supplication. He was asking them to love him for all the gifts he could give them if only he could enter their hearts. Luther was touched. Presidents occupied a special place in the universe in terms of who they were with the red white and blue all around them and in them as well. He would write to him and tell him that he loved him even if there was a war going on.

"Luther, what happened to you?" Pam gasped.

"Someone beat up my hoodlum brother but he won't say who," Vera laughed.

"Is that true? Were you in a fight?"

"I did not kill anyone and no one killed me either," Luther said.

"How's college? Are you studying big things like Amory? Tell us more about this anomie." Pam's act was relentless.

"No, I'm not studying big things. I need to get a job is what I need to do so I can keep my room." His mood was plummeting. He tried to say something to Pam's friend Mona but his words bounced off her and all he knew from the sight of her in her lavender top and suede jacket was that she was above him and out of reach. Feeling out of place, he got up to leave.

"The scholar returns to his books." Vera smiled her victory smile but he didn't retort because of the fire he knew she had waiting for him. I don't care about anomie anymore, he thought. I don't care about anything.

Chapter 5

A letter arrived from the United States government. He had passed the postal service test for employment. The test score number lifted him up. For a short time could feel he had a brain.

That same week he took the subway to Thirty-third Street. Down a set of steps he entered Penn Station at the Seventh Avenue end. He walked the length of the arcade, a route he had taken with Vera and his older brother Luke on their way to Sunday school and then the afternoon service, at which their mother joined them. Still there was the sweet-smelling stand that sold candied apples and fresh-squeezed orange juice and all kinds of nuts, pistachios being his favorite, and the Nedicks should he want a hot dog on a toasted bun coated with pickle relish, as were the store with live lobsters in tanks in the window and the Doubleday Book Store. But gone were a smaller hot dog stand and the Savarin Bar where, beyond the window with the lower pane of frosted glass, men sitting apart in a cloud of smoke had done their drinking at tables and on barstools. And there had been Tie City. And the man who sold the soggy, salty pretzels hanging on sticks. And the plant store with the myriad of seed packets out front.

He was aware of change. Things missing from an earlier time could unsettle him. It was as if, at age nineteen, he had been thrust out of childhood and adolescence into a world he wasn't prepared or equipped for and was already looking back more than forward. At six feet, four inches, he was at his full height. Like a tall weed he was.

Faraway places called to him as he passed through the station. Before the wrecking ball had come several years before, there had been the majestic concourse, vaulted ceilings and floors of exquisite marble and wrought-iron gateways. And those burgundy-colored behemoths of the Penn Central railroad, the engines with the pantographs atop them, that would briefly suction Luther and Luke from their church-bound path.

At the west end of the arcade a set of steps rose to the IND subway line, the A and the B and C trains that ran along Eighth Avenue. The letters and the route were vaguely threatening. The IRT, the Interborough Rapid Transit, was what he best knew, with its glorious red cars, not the IND and its plain silver ones.

He turned right down a ramp into a desolate stretch that filled him with the same apprehension he had felt as a child. Reflexively, he glanced over his shoulder should someone with criminal intent be following him before coming to a long and steep set of steps that took him to street level. How many were the times he had climbed these steps as a child only to fill with worry, imagining his aging mother struggling some hours later up that same set of stairs on her way to meet him and Vera and Luke? How many times had he screamed in his mind no, no, imagining her losing her balance and falling all the way to the bottom and bleeding from the wound inflicted when her head struck the unyielding concrete.

The General Post Office, a mass of granite to match the grayness of the mailmen's uniforms, encompassed an entire block. *Neither snow nor rain nor wind nor gloom of night stays these couriers from the swift completion of their appointed rounds.* So read the motto over the columned main entranceway up a wide set of steps on Eighth Avenue. If it didn't quite now, the edifice had represented the strength and security of the government itself in his earlier years. West along Thirty-third Street, huge trailer trucks entered and left the loading bays. It was the same and it was different. He was different. Once again did it strike him that he was outside the gates of childhood, ready or not.

He walked slowly along the north side of the street. The Horn and Hardart Automat was still there on the corner of Eighth Avenue, where his mother would take Luke and Vera and him for what she called "normal food" after the interminable afternoon service. He stood under the metal awning over the service entrance and its corrugated metal gate, taking in the rank odor of food waste. Some years before he and Vera had witnessed a homeless black man sitting outside crying as he begged two white police officers not to take him into the parking lot adjacent to the Automat. "Please don't take me there. Please. Please." The tears streaming from his big eyes. The officers had their night sticks in hand. The black man's tears said everything about what was coming, but Luther had done nothing. Nothing. He had felt the black man's anguish, but when one of the officers sternly told him and Vera to move along, they did just that.

He was early for his first evening of work, and if he took his time walking that block, he had his reason. This was his history. This was his life. Had he not a thousand times passed those small vine-covered rooming houses where the men on the sidelines of life lived?

The church stood in the middle of the block. A giant neon cross hung at a right angle to the street and served as a beacon glowing red in the night to the east and west. A broad set of stairs led to the nave, on the second level. Flanking the stairway were two street-level doors that led to the rooms where Sunday school was held as well as the Friday Bible studies class he had attended for many years.

Luther had left the church at age thirteen. One Sunday he just refused to go, and though his mother cried, he held fast to his resolve. For too many Sundays had he been shut away from the world and made to endure monotonous sermons by Pastor Horvath while yearning to be at Yankee Stadium or Ebbets Field or simply running about in Riverside Park. "The world has nothing that I want," his mother would say and the word "worldly" from Pastor Horvath's mouth had the sound of an accusation. To be worldly was to embrace a life of sin and forsake God. A religion of renunciation it had always felt like to Luther. No movies. No dancing. Was the mailman to be cast into the everlasting flames because he was not part of the Tidings of Joy Tabernacle? Was Mickey Mantle? Would Willie Mays running out from under his cap and the great Duke Snider with the number 4 so big on his back also perish in the everlasting flames? Would all those men drinking in the Savarin Bar down in Penn Station and the throngs jammed into Yankee Stadium to watch The Mick uncoil into his power-packed swing also be tossed into hell for being beyond the confines of the church? That couldn't be, or so he hoped, as the world was precisely what he wanted.

And yet he could not walk away. His past had magnetic force, drawing him inside the first of the side entrances and up the tight, winding stairway, where he was shocked to see Pastor Horvath, his hair fully gray now, at the pulpit on the dais. That same deep voice. Those same long sentences, seemingly without end. But something, the vitality, was missing. The pews were mostly empty. A few scattered souls here and there in shirtsleeves, not their Sunday finest, as had been the norm for the congregation in years past. No flocks of children.

Luther retreated and took another set of stairs to the balcony, where another shock awaited him. The pew where he had sat with his mother and siblings to the left of Pastor Horvath had been ripped out, as had all the others. Now it would have been a treacherous walk across torn up carpeting. And the flags of so many different nations that had hung from the balcony were gone, including the blue and yellow flag of Sweden, his mother's homeland.

At some point in the sermon his mother would stand in her polka dot dress. Strange, unintelligible words would fly from her mouth as tears streamed down her face. She had been taken over, possessed. Whoever had her would never let her go. Such was Luther's fear each time she succumbed to the spell. Pastor Horvath would have to pause, like a car at a railroad crossing, waiting for a long freight to rumble by. Several times his mother would shudder before seating herself, like an engine sometimes would after the ignition had been turned off.

Behind the pulpit the mural of Jesus standing alone in the Garden of Gethsemane remained, his hair shoulder length and brown but the luminous whiteness of his robe dulled by time. The mural had appeal. It spoke of quiet and contemplation, of afternoon shadows. It always had, even in Luther's seeming imperviousness to the pastor's message. And the faux marble baptismal font was still there as well, though the basin was empty. Luther calling out in his mind, back then, to Luke and Vera, in the robes they had been provided, as they were about to be immersed by Pastor Horvath. No, no, don't let him do that. Don't. He'll make you just like him and all of them. You'll never be the same. Docile and trusting they had been, in a way he could not be.

But the pastor's mother all in white, seated in her throne-like chair behind him on the dais, was not there. Her whiteness a statement of purity. Her white dress, her white stockings, her white shoes, as if no stain of darkness could ever touch her person. And that fixed stare and that fixed position, as if the congregation were seeing a statue, not a person.

A tall, thin man was looking directly up at him, his expression one of meek amiability. Unkindly, the word "doofus" came to Luther's mind as the man waved. Luther returned a less enthusiastic wave and headed for the exit, but the man caught up with him.

"Luther. I'm so glad that you have returned. Your mother will be so proud of you. She is a wonderful woman and praise Jesus for her." He had a sound as soft as marshmallows.

"Hello, Fenton," Luther said. Fenton was a tenant in Luther's mother's building. Room 3D1, to be exact, without a private bath. Probably peed in empty milk bottles during the night. He lived alone and went about his days alone. Luther had never seen him with anyone.

"The Lord has led you here. There are no coincidences. Deep within yourself, you know that this is so. After all, your mother is your mother and the Lord is the Lord." Fenton wet his lips.

"That's not quite it, Fenton. I'm starting a job with the post office across the street. I only stopped by to visit."

"There are no coincidences, Luther. Jesus brought you here."

"Stop it, Fenton. I really don't care for this evangelizing." And he didn't. There had been enough of that with his mother, telling him when he was still a child that they were living in the last days, and that Jesus would come as a thief in the night, and wasn't it time for Luther to take Jesus as his personal savior? She couldn't help herself anymore than Fenton could.

"What you don't like is me as the messenger. You say to yourself, what right does Fenton have to tell you anything about Jesus? Why? Because you see your own hopelessness in me. You see the same inability to have a place in the world in yourself as you see in me. What you don't know is that you don't want the world, any more than your mother or I want the world. You want the Christ Jesus, only you don't know it."

Luther felt a surge of anger.The man was sharper than he had given him credit for being.

"Stop," Luther said, and crossed to the other side of the street. A short bridge over a deep drop led to the main floor of the building. He walked it slowly, reticence in his every step, as if he was about to surrender his identity and be rendered anonymous, simply a cog in some giant machine. Sadness overcame him, a renewed awareness of the gap between his dream for himself and his reality. The constant flow of workers entering and leaving served as a painful reminder of his ordinariness.

A brief orientation awaited him. He was shown the conveyor belt from which to take a bin stuffed with letters back to his stool in a row where he and other workers sat at what the floor manager called box schemes, rectangular structures with slots for each of the fifty states into which to sort the letters.

Some kind of industrial psychology had to be behind the system for extracting maximum efficiency from even the most shiftless, Luther sensed, as the hours passed. With nothing to distract him, compulsiveness and competitiveness kicked in, initiating a race to empty each bin faster than those next to him. The work, though repetitive, was satisfying. Wasn't the essence of life order, putting things in their proper place and, in so doing, disposing of clutter? Had he not been battling clutter and chaos since he was a child in that impossibly messy apartment he had grown up in? Had he not been born with a broom in his hand? Unlike with his college studies, he had been given something that he could do, and do well.

When Luther punched out that night and returned the time card to the rack after his four-hour shift, he left tired but with a sense of accomplishment. Though darkness had come, the light was out in the neon cross that once glowed red in the night. And Fenton, to his relief, was nowhere to be seen.

Chapter 6

The next weekend Vera stopped by again. Could he spare a couple more of those pills? There were more exams she needed to cram for. Though he was running out, he gave her two.

Again she coaxed him into going to The End. This time they had the booth to themselves.

"I have something to tell you, but it's only because I'm feeling so good," she said. She had swallowed one of the capsules with the Coke she was drinking from a beer stein.

"What would that be?" Luther asked.

"Trust me, I wouldn't tell you if I wasn't feeling so happy."

"OK."

"You will probably get a swelled head but someone is interested in seeing you."

"Someone?" He stared at her blankly.

"You don't know?"

"I don't."

"Mona Van Dine." When he didn't respond, she added, "Pam's friend."

"Why? How?" The girl had not said a word to him.

"She wants you to call her."

"Are you sure?"

"No. I'm just making it up. Don't ask me again."

In spite of the happiness pill, her soreness was fighting its way through.

Luther took his sister at her word. She had given him something she wouldn't have divulged had she not been high. In so doing, she had given credence to his concern that she was possessive of him. And now, acting against her own instincts, she had opened the gates and set him free. The scary thing was to think that he might have languished behind those gates if she hadn't.

And what were those gates? A family he wanted to be able to move beyond so he might be part of a bigger and brighter world, one without the pain that was so much a part of the life he had known.

Chapter 7

One night, five years before, in the spring of 1962, he had walked a girl home. He was fourteen and in his first year of high school. The girl's name was Jane Thayer. On the way he summoned the courage to kiss her. Feeling awkward afterward, he blurted, "I want to marry you someday."

Wiser, or at least more restrained, she had replied, "Slow. Slow."

The next night he found himself in Riverside Park with his childhood friend Jerry Jones-Nobleonian. At Luther's prompting, they had bought a six-pack of beer at the Ta-Kome Deli on 115th Street and Broadway. With the church key the deli had provided, they punctured the cans. Luther had never purchased alcohol before. Had his mother not filled his ears with dire warnings about drinking? "Wine is a mocker. Strong drink is raging," she would say, quoting a proverb from the Bible. And there was the story she told, over and over again, of how her mother would dispatch her into the snow-covered fields of the farm in Sweden she had grown up on in search of her father. "And do you know what my mission was? Do you know? It was to find him where he lay before he froze to death and to smash the bottle he drank from against the rocks."

But his mother's warnings and cautionary tale were not with him on this night. The beer just seemed an idea waiting to happen, as if fundamental to his being. And there was something he wanted, even expected, from the beer. Surely it would preserve the elation he had experienced the night before, having met this girl with the strawberry blond hair and the tongue she had shockingly probed his mouth with. Not only would it preserve the elation but it would take him higher, higher than any of the stars that pocked the sky that night. So what that it tasted like dirty coins in his mouth and left him feeling merely sodden? The promise it offered of a change in his consciousness still held.

But it was the girl, not alcohol, that dominated his consciousness the rest of his high school days. He would sit through classes happy to know he would see her that afternoon. And there was that summer following his freshman year that they would lie in the grass on Dead Man's Hill, in Riverside Park, and kiss and kiss the morning away.

Then came the day she said she would be going away for the weekend with her church group. He was stunned. How? Why? It was just a weekend, she said. For her, maybe, but for him the hours were like days. The clock simply didn't move. Come Sunday afternoon he called her at home. No, she wasn't back yet, her mother, with her silky voice, said. Try as he might, he couldn't stay away from the phone. Within an hour he had called again, and then several times more. The last time brought Jane Thayer's father onto the line. His voice was gruff and impatient, not silky. Through the years they grew resigned to his incessant calling. Though he felt ashamed of his conspicuous neediness, the endless phoning seemed beyond him to moderate.

By his sophomore year, he had a plan. He would go on to college and Jane Thayer would go on to a different college and after they had had their lives away from each other, they would come back together forever. But then, in French class, he was asked to translate a maxim by La Rochefoucauld, a seventeenth century author. "Whom one has loved once, one cannot love a second time." The maxim was devastating, a truth bomb blowing the future Luther had tried to construct to smithereens. It was saying that there was no way they could have their separate lives and then come back to each other.

He began to act up with Jane Thayer. "You don't really want me. Why don't you just admit it?" Over and over, he would encourage her to go to one of the other neighborhood boys. It was only a matter of time before she would, after all. Why not hasten her departure? He understood that he was being wildly destructive, but he couldn't stop. When she told him to fuck off, his hand shot out and struck her on the cheek. "You bastard," she said, and took off. He had never slapped a girl before. He stood cringing for some minutes, waiting to be beaten by witnesses to his offense, and slinked off when no such justice was served.

His agony over the breakup was such that his mother would give him a sleeping pill each night. What bliss the pill brought. How quickly it made everything right in his world. But each morning he would wake to the brutal reality of his loss and drag himself off to school. Whether he had predicted the future or shaped it, he couldn't say, but within days Jane Thayer was seen with one of the more handsome kids he hung around with. He had lost her. That was that. And yet, within a few weeks, he began to accept the new circumstances, and as soon as he did, she reappeared and they were back together. It never occurred to him to ask why her new relationship had ended or who had ended it. He was just happy to have her back, until the next flare-up, and there were many.

The summer following his second year they had begun to sleep together. In spite of La Rochefoucauld, he had found a way to believe that they would someday be married, though the word *marriage* and the idea of it made him feel old. "Going all the way" was just a sort of advance on the intimacy they would share when they were wed, would it not? His mother had given him a small room next to the family's apartment on the second floor; he had persuaded her that he needed a quiet place to study. It was there that he would bring Jane Thayer after school to lie with him on the pull-out sofa. From the sidewalk below friends would call up to the window of the small room but he wouldn't respond. He had made his own world with Jane Thayer, and it didn't include them. All their stupid boy talk, their "sounding" on each other, was something to leave behind. After some months, she would come to his room in the morning. They would then go on to school, having slept together.

At the private school he attended, he would hear boys talk of the dates they had been on that weekend. In the locker room he heard an older boy brag about removing a girl's bra. In more ways than one was he in a world apart from these kids from wealthy homes. But as one year turned into the next, his perception changed. He began to feel in bondage to Jane Thayer; the intensity of their sexual relationship had somehow prematurely aged them. How young and free and innocent, by comparison, his classmates now seemed, with their chatter about girls they were dating or hoped to date.

Along with the sense of suffocation, he now carried a burden of guilt. He had somehow ruined Jane Thayer. He had taken away her innocence and made her unfit for the company of others. Who would want an emotionally bruised and sexually tarnished girl? By the sticky summer of 1964 he was proposing that they take a break from sex. To have any hope of achieving that goal, they would need to stay out of his room. She met his earnestness with considerable levity, but if that was what he wanted, sure, she would go along. When one day passed free of the "danger zone," his exhilaration was such that he would scrap the experiment. Once more they were back on his sofa bed. But each such resumption only deepened his pain and came to seem like a relapse. The summer became a succession of such broken resolutions.

A question formed in his mind and screamed for an answer. He found himself seeking the counsel of a neighborhood boy he did not much like, but to whom in desperation he now turned. Could Jane Thayer and he become like new again if they stayed away from each other a while? The boy, after a long pause, laughed in his face and gave him a light whack on the head and walked off. What a fool he had been to go to such a jerk, Luther thought. The boy was limited, a bully who only cared about pumping iron and beating up the other kids. And what a jerk he himself was for allowing his desperation to lead him to such a creep.

The next morning, after a tortured night, the light of heaven seemed to fill his being with hope. He would go to the emergency room at the hospital. He would see a doctor, a man who would radiate his wisdom into Luther with his presence alone. But an obstacle presented itself. The admissions clerk, an older woman with a hard manner, said the future was not a satisfactory answer as to why he needed the attention of a physician. Luther replied that his head was part of his body and it was causing him great pain. The clerk gave him a long look and had him take a seat. An hour passed before he was called to an examining room where soon a man in a lab coat and with a stethoscope dangling from his neck appeared. In truth, he looked not much older than Luther himself with his boyish face. The intern—for that's what he was—proved no more appreciative of the gravity of the situation than the clerk had been. To Luther's immense disappointment, all the intern could advise, after an interminable pause, was to give the situation time before he turned and left the room.

But as with a creature trapped in a cage, he continued to seek freedom from his torturing mind. By the end of the day another moment of revelation exploded in his consciousness. Jane Thayer had a grandmother. She lived in a single-room occupancy hotel, owned by Columbia University, and only a block away. Luther might never have met Jane Thayer were it not for her grandmother, as several times a week Jane came to the neighborhood to shop for the shriveled old woman, who spent her evenings listening to Long John Nebel and his radio talk show guests and drinking carrot juice for the cataracts that clouded her eyesight. Luther guessed she could see well enough to not particularly like what she was seeing when she looked at him. Why else would she say to him, over and over, that God made the small town and the devil made the big city, she herself being from rural Michigan? Well, there had to be a route to love in every heart, and honesty would be the pathway to hers, he could hope. And so Luther went to her that very evening and told her what was what, and while she was too old and frail to break his bones, she did repeat that business about God and small towns and big cities as she showed him to the door.

Nothing outwardly changed as the result of his confession. No death squad arrived at Luther's door. No chastity belt was Jane Thayer made to wear, nor was she sequestered out of reach of him. He returned to school for his senior year, but it was not the normal resumption after summer vacation. In January, he had failed to return to the basketball court of a varsity game after halftime. Driven by resentment that his star was being eclipsed by a teammate, he simply got dressed and left, resulting in his suspension from the team. Subsequently, he began to cut math class, having failed to complete his homework assignments. For European history, he was supposed to read a book and give an oral report before the class, but the prospect terrified him. Had his classmates not ridiculed him? Had they not written, under his photo in the eighth grade yearbook, "We wish for him the back of his head"? Was that not confirmation of a reality that he had lived with since childhood, that his head looked abnormal and deserved the names he was teased with by the neighborhood kids, like "Box Head" and "Squarehead"? Though he had a month to prepare, week after week would pass without him even choosing the book he would report on, so terrified was he of the prospect of humiliation. Then he got drunk at a Friday night frat party he had snuck into, seeking whiskey courage, and was too sick to show up for the PSAT the following morning. His algebra teacher, Mr. Glanwell, had assured the class that the test meant as much or more to college admissions officers than a high school transcript; no amount of preparation would make the slightest difference in their score. They either possessed the intelligence to do well on the test or they didn't. Luther took Mr. Glanwell's words to heart. Cutting classes progressed to truancy. One day became two and then a week and then three before his absence was called to the attention of his mother. Perhaps he could become a truck driver, like those men in brown uniforms who drove the matching color United Parcel Service trucks. Or he could wander about the lawns in Central Park like those men with sharp-tipped sticks spearing stray bits of trash and depositing them in the burlap bags that hung on straps from their shoulders. His dream of an Ivy League college where he would star as the second coming of All-American basketball player Bill Bradley was over. He was just looking to survive now. The school principal, the basketball coach, and several teachers encouraged him to stay. "You need to develop a stronger spine," the principal said, without explaining how. His words stung but what was ruined was ruined. He withdrew and went to a lesser school for the remainder of the year. He did manage to show up for the SAT, but performed miserably. From then on he was quantifiable, a number. There wouldn't be a day it didn't appear in his consciousness as stark evidence of his inadequacy.

He did return to his former school for his senior year, which was surprisingly happy to have him back, and he did manage to graduate, but the sense of failure stayed with him. He saw that it was too late to redeem himself. While some of his classmates were ecstatic to learn of their acceptance at Yale and Harvard and Princeton and Wesleyan and the like, only second and third tier schools accepted his applications. And there was the mockery of his basketball teammate, Tom Smits, whose performance the previous school year on the court had led Luther to quit the team. "You only look smart. You're dumb as dirt," Tom Smits said to him, having pulled the booklet containing his SAT scores from the box outside the principal's office before the booklets had been distributed.

His mother had been crushed to only discover his truancy the previous school year at the parents/teachers meeting. "How could you do that to me?" she said, having come to him that same night in his room. His only defense against the burden of her disappointment and sadness was silence. Did she want him to die? Was that what she wanted? He was already dead. He had learned long ago that he could make his mother cry, that he had the power of life and death over her as well as himself.

And now, at the end of the school year, she was registering her disappointment again when he said he would not be attending the graduation ceremony the next day.

"You would hurt me even more than you have? What is the meaning?"

Only his mother came to the ceremony. His father disapproved that she should spend such money on a private school education for any of the children. Was a public school not good enough? At the conclusion of the ceremony, which he had sat through in a state of depression at his failure and self-conscious at being seen with his elderly mother, he bolted, leaving her to go home alone. But Mr. Sadowski, the basketball coach, caught up with him on the sidewalk. With tears in his eyes, Mr. Sadowski said, "I would be proud to have you as my son."

Luther tried to hide his horror with a smile and ran off into Central Park, as if distance could separate him from the unbearable intimacy of Mr. Sadowski's words. How could he talk to him in such a personal, claiming way? How could he? Mr. Sadowski was nothing and he was nothing. They were bonded by their nothingness. And now Luther had been branded. The stamp of inferiority had his flesh received and for life, his sense of total defeat and humiliation in contrast with the bright and sunny day.

He must separate himself from that school forever and ever. He must sever all connection if he was to have any chance to live.

But it was not all darkness. Some light entered. Jane Thayer was going away. Not forever. Just for two weeks. Her uncle, her father's brother, said she could stay with the family down in Mexico City, where he worked for the American government. His daughter Gwen would be back from her first year of college at the University of Texas and was looking forward to spending time with Jane Thayer.

Luther tried to hide his joy. He had failed at trying to stay away from her; now she would be doing the leaving for them. And two weeks was manageable. They would both be refreshed.

"I love you but I'm not in love with you," Luke's high school girlfriend Nancy Becker had written to him during her first year at Vassar. Luther didn't dare say it was the same for him in regard to Jane Thayer, but it felt that way. She had changed physically. Her waist had thickened. Her face looked puffy; the pertness was gone. It wasn't a matter for consideration in relation to her that he had changed as well. Five feet six inches when he entered high school, he now stood six feet four inches, all of him skin and bones.

On the day of her departure Luther accompanied Jane Thayer to the airport. Her father had driven them in his pale blue Simca. In spite of it being tinny and tiny, sitting behind the wheel seemed to bring out his aggressiveness. "Don't mess with me, buddy. I'll leave you a flaming ruin," he muttered at the driver of a behemoth he was trying to pass. More disturbing, for Luther, was the fact that Jane Thayer sat up front with her father. Luther could only wonder what sort of message she was sending in leaving him alone in the back. It couldn't be a good one.

On hearing the boarding announcement for the Aeronaves de Mexico flight, Luther pulled Jane Thayer to him and sought to give her a soulful kiss, but she wriggled herself free.

"For God's sake, Luther. I'm going away for two weeks, not two years." Her sharp reproach sunk him into a state of shame that lingered for the rest of the day. She had seen once again his weakness, his clinging dependency.

Mr. Thayer seemed to pick up on Luther's emotional distress on the ride back.

"Fly away, little birdie, fly away. Eh, Luther."

"I guess so," Luther replied weakly, as a low-flying jet ripped across the sky.

"You won't be calling her all the time down Mexico way, not the way you have here in New York City."

Like a wounded animal, all Luther wanted to do was retreat into solitude, and that is what he did, softly moaning to himself for the rest of the day and night as he lay on the sofa bed in his little room.

He worked that summer at Sawicki's House of Paperback Books, two doors down from The End. He had asked permission to take the afternoon off the previous day so he could go with Jane Thayer to the airport, and now, back at work, an hour hadn't gone by before Luther confessed to Mr. Sawicki that he was hurting.

"Work. Just work. Work takes care of everything," Mr. Sawicki said. Luther wondered about that. Work was certainly taking care of Mr. Sawicki, but not in the way the storeowner meant. It seemed to be sending him to an early grave. A haggard man whose clothes hung on his wiry frame, Mr. Sawicki was there from morning until eleven and even midnight most days, and seemed to live on containers of black Chock Full O' Nuts coffee. The index and middle fingers of his right hand were stained yellow from the Camels he chain-smoked.

Mr. Sawicki made a face when Luther told him where he planned to go to college in the fall.

"Colby College? Where is that?" he asked.

"Somewhere in Maine. Waterville," Luther said. He had not visited the school. It was too far away, which should have told him something. But it was a small school and maybe he could resurrect his basketball dream if he enrolled there.

"Never heard of it. Didn't you apply to any other schools?"

"Gettysburg and Franklin and Marshall and Muhlenberg."

"Never heard of them either. You'd be better off going to CCNY, if you can get in."

"Why?"

"Better school. And it's free."

Mr. Sawicki was a graduate of Stuyvesant High School, one of the special New York City high schools for gifted students. He had missed out on admission to CCNY by two points, he said. Luther didn't know what "two points" meant, and didn't ask, not wanting to enter the older man's realm of failure. He had a sense that under his tough exterior, Mr. Sawicki was governed by wild and painful emotions and had regret etched deep in his bones. After all, he lived alone and his only relationship seemed to be with his store.

But maybe Mr. Sawicki was right. There had been no discussion of college with his mother, let alone his father. No tuition had been paid. In truth, he was ashamed to even bring up the subject. After all, his mother had done enough to see that he had an education, and then he had let her down. *Better school. And it's free.* And hadn't Mr. Horst-Lehman, the school principal, encouraged him to apply to CCNY. Hadn't he too been trying to direct him toward reality?

And so Luther requested an application, and with the process underway, a sense of great relief came to him. He wouldn't have to go far away, to some forbiddingly cold community in Maine that he had never even visited, and pile up colossal debt. That is, if he got into CCNY. His anxiety took a new turn. Suppose he had missed the deadline and wasn't accepted? Well, he would tell Jane Thayer of his new plan when she returned. True, she might think less of him initially. She had said that she admired him for his desire to leave home and venture out into the world. But he would explain the practical reasons—the costly tuition for Colby College compared with the free tuition at CCNY. She would come to understand.

The day before her return his mother handed him an air mail letter as he passed through the lobby. His whole being flooded with emotion, Jane Thayer emanating through the thin envelope with the distinctive red and blue border. It was nothing to open and read in front of his mother. No, no. This was private. This was his life. He took it up to his room and locked the door and sat with it a moment. She had written to him on three-hole loose-leaf paper in blue ballpoint ink. Her handwriting was rightward sloping and excellent, far better than his erratic penmanship. But what was this he was reading? Gwen, her cousin, knew everyone, and that meant parties every night and tennis lessons and horseback riding during the day and drinks around the swimming pool of her friends. She was having a blast. A *blast,* Jane Thayer wrote. But she had more news, and she wanted Luther to hold his breath. At that point he forced himself to pause. Already, he was at what he thought to be the summit of his anxiety, hearing about Bruce and Greg and Todd and other unfriendly sounding names of boys she had met. When he continued, a minute later, he read that Gwen's parents were only too happy to have her stay with them and finish her last year of high school and her father was in total agreement. Wasn't that fabulous?

Luther folded the letter carefully and placed it in his desk drawer and lay down on the sofa bed. The blow he had received had been delivered so gaily.

"Is that so?" His mother said, later that day, signaling with her brevity that his time with her was over, that caring for and about him was over and now he would be in her perfunctory prayers and nothing more. The realization was an added blow. Now his hold on her was over. No more of those Billy Graham revival crusades and church prayer sessions she would drag him to when trouble would find him, or parents' meetings she showed up faithfully for only to be humiliated when she learned that her second son was a truant. And what did she care about school or girlfriends or his future anyway? His future was with the Lord. The only school he truly needed was the church she had required him to attend until he refused. She had done her work and the church and God had done their work and now he would do his meaningless wandering in a meaningless world until he woke to the reality that Jesus time was the only time there really was. She left him there in the lobby where he had found her and stepped into the elevator. She had places to go and things to do. It was OK. It was in the natural order of things. Sons could leave home even when they were still there.

And Mr. Sawicki? He was ready with his man love, his gruff love, the next day. When Luther, in a daze, finally told him of his wound at the end of his shift, Mr. Sawicki did the father thing. He said to stick around. After locking up, he took Luther down to The Rail, a neighborhood bar and grill. The clock above the bar said 11:30

pm, but that was dinner time for Mr. Sawicki. A tall, slender girl with her blond hair in a ponytail took Mr. Sawicki's order, a $1.99 steak special for both of them. Luther could barely look at her, her beauty as she stood in her black uniform making her completely unattainable.

"You want to sleep with her? You could, but you don't have the confidence. You think the way to get the girl is to be seen as not wanting the girl. She's an apparition, a passing dream, but she is also the summit of God's creation. She is holier with what she possesses than all the church pews in the world, and you're too frozen to do anything but secretly long for her." So Mr. Sawicki spoke to him that night, from the vantage point of his years. And it was true. The world was completely out of Luther's reach. He had been dropped into a hole he would never climb out of.

Fall came and he was accepted, not by CCNY, but by Queens College, another four-year college in the City University system. He hadn't made the grade for his first choice. Another blow to his pride, but still, the crushing weight of all that private college tuition was off his back. A man had to know his place, he had heard or read, and he could learn his, hard as it was.

In this time letters continued to arrive from Jane Thayer. The pages were filled with news of her social experiences—parties in the suburbs where rich kids—boys and girls—would get drunk, shed their clothes, and jump in the swimming pool. She seemed to have a need to tell all, or almost all. Luther's mindset in this time was one of containment. He could only hope that each letter would contain fewer names of boys or none at all, even if the ones she mentioned were "jerks' and "idiots." His own letters were full of reproach for her cruelty in throwing her exciting new life in his face; in contrast to her social whirl, he presented the purity of his solitude and unyielding love.

"The problem with you is that you are afraid to get bitten. Would it kill you to try to make a few friends?"

She could surprise him with her truth bombs. Tom Smits came immediately to mind. He had been Luther's best friend in high school, but had Luther once ever called him? Not that he could remember. It was for Tom to come to him. It wouldn't do to put himself in the power of Tom Smits. With Jane Thayer it had been different. His need overrode his fear.

And now Tom had done more than call. He had tracked Luther down. After years of having only Luther's phone number and the general vicinity of his family's building and of Luther arranging to meet him at some public place, he had shown up in the lobby of the building one night just the week before as Luther was heading out. How? He had asked some guys on Broadway if they knew a boy named Luther. One of those guys was Luke, Luther's older brother.

"So does your brother always stand on street corners with his shirt hanging out of his pants?" Tom Smits going right at him with the shaming as Luther got him off the premises and into the neutral space of a diner a couple of blocks away. Tom Smits came to him in his loneliness and distress but Luther was unable to see it. He had spent the summer with his mother in Martinique, where she was doing research for her doctoral dissertation in anthropology at, where else, Columbia University. She was still healing from her abandonment by Tom Smits's father and didn't want to be "made" by any of the locals.

"So where are you going to college in the fall?" Tom Smits asked, because he couldn't stray long from his wounding nature. All Luther could see was his reflexive mockery, not a boy shaken by his parents' separation.

"CCNY," Luther lied, unable to bear the thought of Tom's anticipated response should he tell the truth and say he had been accepted at Queens College.

"What?" Tom said, incredulous, before recovering. "Well, it used to be a good school."

Tom's "invasion" had pushed Luther to the edge. If Luther was to live, Tom would have to die. It was that simple. Tom was a threat to his existence. Not die as in kill him, but die as a jeering critic of Luther's reality. That night, back in his room, he wrote to Tom—Tom with the 1400 board scores, Tom with the university professor father, Tom with the immaculate Riverside Drive apartment, Tom with the country home to go to in Bennington, Vermont—that one more call or surprise visit and Luther would have to kill himself. A savage glee filled him as he signed the letter and sealed the envelope and even more when he dropped it in the mailbox on the corner. Done. Finished. Free. Now you know who I am, you bastard, you creep, you who made me walk off the basketball court and now walk out of your life.

The previous fall, Tom had invited him to the family's country home for the weekend. "He takes his female students up there," Tom said. "It's his fucking pad. I find girls' panties all over the house." Could such a thing be? An angry, challenging, red-faced man Tom's father was, railing as he drove about protesters against the Vietnam War and chiding Tom and Luther for their pathetic conversations about sports when at their age he had been conversing about Dostoevsky and Tolstoy and Bach and Beethoven. Then the grilling began, as Luther had feared it would. Where did Luther live? Why couldn't Mr. Smits's son know his address? Was that fair? After all, Luther knew his son's address. And what about Luther's father? What did he do? An accountant? For what firm? Skoukin? What kind of name was that? It sounded made up. Tom intruding, saying "Dad, Dad," but Mr. Smits saying, "What? You have a liar for a friend. Get rid of him." But Tom not entirely his father's son. Leaving it to Luther to get rid of him, when he could.

Queens College was the IRT local to Times Square, the Flushing Main Street Line to the last stop, and a short bus ride to Kissena Boulevard. It was the smell of baking bread from the massive

Silvercup building as the train screeched along the curving el. It was laborers in Dickey work clothes with lunch buckets in hand and the *Daily News* folded under their arms sitting impassive at 7 am. It was lugging heavy texts, like Janson's *History of Art,* before he had the sense to leave them at home. It was the dapper lecturer, Mr. Carter-Greeson, with his pointer stick in one hand and a microphone in the other on the stage in the giant auditorium informing them about Romanesque arches and flying buttresses, saying "You're all bright. After all, you're here at Queens College," in a tone of mockery.

Queens College was body counts in the newspapers of Vietcong dead; staring at girls chatting on the campus, books cradled to their chests, and understanding that a chasm separated them from him that he would never be able to bridge; the excessively emotional paper on Eugene O'Neill he wrote for Professor Vance, who had till then regarded him well; the absence of a single friend on the vast and spread out campus; the 8 a.m. math class in which he discovered that he needed to be fitted for glasses because the figures on the blackboard were a blur and in which he despaired seeing the ease with which the young man at the next desk solved complex equations; the sense that in his isolation he was being good, even perfect, for Jane Thayer.

There was a steak house on Broadway and One Hundred Eleventh Street, where he would go to get filled up. The steak came with a baked potato and a small salad and a piece of garlic bread. He would take his tray and eat alone at a table for two. When night came to New York City, he would take long walks along Riverside Drive north past Riverside Church and Grant's Tomb and across the long bridge to One Hundred Thirty-Fifth Street before turning back. Though he had some fear of knives flashing in the dark, he would steel himself to continue forward, as if it were a test of his ability to step more fully out into life than he was then able to do. On these walks he would succumb to powerful fantasies in which he was doing things that had never before been done on a college basketball court He would quickly disappear from the scene of his exploits to escape the adoring crowd and seek refuge in a hideaway apartment high above the street. His ambition was to be famous without being known.

That same fall he saw *The Umbrellas of Cherbourg* at the Thalia Theater, on Ninety-fifth Street, just west of Broadway. Two young lovers sang of their love somewhere in France. All was happiness. All was sunlight. But a war was on in Algeria, and the young man was needed to help quell the Algerians' fight for independence. Such singing. Such love. But all was not the same when he returned. Time had done its cruel work. It had taken her to another love and him to another love. Such was the reality when she pulled into a gas station and he was there to attend to her needs as the owner. She had a husband but it was not him. He had a wife but it was not her. How could such a thing be? No, no, Luther groaned.

A knock came on his door the night of the winter solstice. It was Jane Thayer. She had come not to represent the darkness but the light with her good cheer. She had all the advantage with her surprise appearance. Seeing Luther ruled by moroseness and insecurity, she quickly left, though not before saying she would be throwing a party at her parents' apartment that weekend and he was invited.

The next day, right there on Broadway, Luther saw, from inside the steakhouse where he had gone once again, Jane Thayer walking hand in hand with a young man who filled his jeans so well and possessed a military bearing. The young man's physique completely defeated Luther; there was no way he could ever come close to matching those proportions. He could only thank heaven and earth that he had seen them and they hadn't seen him; he did not want them as witnesses to his pathetic aloneness. Not that he was alone. Not really. Not in that moment. The poet song master Bob Dylan was right there with him, singing about some girl who never went where she didn't belong. And Luther would do the same—he wouldn't go where he didn't belong either. He would not allow himself to be drawn to Jane Thayer's party, where he would be just a supplicant, among other supplicants, before Jane Thayer's throne of majesty. No, no, all he would give Jane Thayer was his absence.

She is trying to be like her cousin in Mexico City. She is trying to create the same social whirl here in New York City. So Luther also thought about Jane Thayer in regard to her party, and it surprised him to experience a feeling of sorrow for her. She did not have a nice apartment. Her mother was a drunk, a self-deprecating woman tied to her bottle. She was not a homemaker. Luther remembered the dust bunnies, the unsightly bulge created by the extension cord running under the worn rug, the stained sofa, the white curtains turned yellow with age from the few times he had been there. He remembered the stale air. Jane Thayer was trying to be something she lacked the infrastructure for being.

Jane Thayer returned to Mexico City after the holidays; he was not sorry that she had once more vacated the premises of New York City. She sat easier in his mind from a distance than in proximity.

If he still held his vigil, he also allowed himself to venture out. Some nights he wanted something more than the footpaths in Riverside Park. One night he heard the loud sound of the Supremes pouring out onto Broadway through the plate-glass window of Benini's Tavern. He looked inside and there was a sultry girl gyrating to "Stop! In the Name of Love," doing her dancing thing in a bikini and go-go boots. Luther might not be able to follow the beat of the thundering music with his feet, but it brought exhilaration to his mind, and the sight of the girl shone a light on his loneliness and summoned longing in every part of his being.

Inside he ordered a beer from the no-play bartender, who buttoned the top button of his short-sleeved knit shirt. He had the physical goods to wear black. His biceps and thick neck were proof of that. Both hands held takeout power and his pissed off expression said he would KO you quick should the need arise.

Luther drank his beer with his back turned to the go-go girl, feigning the same indifference as he had that night with Mr. Sawicki at the bar and grill where the blond waitress had served them. Only now and then would be steal a glance. On his second beer, and with the girl gyrating to wicked Wilson Pickett singing "In the Midnight Hour," he remembered Mr. Sawicki's call to action and sought to screw his courage to the sticking post. He would ask the girl if he could walk her home. But the song ended and the girl came down off the stage in her white boots to the bar, where the bartender passed her a drink and smooched her in a way that could only signify she was his. Luther left without the girl, but he left in one piece, and for that he could be grateful. He saw in that moment that it was dangerous to think beyond Jane Thayer and that only humiliation and possibly violence would be there to meet him if he did.

He was not entirely alone. He had his sister Vera. She too was an aspirant for freedom, having moved out of the apartment to a room right next door on the same floor. Luther was afraid of his sister. He had showed that fear by hiding her schoolbooks back when he was still in high school. He had been seized by the notion that she would surpass him academically and take their mother's love for her own, as she had appropriated their father's love years before by calling on him to smack Luther and smack him good for no real reason, and then gloating when he did. The call for justice was still loud in Luther over that incident. So if his sister was a taker away-er, then Luther was justified in doing the same with her books, though some part of him understood that he wasn't. It could seem that they hardly spoke to each other at all in recent years, except for harsh or cutting exchanges, small but ferocious skirmishes when either encroached on the other's borders.

But with the absence of Jane Thayer and his high school failure, his loneliness and wounds were announcing themselves in his stressed face and withdrawn manner. And so, one day she invited him into her room and made him a cup of tea.

On the wall, she had a poster of the fat-lipped one, Mick Jagger, and his Rolling Stones cohort, and said Luther must give up his crewcut and let his hair grow out. And so he did, because the back of his head was straight as a board and maybe now he would not be called Squarehead and Box Head and Flathead. His hair grew very long and could have benefited from shaping and styling he himself was not able to give the unruly mass.

"You look beautiful," his sister said, which was better than feeling like one of the gargoyles he saw in his history of art book.

A poster of Veruschka, a model over six feet tall, also hung on the wall. She struck a defiant pose, with her feet spread and one hand on her hip. I am tall and I am beautiful, she was saying. Vera was coming to terms with her own tallness, and Veruschka was there on the wall to help her to a confident stance vis a vis the world.

But Luther wasn't fooled. He did not let down his guard. He understood that relations between them could change, that in an instant she could turn cold and dismiss him should she detect anything amiss in his tone or manner or words. Because the women in the family—his three older sisters and Vera—could bury a hatchet in a man's head, and saw it as their right to do so.

And Luther saw something else that he kept to himself for fear that he might die if he didn't. On the street Vera would sometimes introduce him by his name but not his sibling relationship to her, though only if the friend or acquaintance was a young man, as she wanted them to understand that she could have a beau of her own and draw them to her, because she had her own kind of loneliness to contend with.

There was another in Luther's world, though he quietly wished he wasn't. His name was Sean and he had first come to Luther's attention down at the scruffy ball field in Riverside Park when he knocked Felix, the neighborhood bully, unconscious after Felix had dropped dry ice shavings on him from atop the batting cage as Sean took his turn at the plate in a pickup game. Later he was to knock Luther himself unconscious for a reason that wasn't altogether just—Luther had gotten rowdy after losing all his money at a blackjack game Sean had organized and Sean felt obliged to bring him into line with his fists. The power that attracted him to Sean and that he thought he would never use against him Sean did use against him, but that was some years after they had begun spending time with each other, beginning in ninth grade, when Sean came calling on him, having found out where Luther lived.

"It is a school night. I don't want you going out with that man. He does not look normal," Luther's mother said.

"He's not a man. He's a year older than me," Luther said.

"Well, you could have fooled me," Luther's mother replied.

Sean took him to see *Lawrence of Arabia* that night. "I go to the desert because it is clean," he said, over and over, quoting Peter O'Toole in the role of Lawrence, after the movie was over. Both coming and going they took a cab, and Sean paid for everything, even refreshments at the movie theater. Where Sean's money came from remained a mystery. He worked as a delivery boy for Funelli's Grocery on Amsterdam Avenue and One Hundred Thirteen Street.

"I want to see more of you," Sean had called to him, as Luther said goodbye. He had given his rough and violent heart to Luther, and Luther didn't know what to do with it, but he would figure it out. He had seen Sean pound others to the ground since his destruction of Felix, but he somehow felt that was not a line Sean would ever cross with him, and when he did, that night of the blackjack game, Luther vowed that he was finished with him. But it was not so easy. A beating with fists of fury was a kind of love, too. It was just undivided attention of the wrong kind, that was all. Anyway, Sean was just a sideshow in his life by then. Luther had Jane Thayer, and she was his world. How much room could he have for someone like Sean, who treated him like a desirable girl at first before ridiculing him on the beach at Far Rockaway for being a bag of bones.

But then Sean found a love he could call his own, a love he paid to have. No bag of bones was he. Bruce was a golden boy. Sean and he flew all over the country together and fought and loved in expensive hotels. Maybe Sean would go away for good now. But that was not to be. He showed up at Luther's door one spring night. Bruce was gone, at least for now. Sean had beaten him bad for having no class, for going off with whoever wanted him. So Sean said, as if that was a compelling reason for the thrashing he gave his lover.

"Where would you go if you had the dough?" Sean asked. They had gone to a bar on the next block.

"I went to Florida this winter for a week," Luther said. He had taken the Amtrak overnight down to Miami. He had brought his bones to the deserted beach in sixty-five degree weather. He had eaten fried shrimp dipped in tartar sauce and French fries doused in ketchup to get filled up and drank Coca-Cola. An orange-skinned woman with bouffant blond hair had served him. It was all business. She saw his boniness. She saw his loneliness. She saw he had nothing for her but the tip he left. Still, his mission had been accomplished. If Jane Thayer could go away, he wanted to show that he could, too. And, as an added bonus, he had come back with a tan, even if his skin could not hold it.

"Did I ask you where you went or where you want to go?"

"Mexico City," Luther heard himself say.

Though there had been no invitation nor the hint of one from Jane Thayer, they were Mexico bound the next night. Luther had never been on a plane. He arrived at the Mexico City airport drunk from the stiff drinks served by the stewardess. A service road took them from the airport into the flow of traffic and a hotel downtown, where in the bar a mariachi band wearing sombreros played the theme song from "Bridge Over the River Kwai," rousing Luther with their energy and gleaming smiles that only later he worried might have been mocking. Room service was ordered. He lifted the lid on the platter to find a giant steak to get filled up on so he could look normal for Jane Thayer, who was all he could think about in his drunken haze. It was dark when he passed out and dark when he woke up. Had the night no end? And where was Sean?

Luther found a note on the dresser. "This town not for me. Gone home." Under the note were five one hundred dollar bills. Luther was on his own. In spite of his fear, he was pulled back into sleep.

Later he would read that the air was thin at such a high altitude and caused drowsiness until a visitor adjusted.

He emerged in daylight and walked the streets, finding his way on a tree-lined boulevard to the address on Jane Thayer's letters. A thoroughfare with peons sitting out of the sun against the proper residential buildings, as if time had no meaning for them and money even less. Holy wanderers they were with toothy grins at the sight of the beanpole gringo with the out of control hair and anxious face.

He sat on the steps in the lobby, thinking maybe he should move, as he would be right in Jane Thayer's line of sight were she coming from the street. And then what? Would she bolt? Assume he was there to murder her? Even as he contemplated the possibilities, she appeared. Her. Jane Thayer. In a blue blouse and brown skirt. A girlfriend was with her, the two of them shoulder to shoulder and laughing, probably about some boy. Strangeness happened. A possibility beyond his ability to anticipate. She walked right past him, the only sign of recognition an embarrassed giggle as she headed to the elevator with her friend. He understood. She was ashamed of him. It would not reflect well on her to acknowledge him to her girlfriend. Tall, emaciated, with that unmanageable shrub on his head.

He returned to the hotel, talking to himself as he went. Helmetless and death-defying kids tore past on motorcycles. In his room a song came to him, "Sally Go Round the Roses." "Sally, don't you go. Don't you go downtown"? What could that mean? He was downtown, and Jane Thayer was uptown or crosstown or wherever.

Luther picked up the phone. He had Jane Thayer's number.

"Yeah. What do you want?" she said.

"Nothing."

"You come thousands of miles for nothing?"

"I had my reasons."

"I asked you what you want."

"Nothing," Luther repeated.

"Look, I'm sorry if I seemed unfriendly, but seeing you was a shock."

"Why was that?"

"I don't know. Look, I'm having a party tonight. You can come if you want."

Now he wasn't hearing "Sally." Now he was hearing Bob Dylan singing once again about how his artist girlfriend never went where she didn't belong. But he wasn't Bob Dylan and he wasn't a girl. Not yet, anyway. Jane Thayer called to him and he couldn't resist, not like when she had been in New York that past December and before he let his hair grow out.

It was what he had feared. A small gathering of clean-cut-looking American kids with wealthy parents. He sat there conspicuously alone. Seeing his discomfort, Jane Thayer brought him a glass of Scotch, and then another when he drank it fast.

"So what's up with the hair?" she finally said.

"My sister told me to grow it long."

"It looks a mess."

"I guess," he said.

"So why are you here?"

"I'm on my way to Nicaragua."

"Nicaragua?"

"I'm engaged to be married."

Jane Thayer began to laugh and couldn't stop. Soon it doubled her over and drew the attention of the others.

"He…he says…he's headed…for Nicaragua…to get married. He just…stopped off…in Mexico City…to say hello."

"Here for one last fling, eh?" one of the girls said, and she too laughed at the preposterousness of Luther's story.

He had only to wait for the flow of the party to be redirected away from him to steal out the door and the next morning was on a plane back to New York City.

That summer Jane Thayer came back to New York. Her parents had vacated their Upper West Side apartment to live in the remoteness of Brooklyn, where they could have a nicer place at a lower rent. And Luther made a move, too. His brother, Luke, called him to the penthouse to live in the small room next to the suite of rooms he was occupying.

Luke was two and half years older than Luther, built strong, and blessed with mechanical aptitudes Luther would never possess. He was twenty-one now and done with college, having been unable to make a go of it. The Coast Guard wanted him. He had scored in the ninety-ninth percentile on their test, but then they discovered that he had been arrested for auto theft, and though the charge was dropped, as it should have been, the Coast Guard turned its attention elsewhere. The court said that backing someone's car out of the driveway and then quickly returning it to its original place was more like a bonehead impulse than an indicator of a felonious nature. Luke had his flaws, but stealing wasn't one of them.

The penthouse was that much farther from the family's apartment on the second floor. Getting away was big in Luke's mind, or had been, just as with Luther, since they were kids. After high school he did explore Europe on a motorcycle and when he returned he tried to keep an apartment down in Greenwich Village but the rent was hard to meet with the little money he made working as an office temp. He had heard The Animals holler-sing *House of the Rising Sun*. He understood that the building was the sinking sun, but he moved back with the idea that he would leave again; however, the power was not there. He became a street-corner Louie with his shirt hanging out, just as Tom Smits had said. He got up later and later in the day and drank wine with his breakfast cereal and listened to another of his holler heads, Mitch Ryder and the Detroit Wheels.

Luther slept on a mattress set down on the wood floor of the small room. He lay on that mattress for six weeks that summer, having fallen sick. Some mornings he would be woken by the elevator door opening on the landing and hear his mother call out to

Luke when her pounding on the door was not enough. "Luke, I have need of you. Please answer. Please." When he did not answer, the nature of her calling out would change. "Luke, why do you treat me like dirt, like the filth beneath your shoes? What have I done to deserve such treatment?" Because in moving back to the building, Luke had put himself at her service, and being awoken to that reality was painful. "Leave me the hell alone," he would finally shout. And so it went. Soon she would weep. Luther had long since tried to stop up his ears. Her tears, all of it, took him to a place he couldn't bear to go. He had heard her lament before. Many times he had heard her say, "All my children treat me like the filth beneath their shoes."

Jane Thayer did not have any parties that summer, not that Luther knew of. She called to him, not as a lover, and so he went about with her, though he had heard Dionne Warwick sing "Walk On By" in a Central Park concert and heard it as an instruction in regard to Jane Thayer. He even spent the night sleeping on the sofa in her parents' new apartment, down in Brooklyn, while they were away, but he did not attempt to lie down with Jane Thayer. Time and altered circumstances had done that, though the longing could get rekindled by the smell of her perfume and her laughter, even if at times it seemed to be at him.

Then she went back to Mexico City. He did not accompany her to the airport this time but looked for her plane in the sky from the roof of the family's building. The single tower of the Riverside Church and Grant's Tomb and the George Washington Bridge were all in sight but the singularity of her flight did not call attention to itself in the air traffic he witnessed. Suddenly it occurred to him that another shift had occurred and her hold on him might be lessening. He did not fight this feeling. It just stayed where he could find it.

That fall he enrolled at the City College of New York. All twenty-six of his credits had been accepted. He wasn't an A student but he wasn't a C student either. Now he could stay faithful to the West Side IRT local. No long ride to the borough one of his professors referred to as a "residential desert." A couple of subway stops and he was there.

Doctors were on hand at the Wingate gymnasium on the north campus of the City College of New York to ascertain the physical status of the incoming students. Male and female students were segregated. The males walked in their underwear from one station to the next on the basketball court. Everywhere there were hideous white Jockey shorts and none were more hideous than his own, Luther ruefully noted, not because they were unclean. Luther did not wear dirty underwear. It did not fit with who he was in young adulthood. But he was there with all his bones and the meagerness of his thighs and calves showing. If he had gotten filled up beforehand, that could have made a difference, but there had only been black coffee and a sugar doughnut at the Chock Full O'Nuts at 116th Street and Broadway.

The doctors were kind of old. Many had gray hair or no hair. Luther wondered if they were alumni who had been enlisted for this service. In his lab coat and with a stethoscope dangling from his neck, Dr. Hillman had Luther cough and take deep breaths and then instructed him to open his mouth and inserted a tongue depressor so he could see what needed to be seen. He then directed him to step onto the scale and afterward measured his height. The doctor came on hard. He said Luther was malnourished and his teeth were bad and he would have to take better care of himself if he wanted to live.

Luther was glad to get back into his clothes and find a restaurant nearby where he could have some beef stew and get filled up and feel that he was taking action against his boniness. But the doctor's words had some carry to them, like a ball that gets hit and never stops traveling. These doctors. They came from the hard place, the biochemistry and anatomy place. They were statistically wired and so kept away from the soft space where Luther had to live in eternal fear but also admiration of their aptitudes and service. They did more than their share in making the world go around.

That fall was masturbating with a *Playboy* magazine centerfold open in the privacy of his room. It was hearing the elevator winch turning and turning, lifting and lowering the cab attached to it by the steel cable. Luke had bought a Honda motorcycle and Luther listened for the loud sound it made in the night as he tore up the ramp from the basement to the street. Hours later the elevator would rise and rise and its door open onto the landing. Luther would listen for the murmured conversation of his brother and a girl, his catch of the night after trolling the streets of Greenwich Village. The time of vanity, of hair blowing in the wind, was over. Helmets were now the law and he carried a spare so he didn't have to be lonesome in the dark.

Luther loved his brother without always liking him and understood where his lostness lay. Nancy Becker, his high school flame, had given him forearm shiv, she had given him clobber, she was no longer coming to him now that she had her Vassar-ness and the defined parameters of her reading list life.

Luke, before he had his metal steed, had the taverns of Broadway where he would find waitresses with blond hair and black roots and bad teeth and hearts hardened by betrayal. But the Honda gave him mobility. Now he had girls, runaways and castaways called from the isolation wards of America to the imagined magic of MacDougal Street.

Where had they come from specifically, these girls in the night? From farms, ranches, broken homes? Were they seeking stardom or the gift of anonymity the city conferred, and with it the freedom to go where their desires led them?

Evidently they wanted no more from Luke than he wanted from them. They were gone by morning in the shame-proof bliss of anonymity.

Always now it was the next. The door to unlimited pleasure had been opened to Luke. It was a door he must walk through every night. It made his life worth living.

Luther did not explore the streets of Greenwich Village. He did no such hunting. He was still faithful to his own loneliness; it had become, if not his friend, his constant companion. Luke could do his hunting for him.

And yet he had eyes to see. In French class, a stylish girl with hair the same strikingly short length as Jean Seberg and Mia Farrow wore theirs had his furtive attention. She possessed their beauty but not their gentle nature. Wrathful currents seemed to have a hold on her.

"What are you doing with all that scribbling? Trying to pretend that you have something important going on? Because you don't." Saying that was his reward for cowardice, for trying to be more interesting than he was. Saying what Mr. Sawicki had said in the bar that night in regard to the blond waitress with the ponytail. Saying what Jane Thayer had said about being afraid to be bitten. Saying "Get away from me and get away from me for good." In the privacy of his room he had been conjuring her image, but now her spikiness put a stop to that. It was not good to have in his mind someone who had tried to wound him for life.

That was the fall he began to become untethered to the Dodgers. Dave McNally and Jim Palmer and Frank and Brooks Robinson and all the baby birds on the Baltimore Orioles saw to that, sweeping Drysdale and Koufax and Osteen and all the rest. His love for them, as for Jane Thayer, was waning. They, like Jane Thayer, had moved away.

Luke was not committed to the streets of Greenwich Village forever. He soon had a new locale to pull up at called The Cheetah, a spacious disco with strobe lights. There he could perform his moves, and there he met Addie Axelson, in her last year of high school, who had the mettle to meet his mentality, being a big-boned girl who required something similar in her mate. And so he brought her to the penthouse not once or twice but to the point that she became a regular weekend feature. She came from a town called Darien, in Connecticut, which Luke learned was renowned for its upper class citizenry and so she had staying power in his mind and even in his heart. She was definitely not a one and done sort.

Addie Axelson had a friend named Carrie Carruthers. Luke met her the night Addie Axelson came into his life. She was blond and thin, and Luke sensed that she might be a good match for Luther and relieve him of his loneliness.

Maximum effort was needed not to do swivel head when Luther met Carrie Carruthers. She had her slimness but there was amplitude and curvature within it and she had beauty on her face. She had none of the big bones of Addie Axelson nor an expression full of requirement as to what a man should be. She just went on her way with fluidity. Luther stared at her tan moccasins, her brown bell bottoms, and yellow turtleneck and thought, these clothes have been bought for her. They are intimate with her person. Some, unseen, are even resting on her private places.

Some might think that learning was not applicable to Luther, either from books or experience, because there he was once again resorting to his repertoire of useless moves. No, he was not scribbling or projecting detachment from unearthly beauty. He merely sat there dancing with his head to the rough-edged voice of Bob Dylan singing about the vandals taking the handles and Johnny mixing medicine down in the basement. Bob Dylan was having it all his own way and so Luther had no choice but to surrender to the current he had established and let him take him where he would.

Carrie did not do what the woman/girl had done in the French class. She did not call him on his posturing. She did not rake him with verbal nails. She took in the movement of his head at a glance and let her reaction manifest as a bemused smile, as if to say, the world has its share of strangeness that it is not for me to try to fathom or correct but just be a witness to. Luther could see that she had a softer disposition. She was not someone with a voracious appetite for the world but needed to keep it at a distance for her very existence. Blinded by her beauty, he could not see the hurt it hid.

Luther soon had an ally to broaden the communication beyond odd movements of his head. Luke had bought two bottles of gin and two bottles of tonic and Luther had more than his share of both, emboldening him to act on his own behalf. The gin dissipated all disparities between him and Carrie Carruthers while illuminating a world of possibility. If Luke was to have his night with his mate, then Luther would have to clear a space for him, and was it not something that Carrie was acquiescent to retiring with him to his chamber?

In the morning he awoke from a sporadic night of sleep with Carrie lying beside him. He was naked, as was she. It had been a night of strangeness. Several times he had entered her only to feel her hands on his chest gently resisting, to the accompaniment of soft whimpering. To the question what was wrong she made no reply, her answer being the soft cry that accompanied her resisting hands. And yet she was there in bed with him and had not expressly forbidden him to try again. In daylight there was no possibility of shedding light on the mystery. Already he understood that all matters related to their lovemaking were to be discussed, in whatever fashion, in the dark.

But his frustration was minimal. A beautiful girl had lain with him and with sufficient trust to remove all her clothes. More than that, Jane Thayer was gone. Her hold on him was over. Benvolio had been right. Luther had taken some new infection to the eye, and the rank poison of the old had died. Infection, Luther's ass. The light of heaven was shining on him now on even the grayest days.

The next weekend Carrie Carruthers came to him from her home in Darien. He met her at the information booth in Grand Central Station and together they returned to his rooftop room, where they did as they had on their first night, drinking gin and listening to music, though only what was offered on his radio, as he had no stereo. And again he met with the same gentle resistance in bed.

The shadow of Luke was becoming long. Luther began to fear that his brother had an appropriating tendency. The notion came to him that Luke considered Carrie Carruthers to simply be on loan. In a certain mood, Luke could claim a special power to see into the mind of others. He said Carrie had had a thing for him but he had decided to stick with Addie because he had noticed that Carrie didn't always flush after herself, and that was a sign of trouble.

Luther took primal offense to what he heard as possible encroachment and went on high alert. Luke had his peculiar side, as when he would grab his forearm and bring it up under his nose and stay in what seemed like a trance for minutes at a time. And he had his menacing side, too, which he had displayed to Luther in childhood, saying, "Mine is twice the size of yours and don't ever forget it" and "Your blood is bad. It is thin and smells like a sewer."

So Luther took the measure that his fear led him to. When Carrie came to him the following weekend at Grand Central, he took her south, not north, to a hotel on Broadway near the corner of Houston Street. In the lobby stood several shady-looking men next to a cigarette vending machine. The room he rented was starkly furnished, just a bed and a chair, and when he ran down to the bar next door for a bag of ice, it was with terror that Carrie might be abducted before he could get back.

In the morning he was still half drunk from the gin he had consumed in the night and also famished. For breakfast he had a hot dog at a stand in Grand Central Terminal. Carrie encouraged him to have another. All she ordered from the food stand was black coffee before she caught her train back home.

Luther did not know that would be his last night in bed with Carrie, who once again had balked him. When he called her some days later, she suggested that he come up to Darien that weekend, and so he did, in a state of trepidation. Some change had occurred. She was redirecting him onto her turf. Where would they drink their gin? Where would they lie down together?

But he took his happiness where he could find it, in the fact of the Grand Central Terminal itself, with its marble concourse and chattering arrivals and departures board, and its promise of adventure. He was being called north, out of the city, by a beautiful girl and riding on a train of the New York, New Haven, and Hartford Railroad, the engine sporting its outrageous color combination of black and orange and red and white.

Carrie Carruthers stood in a pea jacket and jeans, a red scarf wrapped around her neck and her blond hair aglow under the platform lights. Snow was falling, thick wet flakes that would have no staying power on the ground. She had driven to the station in a VW Beetle, old and green. As she pulled out of the parking lot, she suddenly screamed as her hands lifted from the wheel to her face. The engine stalled out inches before the trafficked intersection.

"Your tires are completely bald. All four of them. Did you know that?" Luther asked, having gotten out and circled the vehicle.

"I do," she said, still trembling.

"But shouldn't you get new ones?"

"I can't afford to."

"Do your parents know you're driving around on bald tires?"

"Leave my parents out of this."

"What would be wrong with asking your father to help out? You could get killed and kill others, including me, driving around like this."

"Don't you dare bring my father into my life. My father does not exist. Not a nickel do I take from him. Not a nickel." No more amusement. Vehemence had swept all amiability aside, if only temporarily.

"But why?"

"Independence. Complete independence is essential if I am to live."

"But how will you pay for college?"

She was a senior, and had let him know, not in a bragging way, that she was a straight A student.

"I'm not going to college."

"What will you do?"

"I'll work, as I do now."

They came to a Wetson's, a Saturday night drive-in scene for the kids of Stamford and the outlying area. It had prefab modernity and inside the fluorescent lighting was bright and white. Luther liked the idea of getting filled up, of feeling substantial, after a couple of burgers and an order of French fries and a chocolate malted. But he had some concern that she would lead him to a table filled with her high-achieving friends and then he might go into his shell and be unable to come out. But it did not happen. They had a table to themselves. He could eat in peace with his enigma of a girlfriend, if he could even dare to think of her as such. He did not say, "Where are we going?" or try to get ahead of the night unfolding, in spite of his concern. Beyond that mask of blandness, he was beginning to think, lay mystery and the cleverness of a master planner.

Soon they left Stamford for the well-ordered streets of Darien, where private houses abounded. Hers was at the top of a hill. A solitary light burned in an upstairs room. She brought him inside, where he sat on a plush gray sofa. Luther had heard the great Dusty Springfield do her inimitable emoting in "A House Is Not a Home." He recognized deadness when he encountered it. He had also seen the movie *Psycho*. He might not have stepped into the Bates Motel, on some lonely stretch of bypassed roadway, but creepiness was in the air.

"Is someone home?" Luther asked.

"No one you would want to know about. Trust me," Carrie whispered, her breath hot enough in his ear that he placed his hand on her thigh. "No can do. Time to go," she said, as if full sentences would put them in peril.

Carrie deposited him at the Stamford train station and drove off quickly. He followed the path of her red taillights till they were gone from sight. In a state of pained wonder as to what had happened, and with the train late in arriving, he was drawn to a phone booth.

"I just had to call." And it was true. He could not just leave. He needed something more from her than she had provided in the oddness of the evening.

"I'm under the covers thinking of you and wishing so much you were here."

"Why are you whispering?" he asked.

"Do you not know where I am? Do you not know?" she said, in that same lowered voice before the phone went dead. When he redialed, the line was busy.

He tried to stay in the atmosphere of her imagined love through the night and into the week, but the peculiarity of their last evening together was too strong in his consciousness not to worry. By mid-week he understood, or feared he understood. He was being left. She was no longer there. The whole evening had been a goodbye, a strange one.

"Can you come in this weekend? I have to see you," he said. He was sure she could hear the quiver in his voice.

"No can do."

"What?"

"This weekend is not good. I have plans."

That word "plans." He felt planked by it. He didn't press her. No strenuous argument. No pleading. He was too insecure for that. A hint of rejection was enough to send him on his way.

He got drunk on gin and Seven-Up that Saturday night in his room, then put his hand through the window and cut his thumb. When it wouldn't stop bleeding, he went to the emergency room. Before he did, he threatened to kill his brother. He didn't believe his own threat, as he didn't believe he had to smash the window pane with his fist. He had room for histrionics in him. Some failure of authenticity. As there was when the nurse began to clean the cut prior to stitching it. He was watching himself. He saw the actor in him performing.

"Shut up, or I'll have the cops come and take you to Bellevue," she said, as he lay there hollering. She was young and tough and saw where his off switch was.

Luther had signed up for Calculus I but all he could absorb were fragments. The sine of the curve, the slope of the tangent line. He saw equations that had nothing to do with the flow of his inner life. He had dropped himself into the middle of the ocean, having hoped to develop a more muscular mind of the kind that real men had and not have to live his life with the shame of paperback novels and a "he said, then she said" world. After a week of torment he dropped the course, without penalty, and sought out a college counselor, a young man with a beard that added the impression of sagacity to his face. The nameplate on his door said Zacharias Wiener, and with him did Luther in that moment place the power of decision as to his future, laying out his board score numbers. Where could he be? What could he be? Luther asked. The bearded young man had a clinician's cold kindness.

"Your numbers have told you where you can be. Just try to live with that," he said.

Luther went away humiliated. He tried to lose the counselor's words but they kept finding him and soon understood that they would be with him for the rest of his life and he must try not to buckle and break under their weight.

A knock came on his door that winter. There stood Sean.

"I need a place to stay. I'm on the lam from the military police. I have nowhere to go. Can you help me out? Can I stay with you?"

He had been drafted into the Army. After two weeks of boot camp down in North Carolina, he had bolted, but not before his head had been shaven. Hammerhead, the neighborhood kids had called him, though never to his face if they wanted to live. A massive thing it was that tapered and curved in the back, much like a hammer. Luther with too much of his head missing, the back of it flat as a board, and Sean with too much.

Afraid to say no, Luther said yes. Sure Sean could stay.

In a confessional mode, Sean told him some of his story. It was not a nice one.

A couple of years before, while working at the supermarket down on One Hundred Tenth Street and Broadway, he had befriended a shopper, an elderly widow. He would personally deliver groceries to her door. Lonely, she invited him in and encouraged by his attention, deluded herself into believing she was attractive to him. Having learned by now that she was a woman with considerable assets, he encouraged her flirtation. After a time he began asking her for money. To his amazement she gave it to him. He now dressed better, and with his newfound financial resources, attracted a beautiful young man, Bruce, to him. They took trips to San Francisco, Las Vegas, Miami Beach. But a notice from the draft board arrived. By now, the woman was tiring of his long absences and the outlays of cash. She called him a gigolo and said she wanted nothing more to do with him.

Gone were the sharp outfits. He still had the fancy leather shoes, but with them he wore a pair of jeans a size too small and an old T-shirt. For protection from the cold he had only a thin windbreaker.

For two days he stayed with Luther in the tiny room. The niceness was the worst part. It was so out of character. No cutting remarks. No ridicule. On the third day Luther returned from classes to find him gone. No greater gift had he ever received. So it felt.

And yet a month later he received a note from Sean. Sean had spelled his name "Garian," but somehow it got through.

I need you now. Down at Fort Bragg. North Carolina. Come with money so I can get out of here. Your friend, Sean.

Conscience had some application to Luther's life. He wasn't without one. He made the long journey down to Fayetteville on a Greyhound bus. He would take Trailways if he had to, but Greyhound had won his heart with "Take the bus and leave the driving to us." In his knapsack he had a wad of cash to make Sean's escape possible.

Outside the bus station was a street full of bars. It looked like a stage set somehow, as if there was nothing but the façade of these establishments. Soldiers were drinking and fighting. A commotion was going on in an alleyway. Bodies piling on. Bodies flying. Clearly it was a place to get primed for violence so the soldiers could take it abroad with them.

I am a girl in the domain of men. I have long hair in the land of shorn locks. So Luther said to himself, in a voice he hoped no one could hear.

Sean was in his barracks. He had toned strength in his body from his boot camp days and weeks. He existed among hillbillies towel-snapping each other's butts as they stepped from the shower. Sean said his parents had just been down to see him. Both his mother and father said it was not the American way to cut and run. They told him to stay the course and make them proud, that this was America he would be fighting for.

"I'm shipping out tomorrow. Gonna go and kill me some of those guerrillas," Sean said, with false bravado. Luther had some idea Sean would have spelled the word "gorillas," Sean being Sean.

"But…"

Luther didn't get the chance to say anything more. Tears had come into Sean's eyes. He threw his arms around Luther so Luther wouldn't see him sobbing. "You don't know. It's so fucking lonely being on the run."

Back in the bus station Luther pulled a book off the rack. *In Cold Blood,* by Truman Capote. He had seen the movie of his short novel *Breakfast at Tiffany's* and it had made him cry, that Holly Golightly should ditch her cat in the rain, just leave the domesticated creature to the meanness of the streets and a life of wet fur and hunger and the entire absence of love. And ditched Paul Varjak too, the one man who was good for her, and it made him cry even more when Holly joined Paul in the search for the cat and cry even more when she and Paul kissed in the rain. And to hear that song "Moon River" while they smooched. A song that might have the power to destroy him with all the feeling it aroused. But the new book was different. It had no play in it, not in the title or the content. The prose was hard and flat and intent on staying on the ground.

Luther fell into a deep snooze. Whole states went by as he slumbered, as did the night. He woke with daylight dawning and the New York City skyline in view. A girl across the aisle with sunlight in her hair was smiling at him, her smile telling him somehow he was in from the cold.

Chapter 8

He was high on speed when he went to meet Mona Van Dine. He had to be. No other way to close the gap. No other way whatsoever. The Riverside Drive address alone intimidated him, as did the doorman ringing upstairs on the intercom for her, saying, "You have a guest" even as he put a dubious eye on Luther. "I'll be right down," he heard her reply over the squawk box.

Luther had found a movie for them. Not a western but something English and proper, because the English were good at proper and Luther didn't want Mona looking down at him for his poor taste. This one was surely proper. So he had read. *A Man for All Seasons.* Historical drama involving whatever. And Paul Scofield was in it, and he was supposed to be pretty good, not that Luther had ever seen him in anything. And one of those nice East Side theaters, near the Plaza Hotel.

An artist, Vera had said Mona was. She would have to be talented. The High School of Music and Art didn't take just anyone. And her mother a Radcliffe graduate, her father with a PhD. And Pam Becker had told Vera about the magnificent apartment. Three bedrooms, and all of them with views of Riverside Park and the Hudson River.

She would be his entrée into a better world, his steppingstone to endless pleasure. No one would tie him down again and walk all over him, as Jane Thayer had. No one. That girl on the bus coming back from North Carolina. The girl with a smile that told him it was a new day.

"Forget about the movie. Let's go to the End Bar," Mona said, and without waiting for a response walked on ahead. As if on her command, the bus was just arriving.

What else could Luther do but follow?

Their evening together started shakily. She had been to the demonstration against the Vietnam War in Central Park earlier in the day. Had he gone as well? Even with the feel-good buffer of the speed, and now the beer he was drinking, Luther was taken aback. No, he hadn't, he said, allowing honesty to be his guide, and lowering his eyes in shame.

"Why?" she asked, not in a tone of reproach, but simply curious.

"Somehow it seemed far away from my life."

"Far away from your life?" Not incredulous. Again, just curious.

"I don't know what to make of the war, to tell you the truth. Communism can seem like an inevitable force, as if it has history on its side. And yet wherever it spreads it seems to impose complete control over people's lives. But I also don't understand what we are doing over there. What would it gain us to keep South Vietnam from falling, unless the domino theory is correct?"

"What domino theory?"

"That the rest of southeast Asia will fall, and then Australia, and soon we will be fighting to keep them from overrunning Hawaii."

"And you believe that?"

"They do seem always to be winning, whether it is China or the Soviet Union or Cuba. Maybe they are stronger, mentally as well as physically. I guess it's not what you want to hear."

As a child he had seen the news footage of Hungarians confronting Soviet tanks in the streets of Budapest. He had heard accounts of the bloody crushing of the revolt against Communist tyranny. And then there was Cuba, and the terror engendered by the missile crisis and the standoff between Khrushchev and Kennedy. The world was a fearful place full of implacable foes, whether the menace came from missiles with nuclear warheads ready to launch from silos in foreign lands or switchblade creatures of the night, like Salvatore Negron, the Cape Man, who had wantonly killed two boys in a Hell's Kitchen park back in 1959.

The war conjured fantasies of heroics like those he performed in childhood games down in Riverside Park with a broomstick for a rifle. It was something he witnessed on TV or in newspaper photos. The media accounts gave him a measure of detachment. He saw the bright orange flame but he did not feel the burn. What did it mean that fifty-nine Vietcong were killed or captured? And maybe we weren't fighting to keep the VC from our shores but out of national greed. Suppose there was some hidden gold, or other precious metals, or minerals we didn't want the North Vietnamese to get. So maybe it was time to bring our soldiers and planes and whatnot home. At the same time you didn't want the Communists coming across the water to Honolulu and then storming ashore on the mainland because they were so unrelentingly pissed off and would stick everyone in reeducation camps. Not knowing as he spoke that the next day would bring the memory of his father emphatically declaring to his mother at the breakfast table that Red China shouldn't be admitted to the U.N. and offering other big opinions. And the next morning would he also hear in his mind the roll call of the neighborhood kids who were over there now—Sean McAuliffe and Johnny "Fat Stuff" Scully and Kevin "Itty Bitty Wittle One" Donnelly and Luis "K.O." Gomez. But on that smoky night all he saw was this girl so pretty and excitingly different from those he had known.

"You know so much. My parents aren't nearly as smart as you."

"No, no, no," he could only murmur in genuine protest. Because he knew that to read the newspapers was not to be a brain surgeon but an idler in the haunts of the commonplace.

The old drunk let fly with his lethalness from his barstool. "He's a bum, Sweetness, a bum. That mop on his head doesn't change a thing. Look at him closely and you will see that he hasn't got the necessities. Columbia doesn't want him. The army doesn't want him. Nobody wants him."

An influx of patrons quickly filled the space between the booth where Luther and Mona sat and the old man. The air thick with smoke and the strong smell of beer. The old man's words had struck like sharp knives and confirmed that a universal truth was currently afloat throughout the neighborhood as to how little he could ever be. But that the attack should come at his time of greatest opportunity.

And yet the universe now offered, when he thought he was done for, a countering voice.

"Don't accept anything that hateful old man has to say. Do you hear me?" There was firmness in Mona's voice. She was a puzzle. Another girl might have been out the door.

"It's getting late. You should be getting home, I guess." In fact, it was just after 11 pm.

"I'm not going home. My parents are upstate."

"Upstate?"

"We have a country place."

Only then did he notice the tote bag she had brought along.

The night was not all pleasure. He had to live with the fear that in touching her, she would remark on his cold hands and realize he was high on speed as well as drunk. For another, he was made to rediscover what he already knew, that a single bed was not meant for two. And so, as she slumbered peacefully, not waking once, he catnapped in the darkness, staring at the lighted face of the alarm clock and dreading how she would perceive the room in the morning light.

When daybreak came, she ran, with a sheet wrapped around her, into the public bathroom. A minute later she returned and jumped into her clothes, then took off for a breakfast date with Pam Becker, but not before saying, "I'm going to be around for a long, long time."

Chapter 9

That spring he dreamt of a house ablaze in the night and of fleeing through the nearby forest from men with guns who saw him as the guilty party. In the dream he ran with abandon and even joy, as if, even in the darkness, new vistas were opening to him.

And school was stabilizing. The only course he dropped was Physical Education because his chest hurt running laps around the track at old Lewisohn Stadium and it was deflating for others to see him in shorts and a T-shirt and his bones showing. No, the image he wanted of himself required that he keep his clothes on. Probably he had taken on too many credits, but he wanted to make up for the paltry nine he had earned in his first semester so he could graduate in four years. For normalcy to have its way, he would have to keep to the schedule that had taken hold in his mind. After college he would go directly on to law school and after graduating three years later be full-fledged in life.

In addition to Vera, he had three other sisters, maladjusted and considerably older. There was Hannah, who was born seventeen years before him and who still lived at home with her seven year-old son. An angry woman whose dark moods could penetrate walls, she smacked with her tongue clamped between her thick lips, saying

"You leave these brats with me. I'll teach them to behave," on those rare Sunday nights that her parents went to church together. An overweight woman who sat in the dark watching "Million Dollar Movie" on Channel 9 on the secondhand TV while eating a quart of Breyer's ice cream out of the container with a tablespoon. And his second sister, Naomi. She, too, with a child, a daughter named Jeanne. And his sister Rachel, two years behind Naomi, who had been, for him, a guiding light with her acceptance to Vassar College and her big job with CBS-TV before she left that job and other jobs and now was an office temp living a rooming house existence some blocks away from the family's building. And there was Luke, his older brother.

His older siblings were a weight, a reminder that he had no margin for error. No one would be there to help him if he stumbled.

Some days he would sit at the top row of Lewisohn Stadium and imagine the amphitheater filled with spectators at sporting events. The gray structure was well beyond its prime, as was the college. The world was awash in grayness from where he sat. The wrecking ball not far away. He could feel it coming. Had baseball ever been part of its past? After all, "Stadium" was half its name and the field provided ample space. If so, it was a ballpark as it was meant to be, an integral part of a neighborhood. You turned a corner and there it was, as he had turned a corner that magical afternoon as a junior in high school after getting off the bus in Philadelphia. He had come to see the Dodgers play the Phillies. There, around a corner, Connie Mack Stadium revealed itself, leaving Luther breathless, as if what he hadn't even known he was longing for had suddenly appeared.

Mona came to him regularly that spring. He would find her sitting on the floor outside his door when he returned to the rooming house after his post office shift.

"But your parents?" Luther said. Like Pam Becker, she was in her senior year at the High School of Music and Art.

"What about them?"

"They will see you are missing and worry."

"It's not a problem. Believe me. They're relaxed about these things."

Or she would arrive in the morning, and he would sleep with her first thing. She showed no anxiety about getting to school on time. Instead they would wind up at the coffee shop around the corner, where some mornings she would eat an enormous egg salad sandwich. At times like that he felt invaded, burdened. She didn't have the same cares and concerns. There was no timetable for her life but to be free of that school and the academic requirements she derided because painting was all she cared about. Her scorn was hard for him to understand. Such a beautiful school it was, that tall tan building on the corner of One Hundred Thirty-fifth Street and Convent Avenue, right across the street from the gated entrance to CCNY's south campus. Music and Art a school that gave its students instant status, unlike CCNY.

Her visits were unannounced. As if in a dream he was. A beautiful girl, so talented, and yet so available to him. Her idea of him so absurdly unrealistic.

"That first night, the way you used a Coke bottle for an ashtray in your room. It told me everything. You were Raskolnikov or some starving Russian poet."

He was going to kill some old lady with an axe? A poet, when the very thought of poetry distressed him?

She took his side when he told her about Marcia, and the folksinger boyfriend he stole her from. She liked that he could act boldly and not be a prisoner of group norms, and dismissed his assertion that the folksinger was the better person for having a social context.

"If he was so great, she would have stayed with him. You have nothing to apologize for," she said flatly. He wanted to believe she was right, and though he couldn't, he did not argue. His thoughts turned to Gresham Dodger, the handsomest boy in his seventh grade class, who said over and over, “We don’t do that here. We don’t do that here,” after seeing Luther punch odious Charlie Hodges in the ear, causing him to scream out in pain, this being several weeks into Luther’s first year at the Claremont School.

Why go where the light of reason cannot shine? he heard himself say, in regard to Mona, words such as his mother would speak.

Chapter 10

He did not care for his political science professor, Bettina Gladstone. At first he had, but then he saw that she was mean, taunting the students for not going to Cuba and helping to harvest the sugar cane the Cuban economy depended on. And when she wasn't going on about failure to support Fidel and the revolution, she was mocking them for not doing freedom work in the Deep South. She herself had the front line credentials that allowed her to chastise the effete white boys in her charge. A woman who looked beautiful from the back row but up close you saw what time had done to her face and hands and what cigarettes had done to her teeth.

As he walked from Wagner Hall toward Finley Cafeteria, a thought came to him that Mona might be waiting outside his room at that very moment. To that point thoughts as to when she would come or if she would come had not visited him. He hurried home, but Mona was not there, neither in the lobby or outside his door. Well, he would stay put. Any minute he might hear her footsteps in the hallway and then that gentle tap on the door. But there were no footsteps and no tap. There was only the silence and the walls and Luther and his growing distress.

He had fallen. He had said he wouldn't but he had. He lay, curled on his bed, seeking comfort from his own soft moaning. The same thing the following day. Rushing home after his last class only to find she was not there, as she wasn't on the third day. He had resolved never to call her. That would only show his neediness. But what choice did he now have? He found a phone booth in a pharmacy on Broadway and in a state of terror dialed her number. She answered on the fifth ring.

"Luther! I'm so happy to hear from you."

"Are you?"

"Of course."

"Where have you been?"

"My parents had theater tickets last night. I went with my father because my mother wasn't feeling well. The day before I had a doctor's appointment. Just things."

"Oh." A play. She had gone to a play with her father. He tried to imagine such a thing.

"Is something wrong?"

"Nothing's wrong. Nothing." It was everything not to slam the receiver back into the cradle.

"Don't worry. I haven't gone anywhere. I'll be back around tomorrow. You'll see."

What he saw wasn't the issue. What she saw was. She would hurt him now. Maybe not right away, but somewhere, sometime. Only a matter of time before she did.

She was at his door in the morning and then once again in the afternoon. As they lay in bed she surprised him. She wasn't liking Pam Becker, she said. She didn't trust her. They had been as close as sisters for a year, but then the change came and Pam could hardly get herself to say hello when they encountered each other. She had found other girls to hang around with, cooler and more popular girls. But now she was back, as if she had never been gone. That wasn't right. She would have to break things off with Pam. She wasn't ready quite yet, but the time would come.

People weren't what they seemed, Luther was understanding. Mona had beauty and talent, but she had loneliness, too. She said as much. She had spent a painful year missing Pam, and now, without a word of explanation, Pam wanted to make as if everything was normal and nothing had happened.

And there was another who had done her wrong, making clear to Luther that she had her roots in pain. A boy named Arnold had invited her to his apartment. They were both eighth graders at the time. She had taken off her clothes, assuming that was what he wanted, and he did sleep with her. But he had meanness in him too, or maybe just fear. He told her to leave. Not only that. He told her she was sick. Mona returned home weeping and buried herself in her mother's bosom. Through her tears Mona told her mother the story. Mona's mother then went and spoke sternly with the boy, saying no one should be treated that way. No one. Mona didn't say whether the boy had words to say back to her or whether her mother went to the boy's parents, and Luther didn't think to ask. He just let the story sit there in his mind and tried to understand what the story was telling him.

Forehead pressed against forehead was the image he had of the boy, not with his mother but with his father, as if the father was charging the boy's battery with his bigger battery so that the boy could better understand what it meant to be born into the world of men and to provide him with the buffer that he required as protection from women. Luther didn't know where this image was coming from. It just appeared as a simple truth.

Mona wasn't done. She had another Pam Becker story to tell. Pam had a boyfriend, a City College dropout and drug dealer named Jake. One afternoon, after school, Pam and Mona went to his apartment, and there Mona was introduced to Jake's friend Ron. While Pam went to one room to lie down with Jake, Mona went to another to lie down with Ron. Mona remarked that Ron had a curved penis, like a banana. She said this as if it was among the funniest things she had ever seen.

Mona went away from Luther that afternoon, but her stories didn't. They had staying power in his mind. That she would undress for Arnold and Ron with no seeming hesitation showed a boldness he accepted in himself but was shaken to learn was in her makeup as well, though she had done the same with him. Her amusement at the shape of Ron's penis was equally agitating. Luther did not associate laughter with the sexual experience. He did not expect that sort of detachment.

Luther felt some fear. What did it mean that someone could just walk in on Mona like that? Or should the question be could just anyone walk in on Mona like that? But he also felt arousal, not only at the image of Mona inspecting a virtual stranger's penis but that the sex took place in a group setting. His mind had only to go there and his entire being was distorted.

Arnold and Jake and Ron. Names that had the sound of masculine hardness, of coldness, on them. Young men whose fathers had pressed their foreheads against theirs that callousness might be in the nature of their offspring.

Chapter 11

It was not for men to come to his room. His room was for him to sit in and sleep in alone, except for the girls he met. However, a man of muscular physique did appear early one morning and promised Luther significant pain if he didn't pay his back rent that day. And, of course, Marcia's father, who had been ruled by outrage. But now, on a night that Mona was fully naked, there came another, his knock gentler than the previous two, but with repetitious insistence. It called Luther, fully naked as well, from his bed and into his clothes. Standing back from the door, as if menace were on the other side, he asked who was there and what he might want.

"I am Peter Van Dine and I'm here for my daughter."

The voice was firm and had an activating effect on Mona. She bolted upright clad in a sheet and whispered frantically, "Don't open the door. Please. Please."

"But it's your father," Luther whispered back, fighting panic.

"Say I'm not here. I'll jump out the window."

"No. No," Luther said, with some vehemence. The drop to the basement was deep. He would not have her legs or any other part of her broken because of such impulsiveness. He would not have her lie badly injured amid air-mailed garbage and armies of rats. She appeared to see the light of reason sufficient that she stayed in place.

When she was fully dressed, Luther opened the door. In the hallway stood a man with hair still blond and thick though he was in middle age. He wore a tan raincoat tightly belted and with epaulets. It went with his tanned and weathered and handsome face. If Mona's father was feeling any aggression, he held it in check and let his silence speak for him. In a short time Mona sped out of the room and past her father, who followed after.

Luther sat with himself in the wake of their departure. He did not see defeat here. He did not see Mr. Van Dine as a nemesis. If anything, he was proud of the role he had played in reuniting Mona with her father and could take satisfaction from the sense that Mr. Van Dine had perceived and appreciated his attitude of collaboration and cooperation. He could even go so far as thinking of the two of them as a sort of team, and what a glow it gave him to imagine that was so.

There had been other windows. His screened bedroom window, so he would not fall to his death on Broadway. The window of the room where he had waited, sequestered, for his mother to take him away following his expulsion for incorrigibility in sixth grade from the Episcopal school he had attended since kindergarten. More than any of them, there was the ninth floor window his sister Naomi emerged from to stand on the narrow ledge outside. How long before she was seen and the police and fire department converged he could not say, or how she kept her balance, or what her mind was telling her that she did not leap and fall down and down onto the unforgiving hardness of the sidewalk far below. He was a child at the time, approaching his family's building to find a crowd had gathered and was staring up. He did as well, and though she was high above and in a white nightgown, he could see it was his sister. A policeman, or was it a fireman, was leaning out the window. Was he telling her that he loved her? Was he saying her death didn't have to happen? Did he speak to her softly? None of these things did Luther know. Only this did he know. Mona Van Dine would be falling from no windows. Her blond hair, her whole being would remain forever and ever. Mona Van Dine was not his sister Naomi, nor any of them, and never would she be.

Chapter 12

He stepped out of the rooming house and looked up at the blue sky. His life was ahead of him if he could only get past his exam that morning. Turning the corner onto Broadway, he glanced at his family's building across the street and the window of the room he had once shared with Luke and Vera and shuddered. A sense of the building's instability came to him. It was there in its crumbling cornices, its grimy façade, the old and rotting window frames and sashes. The building served as a reminder of the harsh consequences of failure. He turned away and paused by the Esso gas station and garage where men in Dickey duds could be men in their gruff but always helpful ways.

"Hey, Luther."

A strongly built young man approached. There was a time when Luther's heart would leap at the sight or even the thought of him, back in the endless days of childhood down at the railroad, in the parks, riding the subways, exploring the neighborhood alleyways, and coming back dark with dirt when it was night. Jerry was the one person that he must never be parted from until it got to be seventh grade and their paths began to diverge.

"Hi," Luther said, hearing the false enthusiasm in his voice.

"You going someplace?"

"I have to get to school."

"What school?"

"CCNY."

"Oh, that's right. You're a college boy now."

"Sort of."

"What do you mean, sort of? You are or you aren't."

"How have you been?" Luther tried to hide the sting of being corrected.

"I'm staying with my moms. Trouble finding a job. People don't want you if you are good. Don't matter. I go into the army next week."

"I'm sorry," Luther said.

"What are you sorry for? You're not the one going."

"No, that's true."

"So why you have to say you're sorry. What good is sorry? Sorry going to do something for me? It going to buy me my life?"

He had been Jerry Jones when Luther first met him. Later, he added a second last name. He became Jerry Jones-Nobleonian. His mother was Latvian, a refugee after World War II who arrived in New York City married to a black G.I. A half-crazed woman with enormous breasts whom Luther would see staring into the store windows on Broadway, transfixed by the bounty of America after the war-torn world of scarcity she had come from. They had lived down the block from Luther in what was then called the welfare hotel. His mother was probably the only white woman in the building. The man who lived with him and his mother and drove a cab was not his real father. His real father had been "runned over," by a Soviet tank. The lie—and it had to be a lie given Jerry's copper-colored skin and wooly hair—became one Luther was protective of Jerry about, sensing, even as a child, that Jerry's parentage was a dark place he must not enter.

Handsome Jerry would have been were it not that the beautiful skin tone was marred by pinkish blotches on his face and hands and all over his body by an allergic reaction to penicillin.

Luther remembering how, some years past, Jerry would say, "Ellie's good, too, don't you think?" referring to Elston Howard, the Negro catcher and sometime outfielder for the New York Yankees, and one of the few on that Yankee team of Mantle and Maris and Skowron and Yogi Berra and Whitey Ford whose skin wasn't white. A boy seeking back then a place for Ellie Howard on the so-white Yankees and for himself in a so-white world.

"Why you got to be in such a hurry for your CCNY? Why it can't wait?"

"I've got an exam."

"You studying to be somebody?"

"I don't know."

"What you be there for if you don't know?"

"So I can find out, I guess."

Jerry laughed his non-laugh. "You crack me up. You really do."

The low-level hostility was painful but maybe inevitable. In Jerry, he had found someone he could feel safe with, someone even lower on the social scale than him, a boy whose family lived in a building white people were afraid to enter and where a corpse was found behind the refrigerator in the public kitchen after the stench of the decomposing body had permeated the entire block for days; a boy who had witnessed Luther entering a West Side private school while he was stuck at the gang-infested public school across the street. There was much to divide them; so much less to bring them together.

Professor Benustifore had a cue ball head and wore a signature red bowtie. His scrubbed and shiny face was full of pride at his own efficiency. Luther, who was speeding strong now so as not to show up ordinary for the test, stared from his desk as the professor made his way through the aisles handing out stapled pages with that blurry blue mimeographing.

"Your genes and your industry—that is, your preparation— will determine your score. Now have at it, ladies and gentlemen. This is your life, and you all have conspired to be here."

Professor Benustifore often spoke like that, so that you had to trail behind the meaning of what it was he said, if you were listening at all. Not for the first time did Luther ponder whether Professor Benustifore had fled an asylum and was only masquerading as an academic, a thought brought short when the professor tapped the bell on his desk to indicate the start of the examination hour.

Luther read the first question but there was only hardness in each of the words and in the totality of them on the slick pages. He looked for the word "anomie" as for a friend he could return to but did not come upon it until question fifty of the hundred that the professor had laid out as barriers to his future. The words so unwelcoming and harshly aligned against him. As always, he began to guess.

He had a friend of sorts in the same class. Her name was Jenna Rosen. A girl with a sweet smile and pleasant manner toward him. Her sister attended Barnard College. Jenna carried no shame that Luther could see that she should be at the City College of New York and not some Seven Sisters college, like her sister. And Luther could understand why. She had the necessities of life, an unassuming confidence in her own abilities. That was impressed upon Luther when, a week later, the test results were given. Jenna had received a perfect score, while Luther answered correctly on only sixty of the questions. That's what happened when you had a mind that didn't stay on the page, no matter how much speed you took, or had a mind with holes in it, so that the facts fell out as soon as they came in. But he harbored no resentment against Jenna. He was just in awe of her genetic disposition toward excellence, not only in herself but in others.

On the subject of minds, he received a letter that very day, and from none other than Marcia Wolf.

It looks like you have spaghetti for a brain. I should have known things wouldn't work out between us. The circumstances in which we met at that horrible party were not great and should have been an indicator of your bias toward bad behavior. Perhaps what happened served me right for walking out on Fred. Still, there was no reason to expect that it would reach the point where you would question me closely about my father's office and the amounts of money he keeps in his safe, just as there was no reason to believe it would end as it did in that wretched room in that seedy hotel with you drunk and stoned and insulting me in the presence of my best friend, who says you are obviously a sick, neurotic person. Are you? You can seem so normal and then you have a few beers and take a few tokes and things come out of your mouth. My girlfriend Edeline says you're a complete loser. And yet I was not nearly so afraid of you as I am of my father. Believe me when I say he is capable of calculated violence. Rather, believe him when he says that if you ever get in touch with me again, he will carry out his threat to have someone hurt you. You were very lucky that night he came to your room and rescued me. Daddy knows people. I do love you still, but you don't belong to anyone. You're the remotest person I have ever seen. Please don't try to get in touch with me, as I don't want to see you have to die.

Luther shuddered, imagining a brutal beating, dismemberment, being tossed in the East River in a pair of cement shoes, all manner of mayhem committed on his person. She didn't have all her facts right, but that was OK. He had behaved badly. That was all he needed to know, and to stay away, just as she said. In fact, he did see her some days later, but from afar, coming out of the End Bar with some guy wearing a Columbia windbreaker. A hunter in her own right she was.

Chapter 13

Luther came to have reason to reassess Mr. Van Dine's appearance at the door. Almost a week had passed since Mona's father took her away with him. Was it possible he and Luther hadn't had a meeting of the minds, that they hadn't recognized each other's sphere of influence? Was the old man holding on when he was supposed to be letting go? Was Mona too much in his image for him to do otherwise? Would war be the inevitable outcome? Or was Mr. Van Dine's victory sealed that very night?

He could barely meet the day. His low grade on the sociology exam brought anew the horror of being inadequate in mind as well as body, how first he could not do the sine of the curve in the hardbound calculus book and now he could not do the texts or the soft covers of the liberal arts south campus either, and even to be a poet you had to be able to do the math of the meter. He lay back down for some minutes with his breath his companion.

When he could, he got up and went about the gray day. Smiling faces, gay voices, the grit of the subway, the old campus buildings—every sight and sound seemed to bring pain. He sat in a corner at the rear of Finley Cafeteria that afternoon bearing witness to the socializing ability of students chatting at the other tables. And then, to his shock, Mona entered the cafeteria, its graffiti-covered walls resembling the outside of a New York City subway car. Her arrival elicited instant panic; she must not see him in such a state of vulnerability. She was not alone but with another beacon of blondness, a tall boy with the look of a Viking warrior.

It was all too much. Luther fled out the back door and past the cluster of kids smoking weed in the stairwell, not relaxing until he was far from the campus because no one should witness him in his emotional nakedness like that, and certainly not Mona Van Dine. Another second in that cafeteria and she would have seen him all skin and bones in his stark nakedness. Aryan handsomeness had savagely beaten him. No way could he defeat someone with his godlike features. Now was all temptation to pick up the phone and call Mona and go down the road to fatal weakness and dependency gone. He would not become a bug stuck on flypaper. Back in his room, he returned to bed and his breath. Soon there came a knock at the door.

"It's me, Mona."

Though she had only come to put the hammer to him definitively, he let her in.

"Why did you disappear from the cafeteria this afternoon?"

"I just felt the need to go." He had been caught. The shame was flooding through him now.

"You looked right at me," she said, seeming to ignore his excuse.

"You were with somebody."

"With somebody? I was with Greg. We had cut class together."

"I guess I had misunderstood."

"I'm allowed to have friends."

"Sure you are," he said reflexively, stung by what sounded like a reproach. He was digging a hole for himself. Saying anything more would only dig the hole deeper and reveal his jealous, hopelessly insecure nature.

He was uneasy with her in the room now. She was looking at him differently. He could feel it.

"Are those your books?" she asked, staring at the small stack on the dresser.

"Some of them," he said, not wanting her to examine them and think his college life was such meager fare. He especially didn't want her to go through his notebook and see his inconsistent, hard-to-read handwriting in the lined pages as he tried to record the words that flowed from the lips of bored professors living for their paychecks.

"Sociology? Political science?" she asked, having gotten up to look at the texts. "You should be taking literature courses. You're my Russian poet."

She wanted him to be better than he was. It wouldn't do to tell her that poli sci and soc., to use the gross abbreviations, were a middle ground between the masculine hard sciences and the effeteness of poetry, and that he could only come to literature when he had been fully beaten. He couldn't tell her that he had to put some meat on his bones if he wanted to live strong.

In the silence that followed, she touched him, and they went where talking was not needed. Afterward she took from her bag a round blue plastic case, removed a tiny white pill from its bed of foil and swallowed it before snapping the case shut again.

Elinore was entering the building as they were leaving. Happy to be seen in the company of blondness, Luther smiled and said hello, but Elinore just brushed past.

"Who's that?" Mona asked, following Elinore with her eyes.

"Everywhere you go, there are delegations of the righteous," Luther said.

"What?"

He told her again about Marcia and the party and the fallout from it, including how Fred threatened to clobber him and how some weeks later Marcia's father actually did. He said he had renegade status and that it was okay with him.

"He got what he had coming to him for being a bore," Mona said, surprising him once more with her response.

They walked south along the bridle path in Riverside Park. The sun was still up and west of the Hudson River. A Circle Line boat was making its way north past a freighter toward the George Washington Bridge. A lifetime New Yorker, Luther had never been on the Circle Line. For that matter, he had never been to the top of the Empire State Building.

"I didn't tell you, but I have a boyfriend. His name is Jeff. But I'm going to break off with him," Mona said.

"Why do you want to do that?" Luther asked, as if the matter did not involve him and to establish, in the aftermath of his flight from the cafeteria that afternoon, that he was sophisticated and understanding of complicated arrangements.

Mona explained that Jeff was an aspiring actor living in an East Village railroad flat, a 24-year-old who worked a day job.

"He writes sappy songs and goes around to bars and clubs with his guitar and sings them. The last time I saw him he threw me out."

"Why?"

"I made fun of one of his songs and his singing and he didn't like that very much."

Luther couldn't find a way to support her disparagement. Jeff didn't sound like any more of a dud than Marcia's date Fred. If anything, he sounded capable and brave, like someone with ambition and direction. To add to her case, Mona said that Jeff was tied to his aging, sick mother, and torn between making a career for himself and going back home to Pennsylvania to help her. Just hearing Jeff's dilemma aroused pain in Luther. He knew what mother love was. He had a mother of his own.

"Maybe you'll change your mind. And even if you choose not to see Jeff, you should go out with other people, don't you think?"

They sat on the steps of the Soldiers' and Sailors' Monument, a cylinder of white limestone rising several stories. Across the way was her block-length building, cream-colored and gracefully following the curving street, with trimmed hedges bordering it. Along the side street a UPS truck was double-parked. The brown-uniformed driver shuttled to and from the lobby with armloads of parcels. Kids were skateboarding on the raised terrace in front of the monument, trying to negotiate the stairs and land upright on the pavement below without breaking an ankle. A jarring, ugly sound as the wheels of the board struck the pavement.

Luther watched as a man in khaki slacks passed by with a leashed golden retriever. He was wearing penny loafers without socks and a blue dress shirt unbuttoned at the top and looking out at the world through horn-rimmed glasses.

"He looks smart, like he went to Yale," Luther said, as the man passed.

"I'll bet he's not half as smart as you," Mona replied.

Luther shuddered at her failure to grasp the reality. "You're way wrong about that," he said.

As if she hadn't heard him, she said, "You know, I told Mommy and Daddy all about you. They said you sound really interesting. Someday soon you'll come up and meet them."

She really didn't know, he thought. She really didn't

He wondered if the wave of fear her words evoked was palpable. No matter. Introduction to her family was a line he would never cross. He knew where he belonged and didn't.

In a time some years before he had found himself in that building, in the ground floor apartment where Nancy Becker and her younger sister Pam lived with their parents. How he had gotten there he could not recall. Luke was present, as were other friends of his from school. In their company, Luther had felt dirty and from another world, in which kids didn't meet in beautiful apartments but on stoops or in the parks or on street corners. He remembered Luke introducing him with a smile. He remembered too a feeling of shame, of being unable to speak, and of leaving soon afterward, abashed and covering his ears in a futile attempt to block out the thoughts in his own head.

Those high school years of Luke's in which he talked incessantly about Nancy Becker. Nancy so smart. Nancy so pretty. How in eighth grade, when she had wire on her teeth, Luke knew she would be beautiful, as if he had discovered her. As if he had nothing but Nancy, and Luther thinking even then that he didn't have her either.

Chapter 14

On the seventh-floor landing Luther found his mother the next afternoon leaning down into the laundry cart, a big red wooden box on castors. He watched as she came up with a load of sheets and pillowcases. Such big arms her short-sleeved blouse exposed, like some brawny baseball players showed off by wearing sleeveless uniform tops. Each week she set aside time for the distribution of linens and towels to the tenants. He didn't let it bother him that she had this humble task, or that she spent time in the basement washing these same items. Why shouldn't she have things to do that she knew she could perform and that made her feel good, just as he had down at the post office slotting letters in the box scheme. Everyone should have things in their day that could make them feel good. Anyway, she was one with the earth she walked. Did she not say, with great pride, like the farm girl she had been, "I'm not afraid of a little dirt, not like some of the women in this building?" Work was honorable. It separated her from those who didn't work, not only the older women living in the building but those men and women in the welfare hotel down the block, of whom she also said, "I work. Why shouldn't they?" seeing only the idleness and intermittent conflagrations and not the more hidden circumstances within and without that kept them where they were. The building had Africans, some in dashikis, and other Third World men and women but only several American-born Negroes, middle-aged and female. "We cannot have their violence," his mother said. "We cannot have that." Violence was like fire. It could quickly spread. Violence was fire. It was for those who had never witnessed the flames to say otherwise.

"Were you looking for me, Luther?"

"I just wanted to say hello." It was a simple truth. To be all right with himself he needed to be all right with her.

"Come with me," she said.

He followed her down a long hallway. Each of the floors had four such compartments, within which there were six or seven rooms. All of the rooms came with a fridge and a stove and some had a bathroom. For all other rooms there was a public bathroom in each compartment. She let herself into room 7B3 with a master key on her giant ring and deposited the linens on the bed. The dirty floor, the mildewed piece of carpet, the old and stained mattress on the stripped bed distressed him. And everywhere the roaches and the lingering smell of spray from the nozzles of the canister on wheels employed to battle them. Whatever the kill count, the roaches inevitably came back in force. A blight was on the whole building—leaky pipes, old wiring, rotting window frames. Since he could remember he had wanted to get away and have a room of his own and so he did, even if the room was smaller and as depressing as the one in which he now stood.

"I want you to do something for me. I want you to run on your long legs up to the hospital to visit with your sister Naomi. She would so much like to see you and needs your support."

He began to protest. She was always rubbing his face in something that had nothing to do with him, family members who were best left to die so he could be free. He could feel the soreness, the resistance, rising. But he would go anyway. Once she told him, what choice did he have?

Minutes later he stood on the corner of Amsterdam Avenue staring back across the street at the new residence that had been built for physicians. Gone was Funelli's grocery, with its half-empty shelves and wilted produce. An after-school hangout it had been. Gone too were the tenements and his Irish friends who had lived in them: Sean and Scully, in his red and white LaSalle High School cardigan, and all the rest. *"Let me cop a smoke, man."* The words came to his ears and with it the memory of the pavement dotted with tiny islands of their spit. Now they were on the warships of Uncle Sam or flying fighter aircraft or on the ground somewhere in Southeast Asia. They were gone and he was still there.

A uniformed guard slouched at his desk chair, his billed hat pushed up on his big head. He handed Luther a jumbo-sized plastic pass with the number 14. It seemed such a small job for a man with so powerful a physique, Luther thought, staring into the smoldering eyes in his big black face. Feeling the charge from the man's anger in his whole being, Luther felt compelled to offer him an improvement plan.

"If ever you're looking for a change in your employment, why not come and work for the post office? All you need to do is take a simple test. Even I passed it. And the pay is pretty good."

But the guard was not in a receptive mood. "Get away from me with your stupid-assed white bullshit," he said, and Luther promptly obeyed.

On the tenth floor he rang the buzzer next to the locked metal door. After a minute standing in the cramped space outside the elevator he rang a second time. Soon a woman's doughy face filled the small square chicken-wire window set in the door. Luther did peek-a-boo behind the big plastic pass. Two locks turned emphatically and the door opened.

"This is no place to be fooling around, son. There are some very sick people here. Who have you come to see?" the attendant said, laying her solemnity on him like a heavy blanket.

"Her name is Naomi and she has a big mouth and never shuts up. She thinks she's Judy Garland but can't carry a tune. And she has a long history of mistreating me."

"She's down there in the common room. You behave yourself with her now."

Patients in seersucker robes and slippers did their medicated shuffle to and fro along the wide hallway, with expressions of unsmiling dullness, as if they did not know from where they had come or have any thought as to where they could ever hope to go. Most had a paleness that came from exposure to only a fluorescent sun. The older ones had papery skin. He supposed the hospital would say their listlessness was a step up from the despair that had presumably brought them there.

Entering the solarium Luther saw a black-haired woman singing a dreadful rendition of "The Man Who Got Away" for a baldheaded man sitting in a pastel chair. The man had his hands clasped in his lap as he stared up at her with an expression of devotion. Seeing Luther, she stopped, though he had a sense that his presence was only an excuse. Naomi wasn't too good with remembering lyrics.

He didn't kiss her. They never kissed or even touched, unless it was her hand across his face.

"Luther, I want you to meet Mr. Horace Valparonicka. Horace and I have been going steady since I got here. Horace is a man of influence and power, an East Coast talent agent who also has offices in Hollywood and Palm Springs. He tells me that he has had lunch in all fifty states, including South Dakota. Horace has been responsible for the rise of many young and not so young prolifically talented sopranos, particularly those who have been overlooked in the vulgar and cheap market that exists today."

Luther stared at Horace's concave chest and the hairs growing out of his ears and the ruins he glimpsed inside his slack mouth.

"Nice to meet you," Luther said, but Horace didn't respond. In fact, he got up and wandered away, but not before showing off some of his talent scout etiquette with a bow.

"Horace says he can help me. He says I'll be his special project."

"Can Horace help himself?"

"You have a cruel mouth."

"Not as cruel as your hand."

"Little Svenska pojka deserved the slaps he got."

Svenska pojka, or Swedish boy. So his mother had called him when he was a child and blond, fairer than his siblings.

"I brought you these," Luther said, handing her a couple of packs of Salems.

The windows had heavy screens on them and signs were posted forbidding visitors to bring in bottles or sharp objects. A game show was playing on the cantilevered TV. The host wore a bowtie and jacket and had a round face full of cheer. The patients stared up at the screen for a minute or two and then would wander off only to return. The thing you noticed was their eyes, the film of deadness that the medications induced. There was no light in his sister's eyes either.

"Are you going to be a gentleman and light my cigarette?"

Luther did as she asked. She pulled on the Salem and blew a cloud of smoke his way.

"I see you looking down at him, Luther, but he's an award-winning man. And you have no awards. You have only the smell of failure on you. The whole family does, everyone but Mommy, and she doesn't because she has God and doesn't care about the world."

"Whatever you say," Luther replied.

"Look me in the eyes. What do you see?"

"I see my sister sitting in a molded plastic chair and wearing a hospital gown."

Naomi blew another slow, steady stream of smoke into his face. He watched her wet her cracked lips with a whitish tongue.

"Listen to me, Luther. Listen to me."

He cupped his ears to show he was.

"Remember when you took that money from Mommy's pocketbook? I asked you what you had in your hand and you said, 'Nothing'? And then I said to you, 'You can tell me, Luther. I won't breathe a word.' I used Mommy's expression. I said to you, 'Give me the money, Luther. I know you've been in her bag.' And you opened your hand, as if you had no choice. That's because I had power over you and I'll have that power for the rest of your days. That's because I'm your big sister."

They smoked in silence. A shy old black man with a missing front tooth and a big white guy with a tremor came over and asked for cigarettes. "Remember who gave you these," Naomi said and winked as she handed out the weeds.

Once upon a time she had a hard, jewel-like beauty, her big eyes sparkling like obsidian glass and shapely features manifesting in her older sister body. But that was once upon a time; the years had brought pharmaceutical bloat.

She lived in room 9C3 with her husband Chuck. He was a drunk and she was a pill head. They had been living rent-free and without jobs for years. She went away to institutions the way some people packed their bag and took a trip. This ward, and wards like it, were her vacation from the life she didn't have. Rockland State, Bellevue—she had been in a number of them, some more than once.

This last time she had mixed alcohol with sedatives and passed out in the lobby in her stained nightgown. It was not the first time an ambulance had come for her.

Mrs. Garatdjian said the only thing wrong with Naomi was the psychiatrists who kept giving her pills. Luther didn't know about that, but he did see his sister as more histrionic than crazy and tried to treat her as a peripheral fact of his existence. He remembered feeling numb with fear that time she went out on the ninth floor ledge that she would fall or jump to the unyielding sidewalk. His capacity for love and compassion when it came to her were lacking. His sister was a source of shame and cause for anger and resentment. His earliest memory was of her calling him to her with a smile. Such love he had felt in that moment only to be met with the hard flatness of her open hand on his cheek even as she maintained her smile. She saying, "This is what you get for being a flathead Svenska pojka. This is all you will ever get for being that."

Their sister Rachel arrived. She wore wraparound sunglasses and her hennaed hair reminded him of car fins the way it was swept back on both sides of her head.

"Hello, Rachel, sister of mine," Naomi droned. "You remember Luther, don't you, our loving brother? He's hard to recognize with all that hair. Don't you remember how Mommy used to say he had all the luck to have such curly hair, and that it belonged on a girl?"

"Don't be silly, Naomi. Luther is a girl."

Luther stared at his sister Rachel. Her face was all done up in mascara and lipstick.

"No, seriously, Luther, it does become you. It hides the shape of your head. No one should have to go around with a head like that. Little Squarehead. Little Blockhead. Little Flathead." Naomi went through the litany of his childhood names. "Do you remember how relieved Mommy was when Svenska got a girlfriend back in high school, Rachel? She was worried about you, Svenska. She thought you might be homosexual. I still think you are. That's all right with Rachel and me. We'll love you anyway, even if you do go to hell."

Luther said his goodbye and headed for the exit. He could say he was done with them for good, but it was a resolve without conviction.

Chapter 15

He had a responsibility to give an accounting of his older sisters' lives. Why he did not know, other than that they were of his same blood and walked the earth for all of the time he was on it. They had to be seen as they were, as he did too. Posterity had to know that they had been here, and the time they lived in.

An early memory was of Naomi singing "Over the Rainbow" and "I'm Gonna Wash That Man Right Out of My Hair" and other songs for which she had the sheet music from the forbidden world beyond the Pentecostal church where the family worshipped. Rachel would accompany her on the upright in their parents' bedroom. They were messengers of hope with their musicality that he would not forever be bound to the bleakness and dread inspired by the hellfire and brimstone sermons of Pastor Horvath and his denunciations of worldliness. Or when they announced that they would be going out to see a movie, he imagined the same freedom for himself some day. For as often as his mother would say, "This world has nothing that I want," the world was precisely what he wanted.

Rachel was a year or two younger than Naomi. He could never quite remember. Along with Hannah, his oldest sister, the three of them were, in his mind, the first set of children, separated from Luke and Vera and himself by years and years. Those brawls they had with Hannah. "Tear her hair out, Rachel… Claw the bitch's eyes out, Naomi." And Hannah screaming "I'll kill you two witches." All of it something other than the baby-voiced Margie *on My Little Margie* or daffy Lucy Arnez on *I Love Lucy.*

The entire floor of Rachel's room a sea of books, many of them open. His shock as a child on seeing the chaos.

Learning that she had to be kept away from him when he was still an infant. A shock that was too.

And Luke telling him of shopping with Rachel at Macy's and how she dug her nails into his hands and when he cried out told him to shut up if he didn't want even worse.

Or the time Rachel asked him what he wanted to be when he grew up, and he said, "I want to be a skin diver," because he had seen Lloyd Nolan on TV in *Sea World,* and she said to him, "Aren't all men skin divers?" causing him shame even though he didn't know what she meant.

And Idlewild Airport, before it was renamed John F. Kennedy Airport. He had gone there with her and Naomi. He didn't remember how. He and Rachel had watched Naomi walk across the tarmac to the plane that would fly her to Detroit, where she would meet her fiancé Chuck's family.

Her brown hair in a single long braid.

And the books she would carry cradled against her chest as she climbed the stairs to their second floor apartment.

He felt no animosity toward Rachel. She had left home. She had gotten away while Hannah and Naomi remained tethered to the building. A lodestar she had been with her scholarship to Vassar College, a stellar institution somewhere to the north that he could hold onto in the midst of the failure in and around him. It had been a point of pride, and anger, for Rachel to be self-sufficient and all on her own. Her first Christmas home from college his mother went to the door to greet her and Rachel shoved her backward into the Christmas tree. The sight of the toppled tree and his mother sprawled atop the gifts had his enraged father chasing Rachel from the apartment in his undershirt, his smacking hand held high with annihilation his intent. Luther and Vera crying, vowing to be perfect for their mother, to make up for what all the others weren't giving her.

What had gone wrong he couldn't say. She had left college short of graduation. Her junior year she had spent at Barnard. That was magical too, a world of excellence secluded from Broadway by a wooden wall painted forest green. Only the very brightest could go there. As a rite of spring, the men of Columbia would gather below the Barnard dormitory and beseech the women of the college for their undergarments. But Rachel did not live in a dormitory. She was unto herself by now.

There was, for a brief time, a boyfriend. Rachel had transferred so she could be close to him. Luther had seen her crying in their mother's arms in the lobby. She just wept and wept. Naomi said that the boy had left her.

In that year Rachel took Luther by the hand and walked with him down Broadway. No nails were digging into him. She had an overdue paper to deliver to a professor at his apartment. Maybe the holiday season had come and no professors were to be found on the campus. For Luther it was beyond wonderful that he should be on this walk with his sister, following the curve of Broadway to their destination. He couldn't say what street they turned west on or what building they entered or the floor. That was lost to him. All he could remember was that a man came to the door and took Rachel's paper and then closed the door.

Luther could not remember another time he had been alone with Rachel outside the family's apartment, except for Idlewild, and so the occasion remained special, even if he didn't understand why, on that night, she had chosen to allow him to be with her.

She went back to Vassar College for her senior year, but she left a month before graduating. Naomi said Rachel's pride was stung that she would not be graduating with honors. Naomi said she was also pained that other girls were getting pinned and she was not and that she was still grieving the man who got away.

The building may have been calling to her, but she did not go to it. She found a furnished room in another SRO, and paid her way working for CBS-TV. That was the world, too, like Vassar before it. Her job was to check the commercials before they aired. Something to do with the accuracy of the words. But there were no words, no written words, only those that were spoken. He wasn't sure. But she was important. She had a place out there. She did not have to inhabit a room in the family building, as Naomi was doing.

Sometimes Luther would see her, at the Chock Full O'Nuts, on One Hundred Sixteenth Street and Broadway. She would go there for their sugar doughnuts and heavenly coffee and nutted cheese sandwiches, and on Fridays for their clam chowder soup and tuna fish sandwiches. Always she was by herself, as she was when he happened to see her on the street. She had a new face and new hair. Gone was the braid and the scrubbed face. She now wore lipstick and applied mascara.

Luther's mother said Naomi was a bad influence on Rachel. She said Naomi supplied her with pills and worked hard to lead her astray. She said Naomi had a demon in her seeking to violate Rachel's innocence. She said that, when still a child, Rachel would stand behind her as she prepared meals in the kitchen and follow her about. She said there was strangeness in Rachel's persistence and what was a mother to do about such a thing, when she as a mother had the cares of the world upon her?

Luther pondered these things in ways that took him around in circles, as if a guiding hand was absent to lift the needle from the record in his head.

About Naomi and her name calling and betrayals and venture out onto the ledge Luther had already spoken. About her beneficence he had not said a word. He wanted it entered in the record of life that Naomi remonstrated with a building worker, Luigi Salvatore, for banging Luther on the head with a frying pan, this after Luther had willfully sat in a newly upholstered chair Luigi had expressly told him not to sit in. Naomi saying, "How dare you hit a child like that? How dare you?" Because strong violence was not in her. It did not go with who she was.

Naomi married Charles "Chuck" Chuckley shortly after her flight from Idlewild Airport to Detroit. The wedding took place in Manhattan. Luther, still a child, was not asked to be present. For some reason, he felt that he was missing out on something beyond the church, even if the wedding was called holy matrimony.

Charles "Chuck" Chuckley freely expressed gravel-voiced grievance against all those who had thwarted him in life, including the witch who had driven him out of the PhD program in chemistry at Columbia University, which he was attending on the GI Bill after service in the army in World War II. His last year in uniform he had spent in the French countryside, where he discovered the wines of the region. While a tenant in the building, he met Naomi. The sixteen years he had on her made no difference. Naomi had found her love, a war hero, former police officer, and now a PhD candidate at a renowned university, as he presented himself.

Five years later a daughter, Jeanne, was born. Staring down at her on the living room sofa in the family's apartment, Luther felt no joy. Jeanne was a beautiful baby, but her parents were not so beautiful. There had been several stays in psychiatric wards of hospitals for Naomi, and Chuck had dropped out of the doctoral program. Unable to support himself let alone Naomi and their child, he lived rent-free with Naomi in the building. To earn his way, he became the night watchman. Several nights a week he sat in a chair in the lobby, a bottle of cheap screw-top wine on the floor beside him. Often he would be passed out drunk and snoring. Those times when he was conscious he would glare and growl at the late arriving tenants. His manner was obnoxious enough that one night Luther's father chased him from the apartment and hurled a telephone book at his fleeing bulk when he couldn't quite catch up.

Concerned about Chuck's drinking and remembering the fate of her own father, Mrs. Garatdjian sent Luther to Dr. Baum, who had an office in the building across the street, which Luther thought of as the house of order because it had a doorman and a beautiful lobby and big apartments and a peaceful ambience.

"My mother wants to know if there is anything you can give him for his drinking," Luther said.

"Have you tried arsenic?" Dr. Baum answered, with amusement on his round and catlike face, as he knew Chuck Chuckley and the whole family. He had made house calls on Naomi and Rachel, arriving with black bag in hand, and they spoke of those visits with titillation in their voices, a fact that embarrassed Luther, because in so doing they were suggesting that they meant more to Dr. Baum than any Garatdjian possibly could.

Naomi had wanted to be a singer. She was seeking a larger stage than their parents' bedroom with Rachel accompanying her on the upright. Sometimes she gave her voice to God, singing hymns like "Rock of Ages" and "In the Garden" at the tabernacle in a voice that could not sustain itself. Often she would fumble the lyrics. But her heart was with Judy Garland. She had seen *Meet Me in St. Louis* and *The Wizard of Oz.* But she did not get to the silver screen or the white lights of Broadway. She got to sing while drugged in the lobby in a voice that cracked and broke.

Luther couldn't say much more about his sisters Naomi and Rachel as they were then. The store of memories was just not there. Though not entirely. One thing Naomi had done was to leave her daughter, Jeanne, more and more in the care of Mrs. Garatdjian because she and Chuck were getting up later and later in the day and the room they had was small and not conducive to raising a child in. So Jeanne came to live in the family apartment. She was a plump and sullen little girl. Often Luther saw her without seeing her, or if he did, it was with some resentment that she was there at all, as she was a manifestation of the spreading unmanageability of her parents' lives. Luther saw both of them in the girl and that was all the more reason not to like her. As a child he had been after his mother to get Hannah and Naomi out of the building and all his mother had done was put her chuckle on him, saying he didn't know what it was to have children. And now, instead of going away, Naomi had brought a child into the world and passed her off on the family.

Many were the times that Luther submitted his bill of indictment, accusing Naomi and Hannah, in particular, of crimes against humanity. Was it not a profound betrayal for an older sister—Naomi—to coax from him when he was still a child that he had taken money from his mother's pocketbook and then, after swearing that she wouldn't, run to his mother and tell her of his thievery? Did it not rank up there with calling him across the room with a big smile and then smacking him hard across his face? Were there not numerous other charges to bring? How many were the times he had come before his mother with these charges only to experience her chuckle? Was justice ever to be found?

Luther could say all he wanted about Naomi, let alone his other older sisters, but Naomi had her own bill of indictment, and it contained only one accusation. "You are cold and cruel and unfeeling. You have no heart," she said, when he screamed at her that he only wished she and Chuck would go away and never come back.

There were others he had to deal with, but that was for another time. It was for him to return to his life as it was unfolding, not as it had been in that murky past.

Chapter 16

As Luther and Mona were crossing Broadway one afternoon, the light turned against them and they paused on the island in the middle of the avenue. When Luther looked to his left, he saw his father sitting on a bench. His father's head was bowed and his eyes closed. Perhaps he was praying, or just resting. Luther couldn't be sure. In front of him was a walker. After his release from the hospital, his father had been fitted with a prosthesis and the walker would provide the support he needed to avoid a fall. As if his father sensed Luther's presence, he raised his head and opened his eyes and smiled. Luther had time to rearrange his face so his father would not see his shock and embarrassment at the chance encounter.

"My good son," his father said, his face wet with tears. Seeing Luther's discomfort, he went on. "These are tears of joy, not sadness. It is a precious, precious thing to live in the Christ Jesus and to be bathed in his love, my son."

"This is my friend Mona," Luther said, unable to respond to his father's enthusiasm for the Lord. His father turned to Mona, maintaining his smile, but now it seemed more a smile of abashment. "Yes. Hello," he could only manage to say.

"Hi," she said, with what seemed a cold lack of interest. Luther felt hurt by her indifference. She hadn't even offered a smile. His father didn't even exist for her. He was no more interesting than any other stranger on the street. Though he said nothing, it was something to remember.

The chance meeting was brief, and not the only one that afternoon. In crossing to the west side of Broadway, Luther ran into his brother Luke as he was heading home with a bag of groceries. Unlike Mr. Garatdjian, Luke was not abashed at all in the presence of Mona. If anything, he seemed excessively admiring.

"You guys should come on up. Mona can check out my Honda motorcycle. It's fantastic. Six hundred fifty cc's. Can go from zero to sixty just like that," he said, snapping his fingers. "Come on, man," he went on, seeing Luther's hesitation. No mention of Maureen or the baby on the way. Just his stupid metal steed. A motorcycle built for a family of three, or for some lone woman he met while out cruising and enticed onto his buddy seat? But it was his nature to be tied to things. The Lionel trains of their childhood, the drums, the shortwave radio, the ten-speed, the bb gun, the hi-fi equipment, the cameras. And now the bike. The hard stuff of life. The stuff where the power was. Luther living in reaction to his brother. In some ways, anyway.

Maureen was showing. She was big with child.

"What's the matter? You've never seen a pregnant woman before?" she said to Mona, whose face had, in fact, registered some surprise. Maureen, from One Hundred Ninth Street and Julia Richman High School, whose father was an all day, all week bar man, a beer and scotch man getting his load on. There were pockets of Irish throughout the neighborhood. They had their hardness, their vitality, their fists, their tongues.

"Sure," Mona said.

"It could happen to you. But not if you stick around him." Maureen jerked her thumb in the direction of Luther.

"Hey. Hey," Luke said, unable to suppress a grin. Maureen's swollen belly an indicator of his potency. The awestruck pride he expressed when he first told Luther of her pregnancy. Luke the one trying to kick himself free of the bars of the crib as a child. Luther in some way his crib, trying to contain him. His younger older brother.

"Hey hey what? Mona should know what she's getting into. No false advertising. Right, Luther?" Maureen went on.

"Sure. Whatever you say," Luther replied, restraining himself from saying that Maureen would see what she had gotten into soon enough. Thinking, with that crafty smile of hers, that she had, at age eighteen, set up her life forever with the shotgun wedding her father had arranged. Their marriage as fated for obsolescence as the washer and drier she dreamed of cramming into the tiny penthouse space. If she hated him for anything, it was because he had a less rosy view of her future with Luke.

"Let's go out on the roof. I'll show Mona my thing. You know, my steed."

Luther didn't need the clarification to know what Luke meant.

"Another time," he said, and led Mona away.

Chapter 17

Mona had a younger sister, Lenore, of whom she was afraid. So she confessed to Luther. Lenore was a straight A student at a boarding school in Vermont, but it was her social ability, the great number of friends she attracted to her, that concerned Mona.

"If she ever moves back home, I have no choice but to move out," she said, desperation in her voice equal to that which Luther heard the night her father appeared at Luther's rooming house door. Quite simply, she could not bear for this sister to see her aloneness. She said her sister was dark and mysterious, and had won the love of an Adonis of a boy whose father raised Kentucky bluegrass-fed horses.

Luther heard this fear about her sister and said nothing. It wouldn't do for Mona to guess what he was thinking and feeling. She mustn't know that already there was movement in his mind in this world without restraints in which he now lived, and maybe always had, toward this dark and magical sister. Mona had given him new territory to enter, and within, he was wild with anticipation.

CCNY was a subway school. There were a few fraternities, mainly Jewish, on the north campus, but, as with Queens College, Luther essentially came and went without connection. That changed one afternoon as he sat in Finley Cafeteria next to a young man he had just introduced himself to, saying he had seen him before, around Morningside Heights and on the basketball court in Riverside Park. He remembered him as quick to the basket and with amazing spring in his legs. The young man was pleased that Luther should remember. His name was Tony Pascual. Yes, he played basketball. He had been a sub on the Power Memorial High School team with Lew Alcindor. No, he didn't play anymore. He was saving himself for academics. His plan was to enroll in the Columbia University School of Business after graduation. Luther liked him. There was a boyishness in his freckled face. He was warm, approachable, and smiled easily. Luther had made a sort of friend.

The mention of Power Memorial and Lew Alcindor put Tony in a mythical realm. Tony had played, or at least sat on the bench as a scrub, among those who could put their elbows on top of the backboard on a team ranked number one in the entire country, never mind the state, whereas Luther had starred for a high school team that would suit up any boy who had all his limbs.

A week later Tony said that he had a room available in his apartment. Forty bucks a month plus gas and electric and the telephone.

"I've freed it up. My moms is out. She doesn't belong there anymore. I'm old enough to be on my own now. Besides, she promised, and a promise *is* a promise."

The apartment was on One Hundred Eighteenth Street and Amsterdam, an avenue on a slant, cars and trucks racing down to Harlem valley or powering uphill. Luther had a clear picture in his mind of the area, which had its share of heartbreak structures capable of triggering potent recall: the drugstore on the corner of 120th Street where he could not sit at the soda fountain without, in any season, sensing in a way that made him ache, a sun-filled paradise that he had once known but which was now lost to him, where whatever of great moment had occurred danced teasingly beyond his memory's ability for retrieval except to sense it as the renewed promise of luminous tropical days and lush nights and the occasional rain shower and men in Hawaiian shirts and the presence of a family who loved him and allowed him to be a child; the stationery store up the block that offered a world of quiet afternoon safety, its shelves stocked with spiral notebooks and fountain pens under glass connecting him with his childhood—the smell of a new leather book bag and the hope that this time, on those ruled pages, he would get everything just right. That much came to him half listening to Tony's gritty reality.

"And she took the bum with her. That was the big thing."

"Bum?" Luther asked, while staring at the wooden Con Ed spool that served as a a coffee table.

"He dared to call himself my stepfather but he's no stepfather. He's just a bum who tried to rob me of my life."

Where were Tony's mother and hated stepfather? Luther wondered. As if Tony could read his mind, he jerked his thumb upward.

"What's that mean?" Luther asked.

"That means they're one flight up, and they'll stay up there if they know what's good for them." Tony punctuated his statement with a loony, gap-toothed smile. Luther could only assume he was expressing joy over his victory in his personal war of independence, strange as that war might be with its reversal of the seeming norm. Was it not for the young man to leave home rather than the parents? But Luther had a sense that Tony's idea of independence had a long history and that it was best to leave the whole matter alone. At the same time it did raise a caution flag.

All Luther had were a couple of bags, loaded onto a dolly, which his mother had permitted him to borrow. Though it was early April now, the day surprised with raw winter coldness. Shivering, he pulled the dolly through the college walk of Columbia University under the watchful eyes of Alma Mater and, behind her, squat Low Library, with its massive dome. The voice he often heard grew loud in his mind, the voice that said he was not good enough to enroll here so he could be part of the sunlight of America and not in its shadow.

The room needed work, but he sanded the floor and applied a double coat of polyurethane; brightened the walls with a coat of off-white paint; purchased an oak office desk for thirty bucks at a used furniture store on Fourteenth Street; and hung new curtains. The apartment wasn't his, but he needed a degree of comfort to settle his mind.

Tony explained things that first week. He said that he was a philosophy major and that his area of study was something called symbolic logic. He pumped his fist and said, "It's real. It's just so real." Luther asked him what was real but Tony wouldn't or couldn't say. "It's too deep, but you know what I'm saying, don't you?"

"I guess so."

"By the time I finish up with business school after college, I'll have a rationalist interpretation of the laws of economics to draw on."

"Great," Luther replied.

Some days later, a rotund older woman showed up at the door. She spoke in great, excitable, Spanish-accented bursts. A stocky man whose sober, intense expression reminded Luther of Teddy Roosevelt stood behind her. "My son has lost all his coconuts. What is it that he cannot leave home like a normal boy? What is all his bullshit? That is what we need to know. Nothing is in the natural order of things with this child."

Luther shared her concern, but a family affair was just that, and once again he cautioned himself to exercise the restraint that Tony's mother couldn't.

"I will tell him you were looking for him."

"Do not even bother. He will only bring his strangeness to our communication," Mrs. Pascual said, and her husband nodded sagely in agreement.

Chapter 18

A man from Luther's past called. Edward had lived in his mother's building, one of the thousands who had arrived only to depart. Blond and from the Midwest and with an expression that appeared slightly demented because of a walleye, he had lived with a beautiful brown-haired woman who, he said, was his wife and with whom Luther had been achingly in love in the loneliness of his nights. While she worked in a midtown office, Edward would sun himself on summer days on the roof in a black bikini brief. Luther knew him as a layabout with an inept criminal mind, Edward having spent the night in the hollow of a settee in the Cathedral of St. John, where he had positioned himself with the idea of stealing all the Anglicans' jewelry from the display cases, an attempt foiled when a guard chose to park himself on the settee through the night listening to his transistor radio.

"Well, old buddy, it's been a long time," Edward said.

"How did you get my number?" Luther asked.

"Oh, I have my sources."

"What do you want?"

"I have a friend I'd like you to meet. I'm sure you'll like her. Many men do like Nora. Nora from Norway is divine."

"That's some word," Luther said.

"What is, darling?"

"Divine."

"Oh, she is flesh and blood. Very much so."

Then it was Vera on the line, saying she wanted to come over with Amory Wooster to see Luther's new lodgings. Luther did not say no, though the thought of Amory setting foot in the ramshackle apartment frightened him beyond his ability to express. He was willing to concede that Amory Wooster was his better. Did any more need to be said than to compare their two colleges? But there was pain in having your ideal self present in the same room with you. It just set off this wounding and debilitating shame that he, Luther, wasn't more than he was. But even if he couldn't change who he was, make himself smarter and more handsome, he could do some tidying up before the visitors arrived.

"Fine. Great. Do it. Maybe having some people over will drive out the stench of him." Tony said, when Luther informed him of the evening gathering. Tony jerked his thumb upward so Luther would know he was talking about the big and stinky enchilada stepfather. Then Tony downed a Coke and crumpled the can.

Edward faithfully delivered Nora the Norwegian that evening and quickly disappeared. If language was a barrier, she communicated just fine with big eyes that promised everything, her short and flimsy dress and fishnet stockings only adding to that promise. She was thin and blond and attractive, a girl who knew her power and what was wanted of her. She eagerly toked on the hash pipe as *Surrealistic Pillow* played, charged urgency in Grace Slick's voice as she sang "Somebody to Love" and Marty Ballin taking them in another direction emotionally with "Today." In this atmosphere of sound and smoke Luther could believe the communication with the beautiful stranger was only deepening.

What followed was beyond his comprehension and control. It was one thing for Vera to emerge from the hallway darkness into the warm light of the living room with Amory Wooster in tow but behind them, inexplicably, came Mona when she was supposed to be with her family for a country weekend. And though Mona looked beautiful in her suede jacket and jeans, he was powerless to leave Nora's side, powerless to forego the exploration of her depths that the evening promised. In a rage at the dilemma that Mona's presence had forced on him and driven by a desire to punish Mona for that dilemma, he drew on the tacit understanding he assumed he had with Nora that she should follow him, his power now on display to the crueler sound of the Stones and "Under My Thumb." One foot was placed in front of the other in a zone of safety from the watchful eyes and they found the darkness of his room where he struggled against any feeling for his action, Nora's body being what he prized more than anything in that moment, she standing between his knees as he sat on the bed running his hands up her legs and beyond. Murderer, murderer, the words screamed in his mind in the room he'd been reserving for Mona. Beyond, there was quiet. Footsteps could be heard in the hallway and the front door opening and closing. And then the lonely sound of those same footsteps in the courtyard leading out to gloomy Amsterdam Avenue. He had done something terrible but it was too big to go near.

Luther turned on the lamp by the bed as Nora slid the straps of her sun dress from her thin shoulders. Her eyes stayed on him scanning for signs of distraction or disappointment as the dress dropped to the floor. There was much to see, the stuff of erotic dreams—Times Square lingerie, a matching bra and panties of black lace with patches of red and a garter belt to hold up her black fishnet stockings. He felt his own thinness in her arms and could only long for what a man with weight and a thick neck and a big endowment could be for her.

In the morning he woke to find her raised up on one elbow, her chin in her hand and her mind set on a fact-finding mission.

"That girl. You know her?"

"What girl?"

"Girl last night. Blond like me. Who else I speak about?"

"I know the girl right here now," Luther said.

"You see her again?" she said, sometime later, as they rode the subway down to the East Village.

"No," he said, though it pained him to say so.

She was staying in an apartment on Avenue B near Tompkins Square Park. The scent of sandalwood incense was everywhere. Her nipples and the outline of her breasts showed in a certain light through the white Indian print top, while from somewhere below came Pigpen and the Grateful Dead with their endless sound.

In the kitchen a cast-iron bathtub stood on claw feet above the creaky floor. Immigrant women had bathed their children in that tub and sent them to their beds in those summers without air conditioning or to sleep on the fire escape. But now Nora was here. In broken English she told him of the continental shuttle between San Francisco and New York she had taken ten times in two years and how she had tripped naked in the Painted Desert and made love at the bottom of the Grand Canyon. She told him of the fever of travel and how it just came over her to go and always there was somebody with the wheels and the money to provide for her and that even in Taos and Boulder, Colorado, there were people being shaped by the experience of smoke so that their brain waves could receive a traveler such as her in a sympathetic fashion. He heard her say that open arms were the answer and that he looked sad and that he did not know how to be a thing just blown about in the wind and maybe he should learn. The worry lines in his face grew deeper but she didn't let him off the hook.

"I think you see that girl again. That I think."

"I am where I am," he blurted, and ran out the door because he knew her heart would not let him in any more.

Not that it ended there. Not that it could, his desire for her being too strong. Within a day he picked up the phone. With much pleading he got her to agree to see him the following weekend. As it approached, he still had not heard from Mona, causing fear that he had gone too far and that she had closed the door for all time. What was he to do? He could not call her—he would only appear weak and penitent and reduce the towering edge that was his only protection from the annihilation sure to follow any perception by her of his neediness.

And yet, on Friday afternoon, the phone rang and an immense light entered his being to hear Mona's subdued, tentative voice.

"Do you still want to see me?"

Just that.

"Yes," he said, though he wanted to say so much more.

"Will you be seeing that woman anymore?"

"I am seeing only myself," he said.

"I've got to go to the country this weekend. Daddy insists. But I'll be over to see you next week." She was saying the past was not an issue and it was time to move on. He felt a wild surge of love for her that brought him close to tears. It was so clear that she was his future from the comfortable way he fit with her. He had brought himself to the edge of the precipice with his recklessness and now he would have to be careful. Now he would have to consolidate.

How perfect. The coast was clear for him to see Nora. He could have his love and his sexual pleasure, too. There was nothing more to ask for in this life. And so Nora did come over that weekend, and there was the hash they smoked and the preliminaries of love-making by candlelight. And then the sound of the doorbell. No, it couldn't be. Now he would be the one to jump out the window, as Mona had wanted to do when her father came for her. It could only be Mona at the door.

"You are expecting someone, baby. Your friend has come, baby?"

"You must believe that cannot be," he said ferociously, even as he dreaded the possibility.

Luke was from neither heaven nor hell but from someplace in between, and there he was when Luther opened the door. Nora had slipped back into her dress and stood right behind him. No, Luke couldn't come in. Not right then. Another time. Luke's mind was not a mystery in that moment. He had a pregnant wife he didn't want and Luther had a pretty blond girl for the night.

"We'll talk another time," Luther said.

"Hey, aren't you going to introduce me?"

"Later," Luther said, and closed the door on Luke's cocky grin.

"He is your friend?" Nora asked.

"My brother. My very aggressive brother," Luther explained.

Shaken by Luke's wolf at the door visit and the fear it activated, he sought to settle down with another joint, which he shared with Nora. After an interlude, they resumed, but the phone began to ring.

"If you want to keep your girlfriend, you'll need to listen to me. I'm not talking about the girl in your apartment."

"What are you talking about?"

"Mona. Your ticket away from all of us. Don't think I don't know what your little plans are all about. I intercepted the girl of your dreams in the courtyard of your building as I was leaving and she was preparing to enter. I'm in the End Bar with her right now. You'd better get over here right now."

Luther hung up the phone.

"What is it, baby?" Nora had been scanning his face.

"It's beyond words," Luther said, as he scrambled into his clothes.

"What's beyond the words, baby? What's beyond them?"

While buckling his belt, Luther went nose to nose with her.

"That some son of a bitch should kidnap a loved one. Even as I speak, there is a mammoth outpouring of support and outraged solidarity. Trust me."

With those words he flew out the door.

Breathless, he pushed through the swinging doors and the Saturday night crowd four-deep at the bar to the jukebox tyranny of Bob Dylan snarling "It Ain't Me, Babe," showering some woman with his cold truth.

He found her seated at a booth. She was not alone. An older man in a wide-lapel jacket and tie was leaning down and whispering to her as Luther slipped into the booth. Luther introduced himself to the man, who turned his watery eyes on him.

"What I care who you are? Don't be talking to a man you don't know." He then turned his attention to Mona. "See you later, Sweetness."

Mona offered the man a shy smile. Luther thought it strange but inevitable that the man could make a crowd part in the way that he did.

"Your brother's here. Did you know that? He's just like you. He drinks so much beer and keeps running to the bathroom. I was on my way into your building as he was coming out. He said you weren't home and that we should come over here and hang around until you got back."

His brother returned with two giant steins of beer in his hand. One he slid over to Mona, the other he downed himself in several long gulps.

"I'm intuitive about women. I can see into their minds and I can pick up little things just from looking at them. Like, I knew that Mona was an artist. I could tell just by looking at her hands. Those are an artist's hands. They're small and strong."

Luther tried not to stare into Luke's grinning, acne-scarred face. He didn't care for the expression that said he was powerful and strong and triumphant. Sooner or later would follow the insecurity and pain that were a truer reflection of how he felt about himself.

Mona excused herself to use the bathroom.

"It's really lucky I ran into her, isn't it? You would have had a real disaster. Tell me I'm not right," Luke whispered, as if she were standing behind them.

It sickened Luther to have Luke crossing the border into his world. It seemed unnatural and frightening to have a brother this near. He couldn't trust Luke. That was the problem. All Luke could induce in him now was gross anxiety.

"Well, thanks for helping out."

"Is the girl still there?"

"Yes," Luther said, reluctantly.

"Look, I'll go over and get her out of the apartment and everything will be cool. How about it?"

Mona returned and Luke stood up so she could squeeze in.

"Thanks for the beer, even if I couldn't finish it," Mona said.

"No problem." Luke reached for the beer and downed it, leaving only suds in the stein.

"Good stuff. See you two lovebirds." He wiped his mouth on his sleeve before taking off.

"What happened? I thought you were coming down on Sunday."

"I couldn't wait. It was too boring being with my family."

"But how did you get here?"

"The same way I always do. I hitchhiked."

"You could get yourself killed doing that," Luther said.

"I just keep my hand on the door handle and if he tries anything I kick him in the balls."

"Great defense strategy," Luther said, genuinely concerned.

"Let's go to my parents' place," she said. "We'll be alone there."

He didn't argue.

Chapter 19

He had come to a crossroads, brought to it by the lust to which he was bound. Nora was a young woman fully uninhibited in the realm of sex, more than willing to go wherever Luther led, or to places he hadn't even imagined. And this he had given up before his exploration had hardly begun. There could be no doubt about that. Luke was a closer. He would put his stamp on her quickly. If Luther couldn't resist Nora's power, how was Luke to do so, wed as he was to a wife he did not want who was soon to give birth to a child he wouldn't have the means, mental or emotional or financial, to take care of?

A painful price he had paid for his freedom, but it was for him to remember that Mona was his freedom, that she, not Nora in her racy undergarments, was his future.

That night, he and Mona had taken the Broadway bus south, away from Nora, away from Luke, away from the End Bar, away from the building. He had lost Nora, and that was painful, but he could only shudder at the thought he might have lost Mona. An hour or two more with Luke in the bar and Mona might have succumbed to his power. Luke might have claimed her for his own. He could have lost both Mona and Nora in one night.

The vestibule was the size of a large room. While she turned on table lamps with big silk shades, he explored. One well decorated room after another with the kind of furniture he saw in the windows of antique stores. A master bedroom for the parents, rooms for each of the children, several bathrooms, and tranquility reigning over all of it. He would be a scholar if he lived there, he thought, in the embrace of an overwhelming sense of peace and security.

She opened the door of the giant refrigerator and removed a platter of sliced roast beef. "It's left over from the dinner Mommy made the other night. I'll make you a sandwich."

He stared at the cut of well done meat. The grass he had smoked had made him ravenous. Still, he said, "Peanut butter is fine." He had crossed one line he had resolved not to by passing through the lobby of the doorman building and entering the immaculate apartment. Didn't he get by on peanut butter and pizza? It was one thing to be hooked on her. It wouldn't do to get hooked on what her family's wealth had to offer as well.

They lay that night in her four-poster bed. Her room looked out on Riverside Park and the Hudson River. Now and then a voice from the street below would rise on the soft spring air. Unable to doze off right away, he stared down from the open window at the Soldiers' and Sailors' Monument below. To the north the George Washington Bridge spanned the Hudson and glittered in the night. Once upon a time he had been one of those park people staring up at the well-kept buildings banking the drive, and now he wasn't. He had been elevated above those desperate, searching souls drawn out into the night and circling the monument. Once again he shuddered thinking about the close call just a few hours earlier and how things could be lost so easily because of the force of his nature. It would never ever happen again. A million miles would he put between him and Luke and all of them.

To the north, near One Hundred Twenty-Fifth Street along the Henry Hudson Parkway, he remembered from his childhood a Chevrolet sign atop the meatpacking plant and how, even then, it seemed to be beckoning him past the narrow confines of his life into the bounty of an America jubilant with song and with cornfields abounding. And now, somehow, he was beginning to realize some of that dream.

When he returned to bed, she was awake. "Are you going to do the same thing to me again?" she asked.

"What's that?"

"You know. Go off with that woman."

"I'm here," Luther said.

"I told my sister Claire what had happened, and she then told Mommy. Mommy says we have a sadomasochistic relationship."

Luther said nothing. If it was true he would find out. And if it was true, what could he do about it anyway?

When daylight came he woke to find his arm thrown across her, as if to keep her from slipping away.

On the walls of her room were framed drawings in bright colors of young men in tight fitting, high-collared shirts with puffed sleeves.

"Did you do these?"

"A couple of years ago."

"I can't draw anything. Just stick figures. Someday I'll get a camera and take photographs. That shouldn't be too hard." He laughed.

Mona made breakfast that morning, and his resolve to hold out against her family and its abundance was further weakened with the smell of bacon frying in the skillet. Forgetting his resolve about the roast beef the night before, he devoured the scrambled eggs and the bacon and four pieces of toast, coated with a smear of butter and jam. What a thing to eat in a pristine kitchen with gleaming appliances and not a roach in sight.

Afterward she led him into a room off the kitchen, actually a set of two narrow rooms with a small bathroom between them.

"What's that smell?"

"Developer and fixer. This is my father's darkroom. It used to be our nanny's room."

Photos of her father covered the walls. In some of them he was nude and proudly aware of his beauty as he stared into the lens. In others he had on a skimpy bathing suit or was fully dressed. There were about twenty photos, from young manhood to the present—lying on a bed of pine needles, standing with legs spread in an open field, against the backdrop of a cascading waterfall. His face in the earlier shots was soft and unlined and weathered and leathery in the more recent ones, but his body remained lean and richly tanned from one decade to the next.

"Your father's a good-looking man."

What he didn't say she said for him. "He has a horse cock," she stated, and did a grotesque pantomime of a man using both hands to keep his huge member from dragging along the ground. Luther laughed nervously as he witnessed the startling transformation.

The vestibule opened onto the living room, large enough to easily accommodate a grand piano. From one of the walnut shelves that lined one wall he pulled a volume bound in buckram. It was a Melville novel, *Typee,* the title stamped in gold on the spine. He ran his hand over the letterpress pages, feeling the bite of the type on the paper. The book had the heft of something valuable. He could so easily slip it out of the apartment. He placed the volume on the marble-topped coffee table and sat on the pale green sofa. The old impulse toward thievery was wild within him. After a while he put the book back on the shelf. The fear of banishment, more than a moral consideration, had swayed him.

Chapter 20

"I'll be right up front with you. I had the best night of my life. You find a woman all alone, deep in her own grief, and you have to help her. You know what I mean?" From a need for understanding did Luke speak to Luther when they chanced to next meet. "I mean, she says she's waiting for you. She looks shook up, you know? The way a person shouldn't have to look. So I ask her if she wants some beer or wine, something to cheer her up, and I go out and get some for us. You know, just something to be sociable. Then we sit around drinking and smoking and listening to some albums. I tell her a little about myself, how Mother comes from Sweden so she'll know that we have a little of Scandinavia in us too. That way she won't feel so uncomfortable and isolated. I'm just trying to help, that's all. You know what I mean?"

"I know exactly what you mean."

Luke lifted the pack of smokes from Luther's shirt pocket and took one. "So hey, she started showing some interest in me. I guess there was just something in me she found attractive, you know? So now we've taken this room at the rooming house you just left. In fact I paid for the room for the whole week so she can stay there and we can be together. I'm thinking that maybe we're really meant for each other. Maureen is so nowhere. I mean, I need a chance to grow too, and how can I do that living with someone like her."

"And pregnant too," Luther said, with a touch of sarcasm. Maureen a woman born to mate and have the home she never had and love her husband as she loved her father, with an unyielding love that would give her a baby and nothing more. But she was not in the fruition field with Luke and why couldn't it be a piece of everyone's permanent knowledge that family was something to get away from or never start at all?

"She had one of those religious fanatic fathers back in Norway. Dragging her off to church, and when he wasn't doing that, he was doing other things. You know what I mean when I say doing things to her?"

"I've got to go," Luther said.

"You're not going anywhere." Luke grinned, as if he knew something.

They were not Cain and Abel. He had a love for his brother that survived the occasional malice in Luke's heart, as when he suddenly wheeled on Luther when they were kids and punched him hard in the stomach, sending Luther to his knees gasping for air in front of the Christmas tree under which they had just placed a gift for their mother. Or air-mailing a bag of incinerator soot from the roof thirteen floors above that narrowly missed Luther's head as he played in the alleyway far below. It was only that Luther didn't want him to destroy his world before it really had a chance to get started, in the way that a frightening older brother could do.

For the most part his brother was a disappointment, not a rival. They had grown up saying how they would not be like their older sisters. They would move away and establish their own lives. Walking the dogs at night, they would fantasize about living in an apartment in one of the well-lighted buildings along Riverside Drive. It would be an apartment as clean as their family's was messy, and they would be free of the violence and unhappiness they saw in their own apartment. Luke three years older and popular at school.

He had the pompadour held in place by Wildroot and the chinos and the garrison belt buckled on the side and he had Elvis, and by the tenth grade he also had the girlfriend, Nancy Becker, only maybe she had him. Telling Luther how smart she was and the beautiful apartment her family had down on Riverside Drive and when she didn't want him anymore swallowing a bottle full of aspirin during the night and lying on the floor moaning come the morning. Mr. Garatdjian was disgusted. It was just another stunt to annoy him and interfere with the breakfast he was having with Mrs. Garatdjian, who frantically called for an ambulance. Because Luke had that kind of relationship with their father. He needed their father's blows. He needed his size thirteen wing tip shoes in his face. *Hatchidor, are you crazy? He is a child. A child,* Mrs. Garatdjian saying, with the horror and the life-affirming and protecting instinct of a woman bearing witness to the violence of the male.

Luke spiraling down in the way that the Garatdjians did as the years passed. Nancy Becker going off to a college of the great while Luke didn't go off to college at all, instead painting rooms in the building to save money for a trip to Europe and on his return he too got a room in the building only it would be for just a little while but the little while kept on and on. Free of the hassle of rent he got to buy himself the stereos and cameras and motorcycles of Japan.

Not that they were truly finished with each other. The euphoria of what Luke had done with the power of his penis to help engender a baby meant he had to call Luther to share in the event.

"Maureen's gone into labor. She's up at the hospital now," he said, of his teenage wife who did not know about Nora from Norway. It had not reached the crisis proportions where he had to tell her just yet. "We should go to a movie. We should go see James Bond. You know, to take my mind off what's happening. Hey, it's a big thing being a father."

Dr. No was playing in a midtown theater, the dark cavernous space smelling of buttered popcorn and roasting franks. On the wide screen smooth Sean Connery won the trust of the sea goddess

Ursula Andress. The movie entered them into the fantasy of a life beyond their previous imagining in which they were blessed with the sleek competence and self-assurance and good looks of James Bond in a life of real if dangerous purpose under the Caribbean sun with a goddess at his side. Reentry into the painful reality of the ordinariness of their lives awaited them as they stepped from the theater.

"You know Daddy used to work there," Luke said, motioning to the curtained window of Jack Dempsey's Restaurant, where no one could get away with brawling without a bruising by the former heavyweight champion whose name was on the restaurant

"I know where he worked," Luther said.

The baby would be given the name Luke Jr. so as to never forget where he had come from and what he would always continue to be a part of. A nurse with a sweet smile stood behind the glass partition in the maternity ward holding up the squalling infant for their inspection.

"That's him. That's my little boy," Luke said, unable to contain himself and infecting others with his joy. Luther stared at the little wonder without delight, seeing him only in the context of the mess that was his family with its tainted flesh.

Chapter 21

May came. He dreamt of a barn going up in flames and of running through endless woods in the dark, ahead of the searchlights of the pursuing party and their barking hounds. He had no certainty of his guilt or innocence. All he knew was that flight was necessary and sufficient to turn his fear of capture into reckless joy.

That Friday, after his post office shift, he departed from his routine of taking the IRT uptown and rode the A train down to West Fourth Street. He wanted a beer. He wanted many beers and he wanted music but free from the intellectual oppression of Columbia University and The End bar that bound him to the prison of self-consciousness.

He found his place on Sullivan Street, the neon sign in the window that said Moogie's drawing him into the softly lit pub. The beer went down like water wherever he brought his feet to rest on the sawdust floor. Sweetly sentimental "San Francisco (Be Sure to Wear Flowers in Your Hair)" and hard-driving "Satisfaction" took their turn on the jukebox. There were to be many others. Higher and higher he went on the beer, the music, the speed. The night was not like the start to most of his days. No devastating insecurity, no thoughts that Mona would find out who he really was, no lament for a state of being that equipped him to feel but never to think. He had found a new home. He would come back.

He called on Mona to meet him there at Moogie's the following Friday night. Such a silly name for such a great place, but also cute and cuddly, like a child's name for a stuffed bear. He just had to share the wealth. He was there before her, drinking up. From the table he had taken at the back he saw her enter and turn the men at the bar into swivel heads as she passed by. Their desire for girlie action confirmed her worth but not his own.

"Come over tonight. Everyone is away again," she said, only sipping from her mug of beer. And she knew he would, speaking as she did from the power of her blond beauty. His resistance was gone, like a sand castle when the tide comes in.

The bathroom wall above the urinal had a message for him:

Screwed maybe a thousand times/It's winter in my soul/

Carrie, we'll never get back together again.

The couplet summoned a reminder of Jane Thayer and the pain and loneliness lost love could bring.

She was lighting a cigarette as he returned. He stuck out his hand, palm up.

"Burn me," he said.

"What?"

"It's OK. I want you to."

"No. " She blew out the match.

"You're regretting that. I can tell. Now light another one."

"No."

"Light it."

"I said no."

He kept after her until she struck a match. But with one quick breath she extinguished the flame. "I don't like this place. Let's go," she said, with summoned firmness.

Chapter 22

The near disaster caused by his involvement with Nora from Norway and the fear he had experienced of losing Mona soon faded. He now felt an internal pressure to add to the count of girls he had been with. *Scoring*, he heard some call it, but the word made him sad, and *had,* as in "he had her last night," was even worse, fully grotesque, suggesting a meal that had been served and digested and then eliminated from his system.

The first that month was a fifteen-year-old. She entered the subway car wearing a miniskirt that showed off her long, thin legs and had a smile that invited him in. At Penn Station, where they both got off, he asked for her phone number and she did not refuse him. She lived out in Great Neck and it was easy to believe with her ballerina's figure that she had just come from a dance class.

"It won't help me," he decided, referring to the phone number. "Meet me." He wrote down the where and when of it on a scrap of paper as commuters dashed for the Long Island Railroad. After they parted he stopped in the arcade for a Nedick's hot dog, heavy with the pickle relish and mustard, and the peculiar synthetic-tasting thing they called an orange drink. Because Nedick's had a bun made firm by toasting that could stand up to the hot dog and not just cave in.

Mr. Ruggiero, the floor supervisor, was a stocky man with an Ernest Borgnine face that told you he was no one to fool around with. And yet there was one, a bearded young man in jeans and a blue work shirt several stools down from Luther who was willing to banter with him.

"My son just got his draft notice. Why the hell should he get his ass shot at by some gook and you don't?"

"I've really got no time for you today, Mr. Ruggiero. I've got to keep the mail moving."

"Answer me, wiseass."

"Is it my problem that Italians don't go to college and have their own way of doing business?"

Mr. Ruggiero seized him by the shirt. "I'll give you some business, you keep this up."

"Intimate, are we?" the young man said, showing no fear.

"If anything happens to him and I hear you've burned another American flag, I promise to kill you," Mr. Ruggiero said.

The psychopaths among the crew had gathered to see if blood would stain the walls, but Mr. Ruggiero walked off without incident.

The young man winked at Luther, before reaching into his bin for envelopes.

"I've been thinking about you," the girl said, the next afternoon, at the End Bar, their prearranged meeting place.

"Me too," Luther replied, leaving out the fever of expectation. He was in the clear, Mona housebound with a bad cold. Even so, the prospect of inviting the girl into the ramshackle apartment was anxiety-inducing. He imagined the well-ordered house where she lived out on Long Island.

"You're a student here?" she asked, as they walked through the Columbia mall.

"No," he said.

"But you are a student, right?"

"CCNY."

"That's a good school too."

Despite her positive response, he couldn't help but wonder if his stock with her hadn't fallen and she was simply hiding her disappointment.

About the apartment she had nothing to say. She wasn't there to evaluate his living conditions. Though young, she had a practiced way in bed, straddling him with her strong dancer's legs and placing her hands on his chest for balance.

Afterward, all he wanted was to be alone. The girl frightened him. He sensed her strength and her intelligence, and her all-seeing eyes were a torment. All his bad, low-board-score feeling came flooding back.

He hustled her out of the apartment and back to the End. He felt as naked in clothes as he had in bed; all he had going for him in her mind was his hair, he was sure.

He asked her if she wanted some food, but she was nix on that, asking only for a Coke.

"Do you prefer to hang out in public places?"

"I'm sorry?" he said, though he sensed what she meant.

"Is this your second home?"

"It does draw me to it."

He went off to the counter. When he returned, four Ethiopians were at the next booth. He recognized them as tenants from his mother's building. One was thin as a pole and wore a yellow dashiki. Luther remembered that after his Barnard girlfriend jilted him, he threw all his possessions out the window of his eleventh floor room, air-mailing them to the street below. It was instructive to notice stuff like that, what men rejected by women could do.

"Hello, landlady's son. When are you coming back to the building? Momma need you very much." The skinny one gave Luther a toothy grin.

"They're friends of yours?" she asked.

"I have no friends," he said, seized with a need for honesty.

He walked her to the subway. "I'm sorry," he said, at the entrance.

"Don't be," she said. "I had a good time." She reached up on her toes and kissed him on the lips and went down the stairs.

The second one he met at Moogie's on a Friday night while Mona was with her family in the country. The girl was attractive and yet suspect owing to her sad demeanor and her listless monotone. She took him back to her studio apartment across the street.

"You can love me. I won't make it hard," she said, a clamp-like grip on his wrists. She had been hospitalized for six months after dropping out of the University of Pennsylvania. Some kind of treatment program. She called it meth-induced psychosis. Initially, she was let out on day passes. Now she had progressed to her own apartment and a relatively stress-free job as a part-time clerk in a bookstore.

He could see no light in her eyes.

"My memory is not good. Someone asks me for a book and the next minute I've forgotten the title. I used to have a genius IQ, but I couldn't put together any of the blocks when the doctors tested me at the hospital. Somehow I know that's a fact that will interest you. You have kind eyes. You don't want to but you do. I write down the customer's requests on a notepad, right in front of them. They think I'm crazy, but so what? Maybe I should write down your name. Would it hurt you to know that when you leave here your name will leave with you?"

"I'm trying not to be too concerned about the future," Luther said.

They had some wine and grass. "You're a speed freak, too. I can tell from the cold touch of your hands and the dilation of your pupils. You're high on speed now, aren't you? You started taking it to pass tests and to talk to girls. Am I right?"

"I'm not here for that," Luther said.

"You look like you're about to cry, but you don't have to. You're not weak. You're just sick. That's what I've been told."

"Why do you call me sick?"

"Because you can't stop."

It was late when he ran stoned and drunk down curving Minetta Lane toward Sixth Avenue and the empty outdoor basketball courts across from the Waverly Theater. The open windows of the litter-strewn A train made for a racket-filled ride up to Columbus Circle. If he could only get to bed with the absolute blackness of night as his cover, things would definitely be all right and the pieces that had flown apart would coalesce into an absolute whole.

"Listen, just listen. Do you hear it?" Tony had his ears cupped as he stood in the living room.

But Luther didn't hear it, didn't even know or care to ask what the "it" was. All he saw was Tony Pascual with his inauthentic smile just this side of deadly rage. Saw sadly too, the simple truth that Tony, perhaps owing to mental issues, could not access the normal avenues of life anymore than Luther himself could. It seemed too much on top of a disaster of a night to have to sit up with his double.

"It's the computer across the street in the engineering building. It can talk. It has that ability." Daring Luther to come straight out and say he was mad when all he could say was "Are you OK?"

"Oh, I'm more than OK. It takes being OK to hear it. That's what symbolic logic is all about, the need to be OK about the ways of clear, precise communication."

"Are you on acid?"

"I'm tripping."

It was a journey Luther had himself had taken a couple of times recently. "Try to stay on the ground. That stuff can make you see stuff that isn't there."

"All wrong. All wrong, man. Makes you see stuff that is there."

Luther turned about in his bed that night. The sheet he lay under felt soiled, and so he removed it. But then the dirt spread to him as well. He pictured Mona sleeping peacefully and the sweetness of her breath and the integrity of her vision. He saw that and then he saw the crummy nature of his own life, and the dirt coating his skin.

He got up and took a shower. The bathroom tiles were cracked, and the tub had rust stains and was in need of grouting. As he soaped himself, he saw the blur of a figure through the plastic shower curtain before it was pulled back violently.

"Now we get to see the reality of you," Tony said. "Turn off the water and put down the soap."

"I'm in the middle of a shower," Luther said, trying to cover himself.

"Do it," Tony said.

Luther did as he was told, paying special attention to Tony's bared teeth.

"What is it you want? I'm cold."

"Don't you ever doubt my word about the forces out there working against symbolic logic, man. Don't you do it. A bowling ball has more sense than you."

"OK. OK."

"Welcome to the real world, man. Welcome to the real world."

Luther pulled the curtain and turned the water back on. He adjusted the knobs till the stream was as hot as he could stand. Still shivering, he ran a towel over his goose-bumped flesh and returned to his room. He would stay up for the remaining tortures of the night. Nobody yet had found a way to sleep with his eyes open and in a state of full alertness. Maybe daylight would chase everything away but you couldn't really be sure.

Chapter 23

Why Tony had the cat was not a mystery, given the love that he was seeking. The plump tabby had a belly that grazed the floor. Tony called the cat Hegel—"thesis, antithesis, and synthesis are all in her, if you can relate. And if anyone hurts Hegel, he has to be hurt in the dialectic that we're all a part of," Tony said, bringing his face so very near.

Luther felt it was pointless to engage with Tony, except with a nod of acknowledgment. It was not lost on him that Tony had failed to remark on the shower incident and may have lacked any understanding of the fear he was causing. Or maybe he did.

Through the dirty window Luther saw blue sky and the shining sun. Memorial Day had arrived, and it was a big one.

He cut west across One Hundred Twenty-second Street, on one side the rich brown buildings of Teacher's College, on the other the high gate leading into the north end of the Columbia campus. Names from the past came flooding into his mind: Bob Buhl and elegant Warren Spahn with his high kick and clever southpaw stuff and spit-baller Lew Burdette and hammering Hank Aaron and the sudden thunder of Eddie Mathews coming out of his nonchalant left-handed stance to top-spin a screamer into the right-field stands, all names he associated with the 1957 and 1958 Milwaukee Braves, and the TV rooms he had wandered into on the Columbia campus to watch parts of the World Series in both years before being ushered out by security guards. And then he was gone from that institutional corridor of quality and the painful peace it gave him and following the tilt of Broadway down toward Manhattan Valley, a subway train coming clear of the tunnel and rising to full exposure behind the dark masonry walls in the middle of the boulevard and following the incline of the tracks onto the el that reached its summit at the One Hundred Twenty-fifth Street Station, Luther noting to the universe that might never know or never care and with all the screaming need of a graffiti artist for just such remembrance that once upon a time he had accessed that station by climbing out onto the roof over the escalator and up through the wooden ties supporting the rails and onto the platform itself before the rampaging metal beast could so much as get near him. It set a commotion going in his blood to be in the city's more roiled and anarchic element, small modest buildings on one side of the corroding el and the sullen experiment of public housing rising boxlike and monolithic on the other, and to sense beyond all of that, far to the west and parallel to the Hudson the railroad tracks and meat-packing plants and a Chevrolet sign over all of it beckoning northbound traffic to the open road and some imagined country scene beyond in sounding the metaphysical imperative of America to go and go and go.

But now another mood, more familiar, came over him. He was afraid. At a stoplight he placed his head in his hands, seeking, in all the brightness, a space just for himself.

"Are you all right?" He heard a woman's voice and took his face from his hands.

"Oh, yes. Progressively so. Strength is my enduring feature, though it doesn't always feel so," he said. "It is just that I am about to take a step forward on a journey whose destination is uncertain at best. Even so I am here and accounted for." The fear had morphed into a surge of energy, a manic boom.

The light had changed. He found himself walking step for step with the woman.

"And in what direction would this journey take you?"

"It is like this, since you ask. There is this mythical paradise, somewhere beyond the city and deep in the Catskill Mountains. Evidently, it is my destiny to be there."

"Well, then, it sounds like you have an adventure awaiting you. And it's very possible I may be a part of it. My name is Lydia Van Dine. I'm Mona's mother."

He gave her a closer look. He was not, in general, terribly curious about older people, having seen too many of them, though how old she was he couldn't say, her face wrinkle-free and smooth and younger than the dead-white hair atop it.

"Well then, you very well know who I am. I am Luther. I kill all fathers and marry all mothers. Just so you know where I'm coming from."

"Charming, for sure. But wasn't it Oedipus who killed his father and married his mother?"

"Do not allow so-called facts to stand in the way of the truth so far as who I am."

Lydia stepped back but she did not disappear. "Yes, absolutely. Anyway, Mona has told me all about you. We have been looking forward to meeting you."

"This word 'we.' Can we hold it up to inspection?"

"Well, there is Peter, of course. And our son, Jeffrey. And Claire, our oldest, will be there, though our jewel, Lenore, is still away at boarding school."

Across the street, in front of the garage and all on her lonesome, stood Mona, a critical eye cast on the two coming toward her.

"You've met already?" Mona didn't look pleased.

"I found Luther with his face in his hands, standing on a corner back on Broadway, Pumpkin. I think it may be how I shall always remember him. I would say I have gotten to know him a bit in the short time we have been together."

Mona didn't say her mother was an appropriating tyrant. She just thought it with her eyes.

The garage attendant drove out with the car, a red Sunbeam Alpine with the top down, and off they went with Lydia at the wheel. The wood-paneled dashboard signaled taste and style but also the heartbreaking yielding of nature to man, nature only being where man could afford to have it, given his capacity to reduce a tree to a plank for the aesthetic fix a customer's driving pleasure required.

The route followed a path full of significance, the ride up the West Side Highway parallel to the railroad threatened with extinction by the rampaging cars and trucks and the entire shoreline a onetime muddy murk of a shantytown in a period he had not been permitted to be born in. Jutting into the Hudson was the One Hundred Twenty-Fifth Street pier, rotting and frequented by toothless old men. A few were on the pier now, moving about in their slow, methodical way, baiting their lines with night crawlers that drew not pristine striped bass from the sewage-fouled water but slithery eels whose evil off-white color alone was enough to make you ill.

"He threw them in the sink," Luther suddenly said.

"Who? What are we walking about? Pronouns need antecedents to be decent," Lydia replied.

"My brother. Not brown, not gray, but a color that defied any words of mine. He caught them in the river and put them in a bag and threw them in the kitchen sink, my mother screaming out her horror at the sight of them still with the movements of life."

But didn't tell her, because he was struck speechless, of Luke diving off the pier and heading off toward the Jersey shore and the terror he, Luther, felt that his brother would be pulled down by the currents that were said to be strong and treacherous and Oh Jesus, come back, Luke, and Luke did, returning with that slow, patient crawl after about a hundred yards.

Lydia reached for the radio dial. "I know how much you are attached to this new music. It says so much about the strength your generation has found, the bold new dimensions we were too timid to explore…" Her mouth a wide gash. But the instrument yielded only static, as if it had grown defective from disuse.

"What does that mean, 'your generation'?" Luther asked. "Are you saying that we have rejected Perry Como and Lawrence Welk? Because 'Love Letters in the Sand' can still bring tears to my eyes. And Patti Page can unleash spasms of delight with 'How Much Is That Doggie in the Window?' Because everybody has had a childhood never to grow out of."

Lydia was momentarily silent, her hand maintaining a shaky grip on the wheel, as if someone had shouted in her ear a hundred times each day the words "women drivers."

"I only meant to say that there is something new in the air that these groups are bringing, something Dionysian."

As the car spiraled up the ramp and onto the upper level of the George Washington Bridge and toward the two massive steel towers, a thrill shot through him, a sense, fed by the motion of the wheels and the sheer spacious majesty of the glistening light-gray structure, that his life was in motion and that a journey had truly begun, if not of the kind in the dream of flight through the woods back at the beginning of the month. But then he had a sudden pang, thinking about Tony languishing through a long holiday weekend with his pudgy cat. He couldn't help but wonder if there would be consequences should Tony take it into his mind to think that he had been slighted.

Once upon a time there had been a station wagon on Claremont Avenue, a strip of buildings on streets running parallel to the great Broadway. The station wagon signified a university professor father and argyle socks and a tweed jacket with an elbow patch and a young wife and children with ultra-white teeth and blond hair that glowed and well-shaped heads. The image was there in his mind and had been for a long time. He wanted to be American, without quite knowing what it meant.

"I do not have the driving skills of my husband. He is legendary in his command of the wheel. No one has or could come close to denting him because he drives with what he calls anticipatory action, the skill of the rare ones who think not one or two but at a minimum of nine to eleven times ahead of what we would have to call the average mind. And is he to be blamed for being partial to excellence on the road?"

Luther took this in and then said, with sudden ferocity, "Listen and listen well, if you please. Driving is a practical exercise, not an art form. Anyone who tries to embellish the essence of this mundane activity, anyone who says it is other than an exercise in going from point A to point B, has dipped into the realm of the psychotic. He has said he has to rule the meager because the daunting is just that, daunting in the full impact of that hard, uncompromising word."

Lydia was rattled. She sought the balance that would give her words the calm she was seeking. "An opinion should be an opinion, not a sledgehammer. Must you break the delicate balance of things with loud arrogance?"

"Arrogance? Where does it lie? Have I sat here and told you I am king of the road? Have I told you that I am world champion at anything? Have I?"

Lydia took the shock of what he said with a shudder. "Well, there was something about killing all fathers," she said, attempting to laugh, before slipping back into a worried sadness. "Be one with us, Luther. Be one with us," she continued, leaving him no choice but to make of his arms a talismanic cross.

They were now on the Palisades Interstate Parkway. Its stone-arch overpasses and broad medians rife with vegetation were a comfort, resurrecting the old childhood dream of nature within reach of civilization. He stared with an ache at the cultivated terrain, and suddenly the city became a cauldron of fire from which he had, if only temporarily, escaped.

And then it was the greater expanse of the thruway. The car did not stall but it did not shine either, taking on hills not as a rampaging beast but at a tired, struggling pace. Despite its heft, a weak engine lay under its hood. The slapping sound of rubber on the spaced cracks in the road through Sullivan and then Ulster (the name cold and forbidding of the sun) County settled him, the curves ample enough to absorb the fastest motion of the speeding cars with no trauma for anyone. The picture postcard scenes outlasting his patience for them and justifying the greed and grasping of the car's ceaseless motion.

And then they were into the intricacy of smaller roads through wisps of towns with names like Willow and Mount Tremper and Shady and Bearsville, a woodsy terrain that spoke of rainy afternoon Catskill loneliness, a territory in which silence reigned and where you had nothing to do but stare at the bark of a tree in the poverty of your days. So it was inevitable that there should be a subdued outrage at New York City and the tidings from the unchallenged TV in these rural homes, some report or other on the newest preposterousness of people packed together to create an environment of decadence and folly without even the slightest notion of how to bait a hook or what a pull on the line truly meant in terms of all it summoned in the senses, because all you had down there now was a bunch of flag-burning A-holes running around with their long hair and their women without bras trying to provoke the country to measure them for death.

All this he didn't understand but would come to.

"I am having big thoughts about a urinal," Luther said. "Is the time coming when I can go? The need is powerfully upon me."

"I will tell you what Peter says," Lydia said, smoke coming from her mouth as she spoke. "The integrity of the individual is measured not by how much liquid he takes in but by how much he can contain and how much hunger he can endure in order to bypass the pit stops of the commoners laid out as traps to further weaken and corrode the souls of men already become as docile as sheep."

Luther thought about the words *bad plumbing* as they applied to the human body and spoke up. "My father pees himself a river each and every day and I'm just like him," he said.

The rocks had ceased their monitoring of the car's progress, being mainly observant on the thruway, where man had blasted his way through. Now the Sunbeam was finding it necessary to be faithful to narrow roads with turns made before civil engineering had become an exact science, with stretches of woodland and then the Esopus River where men in waders and with creels slung over their shoulders waited for the approximation of sex or heaven that the bite would bring, men lost to the dictates of time so far as clothes or the chasing of women could ever mean, men who now lived in wood cabins with only themselves and their fishing rods and the smell of cherry tobacco over steaming coffee and a fire that licked its wood in the most sensually savoring way, the city no match for the country in the goodness sweepstakes, not with the image the latter could present with its tableau of just repose.

Luther thinking, If I could be an artist I'd have something to say about the white line continuing down the road and a beautiful girl doing it with me in an open field.

The turnoff was another matter altogether, a riot of tethered barking dogs in a lot at the edge of the main road, the trailers an ugly kitchen white and the dirty, unkempt children of the hardscrabble adults playing, *brothers and sisters thrown together and excited by their differences and drinking in the wonder of all that was theirs without leaving home,* the scene falling away just as Times Square disappeared from your mind as you escaped cross-town toward Park Avenue because of the distress it entailed to remember it, the brook babbling in its call to one and all of the fishes to play invisible and blend with the rocks in its shallow waters. And then a house quietly dark, solitary in a weedy field, and exulting every minute in its own unself-conscious neglect, the rusting door-less refrigerator on the buckling front porch and the broken tiller sitting tilted and historical as overalls on the crabgrass patch the owner would never lower himself to call a lawn, he the caretaker and not even a remote resemblance to what a man should never be, a bear of a man (so Lydia was to say) who had the daily appearance of etherealness in the friendly, deceptively simple bulk of who he was, a man who could caress a fawn and kill a deer and who would come to know what Luther was in terms of the bottles and cans he left drained in his wake and still remain laconic in describing the endeavors not of the useless but those afflicted by city life or something even deeper which he recorded with assessing and fathoming eyes that didn't even cause him to shudder, having no conceptualized belief in pulling down the thing that went by the name vanity.

The journey ending when the car rattled the boards of the small bridge over the brook, with the bridge, not the car, proving its strength. To the left a pair of swings suspended from the thick, resolute branch of an oak tree, a space where children could pass an iridescent childhood in its shade and where no cries for justice rang out in competition with the birds of the air and the trout in the stream and the overall activity of the woodland surrounding the enclave of civility, the filter of nature removing all folly. On the right was the house, neither hiding nor proclaiming itself, a thing of wood with a cardinal red trim around the windows so no one could miss its welcoming intent. All Luther could see was that it had a porch and windows and a shingled roof and that someone had put it together in a time that he had not been there. The lawn of endless green, spotlights positioned to shine down on it in the night from the bordering pine trees, signified itself as an emblem of aesthetic harmony. In the background a mountain rose with the Van Dine name upon the deed for it and a pool that drew from the cool mountain brook was there at the disposal of summer guests.

The complexity of the day registering in the informal way with formal overtones that Peter stood before the living room fire, hands genteelly behind his back, causing Luther to cover his ears and then to hold his head at the things of life that passed in an instant while really being forever. It was the position in which he would always remember him, legs slightly spread in tan slacks, the beige cotton turtleneck, and the still blond hair combed back with wetness in it and the smile with a hint of warmth and the potential to extend itself further, a look that was blond but not fragile. A man shrewd enough to know he was surrounded by a civilization he had to keep his eyes upon.

"Luther has sharp opinions. He believes it's psychotic to approach driving as anything other than an exercise in getting from point A to point B," Lydia said, indulging what seemed her penchant for provocative mischief.

Peter spoke presidentially through his mind's calibrating filter, saying merely, "Luther looks to me like a young man here for relaxation, not disputation. Perhaps we can all accommodate him toward that end," the light of who he thought he was shining brightly in eyes that laid their claim to wisdom. (Not knowing that in a dark and distant future he would hiss into the face of Luther and with finger bent as if on the trigger that would end it all, at least for *him, Luther*, say, "You are entirely psychotic and destructive of me and always have been.")

And yet Luther could not bow down to a man such as he showed himself to be, in the fetters of academia with his mannered speech, Mona having alerted him that the property was not her father's but Lydia's through inheritance, and if he blew life into it with his Dutch solidity, if he was the anchor that could secure Lydia's foundering boat, he was also the weight that could keep her permanently in place, the information Luther had received locking him into a judgment he could not disown, not at that time, though a river of sorrow would be made of his tears for all he had not then seen in his later years, that her father would emerge pristine and noble, even if flawed, in the character that he had always owned but Luther was resistant to perceive let alone acknowledge.

Mona being equipped with the capacity to speak without a word being spoken and other needed clues being transmitted by his vitally important monitoring devices, Luther could clearly see what Peter was feeling in his bones, that he was a nemesis. And yet he did not say to Luther, "Get out, get out, get out," expelling him as the disaster who would drink all their whiskey and sleep with or try to sleep with all their daughters and ignore their son and assault their values of peace and tranquility in favor of an intense fervor that often amounted to nothing more than sticking his face in their *Time* magazines in pretense of ignoring everything going on in the room. He did not say to Luther, Leave this land of milk and honey and do not darken our door again. He did not say this at all because mastery was the assumed right of the old over the young, a thing the young must not know and that the old must not tell them even as it was being effected through the powerful if feigned tool of reception.

The next day he woke in a red room to a blue sky morning, which he was present for over coffee on the front porch out of a metal mug and the silent, possibly judgmental presence of Mona's younger sibling Jeffrey, whose small eyes spoke of terror and hurt and longing, as if he had been slighted from birth in comparison with others named or unnamed and left too long on his own, the truth being that the pain of neglect made him look older than he was and in need of care and maintenance and celestial light beyond anyone's ability to provide, and as if Peter had already uttered his regretfully spoken words, "He's not as bright as some others."

Luther saying, "There comes a year when we all have to break out and this year is mine for leaving behind the meagerness of who I am."

Jeffrey responding with a derisive laugh and saying, "You sure talk funny."

Luther clasped him with the temporarily bonding words, "Brother of mine," causing Jeffrey to push him away and wave his arms as if warding off mosquitoes come to suck his not so precious blood.

"We have something in common," Luther said.

"What's that?"

"We have hair that needs not a brush but a gardener." He didn't tell Jeffrey that he was too young to have a mop with such deadness to it, as if already it had been defeated by the message that life wasn't worth living with the goods he was carrying.

Claire did not come so easy, seeing that she had the bigger forehead and the bigger eyes and the bigger beauty to go with the luster of her black hair. She had no need for anything but the claim she made on her mother, it could seem, while going through life with the furniture never far from her reach. From the start she rejected him with an insistence all her own and her eyes serving as cameras recording his lack of manners and what it meant to always be falling short of the mark. He didn't call the damage from her smiling stares stab wounds. It was more like being sliced.

"Mona says you're a student at the City College of New York. Does that mean you're poor and ambitious?"

"Even the Titanic sank for a reason."

"Is that supposed to mean something?"

"I'm not at liberty to say."

Claire began to laugh, the laugh of one who has hit a wall obdurate and silly at the same time, in that moment conveying because he was that wall and had dimensions that were thin and possessing nothing whatsoever that she wanted to borrow or steal, that their bodies would not and could not touch and that she would always be shining down on him with that smiling hardness that said *I have something that you want and it will never be yours to have, no matter how much grass or hash you smoke to stoke your dreams.* And she was worth "having," though the word brought him to a place of predictable sadness. She had the cleavage and she had the Ivy League and she had the ability to conjure aching aspiration in every man who set eyes on her. A woman different in her aspect from Mona, bearing as she did the title *oldest sister.*

Luther lost all sense of where he was. It was as if he had gone to bed a Democrat and woken up a Republican. Things were off their moorings in the range of experience he was being exposed to, including the sound of chirping birdsong. Down the way Peter stood on a tall ladder slapping red paint on the front of the garage. The small portion that he had coated gleamed in the sun and he was locked into covering the faded area as the spring project that would define him and save his life and give him peace in relation to the land so he could be strong and relaxed when evening came around and by ritual and never by need had a beer to go with his Winstons. Because the articulation of neatness and craft was his ever-present dream, this being the country segment of his life where the descendant of yeoman farmers (Dutch) could not ascend over but balance out the scholar that he was. Because a barn was not like plotting a book. You had the end in sight even before you began and your mind could drift south to the wonders of a life of freedom born from responsibility.

"He has the balls of a giant but the body of a man," Mona said.

"Oh Mona," Claire replied, dissolving into giggles at her sister's boldness and in that moment defining their relationship, Luther wondering whether it was particular to an Adonis mindset that Peter could set out on the property in only lime-colored bikini briefs, not seeking to hide the bulge so big in the pouch of elastic-banded cotton.

In the afternoon Luther took a rifle from the rack in the living room. Mona said it was for bringing down deer. In a drawer he found ammunition, long bullets with a green casing and metal heads, bullets so adorable that you should have been allowed to sleep with them or eat them or never let them out of your sight. But the weapon was too powerful for what he was being led to do and so he settled for a .22, and with a handful of metal-jacketed bullets found a spot on the rise above the terrace. A sparrow flew over the arboretum. He fired and the thing dropped by the stone fireplace. A chipmunk scurried along the flagstone terrace and he blasted that, too. The idea of wrongness was there, but it was vague, like the premonition that had come to him at age twelve, the shadow on the consciousness of the instant vandal he had in that case been, the plainclothes cop taking him down with a flying tackle in full view of the outdoor concert crowd and pulling him to his feet by his shirt and giving him a boot in the ass for overturning the garbage can in an impulsive moment. There was painful pleasure in breaking the barrier of the acceptable, he thought, as Peter approached, walking in a slow, purposeful manner, virtually naked but in command of his mission, having recognized from the start the miscreant with the meager frame and yet seeking to suspend final judgment in the American way, this being not Nazi Germany but a land where the slow accumulation of fact could be counted on to imbue the final portrait with a lasting truth. Thinking, he's sick. He's crazy. He doesn't know what he is doing. Because who comes upon a scene such as this with a preposterous last name hoping to be remembered as anything but inconsequential? Doesn't he even know or care that entrée to America is on an identity basis? The dead chipmunk there before his eyes on the flagstone terrace and the bird not far away so that he had to turn his face that had seen much and prided itself on reserve to the gun-toting Luther, who had the rifle on his shoulder like the soldier he never would be.

"You thought I couldn't kill but I can, and if they dropped me into Vietnam I'd be knee deep in blood before you knew it. Private First Class Luther Garatdjian reporting for duty, sir. Want me out on point, sir? I'm game. I'm down." He crouched and swiveled in stiff, precise movements and made a visor of his hand to better reconnoiter the land.

"We do not kill things needlessly around here. I will ask you to replace the rifle in the gun rack." Peter said the words firmly so they would penetrate and settle and not just fly away. Then he turned his back and walked to the garage to resume the task at hand.

Luther was shaken. He did not say, It was not I who did these things. He did not walk away from himself as if abandoning a stranger. He heard something crying within him that said he could not go on that way forever.

That evening all was forgotten so dinner could be eaten, Peter now fully clothed in beige dress slacks and a matching turtleneck and with a leather pocketbook strapped to his shoulder. Once again he drove silently along the tight roads, his hair still wet from the shower and forever the restriction of the white line down the middle of the two-lane road and the sporadic houses not yet ready for sleep. The car was but an expression of his will, his mind illuminating the path and communicating it expertly to the steering wheel, as if by some instinct he could invent a route or make the existing one more compliant and yielding than ever it had been or would ever be for any other vehicle regardless of its description. He drove with intensity and even unspoken rage that elements would dare to think of making him lose his composure or fail to control his own destiny. He had seen too much not to believe it could be otherwise, crack pilots shot out of the air because of their American insouciance when all along it was a matter of moment to moment vigilance.

Bernie's had patrons who knew each other and a mellow vibe, just people happy to be with each other after a day of standing among tall trees.

"So Luther, tell us who you are, so we can better get to know you," Lydia said, invigorated by the cornbread and her whiskey sour.

"My earliest memory is of a ranch in Kansas City. My mother was only three when I was born."

"Now wait a minute, pardner. Are there any ranches in Kansas City? Kansas City is a city, after all."

"It was just a dusty little town back then, before the boom times arrived."

"But tell us really, so we can have a handle," Lydia went on, after another piece of cornbread.

"So what is he, a suitcase you want to carry around with you?" Jeffrey said.

"Luther knows what we mean, smarty pants. We want him to feel a part of us."

"I was born in a tree, third branch from the top."

"Ignore him, everybody," Claire said flatly. "He's just trying to be obnoxious. He has nothing else to offer."

She sought to defeat him with her lancing words, but he saw himself as less obnoxious than protective. He would tell them something when he could, when the past was not a firestorm of howling but an obligation. And so he ate in silence, feasting on the leg of lamb and the mint jelly and the potatoes and string beans that went with it. After a while he came out of the silence. There had been a conversation going, but he had not heard it.

"I am the force that will dislodge you and make all that you now own fully mine, assuming—and this is a big assumption—that I even want it," Luther said, addressing Peter and heedless of context.

"And how will you do that, please?"

"Force of will. I am bound to my convictions of who I am."

Lydia spoke up, having quartered and devoured her filet mignon. "Go easy on him, Peter."

Peter's smile had faded into the countenance of one enduring a bad and most peculiar odor. He held this face on Luther for a good minute, in the hope that mutual fathoming would occur.

When he could take no more, Luther wiped his mouth ostentatiously with the linen napkin and stood up from the table. "Separation is so good, so very good. It is what makes the world go round." He placed the napkin on the table and backed out of the door.

"What is the meaning of inflicting this lunatic on us? Have you lost your mind? The young man is verging on psychosis. He is in need of serious treatment," Peter sputtered.

"You're just jealous because he is young and strong," Mona said.

"Poody, you must admit that he is strange," Lydia said.

"Define strange, please. Because he is not like you?"

"Define strong, please. The young man has the build of a number 2 pencil," Peter added.

"Yes, Daddy, and his point is sharp and his eraser is full." Mona sent a visual signal around the table with her raised eyebrow.

Peter stiffened to deal with the affront. "We will speak no more about this matter tonight. We will regard his menacing dialogue as an aberration and nothing more."

The family ate in a silence that could not last for long. "Where did the idiot—I mean your boyfriend—go?" Jeffrey inquired. His father smiled, the word *idiot* having some currency around the table.

"Watch who you call an idiot. Luther *works* and goes to college." Mona made the word *works* the operative one.

"How would you know? He says nothing about himself," Peter said.

"To me he tells everything," Mona replied.

"And what is this work he supposedly does?"

"Not supposedly. Work is work and Luther works."

"Dear, I think your father asked a question. Could we perhaps have an answer?" Lydia said.

"Luther makes sure the mail gets delivered on time."

"Are you saying Luther works for the post office?"

"I'm saying that exactly."

"Luther doesn't look like any mailman I've ever seen, " Peter said.

"No, no. Luther is on special assignment. He works inside the post office building and he had to take a special test to get there."

"A special test?"

"He had to show them that he could read and do figures above the average before they would entrust him with his assignment."

"Dear, are you all right? You've even begun to talk like this young man. We are detecting a faintly ludicrous quality to your speech," Lydia said.

"We? We? Can we come down from the plural into the singular point of view?"

"We can come down from anything so long as you talk to us in a civil fashion, young lady." Peter slammed the table with his open hand for frustrated emphasis, to indicate that the time for fooling around had come to an end and now he was involved in the patriarchal prerogatives of his own power. *Because to run a country was to run a family, and power had its place.*

"All you need to know is that Luther is a magician in full pursuit of his endeavor."

"Precisely. I couldn't have said it better myself," Peter declared.

"Exactly," Lydia seconded.

"Should he even be here? Look what he has done already. He's shot a bird, a chipmunk, and threatened Daddy." Claire was now speaking up.

Outside all they could hear was the sound of parking lot gravel under their feet.

"Has he really gone?" Jeffrey asked.

"I am here, restless and free," Luther announced, appearing from behind the restaurant.

Peter whipped the car around the greensward and the white church—Dutch Reformed, whatever that was in the bewildering hierarchy of Protestantism, except that to be Dutch was somehow to be genial toward all mankind. Masterfully, in Luther's mind, did Peter click from high beam to low with the approach of onrushing cars, then back to high with their passing, lighting the trees and overhead wires like silver strands against the blackness, Luther picturing himself back from the road lying in the concealing foliage undetected by the powerful brightness and safe for all time. All he knew was that a car was moving forward in the night, that an angry silent man was at the wheel, and that he was going somewhere, as he had been since meeting Mona Van Dine, and that he was now surging against the line of family. He closed his eyes and heard an oldie but goodie by the Platters, "Oh Yes I'm the Great Pretender." He heard the song and could apply the title to his own life.

Chapter 24

He walked cautiously down the long hallway of the apartment. In the distance he could hear the pealing of the bells in the carillon at Riverside Church, making a soaring mockery of speech, of thought, of anything but the glory of God in the urban pastoral atmosphere from which the monopolizing and surpassing sound rang out.

A creepy feeling came over him. "Tony?" he called, and poked his head in his roommate's cluttered room. But there was no Tony, just a clutter of badges and books going back to grade school and pennants and piles of clothes and old shoes. He called again, throwing noise on his fear.

A candle burned in the middle of the living room floor. Tony sat lotus position beside it. On an unfolded section of the *Times* the cat was laid out. Dried blood and guts stained the newsprint. The tabby lay stiff, its eyes open. On Tony's face was a faraway smile.

"What happened?" Luther asked.

"Happened?"

"Yeah. What happened?"

"You happened. That's what happened."

"I happened?"

"That's right, baby. You happened."

"How did I happen?"

"With your thoughts you happened."

"Happened how? Happened what?"

"You happened him out the window."

"I happened your cat out the window?"

Tony responded with a dangerous chuckle. "You couldn't deal with my dialectic so you turned your mind on him. I just wanted you to see your work. That's all."

Luther tried to mask his fear. He could think of nowhere to take it but his own room.

When she came for him the next day, let in the door by Tony, she found him face down on his bed. She showed up in a sleeveless summer dress of blue gingham, her arms golden and her hair radiating sparks of light.

"Stop," he said, feeling her hand on the back of his neck.

"Why?"

"Because above my neck is forbidden territory where no one must go."

"What are we talking about here?"

Though he didn't elaborate, they were talking about his world going away should the flatness of the back of his head be revealed to her. Nor did he tell her of the sense of bondage that caused him to fear stepping out of the apartment lest he miss her should she finally come. or how the time had somehow passed when he imagined her arriving as he was thinking of other things. There were no other things.

She closed the door and stepped out of her dress.

Afterward they rode downtown on the Broadway bus.

"I could be doing this forever," he said.

"Doing what?"

"Riding back and forth on the Broadway bus."

A copy of the *Daily News* had been left on the next seat. The headline of the page four article read:

Nineteen-Year-Old Held in Death of His Girlfriend

The alleged murderer, a student, had found himself hopelessly in love with an upper class girl. From a poor, working class family, he had become a frequent visitor at the home of the girl's parents. They became his surrogate family. Then the girl departed for Europe. The trip was her parents' reward to her for graduating first in her high school class and being accepted to Radcliffe. Because he missed her, the young man borrowed money and flew to Paris, hoping to surprise her, but he saw right away that her feelings had changed. Her manner told him what his insides had been trying to tell him on the long plane ride. And then she had to rise up in a state of pomposity, the way she smacked her lips in the enunciation of *too much tongue showing* her plans to go to Greece with Jean *daring to pronounce it like the first syllable in genre.* She hoped that they could still remain friends *in the sudden infuriating action of her mouth* losing his head and stabbing her *so the blood could flow where it needed to instead of having veins and capillaries and arteries controlling it all the time for the selfish purpose of life.* The murdered woman's father arrived in Paris to claim the body and arrange for its return to America. Questioned by reporters, he called the death a tragedy, certainly for his daughter and his family, but also for the accused, who would have to live with the memory and consequences of his rash act for the rest of his life.

Luther returned the newspaper to the empty seat where he had found it, then reached for it again, ignoring the something that told him not to.

"This is interesting," he said, handing Mona the paper open to the page containing the article.

A long minute passed in which he recognized his mistake.

"Why did you show me this article?" Her inquiry came in a quiet voice.

"I don't know." And he didn't.

"I think he's a bastard and I hope he pays for what he did," she said.

"I can sort of understand him." In truth he understood both him and the girl.

She shot him a look, gathered her things, and left. Luther followed after her the few blocks to her building. As she stepped into the lobby, the doorman from under his billed hat cast a cold eye. He went so far as to make a fist and fit it into the palm of his other hand. Luther streaked back up the block, as if trying to outrace his thoughts.

And though days of merciless anxiety passed fearing that he had lost her, she did come calling on him once again. Now his anxiety took another form. Did she not see that she might fall by the wayside if she continued to cut classes and neglect her education? Did she want her future to be the chaos of rain-swept streets with all her possessions in hand? But that was the thing. She didn't see. What her high school offered was meaningless for her life. When June came and it was clear she would not receive her diploma without attending summer school, well, so what? A diploma meant nothing to her.

"But don't painters go to college? And don't they have to finish high school to do that?"

"Not me."

He lacked her lens by which to look at things. He lacked her safety net. He had only his unstable family and his fear. They were in a bar, the Silver Rail. A less collegiate bar than the End, two blocks north, one that drew the local young and older folks. From their booth he could see out through the darkness to the sunlight on Broadway. The smell of frying meat came strong from the kitchen, the double doors swinging back and forth as the waiters passed in and out with slabs of meat swimming in grease. A place for the wild young Irish a few years back. Flanagan. The O'Brien twins. Brawlers. A thumper, a former prizefighter, was in control. He wore a white apron tied tight around his waist and met you with the energy of his bulk, all of him ready to come in low and bang and take a punch as well. His thinning hair was slicked back in an exposing act of bravado and his face shiny. He was sure to make a mess of you if you messed with him. To his credit he made no objection that Bob Dylan sang

"Like a Rolling Stone" on his jukebox because when you grow up on the streets of Manhattan you can grow out of your Catholicism sufficient to breathe.

Bob Dylan dropping out of college and reinventing himself with his name change while Luther wandered pointlessly through an academic curriculum. The folk singer nastiness he was hearing only drove him further down and into aggrieved wonder that anyone could inhabit such starlight while he seemed wedded to his immigrant origins. What would it be to expand and grow into another realm of existence unapproachable so long as he stayed in bondage to his current identity?

He lay his head on the table.

"What are you doing?"

He did not answer.

"Luther, I asked you a question."

"I am feeling the weight of you and cannot speak."

"Let's get out of here. Please?" she said.

His eyes adjusted to the bright afternoon light. She had gone to the restroom. Her stomach was bad a lot of the time. He had to wonder if the birth control pills were the cause. Just because it was a reputable pharmacy where she got them didn't mean she wasn't accepting poison for her freedom.

Two blocks away the family's building rose, not in peek-a-boo style but straight up for the viewing public in the full gloom of its grime, seeking to make you define it by his family's history when it was really just a collection of bricks in space for tenants to be contained in on the way to becoming dust.

He watched the passersby to see if they looked up and nudged each other, as if to say, get a load of that scripture verse on that wall. Must be the last remaining holy rollers in Manhattan living there. And though they showed no signs of noticing, sometimes there were more subtle ways of observation and communication concerning what they knew about a family impaled on its own shame.

He felt a poke in his ribs and turned to find a compact male about his age staring up at him with a big smile.

"Hey, Luther. It's me, Bert. Bert Bach. Claremont High School," the young man felt compelled to say, mistaking the look of terror on Luther's face for incomprehension.

"Oh, right. How are you?"

"Terrific." Bert said, the word expelled with great and emphatic force. And he looked terrific, full of the purpose to which he had been born. He wore a white LaCoste shirt and khaki pants and penny loafers and his brown hair was cut short and parted neatly on the side, just as Luther remembered him. More effusiveness followed. "Dean's list, baby. I'm on the dean's list at Harvard."

"It is good that you are not hiding your light under a bushel but letting it shine," Luther said, forcing a smile and struggling for coherence.

Bert was the son of a Harvard alumnus, but he had gained admission on his own merits. Excellent grades and board scores. He was particularly strong in science and in math, the masculine subjects. Luther remembered Bert's ecstasy when he received the letter. The class was in the auditorium when the school notified him of his acceptance. How sun-kissed and vitalized his life seemed as a result of being chosen. That was the drag about failure. It required you to be alone so people couldn't burn you with their success.

Bert's expression had turned quizzical.

"Why do you look at me that way?" Luther asked, but he knew. Bert smelled his fear and shame.

"I'm just looking at you, buddy. That's all. Anyway, I'm here to see my dad for a week and then I go back to Cambridge. I have this summer internship at a hospital in Boston. I'm pre-med."

Luther was relieved when Mona emerged from the bar. Now he would have something to show Bert.

"Mona, this is Bert. We were classmates in high school."

Bert shook her hand. The gleam in his eye told Luther that he was impressed.

"So what does Luther do besides stand outside of bars?"

"Why not ask Luther?" Mona replied.

"I do some things," Luther said, conspicuously defeated.

"One thing you wouldn't do is tell us where you lived. Why do you suppose that is? All you would say is that you lived on the Upper West Side."

"I had my reasons."

Luther did not lie down on the sidewalk and cover his ears and shut his eyes. He did not run into a building wall so unconsciousness could be his. He stood his ground and endured the shame storm. Yes, the Upper West Side. That was where he lived. Because exactly where he lived would not be good enough for the girls and boys with their Fifth Avenue faces with whom he went to the school of the rich. Because he had no choice but to say what he said in defense of his life so they wouldn't see his sister on the window ledge or the squalor of the apartment and all the rest of who he was.

"Hey look, buddy, it's been nice. I have to be running."

Bert Bach did his running, having a speed to maintain to fit his fast-paced life. He was wall to wall, all day all the time with his activity, and going higher and higher on his energy alone. Going at his own chosen speed, as Dylan sang in another context. Maybe Luther would start to run, too. But not today. He felt tired. He let Mona lead him south toward her family's apartment to a place of safety near but far from where they had been.

Chapter 25

Mona was gone. No summer school. Camp had suctioned her from the hot city streets. The Van Dines did not pass their summers in the city. The absence of air conditioners in their river view windows spoke to that.

All his monitoring devices, such as they were, had been activated with Mona's departure for the country. His treasure had been removed from his presence but not from his mind. Mona would be spending her days at the Art Students' League, she had said. She would be driving the family's jeep to and fro. His fear was great that she would meet someone en route or at the class and serendipity for her would be ruin for him.

The old man so routinely rude was there on his stool at The End with his Buston Keaton face. Moving toward the end of a life that could offer no defense against honesty, he sat sipping his martinis and smoking his cigarettes with no concern for his oncoming death.

"Where's that girlfriend of yours? She finally wise up and leave you?"

"Oh she left me all right," Luther said, one empty stool between them. "She left me for the heaven where she lives."

"What does that mean?"

"It means what it means."

"You don't even know my name, do you?"

"Yes I do. You're Mr. Blood Shot Eyes. You're the man who listens to Frank Sinatra in the dark and weeps."

"The kids in my building grew up and you knew they were going to be something. But you were never going to be anything. You've got all this hair on your head now, but the truth is that your head is too flat for you to go anywhere. There used to be this science called phrenology; a pseudo-science is the way people see it now. You ever hear of it?"

"I've read many books on the subject," Luther said.

"The hell you have," the old man growled. "The point is that you can tell a lot about a person from the shape of his head. And the one outstanding fact is that a flat head and low intelligence go together. Mutts like you are what's wrong with America. At least these round-headed kids from Columbia have some gifts."

"Extinguish me quickly. You can do it if you try. What does my life mean that I have to sit here with a sack of bile like you when youngness is all around me."

The man sipped his martini like the potent potion it was and no one cried that he saw fit to wear a dull black suit on a Saturday night. "Let me ask you something?"

"Fire away," Luther said, and then moved his head like a boxer in a bob and weave as if to avoid the bullet.

"Why are you here?"

"To be in an ambience of pleasure," Luther said, quaffing his suds and ordering another.

"Bologna, wise ass. You think you're here for the girls, don't you?"

"Girlie action. Yes, very much so," Luther said. "I'm a prime candidate for l'amour."

"Let me tell you something, my skinny friend. You think you're here for sex but you're really here for the booze. Ten years from now, the way you're going, you'll be drinking alone in some dingy room wondering where your life went."

Luther crossed his arms to ward off the man's words, but they had already shot through.

"The difference between me and you is that we're both alcoholics but I know it and you don't."

Luther covered his ears but found a better, more pressing use for his right hand in reaching for the beer. "I know what I know," he said sullenly.

"You ever hear of something called Alcoholics Anonymous? A.A.? That's where you're headed if you're lucky, you and all the bums of your generation with your pot and whatnot."

"Yeah, so why aren't you there, with your martini glass?"

"Because it's too Goddy for me. That's why."

Luther was about to ask him what Goddy meant but a man took the stool between them and introduced himself. An ex-seminary student, he smiled a lot, but there was cruelty in his face. Had Luther read Peter De Vries? The writer was howlingly funny, he said. Howlingly. It was a word not generally heard in American speech, as far as Luther knew.

"I'm afraid I haven't," Luther said, letting the truth stand by itself.

The seminary had not been for the young man. His faith had collapsed. "Or should I say lapsed?" he said, applauding his wit with laughter.

"Oh, you can say what you need to say. It won't be held against you."

His name was Justin De Volpe and he admitted to a preternatural sensitivity that kept him on the sidelines of life as an observer. "Would you like to come over? I have some great Panama Red. Would you like to be a moral reprobate with me?"

In the cab, Luther lapsed into reminiscence. "When I was little, a woman opened the gates of the American heaven."

"How is that?" Justin asked, seeking to blend with Luther through the medium of words.

"Her name was Miss Hucksley and she was from the world and I was not. She wore perfume and had the worldly ways which my mother had repudiated and took me to Times Square in her Cadillac, or as near as she could get on New Year's Eve, when all of creation was out for the thrill of life."

"An interesting story," Justin lied.

He had an apartment that would do anyone proud, neat and well furnished and with floors of sparkling wood. And Justin got to be alone in it.

"Hurry with what you promised," Luther said.

"Meaning?"

"The magic of Panama that will make me see stars where there are none and mystery where there are only the plain facts."

Justin produced from his shirt pocket a fat joint that when lit and toked on made Art Blakey and the Jazz Messengers a fabulous trip on a railroad train speeding through a mountain tunnel. Silence and darkness followed, and with it a sense of impending danger.

"I'm here," Justin said, his voice suggesting strength and certainty. Groggy, Luther had slid to the floor. Justin now followed, kneeling to unbuckle Luther's belt and remove his pants. "But I don't love you. I don't even know you. And I haven't read Peter De Vries," Luther called out.

"You don't need love for sex," Justin replied.

"You do if you're old-fashioned."

"Why did you come down here?" Justin asked, not harshly but with a soothing quality in his voice.

"I came here for smoke heaven." He paused. "I came here because I have no friends. Why did you come here?"

"Have we lost sight of the fact that this is my apartment?"

"That doesn't give you the right to do such a thing to me." He thought of Mona and her soft femaleness and the hope she gave him and now it was in danger. He would be left out of some heavenly place from which he had carelessly wandered. He heard himself silently screaming for her and the order she gave his life.

"It won't hurt," Justin said.

"It won't hurt you is what you mean to say." Luther pulled his pants back up and buckled his belt and fell asleep.

When he awoke it was daylight and Justin De Volpe was lying on the sofa with his mouth open and his eyes closed. Luther's head hurt and his mouth was dry and he saw many books but none by the great Peter De Vries, who had brought so much reading enjoyment to Justin.

The streets had a stark clarity in the warm sunlight as Luther headed on foot back uptown. Outside a candy store on Broadway and One Hundred Eighth Street stood a man in a gray smock with friendly white hair and a high forehead and significant jowls. He was all of a piece with what he did, placing scoops of ice cream on cones and then topping them with sprinkles. An unsmiling Howdy Doody he looked like.

"Do you know me?" Luther stopped to ask, remembering the sweet smell of popsicles and creamsicles rising with the cold air of the freezer back in his grade school days. He had a sense that the man should have been gone by now, just like the school down the block from which he had been expelled in sixth grade and the corner pizzeria and so much more.

"Refresh my memory," the man said.

"It's not important and never was, but you were here when I was a child."

"And that's the point, isn't it?" the man said.

"What's the point?"

"You're not a child anymore, and yet you are still here."

"I come to you in trust and yet you hurt me."

"You hurt yourself by not seeing the world as it is. Whoever you were, you now look like a bleary-eyed bum." The man then disappeared back into his store.

Lying on the hard floor had not given Luther a restful sleep. On returning home he fell into bed and woke hours later to a weight sagging the end of the mattress. Tony Pascual was wearing dark glasses. "I can see you but you can't see me," he said. He had this fuzz on his chin and cheeks from trying to grow a beard.

"What do you want?"

"Nothing. I just came here to look. You can tell things about people when they're sleeping." He laughed. A mean, stupid laugh. Luther didn't ask what he could tell. He didn't have to.

"You look like a peaceful gargoyle," Tony volunteered.

Luther sat up. "Get out of here," he said.

"Hegel sends his regards from the spirit world," Tony said. He had finally disposed of the dead animal, but not before it had begun to smell.

He was at home in the Automat, where he now often stopped off before his post office shift. The peace of heaven was there at the sturdy square table where he stared at the revolving tray of condiments over a cup of coffee: the slippery bottle of olive oil, the white pot with bits of dried mustard on its rim. Far below street level the burgundy red behemoths with overhead pantographs of the Pennsylvania Railroad would be entering and leaving the station and only a block west was the great Macy's. His history was right here, with his mother and Vera and Luke. What did it mean that he was alone now in returning to where he had been as a child eating the baked beans from small brown bowls and the macaroni and cheese in its green oval dish amid the art deco-illuminated signage of this dying eatery?

It was late into June now, and as he began his shift the Six-Day War was all he heard talked about by middle-aged men fired up about the conflict. "I'll be over there within a week if those Arabs start up again," one was saying, applying a wet paper towel to the back of his neck to cool off in the bathroom.

"They aren't starting shit. They got their asses stomped," said another one, thick and sweaty, a *New York Post* under his arm.

They looked at Luther.

"I guess you'll be going over too, you with that hair," the guy with the *Post* said.

"Not my war," Luther said.

"A Jew who's not for Israel is an anti-Semite. Believe it," the one with the paper towel said.

"Sorry, but I'm not Jewish."

"With that hair you're not Jewish?"

"Hair makes me Jewish?"

"You with your long hair. You wouldn't fight if you were Jewish. Peace now, burn the flag, all that hippie shit."

"No one's as brave as you, I'm sure."

He rushed at Luther and put a finger in his face. Luther looked down at his bald head and churning mouth and stained teeth.

"I love this country. I fought for it in World War II. We creamed those fucking Germans after those fucking Frenchies rolled over to get knackwursts up their asses. You have something smart to say about that, maybe?"

Luther drew away and went over to the window, where he lit a cigarette with a trembling hand.

"Wise guy here. A long-haired wise guy," he heard his attacker say.

Down below was the red-brick tabernacle, with its stained glass window, in the middle of the block. What a small world that had been.

Luther had nothing against the Israelis. He was not guilty as charged. Many many times had he fantasized about their vanquishing of the Arab armies to the rock and roll music of the Rolling Stones holler singing "Under My Thumb." He exulted in their lightning victory, was dazzled by their military might out of all proportion to their numbers. And Jesus himself was a Jew even if he did not belong to the Mossad or the Knesset. It seemed ingrained in him that the Israelis represented culture and refinement and high board scores and the Star of David, while all the Arabs seemed to offer was intransigence. And as for World War II, it was so heartbreakingly sad that Audie Murphy should, at a young age, lose his mother before joining the army and earning the Medal of Honor for his battlefield heroics. He floated in the concepts of the culture. He knew what Iwo Jima and Pearl Harbor and *The Bridge Over the River Kwai* were. And Luger and panzer and blitzkrieg. But that did not mean it was impermissible to laugh at people in a state of middle-aged bravado.

Chapter 26

"Why don't you come up to Camp? Mommy and Daddy said they would love to have you. You could stay the entire summer."

"May I hear this again, please? 'Mommy and Daddy said they would love to have you?"

"Of course they would. Oh, don't worry. All that other stuff is forgotten. In fact, they said they have been missing you and even expressed a fondness for you."

Luther weathered the inner shudder of horror at their alleged expression of affection and said yes.

That summer was Jim Morrison bellowing "Light My Fire" as if from a mountaintop and harmonic Cream singing "I Feel Free" from someplace in the sky and "Sergeant Pepper" sounding lonely notes all over the lawn, the idea that war could be set to music taking hold amid the bounty of firm breasts invading his consciousness in this wonderland of green. The sheer brazen explosiveness of acid rock that ignored books to come at you with the loud sound that told you number 1 was your reality. A turning point had surely come and Mona and her family and affluence and their manicured property were it.

The war in Vietnam was far away. The napalm showers the Vietnamese received and the constant whap whap of helicopter gunships spraying the countryside with deadly fire did have a place in his mind, but fueled no consistent moral outrage as it did in others. The great events—the war, the peace marches, the torching of the cities, they were secondary dramas to the drama of himself unfolding. So it seemed.

He popped a speed pill the night before leaving the city and found himself flying even as he stood in place, the beer going down like water in Moogie's. The bar was jammed. This would be his lucky night, he hoped. Sure, the idea of spending time with Mona and being out of the city was welcome, but it also meant the confines of family. He would be out of the hunt, away from the endless possibilities on the streets and in the bars of New York City. It was important not to fall behind. It was important to never ever fall behind but to amass the numbers that meant success, that meant safety.

He got weepy hearing "San Francisco ("Be Sure to Wear Flowers in Your Hair)," he got power driving hearing "Under My Thumb," he got a rush hearing "Somebody to Love." He was dancing naked and glorious to the cheers of millions.

And then a woman seated at the bar dared to say, "You look so serious."

"Is the sun so very blinding that you must diminish its glory?" Luther shot back, because she was wearing dark glasses in the dimness of the bar and could it possibly be an affectation?

"Trust me, you are not the sun."

"How about him? Is he the sun?"

"Who could you possibly be talking about?"

Luther nodded in the direction of the pony-tailed bartender with his shirt half unbuttoned to show off his tanned chest.

"Why would he be?"

"Stars are always the center of attraction, at least in their own minds. That's why they must be brought low and punished. Don't you see what he's doing? Look at him delicately moving strands of hair out of his face, as if all eyes are on him. He's just a macho girl."

"So you're jealous as well as serious."

"I have a sparkle in me that lights up the very sky. I'm in harmony here with everything but the bartender's act."

"And what exactly is that act?"

"Have you never heard the words 'live performance'?"

"You worry too much," she said.

"Why do you say that?"

"Because you have two vertical lines above your nose."She motioned with her martini glass to the bartender for a refill.

He got up close to her. "You're not radiating sunshine yourself," he whispered.

She placed her hand on his forearm with a feathery touch. "Close is for saying sweet things, darling. Talk to me about yourself."

He told her that he was aghast at his prospects but that he knew the wealthy if not the famous and so perhaps it did not matter.

She was an older woman, thirty-five or so, and poised. The place was jumping but she sat there detached. Her hand reached out with graceful ease for the stemmed glass at controlled intervals. Now and then her tongue would emerge and she would remove a bit of tobacco from the unfiltered cigarette in her other hand. In her tan silk blouse and black skirt, she was sophistication plunked down amid the bellbottoms and the work shirts.

"You're a tall, envious young man, and you're attuned to women. You can come home with me but you'll have to wait. That's two drinks from now."

He visited the john and peed on the ice cubes in the urinal. He felt special and golden and as if the night must never end. The graffiti poem was still there, the one about having made love a thousand times but now it was winter in the poet's soul. He declared the words as assembled to be a stinky bag of shit, now that he was next to the heat of life and absorbing the bright light of summer even in the dark.

She was a slow walker and placed her arm in his as they waited for the light. Up ahead was Washington Square Park. A police cruiser was parked between the marble arch and the fountain. A kid with his head wrapped in a red bandanna tossed a Frisbee over the top of the vehicle. Another kid, shoeless, barefoot, gave chase. The cop at the wheel nudged his partner. Luther thought the cops would shout out, "Where'd you find the freak, honey?" but they were content to lay their smirk on him.

Adjacent to her building stood a Presbyterian church, dark and gloomy. Behind the massive doors Luther imagined cobwebbed pews and a broken organ and dust-covered hymnals. "Fear and Faith" was the scheduled Sunday sermon, spelled out in white plastic letters in the glass-covered directory.

"Do you have fear or faith?" the woman asked, as she led him up the stairs of the walkup.

"Oh, I have both," Luther said.

She poured orange juice into two tall glasses and then a generous amount of vodka. "It's better when you have control over your own drinks," she said, coming out from behind her bar and handing him a glass.

"We have a bar where I live only we never stock up because we drink everything that comes into the house."

"You have to learn to drink, to control it so it doesn't control you."

"How do you do that?"

"By drinking all the time. People get into trouble when they try to limit their drinks. By giving in you allow the natural flow of your desires to regulate themselves."

"Wow. So why do you go out if you make better drinks at home?"

"To take home what I like that comes along. I'm a fisher of men."

She had turned on a blue overhead light and adjusted it with a dimmer, giving the room a cool, sensual feel. "Do you prefer that awful rock stuff?" She had moved onto the bed and was unzipping him.

"It blasts me to the moon. It takes me to the top of the heap. It makes me number one in all the universe."

"Is that what you want to be? Number one in all the universe? You sound like a very American boy." Several tokes on her expertly rolled joint—she stuck the whole thing in her mouth to wet it good and keep it toothpick-thin—rendered him too stoned for speech, the jazz notes of the active saxophone hurtling him through the infinite reaches of space.

"Nice. Skinny but nice," he heard her say from somewhere down below, his hands on her soft brown hair. And later, somewhere, sometime in the night, the words "If you stay the night, you can come in my mouth."

Strung out and groggy, Luther rushed home in the morning to pack his knapsack and made his way on little sleep through Port Authority to gate thirty-seven. It held no magic, having none of the promise of adventure of a train station. The driver stood outside the Trailways bus collecting tickets. He had a flat-top haircut and a face full of peeve and showed no ill effects from breathing in exhaust.

"I used to have a haircut like yours. My mother wanted me to be an all-American," Luther said.

"We still have barbers in this country. Now get on the bus."

When the driver got behind the wheel and looked into the overhead mirror, Luther was waiting for him with a strung-out smile, to which he added a vigorous thumbs up. Luther had no call to antagonize. He had grown up with men like him, men who now felt betrayed by currents they didn't understand and couldn't be a part of. In sweet sensations moments Luther could even feel love for the driver and his duty-bound life. It wasn't Luther's mission to annoy the man, even though he was.

Soon the comforting motion of the bus, beyond the stop and go of Lincoln Tunnel traffic, lulled Luther beyond all such concerns and into needed sleep. He awoke in time to see the bus leaving Phoenicia and pulling onto Route 28.

"That's it. That's my stop, right before that inn," Luther called out, about five miles down the straightaway.

"You want to get out, you've got to pay."

"I gave you my ticket."

"That takes you to Phoenicia, Anything after that is extra."

"How much extra?"

"Fifty-five cents."

Luther counted out the change into the man's hand. "No free rides on this bus," the driver said, pulling open the door with a long handle.

Gravel sprayed up from the spin of fat wheels as the bus pulled away, the vehicle expressing the driver's emphatic nature and unspoken convictions.

At the bottom of the hollow road he saw the jeep, with Mona behind the wheel. In spite of having showered, he felt dirty. As he approached on what was a perfect blue-sky day, he could only wonder if the dirt showed.

"What's with the paint?" he asked, of the splattered jeans she wore with her blue work shirt.

"I'm working. That's what is with them," she said. She had set up a studio in the barn, where horses had once been kept.

Amid the glories of nature, the tall trees and cultivated land and green mountains on either side, he felt the punishing effects of the night before, the long nap on the bus notwithstanding. He also felt great fear, and sought escape from all that awaited him. Fortunately, no greeting committee had formed at the house, and he was able, with the feeble excuse that his roommate Tony had disturbed his sleep, to fall into bed in the red room and sleep for another four hours.

When he awoke his guilt over the night before had been left behind. He had nothing to confess. He had nothing to feel dirty about. He had done what was right, right for him, right for his freedom. He had found his way. He had knocked on the door he needed to knock on, as when he was a child he had stood outside the rented room of a woman who lived on the same floor in his family's building, stood there without knocking and without words of explanation to speak should the black-haired woman open the door to find him there. He hadn't knocked on that door. He had finally gone away. And he hadn't knocked on other doors during Jane Thayer's reign of dominance over him. And in the long period of depression that had followed he had not knocked on any doors, but now he was knocking on doors and there was no reason to stop. He couldn't stop and he wouldn't stop. There was no life without knocking. None whatsoever. It was all life was about, seeing what was beyond that door. And once you had the tally going, you had to continue. You just had to if you were to stay ahead, stay ahead of the time when she would do the same, if she were to do the same, so you could have the protection of the numbers that you had amassed.

"How was your trip, Luther?" Lydia asked, with glass in hand. The cocktail hour had arrived.

"The driver gave me a hard time. I guess it was my hair. Being behind the wheel can do things to people."

"There is a segment of American society that is entirely repressive and at permanent war with the full idea of freedom, including how it shows itself in terms of dress and hairstyle." Peter spoke emphatically; his right hand chopped the air.

"But Poody, do you have to overwhelm Luther with such a strong point of view? Perhaps he feels somewhat differently," Lydia said.

"Don't worry. He feels just the same," Mona replied.

Luther was content to let Mona speak for him. He had no firmly established point of view about America or its various currents, hostile or benign, to offer, at least at the moment.

"Dad can really crank it up," Jeffrey said, when his parents had left the room. "And you haven't seen anything yet." There was laughter in his fifteen-year-old voice.

"Did you do OK with your courses?" Claire asked. Luther realized she was addressing him. She sat with her legs under her on one of the three sofas. Her skin was darker than Mona's, Mediterranean, and her hair was black and short and tightly curled. Mona said her older sister was a real powerhouse who would someday come into her own. Mona spoke of her as if she were mainland China.

"I am surviving the nuclear attack that was launched on me," Luther replied.

'What does that mean?"

"That I don't have the activity in my mind that you have in yours. That's what it means."

"Can you be more specific?"

All he could really think about were her breasts and the astonishing divide that was her cleavage and of resting his head on such a massive bosom.

"I am deficient in intellect. Ten more points of IQ might bring me within normal range and enable me to do battle."

"What do you mean, 'Do battle'?"

"Intelligence is a form of armor. It makes you impervious to your opponents' slings and arrows while providing you with the weaponry to demolish."

"Some people use their intelligence simply to be useful."

"I wouldn't know. All I do know is that it is definitely frustrating and a wound to live with this lack. The thing I think about all the time is sex. Like what color bra and panties you're wearing and what you're like in bed."

"This is hardly acceptable," she said, her voice rising to the level of her own disgust.

"Maybe. But if I looked like you I'd have sex all the time. In a way it's a total drag having to be a man. You've definitely got the best deal."

"What are you talking about?"

"You don't have to make overtures. You can just wait for the man to come along. And they always do."

"Why are you telling me all this?"

"Because the things you want to talk about bring me pain."

"What things?"

"Barnard and your College Board scores."

"This is so twisted."

Luther sighed. "Right now you are finding me ugly and without merit. But I've already entered your mind and your thoughts of me cannot be disposed of and are subject to change. Anyway, you have to move away from the furniture sooner or later."

"Right. That makes a lot of sense."

"You know what I mean."

"You're disgusting. And to think we have to put up with you for a while." She got up and walked out of the room.

He sat with himself for a few minutes, waiting for the thunder, but only Jeffrey arrived.

"What do you do?" Luther asked.

"What do you mean, what do I do?"

"Having fallen in love with your sisters, I feel obliged to know you even if you do not like me."

"Oh right, why didn't that occur to me?"

"So what do you do? Do you act from desperation? Are you able to do trigonometry? I did OK with math but only to the point that would not make me a man. Do you masturbate with your sisters in mind? I never did, but mine aren't as pretty as yours."

Jeffrey made a face. "Mind your own business," he said, with shut-down coldness.

"I like the way you talk to me," Luther said.

"Well, I don't like the way you talk to me or anyone else," Jeffrey said.

Luther sat silent for a while, something about Jeffrey very much on his mind. "By the way, do you have a big dick? Mona says your father does."

"Jesus." Jeffrey took off, and now Luther was alone again, knowing that somewhere, mostly in the kitchen, the family was in energized action for the evening's gathering, that they would not be content to sit in their separate corners but would be compelled to come together by the force of who they were.

Mona hurried through the living room carrying a large cooler. Baskets of food and other supplies followed, placed in the back of the jeep that in a taxed but dogged way climbed the rutted path. Mona and Luther rode shotgun on the running boards. Spaced here and there were "no trespassing" signs on the trunks of trees with the Van Dine name upon them, showing the power of the word in black and white to impose its will on the viewer's consciousness. From the leafy overhead came the chirping of unseen birds and the explosive racket of a pheasant flying off, while down the slope a deer broke from its hiding place, springing across a clearing, its thin, strong legs supporting its tawny bulk. At the last stretch, virtually perpendicular to the sky, Peter shifted into low low, the jeep now inching along. Luther imagined it tipping over and crashing down the mountain and exploding in a ball of flame.

He had pictured the lean-to as some wooden hovel made filthy by legions of backpackers and maybe a grimy barbecue grill, and so was surprised by its forward-looking design. A thing of cedar wood, it was set on a slate terrace offering a respite from the steep slope three-quarters of the way up the mountain. The interior was large and clean, with a soft spread over a mattress that could accommodate many, and there were easily removable screens to keep out the bugs.

Peter tended to steaks that sizzled on the grill while Lydia served drinks. Luther dragged his deck chair to the edge of the terrace. Far down the mountain you could see the road weaving through the dense foliage along the hollow and the layout of the property: the main house, the barn, the guest house, the solarium, the swimming pool, and up a rise, the meadow and a shale pile. Cultivated land, you saw from that vantage point, rivaled and even surpassed natural beauty.

Their voices carried lightly, easily, on the evening air as the sun dropped down over the mountains. No Tony Pascual or cats leaking their guts, no post office human automaton routine, no subways. Just Mona and her family and him, listening as Peter held forth about the Vietnam War and the hope it inspired in him to see the emergence of a counterculture and widespread opposition to establishment ways.

He heard their chatter and thought of the distance he had come that he should be in the midst of secularism, when, on the other side of the mountain, there had been another kind of camp, a camp of his childhood where old Ukrainian women of peasant thickness and demeanor hung laundry to dry in the fields and a pastor fulminated in a makeshift tabernacle about the eternal flames as punishment for iniquity, and "Bringing in the Sheaves" and "Rescue the Perishing" were sung in the cold mountain air and inedible, foul-smelling food was served and his mouth was washed with soap so cleansing could take place, and if Mommy in her softness would only come up the winding path and take him to her the way that she always took him to her so he could save her from all that was wrong in her life. But that was then and this was now in the secret passageway that life afforded for the miracle of escape to take place and for this family not standing on the sidelines of life jeering at those who had the *worldly* ways and frothing at the mouth at the *backsliding* sinners who had spurned the Christ Jesus. How could such a thing have happened, he could only wonder.

Looking back he would see Lenore's coming as a defining moment, one he had been waiting for. She arrived by bus the night following the evening at the lean-to. Peter picked her up at the bottom of the road serene in the knowledge that she was his for all time. A slender girl with short black hair in jeans and a black T-shirt.

Everett, the caretaker, followed, holding a fawn he had found weak and languishing in a field down by the compost pile only hours before.

"It's a wonder the dogs didn't get it. The house dogs, they form packs and run the deer down in teams." Everett's voice came hoarse from his throat, delivering uninflected words. Luther felt the weight of his woodsman's authority, the quiet and enduring space he inhabited. Like a tree he was, rooted, while presidents and events flew by into nothingness.

Mona made a bed of blankets in the corner of the living room. She fed the fawn from a baby bottle full of warm milk while Everett, in his white T-shirt and green Dickey work pants, looked on.

"You all take good care now. Don't be surprised if her mom starts coming around, if she's still alive." It was rare for Everett to come into the house, Peter would say later. When he did step inside, there was no getting him to sit down, the information saying something about Everett but more about Peter and his complicated awareness of people.

"You try it," Mona said, so Luther did, feeling the pull of the deer's sucking mouth on the nipple of the bottle.

"Oh, he's so gentle," Lenore remarked, entering at the point where Luther was petting the fawn with one hand as it nibbled bits of bread out of his other hand.

Mona had spoken about her younger sister with fear. It was wounding to her that Lenore was more popular than she was, so wounding that she had threatened to move out if Lenore decided to leave boarding school and return home. What was this thing called family where competition ruled?

Luther felt like an actor feigning interest in the fawn. Lenore had not been there to witness his violence against the chipmunks and the birds. Every stroke he now gave it was done with the awareness that Lenore was looking on. *Gentle*. There were worse things to be called.

He heard Lenore speak the name Casey Westerbrook as she talked among her sisters and her brother and her parents. Casey had a brother with an East Village apartment. Casey had been staying with his brother ever since dropping out of boarding school. He had driven up to the school without a license and high on acid just to see her and returned to New York City the same way and the time he threw a piece of chalk at the math teacher. "He's such an asshole," Lenore said, with love in her voice.

On the mantelpiece Peter placed the figures of fired clay Lenore had made—a horse and a goat and a distorted head of herself. The messiness of art, the mold that had to be broken to make it.

Luther yielded the fawn to her. He noted the beautiful round shape of her head and her small wrists. Androgyny. That was the pull of her. She was one and the other both. Her force field was overpowering.

The family played its nightly game of hearts around the small living room table.

"Join us," Lydia said, but he interpreted her words as goading and mocking of his apartness.

"I've got some catching up to do before that can happen." He must read and read to garner the facts they already knew so he could be presentable in their company. Because how could he be at the table without the firm knowledge of the flora and fauna that Lydia possessed? How could you live without knowing phlox from chrysanthemums, peonies from irises?

Peter spread his cards triumphantly. He had shot the moon.

"G-r-r-r-r," Lydia said, in mock anger, as they put away the cards and prepared for bed.

No, he wasn't tired just yet, Luther told Mona. He would stay up for a bit and read. They kissed good night and she went off by herself.

The creaking of the floorboards soon ceased in the upstairs rooms occupied by Claire and Lenore, the only sound now of moths beating against the window panes with the fluttering fury of exiles desperate to return.

He took a heart-shaped Dexamyl from his pocket and stared at it and then he stared at it some more but from all the angles it stayed the same in its innocent pinkness. If he put it back in his pocket he could shortly go to bed, but the pill said it had inquiries to make and places to take him on the road of adventure, that there were lust-filled patches of the night that could not be visited without it. He tried to see ahead to the morning. He pictured himself waking refreshed and peaceful and in a place of rediscovered innocence with Mona beside him. And yet what was that to secret passages leading to unending pleasure?

With one swallow indecision had been vanquished; he would not have to miss his life. For an added boost he went to the liquor table and poured out a large quantity of gin and a smaller measure of tonic into a cobalt blue glass and drank the drink down without the benefit of the ice cubes that would only rattle around in the glass and crowd it up.

Now his ears were alert for the sound of her feet on the floorboards upstairs. Complicity was not exactly reigning and yet he knew somehow the night was not over, and as if by force of will she soon drew near, the steps of the staircase creaking as she descended them, her irregular beauty undiminished in the robe she wore.

"Where are you going?" he asked.

"I want to smoke, but not in the house," she said, pulling him into secrecy with her whispered words.

He thought she was talking about cigarettes but she opened her hand, which held a stick of grass.

"Is that your nightcap?" he asked.

"You could say so," she replied.

He followed her out onto the porch and across the lawn to the pool under the spell of soft moonlight. She lit the joint and inhaled, holding the smoke that her lungs craved. She offered the stick to him but he declined, saying she probably wanted the whole thing for the wonder it could bring to her consciousness.

"I don't need a lot. Believe me," she said, and so he took it and toked up good.

They sat in silence. For how long he didn't know. "Is the work hard?" he finally asked.

"Is what work hard?"

"You know, school."

She erupted into laughter.

"Oh, I've been caught in my stupidity," he said. A feeling of shame came over him but soon passed.

"Uh oh," she said, and laughed some more, as he removed his sneakers and shirt and pants.

A floodlight attached to the trunk of a pine tree illuminated the pool area. Insects hovered inches above the cold stream water. He swam, almost stealthily, gently side-stroking his way through several laps, concerned now that eyes might be upon him from all the darkened bedrooms of the house. To conceal his lustful intent, he tried to assume an expression of innocence and avoided looking poolside, fearing his eyes would signal his desire and she would cut the night right there and return to the house and it would be a close but no cigar affair, every day thereafter taking her farther and farther from him as she saw more of who he was in the singleness of his quest for her.

And yet, when she passed him with a slow, relaxed crawl, the caution lights switched to green.

"Reckless, very very reckless," she said, when poolside he put his arms around her from behind. She turned and he kissed her and she kissed him back with what seemed like equal hunger.

"When Casey comes we can't do this anymore. You know that, don't you?"

"Sure. I know that," he said. They now lay on a mat taken from the pool house. She opened and raised her legs and led him into an open-mouthed kiss.

Glass in hand, he sat afterward in the living room, with the smell of the fawn's flatulence. Her big eyes assessed him serenely. He could only envy the creature's innocence. The pot haze had lifted but the pill, he knew from experience, would deprive him of sleep for at least several more hours. One minute he was in bliss over his experience with Lenore and anticipating more. The next he was trembling in the awareness of the trouble he was now in.

It was well after daylight before he fell asleep. He awoke hours later to the sound of a car rolling over the wooden bridge and the voices of Everett and Peter in conversation nearby. Happy, guilt-free voices, the voices of people who slept peacefully.

"How's the sister fucker?" Mona was standing over him.

"What?"

"You heard me. You stayed up last night so you could fuck my little sister."

"What?"

"Don't lie to me, you bastard. She told me everything. How could you? I trusted you." She ran out the door crying.

He went to the window. Everett and Peter were standing by the jeep, which had a cart attached to it. He envied their morning industry while he had to live in the ruins of where his intrigue had led him.

He fell back to sleep and when he emerged that afternoon, Jeffrey was sitting at the wheel of the mower on the big lawn, the concentric circles growing smaller and smaller, the gas fumes blending with the sweet smell of the freshly cut grass. Mona had set up an easel in the meadow, where she was painting a landscape, while Lydia worked in the vegetable garden and Peter cleaned the pool Luther and Lenore had swum in only the night before with a large mesh screen attached to a long aluminum pole. The dead insects and other detritus caught in the mesh he would fling into the brush. He was showing himself as a bronzed miracle in his black bikini briefs, his long blond hair falling forward over his forehead, as he went about his chore.

The jeep tore over the bridge, a tall slender boy barefoot in jeans and short-sleeved seersucker shirt standing on the running board. A cone of light followed him, and when he stripped down to a black bathing suit and dove into the pool, Peter laughed in astonishment and whispered to Luther, "Lenore has found an Adonis of her own."

Peter left Luther to ponder his words while he clicked Casey Westerbrook with the Nikon F camera to visually capture the fact that Lenore had gone out and gotten herself a teenage version of her father.

Soon a sound different from the classical recordings that had played on the stereo, Cream singing "I Feel Free," was blasting from the speakers secured to the trunks of pine trees overlooking the pool.

That summer was Lydia saying, "We need this time at camp for our rejuvenation. Peter finds working with his hands the perfect and necessary complement to his intellectual labors, being chained to his desk nine months of the year. We have an active social life down in New York. We return in the fall with this zest to see our friends and attend the theater."

The summer was Luther taking what she said personally, as if in elevating Peter and herself she was somehow denigrating him. It was withdrawing from them into his solitariness with the unread *Moby-Dick*. It was being worn down by all they had and all he didn't have and seeing Mona as she stayed back with them smiling and participating in the life of her family rather than enter the darkness that enfolded him. It was the repetitive cycle of punishment for her crime of abandonment.

They had moved to the guest house, a large, rustic space with thick wooden beams in the renovated barn. There were two single beds they pushed together and a pool table and a radio that played mostly static. Separating from the main house had been his idea. The family was too much present, the walls too thin. Distance was required if he was to breathe. The swamp of family was not for him. So he had said to Mona, who did not resist.

That evening, when the family played their usual game of hearts, he withdrew to the guest house, where he lay down, listening for the crunch of gravel or any other sounds of her approach. Every minute that she stayed away increased his fear and anger. She was saying something to him. He wasn't important. He could be taken for granted. In the tug of war that he had now created in his mind, the family was winning. They were pulling her back into their sphere. That she might be happy in their company was no cause for his own happiness. It could only be at his expense. When finally he heard her footsteps and then the door sliding open, he grabbed his copy of *Moby Dick* to pretend that he had other occupations for his mind.

"How is it?" she said, no longer calling him sister fucker. He did not have to answer. He did not have to yield the weapon of his silence.

"I asked you a question. How is it? The book."

He would show her what power was, what it was to take him lightly, the way he had when his mother would go through a litany of names before getting his right, having dared to temporarily erase him from her mind. Withdrawing to his room and refusing to come to the dinner table. When she brought the food to him, refusing to eat and sending her away with the plateful of chicken with rice, his very favorite. Minutes later she would return, but again he would spurn her until she began to cry, saying he and all the children treated her like the dirt beneath her shoes, and then he would have to cry and cry that he had hurt her so, but only after first seeing her tears, the sign he needed that she loved him after all and that he could continue to live.

There in the guest house he held fast to his silence in protest against the annihilating ways of women and when she fled from him once more, she only confirmed her intention to abandon him at every turn.

Back with her family, she would not be waving her arms so animatedly. She would not have that very big smile on her face. She would be learning the price she had to pay for unfaithfulness. Because he was not to be played with. He definitely had too much firepower for that.

When, an interminable hour later, she returned, the smile gone from her face, he held his silence.

"You're still angry?"

He reached for his brown bag and began putting things into it, including the books with words that did not stay in place upon the page.

"What are you doing?" she asked as he continued to pack.

She began to cry and he dropped his brown bag and lay face down on the bed to hide his relief. If he had taken it too far, she would have seen that he could not go anywhere, that he was stuck right where his heart was.

It soon became clear that Casey's looks were superior to his mind. He sought to hide this deficiency behind the sound of Iron Butterfly but still did he make Luther fall down in love for all that he was physically with his long blond hair and perfect teeth and perfect body.

It also became clear that he was dangerous behind the wheel, a teenage fatality waiting to happen. While driving the Sunbeam Alpine Lydia had offered him, he showed no awareness of the rain-slicked road or protective instincts for his passengers in regard to life and limb. He drove with the hood down, the houses flying by and construction workers fleeing his careering path as he sought in motion the power he otherwise lacked. Luther in the front seat, Mona and Lenore in the back as it sped along before veering off the road and spinning around several times. All of them uninjured, though in the spin around the tree the Sunbeam had been headed for, the headlights had been shaved off. There stood Casey with a denying smile on his face as if to say, in the pride and fear that wouldn't let him say any more, "Well, that was nothing."

Some workers who had been resurfacing the two-lane road now slowly approached, drawn by the recklessness they had witnessed. Rugged men in Dickey shirts and jeans who had seen the world from the place of quiet and methodical purpose for a long, long time. They could only shake their heads and offer words of caution—"Lucky, very lucky"—and help to roll the car out of the ditch and leave them there with a resigned reminder that road signs heralding treacherous curves ahead were posted for a reason. Men with truth in their lives, as Luther saw it, as the result of honest labor when all he had was his paperback books.

"I'll drive us back," Mona said, quietly but firmly. Casey slipped into the back seat next to Lenore without argument.

Now when Luther tried to make eye contact with Lenore, she was looking elsewhere. From deep within a directive had originated to avoid his eyes at all cost, as if determined to be true to what she had said, that he could be with her that one time and no more and that now he must live with the weight of the guilt for what he had done. The space she had created for her and Casey to stand in was inviolate. Distance was not a factor; they could be as little as two feet away, and still he could not hear them, his ears being no match for their powers of modulation.

But the voices of Mona's parents were in range that summer, in the morning ritual of Peter holding forth and Lydia gently demurring.

"This most emphatically is not America the beautiful. This is a ravaged, ugly country whose movers and shakers are driven by the profit motive to bulldoze and concretize whatever existing beauty still remains. There are people in this very community who would wrest this property from us and subdivide it and sell it off as lots."

"Oh Poody, you may be right, but must you be so strident?" Not needing to probe the fear that drove his judgmental fury there in the living room in the early morning before the others were up and about listening to him. Both of them in their robes. He had provided her with the structure she had lacked and served as a guide out of her Cambridge torpor and those barroom nights. That shoe he found in her refrigerator because her father had gone away and her mother had gone away and no one had ever come since, only the institutions that gave her the facts she could not put to productive use in the depression in which she lived. Without him Camp was a weedy, neglected place, as it had become when her mother and her grandmother passed from the scene and she had gone on from Miss Porter's to Radcliffe, Peter being the estate manager needed to bring order where none had been.

The ones who came that summer were not principals of darkness nor were they bearers of the light. Frank, Claire's boyfriend, was tall and lean and had no need of the sun to be deeply tanned. He arrived full of himself, with a head of tight, black curls and an attitude as cocky as Claire's was self-effacing.

"We're putting together an incredible band. We'll be doing a lot of clubs on Long Island this fall," he said. He was not in school, having dropped out of Columbia halfway through his first semester.

"The only reason I got in was my 1400 board scores," he said casually.

"Why couldn't I be born with brains like that? Do you know how hard I have to work to get good grades? My board scores went down 100 points to the low 600s when I took them the second time." She turned to Luther. "How did you do on the SAT?"

If he lied, they would never know him as he was and his self-consciousness would simply grow to the point where he would not be able to say two words. He would have to keep his mouth shut; otherwise, scrutinizing Claire would put things together and see that he was really a dumb young man and a liar as well.

"I failed them," he said,

"What do you mean, you failed them? You can't really fail them," Claire said.

"My scores were low, real low," he said.

"Well, you look smart," Frank said.

"That could be a problem, couldn't it?" Luther said. "A person looking smart but not feeling smart or being smart, and then pride factoring in to divide him from his brethren lest they find out how un-smart he is."

"You need to join a rock and roll band," Frank said.

"Oh no you don't," Luther replied. "I'm not going to hell. I'm not going to be some anarchic hippie. I'm going to stay on the straight and narrow and earn my college credits and be what I need to be. Because you can't get intelligent by listening to sounds or even making sounds. You have to have your eye on the words in a book to get yourself anywhere."

"Are you always like this?" Frank laughed.

"I am endeavoring," Luther said.

"Right. Endeavoring," Frank said.

"And don't think I've forgotten that you said you're from Long Island. Let me tell you something about Long Island, my friend. It smells of fish. And do you know why it smells of fish? Because it has made serious inroads into the sea. And do you know the consequence of this little prick of land being surrounded by the ocean depths? Do you?"

"I'm sure you'll tell me."

"The people who inhabit it lack warmth. That is the consequence. They are unduly influenced by cold waters."

"Are you saying I lack warmth?"

"Are you Irish and from Long Island?"

"That could be."

"Then the case has to be closed, because you have been surrounded by water far too long, first in your mother country, and now in the New World. You are but a fish out of water who plays his guitar."

"And you're an ass," Claire shot back, and took Frank away so Luther could have the isolation that he deserved.

A car rumbled the bridge boards that afternoon. An advertising man with his own blender had arrived from New York City to concoct strong and fancy drinks, his name being Sal Duprese and his manner being buttoned down and corporate even when polluted because he could not smile from anywhere within himself. And Luther lived right inside his fear, that terror which created a barrier that could not come down, while the Van Dines had an aerial perspective on their friend, accepting him as he was with no wrenching emotions about his issues.

And Fred Waring showed up, a man seething behind the Howdy Doody smile and the watchful eyes that were a truer indicator of who he was. He had an enormous head packed with brains that he used for the commitment of whole scenes and acts of Shakespeare to memory, and he offered a low, gravelly voice to accompany his smiling ferocity. An actor in his mid-thirties, he too was an advertising man, his company being Winthrop, Shields, and Farberhainey, which had offices on several continents, but Fred was stage-struck, he just had the bug, and was at war with anyone he perceived as trying to keep him from his dream.

"He used to be married to an actress named Sally. Mommy told us that they would have terrible fights. He would get envious of her successes and beat her black and blue. He can be very violent under that calm expression," Mona said.

The personal information gripped Luther. He thanked Fred for being there, for being a success story over his emotions and asked how he had reached that point, but Fred was not partial to Luther and could only bring himself to say, "Get away from me and get away from me now," as if he recognized in Luther someone to be shunned, the self he had been before the modicum of light arrived that allowed the Howdy Doody grin to break free of the restrictions it had placed on itself.

He was followed by an actress, Claudia Flame, an aging secretary who said she represented the lighter side of life. Luther was warned that she had a tongue that served as a whip. During her visit she downed many drinks and said, "Some of us have to work, you know," offering a truth lacking in love, a universally shared awareness of the materially different status of the Van Dines from all others who came along. Claudia Flame then turning her tongue on Fred Waring, saying, in a moment of connection with Fred Waring, "How does it feel not to have your wife Sally to beat?"

Fred just brushed her off with an expression of gratitude for solid bowel movements. "There's nothing in the world that beats it," he said.

All of them going to the graveyard with their own obscurity, where their bones would turn to dust and all memory of them lost.

"She calls Mommy and Daddy beautiful losers," Mona said, Claudia having been a participant in a magical summer when the playhouse in the nearby town of Phoenicia was open and actors and actresses and directors came up from New York City for a season of drama. "Mommy flowered in that summer," Mona said. Her mother had a lead role in *Summer and Smoke* and qualified for an Actor's Equity card. Photographs of her in performance in the guest house testified to her emoting power. Mona was only eight or so but she remembered the guests carousing into the night, the smell of liquor and of cigarettes on their breath and casual nudity and sex a given on the vast estate. The famous before they became famous, their names now in lights and in magazines. But not her mother. "She got cold feet. Everyone told her to continue but she chose to play it safe," Mona said, with the scorn of one with no appreciation of her mother's maternal makeup.

Frank did not go away. He stayed on and on with Jimi Hendrix as his god. Luther admired the attributes of soundness in his body and his mind, and his skin's ability to retain its tan, but Frank also had a mouth that left everything in doubt, because if you isolated it, you saw the way the big teeth were pushing cruelly against the sliver lips. It was by now an acknowledged fact that Frank's father had done a vanishing act from his life, and slowly Luther came to the understanding that Frank might not have been there among the Van Dines in a state of laughing indolence but instead rocketing up to the stars that were his destiny if the power source in his life hadn't been terminated when his father took it on the lam.

"Where do you come from, Luther? Did you just materialize?"

Frank had the courage of bare feet to go with his white cut-off jeans and black T-shirt as they sat on the terrace where dinner was being delivered on heavy platters.

Luther stammered. "I was born in a small town. Republicans were in the majority and they were mean. Varmints filled the land and the virtue of women and the honor of men were being continually compromised. I didn't know it at the time, but this was the reason for my birth. I was there to bring healing where there had been none and to fix wrongs that had allied people against their own true purpose. I was not afraid of guns and not afraid of death and learned to sling lead and won a fierce reputation among real men and the ladies."

"Luther, I believe Frank was asking you a question. Could you answer him more truthfully?" Claire said. She had a smoke in hand and put it to her mouth.

"I was seeking to."

"Do you have a father? Do you have anyone?" Claire pressed the case.

"Of that I cannot speak," Luther said. He sat there among them in his conspicuous silence.

Frank had picked up a copy of the *Daily News,* a paper that Luther was not supposed to read, given what it was in relation to the *New York Times.*

"Hey Luther, how do you spell your last name?" Frank asked.

"Did I say I had a last name?"

"Everybody has a last name."

"Picasso has a last name?"

"Picasso is his last name."

"And his first name, too. That's why he is such a genius."

"I believe Pablo is his first name."

"And do you call him Pablo or Picasso?"

"Where did you say you go to school?"

"I go wherever anybody will have me. I am easy to receive, whether I have a last name or not. So don't cop an attitude just because you have a last name you allow into the air. Not that you have announced your last name, at least to me."

"Dolan. That's my last name."

"Dolan? Dolan?" Luther laughed an unfriendly laugh right in the face of Frank.

"What is your problem today?"

"Leave it to you to feel Pharisee-proud because you have only two syllables to contend with and do not have to deal with consonantal shame. You assume that makes you all-American in your peculiar and foppish darkness."

"Hey, man, I was just asking you for your last name, not your IQ."

"My name is Luther. You know that already. Confront the truth of your own smells before you get into mine."

"Oh deep, man, deep."

"His last name is Garatdjian. G-a-r-a-t-d-j-i-a-n. Mona told us" Claire said, returning to her book.

"People, dig this, I think I've found Luther's grandfather. Here he is, right in the centerfold of the *Daily News,*" Frank said. The centerfold was titled "Summer Fun." There were photos of people on the beach and in the park, the old and young before the lens, and there was his father in a wheelchair on a traffic island on Broadway. The camera distorted his face so his nose had the size and shape of a parrot's beak. The caption read, "Hatchidor Garatdjian finds time each day for outdoor prayer." His father was grinning into the camera and lapping up his temporary fame.

"Groovy first name your grandfather has," Frank said, and he laughed his energy-less little laugh.

Luther had only this to say: "You are not driving me away. I am here for the long haul owing to the rodent class I belong to." He was quivering as he said these words, but he got them out.

"Luther, is English your first or second language?"

"What do you think, you who come from Long Island? To say that one speaks English first is to say that we have never been elsewhere, and that you surely know is a lie."

"Oh yeah, right."

"Leave Luther alone. Can't you see he's crazy?" Claire said, before returning to her book

"I am not finished with you. I will never be finished with you, the way a lover can never be finished with the rock that has its heart," Luther said to Claire. "You define what an older sister could and must be by the smell of your beauty and the power of your cleavage." He wandered off where the air would better have him and collapsed into bed in the guest house.

Chapter 27

He had been there before. Not there exactly, but somewhere over the mountain at the Bible camp to which his mother had sent him so he could have the fresh air of the country, she said. From his cabin window, he had watched the older kids stripping the bark from a sapling, Clementino and Bunny working away with their bowie knives, long, sappy peelings piling up at their feet. Soon the trunk was smooth as a bone and glistened in the sun. Sonia Montalvo and Rosie and Juanita and some of the other girls looked on. Clementino and Bunny had done it because they felt like doing it. From the same window, he had seen old and heavyset women, women like his mother but who weren't his mother, in the rocky field hanging laundry out to dry.

Pastor Chernenko found out. He had his find out ways and confronted Clementino and Bunny by the main house. He wanted to hit them. He wanted to hit them very hard. Luther could see he wanted to hit them because his tongue was clamped between his sliver lips. It was the kind of thing his oldest sister, Hannah, did when she got to hitting and hitting. But Pastor Chernenko didn't dare to hit them because they were bigger than he was and played with knives and had bodies packed with power.

It was frightening to think that there might not be any more trees in twenty years.

"Boys, you cannot treat property in this manner. I bring you up here from New York City so you can have all the beauty that nature offers, not so you can abuse things. I should send you home for this."

Pastor Chernenko's face was red and sweaty, the way it got when he was giving the evening sermon down at the tabernacle. Some of the girls were crying. They didn't want to see Clementino and Bunny sent home. They were the oldest boys at the camp and almost counselors themselves.

That evening, as they did every evening, the children went to the tabernacle, except for Clementino and Bunny. The old people from the main house, who did the cooking and laundry, joined them. They had sad, fleshy faces and served up stinky food. "You don't eat. Skin and bones is what you are," they would say, and run their fingers up his exposed rib cage, as if it were a washboard. Everyone sang "In the Garden" and 'When the Roll Is Called Up Yonder" and "There Shall Be Showers of Blessing," their voices rising in the cold mountain air, but it couldn't take away the homesickness, the incessant yearning for his mother.

June was there. She was young and pretty, with a shawl over her shoulders to keep her warm. She sang "Rescue the perishing, care for the dying, snatch them in pity from sin and the grave." When she looked from her hymnal across the aisle to him and smiled, his heart swelled with the wild pain of longing, her prettiness and her smile signifying a relationship with the world beyond the bounds of the drab religious camp and hope that she could take him there.

Pastor Chernenko was on fire. He waved his short arms and worked himself into a sweat as he moved about on the platform at the front of the narrow tabernacle. Did they know that every last one of them was a sinner? Did they know unless they were washed in the blood of the Lamb that they would burn forever in the fires of hell? Did they know how hot those flames were, that they burned a thousand times hotter than gasoline? Did they know what forever meant?

"Won't you come to the altar, children? Won't you, precious children, receive him, Christ Jesus, while there is still time?"

Reuben Rodriquez. Eddie Gomez. Stinky Pilsudski. Sonia Montalvo. Rita Escobar. Juanita Alvarez. They and all the others flocking to the prayer rail. His sister Vera, too. He watched them as if from a great distance, embarrassed by the spectacle of his sister kneeling on the dirt floor and receiving the reward of Pastor Chernenko's comforting hand on her head as she wept. A whole lot of weeping and wailing going on that night and every night.

Luther slipped away to the kitchen of the main house. The entrance was right under the verandah. Nearby he could hear, over his pounding heart, a coon foraging in the rusty oil drum where garbage was dumped. Nearby a porcupine was noisily gnawing at the bark of a tree. He opened the screen door and in a cupboard found the candy bars. He snatched all his hands and pockets could hold, two rolls of Life Savers, two Mars Bars, a Sugar Daddy, a couple of Milky Ways, and two rolls of Necco Wafers.

On an embankment, at the foot of the mountain, lay the abandoned railroad tracks. He imagined a train, the light from its engine spreading over the trees. He would jump on the back of the caboose and lie on it through the night while the workers slept in their bunks. Every second would bring him closer to home and his mother, who was there waiting for him at the end of the line.

He was back in his room when he heard their voices and the scuffing of feet on the front porch and the screen door opening and slamming shut. Reuben and Eddie entered the room. Their dark eyes were misty with tears, but they were smiling with the glow of whatever they had received in the evening sermon.

"Hey, look, Luther, Eddie and I will never call you any of those names anymore," Reuben said. They were city kids, like himself, from the church on West Thirty-third Street. Squarehead. Flathead. Box Head. Those names.

Their apology so embarrassing. So phony. The sermon had stretched them, but like a taut rubber band, they would soon snap back and he would again feel the sting of their taunts.

Clementino and Bunny had gone off into the woods rather than attend the service. Clementino beat a porcupine with his garrison belt. He had the quills in the black leather to prove it. He had been walking along a trail when the porcupine appeared in his path. Everyone knew he had beaten the porcupine because of Pastor Chernenko bawling out him and Bunny.

Stinky wet his bed that night. Stinky was always wetting his bed. He wanted to crawl in with Luther, but Luther wouldn't let him. He had green teeth and smelled.

'What am I going to do?" he said, in his whiny voice.

"Sleep on the floor."

"But it's cold."

"So sleep on the side of your bed that's not wet."

"I peed the whole thing."

Luther got out of bed. The mountain air so cold. Stinky hadn't pissed the whole thing, but there was this big stain. They stripped the bed, and then they turned the mattress over. "Sleep on that, and shut up," Luther said. Everybody talked to Stinky like that.

Luther got out two Milky Ways from his dresser drawer and gave him one.

"Ooh, where did you get this?"

"I just got it," Luther said.

"This is good," Stinky said, nibbling at the candy bar and snuffling between bites. Stinky had crossed eyes. You didn't really know where he was looking.

They were woken by a pounding on the door the next morning. "Rise and shine. Rise and shine." The small cabin seemed to shake. "You up in there?"

When Luther didn't answer fast enough, the door swung open. Bob Pellalugra, the counselor, stepped into the room. His blond hair stood up like bristles on a brush. Stinky was still sleeping, bare-assed and face-down on the stripped mattress. Bob Pellalugra saw the mound of wet bedding in a pile on the floor. He took a towel, wet it in the bathroom sink, and snapped it on Stinky's ass. Stinky stirred. Bob snapped the towel again. Stinky rolled over and looked at him through sleep-bleary eyes.

"Are you the pig who did this?"

Stinky looked down to where he saw Bob Pellalugra pointing and nodded. Bob led him out of bed by his ear and drove him to the floor. He pressed Stinky's face into the wet bedding.

"Do you like that smell, Stinky? Because that's your smell. What are you going to do for your next stunt, Stinky? You going to take a big fat crap in your bed, maybe?"

"No," Stinky said. It was a tortured, elongated no, as Bob was still twisting his ear. Stinky's eyes were now tearing from the pain. Bob shoved him onto the bedding with his foot.

"What are you looking at?" Bob Pellalugra glared at Luther.

"Nothing," Luther gave the word low energy, not wanting to further inflame Bob Pellalugra and have the ape on him, the way he had been on Stinky. Bob Pellalugra had been in the Marine Corps. He had bulging muscles and a thick neck and looked like he could break a brick with his head. On his right forearm was a faded tattoo of a woman with long legs and big boobs from before his decision for Christ at a Billy Graham crusade. His wife didn't look like that, that was for sure. Ruth Pellalugra was the girls' counselor. She wore thick glasses and was missing a front tooth.

In the afternoon Luther went exploring with Stinky. There was an old house down the hill from the cabins. You walked on this slate path between tall pine trees and there it was, the lawn weedy and the porch in disrepair. They passed through the unlocked door and explored one room after another. A dresser and a couple of beds were all that remained. Stinky began to laugh. He just laughed and laughed. And so did Luther. The laughter went on and on.

Stinky staggered over to a window. "Someone's coming," he said, and bolted down the stairs. Pastor Chernenko had warned the children that the house was off limits. Fear slowed Luther's flight, as in dreams in which he had a healthy head start on his pursuer but froze as the distance quickly closed between them. He had the sudden thought that if he just stayed in place, whoever was coming would hurt him less than if he ran away. But then he too bolted down the stairs, his hand catching a piece of curled wallpaper. He held it as he ran. Hearing the loud tear, Stinky turned before fleeing and burst through the back door. Luther followed in the field of high grass, as afraid now of timber rattlers and copperheads as any pursuer, and trailed Stinky up the hill and into the cabin, where they should have been napping to begin with.

Stinky, sweaty and winded, said maybe he hadn't seen anyone after all and fell asleep on Luther's bed. Bob Pellalugra had thrown his mattress on the roof to dry out. It seemed like a crazy place for a mattress to be.

While Stinky slept, Luther wrote to his mother:

> I want to come home. They give us stinky food to eat and the people are mean. Every day I see you coming for me up the path but you never arrive. I want to save you from the building owner who is hurting you and Auntie Eve. Do you know that I am going to be a lawyer so he cannot treat you like dirt anymore only it frightens me that there may not be time for me to get there before you die.

Once again there were heavy footsteps in the hall and insistent pounding on the doors.

"Children, children. Everyone come to the dining hall immediately," Pastor Chernenko demanded. It was serious business if he was waking them from their naps. It meant trouble of the biggest kind. Luther saw the piece of dangling wallpaper in his mind.

Reuben and Eddie and Stinky and the rest of them flocked out. "Uh oh, someone's going to get it," Stinky said. They filed into the dining hall in the main house and sat at the bare tables. Across the room Luther saw his sister Vera. She too had been roused from sleep. He wished in that moment he could borrow her innocence.

"Children, I have brought you together for a reason. One of you has been bad. One of you walks a wicked path."

Pastor Chernenko paced up and down the dining hall as he spoke, his head down and his hands behind his back. He had pasty skin and fake, orange-colored hair.

"You know, children, it is a sin to destroy private property. It is not Christian and God will not love you for it. You know it is what the evil Communists do. Filthy, filthy people with no respect for human life. God must have his punishment. He must, so righteousness can live in the land, thank you, Jesus." Pastor Chernenko stopped in front of one of the girls. "You know that, Alma, don't you? You know that it is a sin to destroy private property." He ran his hand over her cheek and stroked her black hair.

Alma nodded her head.

"Of course Alma knows. Alma is a good girl. Alma comes to the prayer rail every evening. Alma has given herself to the Christ Jesus. She has been washed in the Blood of the Lamb."

Alma was visited with visions. She had cried and cried just the other night, out front of the main house. She was seeing her family's building go up in flames in New York City. She was seeing her family burning and burning in the flames. She screamed and tore her hair. It had filled Luther with dread to hear her wailing so. Couldn't the firetrucks come? Couldn't they put out the flames? That was the thing that had pained him the most, that the fire trucks wouldn't get there in time. In terror Luther ran and ran, as if to flee his pain and the horror of Alma's family being burned alive in their New York City building.

Pastor Chernenko was so very soft and gentle with the children. He next stood in front of Eddie. "You are a good boy, too, Eddie. You too come to the prayer rail. You too know it is a sin to destroy private property."

Pastor Chernenko moved on to Stinky. "Do you have something to tell us, Stinky? Do you know of anyone in our midst who would do wickedness? Do you know of anyone who would rip wallpaper from a wall? Do you, Stinky?" Stinky stared down at his sneakers. Pastor Chernenko patted the back of his head, smoothed his hair, then lifted his chin with his finger. "Of course you know," he said, in the same soft tone. Pastor Chernenko moved on to now stand in front of Luther. "Tell us, Stinky. Don't be afraid." Luther felt Pastor Chernenko's eyes bearing down on him.

"Luther," Stinky said.

"Luther what, Stinky?"

"Luther ripped the wallpaper."

"And why did Luther rip the wallpaper?" Pastor Chernenko asked.

"I don't know why," Stinky said.

"Yes, you do. You know why. It is because this boy is destructive, because he throws stones and breaks windows time after time after time. It is because he is an ungrateful boy, ungrateful to have this time in the beautiful country. It is because he doesn't come to the prayer altar like you and Alma and the other children. You may all leave," Pastor Chernenko said quietly.

Pastor Chernenko twisted Luther's ear as if intent on tearing it off. In the effort his eyes were reduced to slits and his tongue protruded between his thin lips, as Hannah's did between her thick lips when she beat him. Just when the tears were brimming, Pastor Chernenko let go.

"I should send you home. You have the devil in you." Pastor Chernenko, breathing hard, ordered him to his room.

That week the children gathered with Pastor Chernenko down at the creek. The rocks on the bottom hurt your feet as you waded in, and you couldn't really swim, because the water was never deeper than a few feet. Luther watched from the little bridge over the creek. A dead snake, long and thick as the barrel of a baseball bat, lay nearby under a pine tree. All its skin was gone. Flies in a tizzy buzzed around its whitish remains.

Pastor Chernenko stood in the middle of the creek with his pants rolled up, his pale calves exposed. One by one, the children moved from the bank into the water toward him. He would then lean them backward for full immersion in the creek with the help of Bob Pellalugra. Hair wet, faces shining, they would emerge from the cold water. At one point Pastor Chernenko fell backward, and as he staggered back up, held his hand over his hairpiece so it wouldn't slide off and float downstream.

With each baptism Luther shuddered. The other children were being lost to him somehow, as if something was being removed that made them who they were. Now they would be different, not themselves. He watched as Vera stepped into the creek. How could she? Along with the pain there was pride that he could be strong enough to resist Pastor Chernenko's call. Suddenly, Pastor Chernenko and Bob Pellalugra and the soaked children were staring up at him, as if his time had come. Wearing an uneasy smile, he backed away, and when he was safe from their sight, began to run.

Then it changed. The fiery, beseeching words of Pastor Chernenko in the tabernacle seemed to vanish before they reached the children's ears, or they heard without hearing. No longer were they going to the prayer rail to kneel and weep and receive the Holy Ghost. Now, at sermon's end, they ran shrieking from the tabernacle and down to the meadow, where the boys rolled around in the grass with girls whose lips were like soft rubber. Bob Pellalugra and his wife sought them out with their high-beamed flashlights and their sticks and tried to whack the paired kids apart, but they just found other places to run off to and lie down with each other. On the night air, faintly, could be heard the voices of the old people back in the tabernacle singing "Bringing in the Sheaves."

Chapter 28

Dear Luther,

I am so happy for you that you are in the fresh air. It must be very beautiful where you are. Are you praying? Are you remembering that Jesus loves you and that we are in the last days? Are you remembering that no man cometh to the Father except through his son Jesus Christ our Lord?

If I could just say this. Your niece, Jeanne, has run off. She called me collect from California. I'm worried sick. What can I do but pray for her and for all of us. Naomi is taking it very hard. I feel for her, for she has a condition and cannot take much stress.

Your sister Rachel is in the Bellevue Hospital psychiatric unit. Her drinking causes her to behave strangely. She has such a fine mind. I know it was Naomi who got her started on the wrong road by giving her those pills she takes. It is a painful thing for me to say, but Naomi has been a bad influence. Do keep Rachel in your prayers.

It broke my heart that Luke should throw away Maureen and now is with that other woman. Maureen loves Luke. She sends me letters and pictures of Luke, Jr. It is a very sad thing that has happened.

I love all my children dearly. It is my prayer that we will all be together in Heaven.

Love, Mother

Enclosed with the letter was a tiny booklet with bible verses. Luther placed it and the letter in the bottom of his brown bag.

Chapter 29

Mona was having a productive summer painting landscapes and portraits. Her parents showered her with praise. Luther meanwhile had not made significant headway with *Moby-Dick.*

Jealous and insecure from hearing the attention Mona was receiving, Luther began to brood. She had met Jeff, her previous boyfriend, at a party, and yet, what parties had Luther been invited to? There had been no parties, except for the one he got thrown out of that night he met Marcia. For him it was mostly standing around in bars or wandering in the park to cover the fact that he had no friends, whereas Mona had it all, talent and friends. She was connected in a way he was not. She had only to go to a party and boom, someone claimed her for his own. Just a few days after the party Jeff went and called her. No effort, no nothing. Just called her because he was party material in a way that was universally understood while Luther had to stand alone in a dingy bar listening to "San Francisco (Be Sure to Wear Flowers in Your Hair"). And that's all it had taken, an introduction and then a casual phone call and then the apartment to take her to and to sleep with her on the basis of the phone call, nothing more, just the phone call he got to place after the party because he was no threat, he had all the right moves to get invited to the party and then pick up the phone and invite her over and sleep with her and then sleep with her again, because that's all he had ever wanted to do, all any of them wanted to do, was to sleep with her, and now what was he, Luther, supposed to do to keep them from sleeping with her again and again given their ongoing lust?

He could not take her back to the apartment of Tony Pascual. Tony belonged to another time, a time that was over. He needed a place of his own where he could be alone with her now that there was space in his mind for no one else. It was time to think of the future and adjust it to the fact of her but then it all seemed hopeless given his circumstances and the fact of her parties and the men she met at them who could just pick up the phone and call her into their lives. No, no, he had to put a stop to the torture she was inflicting.

"I've been thinking about it. Really, I've given the matter a lot of thought. I think you should go back to your old boyfriend. I just have the feeling he would be more suitable for you, given that you met him at the party and all."

"Party? What party?"

He laughed the laugh of bitterness triumphant. "The party you're always going to. You remember the party."

"You're joking, right?" She was wearing green bellbottoms and a white Indian print blouse, the outline of her nipples showing through the fabric.

"No, no. He will be very good for you. The parties will be very good for you."

"Stop it."

"Stop it?"

"Please, please shut up."

Because he had been there before with Jane Thayer. Grilling her, insisting that she was interested in one or another of the neighborhood kids. Not that he was wrong. Not that she didn't go off with one neighborhood boy or another, causing Luther to die and die until she began to ease from his mind, which was when and only when she would come back to him. And slapping her several times, a line he must never cross with Mona.

"So what are you two lovebirds up to? Discussing Goethe, maybe? " Frank had wandered over from the pool in his black bathing suit, a towel around his neck.

"Right. Goethe," Luther said.

"What's the matter with your boyfriend? He doesn't seem like friendly people."

Luther answered for her. "We do not have time for you now. We are in intense discussion about our fate. You will just have to go off and kiss the sky, if you know what I mean." Because who was Frank but someone who could play a chord or two on the guitar while unable to carry a tune or present his strategy for being the second coming of Jimi Hendrix, instead lazing around the Van Dine estate smoking Colombian Red.

"Oh, right. I always know what you mean," Frank said, before he went off for another of the small bottles of beer that the Van Dines kept in a metal tub full of cool mountain water out by the tool shed next to the main house.

"So you're going to do it, right?" Luther asked.

"Look, if you don't want to be with me, okay. But don't ask me to go back to him. That's over. Finished." Her saying it was okay if he didn't want to be with her, that bothered him. He didn't like the sound of that at all. It was scary. "I know you want to do it. I know you do. You just need a little more encouragement. That's all."

"I can't listen to anymore of this," she said, and walked off in the direction of the pool to join Claire and her mother. She must have known that he wouldn't follow her where there were people. She would have to pay for that betrayal. She would just have to pay very dearly. He would set the mountains on fire as well as the house and the air too so that it all burned bright.

"We're going for dinner soon," she said to him that evening. He was at the pool table chalking his cue stick. He stank at the game. He had no technique. His arm was like an elongated piston while Frank of the little laugh had a compact stroke and pocketed one ball after another.

"Aren't you going to answer me?"

"Beat it," he said.

She turned and fled.

"Where's Luther?" Hearing Lydia, her voice carrying from down in the driveway, he quickly put his hands to his ears, seeking to shut out those with bigger lives who did not have the anger fever keeping them from the dinners of America.

He stared at the red taillights until the car vanished around the curve. The people of America going to get some eats. In the restaurant Peter would talk his political talk and Frank would say light, witty things, and Claire would laugh helplessly at his jokes. Her parents would be so appreciative of Frank's ability to take their oldest daughter, their budding scholar, out of her seriousness, if only for a moment. And because Mona looked troubled, they would all try to comfort her. They would have a good time feeling righteous and be relieved that the beast was not at the table.

Luther flew across the lawn and into the main house and poured some bourbon and Coke into a glass. He had no faith in his ability to make the old fashioneds they concocted but who needed a complicated drink anyway? He drained the tall glass and made another, then picked up the phone.

"This is the filthy one. I need to speak with Mona Van Dine. It is urgent. The house, the fields, even the mountains are in flame. I have torched the very air." So he spoke to the man who answered. There was a short wait in which he could hear the restaurant hubbub coming through the line before Mona answered. How husky her voice could sound.

"The filthy one is here and getting filthier by the minute," he said, and hung up.

He ran back across the lawn and into the guest house and turned off the lights and an eternity later heard the definitive sound of car doors closing followed by the beam of a flashlight. Luther braced as the sliding door was pulled open.

"What is the meaning of this bizarre behavior?" Peter demanded.

"What bizarreness do you speak of?"

"You are not a guest. You are a nightmare."

"Now you are talking."

"Do you think I am going to tolerate your continuing abuse of my daughter?"

"Abuse?"

"You have been decidedly abusive. Every day you have walked about this property with a long, sour face."

"Decidedly?"

"What?"

"I was repeating your word."

"If there is one more incident, you will pack your things and leave. Is that clear?"

Luther made no answer. He placed his head back on the pillow and fell asleep.

When he came to Mona was sitting on the side of the bed. "Am I still here? Has he escorted me off the property? Am I on Route 28 being run over by the cars of America?"

"You're still here," Mona said.

"Do you want me to go away? Do you want me to crash through that window to my bleeding freedom?"

"I just want you to be quiet."

"You want me to die so you can prove your annihilating power over me."

"Is that what you think?"

"I know the violence of the female mind. It's just a different kind of violence than the menfolk's. It's the violence of the bondage that they seek to impose. Now fuck off."

She ran out the door with her hands over her ears.

Still, he would never be able to accuse her of siccing her father on him the way that Marcia's friend had sicced Marcia's father on him. He could not yet accuse her of being in league with the patriarchs.

The cities were burning that summer. Detroit. Newark. It was not normal, as his mother would say. Not normal at all. But was it normal that childhood day many years before when the muscle-bound white man braked to an abrupt halt in the middle of the side street just a few yards from the family's building and walked slowly back from his car toward the smaller, slighter black man sprinting toward him with smiling fury fueling his eagerness for battle? Where or why the inflammation had occurred a mystery to Luther, and yet inevitable. The young black's confidence bolstered by the razor one quick snap of the wrist freed from its sheath so he could slash and slash and slash some more and soak the white man's T-shirt in his white man blood, Luther unable to fathom the depth of his rage but knowing it was there. The white man grabbing the wrist of the hand that held the razor before lifting him and throwing him through the hood of a parked convertible. The pounding with his free hand he gave the young black man, who still clutched the razor, awaiting his moment. Then the white police officer who whacked the razor from his hand, saying "Fight fair."

How could it not be inevitable that savagery would reign, given these scenes, or his memory of the young blacks arriving with their bicycle caravans from Harlem that childhood summer and beating Luke's friend Whitey to the pavement for provoking them with his white face.

Or the time the black boy—Butch or LeRoy or Winston—said to Luke, "You talking about me? You say some shit about me?" and when Luke said no, because he hadn't, the black boy saying "Why you be lying to me, motherfucking white boy?" before punching him to the ground, where Luke bled into the white snow as Luther looked on, paralyzed.

Or the time the black boy crossed the street and smacked Luther in the face with a piece of board because Luther had lobbed a snowball playfully in his direction. Because the black boy didn't play. The play gone all out of him before it could even begin.

Or seeing those two black boys dying face down on the pavement, having been shot in the back by the retired detective after they had supposedly tried to rob him.

Or the black man on a Philadelphia street landing a blow to his ribs and saying, "You're dead," as if he had a knife. Or the black man as the bus was leaving the Philadelphia terminal for New York saying to Luther, across the aisle, "You spitting at me, motherfucker? You spitting at me?"

Or. Or. Or.

Because you had to know what a time bomb was walking down a city street, whether in New York or Philadelphia or now Newark or Detroit or all the cities featuring acrid smoke and flames and mobs and deaths and beatings of people kept alive so they could be beat some more, of rampaging blacks looting stores and stoning police cruisers and taunting cops on nighttime streets. Luther said they weren't his brothers or his enemies either, that he was split down the middle of his consciousness as to who he was, having heard Martha and the Vandellas, and that he was seeking an intelligent attitude about the disturbances while fearful they would spread up the Hudson to river towns like Yonkers and Poughkeepsie, non-city cities, that soon they would come for him too, honky Luther, and go upside his head with their righteous and unending anger, for all it amounted to in him was a concern for personal safety in the face of the fury of the oppressed and emotionally roiled blacks. Soon the Communists would come to Saigon and all of the world to put it in the order that only they knew how to impose. He confessed to the Van Dines that he looked at the strife as a weak-kneed child suffering the bellicosity of an Armenian patriarch.

"The American government owes an amend to the American people, white as well as black. The American government is acting against the best interests of the country," Peter said that same night, standing on the porch while lightning cracked the dark sky and rains lashed the house. He had to shout his words, to compete with nature for their attention.

"Won't you sign the guest book?" Lydia coaxed, on the day of his departure.

He read the clever entries in the leather-bound book. "The wind/a sigh/Claire and I," Frank had written. "Where keyed-up executives unwind," the gay executive had inscribed. Lydia's intelligent, smiling eyes were on him, compelling him to pick up a pen and record his entry.

"Yeah, give us some of your wit," Frank chided.

"Oh Frank," Claire laughed.

Luther wrote and then handed Lydia the book.

"'The best is yet to come.' Oh, how charming."

"Did I tell you he was a wit?" Frank said.

"Oh Frank," Claire laughed once again.

Chapter 30

Commercial strips, the littered grass of the medians, the ramp spiraling into the Lincoln Tunnel. And outside Port Authority the sun-scorched streets, making him think of the fires of hell. Drifters everywhere living out of terminal lockers and prostitutes in their slinky skirts and dirty underwear and carrying vaginal disease. The lowlife sinkhole action of the street brought home to him what he had left behind.

Mona had come down to the city with him. He stayed with her at the family's apartment. While she napped, he wandered into the master bedroom, spacious enough for Peter to set up an office. Peter Van Dine, Ph.D., the nameplate on the desk said. But who was the nameplate for? Did clients come to his office? Did Lydia and the children need reminding of his academic achievement? Or was it simply an affirmation of his worth? Yellow legal pads were piled high, pages with his rightward-sloping script secured by a monogrammed brass paperweight. Luther lifted the cover off the typewriter, a sturdy Olympia office manual, and hit one of the keys, which clacked against the platen. Typing. That was for the future. For now he submitted handwritten papers. All those hardbound books: Emerson, Thoreau, Henry Adams. What did all of it mean? Was it not love in vain? Peter had been rejected by Harvard when he sought to pursue his doctorate at the university. And he had been a bombardier, not a pilot, during the war. A historian. That meant you couldn't play with equations and formulas. That meant you were lacking like Luther and had to lie down and go to sleep, having been denied the world on the other side of the dividing line.

Though the thought of returning to Tony's place felt like a regression, anxiety overcame him as he thought about the money he might need, even if he could get his job back at the post office. As a child, he had stolen from his mother. There was that one Sunday, before church, when she saw him with his hand closed. Had he been in her pocketbook? No, he said, and when she repeated the question, his hand opened involuntarily. There, in his palm, was a quarter.

"Do you promise never to go in my pocketbook again?" she asked, holding both his wrists and searching his mind. She had humiliated him. She had stripped him bare. But she too had been stripped bare. In her eyes he saw the fear that she could not control him even as he promised never to repeat the theft. He grew excited. He was free. And he remained free after being frog-marched home by the storeowner whom he tried to pay for a model tank with a fifty dollar bill boosted from his mother's pocketbook, as he did when he broke from the prayer circle his mother had organized among the church members to heal him. And free to expand his activity to slipping a key from his mother's ring of keys on Sunday morning and waiting for his aunt to leave her ground-floor apartment for church before letting himself into her apartment. The thrill of finding bills in denominations of tens and twenties in envelopes placed on the floor of his aunt's clothes closet equaled or surpassed only later by the thrill of sex.

The street below the building was cordoned off with wooden sawhorses, as it was periodically. Bits and pieces of the cornices lay smashed on the pavement, startling the passersby and infuriating the shopkeepers. The loose masonry was a reminder to Luther of the decrepitude of the building. In the lobby Fenton stood with his eyes closed and his head bent in prayer in front of one of the framed verses of scripture. Luther sought to slip past him but Fenton's sensors were on high alert. "Just remember, Luther, that there is room for only one master, not two, in the human heart. The choice will always be between the devil and the Lord. Have you made your decision for Christ? Your mother needs a good man. Are you ready to be that man?" There appeared to be no diffidence in Fenton's manner. He was all spiritual business on this day.

"I will think on that, Fenton," Luther said, and moved on, but not quickly enough that he didn't hear Fenton also say, "The hour is getting late, very late, Luther."

His mother was down in the basement, feeding sheets into the mangle with the help of Miss Beck, a smaller woman with a beaked nose. Luther remembered the sewing machine in her little room and her ability to hold pins in her mouth as if it were a pincushion those times his mother would send him to her to cuff his school pants.

The floor boards creaked under their weight and he wanted to shout "Cease and desist" for all the inevitability of what was coming from the machine with the ominous name "mangle," shuddering at the thought of his mother's and Miss Beck's fingers caught and crushed in the canvas rollers.

"Why Luther, is that you?" Mrs. Garatdjian finally spotted him after putting the last of the sheets through.

"You get a little wider now that you are so much taller, and haircut too." A tense, watchful woman who spoke in verbal jabs, Miss Beck wore glasses too big for her narrow face. Her Old World accent marked her as a survivor of wartime chaos in Europe. Her tiny room served as a sanctuary from booted men with guns and a fascist mentality.

He was afraid of Miss Beck. She had a window into his family's life. She saw without saying.

"Make your mother proud. Be a good sonny boy." Miss Beck went on. Both women wore sweatbands around their necks to deal with the heat.

He patted his mother's big arm and kissed her on the cheek, as always not without embarrassment, as if he had come too close.

"Are you back from the country for good now?" she asked.

"Yes,"

"Tell me. Was it very beautiful?"

"Trees and grass are always pretty," he said, not wanting to draw a contrast between the Van Dines' well-tended estate and the laundry room.

"And was the whole family there?"

"Yes," he said.

"How many are there?"

"Three daughters and a son."

"And her parents are very wealthy?"

"They live comfortably," Luther said.

It hurt his mother to ask. He could feel her pain that some could go through life without the trouble that she had known. Her faith was placed in jeopardy and he didn't want to see that faith threatened. His mother's feelings were always a consideration.

"I see," she said.

"It's not as if they don't have problems." he said, seeing that he had disappointed her with the rosy picture of the Van Dines he had presented.

"What sort of problems?"

"Oh, I don't know. Just problems," Luther said, now annoyed that he had given her inquisitiveness an opening.

When Miss Beck stepped away, his mother brought her focus closer to home.

"I did not want to say in front of Miss Beck, but Maureen has gone with the baby to live with her sister in Queens. Luke would not come back to her. He is right now living with that terrible woman on the roof. I cannot tell you how my heart aches for poor Maureen.

She is a fine woman. She loves Luke. I know she does. Is there nothing you can do? Can you not make him see the light of reason?" His mother's rough and callused hands spoke to her preference for the Maureens over the Noras of the world.

"I don't think he would listen to me."

"And then there is Jeanne. She is a thirteen-year-old child. Where can she be? What is to become of her?" His mother's questions sent him into a state of numbness. All he wanted was his own life.

By the cardboard drum of yellow, crumbly laundry soap lay his mother's keyring. He grabbed the ring and ducked down a passageway past the elevator room where blue light flashed from the circuit breakers and paused in the boiler room. He removed the key marked "AE" for Auntie Eve, hid the ring behind the giant water heater and slipped out the small rear door, which he left slightly ajar. Mosquitoes hovered over a pool of filthy water in the alleyway. Avoiding the airmailed garbage and the dog crap, he sped along the adjoining alley.

"You got the four bags of plaster and the two cans of Spackle," Arnie, the co-owner, said, ignoring the cash register and writing the amounts on a receipt pad with a pen he kept behind his ear. The hardware store was a male bastion of hardness. Arnie snatched the man's money and rubbed it against his belly before applying thumb to mouth to wet it so he could count the bills. He then spoke into the microphone. "Benny, get up here and help our good friend down the block with his supplies." Eventually, his wire-haired Puerto Rican assistant arrived. Their work relationship could only be tentative in Luther's conflict-dominated mind. He pictured the worker at night drinking cerveza free of the yoke of Arnie and listening to New York Yankee baseball on a static-filled radio.

"What can I do for you, friend?" Arnie said, looking away as he spoke, as if to convey he sensed Luther before he saw him and didn't even have to officially see him to know who he was and to speak in the cool, unfriendly way he did, only then following up with the armament of his hard dark eyes upon him.

"I need a duplicate," Luther said, placing the key on the counter. His voice was as low as Arnie's was booming. Now it was his turn to look away as he felt the heat of Arnie's disrespecting gaze on him.

"Say, aren't you Mrs. Garatdjian's other son? Aren't you Luke's brother?" Arnie asked, in a voice that carried to the street.

Luther nodded.

"Hey Sam," Arnie shouted. "Come here. I got something I want you to see." A thinner man with a receding hairline arrived.

"What have you got for me, Arnie?" Sam followed Arnie's nod in the direction of Luther. He looked Luther up and down.

"So?"

"That's Mrs. Garatdjian's son under all that hair," Arnie said, disappointed that Sam didn't share his amusement. The building had an account at the store.

"Nice to see you," Sam said to Luther, then turned to Arnie and said, "Give the young man some service," and walked away.

Arnie placed the key and a blank in the vise. Luther turned his back as the machine ground away at the metal blank.

"We got barbers in New York City," Arnie said. He was sullen now.

"And we've got a language that supports auxiliary verbs." Luther addressed himself to a ceiling fan.

Arnie dropped the keys on the counter. "Pay up and get out of here."

"Oh yes, I am going, and right this very minute, you can be sure," Luther said, backing out of the store.

In the boiler room he returned the key to its proper place on the ring. His mother had only to see him now and he would fall apart. No alibi would work on her, not with her mind so powerfully equipped to invade his. As he inched closer to the laundry room, he heard the tub and the drier still going, a good sign, as they wouldn't leave the machinery running while they were away. He lay the ring where he had found it on the mound of sheets and left, exiting through the same back door that led to the alleyway and was about to let himself out through a gate onto One Hundred Twelfth Street when a sharp whistle blew three times. Miss Beck was standing fifty yards back and motioning to him. He had no choice but to abandon his flight and return. She had him dead to rights. She had penetrated his mind as an extension of his mother's power, Luther thought.

"You be a good boy to your mother now. You be a good sonny boy."

"I will see what I can do, Miss Beck," he said, in a dutiful tone of voice.

"Do not be the sickness of America," Miss Beck said. She blew her whistle sharply once again as a signal he could leave.

That afternoon he returned to the Van Dines' apartment. His thoughts had turned anxiously to the future and the things he might do on finishing college. There was social work. You didn't need any special degrees in that field and maybe he could earn $15,000 as a caseworker, as did other graduates of City College. Then he wandered to one of the three bathrooms. He knelt on the cool tiles and began to cry. The tears were a surprise. He saw the horror of his family and the misdirection of his own life, his inability to shape it in a way that would bring security and peace of mind, as if a firm wind were blowing him toward a cliff and he was powerless to resist its force. From far below in the park the shouts of children at play floated up. He stretched out on the tiles and fell asleep with the key that would keep his dream alive safely in his pocket.

Chapter 31

Luther tried to emulate Mona's ex-boyfriend with a place of his own. As for the parties so readily available to Jeff, that was another matter. He rented a studio apartment on West Eightieth Street, just a few doors up from Riverside Drive. Such joy flooded him at the sight of the black-lacquered, cantilevered desk and an overhead lamp where he would be able to sit and read the Harper Colophon and Anchor paperback books and Signet classics and all the rest, books that never added to his substance sufficient to remove the stain of his one unforgivable failure. Twenty-four dollars a week, the elderly landlady said. Still, he should be all right with the sizable student loan he had received and, of course, the key.

With Mona's help, he picked out an Indian bedspread, yellow with brown and red patterns, and a cheerful red throw rug. Alone in the new place he lit a sandalwood stick of incense and played a Donovan album on his newly purchased portable record player. He promised himself he would stop at the end of the album only to replay it. What a thing, to *wear your hair like heaven*, Luther thought, soaring with Donovan and then with Joan Baez singing "Silver Dagger." The pain grew. It became too much. Donovan and Joan Baez were singing for people whose pathos-filled lives were worthy of being set to music, not bottom dwellers in the hell of their low numbers.

Something had changed. Even fully clothed, he felt naked in his need for Mona and conscious every second of her absence. And yet as much as he thought of her when she was gone, once she arrived and the sex was done with, the pain found him again.

A third party was a fixture now when they were in bed, a figure with an enormous penis. This Luther could know but she mustn't. And she mustn't sense the anxiety that now consumed him about money and the future. The punishment that would await him if she did would be brutal. Fall crispness could be felt in the August air, with all the dread it summoned.

"Mommy wants to take me to Europe for six weeks in October," Mona casually remarked in this time. He heard the names England, France, Switzerland, and Italy. It was like receiving a surprise punch to the stomach. Mona had succumbed to the corrupting power of her mother, who was now methodically moving in for the killing of him with the appropriating power of her big fat pocketbook.

"I won't die, but that doesn't mean I will live either."

"Stop it."

"You've left my future to create your own. Is that it?"

"I have to do something."

"Something?"

"Maybe there's an art school I can get into in January without a diploma."

January. Winter. The writing on the bathroom wall of Moogie's Bar was turning out to be prophecy.

She was strong, uncontainable, different, even in the way she read. She devoured books. *The Magic Mountain, Joseph and His Brothers, War and Peace, Dear Theo,* whatever. She sank into them while his mind flew everywhere as he tried to read, the world not orderly enough for him to take his eye off it and give himself entirely to the page.

I'm going to be around for a long time. Hadn't she said that after their first night together? The words had been a buoy that kept him from drowning; they had been a source of light and happiness.

They told him who he was and when he felt low he could draw on them. But lately he had been seeing what she said in a different light. Because while a long, long time was just that, it wasn't forever. What she was saying was that someday she was going to leave, that the long, long time would be over. And so, though he feared the annihilating consequences of showing himself weak to any of the women of power, he had to bring the matter up, to ask about those words of hers and what exactly she had meant.

"I said that? Well, I guess I meant just what I said. A long time."

"You didn't have a length of time in mind?"

"God, that was months ago. Look, Claire had a boyfriend for three years. That sounds about right."

He lay still, feeling the continuing transfer of power to her and hoping she wouldn't notice. But how could she not? It was not a matter of making her very sorry for talking to him in this way when he was down. His arsenal was useless, nonexistent, in the moment. It was a matter of not dying from the pain of the finiteness she foresaw when eternity was his need.

Still, he had his key, and in his fear he talked to it and slept with it under his pillow and then made copies so his future could not be lost. It sang to him of books he could make his own and bathrooms he would never have to share. It would keep him safe from the unbearable ticking time bomb threatening dispossession into the streets of New York City.

He walked along Broadway on his mission, stopping to dawdle in front of store windows to ease passersby of their suspicious minds and continually rearranged his face to approximate blankness for the same reason. But as he was about to enter the lobby, his mother stepped from his aunt's ground-floor apartment. He stepped back out of her sight, then headed quickly down toward the park. On the way he casually dropped the key into a street drain. Later, he did the same with the copies. His mother's oblique notice had been received: Do not return to the treachery of the past.

His neighbor was an elderly Chinese man who even in summer wore a loose-fitting double-breasted suit and a Stetson hat on his bald, shiny head. Luther would see him climbing and descending the stairs of the walkup and considered him a model of patience and acceptance, of still waters running deep in the holy, all-enveloping now. Always it was for Luther to say hello, which the man would acknowledge with a nod, as if to say he had only the slightest space for Luther in his universe.

"You inhabit the center that will not have me, the Buddha center of completeness," Luther said to him on their second encounter.

The man showed no interest in Luther's blandishment.

"Please save me from who I am," Luther went on. Startled from his calm demeanor, the man hurried inside his room and locked the door to secure himself from his strange neighbor.

The landlady sat peacefully on a bench in the park, tossing bits of moldy bread to the cooing pigeons one afternoon. There were sailboats on the river. There were jets in the sky. There were buses going north and south. Life was in motion for some folks.

"How is it that they don't die, feeding them what you do?"

"You are the college boy. Do you not know anything?" the landlady asked.

"I know they must be saying something to us of the way the world works, with their cold, neutral eyes. They are teaching us something about realism and what the real task of life is."

"Do you have any real knowledge, son? Do you have any facts?"

"I really don't, but I have strong feelings."

"You will have to do something with your life, starting with your hair."

"My hair I can do nothing about. To cut it would be to reveal my head's flatness," Luther said. He was full of wonder that all anyone uld need for peace of mind was to keep tabs on the tenants in a small building and feed the filthy pigeons of New York City. The landlady's acceptance frightened him. How different from the worry his mother showed.

"You know that I was born to do this too, even if I fear it."

"Do what now, son?"

"To sit on a park bench and just watch, from the plateau that I cannot move beyond, all that is happening. I have only so much torque to draw on, and it is not enough to go higher."

"How's that girlfriend of yours? Has she gone away from you?"

That girlfriend. The words drove him down. She was saying he would wind up alone with just her, the landlady, sitting on a park bench while the girlfriend elevated to a life of bigness.

"You don't see her because I go to her parents' apartment. Because my place has nothing to engross her and she picks up on its emptiness. I need to ask if you would have another room for me at some point, something less expensive where I could afford to stay for the longest time, my fear being that my girlfriend is going away and I cannot hold the future in the shape that it needs to be."

"What's the matter, Sonny? You can't pay?"

"I can pay. I have more money than there is time to spend it," Luther said, in full contradiction of himself.

"You look worried, Sonny. You look like you just told an untruth. Are you afraid that you will be put out on the street, that the rains will come and pelt your possessions, that your earthly goods will become water-soaked and useless in the filthy streets? Are you afraid that you will fall far, far from your dream? Sonny, are you worried about your girlfriend? When I see two people such as you, I can tell in an instant who will win and who will lose."

"Jesus," Luther said, aghast at her unsolicited analysis.

"That's right, Sonny. Jesus."

Luther passed out. When he came to, the old woman was gone. So too were the pigeons. There was only the squirrel at his feet. In that moment all the squirrels of New York City lost their cuteness; he saw them for the bushy-tailed rodents that they were.

Chung Lee was his neighbor's name. So Luther learned from a stray piece of mail left on the staircase. An idea seized him. That evening, after several false starts, he knocked on Chung Lee's door. When there was no answer, he knocked a second time and again received no response. And so he knocked a third time and heard footsteps approaching. The door opened, with the chain lock still on, Chung Lee's face there in the crack quivering with anger and sparks flying from his eyes.

"Good evening, sir," Luther said.

"No good evening see your stupid face. What you want?"

The verbal blow knocked Luther back, but he quickly stepped forward again. "Could you open yourself up to me a little more so your life is not so small and my own can be expanded, too?"

"I open nothing."

As if he had not heard, Luther went on. "Let me say first that I am dying of acute anxiety..."

"I carry gun. I have license. I shoot you bang bang you try to come in here."

"Don't try to distract me from my pain. I must establish new lodgings here or perish," Luther replied.

"What your stupid face not saying?"

"I want your room. There is no other place in all of Manhattan that I can be. In exchange you can have my bigger room."

"Go back your room. Go now, and listen your stupid music with your stupid face." Chung Lee closed the door emphatically.

Luther sped that night to Mona's canopied bed, but it offered no refuge. Her family's home, with all its amenities, was not his. He needed ground of his own to stand on if he was not to terminally weaken. As if it were a test of his own independence, he left at midnight, streaking past the cruising men in tight jeans drawn by loneliness and hunger to the Soldiers' and Sailors' Monument. He would return to his room and master his anxiety, the obsessive and savage focus on rent every second of every minute of every hour, so he could settle down to his paperback books.

As he was nearing his building, another idea came to him. He raced to the corner newsstand on Seventy-ninth Street and Broadway, and bought a copy of the New York *Times*. The paper had tradition. It had status. He sat on the steps of the grimy old Baptist church and turned to the classifieds. The *Times* would not let any joker advertise for a roommate. He would find someone to share a place with, someone more stable than Tony Pascual, so he didn't have to be alone with the burden of being responsible for himself.

Over the next two days he went down the list, but the men he spoke with turned him away, saying the rooms had already been rented. Young, hard men who projected no warmth. He was not disappointed. They were not men with whom he would feel comfortable sharing a place.

He still had words he could speak. He didn't need the classifieds for that. Words he could use to nail down the future, saying to Mona, down by the marina at Seventy-ninth Street and the Hudson River, "It's like this. In a few years I'll finish college. Then I'll go to law school and success will be mine." Science and math would not be a barrier, the law being all chatter and seeing from different points of view. The tallest buildings would bow down to him.

The yachts bobbed gently in the water but kept their place, unlike the pieces he had positioned in the air. The Communists had five-year plans and they were progressing. Why couldn't he do the same?

"You'll make a very good lawyer. You have a fine mind."

"Not fine, not fine. Do not use the word my mother uses for the mind of my father."

The anxiety was back and it was relentless.

Chapter 32

Some months had passed since he had last seen Vera. He had acquired a new family to go with his family of origin, a father who read Henry Adams in addition to one who read the collected works of Oral Roberts and A. A. Allen and other preachers who in their fine suits slapped their Bibles so very well. But now there she was on that early September afternoon. A chance encounter on Broadway. He had expected to be spurned, given his absence from her life; instead she received him warmly. And why wouldn't she? After all, he had arrived not on the wings of triumph but on the verge of a nervous breakdown. And so she listened sympathetically to his burden of pain about the room beyond his means he had rented and Mona's coming departure for Europe and how the two things had destroyed his ability to think.

Her placid demeanor confounded him. Following her graduation, she had taken a job with New York Telephone Company in Inwood, at the northern tip of Manhattan, and in the spring would enroll in SEEK, a program for those high school graduates who required remedial work before going on to a four-year college in the CUNY system. How different her patience, her acceptance, were from the race he had imposed on himself and the chronic shame at his low numbers and his rejection by elite schools. How had she gotten to such a place of humility? Could it be that she had a long-range plan for excellence and that starting at the very bottom took the pressure off? His mother had that quality. Had she not been a humble domestic for a Park Avenue couple? And there was the somewhat menial nature of part of her job even now, providing bedding and towels for the tenants.

"Come stay with me," Vera said.

"What? How?"

"I moved out. I got away."

"Got away where?"

Like Luther, Vera had her own aspiration for freedom. It had taken a toll on her to witness the struggles of her older siblings. She too had a fear that the building that had snared Hannah and Naomi and was now snaring Luke could trap her as well. Her step toward independence was to rent a room in an apartment on One Hundred Eleventh Street and Broadway, just two blocks south of the family's building. A small step, but a step nonetheless, as Luther's had been. He was happy for her. He saw her as a flower blooming in new soil.

What he was thinking he couldn't say, after leaving her. There was no thinking, just the obsessive focus on the number twenty-four, his weekly rent, and the crushing weight of anxiety that it brought. He had nothing, nothing. There was no place but the street or the building. He had to get free of the hellish burden of that number.

He arrived at Vera's door with his things in several boxes. She led him to her room, where she played the Mamas and the Papas on her portable record player, "California Dreaming" stirring in him a longing to be on the West Coast while reminding him of the gap between his present state and his goal of excellence. The song felt painful and reproachful. A world of light existed out there, yet at age twenty he was listening to "California Dreaming" in his sister's room only two blocks from home.

"The sofa's a convertible. Don't worry. There's plenty of room for both of us, seeing that we are both so skinny," she said. It would be like old times, she was saying, when they were together and no one else was there.

But he didn't want the sofa. He wanted the floor, even with its hardness.

"OK," he said, trying to keep her anger at bay.

She left him to take a shower and returned some minutes later in a slip and moved a drier over her long and wet brown hair.

"Let's go downstairs to the diner," she said.

"I can't."

"What's the problem?"

"Mona. Mona is my problem." He could not tell her directly that his life was elsewhere for fear of the consequences that could bring.

"Mona?"

"She leaves tomorrow for Europe. This is my last chance to see her before she goes."

"Do what you have to do," Vera said.

"I'll be back in a couple of hours."

She clicked on the hair drier again, allowing its electric whir to be her response.

Mona was waiting impatiently downstairs in the coffee shop. "I can't stay long. I still have packing to do," she said. He could tell when he called that she didn't want to meet with him. There was no point to his anger and his threats. How did you threaten to leave someone who was so clearly and emphatically doing the leaving? They left without ordering and he walked her home through Riverside Park.

At Ninety-sixth Street stood a bridge spanning an entrance to the West Side Highway. He stopped and examined the small space between the patina'd base of the lamp resting atop the bridge's retaining wall.

"What are you doing?" There was annoyance in Mona's voice.

"Take a look."

"So?" she said, after a quick glance.

"You didn't see the two coins?"

"I saw them. So what?"

"So nothing." He began to cry. A real waterworks. It came on so quickly, and now he couldn't stop.

"Oh come on, Luther. It's not forever." Not joining in his tears but standing in cold disapproval of them.

He wiped away his tears on his sleeve and walked with her to her building some blocks away. "Don't worry so much," she said, and gave him a quick kiss before disappearing past the doorman into her building.

He returned along the same route on Riverside Drive, the song "Blue Moon" playing in his head. Two pennies Luke had placed under the base of that bridge, as if to seal his love for Nancy Becker in their high school years, thinking coins could keep her from moving on. Not having a key, he had to ring the bell to the apartment where Vera was staying. When there was no answer he rang a second and third time. The door finally opened and a young woman wearing a long nightshirt looked up at him.

"What do you want?" she said.

"I'm here to see my sister Vera," he said.

"You know it is late," she said.

"I do," he replied, as she stepped aside. There were four of them sharing that apartment, his sister had said. Four brainy women working toward doctorates at Columbia University. Vera had found the sisters to model herself after.

Vera lay in bed with her back turned, as if to say she was closed to him forever in the anger that was her birthright as a Garatdjian. "I really don't want you here. I want you out by the morning."

She had left a space for him on the bed but he did not take it. Instead he lay down on the floor. How easy it was for him to see and feel that anger, as it was only the way he could be with Mona.

Chapter 33

From down the hall came the smell of paint. Little Tommy was applying a fresh coat to the room next door, giving it the pale green treatment that all the rooms in the building received. Little Tommy, as opposed to Tall Tommy, the handyman Mrs. Garatdjian called upon to replace blown fuses and bulbs. Little Tommy, from coal country in Pennsylvania, with the bad temper and the Pall Mall cigarettes and the little joke when he went to the renting office, saying to Mrs. Gladwell, "Give me ten dollars on account" and then pausing before adding, "On account that I'm broke." Little Tommy had a woman in his life in the way that he could, but he also had his anger and his violence, and so the woman could come to his room but his temper was too much and she had to leave him to the ponies he fixated on and his days off at the track and his evening vigil waiting outside the luncheonette around the corner on Broadway for the *Daily News* truck with the racing results.

Luther was mindful of him as just another man who had to be handled and not wanting to see him for the shame that would engender. But his bladder felt like it was about to burst, and so he did see him on that morning. It was unavoidable, Little Tommy intercepting him as Luther made his way to the public bathroom down the hall. Little Tommy saying to Luther, "Moving up in the world, are you?" meaning Luther had risen from the second floor apartment where his family lived to the seventh floor. Little Tommy laughing, laughing at him for being like Hannah and Naomi and Luke, for being like all the weak and fumbling Garatdjian offspring. In his pain Luther too stricken to mumble anything more than "I guess so."

Broadway was visible from the window. How clear and bright the early fall day was. Luther stared down at the pedestrians, watching to see if any would stop and look up at the verse of scripture on the south wall of the building. No one did, but that didn't mean they didn't know it was there.

The room was chilly. He paced back and forth, trying to warm up but also to walk off the pain. There was a knock at the door. "I have so many. Wouldn't you like a kitty to keep you company?" The cat woman, Miss Hansen, was standing in front of him with a little tabby. A woman with a German accent who spoke in an imploring voice and looked like a cat herself. Luther took the kitty. Like a feather it was in his arms, with big paws at the end of such skinny legs, its claws seeking a hold on his shirt.

"I remember you when you were just a hanging string. You are still a hanging string. You are not at peace because you have nothing to care for and nothing to call your own. You go where you are not wanted and eat candy bars and this is the result."

"What is the result?" In his stricken state he had no defense against her.

"Destitution, of course. What else could explain such a look of impoverishment."

She was one of many women in the building, women who had been driven off by men or who had fled for their lives from them or who, because of formidable wounds or simple intelligence and strength, had never been with men.

"I'm not so impoverished."

"You fool no one with your nonsense. I think Schnell will help you, but whether you will help him is another matter. I must ask that you take the very best care of my little one." She instructed him about the kinds of cat food he would require and the regularity of feeding.

"What's a Schnell?"

"Schnell means quick. He is quick, and you are not quick enough. You must do things to improve and not listen to the messages that are talking to you." The Cat Lady took the kitty and put him on her shoulder so the two were staring at Luther as she spoke.

"And you are so great?" Luther was growing annoyed. He wanted the woman gone so he could get back to his pain in an undistracted way. Pain did have a purpose. It was an expression of faithfulness.

"Did I say anything about greatness? When I say that you are a hanging string, I mean only that you will have to do a lot of dying before you can live in peace in the quiet of your little room. Poor little Schnell," she whispered, placing the tabby on the floor. "Poor, poor little Schnell."

Luther sat with his new friend on the bed. Schnell showed no sign of missing his Cat Lady mistress. It was frightening to think of anyone or anything being so adaptable. Luther lay back down in a fetal position, while Schnell kneaded the blanket.

Mommy. He whispered the word. Then he said it again and again. Then he said it again and again and again and again.

Mona had provided him with a copy of her itinerary on the letterhead of the travel agency, all the mailing addresses of the hotels in London, Paris, Zurich, Amsterdam, Venice, Florence, and Rome, cities intent on causing major trouble that would wash up on the American shore, trouble that he could only contain with abiding concentration on the threat his mind was warding off with vigilance.

> Mommy is a nervous wreck. She chain-smokes and drinks and consumes tons of food, her mouth so wide and devouring. She is unable to lose herself in the moment. She wants to, but fear rules. The bellboys and hotel clerks and busboys and waiters dominate. She pleads with them not to hurt her. Home is the source of her strength. She draws her power from

kitchens and grocery lists and innumerable itemizations of household duties. The English are a perverse, private people. They eat bad food and they are also unclean. You get the impression of soiled underwear under their soggy woolen clothes and of dirt behind their ears. They really have no handle on painting. Their art form is literature. They speak beautifully from mouths full of green teeth. Mommy says she will hit her stride (her word) when we reach the continent. She says France is where she experienced her awakening as a woman. Well, the trip has begun.

He opened the window and said out loud to the wind that he was not one of them, that he was not Hannah or Naomi or Rachel or Luke, with his street corner ways and his shirt hanging out of his pants. He told the wind that he was only there temporarily and that the gates would not close and keep him in and that the ghosts of the past would not surround him and keep him down.

Though it was morning Luke had a can of beer in his hand and the pungent smell of dope filled the room. He was wearing jeans and the V of his T-shirt revealed angry red pimples on his chest. Acne craters covered his face as well. "There was this one day during the summer I just got aggravated with her. You know what I mean?"

"Irritated."

"What?"

"Irritated, not aggravated. Unless you want to sound like Daddy."

"I got fucking aggravated with her, I was saying."

'Who?"

"Who do you think? Nora. Hey, you're not still upset about that, are you? I mean, what else could I do? Things just clicked." A smile of triumph now showed on Luke's face.

"That's good when things click," Luther said, staring at the disconnected washing machine and the half-used box of diapers that served as Maureen's legacy.

"So we were over at Mama's Deli across the street getting some cold cuts and beer. She goes and gives this huge guy wearing shades this big smile and he smiles right back. So after we're back in the room I say to her, 'What did you go and do that for?' I mean, I have a right to expect some kind of loyalty from the people I'm with. She pretends she doesn't know what I'm talking about, says she has a right to smile whenever she pleases, as if I've a narrow attitude. So I yell at her. Next thing I know she's working for some guy who says he's a filmmaker. He gives her money to sit naked in a bathtub and who knows what else is going on with them. It's like she's closed down on me, and here I've left my wife and baby for her, you know? I left my home just so I could be with her in that dump across the street. I don't know how you ever lived there. By then Maureen had split with the baby so why should I spend money for rent when I can live here for free? You know what I mean?"

Leaning on him, Luke was, as he always eventually leaned on him to say what was wrong was right so he could live with himself. "Sure. Sure I do," Luther said.

"Sure you do what?" Luke having to be certain the receipt he had received was proper and suspecting that it wasn't.

"What you said."

"What I said what?"

"Huh?"

"You're fucking with me again. I know you are. You're here, too. Remember that, just like Hannah and Naomi."

Luther went out onto the roof and climbed the ladder up the side of the penthouse. The smell of burning trash came from the incinerator chimney, charred embers floating up against the screen. He pressed his hands against the warm chimney bricks. Behind him rose on legs of black steel the cedar-shingled water tower. The thought of decomposing rats inside triggered a wave of revulsion.

Maybe Luke was right. Maybe he would be like Hannah and Naomi and his brother. Maybe he was back for good.

One summer night some years before he had sought refuge in that same spot. As he lay back, a luminous disk making a low-level whirring sound appeared in the dark sky. For some time it lingered, hovering perhaps fifteen feet above him. How long he could not say, but long enough to know that aliens in their flying saucer had come just for him so they might be known to him as he evidently was to them. Though frightened of abduction, Luther had remained in place. And they showed that he had no reason to fear. Contact having been made, the aliens continued on their rounds, Luther's sense being that they had other destinations, on what could only be a long, long journey, even for extraterrestrials traveling at possibly the speed of light. And yet a promise, unspoken as it may have been, had been made. They would return. They would come for him so he could have a home away from home.

So Luther had believed, but now, with the passage of time, doubt had all but erased from his mind the possibility that the universe had singled him out for specialness. And anyway, where would these aliens take him. Far away from Mona and Camp and all he had come to hold dear? No, that couldn't be. That could never be. Not so long as he had Mona. She was his lifeline, a lifeline he must never let go of. She might not take him to outer space, but surely she would lift him onto higher ground.

Chapter 34

Mona's strong sentences frightened him. They had vitality sufficient to make them hop on the page. Her writing was a reflection of her adventurous nature. Whatever fences he put up around her she might easily jump over. Her letters induced insecurity rather than reassurance, while his own showed panic and impotence. He threatened, lashed out, and then wrote once again to apologize. Dignity was lacking. Across the ocean, in hotel rooms across Europe, he imagined Claire's cold eye on his letters—the dismal handwriting, the ranting devoid of insight or style of a desperate soul—and imagined Claire and her mother trying to subtly influence Mona away from him by opening her eyes to new possibilities. And Mona herself not relishing but embarrassed by each new postal arrival, seeing each letter as just another expression of his clinging nature, as if he were some desperate child it had been her misfortune to involve herself with.

The roaches were intrepid. They were in Schnell's bowl of dried food and swam in his bowl of milk. Their swarming numbers created a sense of helplessness, like the lightly clad VC besting the heavily equipped American army and air force.

During the day he would look forward to the little blue over-the-counter sleeping pills he had begun to take at bedtime. Such relief they brought. Mona would come back unchanged, he would leave the wretched room and the building, he would bring a new confidence to his coursework. Freed from the tormenting waves of anxiety, his thoughts would turn, as he lay in the dark, to Lenore, the pills awakening him to his true desire. He pictured her with him now, not Casey, who had ditched her for the East Village girls who knew how to move their boxes, in Casey's words. She came to him darker than the night with her ruby lips and laughing eyes.

Recalling the fantasies of the night before in the morning, he repudiated them and swore allegiance to his pain once more. Mona represented love and health; Lenore was nihilism and drift. He tried to get through the day in a state of chemical-free righteousness so he would not have to be as those stuck to the building like flies on flypaper. When bedtime finally came again, he could take the pill he had been so longing for through a dreary day of classes and there Lenore was, showing the same passion as in their one time together. "I will follow through in the morning. I will persevere with my dream," he murmured in the dark, but when daylight came, all he felt once again was dread and horror at where the pill had taken his mind.

And yet that afternoon he did set forth in the hope of a chance encounter with Lenore. She was now enrolled in a fortress-like public school just off Columbus Avenue on the West Side. That much he had learned from Mona. His plan was to walk along slowly in her neighborhood and just run into her. His intent would be too clear were he to position himself directly outside her school. She would turn and bolt. But with every step he took, the futility of his ruse became clear. The sight of him in whatever circumstance would expose him as the grotesque stalker that he was, and so he hurried away.

Vera showed up at his door as if her false promise of shelter had meant nothing, but it was not for Luther to take issue with her, as he continued to discern in Vera a strange power, a verbal fury, which if tapped could leave him dead, or wishing for the end. Anyway, the idea of the two of them sharing a room had been absurd. Better to have a roach-filled room in the building than to be sharing a bed with his younger sister.

She ordered more than coaxed him to the End Bar that evening, where she spoke of Amory Wooster, wrapped in ivy, as the object of her affection. Luther kept to himself that Amory seemed high above her in his Columbia-ness. He did say that Columbia was a tyranny and that it had been warring on the family's belief system since they were born, that the verse of scripture from the Gospels on the side of the building was a refutation of everything Columbia University stood for and was deserving of the highbrow elitist laughter it provoked. He said that shame— shame shame double shame—was the family affliction but that it was necessary not to be driven into the ground by it. He said too that Columbia had legions of able men and women to unleash their laughing thing on the family for having dared to suggest there was a life of the spirit beyond the mind that would seek to keep it out and maintain the facts of the world in place and that not even Jesus could counteract this so long as the planet adhered to the concept of time. In any event he said he would give his kingdom for a speed pill and a pitcher of suds but that he didn't dare to indulge while living in the family-of-origin premises where Hannah, Naomi, and now Luke were chained to their turmoil because that would blow his chance of ever leaving there again and mean he was no better than them.

"You are becoming a mental case. You know that, don't you?"

"Or a moody blue. Or both." He took a bite of his cheery cheese Danish and winced. "Jesus, my tooth hurts." He pushed the Danish toward Vera.

"You have to see my dentist, Dr. Berman. He's wonderful. Luke has gone to him, too. Tell him I sent you."

Dr. Berman was able to see him the very next day. Luther's feet flew over the fallen autumn leaves on the pathways through Central Park to the dentist's office on Sixty-second Street and Madison Avenue. Such an office it was, the waiting room furnished with sleek modern sofas and chairs all color coordinated and several abstract expressionist paintings and mood music for a sedative effect. Out of sight and earshot was Dr. Berman's whirring drill.

"What's the matter? You don't like dentists maybe? Your sister talks. How come you're so quiet? We're bad people or something?" Luther was numb with fear seeing the drill dangling from its cord and the ghastly implements arrayed on the porcelain tray.

Dr. Berman fell quiet as he explored Luther's teeth and gums with a Sickle probe. The intimacy of it. Luther closed his eyes. Those horrible experiences with the Rockefeller Center dentist back in childhood, the shocking pain of the drill striking a nerve, had stayed with him. He tried to hold on to Vera's assurance that Dr. Berman would be different. And, in fact, he was liking him already, in spite of his verbal aggressiveness. An intense man with a big nose and a comic way to go with his serious face. The Cornell University degree framed on the wall was reassuring of his worth. What more could he ask for than a smart Jewish dentist?

"You need to take better care of yourself," Dr. Berman said, as if offended by the neglect he was witnessing.

A wave of shame passed through Luther. Thinking, I am not a Jew. That is my problem. I lack the intelligence to sort out my life. I can only leave behind soiled tissues where there were none.

Dr. Berman took care of the problem tooth that day. Though Luther squeezed the armrests tightly and braced for the shock when he struck a nerve, it didn't come. A strong injection of Novocain followed by the placement of a small rubber mask over Luther's nose and the administering of nitrous oxide took him to a place of bliss.

A white-clad aide had entered the room to assist Dr. Berman. Lola was her name. She was dark and petite and too womanly for someone such as him, though now the gas had charged him with a confidence he previously lacked.

"You're a goddess," he murmured, Dr. Berman having left Lola after filling the tooth.

"What's that you said?" Her voice was challenging. It had an edge. Not the voice of a goddess but of a tough woman used to keeping lecherous men in line.

"Nothing. Nothing at all."

"You need to take care of your hair and your body, too. You're too thin," she said. She *had* heard, and she was answering him. She was laying out the reasons he didn't qualify for her love or her lust.

Chapter 35

That October the antiwar demonstrations planned for Washington, D.C., called to him. He was neither part of nor apart from the masses that gathered and crossed the Potomac to levitate the Pentagon or of those who in the full adamancy of their resistance burnt their draft cards. He simply drifted along in the cool fall air trying to take in the bigness of the world and dizzied by the size of the gathering. Celebrity was present as well—organizers like big David Dellinger and big Jerry Rubin and big Abbie Hoffman, and there were the established intellectuals with the bulging brows like big Norman Mailer and big Robert Lowell. All had joined forces to galvanize and amalgamate the consciousness of the nation, having gone with the assurance that images of them would extend to the country's borders and beyond.

And Luke was there with him. "Maybe I'll come too. Maybe we'll meet some girls," Luke had said.

Luther was going for Mona so she would think he was in the thick of things and love him good when she came back. They had gotten a ride down to Washington, D.C., in a VW Beetle, part of the motley motorcade heading down the interstate. Luke was uneasy during the ride. He kept silent and avoided eye contact. Luther shared his uneasiness. Why wouldn't he? They were outsiders in a car with two idealistic students driven by moral outrage Luther and Luke did not possess. A young man who wore a headband to keep his long brown hair under control was at the wheel. His girlfriend sat up front with him. Luther was in love with her already and couldn't help staring at the barrette in her auburn hair.

"Do you attend Columbia too? I think I've seen you around the campus," the man asked.

"Only to pass through. It is not for everyone. Not to the likes of me, anyway, though I can't speak for my brother," Luther said.

"So what do you do?" the girl asked.

"I attend the City College of New York. I'm trying to get away from the life I come from. I live with failure at my door every day."

"That's a hard way to live. But the City College of New York isn't failure. And participation in the demonstration today isn't either."

"Oh, I'm just drawn to it by the pull of history and do not want to be left out of the currents of our time. My girlfriend is a demonstrator, just like you. Mona's her name. She went to the antiwar rally in Central Park. She has good breeding. She represents the excellence I myself can't seem to achieve, but at least I can be close to it through my connection with her. To be honest, I sometimes feel like a bum."

"Really? A bum?" The girl laughed.

"My brother, too. He's even more of a bum. He stands on the street corner with his shirt hanging out of his pants. We both do a lot of chasing after girls in a needy way. It keeps us alive." His eyes were still stuck on the red barrette in the girl's brown hair.

"What the fuck? I should punch you in the fucking face for talking that kind of shit in the car," Luke muttered. "Calling me a bum. Calling yourself a bum."

Luke was right. He had been cruel, Luther thought, remembering the savagery of their fights back when they were kids. The time at some miserable bible camp he had flown into a rage at Luke and wrecked their room and tried to wreck him, his anger feeding on itself in a wave of unchecked destructiveness.

Luther didn't want for Luke to be a bum. He didn't want to be a bum either. He had a theory, perhaps shaky, that the blows their father had dealt Luke were received, punishing as they were, as the only form of love that he could give. Those beatings, which Luther had mostly escaped, had made his father a part of Luke that he wasn't to Luther. Like their father, it would never be for Luke to disrespect the institutions of government or burn the American flag or his draft card. For better or worse, Luke aligned himself with power. He would see the demonstrators as anarchic children who deserved the severe punishment that possibly awaited them.

Luke couldn't let it go, what Luther had said, when the ride was over and they had reached their destination and were alone.

"What the fuck is wrong with you?"

"Same thing that's wrong with you. We're Garatdjians. Got to be something wrong with that."

"There's something sick about you, man, to be talking that way."

"I made a mistake. I'm sorry. You say things too, sometimes."

"Not like that I don't. I don't disrespect you to the point of death."

"What's that supposed to mean?"

"It means just shut the fuck up."

Luke had brought along a Yashica 2 ¼ box camera. He was keen on photography, as he was for gadgets and equipment in general. Stereo systems, motorcycles, and back in childhood, shortwave radios and Lionel trains and BB guns. With his camera he photographed the Lincoln Memorial and Luther standing at the edge of the reflecting pool on the National Mall.

Luther was moved to tears by the Gettysburg Address and the Second Inaugural Address. His mother worshiped Lincoln. He was her ideal of a handsome man. She didn't care for a man who laughed too much. She said that seriousness of expression had its place. Luther took strength from his mother's conviction. Already had he fallen victim to the face police of America and their constant war on a grave countenance, unwilling and unable to let it be, as if the true enemy was pain and the need to extinguish, abolish, or at the very least hide it. Did these face police not time and again zap him, saying, "Would it kill you to smile?" but never asking if it would kill them not to.

Lincoln, his stovepipe hat removed, smiled down benignly and clear-eyed from his lofty perch. Would that the Great Emancipator who had freed the slaves would take him back to the last century where he could live in peace and happiness and avoid the turmoil of who he was, or could Abe at least take him back to seventh grade, where Luther first read about him?

But Abe held his silence and it was just big Dave Dellinger and big Abbie Hoffman and others who were American but not as American as Abe, with all the wisdom he could bring to a situation. Luther's attention not on the amplified words he heard, words blown away on the October wind, but more on his brother's discomfort, even paranoia. Luke didn't operate well in daylight. Apart from the photograph of Luther Luke had taken, he couldn't use the camera, so fearful was he of what the placard-bearing, chanting demonstrators would think. Afraid to ride the New York City subways, for that matter, for fear of people staring at him. Meanwhile, Luke thinking, You weak, love-drenched hordes with your flowers for the soldiers' guns and your words and more words. Or so Luther imagined.

In fact, the protesters were faced off against helmeted soldiers. They carry guns and yet they are good, Luther thought, of the uniformed young men holding rifles with fixed bayonets against the crowd. There was no figuring it out.

In the halls of Congress he imagined men in suits looking on and LBJ too staring out from behind a curtained window as the gathered began to move across the bridge over the Potomac toward the Pentagon. Soon there was a bonfire of burning draft cards. Luther came undone. To be present at something so monumental and yet feel so insignificant and irrelevant. He had not risen to the event's level; he had come with no moral purpose. His ambivalence had accompanied him. He was the soldier with the flower in the barrel of his M-16 and the flower power demonstrator who had placed it there. All elements of America were in him, war and peace. He was not a foreign substance. He was native born, so how could they not be in him? He was the sum total of what he had been fed, and what it amounted to was a ball of confusion that equaled paralysis. And yet the granite face of the Pentagon did not fool him. Emblem of strength it might be, and the hippies would have no success in elevating its mass, but it too would give the lie to its image of permanence.

"Oh man, I'm so fucking hungry," Luke grumbled, and so they hustled themselves away from history in the making to get cheap hamburgers and hitchhike out of town before dusk.

Chapter 36

Bum. Luigi the Sicilian had spoken it first, back when, saying, "What a bunch of bums you a gonna be," his words summoning in him tears of laughter. Luigi might have been dark and combustible at times. He might have split a policeman's skull with the officer's own nightstick, but joy was his natural expression. And joy it had given Luke and Luther to descend into the basement to be with Luigi in the space Auntie Eve had given him for an upholstery shop. There he reupholstered Auntie Eve's stuffed armchairs and smoothed and refinished her wooden furniture.

Beyond the space he had cleared was a forbidding wilderness of furnishings piled to the ceiling. Though he had not seen any, Luther was certain rats abode in that chaos. The understanding came to him that Auntie Eve did not so much manage the building as it managed her. A decrepit, out-of-control beast it could sometimes seem.

"You no good sumbitches, get some a sausage from the store." Fat sausages that Luigi would split in half and fry on his hot plate, the meat sizzling as it browned.

"How's your little dickie," Luigi would say to Luther. "Your aunt is an old pussy," he would also say, which made Luther sad and uncomfortable to hear. Luigi shouldn't have been saying things like that about Luther's aunt, not about anyone. It wasn't right.

Luigi took them by subway to the edge of Manhattan, where the waters of the Atlantic met it, and over the Manhattan Bridge, Luther staring out the window of the lead car alert for trouble should the structure give way and the train fall and fall and they all be drowned in the ocean's depth. He had heard about the pharaoh's army and the trickery that God and a body of water could do. Only when the train made it across to Brooklyn, the water testing and testing that borough too, could he relax his vigil and peace be his once more.

Vera was not allowed to be part of the outing with Luigi. Mrs. Garatdjian would not have it. She did not have to explain. Luther had his understanding and Luke had the same understanding as to why.

Brooklyn was outdoors for a long part of the ride on the BMT. It could not forever be contained in any tunnel but had to be seen in all its mystery. That wall that rose alongside the tracks and above that wall glimpses of people and houses, the senses overwhelmed that they should be there in their state of happy anarchy, that they did not need a tall building to contain them for safety's sake.

At Stillwell Avenue a ramp led down to Surf Avenue. The damp air called them to the ocean's edge, though first there was Nathan's for franks and French fries, Luther eating so he did not disappear when he stood in only his bathing suit on the hot sand. After the beach there was the Whip, the Cyclone, the Wonder Wheel, the House of Horrors—there was no ticket Luigi would deny them.

Mr. Garatdjian may have seen what Luigi was doing and what he had become to Luther and Luke. He too wanted to be part of their lives. They were his children, were they not, and so Mrs. Garatdjian pleaded with Luther to make his father happy. Already she knew of his distance from his father and his fear of him. She knew, as Luther knew, that Luke absorbed his father's blows because if it was the only love he could receive from his father then he must take it. But Luther was not like his brother. He had a line of apartness from his father in his head because of the fire his father had been made to display when made to get up because of the aggravation (never irritation, never) they caused him, his father saying "You do not know what I will do if I lose control. I do not know what I will do." But Luther knew and Luke knew of his smacking hand and saw it in action that very morning the three of them set out for Brooklyn, saw the smack his father dealt before they had turned the corner onto Broadway, saw his father's fear, saw his father's vigilance soaring, saw how his father pressed him and Luke against the tiles of the Cathedral Parkway station as the IRT local roared its approach, lest they all fall onto the tracks and be crushed by the merciless action of moving steel rending flesh from bone and bone itself. And saw and smelt the saliva his father wet his handkerchief with to dab their faces free of any dirt that had gathered.

His father standing pale and hairy on the hot sands of Coney Island in a black bathing suit, his legs sticklike and his belly swollen and his chest sunken. His body a thing of different parts that didn't go together and that called out to be hidden away so Luther did not have to see his own future exposed to him so brutally. So old and decrepit his father was. Luke fled into the water, beyond the breakers and heading for the horizon, as if the ocean's depth and indifference to his life were of no consequence.

And there was no Nathan's to get filled up on beforehand so Luther could stand substantial on the sands, Mr. Garatdjian saying, "Why must you always be asking for things? Did Mommy not feed you before we left? Have you no gratitude?" And stingy about rides after the beach. His father's anger like the cogwheels of the Cyclone slowly pulling the cars to the summit before the reckless plunge and down and around the track at breakneck speed. His father's anger a building thing, like a bomb that bulged before it blew. His father's anger not to be compared with but run from.

But a different side of his father showed itself that day. While Luke was but a speck in the ocean, two young black couples came and lay on towels and showed themselves conspicuous on a beach where all around them was whiteness, and from that mass of whiteness came four young men in the briefest and tightest of bathing trunks that they might show off their bulge and their powerful builds and for whom their pompadours were their crowning glory. They did not come to introduce themselves or to chat but to encircle the young black men and women and insult them and beat the two young black men back into the sands as they rose to defend themselves, punching and punching and kicking and kicking to drive them even deeper into the now blood-stained sand before bashing their fallen bodies with a big wire trash basket, beat them until the only movement from their victims was the occasional twitching of their limbs. Not a hair of the muscle men's hair had fallen out of place in the exercise of their power, and now that they had done their filth they could go back into the mass of whiteness.

What must be said is that Mr. Garatdjian, now a witness, was made to get up and to run on his stick legs toward the scene of destruction, calling out as he went, "What is the meaning of this? Have you lost your minds?" before himself being cast down into the sands by a powerful shove from one of the muscle-bound men. And where did Luther go? Did he go toward the muscle-bound men? No, and no again. He backpedaled toward the water's edge, lest the violence find him, praying and praying that his father's blood not be made to flow.

And so you know that Luther had Luigi as well as a father who was present even in his absence. And that there were other fathers as well.

Chapter 37

Vinny did his thing behind the stick in a bar the college boys and girls did not go to. He showed himself not to mind that they went elsewhere to hear the Beatles and the Rolling Stones while his jukebox played Mel Tormé and the great Jack Jones and Frank Sinatra and Connie Francis and Vic Damone and a touch of Patti Page. Vinny could simply exist being himself in fidelity to the culture he had grown up with that required you to be a fireman or a cop or a criminal and to work with your hands and to take the blows that were dealt you without crying. He had a built body that did not need words to go with it.

Luther tried not to be caught staring at Vinny. It wouldn't go well if he was. Vinny might see it as a transgression and be obliged to say, "What the fuck you staring at?" or some such. And yet working the stick was his stage. He was there to be admired, just not by the likes of Luther. Why else would he perfect that fifties pompadour as a statement of indifference to what was happening in the hair department nationwide while practicing the art of sleek containment of his muscular heft in the black knitted shirt he buttoned at the top and the pressed black slacks to go with it and the sharp leather shoes, the totality a promise of the kind of goods that were deliverable beneath the fine threads that he wore so casually and with the unexpressed conviction that words would never be part the arsenal he would need, the powerful physique that the dark threads could not conceal elevating the status of his existence into a thing of beauty profound.

Luther thought-streamed Vinny with an untruth. "We were in Washington, D.C. We levitated the Pentagon all by ourselves." Vinny was putting on a show washing and drying the dirty glasses while managing to keep his clothes out of trouble. "You don't give a damn about any kind of peace demonstration. You live outside history," Luther continued. "You have the body parts that I've always wanted, but that Santa never brought. A thick neck would be at the top of the list. Almost at the top, if you know what I mean."

Luther broke his silence to order another beer, while wondering why he hadn't been able to stay in sync with his generation down in Washington, D.C., why, that is, he was in a dark bar watching handsome Vinny wash and dry glasses instead.

"Do you have the answer?" Luther asked.

"You say something?" Vinny said.

"No. Nothing." Luther looked out the window. The building was still across the street in all its painful commitment to being there.

Only later, in the far reaches of the night, did he wake and wonder with a fright if Vinny had been among the pompadours who drove the two black men into the blood-stained sands of Coney Island those years ago and why he, Luther, would think that meekness could neutralize the danger he represented if he was. And then wondered if Vinny was one and the same with the pompadour who had lifted the sprinting black man with the open razor over his head and crashed him through the hood of the convertible back those years ago as well.

We took the ferry from Dover to Calais, a cold October crossing on which I received my first experience of the French. Even the waiters and the busboys are, you can quickly see, convinced of their innate superiority. They make you feel very much the outsider, which only increased when we got to Paris. There they try to daunt you with their social intelligence even as they walk triumphantly along the boulevards. Despite all she has said about the wonders of France, Mommy's anxiety is evident. She takes it into the Louvre with her and along the Champs Elysee and cowers in Notre Dame. Fear impedes the flow of her words and I am still looking for her vaunted savoir faire. If the trip was meant to demonstrate her independence, it is revealing the opposite. Last night Mommy and I went to a café on a nearby boulevard and sat at an outdoor table where, after several glasses of cognac, she said she would be going back to the hotel. "I want you to have a good time. I want you to have a rich experience that you will always treasure." What she meant was that she wanted me to be picked up, which she counted on happening once she had excused herself. I don't know about Mommy sometimes.

Luther was outraged. Mona's mother had been revealed to him as the person she was—a pimp, a panderer. Her greatest desire, her single-most ambition, was to arrange for the fucking of her daughter. She was a woman intent on coming between them and destroying their goodness. He could see her laughing back at her hotel room, her head tilted back, a long, malign laugh.

But there was something else, equal in strength to his fury. There was lust. Images flooded his mind of Mona being taken by a stranger with a massive member. A cycle of fear and anger and titillation repeated itself through the day.

A bulletin for all concerned: be aware of the mother who would do you harm. Be aware of her alleged might and her naughtiness that risks being evil. Be aware of women who want to fly not to heaven but plunge straight down to hell. Be aware of what Paris can do to the souls of the just and the unjust alike. And of course be aware of the supreme power of the supreme allied commander with operational headquarters here in New York City and that the invasion that came once can come again, with force invincible smashing through by land and sea and air bent on full liquidation. Be aware that beauty and justice must never be tarnished, even what exists in such a degraded soul as I. Best to be on notice that my reach is global.

Miss Hansen held a lighted candle. "I have come to reclaim little Schnell. I am afraid you do not look after him properly. The poor dear may very well have rickets as a result of your neglect. I suppose I should not have expected so very much since you hardly look after yourself. I am afraid you really are nothing more than a piece of hanging string. Do you remember that I would see you with your sister out on the street when you were children and you would come up to me and say, 'Please, Miss Hansen, could we have a quarter? We are orphans'? Do you remember that? You said the same thing to all the women in the building. The question is how long you will remain a piece of hanging string."

Luther looked at little Schnell and how he was rubbing up against Miss Hansen's leg and not his own. "He is just like me. He prefers women to men," he said.

"He prefers good women to uncaring men," Miss Hansen said, bending down slowly to scoop up her skinny cat and take him home to momma.

Luther was not branded by Miss Hansen's words as by a hot poker. He had not been uncaring, as she claimed. But he did take in her words, repeating her assertion that he was but a hanging string many times in the privacy of his room.

Chapter 38

She was back but she wasn't back, seeking to frustrate him with a supreme dawdling technique. If he was to believe the itinerary from the travel agency, her trip was over, so where was she?

"Stay in your rooms, all of you. You are nothing and she is everything. Do not dare to ruin my life with your oppressive presence," Luther shouted to the tenants in the compartment who shared the public phone, frantic for the relief that only her love could bring.

He lost count of the times he called her apartment and was now at the breaking point. Her humiliation of him was complete. Surely she knew, as she had always known, that she would inevitably sweep away his pathetic resistance and reign supreme over him. Pain was his for the asking, and she would give it to him with American gusto.

The flight had been long and difficult. She was exhausted, she said. Could he not wait to see her until the next day? But no, he couldn't.

She put a power move on, showing up in a black evening dress and black stockings and high heels, even a black cape with a gold chain and a black leather bag with its own gold chain. Her hair even lighter, more brilliant, more blond, as if Botticelli had chased her off the canvas and into life. The physical ache was too much for him. Quick, frantic lovemaking followed, as if he had been given the chance to release from all the anxiety stored in his body for all the weeks she had been gone.

Afterward, he spoke his fear in a simple tongue, said what he hadn't the courage to say before, that if she left again he would disappear into nothingness as just another family member captive to the building and that she must never again leave him at their mercy.

Mona was receptive in the way that she could be. She was not out to destroy his mind, but she had been reading Anais Nin.

"Mommy and I have talked about going to art school in Boston this January if I can get in. Probably I won't be seeing you if I do go away. I had a chance to think about us while in Europe, and maybe things are just too crazy. That doesn't mean you have to kill me. Boston isn't Paris, and I'm not going off to a Greek isle with another man." She copped a smoke to signify her settled triumph while he lay curled in all the fear her words engendered. She swept her cape around her shoulders and departed with the goddess-like image her father had taught her to embrace.

A week later, shed of her European finery, she had an acceptance from the Boston Museum School of Fine Arts on the basis of her portfolio. Luther stood by looking downcast as the family basked in Mona's success.

"Have you ever seen a happier-looking man?" Lydia asked, and he knew her light laugh was meant to assassinate him. He staggered around their living room as if he had been stabbed. Finally he spoke.

"Do you know what it means when my lifeline is threatened? First there was the tidal wave of your European tour, and now there is the tsunami of four years of art school in another state, when I have not been able to leave the borough in which I was born and raised. You have me on the ropes. You are annihilating my presence in this very moment. But I will establish myself on the path of perseverance and clear the way for my own rising star."

Luther withdrew to Mona's room with a bottle of bourbon from the liquor tray and drank from it. The more he drank the more it all made sense to him. Life was communication. If they had stared into his emotional nakedness, they must now see his flesh so the picture could be complete, and so he emerged in his birthday suit that full disclosure might have its day.

"You will leave this table immediately and not return until you are fully clothed," Peter said.

"I have been shed of my clothes," Luther said.

"Where are your clothes, please?" Peter demanded.

"What?"

"Your clothes, young man. Your clothes."

"I have no clothes. You divested me of my garments and threw them out the window onto Riverside Drive. Do you not remember how I begged you to spare me my underwear, but even that last vestige of pride you stripped from me for humiliating inspection by the general public."

"That is an outrageous lie."

The family went into a huddle, of which Mona was conspicuously a part. He heard the word "Bellevue" and he heard the word "police" and he heard the word "psychotic" before retiring to Mona's room.

He was lying spread-eagled on her bed when she entered.

"Asshole." She threw the clothes at him that she herself had retrieved.

"Flush me down the toilet and flush me down it good."

"You've got to go. Otherwise Mommy and Daddy will call the police. Everyone is very upset."

For days he stayed in bed, doing little more than getting up to relieve himself. He had been crushed by the larger forces he had tried to harness himself to, and was left with only his breath to keep him company. Now and then he would hear tenants passing by his door, and they only served to deepen his sense of hopelessness, as they, like himself, were pathetic by virtue of where they lived. With savage judgment driving him, he posted a sign to the outside of the door that read, "LOSERS STAY AWAY !!" but they paid him no mind, given their need to get their business done.

One morning, in early January, she was gone. He could tell. The entire building shaken by the torque the master driver demanded from his black beast told him so, Peter having sprung himself from his study to situate Mona two hundred forty miles away in Boston.

He fled into Riverside Park, a wintry glaze upon its lawns and stripped, skeletal trees, and entered the railroad tunnel of his childhood, while on the West Side Highway running parallel to the tunnel the rampaging cars were having their way. A snapping sound the tires made as rubber met the cracks in the road, causing you to listen for it, the sound neither a comfort nor a torment. He slipped into the tunnel through the semicircular window where a vertical bar was missing. Up above were spaced grates to allow the diesel fumes to escape in the progress of industry over nature, and after a while the train heralded itself with rays of light from beyond the bend far down the straightaway.

He stood and saluted as a tandem of black New York Central switchers passed, and had no heart to chuck bits of track ballast at the string of boxcars and gondola cars in their wake. Some things, like banging the rocks off the freight cars signifying the might of America, were left in childhood. He was just grateful to be in the presence of power where he could find it.

"Son, the Holy Ghost has been looking for you. Did he find you and did you let him in?" his mother asked that same night, having come to visit with him.

"Mother, let me go. I am full of my own filth and desperate for my own cleanliness, which I must be alone to obtain."

"You must cease this world you were not meant for."

"Oh yes. Oh very yes yes," he could only say, feeling the anger she engendered in him with her words.

The cat lady entered following his mother's departure. Luther did not fight her presence.

"How do I get old like you with all the peace you exemplify? How do I get past this longing for all I do not have?"

"You have many days and years to continue as a hanging string before you can hope for a change to come. You treat yourself no better than you have treated little Schnell, and that is the great iniquity." She spoke to him from a place of peace with her whiskers on full alert.

When she went away, he thought of the tunnel, and could only wonder if some great truth awaited him down there.

In the morning he was woken by a pounding on the door.

"Who the hell is it and what do you want?" Luther shouted, struggling to get his bearings.

"There is phone call for you, strange and stupid man," a voice replied.

He came to the hallway phone in his underwear and picked up the dangling receiver.

"Go ahead, universe. I am listening," he said.

"It's me, Mona. I miss you."

"Are you giving me fishy talk? My teeth are bad. I have no mind. I am just skin and bone and regret."

She began to cry, as if she hadn't heard. "I couldn't bear to leave you. I couldn't. I can't. You'll come up to visit. We will be just fine. You'll see."

For days thereafter he wandered in a daze of bliss, having been rescued from forever darkness and perpetual sorrow. Or was it a dream?

Chapter 39

In this time an odd and inexplicable thing happened. Amory Wooster, Vera's Shakespeare maven friend, went crazy, or so she said. He was found running naked through Central Park on a brutally cold January day.

"They have him in Bellevue. He's on a special medication. He's going to have to be on it for the rest of his life." She spoke from a place of radiant happiness that her supposed sorrow could not mask.

"A lifetime is a long time. How do you know what he needs for the rest of his life?" Luther tried to inquire, but his words got blown away by the force of her will as she bowed down her head in falseness, asking him to feel not for Amory but for her, everyone being a target for her conquest.

And then Fat Man had to arrive from Cambridge, Massachusetts, the world headquarters for Harvard University and Boston University, the latter not a place of learning in Fat Man's mind but a mill for future has beens who never were to begin with. He came with the scintillating quality of his own exam prowess. Vera said he was a good friend of Amory's and had been in love with him for the longest time, though she did not mention the word *consummation*. She did disclose that Fat Man was a doctoral candidate at Harvard in something called philosophy of education. But he was not simply a lowly graduate student listening to the Beatles over pizza on a Saturday night. Firstly he tuned in to Bach and got out of the house and the state to groove on cool jazz at Small's Jazz Club, in the East Village, and while in transit from Cambridge appreciated the majesty of the Supremes in his five-gear Porsche speedily closing the distance between him and the things he needed. He also had a Great Dane he tongue-kissed and wore expensive suits and flew to Europe every other month on buying binges, his purse open for the people he loved owing to the bounty of America he had access to and driven by his insatiable hunger for all the foreign capitals so he could be abreast of what was going on. He was a man of deep feeling in his Sulka ties, and even if the only thing he could truly love was excellence, he was prepared to tell you why.

And in fact Fat Man considered Vera the most excellent young woman he knew. And because she saw the Fat Man loving Amory Wooster so good, she thought Fat Man should love Luther as well.

Luther had nothing for Fat Man when they sat face to face in the End Bar with Vera, particularly since Fat Man had put on the table an intelligence meter whose needle always remained in the highest zone whatever babble Vera uttered but which plunged as soon as Luther opened his mouth. Being who he was, Luther finally snatched the instrument and threw it to the floor and asked did Harvard have any long-term plan for saving our true national heritage so the past could never be gone from us and we didn't have to be at the mercy of heartless aircraft and soul-destroying trucks? Fat Man could only respond that Luther seemed remarkably insulated from reality.

"You should follow the example of your sister and embrace life."

"Oh yes, oh very yes yes yes. Only a fatso like you would think so."

"Your bad teeth are a match for your bad manners. And don't ever talk to me that way again."

Luther leaned forward across the table. "Lick my steaming cunt," he said.

Fat Man laughed and turned his attention exclusively to Vera with a stream of Harvard talk. Luther hung his head, understanding that reality once again was setting in and there could be no protection from it.

"Luther is smart, too," Vera said, a picture of smiling largesse. "He attends CCNY."

"Not for the mentally defective, but not for the top echelon either. He might consider transferring to Columbia."

Luther held himself in check. No need to tell Fat Man that he couldn't go where his intelligence did not permit him to go, that he had to stay low to the ground and live within the numbers that had been assigned to him while fearing all those who had been blessed with large gifts.

"Luther is dying," Vera said. "He thought he had the power to leave home but he really doesn't. Arthur, you take over now." She did not call him Fat Man to his face.

"Take over?" Fat Man's voice registered his surprise.

"Take him over, and take him over now." With that Vera jumped up and fled with her sudden crossness.

Fat Man had a friend to see that evening, a gifted musician. Reluctantly, Fat Man invited Luther along. Not having many stories, Luther told him the one he had shared with Justin De Vople, the Peter De Vries man.

"Once upon a time a woman took me in her Cadillac. It was New Year's Eve but she took me anyway, and when the crowds in Times Square saw us they parted and were joyous, so happy were they to see us. And I was so happy to see her, because I had never seen her kind before, with her laughing Texas voice and the smell of worldly perfume upon her, and the drive down Broadway in her worldly car so we did not have to walk or take the subway, and what it meant for a child to witness such a thing, to be able to step into the night-time beauty of America. I am reaching for that same feeling now in your vehicle but I cannot find it, even as we take the same route to whatever the destination."

Fat Man parked his Porsche on Seventy-first Street, just off Broadway. He exited slowly and Luther followed him through an open iron gate and a courtyard into a building deserving of respect. A brittle man named Charles stood in waiting for them at the door of his ground-floor apartment. When Charles saw through eye contact and all the other sensors given to man that Luther had nothing artistic or of a personal aesthetic to offer, he showed him his back and plucked the necessary chords and notes from the universe and summoned from his harpsichord "Three Blind Mice" for his guest's musical appreciation, and when Luther could take the ridicule no more, he bolted out the door.

Chapter 40

Luther had kept his distance from Tony Pascual since moving out. Over those months he came to realize that his room in Tony's apartment had been a good deal. He had only hurt himself by leaving, given that he lacked the resources for anything more. And so, in a state of anxiety, he approached Tony in Finley Cafeteria.

"I knew you couldn't make it. I knew you would fall flat on your face. So come on back. Just come on back. I'll play beautiful music for you with my Janis chick to keep me company." He did a few riffs on his imaginary guitar, punishing the strings, to tempt him.

Luther's return was not what he expected. Shouting came from the room at Tony's place that had been his. "Fuck" and "Shit" and "I'll kill your ass." The door was ajar and Luther could see a man's bare feet as he lay on the bed. A simple fear came over him that the man would go berserk, if he wasn't already, and would fly out with a long knife and kill him and anyone else that he could find.

Tony Pascual joined Luther by the door. "That's Billy Riley. He is my very best friend and has been in Vietnam killing the Vietcong. And now they have almost killed him. That is the essence of symbolic logic, the equivalence factor. Do you understand?"

"You bet," Luther could only think to say, paralyzed by the seeming threat of pandemonium.

Tony Pascual led him through the French doors beyond the living room.

"This is where you will be until the logic of the reorganization becomes apparent and requires you to leave."

"Leave? I just got here," Luther said.

"You have to obey the necessity of the historical imperative. Have you got that in your knowledge?"

"What historical imperative?"

"The historical imperative of J. J."

"J. J.?"

"Janis. She's right next door. We're taking it slow before she moves in."

"Tony, maybe you want to think about that. I mean, she may not be your type."

"She's my type. I play all the right chords for her." He erected his guitar at a right angle to the sky and plinked out his message of power delight.

Luther closed the French doors and took in the fragile solitude. Although aesthetically displeasing, the small glass panels in the doors had been rendered opaque by paint, and for that he could be grateful. He began to cry for Mona and the pain it brought him to be away from her and the nightmare of a life without her and only the telephone to bridge the gap and only his mediocrity to keep him company. He cried out for warmth from the frightening spaces around him, but the air was cold and he was cold and nothing was at hand to provide the heat and comfort that were requirements for living, and he was just a bum de la bum like demented Tony Pascual. He cried at his low-number inadequacy to the tasks of life while across the street the School of Engineering Building of the great Columbia University hummed with efficiency.

He lay down with the great *Bleak House* at his side and asked it to take him between its bright Penguin cover so he could feel nurtured by the words that had been produced on the fine paper and asked it too to protect him from the wintry gray streets that were calling to him. He asked the great *Bleak House* to remove him from the trap of his own life because he couldn't go any farther than where he was no matter what he did, movement no longer a function of changing his shirt or his jeans or his room or anything, the rays of life itself conspiring to keep him in place under the weight of implacably unyielding numbers. Once again he just wished that he could die, being in the condition of life that he was.

He fell asleep with the book on his chest. When he awoke a man was standing over him. His feet were in rubber sandals and he wore a black pajama suit with air holes in the armpits.

"I took them off a dead Charlie. Blew his face off while on patrol in the Mekong Delta. Pussies, all of them, Charlie was. The NVAD were something else. They'd do anything for your blood."

He was hard to look at. It was his head. It offered shock value, what with the fact that it was completely shaved. A jagged scar banded the top of his scalp. Luther inwardly recoiled. It was like someone had ice-skated on Billy Riley's head with a very sharp blade.

"Do you want to kill me for not being you? Am I allowed to ask some questions?"

"Go." He clenched and unclenched his hands and streamed his energy into the room with an intense hum. He was short—about 5'4"—but powerfully built and nimble as he moved about on the balls of his feet.

"How do you get to walk around in a dead man's uniform?"

"You fucking kill is how you do it."

Luther was blown back by Billy Riley's response. "Do you know who you are, with your extremely shocking scar?"

"Tell me who I am."

"You are my hero. You are the one for whom 'Sally Go Round the Roses' was written and sung. You are LaSalle Street in the summertime and the street battles with the kids from the projects. You are, all 5'4" of you, where it was at on the basketball court as you took it to the hoop among the tall trees. You are the action of life and I am the man who stands around watching you. And now you are free to be yourself and to be organized around a principle of existence called survival. All I can do is talk and all you can do is do. Only I have to ask you one other thing."

"Say it."

"Please, never come in on me when I am dressing. That goes for Tony, too. It would shame me no end for you to see me as I truly am, though when I am sufficiently drunk, you may then feel free to feast your eyes on the poverty of my body. It is just that you put me in mind that I am minus my manhood even as I hear voices that say you are not good enough for me. The truth is that if I get too close to you I will lose Mona. At least that is my fear. Because in my mind, while I love you deeply more than you can ever know, if the fidelity of memory and the feeling that attaches to it can mean anything, I cannot be with you owing to the divide between who I am and who you are."

Billy Riley stared at Luther with his battered head tilted, trying to get an angle of comprehension even as he rocked back and forth on the balls and heels of his feet. His head and internal distress hurt too much for quietness and there were the erupting noises of the jungle and flashes of the Charlies he had seared and the ears he had clipped, passing the litmus test of killing far from LaSalle Street and the mother and father who were not there owing to the alcohol they drank and the beatings they inflicted on him and each other and the Catholic brothers imposing their bruising ways driven by their particular understanding of The Christ. He had seen the corn-fed men of America with their gaping wounds calling for their mothers and death, this outside the confines of the great *Bleak House,* having dropped out of community college with the draft awaiting him.

"Because the wounds of life are too great to countenance, and they come so early on. What I mean is, how am I to respect myself reading the great Charles Dickens in the presence of such as you? Tell me, if you will, what right a person has to even live knowing that is the case? Do you have an answer? Do you?"

Billy Riley had gone down on the floor. He lay on his back with his arms locked around his bent knees and rolled from side to side. Luther put aside his Dickens novel and aspiration to sooner or later link up the nineteenth with the twentieth century. So what if he couldn't just then sink into the thin pages, a world of words and more words but no equations, his mind drifting into the default gulch of deficiency. So he joined Billy Riley on the floor and rocked in his own kind of pain and made his own noises, causing Billy Riley to jump right up onto his sandaled feet in astonishment at the intimacy of the imitation. Billy Riley just left him there to deal.

Not that Billy Riley was finished showing himself in the way that he could. Luther had only to leave his domain behind the French doors to find that out.

"I'm having a good time on the shit can," Billy Riley yelled out, as Luther ventured down the hallway past the bathroom door. "Hey man, don't walk away. I'm talking to you," he went on, putting a verbal check on Luther's progress.

So Luther felt compelled to draw near to Billy Riley's bathroom smells and witness his new roommate wiping himself, then tie his baggy pajama bottoms with a piece of rope. Once again, Luther experienced queasiness at the sight of Billy Riley's gruesomely wounded scalp and the whole thing of him.

"I am not in the word department right now. I hardly know what more to say," Luther said, as Billy Riley moved him out of the way with a roar and headed for his room.

Chapter 41

In the months that passed Luther and Mona became weekend travelers on the New Haven Railroad. Since she was the one to go away she should also come back, but then his heart melted at the unfairness and the shame of asking her to abort her process outward and so he went to her on alternate weekends, which gave him a chance to ride the rails and fill with the happiness that motion brought. In all this time the words "I love you" filled the air, both of them singing in that key.

Amid the change he managed to pick up the thread of his old life, finding his way back to the post office and the power of big-toothed Mr. Ruggiero of Queens, New York. En route to the P.O., longing for Mona came over him in Pennsylvania Station. From a phone booth he called and got the landlady of the rooming house where Mona was staying. She was not a friendly landlady, telling him coldly Mona wasn't in her room and maybe he didn't need to call so often, that in fact she would have the police on him because the telephone people were making inquiries about illegal credit card calls, Tony Pascual having obtained and shared with him one such credit card number, which Luther would then give to the phone operator. His mind went blank to everything but his need for her in that moment. It was close to six, the rush hour, and all the dashing

Dans were streaking for the Long Island Railroad with their empty attaché cases.

He arrived at work fearing the loss of Mona to the bright world she had escaped to and worried that he would spend the rest of his days as the human automaton the P.O. had turned him into along with the other automatons. The more he heard about her world the less comfort he could find in his own.

That evening Luther told Mr. Ruggiero the truth, saying that Mona was headed for the cover of *Time* magazine as the foremost artist of her generation, a woman coveted by men of wealth with all the obsessive fervor of collectors after a priceless painting.

"I never had two thoughts about art but since meeting Mona I see it as a higher calling because she's doing things with her hands while I look at myself and the students around me with their paperback books and little term papers and puny ideas and meaningless classroom discussions. What I am saying is that she reads the great *Dombey and Son* for pleasure while I struggle to read it at all for credit. Because she doesn't care anything about grades or cumulative indexes or graduate school, and she has no need to place books on the shelf in proof of her knowledge. Because what she does with her hands is an expression of her being, while what I have are bored professors with jobs, not callings, and for whom the paycheck has become the primary thing. Do you understand where I'm coming from, Mr. Ruggiero? Do you?"

Mr. Ruggiero finally spoke. "Why did you have to come back here? Can you tell me that?"

"For one reason, and one reason only. So Queens can come to love Manhattan, Mr. Ruggiero. I feel bad about your son, Mr. Ruggiero, but he's still fighting valiant and strong, isn't he?"

"You leave my son out of this before I break your bones."

Luther saw the clock upon the wall. "I must be faithful to my pain," he shouted, and raced to a phone on a lower level and called Boston. The landlady answered and was clearly stoked on Boston baked beans. "Leave the poor girl alone. She's just trying to get away from you," she said.

"Be careful who you're talking to if you value your mail. I have the entire government behind me. I am very, very powerful in my—"

The landlady did hang up on him. Luther ran back to his post with his hands to his head, unable to see how he could get through the hour without calling once again, in violation of the schedule he had set for himself.

Mr. Ruggiero was waiting for him. "You got a problem, maybe, running off the floor like that?"

"Do I have a problem?"

"Do you—you—have a problem?"

"What's a you-you?"

"I will be watching you." Mr. Ruggiero said, pointing a thick finger in Luther's face before walking off.

His distress mounting, Luther turned to his box scheme brothers: "I have always feared the world of men. Men are a lonely bunch. Their suffering makes them mean. Men without women are nothing. My girlfriend's father? He would shrivel up and die without his wife. My own father? Lost, completely lost, without my mother. The truth? Men without women sit in Chock Full O' Nuts, their fingers smudged with newspaper ink. Men without women do not change their underwear or brush their teeth. Men without women have cojones like shriveled peas."

But they paid him no mind, and so he suffered at his post, waiting for the minute hand of the clock to complete its torturously slow hourly rotation. But his rush to the phone was again all in vain. She was not there, and the landlady was not there. Perhaps there was even some collusion and she and Mona had become partners in engendering pain. All he knew was that the phone rang and rang and that the ringing went unheeded.

"I must leave you now," he said, when his shift was mercifully over. "I must take my time card and punch out and run into the great Pennsylvania Station, through which years ago my mother delivered me to the church across the street. I am not Jesus. I cannot live outside of time, I cannot perform miracles of transcendence. I must abide in the flesh. The only peace I know is when I am connected to her. She is my dream so big, in which I have lost myself. And you, the very sight of you, are the spectacle of a life so small, so do not come near me. I have hitched myself to a star, and while the journey is painful, it must go on so death cannot occur. Are we entirely clear about this?" But once again they heard him not.

And so he hurried on his long legs down the long flight of stairs into Penn Station, shouting for the men of violence not to do him, all his senses on full alert. Arrived in the arcade, he screamed,"Mona," the sound of her name taking the roof off the structure and causing her to call down from Boston that she was home already and what the hell was wrong with him that he needed to be so *loud*?

"Who I am and who I am striving to be are two different things," he shouted back, before normalizing the channel of their communication with another credit card call. "Just know this. My nose for duplicity is very strong."

Mona told him to shut up, that she had been out visiting a friend, and rendered him calm with her explanation. He was free now to devote his energies to a nocturnal search. Entering the waiting room of the Long island Railroad, he saw a girl sitting alone and addressed her as he needed to. "It's not about scoring. Scoring is an ugly, cheap word. Call it rather a simple necessity, an obligation to myself to improve my security, to get that much farther ahead of her before the betrayal that must ultimately come."

"Don't think I can't relate to where you're coming from," the girl said, rising to give him a full kiss while pressing the bounty of her bosom against him. She had a boyfriend who was in a nearby facility for drugs, she said. She had just come that night from visiting him. He poked his neck veins. He poked his arm veins. He shot between his toes and in his thighs and in his sorry stupid ass. She said she was full of anger and wanted Luther to take her home and that her boyfriend needed to be attacked for all he had done to her and she herself needed to be attacked and that Luther, on the basis of what he had said, also needed some attacking in his life, so maybe they should get moving already.

Luther was in a state of supreme happiness as the train racketed its way uptown. The girl's breath smelled of alcohol and she said she wanted to go and get some more, beer and Southern Comfort being more important than anything, And when he asked her why some people had to go and be made so perfectly in terms of their skin and nose and hair and teeth, and others had to go and be made like him, she could offer him nothing but another full kiss of reassurance.

Behind the French doors, he told her all the mystery of the world was in how people made love and how, in that act, they showed sides of themselves that couldn't otherwise be seen. She shushed him and took what he had and didn't laugh at his body parts and in the morning she woke up beautiful and he woke up with cottonmouth and the awareness of movements on the other side of the door.

"I have a roommate with a shaved head and a brutal scar. He's just back from fighting the Vietcong."

Beyond the French doors Tony Pascual was not to be seen though Billy Riley was, but she merely walked on by and out the front door. If Luther had not made a proper introduction, it was because he couldn't, in the moment, remember her name though he had written it down with her phone number.

It was not always Penn Station and his mother. Times Square had its place too. There had been a man. Mr. Urgent Urgent. Hurrying Luther into the phone booth with the promise of a quarter if Luther would only help him with the task so desperately needing attention. And Luther immediately caught up in the drama and wanting to do right by Mr. Urgent Urgent, wherever it was he had come from, when only a minute before Luther had been thinking of his third grade friend Richie—Richie who hit the softballs so high and so far with his effortless swing of the bat—whom he had gone across town to see. Such a tight space the phone booth was with the door closed on the two of them. The man reaching down and unzipping his zipper and saying, in a different voice, a harder voice, "Take it out. Take it out now." Like a long thick piece of firm rubber it was. "Pull on it now. Back and forth. Do it," the man instructed, in the same voice. Like magic Luther had never seen before stuff flew from the man's thing, sliming the black phone and the booth with white and dripping gloop. Then Mr. Urgent Urgent dropped coins on the floor so he could be more than good with his word and was gone. Not that Luther gathered the coins, not with the gloop everywhere and the terror embracing him.

But Mr. Urgent Urgent was not done with him. A week passed and Luther was sitting peacefully in the church pew trying to follow the disappearing words of Pastor Horvath when a commotion started in him on seeing the face and everything of Mr. Urgent Urgent, a commotion he had to heed, and so he ran on his long legs from the church and from his mother and Pastor Horvath. Through Penn Station he ran, with no time for his mother and no time for the trains of the Pennsylvania Railroad, and no time for Penn Station either in his rush to get to Mr. Urgent Urgent, only one stop away at Times Square, lest he miss him, but when he arrived on the IRT Mr. Urgent Urgent was not there. He was not there. Nor was he there the week after or the week after that, nor was he there in the stinky subway bathrooms, the many subway bathrooms, Luther having extended his search, but other men were, standing beyond the time of peeing with their things out. Everywhere the men were with their things out or outlined hard inside their pants on the subways and in the libraries and on the streets and wherever it was that men went, and Luther was there among them, heeding the call he heard in his head when the call that always came happened to come.

Chapter 42

The rooming house was on Huntington Avenue. She had made her little room cozy by filling it with good things from her good home: a beige throw rug, a standing lamp, a small set of shelves, a pretty afghan for her bed. On the corner stood McGuffy's, a drugstore with a fountain that warmed Luther's heart to see as he watched the soda jerk do some serious stick work. Though she had only a hot plate, Mona had no need of McGuffy's, where the men and women with serious tooth decay went for their coffees and English muffins and greasy lamb stew. Because it was her birthright not to be driven by aloneness to sit at the counter in eating places where people went to get filled up.

The landlady had some things to say to him when she saw the two of them together exiting the premises. "Is this guy from New York? Because if he is, he's a criminal." Her gray hair was pulled tight in a bun to show off the severity of her angular face.

"I am from the great state of Hawaii, where we say aloha all the livelong day in an environment of great peace which does not mitigate against great industry," Luther offered.

"Hawaii? You look like you've been in prison, you're so pale."

"And you look like you've been in Boston, you're so very angry."

"You have that same snotty voice."

"No one has ever characterized my voice as snotty," Luther said.

"Well, if you're not him, then who is the jerk who calls at all hours from down in New York? The telephone people are after him."

"That is the question, isn't it?" Luther replied, closing the distance between them.

She waved her hands in dismissal. "Stay away from me, whoever you are," the landlady said.

On the sidewalk Luther turned and saw the landlady had followed them out the door, and that her eyes were on Mona, as they had to be, for the landlady was looking at quality. She was seeing it before her every eyes.

The school was situated down from the museum on a street sometimes called Paradise and at other times Childhood but most often Sadness, in sweet acknowledgment of where it led. To add to its nature, and to allow the children to play memorably in the arena of art, there was across the way a park with a little wooden bridge over a duck pond and a big athletic field and light towers rising gracefully over concrete stands and a strip of restrained dignity on the other side called Park Row, where there would come a time that she would live as she expanded into the world of troubled happiness.

She took him around to rooms filled with the smell of paint and turpentine and students at their easels and pottery wheels and etching presses, all of them involved with the messy stuff of art. He noticed the men especially, in their paint-splattered pants. He saw them lower their brushes to their sides and stare at him coldly, and saw that these were the men who would try to claim Mona for their own.

"I am not prepared to burn your houses down. I am not prepared to cancel your young lives. But I am afraid, and that you need to know, for you are standing in a place of hostility toward me, with not an iota of warmth being manifested," he shouted, but they dared to act as if they had heard him not.

After the tour, they sat in the park. Seeing Luther shaking, she spoke directly of the matter on her mind.

"Luther, do you want to be something? I mean, are you anything but sensitive? Do you have any intelligence?"

"Why are you talking to me this way?" he asked.

"Because you looked so stricken with fear inside the school," she answered.

"I have the necessities," he said. "I have all of them except for geography. Some of those islands I can't remember. And economics and science. And mathematics. But I can read. I can go line by line down the page of any paperback book."

Mona had grown large. She had gone over the tops of buildings in height. At the same time he was increasingly shrunken.

A tandem trolley, a monorail thing, took them through the underground to Park Street. The trolley had been there for many years, faithful to its route, and lacked the metallic screech of the New York City subways, Boston showing itself to be a city on a different scale. A more modern subway did the job of taking them into Harvard Square in Cambridge, where, to buck him up after deflating him, she now said, "You're as bright as those Harvard students," pointing to the dormitories that housed them, words he could not let her get by with lest they destroy him.

"You are wrong. You are flat-out wrong. But I will not run out into traffic to make you see it."

From Harvard Square they headed past the Coop to the Brattle Theater, finding downstairs a poster shop and the scent of incense and the Casablanca Bar, a dark space in which the bottles glowed. *Duck Soup* was playing and offered comedic fare to the Harvard throng that filled the seats. Their laughter at the Marx Brothers' antics made him happy. It pleased him that they found the film appealing in spite of their intelligence.

"I can't say why," he stood up and said. "It's just that when you are armed with such intelligence, what can possibly be good enough to fend off the mocking Harvard laughter the world knows you to be capable of? Because you all have fine minds and nowhere is it written that we are to do otherwise than to bow and scrape in deference to the fact of it. Which doesn't mean at bottom we truly want to, that we aren't ultimately tired of your Harvard irony that keeps us intimidated. Because you have forced my own laughter to be restrained, as if all eyes might be directed to me if I were too loud. And I will tell you this—Boston and Cambridge are like being in a house full of people such as you, and I so fear your bright laughter. But the time will come when the hegemony of your minds will be broken and the light of sincerity can come shining through and I can simply be myself."

"Throw a net over him," someone shouted.

"Make that two."

"Is Dr. Freud in the house?"

Luther fell asleep. Mona shook him awake when the movie was over and the lights had come on, exposing him and worse, exposing them, the ones who had been in the seats, and he shielded his eyes from their collective gaze, because now the darkness was gone and with it his courage.

When Sunday evening came, he made the decision to stay into Monday. The Boston Museum School of Fine Arts had defeated the City College of New York, and art itself had defeated paperback books.

"I will not be in the way," he said, seeking to reassure Mona. He saw the discipline she brought to her calling and sought to accommodate himself to it, the Rolling Stones' "Under My Thumb" having no application whatsoever at that moment.

In the morning Mona harnessed herself to her art school schedule while Luther wandered about the city, the question never far from his mind as to what exactly he was doing.

The light towers of Fenway Park rose above the neighborhood buildings. The BoSox would have Lonborg. They would have Yaz. But they would not have him. His interest in baseball had waned with the end of high school dreams of athletic glory.

That afternoon he sat in a Park Street theater watching *The Sound and the Fury*. The Technicolor was jarring; the film seemed meant for black and white. Luther loathed Jason as the domineering uncle and was sad for Caddie, trying to find herself after getting lost in the world, all this in the post-Civil War ruins of the South, The afternoon was passed in virtual solitude, there being only a few other viewers and row after row of empty seats. "I know you, Jason, I know you as myself, for I too have the capacity to try to block a woman from her rightful place in the world and I too have known lack of compassion for fallen sisters." So Luther said to himself.

But he could not stay with Jason or Caddie or Benjy or Quentin, who wanted to stop all the clocks of Cambridge because to come from a family and to leave a family was to go where you were not known and to live in your mind with what you did know, Caddy's muddy drawers, the two worlds being enough to build the wall that ultimately killed you. He had to go to the restroom. He had to go there in the afternoon quiet and stand over the urinal waiting for the man to come who didn't come, the man with the big member who would make it all right for him there in the illicit afternoon. And when it didn't happen, when he didn't show, there was no point to going back to his seat. There was only the need to vacate the premises and take his fire for sex out into the street.

At the corner convenience store next to the Harvard Coop he was stopped by the cover of a paperback that showed a naked brunette woman sitting in a chair with her legs crossed and embracing herself with both arms to cover her breasts. Was it truly Victorian pornography or a spoof of a bygone era? Spendings, comings, gamahuching, flogging, the seat of love, Mr. Priapus, Lady Pokingham. The publisher was not Smut, inc., but the estimable Grove Press. Self-consciousness prevented him from inquiring about the book, as the store was filled with Harvard students and once again, as in the Brattle Theater, he was cowed by the fear of their annihilating laughter. And so he brought the book to the cashier as if it were just another item along with the Granny Smith apple and copy of the *Boston Globe* he also purchased.

Aroused by the little he had read about quims and bottoms, he continued his wanderings. Somewhere in the city was an available girl on a streetcar or in a pizza parlor or wherever. He saw a couple of prospects but couldn't manage to approach them. The logistics weren't right. He would have to depend on them having a place of their own, and even if they did, how could he get back to the room and Mona in time?

The wind blew. The women seemed to be walking in a direction away from him down Boston streets lined with buildings notable for their bulging bay windows. Tomorrow would be different, he told himself, turning back. Tomorrow there would be the return trip by train to New York, and for sure he would meet someone then, someone who would provide protection from all the power arrayed against him.

Chapter 43

Fat Man brought his love to Tony Pascual. He wined and dined Tony and spoke of the many doors of opportunity he could open for him. Fat Man's impulses were generous. The Ivy League. A career in modeling, Tony's handsome face and impressive physique in the pages of *Esquire.* Tony wanted a BSA motorcycle? Not a problem. On his next trip to England Fat Man would arrange it. Fat Man love could do anything.

Luther understood that he was, to Fat Man, a scarecrow thing, just as, to Luther, Fat Man was an overly abundant thing. But Fat Man did offer mild approval of Luther's room.

"I see you've begun to master your interior environment. Perhaps now you'll be able to do something about the external as well."

"Do not burden me with too much, even if I am the savior of the world," Luther replied.

An anonymous letter appeared in the school newspaper.

> Sex at this college is off limits to me. Too many eyes are watching. Too many people see into the quality of my mind. But that does not mean I don't think about it and hope and

pray that sometime dream lover will come my way, just for the day, so she can never disturb the eternal vow I have taken with Mona Van Dine, very much in Boston now and very much on her way to a fame that will fill me out or make me perish. Because when you have an ideal mate everything shines better in your life, even if you do have to heed the call of adventure and go off into the unknown. Speaking of which, nothing is colder than the showers of doubt that rain down on a man. Nevertheless, I will be in the cafeteria every weekday.

P.S. I have been poisoning my mind reading and rereading *The Pearl*. Lady Pokingham says they all do it, and I believe you know what she means.

He no longer wondered if Elinore of the sad face would come to him from the rooming house. She did inform him in a dream that she had consolidated her hold on the boyfriend, who was transferring to the University of Chicago. Being from New York City and of a certain era, she sang "I Will Follow Him" and sang it well, Luther too succumbing to the irresistible lyrics. After the temporary high, apathy returned, the two of them acknowledging silently that they had hitched themselves to shooting stars. Together without them there could be no spark of life, as they had nothing of value to steal from each other.

Luther's attention was drawn to an angry Bronx kid with agitation against the system who got himself expelled for campus ruckuses and slept on the campus anyway. He was working-class Irish and handsome and had a perfect grade point average. It filled Luther with pain to see the young man going down the failure road, given the gifts that he had. He wondered if the young man was showing off, in some way, performing for the girls on campus? Was he simply shy and did he believe his only way of communicating was a show of recklessness? How Luther wanted to love the young man back to health, having seen his kind before in himself and others.

There was another who roamed the campus, a Frank Zappa look-alike with his handlebar mustache and Jesus-length hair, who held court in Finley Cafeteria. Luther was hurt and offended by his denunciation of CCNY as a cheap factory and listened coldly to his revolutionary rhetoric. For him Luther had no love.

No one came to his table as a result of the letter, and so he was forced to continue his seeking, given that Mona was determined to keep him in a state of high anxiety while she performed her art world wonders from the center of who she was. Because he could not find safety in the company of men or sitting alone in Chock Full O' Nuts with the seconds and the minutes and the days and the years mounting in his life. Seized by an impulse, he would check out the diners up and down Broadway or race off to the Museum of Modern Art on a hunch that *she* was there.

He fell under the spell of a young woman in a literature class with red hair excitingly short, as were her skirts. Sitting next to her at his desk he would pass her notes to stimulate her curiosity. Possibly she would think there was something to him, some gifted dimension. But she was having none of it.

"You could write till your pen ran dry and it wouldn't generate my interest."

The blaze in her eyes and the fury of her tongue told him she was vehemence itself.

"The price you ask to enter through your gates of hell is extinction. To withstand the contempt is to pass through roaring flames."

She got up and changed her seat, but that was not a deterrent to her living within him.

There was also a girl, Addie, who befriended him and whom he liked but had no passion for. Some months later she would be left by her boyfriend, Amos, who had the wherewithal to see the meaning in a PhD in English literature and able to do the work to secure one. Whether it was privileged information or not, she informed

Luther that Amos had no less than thirty-seven pairs of underwear. For some reason Luther could not explain, this bit of news sank deep into his consciousness. Her pretty face and slender torso were appended to unusually thick legs that deprived her of unqualified physical beauty. Luther could not help but wonder if that flaw in her physical being drove her more deeply into the poetry of T. S. Eliot, whose collected works she walked about with clasped to her chest. She related to Luther in a laughing, nervous way and without an expression that challenged his existence. Was it that like found like? Addie had her tree trunk legs and Luther had his tragically shaped head.

"Is your father missing? Is that it? Is that why you hold dry, brittle, reserved T. S. Eliot to your chest?"

Addie began to cry tears of grief, causing Luther to cry too and swear never again to be unintentionally harmful to her peace.

Addie brightened up and said the words "burnt umber." Luther, searching through the contents of her book, said the words "East Coker." He was sure they could remain friends until he ruined everything with complete inappropriateness, and that even then her soul would understand and receive him.

There was one other from the CCNY world, an older man—he gave his age as thirty—whom Luther met in a European history class taught by professor Ralston Gert, who said that technique was everything in getting the success that had come to him through the series of bite-size texts he had authored. He said it was necessary to chomp down hard on history and then sanitize the mouthful of all its impurities before shaping it into a book. He said it gave him enormous satisfaction to kiss his books each morning and then drive over the George Washington Bridge from his hamlet to the "stirring" metropolis and to know that he was being paid for shining forth in the way that he did for the students of the college. He had very white teeth and he pulled his lips away from them while demonstrating his technique of the careful bite followed by the sanitization of the morsel being prepared for the readership's delectation. Luther had too much fear and depression to wonder how someone could be so proud of so little. In fact he collapsed onto the floor after the lecture—something about a man named Metternich—feeling the weight of the world too much upon him.

A man with a Howdy Doody smile and a glass eye was there for Luther when he came back to consciousness. "I'm tending to you because I know what it means to be down. I fell incredibly low in this life. My existence was the absolute dregs. I ran away from home and became a male prostitute. Filthy old men did me dirty. I drank and took drugs and pissed and shit all over myself. I committed incredibly violent crimes. Do you understand what I'm saying?"

Luther did not have it together to speak. From his place on the floor he saw Professor Gert streaking out of the classroom with attaché case in hand. The professor did a freeze at the door and then an about-face so he could get himself next to fallen Luther. With their faces almost touching, Professor Gert said, "Bite, young man, bite. And when you have bitten, know what to do with the morsel in your mouth." The professor raised a stern finger and then fled down the corridor.

The man's name was Lou. He helped Luther along to Finley Cafeteria and bought him a 7-Up.

"My whole ambition is to be accepted to a graduate program in clinical psych at a topflight university. Toward that end I am amassing one A after another. In three years of college, there has been one B, leaving me with a near-perfect grade-point index, and I killed the professor who withheld from me and threw his body in a lime pit so no flies can ever be upon me in regard to the disposition of his case. Academic success is all technique and discipline. I am proof of that, since I have a very average mind." The man never lost his strange smile, as if he were detached from the universe.

"I believe everything that you are telling me, but at the same time, you are clearly not part of the national zeitgeist in terms of your clean clothes and short hair and industrious ways. What is the point of your act?" Luther asked.

"It has no point. I simply do not drink or take drugs and I have no act. Perseverance is everything. And where that has led me is to you. Let me say this. I am incredibly horny. I would like nothing better than to suck your dick."

Luther's mind had been back on the lime pit but now he was jolted back to attention.

"Your sexual hunger is my own. The barrenness of your life is my own. Your preoccupation with grades is my own. But for the very life of me I must tell you to leave my front door, if you catch my drift." Luther jumped up. He clasped his hands to his head and ran away from glass-eyed Lou.

Later came Jesse down the aisle at the post office with his Walt Whitman beard and bearing, not unscrewing the locks from their doors and the doors from their jambs but simply displaying what purported to be beaming Olympian awareness. Because Jesse was on a mission to reach the cosmic from the perch of his high intelligence/high board score life, he was augmented by drugs but could not be said, at least by Luther, to be the product of them. Seeking to share his wealth, Jesse opened his big hand, and there, in his palm, revealed a purple pill with a triangular shape, allowing his treasure to speak for itself. In blind faith did Luther swallow the pill and soon the experience of bliss was his, as it was when he took those speed capsules. Oh Jesse, bringer of joy as Luther's own brother could not be. Jessie with his hair pulled tight in a ponytail and clothed in a blue work shirt and a pair of jeans. And, oh, Mr. Ruggiero, to whom Luther beamed his love down to the foreman's parochial school beginnings.

It was not enough to stay at his box scheme station. He needed to share the universe of joy he now inhabited with Jesse, himself a box schemer though in a different aisle, and found him in the bathroom smoking a joint by the open window.

"Time for some mellowness," Jesse said, offering Luther the joint.

The "ness" was a little much, but at least he had broken from his silent Buddha pose.

"Grass isn't odorless. They could bust us for smoking it. This is government property. And besides, we need vigor and alertness and focused dedication to attack the box scheme. Because when we give order to the box scheme, it gives order back to us so we can have a purpose to our life. Smoking dope on the job leads to confusion and inefficiency. Can you see where I'm coming from?"

"You have the contours of the truly innocent."

"Speak English to me, longhaired man." Because he did not want Jesse sealing him shut with definitive description. But Jesse went on about his business, independent of any words that Luther spoke, and finally gave the roach a powerful flick out the window.

"You could burn down the city like that. The roach could land on old newspaper and alter your karma for the next century." Luther leaned far out the window to see where the roach had landed, but no combustion showed itself.

"Friend, friend," Jesse sighed, too mellow for further word engagement. He slid down onto the floor, using the wall for support, and Luther did the same. Jesse went and told him his whole life story, starting with Brooklyn Tech and the colleges that had lusted for him. He spoke about his pitched battles with his rabbi father, and the form it impressed upon his life, and about his coddling mother, whom he blamed for crimes against his own humanity, and about the two older brothers studying to be doctors so he could be free to place his large self in the sandbox of an infant's eternity.

Minutes or years could have passed. It was hard to say, and with smoke and speed heaven escalating, who could really care? Jesse broke the silence that had returned, saying, "Someday I'm going to kick that foreman's ass."

"No man, I really don't think so," Luther said, his words delivered slowly in his desire to impact as an ambassador of truth. "You are a gentle giant, I suspect. I also suspect your intelligence gives you the belief you have nothing to prove and so every right to fail."

"Who said anything about failing?"

"Then why do you appear to be a hippie bum like me with your blue work shirt and jeans and your ponytail?"

"I said someday I'm going to kick that foreman's ass."

"Do not go down the path of repetition with your mind so bright."

Luther erected himself and tried to explain the futility of going up against Mr. Ruggiero because Mr. Ruggiero represented the Italian-American nation, Luther remembering the toughness of the Italian kids from his childhood, the only ones the black gangs were afraid of because of the stone cold ferocity they wielded their chains and zip guns and stilettos with, consigliere and lieutenants joining in with Cosa Nostra panache for street level bashings. He delivered the news of what Mr. Ruggiero represented with passion, but Jesse just sought to rise above him with an amused smile, causing Luther to ratchet up his plea for peace, saying, "I thought you were the Buddha with your aura of serenity, but now I am wondering if you are from the land of the stupids, just like me. Because I see it all right now in the illumination that is happening. I see you too wandering in the aimless, self-destructive regions of those at war with the father." Luther had no choice but to be disappointed in his newfound friend.

"Logic and dope don't always go together," Jesse said.

"Oh yes. Oh very yes. I hear you."

Jesse went in another direction. He had a girlfriend named Fran who was sleeping with their philosophy professor, whom Jesse and his circle of friends had declared a genius.

"Have you done anything to overwhelm the situation?" Luther asked, still stuck in his pot haze.

"She's going to do what she's going to do."

"But how do you sit there like Buddha breath with all that going on? Are you finding pleasure in your pain?"

"Stop," Jesse said. He was about to light another stick when Mr. Ruggiero entered.

"I've got you bastards now. You've been smoking marijuana and you are dead meat and the maggots will eat you without pity." He showed them his Ernie Borgnine grin and malignant teeth.

"What does the word 'Borgnine' mean?" Luther asked.

"What?"

"Borgnine. It's a deep name. Sit with us and discuss. Because you wouldn't necessarily know from its sound or spelling its origin. The name isn't Borgnini or Borgnino, it's Borgnine. Do you see what I mean? And that's the beauty of life in some of its aspect. We sit here accepting everything around us, and then suddenly, the familiar strikes us as odd. We realize we don't know what we thought we knew. We suddenly see the thing, like a name, in a new way, and it's never the same again."

"Shut up, moron. You son of a bitches have been smoking marijuana in a post office bathroom."

"I've got it. I've got it," Luther said. "Borgnine, as in Carmine. Italian, right? Oh yes. Oh so very yes yes."

"Didn't I just tell you to shut up?"

Jesse stood up. "Hi," he said, with exaggerated cheer, bringing his face right down into Mr. Ruggiero's.

"You two freaks get back to work now," Mr. Ruggiero said.

"Jesse, let's do as the man says," Luther implored. "He's Italian. That has a world of meaning, as we have been discussing." Luther led his newfound friend from the danger zone.

Jesse's experience with Fran, his wandering girlfriend, served as a cautionary lesson for Luther to be on full alert for any insurrectionist anarchy Mona might have in store for him, that he might quell it instantly so perfection could reign in terms of Mona not being physically intimate with any of the eligible men of Cambridge/Boston. Because now that a little time had passed since she had fled, his panic had abated. If he kept a sharp lookout, the miracle could happen. she could be back in New York City in four years or less to make everything all right for him because it was clear that he could not go outward from where he was and so the finish line would have to come to him.

Jesse was tight with Sid Nizer, a mustached young man also from Brooklyn and Brooklyn Tech with loud ways and big, gleaming eyes and a mind searching beyond the confines of the classroom. They went all the way back to childhood, and Sid said Jesse was legendary beyond belief in terms of the intellect he had no need to show, and both attested to the reality that Brooklyn was a state of mind as well as a borough where people rode subways into forlorn stations and the buildings were small and the churches were many and that while you could wish you lived there, you somehow always went away for fear that you would otherwise lose your grip on the march of events that somehow you needed to be a part of. Not that Brooklyn was a retirement home but just far away.

This is what Luther came to know about Sid Nizer: that he had been raised exclusively by his father, that his mother had never been in his remembered sight, that he had an older brother in medical school, just as Jesse had two older brothers studying to be doctors; that he lived outside of all systems in terms of the energy that he put forth on the earth; that some might be classroom-bound but he, like Jesse, could only be partly there for the curriculum offerings of the professors so very tired and thinking ahead to a night of prime time TV. Of importance was that while both Sid Nizer and Jesse Kohn came from Brooklyn, they did not go back to it in the regular way that they had once been immersed in its long streets of both sorrow and joy because now Manhattan was in them and they were in Manhattan but the influence of Brooklyn was still there as a base from which they had come to build their lives, Brooklyn having been an event that was now becoming a memory but not in a way that would yet involve them with conscious sadness, as they were too young and vigorous in terms of the hormonal urges that kept them tuned in and tied to what was new, so no, not by any means turning their backs on DeKalb Avenue and Nostrand Avenue and President Street and the social club the Jewish kids could walk by safely only sometimes, Vinnie sitting back to front on the chair out on the street shooting the breeze with the monosyllabic utterance of the truly tough with the other men of toughness who could break your face and your chest into the parts it needed to be in for death to arrive, the business all done and the money collected and the pasta sauce simmering with just the right amount of garlic, everyone having a feminine side, even the Chinese. And the blood washed off the hands before sitting down for the evening meal so respect could be maintained. The long ride on the BMT to Coney Island with the houses up above the tracks on the embankment, once again Vinnie now with his friend Sal in undershirts on streets with grass growing in the cracks, Brooklyn showing the fortitude to claim its own regional distinction, never able to forget about Manhattan while having its quiet strength even if Manhattan could sometimes forget about it, but still the route you had to take in order to gain the sea and all those quiet lives in the shadow of the taller neighbor, wrenches and other tools put away on pegboards in basements no one even suspected of existing and then the heartbreaking car lights in the night and the child's adventure on his bike stopping for a drink from the park's own water fountain before the darkness came to lives unfolding in the borough's embrace.

Because Sid Nizer did not live at home anymore. He had his own place in the west Fifties in Hell's Kitchen, a fourth-floor walkup that he could find because he was always in motion, doing the things he needed to do for himself, grabbing at low-rent apartments as you stood by watching his show. Luther saw something jeering about Sid Nizer over and above the rough chop of mustache and the slash mouth it tried to hide and the eyes that stared at you with mockery. There were no soft parts to him but only his hard masculine casing.

And yet it had to be understood that Sid Nizer was the thing that made America great with the sideline activity, the entrepreneurial endeavor, he performed (when he could put aside the collected works of Kenneth Rexroth and the other Kenneth, Patchen, of New Directions fame). He sold ups and downs and hash and grass. Some said he had respect for the living only insofar as he could make them dead. Others said he missed his mother. Others, like Luther, just looked on at the energy he marshaled. No one heard him crying because he did not have time for his own tears.

He got you nickel bags and ounces too, and used the very drugs he sold, so as not to be apart from you. And everywhere the drug cops were, he was not, on account of who he was in his enterprising life. His sleep was noddy time, for the smack he took brought him close to his departed mother and out of the hardware store where he too often lived.

What Jesse said to Luther, after demonstrating the extent of his CCNY campus connection, was: "Most of my friends are very bright, but that's not why I like you."

Luther fell down in shame and cried for an hour. He did not know where to go or what to do with Jesse seeing into his lack. Jesse made no effort to pick him up. An intelligence god did not do things like that.

Nonetheless things went on, with Luther feeling the need and the inspiration to show Jesse some of his life, now that Jesse had shown him sides of his. He told Jesse he had a girlfriend in Boston and described her in the superlatives she only deserved. He also let it be known that he was always finding girls or looking for girls so he didn't have to ever fall behind in the race for supremacy and safety. He said he needed two a week to feel he'd done his homework right and to garner the As that no one else would ever see. Jesse did not fall down in shock but he did register surprise that Luther would approach strangers on the street and ask them to lie down, Luther having leapfrogged over his inhibitions to come to such a radical solution for his own desperate need. Jesse, by way of contrast, met people like his girlfriend Fran through a social network finely calibrated to appear wherever he was and to disappear wherever Luther went, Jesse having the goods to merit such social bonding.

The sense grew in Luther that Jesse liked his manner of social interaction, and so he took him to the apartment of Astrid, a speed freak woman he had met some days before. There were smelly garbage cans in the hallway and the stink of decomposing rats coming through the walls but she was where he could expect to find her with her one-expression face, a somber mask of speedball deadness. Luther was high on speed himself, another gift from Jesse, after another box scheme night. Astrid told him she was his future and that he could also be as she now was if only he kept on with his joy-pill course. He agreed that pills were the necessary solution for one who suffered a lack, his dream of academic success dependent not only on cracking the books but sealing the content into his mind so it would not drift off through his eyes and ears and nose and mouth. Astrid said, flat out as the plains of Texas, that it made her heart sing to be with someone so stupid.

Jesse could not be there very long amid the unwashed pots and dishes in the sink, and when Luther tried to follow him out the door, Jesse blocked his way and simply said, "Finish what you start, my friend. Finish what you start."

And so Luther lingered, but Astrid could not claim him for herself. Where life no longer was in its animated form he could no longer go, and so he waited for the opportune moment to slip away, knowing that she saw what she saw, that under Jesse's influence, he was abandoning her.

And this was where he stood in relation to the student body of CCNY, into which he could not merge to a degree that would recommend itself to anyone intent on wholeness and peace of mind, the idea acting on him that he would have to wait for the better thing to come along.

Chapter 44

The End Bar was jumping, with the men who wanted to be from Columbia seeking Ivy League women to bed down with on a Saturday night. Mona was in from Boston, and her miniskirt and tight blouse revived his fear that all the sexually able men on the East Coast were massing to have their way with her. The sexualized atmosphere of the bar only added to his anxiety.

Men flocked to their booth. They said they would be her slave, or told her that she could be theirs. An old feeling came over Luther, a feeling of helplessness, of being a hanging string in a strong and relentless windstorm.

"I am not enough to keep the wolves at bay, these wolves who have come to devour you. I must leave you to your own devices."

"What are you talking about?" She looked astonished but he assured her she was just fighting the truth of his words, and so he slipped away, as her mother had slipped away and left Mona alone at a café in Paris that past fall.

But the End Bar wasn't Paris. Mona followed after him into the street.

"You sick, pimping bastard. What the hell is the matter with you?"

"I don't know," he said.

She had a gift for friendship, more than she knew. A fellow student from her school asked to go to a movie with her, she said. She described him as homely and said his name was Rolfe. He had taught her a better way to stretch canvas over a frame and had directed her to a good art supply store. Luther felt insecure. Rolfe might be homely but wasn't he himself homely as well, and if it hadn't stopped Mona from bedding down with him, why would it stop her from doing the same with Rolfe?

"But I bought us tickets to see the Doors," Luther said. They would be performing at the Fillmore East. All light seemed to go out of Luther's life, even as he recognized the damage he had inflicted on Mona with his possessiveness.

"Why don't you take Lenore? I'm sure it would cheer her up."

Immediately the light went back on, an even brighter light.

"Well, all right," he said, seeking a tone of reluctance to conceal his astonishment at the gift he had just received.

"Look, I'll come in next weekend. I promise," she went on, making things still easier for him with the reassurance that they would not be away from each other forever.

That February her parents had sent Lenore back to the boarding school in Vermont where she had met Casey the year before. Casey had since dropped out to live in the East Village with his brother. Mr. Hodgkins, the headmaster, had welcomed her back, as did the faculty and student body. She was an intelligent, creative, and popular girl. But it was a serious matter, one month into her return, to swallow all the sleeping pills she could lay her hands on. Lydia and Peter were summoned for a face-to-face and, terrified beyond description by Lenore's close call with death, took her back home for safekeeping.

Lydia loved her other children but Lenore held a special place in her heart. Her third daughter was not burdened by intellectualism and a cautious temperament, like Claire, nor marred by narrow, insecurity-driven ambition and competitiveness, like Mona. Lenore did not fight her mother. Rather, she accepted her love. But it was not a love that could sustain her. You could love Lenore, but then she would get sad again. She was stuck on a young man in the image of Peter, and that deepened Lydia's love for her. Lydia knew what it was like to feel that everything good was with the other person. Claire and Mona would find ways to control their men. Lenore fully surrendered to the strong current of her love. She would be the freest of the three girls sexually, Lydia was certain.

She returned to the same neighborhood public school and resumed her sessions with a psychiatrist. Every day she took at least four green and black Librium capsules. They dulled her, but she didn't mind. Anything was better than her own natural state of consciousness. And yet, even with the medication, Casey seemed to be alive in her in a growing, not a receding, way, the call she had been hoping for not coming but instead her girlfriends on the line with updated reports of Casey sightings with girls formerly from America, all states of the Union fully represented, but now of the East Village in full abandonment of who they had been for who they could be with rock and roll anthems of mind expansion going on all hours of the day.

The therapist, Dr. Justin Jolper, said his life was devoted to overcoming obstacles. He mentioned his skinny calves, about which he had not been able to do very much except in the way he now thought about them. He said he had come to love his calves in something of the same way he was coming to regard her, with the understanding of course that she was beauty itself and his calves were not, and could it be that her laconic ways, her amiable smile, meant that she was responding to his award-winning method? When she did not answer, he got up from his chair and started toward her and so she fled as if from Frankenstein.

Some mornings she couldn't make it out of bed and lay there feeling far away from her life with her boarding school peers as her father held forth to her mother in a repetitive, furious rant about the coarsening, destructive effect of the American ethos on individuals like himself. During the day she would hear the sporadic clacking of typewriter keys against the paper and noticed, not for the first time, how her mother gave herself over to sleep in the afternoon and the sense of the disquiet and anxiety that announced itself in the silence of the vast apartment. Their lives seemed made up of sad routines. Her father's efforts at discipline were so pointless. Why didn't he break down? Why didn't he accept that he was lost? Why didn't he stick his head out the window and holler and just accept that his existence was meaningless?

All this was given to Luther to know in the time that he was living and Lenore was living and all of this was going on.

His sister Vera had not yet given him a song to sing in the envy key. He did not feel any threat from her at this point, any encroachment on his life that would summon rancor and the hurt that comes from being beaten. She had moved some more blocks from home to be in a Riverside Drive apartment away from the women soon to be armed with PhDs and assuming their rightful places in the world. Because Riverside Drive was an essential element of her success dream as well, the thing that would make right all the deprivation of childhood and the wounds that were now part of her. There was no time and no place for impediments; she stepped over and around them in her laughing way.

The building was old and the carpeted stairs creaked as he mounted them and he filled with longing to live in such a peaceful place away from the noises of the world with the Charles Dickens novels he could not always read but knew someday he would, seeing that they were from England in their quality Penguin covers. Vera continued to hold her job with the phone company and was now taking college courses through a special program and laying the groundwork for her own delayed advancement. Luther did not have to say down down, stay very far down, as she was showing no signs visible to his eye of rising up in a way that could smite him dead. Once again did he marvel that she kept moving, undeterred by low numbers. She did not have to call herself vile names, at least within earshot of him. And he did not have to ask why it was he did, because the only answer was that he deserved the dirt he dished himself. But he did say to her this on that night, "I do not understand how this can be, given the afflictions in my mind, but there is definitely an unstoppable force operating in you. Is it that you do not hear and listen to the winds of opposition?"

"Or is it that you are too sensitive and do?" she replied.

"Oh. Oh," or some such fearful noise he made in an effort to block the pain.

Ignoring him, Vera said, "There's this wonderful man who lives on my block. I'm trying to get him interested in me. He looks like Albert Einstein and goes to Columbia."

All around were her books and plants and the poster of the model Verushka on the wall with her big lips and her tallness, Vera too having big lips and tallness. Lenore would not have had that kind of narcissism, Luther could not help but think.

"Lenore has worth and thinks she has none, and you perhaps have less and think you have abundance. How can this be?" he suddenly shouted, causing Vera to hurl him onto the street, where the speed pill he had dropped had a chance to do its work in the open. Despite his ejection he could be grateful that the feeling of well-being growing in him would not be dissipated in the confines of his sister's apartment. What could be better than to be American and to have joy spreading throughout him and a date to light up the darkness of a Saturday night that had to be set on fire and extended in a way that the idea of an end could lose its very meaning. "Yes, oh very yes yes," he said in a muted voice so nobody could suck his happiness from him. He was moved beyond his inhibitions and doubts, noting as he boogied and bopped along the bridle path in Riverside Park with an invigorating spring breeze in his face. The concert was one part of the night with the real goal being to enter Lenore's darkness. Sure, Jim Morrison would be something to see and hear, that unsmiling face and booming voice, but Lenore was the real deal.

Luther checked the pocket of his pea jacket to be sure that the tin foil containing the tabs of acid were still there, the acid being for later. A silence would reign. A single candle would burn and bear sole witness to their coupling, America not a word but a concept with its feminine ending of womanly love promised by the Statue of Liberty itself, America a country of long hair and bedroom eyes and the so soft surrender of her sex.

Peter met him at the door with his still-blond hair flowing from its source and gave a bark of angry yet cultivated recognition that said it all in terms of this being his family and Luther better not fuck with it. Luther was knocked to the ground by the vibration but was able to get up with the thought that someday they should have a discussion about the very idea of family on a mountaintop with a strong wind blowing.

The scene spoke of family, Lydia and Claire gathered around the TV in the comfort of their home.

"I am back and feeling like love itself in the present moment," Luther said.

"If you hurt my little sister I'll kill you," Claire said. She made a line across her throat.

"It's good that you are moving forward. The status of my peculiar development is that I am negotiating the waves of my own progress through the aid of a synthetic reality. But I cannot sit and watch the evening news, as you are doing, with the men of full earnestness coming forth with their important papers to keep them company. Like any Third World country, I simply have too much development to undergo before I can hope to join the ranks of civilized nations."

"I hate him so much, Mommy."

"Get rid of the diminutive. It will keep you small if you do not," Luther said. He raised an unctuous finger to further draw revulsion from her with the intention of savoring it in his own world.

"He's either stoned or drunk, Mommy."

"As I said, I am love itself in this aggrandizing moment."

"Luther, we are happy for you. We don't regard you as delinquent or deficient. We regard you as a member of the family and respect you for all you are trying to do." Lydia said.

"Don't get too nice on me. I will only have to hurt myself," Luther replied, after bowing from the waist.

'We are just glad you are taking Lenore to this concert. She is our scrumptious one. She has too much to be held back by life's circumstances." Lydia went on.

Luther was suspicious of Lydia's "we." Did that include Claire, with her abnegation of him and Peter with his bark for a hello? Suddenly he cringed and held his head and shouted "No."

"No?" Lydia repeated.

"No. I must sit down." He fell onto the sofa, causing Claire to pull herself tightly together.

"What is it, Luther?" Lydia knelt and put her hand on his shoulder. He could hear no sign of the theatrical in her earnestness.

Luther got back up. "I'm OK. I really am. Some things must simply remain private." He could not tell them that he had received an image of himself as his father, old and decrepit and predatory.

Lenore had put on a black velvet sleeveless dress and black fishnet stockings and had made up her eyes to look like burning coals.

"Has his deadness arrived?"

"Oh yes, I am here and reporting for duty," Luther said, trying to recover.

"You are so depressing. You are even deader than I am. How did you get so ugly and so wrong?"

"We shall talk about it," Luther said, the lingering image shutting him down, making him unsteady.

Peter escorted them to the door. "If he begins to act vile, you can and must leave right away. The ship of state must remain intact."

Luther thought of the high seas, and how scary they must be until you gave yourself over to the idea of death. "I was on a ship once—"

"We will hear this another time, young man. Another time." Peter closed the door in the manner of one accustomed to finality.

Outside the building Luther sat down on the sidewalk. Lenore looked at him with a quizzical smile. "Are we having a problem?" she asked.

"A very definite problem. I am carrying an excess of weight and do not know how to be free of it."

Lenore laughed, from her land of apathy. "You're about to disappear into thin air."

"Weight can have a dimension not apparent to the eye. This is another kind of weight. The weight of the father and all he wants to be in my life in terms of the secret society he inhabits within me."

"Shut up and let's go," Lenore said, leading him up by his hair.

"Oh very yes yes," Luther said.

They spoke not a word to each other in the subway, the time for silence having come, but it could not last, not with her eyes upon him. "How far have you reached? Are you in Guatemala yet? Have you crossed all my borders?"

"I'm already tired of you."

"And I am so taken with you. Even if you are shrouded in mystery I want to follow you forever."

When they reached St. Mark's Place all the young people of America seemed packed into that tiny strip, with more arriving by Greyhound bus and by any means necessary from the America they could not be in anymore. The boys had hair so fine and long and Luther gave a crisp salute to one in an Army long coat with chevrons on the sleeve. The boy ignored him in the imprisonment of cool and passed a joint to a girl wearing a granny dress and a shawl, the two of them sitting on a stoop.

"Do not drop too far. You will never get back up. I am the son of immigrants who swam great distances to get to these shores. Heed my words before I get too ashamed to ever speak again."

The girl offered him the joint with a mocking silence.

Even stoned on the joy pill, he did not entirely like what he saw, the treasure of America running naked in the streets with the psychology of their escapism untreated.

"I must enroll at the University of California at Berkeley law school right now to be safe and secure in the way that I need to be," he said.

"Can you postpone your flight until after the concert?" Lenore asked.

"You give me such hope."

Outside the Electric Circus, a man on stilts in Uncle Sam red, white, and blue and top hat towered precariously over the crowd. Luther waved to him but Sam was too busy with his sternness to wave back.

"Why is it darkness reigning in this theater?" So self-consciousness drove him to say when they had taken their seats, but she merely cupped her ear and said "Eh?" as a defense against the words he spoke.

The theater was old and in a state of smelliness, having been reopened by a man with long hair who had a vision of the buck and getting famous performers into his home so he could be a part of them. And if he was now (as of this writing) in a nursing home with no knowledge of where he had been or who he was, back then he knew himself as a man with a pronounceable last name. Luther had his share of gratitude for the man for saving what had been lost, even if it was destined to die all over again, and for making it possible for him to sit back and view with pleasure, and also some concern, the spectacle of the mighty Doors. Morrison man was his very self in his black leather pants, signifying his aspiration to be an adorable little girl with his finger delicately to his hair after emerging out of darkness (and one or more of the fifty states, Luther didn't know which) onto the stage.

"I too want to be that same little girl," Luther confided to Lenore, who would not be diverted from looking on impassively at the stage.

Morrison man had her attention, but Luther couldn't be sure he had her approval or what it took, beyond Casey, to win her heart.

Luther had no awareness that night about Lenore and the future she was shaping for herself. He did not see the spaces through which she was falling into the places where she had to be. He just had the scale of action and perspective he could have at that time of his life.

It bothered him that she would not turn her head, that he had always to swivel-head his toward her, but he had no way of keeping his in the straight-ahead direction she had fixed on and was so expertly maintaining, when all he wanted to do was be sure she was in the mood of the music and for her to signify that The Doors were good enough for her to see.

"Dang," he said, from a place of vexation at Lenore's iron-willed detachment.

Worried that a failure of his good mood might be coming on, he took the action that was called for and at the break popped another speed pill in the bathroom. This way, he said into the mirror, the night will go the way I need it to go without in some way having my having to be present for it in terms of the feelings that could otherwise come up.

By the time the concert let out, his hands and feet felt cold.

"I am calculating that your parents will still be awake if you go home now. I want to be able to stay up all night with you, to drop acid with you, to feel every part of you. Let's hang around down here past their bedtime."

"I have to call home first," she simply said.

As he stood waiting for her on the corner of Second Avenue and St. Mark's Place, the hippies began to call attention to themselves. When Luther looked around, he saw them looking in on him from their place of massed strength in the windows of the nearby buildings as well as on the ground. Others were in idling cars and still others had the vantage point of lampposts from which they hung. A few in dayglo-colored construction hats stared from manholes, the covers having been removed. Luther looked for Casey as for a savage, loin-cloth-covered leader of the tribe, but he was nowhere to be seen. And when they brought no words to him, it was for him to put the words on them: "You think you have me dead to rights as an impostor, but I am Luther and I am looking hard at the very word 'hippie' itself. What is a hippie? Where did the word come from, and why the diminutive, as if we would never grow old but curl back endlessly into the youth that would flee us? What is our mandate but the recognition of apocalypse tied to the steel girders of industry and so a return to the playing fields of childhood with the exception of our carnal pleasures? And what is the level of corruption amid all the flowers?"

He received no answer, and when Lenore hung up the pay phone, she had this to report: "'You come home right now, young lady,' Daddy said to me."

Luther closed his eyes. "Desire must always win out over patrimony. Do you get my drift and do you see the need for a plan around the workings of his containment policy? Open up to me, flower. Open to me. I want to kiss your toes, your thighs, your ass, your cunt. I want to live inside you. I want your deepest thoughts and long to watch you pee. I am all drugged up just to be with you. Can't you see that I have crossed oceans for this event? Oh light that was lost in inaccessible heaven, you have come back to me."

They descended into the subway, where no talk was attempted, though her father's posture of the no-nonsense family man continued to sting.

As they walked the long last block to her building, someone called out "Lenore." A girl behind them came running up. "Jenny," Lenore said with false brightness, as Jenny threw her arms around her.

"Why did you leave?" Jenny asked, and as the conversation continued, Luther came to understand that they were friends at boarding school.

"My name is Luther, and I will just stand here and listen if you don't mind."

Jenny had not looked his way, and maintained fidelity to her obliterating purpose by going on. "Are you still seeing Casey?" Only then giving Luther a flicker of a disapproving look, for which he was ready with his arms positioned like a cross.

"That's over, I guess," Lenore said.

"He's such an asshole, if you don't mind my saying so," Jenny said, and they both laughed, though Lenore from the place of pain and sorrow.

Luther could do nothing but express his growing concern. "Please don't crush my dream. Please don't come between the thing Lenore and I have going on as a result of my orchestration. Take your hard, grasping ways and leave us to the tenderness of our night. I see your skin of leather and your ways of calculation and know you will survive but you are outside Lenore's realm now and so we must leave you so she and I can lie down in our pleasure right under her father's very threatened nose. A dynamic that you are willfully oblivious to is calling us and we must be faithful to that purpose."

"My father has me on a curfew, " Lenore said.

Luther had been studying the black-haired girl. "I know you think you have me dead to rights in your assessment of my unworthiness, but perhaps we could meet again when your lust is more in evidence."

The girl kissed Lenore good-bye and gave Luther the finger, and so they could all now be on their way.

When Luther and Lenore entered the living room, the TV was still on, Peter and Lydia and Claire watching the mighty dragon slayer Eugene McCarthy, his Irish pride intact, polluting the air with the poison gas of his ponderousness.

"No one knows how truly hateful he is," Luther said.

"He's challenging for the presidency and you call him hateful?" Claire said.

"Put an instrument on him and it will pick up the gases coming from his eyes and from his very skin. He is a small man of very distinct peeve. And it doesn't help that he writes brittle poetry that goes on the page without full lips and warm blood."

"What single thing do you even know about poetry?" Claire challenged. "I don't think you can even read and write."

"I know it is the disconnected words of sleaze bag men who masquerade their incoherence as art with the sole intention of getting women into bed with them. I know it as the effeminacy of America that must at all costs be stamped out in favor of muscular science, which, along with killing, is the only measure of a man."

"Luther, what can we do to broaden you? How can you grow from such a point of view? How do you come to have such wrongful ideas?" Lydia asked.

"How do I come from the tradition of God that says you are all sinners and must burn in hell, love you though I do in my annihilating way?"

"Luther is right in the sense that politics as it is practiced in America would have to corrupt the artistic impulse," Peter said gently.

"You see," Luther said.

"The thing I see is that you're headed for the nuthouse," Claire said.

Peter and Lydia asked about the concert before retiring, doing their part in acquiescing in the miracle that had to unfold for Luther's life to have meaning. Yes, fatigue could be a generational thing and remove barriers to the plundering of the night he was planning. Claire showed more staying power, but could not outlast the pharmaceutical power of the pills he had taken. Lenore she kissed good night. Luther she ignored as a way of bidding him adieu.

"She can say what she wants to about me with her nose upturned, but I am going to persevere," Luther declared. "The question now is whether we want to go on the trip of our lifetime or succumb to the ordinary darkness of another night? Do we, that is, want to do the Morrison man thing of setting the night on fire?"

The tin wrapper with the two tabs of acid making its March debut, Lenore showed the amorality of her girlhood by lowering her head and licking the tab off the foil in a way that said she could be moved by circumstance out of the drabness of circumspection. And so they could have a space for themselves that enhanced the environment in which they sat, the vertical stripes on the living room wall rippling in a capricious motion, a sexual undulation of great significance as it stripped bare the sensual essences people were directing at each other below the chatter.

"Do you see how the green velvet of the chair in which your father sat is acting up? Do you see what he has done to it in terms of stimulation?" Luther asked, pointing at the vacated wing chair that doubled as the throne of justice.

"Oh yes. Oh very yes yes," Lenore said, collapsing into peals of laughter at her own mimicry.

Down below the headlights of the cars were revealed as streams of celestial light in coordination with the sparkling bridge far to the north. "Do you see how the bridge does its manly job without complaint?" But he fell away from the window back onto the sofa, feeling joy indescribable coming over him far beyond what the speed had ever offered, and placed his hand on objects in a new and discovering way: the coolness of the coffee table's marble top and the softness of wide-wail corduroys as he ran his hand over his thigh.

"Somewhere in China people are working right this very minute," he said. "Can you imagine such a thing, that earth continues its spin and yet we never fall off? The thought makes me want to hold onto something for dear life or let go absolutely. Oh man, that voyages could get going in such a way that time could stand still. Are you parting the waves with me, sister?"

"Sister?"

"Do not make me meditate on that. Do not send me down that road I cannot get free of. Do not tell me they are there within every girl I seek out. Do not tell me they are defining and confining me.

Do not tell me anything that will abolish this night of dreams," he said, placing his hand on her thigh.

"Uh oh, more criminal intention," she said, raising her left index finger.

But there was no response to his touch. She simply stared at him with eyes that were all-seeing and plunged him into the lake of shame when he saw her complete passivity.

"All evening I had been drinking you in with my eyes. 'She is sipping a soda,' I would say, or 'She is now lighting her cigarette and smoke has been in her mouth and around her perfect teeth,' I would say. Do you understand where I am coming from?"

The avowal caused no change in her. Even with the speed and acid combo, he was now aware of wanting something from her that would elude him. And yet the more she gave him of nothingness, the more his hunger increased. He tentatively touched her silky black hair.

"Are you done?"

Such a concise, simple question."I guess I have to be," Luther said.

"There are only two of us who are going to get away from this family. That's Mona and Jeff. Claire and I are not going to make it."

"Why is that?"

"It's the way things are," she said softly.

"Are you saying that families are death traps?"

"Mine is."

"Could you ever love me? Could you ever take the leap of faith and amalgamate yourself to me even as I maintain your sister as the source of my stability from which to explore the mysteries of deathly darkness with you? Could you be my profane love that is love all the same?" he asked desolated Lenore even as she faded away, off in the forlorn ambience of her mind. The night had its own rhythm and she did as well. She was beyond words and into her own intense and consuming sorrow. The magnitude of her loss, the shining sun of Casey, was there before her in the darkness. All she had been left with was Luther, his blather and posturing and incessant pleading just a quickly passing shadow over the main course of her life. Because now that he, Casey, had fled and the things of daily life had fled and illusions of what a family was had fled, what was there to do but to sink into the lower depths and speed up her appointed time for vanishing?

"Can I take some credit in helping Mona to get away? Can I be seen as a key figure among the anti-patriarchal forces enabling women to advance?"

"I just want Daddy to break down. Instead he goes on and on, as if he doesn't know how hopeless it all is," Lenore said, and as if she hadn't heard Luther.

"I am very confused. Because typewriters cost money and are heavy and people need to have things to do so the structure of life can be maintained and purposes fulfilled."

"He's not a real person the way he lives," was all she would say.

Had they left their beds? Had her parents and Claire been there all along? Possibly they were in their rooms, straining to hear, but possibly too they had come out of those rooms in their bare or slippered feet and now were inching closer.

"You must see me to the door. Things are currently escalating," he said.

"Are you afraid for your life?"

"I am who I am," he said, seeing the sudden animation in her face. "Now will you please lead the way, for forces have assembled against me."

"Only cowards are afraid to die. What are you hanging around for, more of the same?"

He followed after her into the vestibule, where most definitely they would be lurking, Lydia in particular, a very different Lydia from the one they all knew, the woman who ate and laughed and drank and smoked her many cigarettes with her head full of nature. Her smile would be gone. In its place would be a severe expression. At her side she would hold a knife.

Luther removed his shirt. "Stab me good, power woman. Stab me good, woman so false, so my function can be realized to draw out your anger and liberate you from your reasonable *stuff.*" But if she was there, as the goose bumps on his flesh told him she was, she did not step forward.

Lenore held the door for him. He moved forward slowly onto the landing, shocked by the bright light and imagining himself a slithering snake. "On different levels I have harmed you. This I know. I will go now, never to be seen until the next time." He couldn't be sure she had even heard him.

He righted himself for the street and walked along it buttoning his shirt with his back to Riverside Park. "I have a leg up on you," he said to a lone passerby, as if in the lightness he was now experiencing he could lift right off the ground. He had the sense that he had been recreated on that night, that glimmers of possibility were surfacing through the drabness of entrenched and mediocre routine, that he could possibly be somebody and didn't have to die because he was academically deficient. He saluted crisply the sleeping New Yorker bookstore and the sleeping New Yorker movie theater. He said hello to the southbound Broadway bus and the cruising taxis and expressed his admiration for the old buildings and the fidelity they had shown in continuing to line the avenue. And then he made a point of minding his own business, adopting the circumspection that was needed to survive on the northbound side of Broadway the rotating light on the hood of a police car and the wail of its goofy-sounding siren. "I am not here to be arrested. I have done nothing wrong," he murmured in the doorway of a pharmacy. "Please pass me by so I can be free of you. I am closing my eyes. I am turning my face to the wall. I am adopting the innocence of a child. Please do not crush me with your powerful apparatus."

But then he went and peeked, and beheld the naked reality of the aroused squad car advancing in a zigzag pattern on the sidewalks of New York City, shouting as it sped "You're the one, you're the one." Even in the recessed doorway he couldn't be assured of physical safety, given the vehicle's animated display of its own prowess. Suppose it had adaptability to nooks and crannies to go with its vocalizing feature? Suppose nothing on earth could offer him the protection he required? Terror was on him once again when he had given himself reason to believe the open air would be a restorative. Was it possible the car itself was imbued with a sense of smell as keen as a bloodhound's and that he must beg for mercy? Because it wasn't normal that a car should make a mockery of driving regulations with its zany patterns of progress, nor that it should come to such a knowledgeable halt at curbside with its sudden silence abounding. The thing defied logic and created painful mystery in his mind, leaving him no choice but to surrender. The burly officer in the death seat looked him over coldly from his sneakers to the top of his hairy head.

"The thing I want to confess, while not earth shattering, goes to the root—" Luther began to blurt but the squawk box erupted, dispensing voice crackle. Speaking over the racket, he went on, "It's the acid I want to talk to you about and the murderous impulse on the other side of civility that I have witnessed on this night and the molestation of the innocents who are, in our lunatic society, not always so innocent. There is no need to apprehend me in a ruthless way. I will go quietly on the journey of suffering and dare you to make a man of me." He then held out his wrists for their handcuffing pleasure.

A poke in the chest with the officer's leaded billy club drove Luther back. They had bigger fish to fry, the officer seemed to be saying, as the siren wailed to life and the red light on the hood lit up and began to rotate.

How very bright the Broadway bus was. Luther found himself laughing uncontrollably at the elderly man who sat facing him across the aisle. In spite of the rudeness, he could not stop, as if a lunatic were loose in him.

The Columbia University mall was almost deserted. To the north was the massive dome of Low Library and the steps you had to walk to get to it and to the south the names of the historically great banding the equally great Butler Library and calling out from the past. A sense of liberation had come over him. The weight of his low numbers felt not so crushing, even in this Ivy League ambience, as if Lenore or the acid or both had rearranged his insides and he could now go free from all that had been holding him down.

A man and woman sat on the sundial reading *Pére Goriot* aloud, championing their intimacy by taking turns. The Penguin edition, no less.

"You are loved. You are warmed by the sun of academia. You have been accepted and certified. You have all that going on as the foundation for your exploration. For myself there are large and ugly rocks in my garden, but I think that tonight especially I have found a way to break free from the tyranny of all that would shut me down. Let me, if I may—"

"Excuse me, but we were reading." The man spoke up. He was bearded and strong in his look of appraisal.

"Yes, OK, I understand the pull of a book, especially when it is a Penguin, and someday I hope to live safely between their covers." He began to walk off, but the woman called him back.

"What is it you wanted to say?" she asked. Luther turned. She had a pretty face that came with glasses and an uneasy smile.

"I thank you for the reprieve you've given me, and I have no intention of advancing on you if it is within my power not to do so, although on this night in particular the pull of sex is strong in me as is the belief system that I cannot know a woman and she cannot know me until and unless we sleep together. You see, I am failing on the academic path, as you and your beau so clearly are not, but on this night I have been warmed by the sun of acid and a remarkable turning has taken place where possibly I can leave behind the number I am not and live with what I am but not as a drowning man. Evidently this university was here before you two or I ever arrived, and so it had a head start on defining itself as the footpath to success for anyone who wanted to live in the bright spaces of

America. But now I can have my own life, if the structure of my mind holds together and the low numbers do not win out again."

"How low were your numbers?" the man demanded.

"I cannot reveal state secrets, and do not bring me down from where I am trying to be," Luther quickly replied, in anguish at the hardness of the man and in escalating interest in the potential softness of the woman.

"What are you trying to tell us, anyway?" The man was clearly impatient.

Luther smelled the air. It smelled so very good. "I have nothing more to say, given the constraints of your austerity regime."

"No, tell us," the woman said. She had wrapped her lovely self in her own arms in the chill of the night.

"I could wish those arms around you were my own, and that I could live forever in the embrace. Do you know how my heart fills with longing?"

"Cut this shit out," the man barked.

"Let him speak, Cliff."

"And let there be no dissension, no dissolving of your unity, even as I come between it. That is the painful marvel of America, that I come to you to say one thing and say another. As an aside, imagine, just imagine, what it would be to live and speak with an obligation only to the truth?"

The woman had no features that were not in keeping with the quality of America. Her glasses were not a detriment but a boon. As for the young man he remained rigid in his judgment of where the vermin was to be found, and so Luther addressed him directly.

"You are a wall of silence and moral probity such as can be activated in the least of people when the vision before them is anathema. What can I do to make things right between us?"

"You can go away."

Luther turned and removed himself from their company, but the woman ran after him and said, hotly, in his ear, "Cliff has all the requisite numbers for our future and you have only the poverty of your own ways. The home I came from was cold and preached the doctrine of calculation, so what could you and I ever hope to achieve?"

"Don't bring me down from where I have been. Don't make me go where I don't want to go." He looked past her to Cliff, now standing on the sundial with legs spread and arms folded in a posture of fortitude, and also showing a fixed gaze that worked, for the woman was drawn back to him, much to Luther's relief, and now that the door had closed he could go on his way.

The night was a turning in his mind of what his time with Lenore had meant, with a new vision emerging of what his life could be if free of the domain of paperback books. He could put on some weight and get prettier and become an actor on the stage with no haunting numbers to inflict their wounds on him. In deep gratitude and wonderment was he for this new path that had opened and that promised freedom from the torment of his mind.

He spent the hours before dawn catnapping on the mattress in his room. The speed and acid still had more work to do.

He heard the lock turn at the other end of the apartment and then footsteps. He followed them with his ears into the living room. "We going to have to visit with those chicks again. They got some hungry ways." The voice was not that of Tony Pascual or Billy Riley. The man laughed a constricted laugh.

"Fucking A. Alice was all over me." The voice of Billy Riley.

Luther clamped his hands to his ears to block out their sleazy talk and for daring to mirror his own lust, but his bursting bladder drove him beyond the French doors and into their company. A black man was parked in a chair, his legs spread. His laughing eyes saw right through the disturbed thoughts in Luther's white mind. He gave his little laugh of recognition, as if he had seen the same thought a thousand times before. Poor little white boy don't like the presence of a black man. Poor little white boy afraid black man going to stick his big dong in white boy's girlfriend's pussy.

"You don't have to ask me to deny my every last thought. You don't have to ask me to deny my life," Luther countered.

"We didn't wake you with our sound, did we, man?" Billy Riley now had a topping of fuzz on his scarred head.

"Yes, you did," Luther said, growing small and girlish in the presence of such men.

"This is Darryl. Darryl, this is Luther," Billy Riley said.

"Luther?" Darryl mulled over the name with his mouth and chin and stroking hand collaborating. "What you doin' with a black man's name, white boy? You ain't done enough absconding with our heritage?"

"I am named in honor of the great Martin Luther, who put the Catholics on notice about their mercenary ways with his ninety-five theses nailed to a church door. I am the spirit of rebellion itself. I am also full of piss," he said, before streaking for the bathroom.

When Luther returned, Darryl said, "You be shaking my hand before you go behind those doors again. You up for that, mother-fuckin' white boy?"

"I'm up. I'm down," Luther said, beginning to rejoice in the freedom Darryl's language gave him.

"Shake my hand, brother. Shake my hand."

Luther went for the unity offered with full vigor only to fly backward against the wall when Darryl pulled up from the side of the chair a mechanical claw.

Darryl responded in the way that he could, saying, "They got them some mo'foing chunkers over there. They chunked me with one of our own claymores. I be chunking them right back all over that mo'foing country."

Chunking. Luther had never heard a word more vivid. It spoke of process and packaging and neatness. He saw cubes and squares being sectioned out of the shocked, aggrieved Vietcong, who only moments before had been chunking them.

"I am trying to love you even as I recoil from everything you are. But do not ask me to shake the metal contraption. And please do not pinch me with the clippers at the end of it. Things having to do with a body gone wrong disturb me no end."

"Fuck your disturbance, you stupid-assed mo' fo'. Suppose I stick my metal boy right up your goddamn ass?"

"Then you would be taking me in a direction I do not want to go," Luther said, cringing at the threat.

"You go out tonight?" Billy Riley asked.

"I went to a Doors concert with a friend," Luther replied.

"That's some good shit, the Doors. They got some tunes that play with your head. We were just saying how we got our fires lit tonight. I just be speaking an unrighteous truth tonight," Darryl said.

"What's the name of that girlfriend of yours?" Billy Riley said.

"Her name is Mona, and even the wind is brought to sighing when you speak it."

"Right. Mona. He's got himself a good-looking girlfriend, Darryl. Classy, too."

"That's the way to go, bro. Get with some class," Darryl chuckled.

Luther cried out, "You are filled with a fortitude I cannot imagine. You exist on a syncopated rhythm all your own with your black heart a mystery. A limb was taken from you but you talk away from it, as if nothing impacting your body is central to the main event of you. In that way you show your endurance."

"White motherfucking asshole, what you be talking about the endurance of a black man for? You ain't earned no insight into blackness, into the otherness of the way we think about and watch you."

Billy Riley had a focus all his own to stay with. "You said she was an artist, right? You said she goes up in flames for her art. You said she goes to some school out of the city, right?" Billy's mouth was opening and snapping shut with savagery now.

"Yes," Luther said, "though I offered nothing about flames," seeing himself now as prim and fastidious in the face of their mammoth decadence, as if seedy Times Square had come to 118th Street and he must draw a line against it or live forever in raunchy tumescence.

"So where is it? Where does she go? Keep me on the track of this."

"My mind is in collision from the night's events and you have taken me from my groundbreaking reflection on them. I will tell you only this. She attends the Boston Museum School, and only people of the finest stock are allowed through its doors."

"The Boston Museum School? What do they do there, study museums?"

"It is an art school of the very great," Luther said, keeping it simple.

"Damn, Billy, wasn't that blond fox tonight from some art school in Boston?" Darryl did some hateful laughter, like something tearing in his throat.

"I will go and lie down now, but that does not mean our communication has ended. You have both seen death and committed death. You have achieved intimacy with expiration, and so you are now consigned to being apparitions on the earth, the truth being that you left so much of your life over there, and must for now exist in the confabulations of your brutalized minds. As for me, I have my own confabulations to deal with. I must cling to the belief that someone does want me, and I must hold onto her to prove that I am not nor ever could be but a ghost upon this planet."

He lay on the mattress with the pillow over his head to muffle the sound of their ongoing voices. Sleep finally came and he woke several hours later to gray dawn light. Darryl, his legs spread and his head back and mouth open and his claw resting on his crotch, was asleep in the chair. Luther thinking, I have *Dombey and Son* to read, but what retreat did Darryl have? Billy Riley had been in the crucible with Darryl, and could love him as a brother, while I have my whiteness divide.

Darryl, startled out of sleep, raked Luther across the arm with his claw. "Get away from me. I ain't your friend. I am a black warrior and you are a white boy so fucked up the army wouldn't even consider you worthy to die."

Luther ran into the street to a phone booth, where in privacy he would tell Lenore of the new door she had opened for him even as Mona remained the foundation for his survival. Claire answered with a terse hello, as if on Luther alert.

"Yes, here I am, and good morning to you. A word with Lenore, if you please. Do proceed with dispatch."

"Asshole."

"Just so you know, the war of liberation is on."

"She can't come to the phone."

"Tell me why, please, so I needn't feel afraid and be hurled into the cold place of rejection."

"Because she is fast asleep. That is why."

"I have brought disorder to a smoothly running democracy by my presence. I will go then. It is raining in my heart and soul, but I have Charles Dickens to go home to, and instant coffee to drink from a plastic cup deeply stained."

"Try not to call again."

He did just as he said he would, settling down with the great *Dombey and Son* and sinking into its pages so a sense of purposefulness and order could flow through him. It was as if, for the first time, he was discovering the centering effect of reading. And yet, a few pages later, he realized that he had lost the narrative entirely, that thoughts about Lenore had carried him off even as his eyes stayed on the text, the way it always was and had to be, with distractions having their way while the supposition held that the book was the worthy thing indeed to focus on and not simply an artifact rife with deadness, the packaged distraction of yet another mind at work.

"I will get back to you, Charles Dickens. I will grow strong and warm and cozy with you, for nothing is nicer than a Penguin paperback with their fine pages. I will grow strong as my shelves fill up, even if English is for sissies and real men do fractions, without which the words can have no logical relationship to each other. But now is not the time to settle on England and all the coziness it has to offer, not when she is in my blood and the thing from last night lacks full clarity." Because now he was hungry for Lenore again in the deadness of a Sunday morning and had to have her and maybe Claire didn't have to be an impediment of stone to his success after all. Maybe the night had a way of sweeping away all concerns about him so that he was pristine to their eyes in the moment and could strut back into their lives. Yes yes, they were not weeping over the stain he had left on Lenore; he wasn't even a shadow on their collective mind. And maybe, just maybe, he had to call her for his own survival, because it was March and cold and wet and she had felt so close and yet so far while they sat together on the sofa. Maybe now he could bridge the gap, close that distance forever. He was America rising in that moment, strong and undefeated. Because, having been directed to the right path as a future actor, he could augment his being by aligning himself with his heart.

"Van Dine residence," the male voice said, emphatically and with the power he dared to believe attached to it. So male, so strong, that the receiver set Luther to vibrating. As if the voice had known who would be calling and was waiting all along to give thrashing power to the words he spoke and to drive away the interloper who would seek to interact corrosively and with overwhelming need with his daughters.

"Do you know who I am to take the tone of voice that you do?" Luther finally said.

"I know exactly who you are," Peter said.

"Exactly indeed," Luther replied. "Be warned that I am in love on different fronts and that fifth columns, insurrectionist forces, are mobilizing against your power and that I am serving as legendary field general in the campaign to bring down patriarchy in all the realms it dares to exist."

"Your only campaign should be to undo your insanity," Peter hissed.

"Don't you dare hiss at me," Luther answered back. "I read twenty pages of *Dombey and Son* this morning. And I could have kept going. That's why I stopped. So I wouldn't wear it out. But I'm going to go back and climb right into it all over again."

The phone went dead. Luther banged it against his head before hanging up the receiver.

Chapter 45

When Mona arrived in the city the following weekend, she came wrapped in her own success and showing signs of becoming the creation she wanted to be. Her parents had no choice but to admire her, her father willingly and her mother with the reluctance of someone with whom a war was going on that she was losing to the younger opponent whom she herself had summoned to life to be a shadow on her existence as part of the perplexity of human involvement, or so she understood owing to the expertise of the Carl Jung Bollingen series she had set up for herself as a source of understanding where subjectivity could have its say in a house of historical fact. And because she, Mona, threw her arms around Luther and gave her sister Lenore a big hug too, it had to be clear that she was arriving on the wings of victory with all foes temporarily vanquished and her baby sister reduced to a shell of who she could have been and no sense of betrayal in the air.

"It was so great to get your letter. I want to do acid, too," Mona said to Lenore. It was just the three of them, Lenore and Mona and Luther, by the following day, the rest of the family preserving their rite of spring, the opening of Camp.

Luther stared with feigned concentration at the hardbound books on the living room shelves, his bell having been rung by the mention of the letter. It took a while to realize that if Mona had given hugs, then the contents of the letter couldn't have been incriminating, Mona knowing anyway that Lenore had done the tripping thing up at boarding school with Casey, that in fact the whole school had done the tripping thing, the classrooms emptying out and the entire student body wandering around in the nearby woods weeping and grooving and whatever, and now Mona herself wanted to make forays into new realms of experience so she could see like van Gogh and not be looked upon as an uptight sister, and Luther was there to oblige her. A tab of acid wasn't the same as a speed pill in that it was mind-expanding and not corrosive to the brain cells. And he just happened to have a batch with him.

Though the idea had been to focus on Mona that weekend and consolidate what he had before even contemplating once again touching what in lucid moments he saw clearly wasn't his, the evident happiness Mona displayed made revision of his thinking an imperative, which led to a proposal, its urgency carefully muted, that Lenore be asked to share in the wealth, an extra tab of acid being available should she be persuaded to want it for its mind-altering pleasure.

"Sure, sure. We can do that," Mona said, there in the rooms of cleanliness and order that her parents had presented to the children, with the shelves stocked with canned goods but the refrigerator crammed with cheeses and cold cuts and all manner of delicious fare. And it had to be noted that Mona had grown more secure. No more threats to move out if Lenore returned home from boarding school. No need to fear her sister now, since she, Mona, was the one out of the house, the one expanding (the very pretentiousness of the word notwithstanding). No need for any difficulty in being generous with her younger sister, driven hard, hard into the ground. No need for it at all.

He watched Lenore lick the acid off the palm of her hand and saw the sullen spirit her eyes expressed in meeting his, eyes that said trespass and violation and oppression and outright clumsiness were going on. And yet he could sweep away what he saw with the currents of his own mind, her willingness to join in being a sign that she really didn't want to be through with him after all, and that further sparks from the journey still had to fly. Another strange adventure awaited, the night now a long and never ending promise.

The acid was unkind to Mona. Where initially there had been bursts of pleasurable color, moroseness now set in. A change of scene was in order. From the book-filled apartment to the park they were called to be among the dancing trees and near the trains in their underground existence and a river continually flowing over its own history in what only appeared to be a seamless flow of calmness. Her funk having lifted, Mona did cartwheels down the hill, Lenore joining her, the playground their destination. They went right for the swings and soon were extending out on the backswing over the high wire fence that encircled the playground. Luther saw smashed skulls and broken limbs, he saw tender lives erased in sticky pools of blood. He shouted for them to stop but they did not hear him in their laughing thing free of the fetters of power with their teeth bared.

The thing being that they were out of step with their environment in a way that only Luther thought he saw. Did they not understand that their delirious laughter was but a summons to the deprived of the city, those who lived to stab and stab to assuage the pain of their low existence?

"Shush," he whispered, when finally they were back on the ground. "Do not provoke them with your gaiety. Do not do that. They are all around." His wild flock ran from him screaming "All around. All around," as he tried futilely to shepherd them toward home, but they coalesced as a taunting thing thrilled to be in active alignment against his puny power and sent him down into the grass.

"Behave yourself, young man," Lenore shouted, her command triggering centuries of laughter in them.

Back in the apartment he did not wonder why it should be that the darker one's touch thrilled him more than his love's. It was only a matter of accepting the duality of love and making it one. Mona had regressed into her funk, and so Luther sat with her, offering reassurance that the bad feelings would pass. No, she wasn't an awful person, no, she hadn't hurt anyone, no, she did not have to die before she had even lived.

He left Mona with her head in her hands. The heightened aesthetic seemed to have passed. Dancing objects had given way to simple lust. He found Lenore lying on her back in the middle of her parents' bed. "Have we come? Have we arrived? Are we looking for girlie action, a girl to move her box even if she is dead?" She taunted.

He climbed onto the bed and kissed her full on the mouth.

"You're so crazy," she laughed. "Bad. Bad," she went on, when he felt between her legs. Her voice mocking, as if she were seeing from far away. And so he returned to Mona.

The second time he came calling, Lenore stuck out her tongue and made panting sounds. But by his third visit her mood of sarcastic abandon had passed. "Why aren't you with Mona? Do you know what you're doing? Why are you laughing? She needs you," Lenore said, tears filling her eyes. Her sudden earnestness threw him.

"She is in a holding pattern," he said, his hand reaching between her legs.

"Is the party in here? Does Luther have his hand in the cookie jar?" Mona stood by the door and spoke as an all-seeing presence.

He quickly removed his hand and called on elements of magic to rearrange her vision as he left the bed.

"I'm feeling treachery in this room. Do you know where it's coming from, Luther?" Mona had moved to the bed to sit beside her sister.

"I see nothing." Luther got up from the bed as Mona sat down. "I have seen only the disturbed elements of love, but they have come and gone."

"How about you, sister of mine? Do you know where it is coming from?"

"I'm so glad to see you," Lenore said, and pulled her sister to her.

"I feel so ugly," Mona said.

"Me too," Lenore said.

"How about you, Luther? Do you feel ugly, too?" Mona asked. She laughed tentatively at first and then more, emboldened by what she was seeing, going up the laugh ladder with Lenore aiding and abetting with sisterly esprit. Because suddenly there was no stopping the power of their derision. Where he had been lusting for Lenore only minutes before, there was now a growing fear that she was taking Mona away from him and that she was the enemy coming to iniquitous life.

He ran to the other end of the apartment and stuck his head out the living room window. "Once again is it cold in my heart. Once again has terror struck. Once again have my sisters emerged in the place where I least suspected them in a band of solidarity defined by an exclusion."

Having made his announcement, he raced back into the bedroom. All was sisterly subterfuge with the long lingering kisses he witnessed and with no thought of the male in their midst. Once more he ran to the living room window to shout out the return of the old in the form of the new. He then waited for injustice to be explained and perfidy justified.

When Mona came to bed, her laughing spell was over.

"Did you go and fuck my little sister again?"

"I have done nothing that I was not supposed to do."

"Don't be more of an ass than you are."

"Am I in her bed or am I in your bed? And does this not speak sizable quantities of the truth?"

"Shut up," she said.

The next day, there was a lingering sexual frenzy, and when Mona stepped out, Luther once more approached Lenore, only to encounter the wall of apathy she presented. He fled her knowing eyes out onto the street, and yet he had the sense of being in a strange new place. Walls that were supposed to be up had come down. On a walk around the block he gazed at women with an entirely sexual focus, as if he knew and they knew where the heart of the matter stood.

He had not thought about Lenore's letter to Mona since Mona first mentioned it, but now, when he returned to the apartment, it entered his mind with compelling force that Mona had brought the letter with her from Boston and that it was in her bag, which sat on the dresser in front of him. He was quite certain that all his answers were in that letter. And there it was, next to her wallet and a chaos of papers he himself would never have been able to live with. He pulled out the sought-after envelope with Lenore's small, neat handwriting, removed the folded loose-leaf page therein and, behind the locked bathroom door, began to read:

> I admire you so much for moving out and going after what you want. It is so brave of you to go off to Boston and to seek success. The whole family admires you. Daddy is always talking about your strong spirit and your beauty. You're his favorite, that's easy to see, from the expression on his face when he speaks of you. I wish, though, that he would break down, don't you? He just tries and tries to keep so much in. I'm hoping that your life will continue to expand and that you won't let Luther—Jesus, is that really his name?—try to confine you, which is what he is trying to do. Mommy thinks he is a certifiable mental case and Daddy thinks it might not be a bad idea to shoot him dead for the sake of all concerned. The concert was all right, but his talk was depressing. You could do so much better. I know for a fact that Mommy and Daddy find him repulsive and Claire and Jeff want to kill him. Even the cats stay away from him. I'm saying so much, I know, but I want the best for you.

More than hurt, Luther ran to the nearest window, outside of which he hung by one hand so the threat of death could supersede all other thought. When he had had enough, and that time arrived quickly, he found he was unable to pull himself back in, and his strength diminishing, it began to feel that his arm was being torn from its socket in supporting his impoverished weight and it would be easier to give in and just plummet to the hell of lonely and permanent unconsciousness when a powerful force for change pulled him to the safety he would not have been able to reach on his own, that force being none other than Peter Van Dine, who had seen the spectacle from down below.

"Are you crazy? Should Bellevue be on your itinerary?" Peter demanded to know, but Luther could not speak, he could only hug the man for dear life and then ran into the living room and sat slumped in a chair with his legs spread.

"Is there nothing you won't do for attention, young man?" Peter asked, having followed him.

"Young man?" Luther repeated, throwing away tone and added content to seize on the words, and tears welled up in his eyes as he once more hurled himself on Peter, who now had to physically push him away, Luther dropping to the floor.

When he could right himself, he escorted Mona to the East Side Air Lines Terminal, where she could get a bus to the airport and fly back to Boston, the urgency of time superseding the romance of the rails.

"You have been drawn in, deep into the bowels of family," Mona said. She was not broken in half. She was just tired.

"I will fight any war that you commit me to wage," he said. "So long as it is pointed in the direction of illusion."

"Do you have something more to tell me?"

"Only that I cannot always abide my feelings. I don't want you to think that I will die now that you are leaving, but I don't want it understood that I will necessarily live either. Is that clear?" His earnest words about rallying behind the law school dream and the stature it conferred had meant nothing to Lenore. He had given her his best only to find it right there in the garbage.

"Oh shut up," Mona said. She looked tired and yet luminous from the ordeal of the acid.

He kissed her goodbye and could breathe a sigh of relief amid the exhaust fumes that the letter hadn't been worse, that her despairing younger sister hadn't told all. The last part of the letter was what stayed with him, the idea that her family was looking at him funny. Somehow he knew it was too late to sway them from the poor opinion in which he was held and that, in future, he would only be giving them more reasons for their reservations as life went on heating up and ideas for living continued to come.

Chapter 46

Lyndon Baines Johnson was crying, and nobody even tried to cease his tears. Lyndon Baines Johnson was crying for the country that had rejected his love, a love that had somehow gone wrong. He was on the television, his sliver-lipped, sad face and floppy ears filling the screen. He said, in his earnest way, that he would not run for reelection later in the year. He said that he had had enough. The patrons in the End Bar cheered and whistled, giving LBJ (from Southwest Prairie State Teacher's College) icy blasts of Ivy League intelligent derision. Luther felt a hurting in his heart for the falling president, who suddenly seemed human and fragile, and a tender yearning for the years 1963–1968 that he represented. Lyndon Baines Johnson was big cars and big steaks and petite women to accommodate him. Luther wanted to grab someone and explain: Lyndon Baines Johnson had been with him when he had been in a blue blazer and charcoal gray slacks at the Claremont School, waiting for the number 4 bus on Fifth Avenue and Seventy-second Street. He had been with him when he was seeing Jane Thayer back when. He had been with him when he was doing long-range bombing on the basketball court. He had been in the realm of the fathers in a thousand newspaper photos. Luther had grown comfortable with Lyndon Baines Johnson and Lady Bird and their daughters, and fear swept through him not to know who would come next.

"My home is not Broadway but the Mekong Delta," he suddenly shouted, from atop the bar. "My home is the helmeted soldiers doing the hand to hand with the NVA at Ia Drang. My home is General Westmoreland assuring a safety he cannot deliver and all the news brought to me on television and in the newspapers. I am just a watching little boy, living in and through the images that are presented to me and that I do not know how to rise above and move away from. And you are a jeering horde ruining the world with your Ivy League laughter. The very vibration of it travels through walls as well as skulls and shuts the systems down that it dares in its assumptions to touch without love as its guide. Because the truth that your laughter would seek to assail and override is that the president in the flesh would overwhelm you, that he has world power within him and would dry up your laughter and lure your girlfriends from you. Because the president—yes the president from Southwest Texas State Teacher's College—would not have time for your barroom ways, seeing that he is too very busy doing. And now you are so very eager to love Robert F. Kennedy and his white-toothed, shy smile as he tries to be the darling little girl so many American men need to be. I will tell you this, my very dear and beloved friends, for I am very close to you even in my fear, strange forces are affecting the top echelon of the country, and there is nothing for us to do but weep as we witness the perils of our time. Look, just look, at our political landscape and note the running dogs in the fields of ambition and power. Pay attention to Robert F. Kennedy, Jr. Pay attention especially to the junior and what it can potentially signify for one living in the land of the diminutive. Pay attention to where our hearts go when they go nowhere. Is it not a darkly fated candidacy that announces itself after the strong showing in the snows of New Hampshire by another Irishman, a man with white hair and rancor who does not live in the land of the diminutive but who dares instead to answer to the uncompromising name Eugene, thereby saying that he seeks not warmth but life in the land of ice and early morning rigor. Let us talk about this Eugene, this Eugene

McCarthy, come let us reason together about this man of ice, this man driven by pride and with poison gas in his soul, this public man with a private grievance, an unrelenting rage that pulls the skin on his face so tight and that we all dare not admit, stems from a stingy heart and an ineradicable awareness of his own all-around smallness and inveterate meanness, being of course the vicious dog who bites without barking. And so we are driven back to Robert F. Kennedy, Jr., and what do we see? White teeth and a loving heart for his country and the effort to tutor him out of parochial rancor by his New England Ivy League mentors that he might be better than he is. Does he not hear the same voice as me? Does he not hear it asking why he couldn't have been born smarter? Why he couldn't have a more supple brain? Because his reading—he reads the Penguin classics at night, including Thucydides, for their fine, fine covers—is compensatory, a sad, desperate attempt to bring himself within range of his acknowledged superiors. Because he is crying inside at what he lacks. *Because he is little Bobby Kennedy in the terminal cuteness of the diminutive within which he must live and die.*"

They bowed in mockery. They kissed him falsely and called him a longhaired lout and some who knew him from back when called him *blockhead.* But he hopped on the bar once more. "My long hair falls away in the face of my awakened fear. The rallies and demonstrations against the war and the Washington, D.C., peace march fall away. All those offered words of agreement with those who say the U.S should withdraw its troops fall away in fear of a final Communist victory, now seemingly inevitable following the Tet offensive at the beginning of the year and with the bombing halt. Because they are always there, the Communists, an implacable force. And if the North Vietnamese flag finally flies over Saigon, then where will the progression stop? Sooner or later they will come and take Mona from me and place me in a reeducation camp. Do you understand? Because there are people who want to punish America and punish her severely, and we are those people."

An attitude of grievance by the more radical patrons had him tossed through the swinging doors and out onto the sidewalk. He struggled home only to find that Darryl was gone. But Billy Riley was there, grinning as if at a distance from everything earthly going on and self-contained in his perpetual youth, Billy Billy to Robert Jr.'s Bobby Bobby, as if some lock had been imposed keeping him from the realm of adulthood in every way except the body, a man-child with roots that tied him to the neighborhood: the basketball, the girls, the thrill of early morning spring, the meaningful voice of whomever singing "Sally Go Round the Roses" with lyrics you didn't have to comprehend to summon the remembrance of bliss while drinking from a Riverside Park water fountain.

In the face of Billy Riley's cool knowingness, Luther had no choice but to take off his shirt and his pants and everything else that covered his nakedness.

"Because you wanted to see, did you not, to claim your superiority? Is that not your American way?" Luther stood for inspection as Billy's laughing eyes roamed his frame.

"You're skin and bones, man."

"My growth is in my hair, and in all the parts that need me. Though yes, in my dreams I do have more of everything." He lowered his eyes demurely, so Billy Riley could see him as he really was.

"Why do you talk so funny?"

"Why do I have to look so funny, in the approximation of a gargoyle? A language has to match who you are. There has to be a dovetailing of appearance and sound."

"What are you reading, man? I mean, what do you do?"

Because Billy Riley was short and he was crying inside and he had gotten his head experienced and he wasn't in college and he wasn't easily getting laid. Luther understood the advantage that had been conferred on him to be in college and have long hair while Billy remained invisible to the women that he wanted because his experience was not right for the time nor was his hair. And so he had to fester the air with his lustful longing.

"I am dying in my own way, not as honorably as you in the service of your country. But I am dying nonetheless, and if you must know, I am involved with the very great Charles Dickens, who does remind me of England at its very finest and the quality of the stock that I do not come from even if I do not remember the pages that I've read."

"What do you mean, you don't remember? Why do you read if you don't remember?"

"Because I cannot afford to die, given the direction that my family is going. To die would mean that I would have to live with them all over again, and that would be a state unbearable. And so apotheosis is the only firmament that I can inhabit, making a legend of myself in the mind of America. And if you just keep reading the words that are on the page, something has to stick if only it will love you enough."

Billy Riley tooted loudly through his pajama bottom, the windows remaining open against the threat of any smell-rich contaminants.

"Is that a comment on what I am saying?"

Billy Riley pushed away all talk of that. "I was in college. You know that, don't you? I cracked the books."

"Yes, of course you cracked them. You cracked them as in attacked them, because you did not see fit to lovingly hold them. You had, in other words, to be manly in your approach so that they would not turn you into a shy little girl. And very well did I see you in your days of learning acquisition. I saw you outside the very famous Take-It-with-You Deli, there on 115th Street and Broadway, the snacks and more king to the great Columbia University. Even back then I saw the odd juxtaposition of who you were with who you could be against the backdrop of the tyrannizing institution that would have neither you nor me, the admission of which cast us far far from the winner's circle and the bright lights of America."

"What are you talking about now?"

"I am talking about closeness that comes from far away, the elements of your life that seep into my consciousness and give my blood a start every time I see you because of the freedom of all your parts working together for the goal of action and the consciousness of what it is to be hip and at the same time unto yourself. Because I have the capacity—we all do—to fall in love and cry ourselves to sleep over what we cannot have so that the country itself and all the life in it becomes a boiler of emotion that cannot sustain itself. You have an older brother. He leaped into my mind as all a young man should be as he sat on a stoop on LaSalle Street, where the Catholic domination could be seen in Corpus Christi High School and the smart uniform it turned you out in. You were some blocks north of where I lived, the two of you objects of wonder in the way that you went about your lives. Because he had long straight hair and a legendary reputation as a street fighter, that is, he had the savvy attacking fists that could take you out with a left or a right, being that they were driven by an anger source that would not tolerate defeat the way a riled hornet must sting and sting and sting with consummate and vindictive dedication to the task. Nothing can explain attachment like the relation of the younger to the older, because your Irish brother was to me in the tradition of the heroic gunslinger going down manly in a blaze of glory and nothing could defeat the legend that grew even if it had to be bottled up in adolescent time and the passages of life would not wear well on him. No, he could only live on the edge of extinction, but you, being in the realm of younger brother, took note and were softened by the awareness of his excesses, as you clearly needed to be. Because the savagery of what we have come from apportions to us the life that we now know."

There was a quiet in the air now, *Dombey and Son* lying open and page down as if in shame over its questionable relevance in a sensitive display of its Englishness.

"I was in college. You know that, don't you?" Billy Riley said once more.

"Is your repetition a declaration of war or simply the laying on of fact?"

"Manhattan Community. It's the same thing as City College, except that it's two years. You know that too, right?"

"Right," Luther said. "You are saying that you have smelled me out. You have sniffed my attitude of unearned superiority and now you are asking me to pay the price."

"Yeah, but then I went to take care of some business overseas. You know what I mean?"

"Oh yes. Oh very yes," Luther said.

"Talk me some motherfucking Vietnam talk."

"Do you want me to cry because I have not been there? Do you want me to fall into the trap of spouting off about something I did not partake in, so you can brandish your Zorro sword and run me through at the place of my own falseness? Do you want me to talk about the mindlessness of the domino theory and the incoherence of our response to the internal affairs of a country across the globe? Underweight Luther lecturing battle-tested Billy Riley about the folly of our involvement in Vietnam so you can hate me into perpetuity?"

Billy Riley bounced on the balls of his feet. He clenched and unclenched his hands and ground his teeth in having his own experience. Luther could take the scene no more. He collapsed onto his mattress and covered his face with *Dombey and Son* before putting aside the book so sleep could come.

Chapter 47

A Friday night and the joy of love was in and around him in the sleeping department stores and the subway trains keeping faith with the rails they ran on as he left the post office dear, feeling restored to a sense of purpose by the box scheme that he had faced for four hours. He would now go home and study for the finals that awaited him the next week, but first there was The End. And yet, on One Hundred Fourteenth Street, just west of Broadway, he saw a gathering seated on the street itself and police officers surrounding them. A young man strategically at the top of a stoop shed light for the multitude through a bullhorn on the manifold nefariousness of the university and spoke passionately in defense of the legitimate and just interests of the working people of the neighborhood suffering such affliction from the academic behemoth. A huge sheet with the words "Rent Strike! Columbia Unfair to Tenants" written in red paint hung from a second-floor fire escape. "This university tries to use its power to evict tenants who have lived here for years simply because they are not part of the university. Let us say no to the oppression of working people. We need to stay together and fight the power."

Luther stayed abreast of the speaker's words as he weaved among the crowd, knowing one false move and an explosion of mocking Columbia laughter would be upon him. He was wary of fight the power agents. They too were power seekers and possibly had too much iron in their temperaments and natures a tad too unforgiving. Still, the cause seemed just. Because Columbia had a big belly did not mean it should push people where it pleased. He spun round and round and when he stopped, he announced himself. He said he saw them watching for what he would do in the way of committing to their ostentatious cause. He told them further that he was really planning on going home to read Charles Dickens. "Because I was born just a block from here and have to be able to get away. I did not come from elsewhere to have the perspective such as you have. I am mired in my own experience and must find my way out in any way that I can. So even if the words fold back upon themselves and disappear for all eternity without retention, I must put my face on the pages to get what absorption I can." And though he talked loud, they had nothing to say and only smiling incomprehension or possibly indifference showed on their faces.

Even the top brass were on hand, the captains with their white gloves and medals and gold braid on their uniforms, as if they had been tested through the years and their mettle now showed on their florid faces. Luther assumed they had families in order and homes in order and the hierarchical structure of life in order and intact for them to lie down in, their comfortable lives in part dependent on quelling the anarchic forces with whom they were now dealing. Luther wondered how he could discreetly kiss their power and manifest approval of their uniformed handsomeness without succumbing to the notion that they were right in where they stood, so he could go home and read the great Charles Dickens.

The night had a way of calling and the crowd a way of calling, together calling attention to the meagerness of one's life of apartness, and surely it was so with Luther on that night. To be among the Columbia ones ringed by the uniformed ones of proletarian origin drawn from the streets on which he had grown up was too much. Surely this was everything he could ever care for, the chance to step into history and oneness.

"Do you know what they have gone and done so progress and stability and excellence of their own kind can be prolonged into eternity?" he suddenly shouted, throwing his self-consciousness onto the street. "They abused, yes they very much abused, my high school girlfriend's grandmother because she had the gall to remain in a rented room in one of their wretched residences past the time when they wanted anything to do with her because she was not of Columbia in what she did or in her elderly age. Their sole desire was to throw her into the street. Big Blue resorting to the dirty stuff of shutting off her hot water and failing to give her linen or to make basic repairs. It is hard to go against the Columbias. Because the Columbias are refined, white-haired men in oxford shirts and rep ties who command a cab or a waiter with a single wave and can turn a single room occupancy filled with blackness so very very white. Do you not remember the Mayflower Hotel with its very own blackness on 112th Street and Broadway? Do you not remember the agitated, tormented blacks of that very building standing on street corners with brown bags over their green bottles from which they got their taste in an attempt not to deny God's presence but to take care of business on their own since he was so willfully distracted and how the Columbias drove them out and put in their place the men of khaki and penny loafers and argyle socks, men who knew how to walk with one hand in their front pocket, as their fathers had taught them to do? Facades of buildings they sandblasted to erase all the grime. Because that is what the Columbias are saying. You can have it on our terms or you can have it on the brown bag 'Let me get a little taste' terms of anarchy."

The police terminated his messaging with a bullhorn blast—disperse or face certain arrest for disorderly conduct. For the Columbias had come to sit in the street and preserve the neighborhood in their ephemeral way and seduce the world with their youngness bold and so very sexual. Huge paddy wagons rolled up and the policemen tapped their leaded nightsticks with repressed frenzy, waiting to hurt the Columbia young men in their heads and bodies and have at the Columbia young women. Because once you were in their power they would show you what that meant.

Luther saw once again that he had a chance with danger in the air and on the ground to be part of something big and forget exactly what he was in his apartness. Because the Columbias would not mind his staying if only to ride in the paddy wagon with them. It was not the time to be going home to Charles Dickens and turning your back on history itself. You just did not visit England and the nineteenth century on a Friday night in spring.

"I don't know what to do. I'm so confused. I played stickball and loadsies on this block as a child and fell in love with Mara Sandberg, who took my breath away in sixth grade but lost her looks by high school, and saw Johnny Antobelli, the super's son, beaten senseless by Arnold, the angry black boy. Do you hear me? I was here before you on a day of infamy, shouting out, 'Ching Chong Chinaman sitting on a fence' and he came stealthily from the basement and his old man's legs were faster than you could imagine, fueled by slights ancient and current, and I ran, while looking over my shoulder, straight into a lamppost and fell in a daze to the pavement but even this was not enough for him, he with his hair in a long braid had to bend low and drop a load of spit in my face and curse me with the words 'lo fan,' and yes, the sliminess of it was unspeakable."

As the bullhorn overrode him with another warning, Luther was startled that his eyes should meet those of the girl from his literature class, the sexy one who wore the miniskirts and scolded him for his oddball scribbling, only now she was with a surly student in a Columbia windbreaker who, with his jet black hair and model's looks and eyes that established themselves in your mind, read Luther quickly and saw enough to then ignore him, prompting Luther to scream, "What's your mind on now, Don Juan? Your next fucking shirt ad?" The law had begun to lift limp bodies into the vans, and now came for the annoying one. Luther went running after him, shouting, "You have your movie star looks and Columbia intelligence and though a scowl has permanence on your face it does not keep the women from running to you. Do you know the envy this summons in me?"

A last warning was given over the bullhorn to leave or be arrested, but fear of ridicule kept Luther in place and so there he was in the paddy wagon with the Columbias who so frightened him, listening as they recited huge chunks of Yeats, while from the paddy wagon of the Barnards could be heard equal portions of Sylvia Plath and prose passages from the finest works of Doris Lessing, no one bothering to sing "We Shall Overcome." Luther could only be quiet in the presence of such erudition. Was it possible that the wrong choice, not newness, had opened itself to him, he now wondered, amid the crush of bodies worse than the rush hour subway, as the wagon rumbled down the West Side Highway?

He could have these reservations in spite of the presence in the paddy wagon of golden Mark Rudd, wearing a sports shirt and khaki pants, who had addressed the gathered with his customized bullhorn, painted a brilliant May Day red. Luther knew every last thing about Mark Rudd, that he had big eyes and a strong chin and short blond hair, which he did not need to grow to a long length to hide the missing part of his head because his head had no missing part, it was so perfectly round, and that the word "underweight" had never been applied to him. And he knew that Mark Rudd had a handsome All-American face and that he had been born in the state of New Jersey with no ill effects and into a house that had a high level of order and that he was an honors student and high board man and even had the necessary qualifications for acceptance to Harvard and despite his fame was a just folks everyday sort of guy with a girlfriend who sometimes gave him trouble and when his parents came to visit, they would bring along sandwiches which they would eat with their son in the family car. (And that even if Philip Roth wanted to get upset with Mark Rudd for living the life he did many years later, it was no reason to trash the Sixties for what they were in the ongoing development of the country and the world in the way it would have to cyclically be.) And because his parents accepted their son as he was. He was just their Mark, the same Mark who had been a model Boy Scout. It had brought tears to Luther's eyes to read about Mark Rudd and his close family ties. And now he was there, in the paddy wagon, in the presence of Mark Rudd, born Mark Rudnitsky. And suddenly, springing back from the depths of his recoil, it was necessary to shout out the truth: "I love you, Mark Rudd. I love you so very much. You are so perverse and so all-American at the same time and not even girls can make you cry. Oh know only this—I have read every last magazine article about you, even if I haven't finished *Bleak House.* Because the truth is that through your persevering action, you make living history far more appealing than anyone or thing that ever came before, excluding Ebbets Field. Mark, I want to ingest your essence. I want to do something abnormal in your midst." But he could not interrupt their intense bonding, or bridge the gap that made him a stranger among them. He had only his words coming back to shame and humiliate.

Officer Harry Connelly of the NYPD was the man he most remembered from that night. Patrolman Connelly was there at the Fiftieth Street Precinct, where they were booked on disorderly conduct charges. And he was there at their final destination, the Tombs, where they slept six to a cell, Luther wishing for some of the darkness of the paddy wagon to escape into so they, the gifted ones, would not see who he was and shame him. He remembered the caked toilet and the damp cement floor they slept on with only thin blankets to keep off the night chill while electrical storms flashed outside, as if in triumphant dismissal of who they were, causing Luther to be drawn to to the barred window. "Lightning does not overrule judgeships. Class distinctions set even nature in its place. These are the sons of the ruling class you are seeking to negate. Good luck, chump, and watch your ass," before falling back to the floor and the cover of his smelly blanket, what conversation there was flowing away from him with their high numbers and overachievement and aggressive personalities and large chests. There was Bryson, who would rattle the bars and call out, "Yadda yadda warden," whatever that might mean, with all the tears of heaven being shed for their youth misspent in the folly of struggle with existing power. Was it a line from some prison movie? Was it a dazzling piece of irony? Or the other one named Fletcher. Why couldn't they have normal names? Why should they attack with last names for first names and bully you with their differentness? The one who dared to call himself Bennett quoting some line about teaching us to care and not to care. Suddenly Luther rose up again, with the blanket over his head to provide cover. "For sure, you Fletcher Fletcher and you, Bennett Bennett, and you, Bryson Bryson, have fathers on the line right this minute, exuding their silver-haired boardroom power to the appropriate authorities. Or maybe they don't even have to pick up the phone but only to will it to be so and it is done. Have I got my facts straight? Are you aligned with power while pretending not to be? Is this your one chance to see how the other half lives before torquing up to higher ground? Because all I care about is *Bleak House* and I have nothing to read in order to catch up with you." Again they did not answer him. Again they did not find him on the power grid they were part of.

And so morning came and they were released from their cells into unavoidable interaction with Harry Connelly, from Queens, with a parochial school education on his face and in his brain, the fist from the brothers and the ruler to the hand from the nuns, Harry with the understanding that came to him that you live in your physicality and hate all those who don't, all those with their books and their *New York Times.* A pulsating presence in his blue uniform, he walked back and forth along the line of them as they were shepherded to arraignment. The thick neck, the rounded shoulders, the bulk that he carried quietly while living for the times that he could do things physical to people in his Harry Connelly way of expressing himself.

"Was you one of them that beat up on one of my buddies the other week?" Harry Connelly stood nose to nose with the "Yadda

yadda" Bryson man, going at him with his bad grammar and not giving any kind of shit about correct speaking in the presence of the Columbias, referring back to a prior campus ruckus in which a cop had been hurt, and although the cop had not been hurt bad—he had not been beaten up but knocked down as the demonstrators were attempting to flee—Harry Connelly held on to the injury as an incentive to do some serious pounding. Bryson shook his head, knowing who he was talking to and so took all the smartness out of his expression and emitted not a single bit of Ivy League laughter. Officer Harry Connelly then fell into a more joking way with them. How did they find time to study with all this demonstrating? Did the university give courses in student demonstrations? Harry Connelly got on easy terms with them, the Columbia men who basked in the sunshine of life wearing the light blue of their exalted university, which gave peace and wholeness to all those who entered its gates and smelled its freshly cut grass.

Down the line Harry Connelly went, before he stationed his powerful 5'10" body in front of Luther. "What's the matter, Muscles? You don't like to talk?" A wave of involuntary laughter passed through the group, for Harry Connelly seemed to be partially speaking for them as well. Muscles. He could feel the eyes of the others on him. Fletcher and Bennett had tried to engage him in conversation that morning when watery coffee and sandwiches, the meat unrecognizable as bologna, were passed out. Where did he go to school? But he had brought his head out of the blanket only long enough to make a zippering motion with his lips before heading on to the wild blue yonder of his thoughts.

"I talk. I talk all the time in my mind, which has its own sound chamber."

"Is this guy all right?" Harry Connelly asked. "Maybe we need to take him to Bellevue."

"I am more than all right when I avoid the trail of iniquity."

"Something tells me this one's coming back. He has that look to him," Harry Connelly said. Luther could feel his comment resonating among the gathered.

They were led into the courtroom, where Luther looked with longing at the elderly bailiff sipping his morning coffee in the full knowledge that he was on the right side of the law. In full deference to the judge, who appeared from behind a closed door with his emaciated frame lost in the black robe, the bailiff barked, "All rise," that order might be established and maintained.

Maybe this is his off-day, Luther could only think. Maybe this is his day for watching Yankee baseball. Maybe he was pressed into service because of the ruckus the night before. Whatever, the judge worked his gavel with authority beyond his thin bones, and the defendants were seated only to rise shortly and be dismissed on their own recognizance.

The sun was friendly, offering gentle warmth to ease the chill from the long night in the cell. He was back in life, all around him a swirl of energy and commerce on Canal Street. Despite his fatigue, he went straight for a phone booth.

"You won't believe this. I've experienced the mecca of protestation that needs only the history books of the future to chronicle it."

"Talk to me," Mona said.

"I will tell you true. I am standing on the corner of Canal and Mott and the trucks of America are rolling past with the arrogance to which they are accustomed. I have a new role, Mona. My name is now Rampart. I am a revolutionary come to set fire to the world. I am Trotsky and I am Jesus, too."

"Talk to me, Luther."

"I got arrested. And with Mark Rudd, too. There, I've told you. And now I am famous, if only anybody will see me."

And so, on that warm May morning, Luther told her of the glorious event, how he had gone without sleep the night before, and of the inedible slab of repellent meat he and the other detainees had been served.

The sound of a paintbrush swishing around in a can of turps told him that she had already started her day and that he was barging in. She told him through the vibration coming through the line that she saw through to his real motivation for being part of the protest.

"Is it that I am imposing on you? Is it that I have become simply a hanging string in your mind? I will get off the phone now and leave you to your life. I will sit down with a newspaper and then try to read a book. I will do whatever it takes to get free."

But he also knew his truth. She was just competitive and envious. If he did something bold and positive, she had to try to undercut him. He knew his truth in the moment he knew it just as he knew the streets of New York City.

Chapter 48

He read the first sentence of every paragraph. Then he read the first sentence of one paragraph on every page, then on every other page. Sometimes, to vary things more, he read the last sentence of a paragraph or even just the first word if it was a long one in the ongoing project of distilling the very essence of the great *Bleak House* so he could nail it to the floor and place the book on the shelf. And sometimes, of course, the luscious kernel of truth was right there in the very center of the paragraph to be gobbled up with the rest left discarded as mere chaff. In this way he could get at least some of the words that the great Charles Dickens had written into his mind, starting with "Pip," so he could have a thing or two to say on the final exam as to who Charles Dickens was in that time that had disappeared except for his book. He did it with small quantities of speed and so put finals behind him and zipped up to Boston to visit the girl that he loved with the first week of June upon him and the promise of summer ahead.

But vigilance was a factor that could not be overrated if he wanted mastery over his life, only it seemed to Luther that he might have to send away for additional parts to achieve the performance level required as just when he was about to knock on Mona's door, he heard voices inside that sent him flying backward and to the floor. And who came to almost step on his face but a man from that very same room with the mystery of who he was attached to the fact that Mona was just behind him.

"I'll see you in hell for betraying me, not that it doesn't cause a painful thrill as well," Luther said from down below.

Mona grabbed a handful of his hair and raised him up. "Luther, this is Gordon Brooks, my painting teacher," she said, forcing a restrained and civil tone.

Luther tried to stop shaking so the man could come into focus. In his fifties, with flecks of gray in his long wavy brown hair, and with a steadfast, level gaze that turned Luther away.

"I am pleased to meet you, now that I know who you are. I have just finished with *Bleak House*, so I know my life is ahead of me."

"The world of Dickens is a wonderful one to enter," Mr. Brooks said.

"Right. He does bring some good loving to the page," Luther agreed.

"Well, I'll be going now," Mr. Brooks said, after staring at Luther with some perplexity, and headed down the stairs.

It was a happy time. It was June of 1968 and the sun was shining.

"Is he a home run hitter? Is that how you would characterize him? Does he hit them deep to center field, showing his contempt for the daunting spaces, or does he dink them straight down the line like a cautious, stingy Nellie afraid of using or developing his full powers?"

"He's just an art teacher, silly. He's very sensitive and very smart. He knows everything anyone could possibly want to know about the technical side of painting. But his knowledge is superior to his talent. He brought a few pieces into school. They were sadly lifeless. He's just a teacher now and the other is a slowly dying dream."

Luther felt bad, hearing her talk that way about Mr. Brooks. It wasn't right to take away people's dreams and leave them to die in their grayness. He wondered why Mona had to speak such a sharp-edged truth and why she couldn't live with the obscuring softness of his very own mother. He could only guess that clarity was the price you had to pay for success if you weren't to step out of the race into the mushy evasions of low-grade love. To advance you had to be ready to kill, to hurt, at least with words. He didn't know that he ever wanted to come to that place.

Luther requested the details of Mr. Brooks's life, and Mona fed the morsels to him, which he snacked on hungrily in her room, while lying down. They were not a taste delight, but rather like bland wafers. A wife and two daughters. A house in outlying Brookline. An MFA from Yale. A reputation for being a romantic who took an interest in his female students. Not a feast, but still something to ingest. Luther worked on a way to neutralize the elements of Mr. Brooks, coming to see him as someone who was more interested in appreciating Mona than in sleeping with her. He had a sense of a man with much aesthetic refinement but little sexual fire. Luther could stop vibrating. He could bring his engine to a shuddering halt.

The following day a boy from the Adoration Council of Greater Boston stepped forward and made himself known as Luther and Mona approached the Brattle Theater in Harvard Square, for it could seem that they had no place to go other than restaurants and darkened theaters and other public places, there being no room in the relationship for anyone but Mona, the queen of art, and himself, the thing in hiding from the face of manhood. The boy he saw that day was no chthonic vision but an apparition of the earth with hints of illustrious antecedents in the liquid glitter of his big dark eyes. He came with a compact body and neatly combed black hair evenly parted in cool defiance of the hairy norm.

He had in tow a girl who commanded many looks with her hair so black and short and fine and her facial features of perfection including luscious lips. She could have been his female double. But her beauty could not hold him within her borders. He had an appropriation frenzy going, seeking to peg Mona to him with his gaze of smiling intensity.

"That's Lane," she said, not volunteering the information but answering his question, as they stood on the ticket line for the movie theater. "He's brilliant. I get depressed looking at his work. It's so bold and original even the teachers are intimidated by him. He's a wild child who tries to sleep with all the girls. He's also incredibly wealthy. His father owns half of Boston, someone said. My first day at school I climbed a tree and he climbed right up after me, looking up my skirt. That's Lane."

Luther reeled at the information onslaught before settling into acceptance that Lane had now entered both their lives with the powerful energy he exuded. Luther did not hate him. It was more that he longed to be him, to have looks and talent and a pappy who owned so much of Boston. "Oh I don't scorn you, God, so much as I don't have anything to do with you, given the injustice of your ways," Luther exclaimed, leaving it to Mona to silence him as the movie was beginning.

Because Mona was having her end-of-year review, normalcy had to reign, and so Luther sat in her room reading Norman Lewis's *Life in Death,* a very famous book that he didn't understand though he did read each word before turning the page. Mona was entirely encouraging. "I love to see you read. You have a lot on the ball," she said.

"Oh yes," he replied, and had his third cup of coffee because he could never be without something to drink at hand.

The self-addressed postcards he had left with his professors started to arrive as a way of reintroducing Luther to reality. In the morning Mona would bring the c/o correspondence to the room from the table downstairs, where all the mail was left. And wasn't it just their way to go and savage you when you had already been savaged? You got punched in the mouth on one block, all your teeth were knocked out, and then they broke your head on the next and rolled back and forth over you with their cars on a third. They couldn't help themselves. It was just malignancy. His Dickens grade had come and his philosophy grade on the temerity of a poet going by the name Bysshe and what it meant for the world to have an ode written about a bird that never was.

"Now you have seen who I am in black and white," Luther cried, but Mona continued her day with a quiet sense of purpose and after an hour some hope returned that better days were ahead.

He tried to reconstitute himself and thought of Mona at the little school on the Fenway, with the ducks in the pond across the street and the lights of Fenway Park in view, rising above the residential buildings, a field of green inside the heartbreak structure where men could be boys so time didn't ever have to end. He saw that while his dream of athletic greatness had died, Mona got to be an honest laborer with her vision intact. She didn't have to summon great thoughts. She didn't have to be bitchy. She just did and she just was. He had only one outburst that whole day, running to a window and shouting into the Boston air, "I would be so free like the rest of you if only I hadn't failed them." But he had, and the gates of grayness were always a threat to close on him.

And to show that miracles could occur even in the Greater Boston area, Fat Man called Mona to tea with the request that she bring along any of her set who had the imagination to be with him, having received from anonymous sources the names of all who were newly arrived and worthy in the area, and for sure her reputation had preceded her.

"I bought a few rugs and some vases in Morocco. And when I go to Europe next month to conduct a seminar on the logistics of the educational structure in the ongoing reconfiguration of quantum analysis, I'll probably purchase a new Porsche and have that shipped back here as well." Fat Man was sitting in a velvet robe in a throne-like upholstered chair in his apartment near Harvard Square. The living room already had a nice oriental rug and a few large vases, but Vera said he had a buying mania, that when he came to New York he would hit all the expensive stores and suction goods out of them with a powerful hose and return to Cambridge with Armani suits and Sulka ties and Tiffany jewelry. If Luther understood properly, Fat Man was a doctoral student at Harvard and taught undergraduate courses at a local business college. He was just a whiz with money, Vera had explained. And surely Fat Man appeared to have it all his way, throwing off big names and waving his Ivy League pedigree while he sat like a pasha in his silk robe.

"I have no relationship with you, so don't even say anything to me," Luther said.

"Your friend looks mentally beaten," Fat Man said to Mona. "He looks like someone for whom the game is already over."

"I like him," Mona said. "And besides, he is earnest in his love-making, and he protects me from having to look too closely at my own craziness."

Luther nodded his head up and down in a wonderment of assent.

"Lots of men can make love. I could introduce you to more than a few," Fat Man said. "Anyway, women's interest in sex is as indiscriminate as men's, only they are afraid because of their conditioning to acknowledge it. In the realm of sexuality, everybody is a whore."

"No, no. You've got that wrong. Women are not whores. Our bodies are not for everyone."

"I am so confused," Luther offered.

"Shut up. We're not talking to you," Mona said.

"Yes, well, if you want to spend your life with a reclamation project..." Fat Man didn't get to finish his sentence.

"Watch your mouth," Mona warned.

"That's right. Watch your mouth," Luther added. "You'll be lucky if we don't reclamation all over you."

Fat Man shifted cheeks in his Fat Man chair. "So where is it that you go to school?" he said, still addressing Mona.

"She goes to the Boston Museum School, and she got in on the basis of her strong portfolio while others by the hundreds were being turned away."

"Why not Boston University? It's probably better."

"Because she goes where she has a right to go, so don't try to interfere with her plan for living," Luther piped up again. "Are you familiar with the word *foremost?*"

Fat Man looked to Mona for the help she would not give. "A common adjective, I believe," Fat Man said, finally turning to the one he had been trying to avoid.

"Then you know precisely who she is about to become. And so I need to say no more, because the case is certifiably closed."

Fat Man sighed, as if to brace himself for an odious task. "And tell me again what institution of higher learning are you enrolled at?"

"Don't think for a minute I do not hear the dubiousness in your voice. CCNY, if you have truly forgotten. I am taking courses in philosophy and the great literature of the world."

"Then I'm sure you're knowledgeable about the Socratic method and Aristotelian logic."

"Without a doubt, but my real focus has been on Percy Bysshe Shelley, in particular the brazen peculiarity of his middle name and bird thou never wert."

Fat Man gave Luther an appraising stare. "It may be that you will have a problem in this world, seeing that you are not strong enough for manual labor and not fit enough for productive mental activity."

"Yeah yeah yeah, but CCNY has Dr. Jonas Salk, and he knows more than you ever will about injections that can make you live."

Fat Man erupted in a great chuckle, his folds of belly fat undulating and sending ripples throughout the universe and to demonstrate that he could elevate above any label that might be stuck upon him, starting with *conspicuous consumer.* Having long since discerned the essence of Luther, he could now, in emulation of the levity that stood as a feature of the great master of acquisitiveness Sidney Greenstreet in analyzing the chessboard of life, he now turned to the one and only Mona and dared to say, moving the progression of the game to where it had to be at that hour, "Are you familiar with the word *pander?*"

"Many times I have come across it in my reading sessions," Luther interjected.

"Be quiet, Luther. Of course I am"

"You will make very good material, given that he likes intellect as well as beauty," Fat Man said, causing Luther's ears to twitch.

"Where are you going with this?" Mona asked.

"I will be quite plain about my intent. Neither of you has the makings of a social butterfly, if I may be free to speak candidly. You are clinging and fearful, though you, Mona, have greater possibilities of flowering based on the richer, more fructifying gene pool from which you have come, which one can see in your total affect as well as your skin and teeth and hair and your luminous presence. Luther, on the other hand, is dull and of the street. An American mutt, forever spraying fire hydrants. The point is only that next door lives the great American stud, a young law school student with curly black hair and the physique of a Greek god. His name is Reginald Bolt and he has over his bed a big leather belt with notches in it, and goes for months at a time averaging a woman a night, his theme song being that stirring number by the Supremes, 'There's No Stopping Us Now.' Are we starting to get the picture?"

"I am and my sensing apparatus is on high alert," Luther said.

Fat Man went on as if he hadn't heard. "I am myself wooing Reginald Bolt but first must win his favor, and with that I will bring in the show." Fat Man rang a bell three times, and before Luther could ask what the story was, the heralded one entered in only a loin cloth.

The nearly naked Reginald Bolt positioned himself in front of Mona, his crotch in her face, as if some moment of truth were arriving and no one must try to get out of its way. He stared down at her with concentrated rays as she stared at his bulge. Luther, stricken, could not cry or call for murder. He had only to stay where he was and watch as Mona undid the wrap and beheld in wonder the fully aroused thing. The law school student then lifted Mona up and took her away, driving Luther to the fetal position, where he stayed after the door had closed.

Fat Man said Luther would have to leave, but that he hoped his eyes had been opened to all that life would continue to deprive him of because of his lack of excellence. Luther said his only hope was to come back and shit in Fat Man's face as he slept. And then he would call on the law school student and deliver the same gift.

Luther wandered the streets, seeking to walk off the effects of what he had seen and heard. By nightfall he had returned to the scene of the crime, where he shouted up to the windows of the accomplice and the assailant, "How dare you seek to exterminate me?" Because a good lawyer was supposed to help unfortunate people, not run around in a loin cloth. And for that the law school student's punishment would have to be severe, Luther vowed, as would his own, for having the audacity of the hypocrite to live upon the earth with his own distortions of the truth.

About the law school student she would only say, when she finally returned, that he had expanded her, and in so saying consigned Luther to the depths of hell. He managed to continue his life in approximation to her, full of wonder and grotesque stimulation knowing some other man had invaded her so suddenly and with her acquiescence, the beckoning call for revenge intensifying in him the wild need for nocturnal adventure.

With a hunter's resolve he hit the streets with a joy pill operating to alleviate the pain. In a sub shop with a jukebox playing the laughable "Tommy," he found her at the pinball machine, a high school girl struggling against the fetters that her parochial school sought to impose on her senses. A tall girl with her black hair in a ponytail and an acned face but a packing figure that made you hers in her black mesh tights and short skirt and button-popping bosom.

He struck a pose of innocuousness, the kind made famous by Norman Bates in the detention room of the police precinct, where he did not swat the fly, knowing all eyes were upon him so of him it could be said, "Why, that Norman Bates, he wouldn't hurt a fly." Best to wait until she left the shop. You never could tell. Her boyfriend might be on his way or even one of the feral teenage monsters piled into a booth. Or a horde of girlfriends might suddenly descend on her and become his sisters' chorus of shame. No, one on one was all he could handle.

When she had had enough of the pinball machine, Luther approached as a supplicant and asked her to administer to his wounds in private. He said she was just a girl, and he was just a young man, and because it was June of 1968 and even Boston was experiencing warmth, they should make the most of it. She responded that she too felt the night calling. Still, he needed to draw her out, to have a fuller context for her being. Her father was a postal worker and she had a brother who played football for Holy Cross and a mother who grew old early. She wanted to get away. She wanted to do something. She didn't know what. Her mother on her case all the time. Home too late, dressing like a whore—she ticked off the grievances and lived in her soreness.

"What's your name? Do you have a name?" she suddenly asked.

"My name? My name is Lawyer. Counselor. Stud. So women call me."

"No they don't. They call you Stupid." She finally laughed. It cheered her up to to give him a verbal whack.

"Do not doubt for a second that I possess a glowing intelligence," he said, summoning a strong refutation.

"The only thing you're glowing from is what you're on."

"So you say. And I have an enormous penis. It makes up for everything."

"You have pencil written all over you," she replied.

Somewhere in Boston Common the ducks were resting while the trees caught the light of the full moon. There on a park bench Luther smooched the girl, who had given her name as Mary Beth.

"Is this where you live?"

"It's where I have been led. I live far away, in a place called New York City."

"Led?"

"Love led."

"You talk funny, mister."

There was no consummation. The space too public and his animal content not that high. Without the physical, there was nothing to hold him to her. His emotional dependency on Mona was complete. And so they parted.

Back in the apartment, he cried out, "I can't stand the pain. Kill me quick. You were supposed to stay with me forever. I don't know if I can live. I don't know if you can live."

She turned back to her easel while he lay in the fetal position.

Fat Man was not finished. He arrived in his Porsche and said it was party time for all of Cambridge, time to bask in the glow of brain-packed Harvards gathered together to celebrate their graduation from the world's preeminent center of learning. The featured guest at the gathering would be a poet from the university. People saw him and didn't know what to say. Some called him a nutty fruit cake. Slight and nerdy-looking—Woody Allen with a mountain of hair and a face full of pimples—he caused that kind of reaction.

"Don't use the P word in front of me," Luther said.

"The P word?" Fat Man inquired.

"You heard me," Luther said.

"Do you know what he's talking about?" Fat Man asked Mona.

"She knows very well, el pimpador."

"Poet. That's the word he objects to." Mona shrugged.

"And will stay on my guard against with all the life that is in me."

"Well, I'm going. I could use some expansion," Mona said.

"Can I bring *The Pearl?* I must bring *The Pearl,*" Luther said.

"The what?" Fat Man asked.

"*The Pearl.* It's about men who go with women and women who go with men in all the glorious comings and spendings that any printed page could ever hold. It's the true story of England."

Mona said nothing and Fat Man didn't either in tacit agreement on the need for silence. Fat Man just did his job of whisking them to the necessary destination.

Luther went to the poet. He didn't dawdle in the least.

"I won't assault you. That is a promise. It is just that I am in a state of urgency with my insides bleeding. The pretty girl that you see me with? She went off with another man, a dog with dark curls and teeth of unmatched whiteness, a man who ascribes to himself the power of the universe based on what his moms and pops told him he could and must be, snatching here, snatching there, so that the world becomes his candy store. For me as I am, dignity is a farfetched leap. I do not know what ails me but I do know that I do not have a center. What can you tell me about the power of the word to locate me and do I need to have mathematical precision to put the word on paper? That is, do you need a prerequisite to be a poet? That is my concern. Are you about to speak, or are you just here to listen to your wretched Mahler?"

He was not a surprise in the physical realm, Fat Man having aptly described him, nor did he have a soul on fire with generosity.

"Go away. Forget about being a poet. You'll only ever be destructive."

"That's OK if it has to be. It's a reprehensible calling anyway Still, why do you slam me with your judgment profound?"

"Because you are governed by the moronic idea that poetry is effeminate and has to be bashed so you can cover up the little girl that you really are."

"And what kind of little girl are you that you should look the way you do?"

"I may be a poet, but I can also be violent. I have hurt many people with physical blows before I learned to punish them with words."

"My violent little fruitcake."

"Do you want death, that you talk to me this way?"

"I want truth, Mr. Harvard. How did you get to such a sissified place, that you offer lines incomprehensible, the reader lost in your vapors?"

Through clenched teeth the poet said, "By understanding that I couldn't do anything else."

"But you are Harvard. You can rule the world, or at least the CIA."

"Please be quiet now," the poet said.

"OK, but even in my silence I will remain strong and vigilant."

Mona was across the room, engaged in conversation. Luther lay down on the sofa and closed his eyes. He heard much talk about the movie *2001,* how fantastic it was. Hal this and Hal that. He entered a delirium of fear in which he imagined himself a sliver of paper hiding between the books and heard that Dylan line, something about a girl being an artist and not going where she didn't belong, and kept his hands to his head for his own protection.

When the black station wagon showed itself, a man of prominence was some hours dead but that had not stopped its wheels from turning, Peter Van Dine driving without the distraction of news coming through the dashboard radio so he could be one with the elements that had made him in the life he was living with his hair combed straight back and the open road ahead and the sweet sadness of his middle age right there in the rear-view mirror to reflect upon. And even he had to laugh at the strangeness of being a historian looking back while having a face that had to look forward while at the wheel, something he conceded was not a puzzle for greater minds, those that Harvard had accepted while excluding him. Well, human beings were just like trees with lives of whatever duration before returning to the earth and if Massachusetts had them, so too did Connecticut and New York and even Delaware, should anyone choose to ever go there and take a look.

Boston was not the prized destination, his daughter was, for with her was his dream of a real and rejuvenating communication there in the bed of family he was preparing to lie down in. For this reason did he emerge from the vehicle in his morning glory, ablaze with anticipation of gathering her to him, all the pain that she could inflict long gone from his consciousness unless she wanted to bring it back. The sun was present as were the small buildings on a street of plainness that even had a garage, Boston finding a way to keep things right size.

No father takes a daughter's life for granted, Peter Van Dine saying not once but thrice in the active spaces of his mind that Mona was a jewel, the manifest splendor of his regime on display, even if he now had to deal with Luther, not quite gone into the dusty traces of the past but in fact noisily active in defense of his own being and jabbering on, something about how, even if tragically wounded by the treacheries of Mr. Van Dine's second daughter, he remained in her service and so was deserving of the love that should come to any mother's helper. Luther sensed that whatever meaning Boston had for Peter Van Dine he would have to remain quiet about, for Mona's father was in the locale where the ashes of his future had been buried for him to grieve upon, the deed done by the letter containing Ivy League words saying he was not wanted in Harvard's PhD program, causing him to fall into Lydia's arms and the comfort only she could provide. And was Peter not for her a way out of a landscape of bleakness where once there had been light? Stuck behind the walls his ambition had placed on him, he ultimately strove for escape into nature and solitary splendor in which to expose the excellence of his physique. Because the letter had sealed him into quietness and caused him to live in reflective, not triumphant, spaces, the world of glitter having turned him away. To be seduced by the world is to have the steel fist sheathed in velvet smash you in the mouth, he said, finding solace in the trees that offered their meditative stillness and all that rose from the earth to grow strong or edible or to simply adorn. Because he was in a holding pattern against the hustle and bustle life all around him, an agrarian, while Lydia wanted to surge forward on the juices that drove her into the land of newness and adventure. But he was still the man whom she could throw her arms around even as he struggled with the essential untidiness of human contact, and they had that thing to go to—husband and wife—in the comfortable eternity of their togetherness.

Such was Luther's understanding.

Luther showed himself strong, emerging from the rooming house with a boxful of Mona's possessions so he could stand tall in front of her father as her number one helper. He expressed confidence in the logistics of the operation before running back into the building and returning a minute later with two heavy suitcases for loading into the idling Chrysler, so her father could remove her from a demented world and back to Camp, a place where childhood was long and beauty was strong so long as it stayed intact within itself rather than risk the pollution of lackluster genes. Because to be a father was to be supreme within a realm of justice all his own.

Boxes of art supplies, large drawing pads, paintings removed from their frames—soon, all her possessions were on the street, and here Peter himself swung into action with his packing expertise so the car could be free of the disorder anathema to his domain. A fire is blazing in my blood, he was heard to think, as he showed the angle of vision to recognize where things went and what the spatial relationships needed to be, and with this task he could be considered to excel. Where others could disappear themselves in the flames of love, moving from one burnt out drug hearth to another, Peter remained the aficionado of the structured scene.

"Her review went really well. She was the true star in the realm of art," Luther reported, now that the road had smoothed things out.

"Review? What's that?" Peter said, bringing more perplexity to the word than it warranted.

"Nothing more than what it says. Her artwork was the hit of the school, and she is now on her way to famousness." Because if he didn't mention it, she wouldn't either, and it was necessary that her father know all the wonderful things that were happening while the car was in motion.

"Well, isn't that marvelous?" Peter said, when the facts were in. The voice was cultivated, playful, but was it his own?

And when they made an emergency stop, owing to Luther having to pee with canine frequency, thus abusing Peter's vision of road mastery, they decided to indulge in a thruway snack, Peter saying, out of earshot of his daughter, "Doesn't she look splendid, just splendid? Is she not decidedly blooming?"

"Oh yes. Oh very yes yes," Luther could only concur.

Not knowing that they were walking into a state of shock, people gathered at the concession stand for the newspapers of the day and the advent of death for RFK, the bullets from the man with the double name Sirhan Sirhan terminating his physical force and presence. Stunned at recognizing himself as a member of the American family of man, Luther launched into a vilification of the poison gas man from the upper reaches of the Midwest, saying he had never been a Eugene McCarthy man, not even after he nearly defeated LBJ in the New Hampshire primary, that there was something vicious about *Eugene*, something vain and turned against himself. Surely he had a streak of perversity and anger sickness in him. And Luther did not believe in his intellectualism. It was a pose. His true ambition was for a politics of endless paralysis, to shove everything into the realm of ideas and make war on *doing*. For that reason he had wanted him to get the hell out of the way of Robert F. Kennedy, Jr., latecomer to the primaries or not, cautious tester of the winds or not. Because Eugene McCarthy secretly did not want the responsibility of winning, he would do a dawdle dance inches from the end zone while holding the ball aloft and find himself caught from behind. He just wanted to get in the way of those whose purpose was to win, while dribbling endless non-thoughts made up of tired, far-between words, recognizing no one but himself. A man with high solipsistic content beneath that peeved facade of intellectual rigor and high purpose. If his life depended on it, he could recognize no one but himself.

Luther held forth to Peter while they were motoring down the Mass. Turnpike, the trees now decked out in funereal black bunting owing to the devastation to the land brought on by the assassination of Robert "Bobby" Kennedy, brought low by the weaponry of his assassin. And yet happiness was in him being there in the car and in the moment in love with Peter Van Dine, in love with the history, the American history, that was in his genes, his Dutch yeoman farmer antecedents in south Jersey, red white and blue and Main Street America abounding in him. "You come from the lightest of countries, where creamy cheeses are made, while my father originated in the land of rats, a land of carnivores in which men picked their teeth clean of the veins and shredded flesh of the children they devoured. You are the sun's golden rays warming me through the windshield and the lightness of America is in your still blond hair and has been passed on through you to your sunbeam of a daughter. But this you should also know. All spring I had been championing RFK and watched him gain momentum. RFK was a roll up his sleeves kind of guy. He wanted to make things happen. He was not a turned against himself type. He was not a dweller in affected ambiguity nor a man of cold parts and self-centered meanness. And he was becoming the express. He had won California. His father and mother had taken him aside. They had measured the size of his teeth and said his canines were big enough to get the job done, to hurt the people he had to hurt. They told him to get out there and do things to people, Kennedy things. They continued to call him Bobby when he had grown to full size and his hair had flecks of gray in it. They kept some part of him in shadow and stunted with the diminutive. Such a shock to see, at the rest stop, the front page photo of him spread-eagled on the floor of the hotel and gone away from everyone except in body. All this from the gun of the Sirhan Sirhan man, who from his name and his lethal mission seemed an arch villain come to life from the pages of a nightmare comic book.

"Mona, to be honest, hasn't seemed so shaken, hasn't heard the rumble of tanks or whiffed the intrigue behind the newspaper headlines as to where the forces of government are appropriating and consolidating their power. Frankly, she has had the centering discipline of applying paint to canvas, in this way eliminating from life all but the thing in front of her. Plus she has had the advantage of expanding—a word I detest—her horizon of sexual destruction under the laughing malevolence of Fat Man of Cambridge, but I can't get into that. In any event, she does not dissipate herself with pointless speculation about the secret passageways through which the rogue elements roam in rearranging the structure of power. The plain truth—and it does not raise or lower the iniquity bar but leaves it right where it is—is that I have appropriated the tragedy unto myself. I have made it mine when it isn't mine, and she has been silently rebuffing me for trying to horn in on a special moment in history. She sees me trying to enlarge myself on his famous corpse. She sees my longing to be part of the tragic American landscape, and she is not buying it."

Peter saying, "There's not a chance in a thousand of gun control in this country. The gun lobby is simply too strong. Violence will always be part of our culture. It is part of the national psyche." About RFK and the home run he had been trying to hit he had nothing to say. RFK was just a political personality, a lightweight serving vested interests who would beat him down with their own greed and put him fully at their service.

For long stretches, when his silence wasn't invaded, Peter just did his driving thing, talk holding no real interest for him when he was behind the wheel having his complicated interaction with the road and the other vehicles he was surpassing, now flicking on the directional to pass a slow-moving van with a treacherous intent to its moseying way, trying to bring Peter down to its retarded level. The look of steady intensity on his face seemed to build and to saturate every pore, Luther becoming bothered by the weight of his focus. He wanted to shout at him what he had said before, that driving was not a science but Point A to Point B stuff, and the rest was psychosis fueled by rock and roll music. (Always the violence waiting to follow the soft stuff, the broken sternum and smashed teeth and pulverized jaws, scented tissues no deterrent to gasoline, which burned hot.) Not that Peter would ever deviate from Beethoven to rock and roll music.

Luther's high feelings were gone by the time they reached the outskirts of New York City. Everywhere he saw the same thing, people taking baths in gasoline and lighting themselves on fire or positioning their heads for crushing before the wheels of the buses of mass transit. It was only the same thing that had been going on for a long long time in a city that could be arrived in but never left.

When Luther's eyes met those of Peter in the rearview mirror, he saw starkly the disfavor in which the older man held him. And when, at journey's end, Mona and her father, with the help of the doorman, unloaded her possessions and entered the family's building, a feeling of desolation overcame Luther as he found himself alone again on the streets of New York City.

Because she had an unresolved hunger for the world, Lydia sought to speak to a side of Mona that didn't exist and suggested to her in an exhorting manner that a summer job might be in order to free her from the confines of art and place her on the plane of the life around her. In Lydia and Peter's circle were friends who were part of the business fabric of the city, Lydia's dream being to bridge the gap between her and her second daughter and at least abate the shadow self she perceived Mona to be. Her second daughter seemed bonded to a sphere other than Lydia's own. Talking to Mona was like talking to a stranger she did not care for in all her aspects while weighing the consequences of what would be destroyed by cutting loose with a sharp tongue. And yet she did not want the infection of entitlement to take hold in her second daughter. She did not want her growing up with the idea that the world owed her a living because she could fill a canvas and use the word *turps*. She did not want Peter's dependency to be his dominating legacy to her.

"My mother goes and arranges some stupid job for me when all I want is to do my own work. She has some crazy idea this is good for me. I'm an artist. What do I care about helping one of my parents' boring friends at his design studio?"

"Yes. Yes yes," Luther replied, not in assent but as a means of distancing himself from her vehemence. With the parents gone he felt frightened and alone. Why should it be worse when he and Mona were together in the city than when they were apart?

Was it a sign of trouble that Mona had not unpacked her bags? Indeed, it now seemed a lot to ask of her, to be a working stiff just like him. Where did he get that right? Luther saw the danger he was in. He remembered with concern the words he sometimes threw at her, how someday her trust fund money would run out and then she would know on a deeper level the meaning of Dylan's question as to how did it feel to be a rolling stone and have no direction home. He felt himself buckling under the weight of his own master plan, and she was not helping him with her fury evident at the thwarting of her artistic will.

Luther had to struggle to keep up with her as she streaked along Broadway headed for her job, and when he tried to stop her, she simply pushed past him and down into the Eighty-sixth street subway station, making her life all his fault forevermore.

He wandered over to the public library at Forty-second Street and Fifth Avenue, stopping to say hello to the stone lions in the entranceway and thinking that he had been born and would die in this city, whatever the plans of others might be. In the reading room he fell asleep holding a book on Aristotle. The man to his left nudged him awake, saying he had begun to snore. Luther said he was going to read everything worthy that had ever found its way into print, and the place to start was with the letter "A."

"Aristotelean methodology could definitely be my strong suit, if I would only let it wash over me. I have a friend who baffles me talking about symbolic logic, but the Greeks were different. They had their sandaled feet on the ground and wore loose garments." Luther leaned toward the man and whispered in his hairy ear. "Would you like to go into the bathroom and have homosexual sex with me? I am very willing and very able. I am also very frightened of and angry with my girlfriend, and this activity would not be without precedent. As a teenager, while going steady for four years, I gave men access all the time."

Luther gave a dismissive wave of his hands as the man made a fusspot thing of gathering his papers and changed his seat. Libraries were like that, furtive liaisons in men's room stalls, longing for the girl at the next table or the one swishing her stockings in the stacks, the blood heating in the hush amid the shelves stuffed with tomes and the dust motes floating through the dry air. It was that Columbia guard from his long ago past taking him into darkened Butler Library to have his way with him once he put down his flashlight and time clock.

At five p.m. he stood on a pretty Greenwich Village side street in the dappled afternoon light across from the New School building. It has no entrance requirements. It can't be any good. You have to have solid credentials to make it in this world and a genuine ability to put the blocks together. Otherwise everything is hopeless. We do nothing with our lives but stave off that crushing sense of inferiority. So his thoughts went.

Mona descended the steps of the walkup and blew past him without a word, and in that moment he more fully understood that he had been trying to buck the path she had set for herself. He was now willing to assume full responsibility for her rage and accept the current pulling her back toward Camp. If he had any doubt as to her resolve, that was eliminated when he caught up with her.

"Let my mother show up for that job. I'm supposed to sit around all day pasting down pieces of repro on some damn mechanicals? And then one of the creeps tries to pick me up? That's it. I'm through. I'm an artist, got it?" Her will expressed with uncompromising force, she once more disappeared into the subway before he could respond.

The next day he carried her bags through the steamy Times Square streets and into the lower level of the Port Authority Bus Terminal. If he could not block her, what choice did he have but to offer assistance, as he could not leave her.

"Are you planning to see other people? Are you planning to kill me dead with the dictates of your body, as per Cambridge? Are you going to stretch yourself far and wide as a social extension of your gifts? Are you going to leavc me in the dust, never to be seen again, while you hold all the cards? Is this my one and only life, to try to contain you while in pursuit of insurance in anticipation of your leaving? And do I have to stay here forever in the seediness of Times Square while you depart for the leafy bower of bliss you call Camp? Are no miracles of resurrection available to me to torque up to the level of survivability?"

"I'm not planning on any action of that kind, but the door is not exactly closed," she said, planking him with her frank yet pompous use of the word *action*. From the land of no regard for him she spoke, no mindfulness of the security of the vault that he needed and instead assigning his health to the fluctuations of her mind. He scanned the bus line for his possible replacement. Was it Mr. Lewd Mouth? Was it Mr. Heart of Stone with his cold blue eyes? How about Mr. Ponytail? All three had run their eyes over her.

He followed her out through the swinging door to the boarding area, the bus driver copping a smoke and unfazed by the exhaust fumes, as if to say in his gray uniform that he was solidly behind all vehicles and the means necessary to power them. His hacking cough and his cancerous skin he embraced stoically. He stood there in a world he no longer knew with longhaired kids he wanted to take a stick to for burning the flag and for their bra-less women.

Luther imagined the three men getting up during the ride to use the bathroom in the rear and tapering onto conversation with her as he wandered through Times Square, his fear-driven vengeful lust sparked by window displays of garter belts and half-bras and lacy panties along Eighth Avenue. It was time to get moving again and increase his lead lest Mona destroy him.

Chapter 49

That summer, in order to affirm his commitment to a life of progress, he took an English course with Professor Hastings Buckner, who operated out of a Quonset erected to compensate for the lack of space in the college's more permanent and traditional structures. Luther visited the professor's office to find him with a smile that turned out to be a permanent fixture, though the Meerschaum pipe was not, the professor removing it from his mouth to greet his new student before returning it to its rightful place.

"I believe it is time for me to make my debut in the twentieth century, as I have been wandering in the weeds with all that has gone before for long enough. A break with the lingering tortures of the vestigial past is essential. I want to be involved with truth, justice, and the American way and cannot endure Beowulf and Sir Gawain and the Green Knights for one second more. Besides, I have thought enough about the word *anomie* so that my head hurts."

"The twentieth century is an open field, and America has a slice of the literary pie, as it were."

"Enough with the 'as it weres.' I know what the words *dactyl* and *anapest* mean without being able to penetrate to their essence in the way that I know about rhombuses and parallelograms without being able to incorporate them in my daily living. I am counting on prose to be more forgiving than poetry and math so I can have some place to go that does not need signposts of classic intelligence, which I am without, for I seek to hide my stupidity as I do the box shape of my head."

'Are you stupid?" Professor Buckner returned the pipe to his mouth, not in a devouring way, but just so he could savor it along with the words that he had spoken, words that came from the mountaintop of his equable age.

"Certifiably so, but my main problem is with the girls on this campus. They go into a room and talk about me and then come out and set up a wall of universal rejection."

"Do you have sisters?"

"Do I have what?"

"Sisters, I believe I said."

"The whole world is my sisters. It is peopled with their deformities."

Professor Buckner came close and pointed the wet end of the pipe near Luther's eye. "Faulkner may be your man. He is the only writer in America who knows what it is to have sisters and the force field of inhibition that gets generated."

"I want to have a higher aspiration that will give me a liquefying purity in the face of life. But I have to warn you—I think poetry is effeminate and English is restricted to those who can't do math. Can I ever get past the gates of your observant smile to the place where you can help me?"

"Why don't we do this, Luther? Why don't you read those novelists you just mentioned and come back and discuss them with me in two weeks?" Professor Buckner reinserted his pipe and greedily sought to suction smoke from it.

"Just remember that I am not afraid of lewd acts, if it should come to that," Luther said. "And let me further say that I believe I can knock you off. In fact, I think I can take you within the first round and that you smile more from fear than from love. I also did my homework and saw in the catalog that you received your B.A.

in 1950 but it wasn't until 1961 that you actually got your Ph.D. Do you have anything to say in your own defense?"

"Do the dates need defending?" Professor Buckner double-sucked on his pipe and arched his eyebrows.

Luther paused to consider whom he was talking to before going on. "My mission in life is to surpass all fathers. So far as I know, I have surpassed my own, though my mother is still with him in the act of appropriation that he maintains. Your interval between degrees gives me hope that I could catch and move ahead of you. I have also been seeing that the schools you attended were not of the highest caliber. Though I am not off to a good start, being here at CCNY, maybe I can make some advancement on my grades and go on to a university of stellar quality and earn the fame that you are lacking. Would that be too much to ask, to sleep with more women and to be able to beat the likes of you?"

"I think Norman Mailer will be a very good reading assignment for you," Professor Buckner said, intensifying his relationship with the pipe through the sucking power that he applied to the stem and the death grip he put on the bowl, causing wonder as to whether he was seeking something from the pipe that it could not yield and would he break it all to smithereens in the attempt.

"How so?" Luther asked, imagining the damage beyond the bearded face that the pipe had done, the image versus the yellow teeth and caked lungs past which the professorial words flowed.

"In the sense that he is driven to scale mountains and winds up in the desert instead. He is very American that way."

Luther felt compelled to sniff the air, as if something suspect had been spoken. "Is this envy or truth you are expressing? In any case, I am compelled to invade the twentieth century in acknowledgment that time is running out and that a man cannot train to swim the English Channel by reading Proust."

"Precisely," Professor Buckner dared to say, biting off each syllable with no display of conscience whatsoever.

Luther could wish that he had the courage and the stomach to crawl right inside the professor's mouth with a lamplight on his head so he could begin to get to the truth of origins. "Where do words come from and why is it necessary to worship them? Is it so you can make a living by relying on worldly sermons?"

"That is what a teacher does? He sermonizes?"

"Your words come out like pellets. They are not free flowing. Others ride the rivers of their words downstream and straight over the waterfall, not knowing that the rocks in the shallows below will crack their heads into a thousand pieces. But where do the words come from? How do they travel from the mind to the hand that writes them, and how do they come to have meaning sufficient that empires can be built on them? Who is the word maker who makes the words and what is the face of him and why are some words so constricted while others have the run of the land? And what is it all about, given that it is a paperback book you cannot put between two slices of bread?"

"Words are of the intellect. They are fashioned in the secret chamber of our own merit," the smiling professor said.

"Words are not of Jesus, the song he sings to himself?"

"Anyone who has a real mind does not concern himself with Jesus," Professor Buckner said.

"Can I pull your face off to see who is really there? Can I do that, Mr. Buckner?"

"Professor Buckner."

"That is your name?"

"That is my title."

"Well, I will do my best with Norman Mailer and the twentieth century, since they insist on being known."

"I'm sure you will do just fine," Professor Buckner said, directing Luther to the door with the stem of his pipe, his mouth relinquishing it if just for the moment.

Note to Professor (formerly mister) Hastings Buckner, B.A., Occidental College 1950, Ph.D. Boston University 1964:

The novels of Norman Mailer were written while he was very depressed and chewing great quantities of glass, having seen, not for the first time, the limitations of perspective even while wearing a fine suit of clothes. He was sunk into low spirits by the fact that he had to make his words and didn't know what he had gotten himself into, even if he did have heavy thighs. And because he didn't chew gum he had to drink, thinking of all the things that would be kept away from him if he couldn't live, and dreaming every night of his mother, both repudiating her and loving her at the same time, for how else was one to approach a woman who called him 'Normie" and had seen him when he was very small, as did her husband, who after all had a role to play, too. Because while Norman Mailer grows fat, there are still women, in America and abroad, who are willing to slide their bra straps from their slender shoulders, and look at you with eyes of allure. This must be a source of torture to him if they are free of his possession, and yet his odds change if he continues to fashion his words and has the will to drive them into print. As Picasso paints with his penis, so too does Mailer write with it. The energy source is the same. For that reason he had to kill women, because he couldn't get better before he got worse. The other thing is that he grew up in Brooklyn, and in Brooklyn there is nothing to listen to. All devices are geared to the sounds of the City, meaning Manhattan. So if you are in Brooklyn you definitely have to look north and have a longer reach to be fed your desire. There is no lack of great women in Brooklyn; it is more that Brooklyn is the place of people who never left or came because they were driven from where they were. I mean this as only a partial explanation of all that has gone before him, with the mystery of more to come still in great need of respect. I will be back with the full scoop after further digging.

That summer a work-study grant was issued to him with an assignment to an office in a building on Thirty-fourth Street between Eighth and Ninth Avenues. Already he was seeing that if you lived in New York City you were sentenced to the phrase "between Eighth and Ninth Avenue" until you wanted to cry at the limitation you had placed on yourself.

The trains of New York City were consistent in their approach to life. They came into and out of Pennsylvania Station far below the Ninth Avenue street level so that you thought you were looking down at a speck , an HO layout, from some mountaintop. You could not get the full flavor of the trains from the perspective you had been given, but even so, the intricacy of the rails and the overheads was enough to make you hope the entire scene would live on, its essence of forlornness and the promise of adventure incorporated forever in your being, the men in flannel shirts with their lunch buckets some part of the emotional tapestry that could only be understood as pain and longing. Luther ran to the view down with profound thirst, as if he could drink of the past and make it holy, and after a short while there was nothing more to be extracted from what had given nothing in the first place, and he turned his attention to the storefront at the corner of Ninth Avenue and Thirty-fourth street where the Whelan's drugstore had once stood, and saw that the past was still with him in terms of ice cream sundae afternoons on the break from church and all that it represented just around the corner.

About the New Yorker Hotel, the General Post Office, and the Automat, all nearby and threatened by the negations of change, he had nothing to say except that they must persevere in their mission of keeping his landscape alive so he could know where he was and not be a nomad in Manhattan.

It wasn't nothing to be alive in your childhood so you didn't have to walk around dead.

The job was a make-work kind of thing and you had to go inside a building to get to it. In that building, where once there had been honest energy abounding, there was now a city-run start-up program to revitalize the numbers of the borough in terms of assessing the feasibility of more residential housing vis a vis the commercial enterprises in the Clinton area, the fact that dozens of such reports were buried in city archives having long since been forgotten. The instructions were that he should start with Macy's over in Herald Square and ask the management if it wouldn't rather be a housing project for the poor, because people had been there before it ever was, or whether retail purposes should forever hold sway when we did have Cuba a mere 90 miles from the continental U.S. Luther was sure the instructions had come to him just right amid all the paperwork management could create.

Pentamente Zualo, Luther's name for Brewster Bill, the director of the project, showed little space in his being for feelings. He was very much about the task at hand and very American in his Wonder Bread way, willing that a smile be on America's face in its march toward ever greater prosperity. A prelaw major at Williams College, he had this to say: "I'm not all that bright. I make up for what I lack with hard work. I won't do all that well on the LSAT, but if I keep up my GPA and stay involved with interesting stuff like this challenging task, then I'll get in somewhere decent." He came from Fairfield County, Connecticut, spoke well of Dad and Sis, showed up to work in jacket and tie, and exuded an upbeat manner.

"I am an entrepreneur at heart," Pentamente Zualo continued, Luther struggling with his fear to listen and once again yearning for the softness of Mommy to cushion him from a world that would not have him except on the terms of this new young captain of industry. "It goes against my grain for a city government to be deciding on a housing policy when that is the province of the individual realtor gauging the demands of the market. From all my reading and intuitive understanding of the situation, bureaucracies bring in layabouts, chronic alcoholics, and ne'er do wells of every description. But I am here to demonstrate that a commitment to excellence can invigorate even the most slothful agency, and so I must put the whip to you and drive you forward into the streets of filthy Manhattan." He called attention to an area map on a bulletin board. Pins with little red heads dotted the map, and while Pentamente jabbered on, Luther began to doze, pulled into drowsiness by the sweetness of the cherry cheese Danish he had devoured only minutes before. He dreamt of women singing softly to him while he lay in his swaddling clothes. When he awoke he saw with some disappointment that Pentamente was still attacking the board with those little pins and talking of areas of deployment and strategic maneuvers. Was there any way to love Pentamente? Was there any way to cross the line and embrace his short hair and jacket and tie and have his same sense of purpose, not the Automat mentality of Luther's father or the laid back stance of his generation? How had he come so far into the region of long hair with all the demands it placed on him and was Pentamente Zualo a time warp baby or the real thing? Luther could not contain himself anymore. "The point being that I was born in New York City, not Connecticut, and so have been without the grid of constructiveness that lifts up those who inhabit your less urban spaces."

"You're a bum with long hair. That's what you have to face," Pentamente Zualo said, sticking another tack on the bulletin board to continue the purpose he had come for.

Luther stepped out into the district he had been assigned, the sight of beautiful girls all around causing him to exclaim, outside the Automat on Eighth Avenue, "Oh for a heart that is not pained by its own longings," and witness the ghost of his father in that same Automat his mother espoused before stepping forward into Macy's with all the vigor he could summon.

Clerks were scenting the air with perfume as Luther wandered over the hardwood floors and the elevators made that delicate, feminine sound signaling their arrival. To contemplate the commerce was dizzying: the ringing cash registers, the bookkeeping, the tedious product inventory and the sadness beyond the glitter of the store's displays, cardboard boxes stacked on concrete loading platforms with steel-reinforced edges daring to exist under ribbed metal awnings, all of this in permanent shadow and in proximity to the ever-present time clocks.

"I need to see the manager. It is urgent. They will kill me unless I get the assignment done quick."

"For which department?" The saleswoman unable to tear herself away from her scents bottle and admiration of her long red nails.

"The world manager. The one who looks down from above and sees the whole thing as comprehensible, as I can only pretend to do by being tall."

"Comprehensible?" the woman repeated absently, as if suddenly vacating the premises on which she stood.

"I could so much lose my head in here," Luther said. "The smell of perfume conjures for me a woman in an evening gown with a thin neck and a full bosom and a narrow waist. I lose myself in the pleasure of the smell and then I lose myself in the pleasure of the night where it enfolds me so that I hardly know my country of origin. I want only the dream that the enticing scent entitles me to. All sense of mighty purpose that attaches to a man gets lost, and I cannot be Magellan or even Pizarro. I am just Luther standing in a Manhattan department store seeking relief from his desire."

"I think I understand you," the woman said. "You're enveloped in a dream of your own longing. You want the winds of change to never leave you and at the same time you want to stay right where you are."

A lull in customers allowed them to chat. He could hardly stand when she whispered the words "secret passageway" into his ear, such was the power of her warm breath to crumple him. He wobbled toward a far door she had indicated with a nod of her head and passed through it. As he mounted the stairs he wanted only the warmth of her, not the assignment that the false Pentamente Zualo with his insane American energy had burdened him with. After a brief minute of struggle with the stairs he collapsed and lay on a cool landing.

Flat on his back he came to staring up at a space painted white with windows in the ceiling and nowhere else, through which he could see the sky above and only that. A man in an engineer's cap and striped bib overalls big in his face and his body sat at the controls of an enormous transformer. A model train layout covered the room, with Lionel freight and passenger trains crisscrossing the board over trestles and mountain passes and through tunnels. The trains of America were going everywhere that trains could go, to the far edges of the board and back. Switchers and coal-burning locomotives and twin unit diesels, rugged freights with the worn, glorious, proclaiming insignia of America, trains that rambled through every state of the nation—Wabash Line and Rock Island Line and Illinois Central and Norfolk and Roanoke and the Southern Pacific shouting its swamp green colors and the Lackawanna Line not far behind asserting the endless variety of America in its ascension beyond innocence. Crossing gates lowered as the sleek coach cars of the New York Central Chicago Zephyr passed by, providing its passengers with a cushioned ride, in that moment of time the black staff in their livery on board navigating past the white love/hate thing of America, trying to believe that even as they walked toward the rear they were moving forward on the iron rails.

Luther sought for answers from the railroad master, who from a need for panache wore a red kerchief around his fat neck as if he were Casey Jones at the controls in the heated cab of a coal-devouring locomotive.

"Where are we going, mighty master, you who are so much in control?" Luther inquired, but he was unable to shout him out of his complacency. Provoked, Luther climbed into the cab and reached for the man's face to pull off his mask, should he be wearing one, but

Master Man casually slapped him with a backhand sending Luther around the corners of the room like an iced hockey puck.

"No one stops me from the truth, Master Man. No one," Luther said, rising with the sound of his own voice. Again he lunged for the man's face, seeking to pull it off so revelation would be at hand. Again the man backhanded him, gave him the short sweet motion of power that he had willed to be accrued to him. This time Luther's mouth filled with blood and in a rage he grabbed the Lackawanna engine from its track and hurled it at Master Man, who only distended wide his jaws to swallow it whole and spit it back onto its route. He tried tearing the trestles from their foundations and stomping the tunnels into flatness, but they only returned to the shape that Master Man had given them. Finally he unzipped his fly and tried to pee on the speeding Boston and Maine freight but the control man without a flicker of effort dissolved his emission. Master Man was simply obdurate and iron-willed in his singleness of purpose, and Luther was feeling crushed and unable to breathe in the confines of such hegemony when Master Man dealt him a knockout blow.

Luther entered a dream world under a scorching, brutal sun, a foretaste of Hell's eternal flames. People wept and pleaded with God to allow their lives to be taken by the cold, not the sun's tormenting rays. What sort of mentality did they possess that they wandered about in dark clothes in such heat? He looked down at his corduroys, his apparel for all seasons, since shorts in summer were for men with the right knees and calves.

He came to and staggered through the revolving doors of the Automat, where he bought three iced teas, which he liberally sweetened. With his head on the table he snoozed away the rest of the afternoon.

"Both Mommy and Daddy say it shows real drive and ambition," Mona said over the phone, that he should be in summer school while maintaining a job. And then for Lydia to get on the phone and say, "We hear you're doing great things down there in the city, Luther. We hear that you've been working terribly hard. What's it going to take to get you up here?"

"I will grow stronger and stronger," Luther said. "I will keep this feeling of confidence. I will be full of myself and in reach of American glory."

"Of course you will, Luther. Of course you will," Lydia said.

The approval sent Luther soaring. It was hours before he could begin to come down, and in that time all his mental fulminations against Mona for leaving and for the privileged life the family led had vanished. He understood why he had felt such insecurity when he and Mona had been together alone for that brief time at the beginning of the summer. It was too much of a burden to be together on their own. He wanted to be a part of all of them. And they wanted him too, or so it appeared.

Dear Hastings Buckner:

I have not been killing Norman Mailer. I have simply been reading him along the edges of the text, the way a child will nibble at the edges of a sandwich before biting deep and savagely into the heart of it. I believe I have him surrounded, that his stab wounds, while slight, are multiple, and that he is slowly weakening. The thing that leaps out is that he has done surgery on his name so it could usher him into the realm of where he needed to be independent of any differentness, which he can deal with on his own. So he has showed himself to be a man of success in a suit, with no mind for the common man but no mind for the exemplary man either, just a man chewing on his words before releasing them so they can arrive masticated on the page and full of egotistical need for the appropriation of sex within the realm of higher echelon experience. This he certainly sought in the early

1950s with a body full of salts, while what he really wanted, with his small penis, was Marilyn. All this sent him not into areas of failure but of pain. Am I making myself clear?

Because she was his confidante, Luther reported everything he could about Master Man to Mona, how he had made the trains to run on his time, augmenting their reality with dazzling routes. Mona left him nowhere with her response, saying simply that he should write about it, that he had no choice but to go with such a thing to paper.

He hadn't gone nationwide in his search. Filled with fear-driven desire, he wandered the streets, reaching for girls as a child reaches for candy. Because Mona had given him her heart on the condition that she could take it back. Because he was who he was. Lacking a social context, he relied on random encounters in public places. The thought of dating brought overwhelming conflict and guilt.

One night he headed down to Greenwich Village, knowing *she* would be there. Seeing a girl walking east on Eighth Street, he followed after, willing all anxiety from his face that he might appear to her as innocence itself and far from criminal intent. In front of the E. S. Wilentz Bookshop, closed for the night, he made his approach.

"They sell poetry in there, and I am not so much an enemy of the form as ignorant of its intentions. I have heard you need a high aptitude for algebra to do it right."

"Not so. You just do the thing and your voice finds the form it is compelled to take."

"Yes, that gives me hope. Do you think we could talk at depth over coffee? Do you think that could happen?

The girl was wearing a wristwatch. She brought it to Luther's face. "At two in the morning?"

"I am most sorry. I am so deep in shame I can hardly speak."

"This is quite extraordinary. I do believe you approached me the same way only last year, right on this street."

"Oh, I would remember that if it ever had happened. You are too much the sight bonanza for memory not to hold," Luther replied.

"Of course it was you. An ectomorph with unmanageable hair."

"I am Luther, but my real name is Shame."

"You need to ask yourself some questions, but you don't have the strength."

"Questions?"

"There's something wrong with you. You need some help."

"Could it be that you would be the one to help? I could very much benefit from your expertise. You could take me home right here in the dead of night. No one would know, and that way I would not have to sleep alone having failed to up my total."

"Upped your total? What, like notches on your belt? You are no stud."

"No, but I am implacable, and need can get you where muscle won't."

"And why do you need to up your total, as you say?"

"So she cannot kill me in the tracks where I lie, that is why."

"And who is this she?"

"Oh, she has world stature in all her features and the forces are formidable she can marshal to remove herself from my life as her journey upward bound continues. Botticelli went and painted her ahead of her time for installation at the Met."

"You are a needy dope. Now good night."

Oh, the coldness of her strike, and on a hot summer night, to leave him for dead on a West Village street.

Chapter 50

They were not a part of him but they were a part of the twelve tribes and would come from New York City not to be with him but with the land that he had claimed to be of milk and honey set down in the coldness and deprivation of the Catskills.

From the front porch at Camp, where he sat with Mona, Luther could hear the howling autonomy of Sid Nizer's desire and his affirming, aggrandizing belief that he should be seen in the nakedness of his aspiration as a son of Brooklyn with a motherless childhood and a scale-master soul. Even out of sight Luther saw Sid Nizer in the distance maintaining the lascivious wetness of his lips with repeated licking and patting his mustache relishing the fact that it was for Luther to provide the necessities for his pleasure, because it had been for Luther, friendless Luther, to say that they—Sid Nizer and Jesse—should just very much come on up, offering them a stay at a place not his own.

Not that he had been expecting them so soon on that August day at Camp, even with the invitation that he had extended, following Lydia's open invitation to him, which he had acted upon when his work drive had diminished to the point that he was lying down on the benches of Herald Square Park in the company of the pigeons, able to rest assured that he had the regard of Mona's parents as a truly toiling person and could bank on their love and esteem. In his neediness he failed to see that they had other concerns that mitigated against receiving him deeply. In fact, they weren't even there when Luther arrived, having driven to Saratoga to visit friends.

He sat with Mona on the front porch drinking coffee and saw with some horror that in spite of the vigor she was blessed with, she too was now having cups of coffee during the day. What a low thing it was, he could only think, to have the power to infect and corrupt even the worthy with the affliction of lassitude and diminished sense of purpose.

The family cat Ambrose caught Luther's attention as he headed down toward the garage. Angry starlings buzzed the Siamese for the effrontery of his intrepid resolve. Luther could only admire Ambrose's stalwart nature and sangfroid, as if he were an aircraft carrier being buzzed by gnats.

"Why do they have to act like that? Ambrose is just out on his constitutional. Those birds get to fly about. Why doesn't he get the right to walk about?"

"He's after the nest up in the garage. That's why."

"I don't think I like that," Luther said. "I do not care for nonchalant killers manifesting singleness of purpose and a bent for destruction. I do not want for Ambrose to have his way in the world of nature while under domestic auspices. That would seem unfair, uncivilized, and other words I cannot find. Kill those birds and you kill me," he called out to the stalwart cat.

"Leave Ambrose alone. He does what he needs to do," Mona said. "Besides, the birds are out of reach. And double besides, you were killing birds up here just last year."

"Desire places everyone and everything within reach. Must I intercede with a killing of my own, just when I have outgrown the need? Must I eliminate Ambrose?"

"Stop with your talk of killing."

"I will trust you this one time. We will see if you have the necessary outlook for all creation." With that he got up and started walking toward the garage.

"Where are you going?"

"I am offering myself as an international observer should a war crimes tribunal ever need to be held."

"Sit with me. Just sit with me," Mona said.

"We will see what normal is before the day is done, extending our exploration to the far corners of our shadowed minds."

The nest was halfway to heaven in the rafters of the garage. The rich smell of motor oil from leaky vehicles rose from the concrete floor. The black Chrysler had vacated the premises for the trip to Saratoga, but the jeep remained behind, loyal and local and suddenly spooky in the shaded space it occupied, as if, its olive drab metal notwithstanding, it had thoughts of its very own. Luther patted its hood, wondering now if it were a metamorphosed horse with one powerful, lethal kick left from its previous life in payment for his unwanted, fearful touch, while seemingly far away, Mona continued to sit in her world of current sunshine. Seeing Ambrose inexorably headed his way, he knew he could not call on Mona for assistance, that he had entered a world of confrontation all his own and that he would have to handle it without armed might.

Ambrose had a tan, chunky body and a head in chocolate darkness. When Ambrose walked he walked with a mind of his own and with a center of gravity and focus removed from external event. To hold him was to know warmth and experience a purr that vibrated through your being. These should have been factors in the way Luther now saw him, but the cat had stepped outside his role when he crossed the line into the garage and made revealing eye contact with Luther, a moment when the truth of crossed purposes made itself known; understanding came instantly as to where they stood vis a vis each other.

"Are you going to snuff out life before it has even begun? People must be safe in their homes, and if interventions are necessary, so be it," Luther said, unable to take the inexorable needs of nature anymore. He then rushed at Ambrose, who darted into a rhododendron bush, and while the starlings did not cheer, they were not opposed to the aid they had witnessed.

Mona was not on the front porch when he returned from his hero's journey, but her cup remained faithful to the spot where he had last seen it on the porch railing. She emerged shortly through the screened door with news of significance that would seize hold of any day.

"Your friend Jesse is down at the inn at the end of the road. He says he's here to bridge the gap between two cultures. He says he's not alone but has half of New York City with him. The question is: Do I kill you now or kill you later?" This she said with him right in front of her.

"Stop with your killing," he said, repeating her words to him.

"Can I know what you are going to do about these friends of yours."""

"I will tell you what I will do. I will run straight into the woods and never be seen again," he said.

"Suppose you get in the jeep and take a drive down to meet your friends instead? Afterward you can run into the woods never to be seen again."

Luther rushed to the kitchen and grabbed a box of salt. Then he ran to the pool and took off his sneakers and socks and wet his feet. Then he sprinkled salt heavily on both feet, the salt sticking to the wetness, and soaked them in the water again so they would be beautiful for the men and possibly women of New York City who had come to see everything he now was tentatively a part of.

He drove the jeep slowly down the hollow road that morning, oblivious to his surroundings, a hushed house here to the side of the road and a hushed house there, dwellings that grew as if from seeds in the imaginative earth. Minutes later the jeep was rolling over gravel in the parking lot of the inn.

He found them around a table by a curtained window overlooking Route 28, bearded Jesse and scale master Sid Nizer and others he didn't recognize, terror driving him to say, "No one enters my home. No one."

Sid Nizer rose and spoke. "We've come all the way up here to meet this girlfriend of yours, the goddess we've heard so much about from Jesse." He gave his mustache a pacifying pat, as if it had become agitated at the very prospect of Mona.

"I have lied. I have deceived. From a sense of demented largesse I have made available a property I don't even own. That does not mean I cannot recognize when inappropriate extension has taken place."

High in the sky at noon was the sun tormenting in the spaces free of shade, and so the pool became a magnet for them, a thing they did not have in their city-dwelling days. Pretty women with tough exteriors bonded to laconic and laidback smoke-head young men sporting the obligatory chop of mustache their fathers had commanded. And yet Luther's focus was on high board score Sid Nizer, who was all over Mona, dancing around her naked with his big dick dangling.

Luther wandered away to the guest house, where he found a young man and his girlfriend.

"What is calculus, anyway? Is it God? Why does it keep some people outside its gates while claiming others for its lovers?" Luther asked. Jesse had said the young man was a math whiz.

"Can't you see he's cooking?" the girl said.

In fact the young man was heating a spoon with his cigarette lighter. Luther went to the window to check that the leaves were still green and that they were still in summer.

"I'm locked out of your hearts forever. Is that it?" Luther asked, as the girl tied the man's bicep tight.

"You only look like a folksinger," the girl said coldly.

The young man had placed a strip of rubber around his arm and held it tight with his teeth as he injected himself into the exposed vein, a ritual for him not grisly but rewarding, having gone beyond hallucinogens and hashish and grass. The girl then did the same, that she might follow wherever he might lead. He saw that they were exclusionary in their natures, as he himself generally was.

"You have drawn your circle tight," he said, and walked out.

Through the shielding pines he glimpsed Mona in bonding conversation with the iniquitous one while high above Jesse made the solarium his own personal watchtower.

Perhaps sensing the perception of impropriety, Sid Nizer left Mona's side and approached Luther across the lawn.

"You see Marilyn lying over there by the far end of the pool?" He pointed to a woman lying on her back on a mat thrown over the slats.

"I do," Luther said.

"She's after me to sleep with her, but I can't get into it today. Maybe not ever. There are too many variables."

Luther held his tongue at the complexity Sid Nizer was sharing and watched Mona raise up out of the pool like a goddess.

"Peace, sister." Sid Nizer said.

"Peace to you, brother," Mona said.

"This is not an alliance of the blessed, and killing may have to be done," Luther blurted.

"He's been threatening to kill me for a long, long time," Mona said, Sid Nizer applying all his listening devices to the conversation.

The day seemed to be moving farther and farther away from him. Mona was finding a way to be at home among the smoke heads and the mainliners, that home truly becoming where Sid Nizer was. Luther wandered into the kitchen and filled four pots with water. Then he turned on the gas jets and began to boil the water. When Mona came into the kitchen, she found it full of steam.

"What are you doing? Are you insane?"

" I am steaming the poison of hate out of me for all that you are doing."

"I'm thinking of driving up to the lean-to with your friends, since you are absolutely useless as a host."

"I have done my very best not to die today."

"Very good. Very very good," Mona said, turning off the gas jets and emptying the pots of water. "Now are you coming along?"

"I do not hear invitation in your voice. This sounds like a party of the chosen."

Somewhere outside Jesse was singing, bellowing really, "Climb Every Mountain," daring to make fun of the glorious Von Trapps.

"That's all the invitation you're getting." Hearing her words so hard and strong and emphatic, he slapped her hard across the face.

"Bastard," she said, ignited by the epithet before she fled.

Conclusive proof was at hand. She wanted to make it with Scale Master Sid Nizer. Make it. The language of the cheap and the lost. A sad, ugly term. He said it over and over silently, letting his mind hurt him with the words.

In his mind too he saw clearly the progression from the spring of the previous year, when he had been a laughing thing only to meet her and find himself rushing home in anticipation of her arrival. His resolve never to set foot in her family's apartment and then when he did, to only eat peanut butter from their refrigerator. Quitting his job for the stay at camp that summer and his inability to leave after Mona's father had given him word storm. His abysmal showing the rest of the summer at the apartment he briefly rented, and his complete collapse before, during, and after her return from Europe. And now this. Line after line after line crossed into abject slavery.

It was hours and hours before they returned, and in that time his mind tormented him with images of Mona having it done to her, images that also fired his lust. He found himself in a bewilderment of emotion and could only hold his head as he wandered about, fit for nothing but the roar of anxiety like an untamed ocean within his being. By the end of the day they had come back and gone, leaving Luther and Mona with the violated nest down in the garage, because nature had to have its way.

Then the other thing went and happened when it could, to give the summer further and shocking and long-lasting impact and new and conclusive proof that the world offered no protection from reckless resolve, a falling tree failing to strike the Pine Hill Trailways bus, if only by inches, not from forbearance but only because life had other ways to let him know what was what, this on a storm-filled day that didn't drive the fishermen to leave the Esopus for indoor pulls on their pipes. Because the fishermen were old enough to know what was needed to get to the end and not induce it. They might not be doing their business on the avenue, but no one could say they were ghosts in their own placid plaid shirt existence either.

The bus sometimes spinning, sometimes planing, sometimes parting the waters that the heavens had bestowed, the driver obdurate in his will to see the vehicle through, all along holding to the American fiction that metal was tougher than anything the clouds could bring.

Mona had not banished him. A council of the righteous had not formed. No decree of ostracism had been proclaimed. The disgust she showed on the day of the slap had faded, and now he was back in reasonable standing with her in the life he had to have. If Scale Master Sid Nizer had gone and done his thing on her, she wouldn't say and was fiercely resistant to his attempt to launch a fact-finding mission.

Later, he would say that he had experienced a premonition, had seen her face in the branches of the trees as the bus followed the curving road along the Esopus River. He would claim this vision in a rush of intensity to signify what? That he had special and prophetic powers? That he was simpatico with her? What he did not say was that he had been the very picture of a swivel head, drawn to the swell of the melon breasts under the Indian print blouse of the girl across the aisle.

Luther's thoughts turned to the driver, and more specifically his flattop head of hair, by which he signaled himself as a bulldog-faced symbol of resistance to the hairy horde. "I do not mind your stance of resistance. In fact I have roots in who you are and see the wound your heart has received that the young 'uns cannot hold the country dear in their hearts as you do. Your fury is your song of love, you who have paid the price in service to your country and sequester yourself in peeve outside the bounds of young love."

The bus passed the jeep at the bottom of the hollow road. Mona sat at the wheel with Lydia beside her. He did wonder that Mona's mother should be part of the welcoming committee but let the thought go.

The storm having spent itself, Luther lit a cigarette as the bus tore away from the shoulder. Mona was now leaning against the jeep, her arms tight around her. Fear found him that he was a perfect stranger to the one he loved and the hint of fall coolness in the air hinting at the hammer blows the new season might bring.

Lydia came toward him. In that moment there was nothing for him to contemplate, the universe simply compelling him to bear witness to her arrival.

"Dear sweet architect of our adversity, you who are so profoundly implicated in the unfolding, our Precious is dead, dead, as dead as the flowers of yesteryear yet fresh in our memory. Forever, I said. Forever and ever. Do you understand?"

The cigarette he had only just lit fell from his mouth.

"Your mouth is agape and so is your mind as it absorbs the truth that reality imposes on all of us. Actions do have consequences." She picked up his cigarette and dragged on it.

"We are talking about what now?" he asked, because she was not coming at him plain.

"My baby Lenore, gone," she said, giving him the plainness he had requested.

A sleek ambulance hearse, black so there would be no confusion, and with curtained windows, at that moment glided down the hollow road, as if on a cushion of air, should a visual be needed to affirm the veracity of her statement.

Here is the history as it was presented to Luther. There had been Lenore's trip to the city the week before in the hope that Casey would resume seeing her so 1968 could be 1967 all over again. She had not seen the *Umbrellas of Cherbourg*. She had not read that dreadful maxim of La Rochefoucauld—"Whom one has loved once one cannot love again." She had no mind for the remorselessness of time at her young age. She was the full captive of her blind longing. She stayed at the apartment with Claire and when Casey came calling she left the door of the medicine chest in the bathroom open, thinking he could see the darkness in her mind casting a shroud over the entire premises and a red light flashing on the amber bottle of barbiturates in that medicine chest. He was more circumspect. He did not talk in his boastful way about the East Village girls who could move their boxes and showed a sober face when he said he could not see her in the old way. Reader, you must understand that she could not get relief from a book or TV or the sky or the trees of Riverside Park that were awaiting anxiously her inspection. Nor did she need rock and roll to be an accomplice to her pain in the bottom dwelling sphere she now inhabited. She spoke of taking her life. She called it going to sleep and Casey recounted that the room filled with a black cloud that prompted him to dash out the door. That was Casey's testimony when Claire called him with the news. Great rivers did he cry, she said.

The morning of the afternoon Luther arrived at Camp Lenore had gone missing, some days after her trip to New York City. Claire had seen the open medicine chest in the cabinet. More alarming, she had seen the open and empty bottle of sleeping pills by the sink. The family searched far and wide on the property.

Everett, the caretaker, found her passed out on a bed of pine needles, what Peter at another time called coniferous duff. He tried mouth to mouth resuscitation but she was gone.

"Don't feel obligated to stay. We would be pleased if you would, but you are not a war criminal." Lydia turned her cigarette into ash with a strong draw that left her with only the filter, then blew out a complicated pattern of smoke, leaving Luther time to think. His continued presence, she seemed to be saying, would be appreciated. But was it enough to be wanted? Did he not also need to be needed?

Death had its own slow unfolding. Sometimes it was there and then it left you to stare at the clouds but you were never really free. You were still in its province. It lifted you out of your normal context. You were allowed little journeys and then you returned. Someone was dead. What did it mean? It was like trying to put your arms around a greased beach ball. It was like nothing.

The phone rang and rang, people calling, legions of the innocents offering their tender expressions of sorrow, all of them drawn by the Radcliffe radiance of Lydia. She showed phone excellence, handling the condolence callers with grace and appreciation, having the need to stay up before she could go down down to the ground of her sorrow and be able to build to self-perpetuating rage. Ethel Kennedy came to Luther's afflicted mind. She had lost her boy, her tiger that only she could tame with the receipt of his sexual energy in their matrimonial bed.

"What is this sweet pain?" he inquired of the apple tree. "One thing gets in the way of my understanding. She was the smart one and he the dumb head. She could have gone to Vassar and he was only Slippery Rock U. material. How is it she didn't trounce him?"

But the tree stood strong and silent, continuing to offer its presence and that alone, as predictable as the taste of dirt. Mona was not weepy—she shed no tears that Luther could see—but neither did she pass under the triumphal arch and proclaim herself number one in all the universe. She too had been a searching streaker supreme when the call went out that Lenore was missing. She had no strategies in place for home rule. Desperation was her fuel, as it was for the others. Even slow-motion Everett had quickness in his step. Was it not enough that she had been roused from her oils and turps, that she had been able to establish priority even without the shattering aspect of eternity to bring her fully sober? She was only aware of the gruesome suddenness of it all.

"We all killed her," Mona later said emphatically. She had no need of written reports or studies not yet made.

The Van Dines had no church affiliation, but they did have a phone book, and the call went out to a man who had spent many years in the empty spaces of a Catskill Mountain house of worship. He was often visited by the unwelcome phrase *the sad rituals of perfectionistic children.* Loneliness lived in his thin white bones, but he did have a car from which to cast a desultory look at the life he had not lived, and so it was with some eagerness that he drove over and rattled the little wooden bridge and conducted a service for the girl he did not know.

"Blessed are those who mourn, for they shall be comforted.They will walk through the valley of death but fear no evil." So Pastor Jenkinsby spoke, there in the living room, while keeping his whiteness and his Adam's apple and his gray hair intact, Peter not failing to observe him through his silence and seeing the man's dispirited faith that only confirmed his own, because if God did not exist, then time had to, and the only way to handle the canvas of the unfolding thing was to nail it to the wall with the tacks of fact.

The meditation on life and the absence of life brought on in Luther the need for a good pee, one that he sensed would give him real pleasure despite the awkwardness of excusing himself in the midst of such an occasion. (This was not a gathering for the sitting.) Though he did arrive back in time for the conclusion, his return had the sound of a still flushing toilet for an accompaniment. This was not right, Luther understood, his disregard of decorum going on while the urn rested on the mantelpiece, waiting to be dealt with so they could look elsewhere for her return.

> Daddy, do not think I love you just because you have blond hair. I could love you very much without it. It is not personal to you that I am going away not to think. I am with you always even if you think you cannot find me. But Daddy, you must break down, and Mommy, you must break free

and Claire and Mona and Jeff, you all must run toward your own survival.

From the urn she said that the cremation had been purifying and that everyone should be reduced to essence. A plain stone marker marked the woodland spot, though a headstone had been ordered. There was nothing, not mountain peaks or low-lying valleys, to save them now, a voice was heard to say.

These were those who came to the service and the burial, very much fewer in number than the callers who had expressed heartfelt sorrow. Fred Waring and his wife Alicia drove up in a VW bus, the roomy interior suggesting that it would someday soon be filled with family. Fred said his past was full of strife, but that his new wife was a game changer. The ex, he said, he had pummeled and blistered with his tongue in fits of professional envy. When questioned closely, he said he beat her black and blue and threw her down stairs and found it most effective to bang her head against the walls. This he acknowledged in an exclusive interview with Luther.

"You see," he said, in an expansive moment, "I do not have to assault my new wife. She is blessed with a high IQ and has a penchant for chess but no career ambitions, and so poses no threat to me."

Luther shared that he deeply understood where Fred Waring was coming from, that he too had experienced feeling ugly on the inside and on the outside as well, with a misshapen head like Fred Waring's and the face of a squalling baby, also like Fred Waring.

"You look, if I may say, like a man in the middle of an excruciating bowel movement," Luther went on. "But the thing is that you have a real man's experience." Fred Waring had been in the service in Korea when the country was at war with itself and the United States.

"Would you run your name by me again?"

"Luther. As in Martin Luther. Lex Luther. Lucifer."

Fred Waring seemed to have stalled in his desire to come forward, but Luther heard him rise out of his momentary torpor with the following: "Don't you have any life of your own that you have to be around these people all the time?"

"That is a question to be asked, if at all, after I do have something more in my life. For right now I am in the totality of my existence."

Luther took a healthy gulp of the wine he had been drinking, keeping an eye on Fred Waring as he did. Fred Waring, despite his doughy face and receding hairline, took this as a cue to move further forward with the truth of his life, the dialogue deepening as Alicia stayed out of it, large in her frame and ready as she was to have his baby, something his ex-wife could not provide, not because she got thrown down stairs but because she didn't want to, having sealed herself off from motherhood in the way that Mona swore to as well.

That evening the nature of Fred Waring further manifested, Luther going into deep shock over what he saw and astonishment that others weren't seeing it as well. Fred Waring, a job man, was acting with false deference toward Peter when posing questions about national and international affairs; he was only feigning interest in Peter's predictable answers. Luther, his listening devices in place, heard Fred Waring think: "I have a job. Why don't *you?*"

Luther put his hands to his ears and shut his eyes, the only alternative to Fred Warning's derision being to bolt from the room. It made him want to die to witness people from the world, people who had jobs, being mean to the Van Dines, who had no jobs, especially in their time of tragic trouble.

Finally, when he could take it no more, he jumped up and confronted the falseness of Fred Waring. "Change your face and change it now, buddy. Otherwise you and I have to fight, and I am tough from way back."

Fred Waring looked to Lydia for help, and Lydia was forthcoming. "He's just upset. He processes information in the way that he can. Luther, maybe a walk in the night air would help you."

"On the contrary, I must very much stay here if I am to monitor events."

"Very good. Then maybe you could be seated. You're scaring Fred and everybody else."

"He doesn't scare me. He does something else, though," Claire said, causing Luther to pull up his shirt.

"Am I bleeding, or do I show myself still whole?" he asked. And when no response was forthcoming, he could say with confidence and satisfaction, "Case closed. Case very much closed."

"Luther, do sit down now." Lydia had added sternness to her voice.

Luther did as he was told, but sat on the chair's edge to convey that his vigilance level was still incredibly high. "Don't go there, baby. Rearrange that thought," he instructed Fred Waring.

"No, Luther, no," Lydia protested. "I must ask you to leave the room if you won't behave."

Luther stood up and backed away. "I'll be watching you, Mr. Waring, from wherever I am, whether from the lonely height of the man on the moon or the very next room. Neither space nor walls will protect you. Think about that. Because I come to you with knowledge of what the word *mockery* means."

All that night Luther sat on the front porch, hearing the raccoons scrounging about and the porcupines snarfing up the garden hose and the constant grasshopper chorus. The stars were out, only giving the appearance of closeness. He was waiting for some sign, having heard the term "particle physics" but Lenore was not to be found, not in any of the places that he could think to put his eyes.

At dawn he was shaken awake by Lydia, who found him asleep on the porch sofa. The morning coolness had brought him to shivering, and he followed Lydia inside to the kitchen, where he sat with her over coffee, she needing to prepare her mouth for the first of the morning's smokes, which she was in no way ready to do without.

"I'm a bum. I exist within all the parameters of bumminess," he said, drowsily.

"Are you really a bum, Luther?"

"Everyone's a bum. God is the biggest bum of all."

"Why is God a bum?"

"Because he's never around."

"Talk to me, Luther. Talk to me. Life is about more than attack. Life is about love."

"Don't kiss me when you speak."

"What can that possibly mean? You are a good person, and must learn to act like a good person. Some plants or a pet would help you."

"I can hardly take care of myself."

"You must give to survive. You must keep giving. That is how we grow."

"I feel you weighing in on me with your softness. I feel it all the time."

"Are you trying to say something to me, Luther?"

The coffee captured his whole mouth. Lydia made fine dinners and desserts but everyone was on his own when it came to coffee. Only instant was on offer. Was she saying who she was by this act of incompletion? Luther didn't pretend to know.

"Where is Lenore?"

"What?"

"I am a detective of the truth. That is all. They say that the good die young. That can only mean the bad live on. Because you have to have the blood of rats to keep going. You have to be able to exist on offal. You cannot be delicate and survive. Lenore could not live on offal. She was not born for offal. And so now she has to sleep with the dirt."

"Why don't you talk about yourself, Luther? Why don't you tell us who you are?"

"I am strong, and I make men less strong than me cry."

"But that's not really saying anything, is it, Luther? Tell me about your father, for example. Do you love your father?"

"I killed my father long ago and hid him in a place where no one could find him. That's why I'm with Mona. You know that, so all the fathers in the land can be in a state of fear and trembling."

"But you mean that you killed your father symbolically. It's not as if you actually are Oedipus."

Luther looked at her blankly, having forgotten his initial conversation with Lydia the year before.

"You've heard of the Oedipus complex?"

"Sure I have."

"It's always useful to have insights into ourselves, Luther, to know the forces that drive us and the things that hold us back."

"Would you like to kill Peter? Is that it? Is Peter the thing holding you back? Because that is the thing that separates you from Mona. While she is at war with the patriarch, you are in collusion with him. Is it painful to know that you are a patriarchal woman?"

"My baby is dead and you talk about killing." Lydia's hands shook. They had been shaking all along.

"You told me when I got off the bus that I had killed her."

"Yes, that is true. All you men killed her by taking a piece of her and not putting it back, and for that you are responsible, the reason women exist at all being to make men feel guilty over the callousness of their actions. What other wound is a woman to inflict on a man, unless she is to murder him in his bed or poison his food?"

"Yes, yes, I fully understand where you are coming from," Luther said. "And it is heartening to hear that others have been implicated as well."

"Others have been implicated, and the consequences will run deep and severe for them," Lydia would only say, married now to her cigarette and the complicated smoke her wide mouth was able to expel.

He watched her devouring mouth with nothing like detachment.

"Feed the face, Luther. Feed the face," she said, sensing his attention to her thing of prominence.

"I feed it with liquids. They help me grow strong all different ways."

"Don't be afraid of me, Luther. I won't kill you. I was not standing there with a knife and my hair down that night you got so frightened. It was just your LSD imagination, dear emaciated young man."

Luther jumped up, only to sit down again, captured by the terrifying truth of her. "I am ready at all times for your action. I am up to any challenge you can muster. I see in my sleep. Get no funny ideas about what you can do with my life."

"You're afraid of needing me, Luther."

"I'm afraid of nothing. I kill everything that gets in my way."

"It's called youthful bluster. That's all it is. I won't swallow you whole."

It was true that he had been pulled toward her by a need for understanding and was seeking the softness of her, even if debilitation awaited him.

"I know what it was for Lenore to need to die because her boyfriend had left her for the girls of the East Village. I know what blackness would look like if Mona left me."

"Perhaps you will see a therapist," Lydia said.

"I will not have people playing with my mind, since my mother says they are full of their own foolishness and worse."

But the thought of someone to talk to about his raging anxiety was comforting. The money was another matter. "You should not tell me of the things that are out of the reach of my own life," he said.

"Why is that?' she asked.

"Because I have listening devices that pick up the sounds of hope, and that is so very painful."

"Yes," Lydia said. "Very yes yes." A pained smile came to her face when she finished with her mockery of him.

Chapter 51

After the bells had stopped tolling in his head for Lenore and before she had locked him into silence for the long run toward meeting her once again, he had an urge to talk of her in some way that would call attention to his life outside the normal flow of what it was, as if death had conferred on him a specialness that could put a halt to action and allow him to just be. And so, with the fact that the trains from Penn Station were running on or close to schedule, offering themselves as aspects of the puzzle, and Pentamente Zualo continuing on the scene as an exemplar of ambition, Luther could come forward, bridging the gap between Connecticut and New York with the reality of Lenore. Because a middle class girl with the laughing intellect to augment the physical had vanished from visible existence even as a banner reading *August* flapped strong and prominent in the Manhattan wind.

"Well, that's something, all right. It would be hard to top without pulling out all the stops, so I have to concede that you're number one for right now, but I'll tell you what. I believe in decisive action and it is my firm conviction that there is nothing more profound than the sweet power of work. Karate chop all unpleasantness out of your mind. Forward is the only motion. That is my motto." That was Pentamente Zualo talking, strong in the gingham shirt and tie he wore with his jeans and command post blazer, as if he were the highway itself as well as the things rushing past on it in the express lane to nowhere. He got back to the task at hand, calling a meeting and sweeping the indicator stick over a map of the area.

"I've got three words for all of you. Just three words. Full court press. Full court press.. Let's bend those knees and keep our hands up," he said, offering up a dream for the benighted, the shiftless, and those who just happened to be there.

Luther wrote a note on thin air to Pentamente Zualo.

> I must have left you behind in another time and place. I would surely be you if I hadn't grown this way to be, the drum of my generation beating very loud with its askance look and causing me to stand apart while recognizing your industrial strength, so that I cannot love you, except in the secret admiration society place.

A letter of the personal kind, not a utility or phone bill, came to him, with handwriting proclaiming its importance.

> I want you to have this check in a modest amount for the priceless support you gave the family and me, and in spite of the crime you acknowledge yourself to have committed. Frankly, I give you this check in contempt for all I have ever owned and the pass that it has brought me to in having to reckon with my child's departure. Because this has been wrought, the lash must be severe, and no one will consider it the crime of the century if I ask you to take your share of the punishment. Let it also be said that I have registered your use of the word *patriarchy* and am filing it in my system for future use. I will always be at the service of men; my needs are too great. No one should ever be asked to join your lost

and unnamed cause. Left to your own devices, you can only end up sleeping in the rain while believing, with your delusional tendencies so strong, that the sun is shining down.

The name of the doctor I have in mind for you is Bertram Z. Bernard. His education has taken place in Basel and Vienna and Cambridge (England *and* Massachusetts). His speech is not fiery and in manner he is not flamboyant. He is simply a steady seeker of the truth, and a special ball bearing system keeps him in constant equipoise as he mines your case for aspects of preciousness to build the new you that is in need of if not seeking to come out. You are not my heart's desire. You could never be any woman's first choice, given the reediness of your neck and the other impoverished dimensions of your physique. Your birth was clearly the afterthought of a tired man and woman, who had spent themselves more generously on the ones who came before. Nevertheless, you have a serious if demented quality, which could under some circumstances, if no one else were around, exert a pull. The good doctor's office is 890 Fifth Avenue. I am sure he will give you a free consultation if you simply mention the family name, And I will be greatly insulted if you do not get well, now that I have given you permission to do so. Lydia

While waiting to be called by Dr. Bertram Bernard into his office, Luther sought to get composed in the event the doctor was observing him through a peephole in the wall, it being a beautiful day on Fifth Avenue with the air conditioners in place and doormen maintaining their positions. Luther held the *New Yorker* close to his face, peering over the top of it when a tall, elegant woman in a black dress and heels and stockings that swished emerged from behind the door, behind which the dark things of life could get discussed so she could have the face she now had.

"I wouldn't need him if I had you. Take me home immediately and cause me to be your slave," Luther said to the startled woman. "Because a bra is a thing of endless mystery and I haven't yet seen yours and a mission isn't complete until the objective is reached." He let his tongue hang down as far as it would go and the woman rushed off, leaving him in a state of longing for her imagined warmth.

The doctor wore a French blue shirt and black blazer and a tie with a fat knot and a dimple to show it off. The equally black frames of his glasses came on strong to flatter his face.

"Mr. Garatdjian? Have I pronounced it properly?"

"You are doing fine. My father's name is a source of trouble beyond the pronunciation of it."

"How is that?"

"It brings with it all the annihilating forces that came before him in the turmoil of the world."

"Your father is alive?"

"He says he is ready to die at any time so he can step into life everlasting, because the bodies of his kin were left to rot in the burning sun on the trek to Damascus in a time that does not have to exist if I stay within the bounds of America and simply hug my box of Tide. Because we talk the language of Houston control, not naked men and women and children baking to death in the deserts of Aleppo."

"So your father is Armenian?"

"He says he is from the land of rats."

"Why do you call it the land of rats?"

"Everyone knows of us, and that is why we have been so badly beaten, because who wants a squealing, tottering rat around given the insatiableness of their drives? Rats need to be poisoned, stabbed, hacked, sliced and diced, defenestrated (this does not always work), and burned on large fires."

"Why are you here?"

"Unlike Lenore, I do not have it in me to decease myself."

"And who exactly is Lenore?"

"A young family member who left them unannounced."

"She took her life?"

"To disappear forever is a savage thing."

A brief silence followed. 'What can I do for you? I still have no clear picture of how I can help you. The girl Lenore. Was she your girlfriend?"

"Oh no, that she could never be, but she was definitely an object of my lust and love commingled."

"And you are grieving her loss now?"

"Do not lead us into sissy talk. I'm angry that she went away. What a waste. But I also understand what it is to feel that you can't live without some person, the way she could not live without her Adonis boyfriend. You see, he left her so he could be with the girls of the East Village."

"Are you in a relationship that troubles you?"

"Oh very much yes. Mona is America and I am not and how to keep her within the confines of my own borders is always a problem, seeing that she lulls my guards to sleep and breaks free to have the action that she wants."

"Would you say that you have this fear a lot?"

"America is America, and to be so gloriously connected to it through her makes for the possibility of a loss I could not bear. Her power over me is frightening and finding other girls only temporarily relieves this fear. She has taken over my whole life. I don't have a minute when I'm not thinking about her—where she is, what she is doing, what she is going to do. Just last month she went off with the Scale Master."

"Scale Master?"

"Brooklyn Sid Nizer. He was born without a mother so he could grow strong and wear a mustache with impunity."

Again a strong silence fell. Dr. Bernard had gone into noticeable hand action, with both doing the mushy against his well-shaven cheeks to heighten the sense of concentration coming from his presumably engaged mind. There was no boldness to the look, just a meditative quality.

Luther went against the silence. "I feel very weak and afraid most of the time, and that I should change my name to Hanging String and attach myself high up on a lamppost where no one will look to see me. I have never gone public with this fear before, and so it is very good to be able to say it. I do so very wish I could rip it from my essence."

But the doctor had a mighty fortress for a mind, his hands now part of his face and his glasses coming into greater prominence. The eyes small and hard behind the treated lenses saying he could put Luther in the confines of his knowledge and keep him there.

"You suffer from a condition I will call morbid dependency."

"You have named what ails me, and in truth it brings me great comfort. But what do I do about such a thing?" Luther asked, hearing an echo of his mother in his words.

"You can see me once a week. My rate is thirty-five dollars per session."

"Sir, I am from the B class of life while your glasses and your tie mark you as a man of distinction."

"You are in need of a major personality overhaul if you wish to go somewhere with your life."

"Sir, you are crushing me with your words." Hearing himself, Luther flared up. "You are not God in the focus you would apply to my life, nor are you the whore of Babylon. You are just a well-dressed soul who eats sandwiches and hot soup on his way to death."

"Our time is up," Dr. Bernard said, and showed Luther to the door.

The next week, Luther received in the mail a windowed envelope that contained a bill that made him cry and cry, for the bill was from Dr. Bertram Bernard in the amount of thirty-five dollars, with the handwritten words "Fork it over pronto" written in thick black ink and underscored. Luther's tears were prompted by genuine sadness and hurt that Lydia Van Dine could somehow believe the business of America would be suspended and Luther would not have to pay a consultation fee simply by the mention of her name. If the Van Dines had no lock on reality, then where was it to be found?

Chapter 52

Luke was ready for Luther and Mona with a mug full of wine in his hand. He offered Mona a pour but she declined. It was early afternoon, and plain from the warmth of the unmade bed where Luther and Mona sat and the sleep smell in the close air that Luke had just gotten up. Luther could only watch as his brother positioned a chair next to Mona so he could face her eye to eye.

"He worries about you, you know," Luke said to Mona. "He thinks you're going to leave him. It's something he tries to hide. You see, he knows you have all the power. It took him two years to get over this girl he was seeing all through high school. He lived like a monk after she broke up with him. The one in the family he's most like is my older sister Rachel. She's smart but she's crazy. Every year she winds up in Bellevue, which is where he is headed. You should think about being with someone more stable and with a pad of his own and a little more to offer in the physical department. You have to know by now that he doesn't have the right apparatus."

Luther had been rendered silent by his brother's boldness.

Mona jumped up to increase her apartness. Luke took it in stride and with the understanding that his time would come. His Adam's apple bobbed as he downed the contents of the mug.

"Let's go out on the roof. I want to show you my thing," Luke whispered.

From the chimney came the acrid smell of smoke from the basement incinerator. For a moment Luther stared, as he often did, at the Riverside Church and its huge bell tower, and beyond to the silvery George Washington Bridge. It was always best to look north and west, to that which would take him away from the city and toward the full adventure of America, especially golden California, even if he hadn't gotten there yet.

Luke removed the tarp to give the bike its full exposure, a 500 cc. machine of silver sleekness on its kickstand. Luther's mother arrived from nowhere to plead with Luke to remove the motorcycle from the roof. The fire marshals would come, she said, and give the building another enormous fine. Luke merely laughed at her distress and threw her off the roof, but she came flying back and so he had to throw her off in another direction. No one could account for the turmoil of their relationship, and violence only temporarily gave him the upper hand.

"Every night I bring it up here in the elevator. I can't sleep knowing my baby's down on the street at the mercy of thieves." He downed some more wine, having brought the bottle along. Luther saw the wine dribble on Luke's T-shirt as his brother opened the gas valve and primed the engine and brought it to life on the second kick and did a terrifying wheelie, the machine almost perpendicular to the ground and Luke's spine, the totality of it, on the line, before coming down from his zone of reckless pleasure.

Mrs. Garatdjian flew back over the roof to stand before them, saying, "We cannot have this here. We cannot," meaning the fire department, the threat of life falling apart, the looming street, the hooliganism and anarchy she sensed in the loosened fabric of city life. Once more Luke disposed of her, jumping onto the parapet to laugh and laugh and beat his chest at the temporary liberation that he felt.

"Now get on," he said, grabbing hold of Luther and hoisting him onto the seat of the motorcycle.

"What?"

Luke shoved the machine off the kickstand. "Now pull in the clutch and turn the throttle. Gas it. And as you do, hold in the clutch until you've slipped into first gear with your foot."

Luther heard the click as he depressed the gear pedal. The machine flew forward, the distance between him and the low retaining wall vanishing. He saw himself as a human projectile going over the roof because impact was sure to send you forward into a thirteen story plunge, but his hand had locked onto the throttle. The front wheel slammed into the three-foot retaining wall. It was beyond his imagining that the impact would jolt his hand free of the throttle, that the bike would stall out, and or that he would fall sideways, not forward, with the bike on top of him.

"What the fuck, man. What the fuck. You all right?" Luke pulled the bike upright as Luther slowly got to his feet. Seeing the grin on his brother's face, Luther stepped back and grabbed Mona's hand and ran with her back inside the building and down the stairs to a lower floor, where they waited for the elevator. He had received his warning. Now all he wanted was to be free for his life.

Chapter 53

It was not for Luther to take his rooftop debacle lying down so he would live as a traumatized doormat into eternity. He got strong and did a perfect figure eight to earn his motorcycle license and bought himself a copy of *Buy-Lines* so he could have the merchandising information that he needed, people selling so they could buy some more or people selling just so they could live. He did not begrudge them their involvement with the world of commodity. He too was suddenly eager for a vehicle rugged and shiny that could take him great distances while giving him power to boot. The ad he saw, for a BMW R-60 motorcycle in excellent condition and with low mileage, claimed him for its own with its stamp of authentic quality.

The seller, Delray Duncan, drove up from Brooklyn, chunky and aggressive in loose-fitting denim overalls. He spritzed Luther with talk about the overhead camshaft and bore and stroke and transmission ratios. Luther sat on the buddy seat and told him how his brother had sent him on a mission of death. Delray dragged him off the machine by his hair and banged his head against a lamppost. "It's the way of the world, man," he said, there by the Henry Hudson River Parkway.

They watched a giant gray rat feed on the face and neck of a giant turtle, before squeezing its cartilaginous self into the shell to feed on its innards in a demonstration of what it meant to live on the earth. When it came back out of the turtle's shell, the man booted it over the revetment and into the river with a powerful kick that sent it kerplop into the scuzzy water to take its place with the scumbags and the fecal matter and the urine of New York City.

"Sooner or later it will be coming back for you. It will track you down to your home and gnaw on your nose as you sleep and devour your lips and enter through your mouth and come out through your ass, eradicating your digestive tract as it goes."

Delray gave him a hard and disdainful nougie to the back of his head, causing Luther to yelp and rush with a tender hand to the aching spot. "Why?" But the man was from Brooklyn. He knew the power of that one word, the *r* sneaking in and fortifying the *B* and the double *o* offering a sleek Modigliani belly and then the chunky *k* to trigger the cataclysm of consonants to elevate the name out of the category of word and into the realm of something else—Midwood, Bensonhurst, Bay Ridge, Cobble Hill, Montague Street—that no one could fully explain, only sense in its rich differentness from Manhattan. Luther scanning Delray's pockmarked face and wanting to kiss his worldly-wise eyes. "Oh yes, you are very much from Brooklyn in the action that you show me, while I am just a tall and decorative tree with Manhattan roots. Indians once roamed this land. Why are we now blowing exhaust on their unseen burial sites?" The cars ferocious in their assault on the roadway.

The man grabbed him hard by the shirt, causing a button to pop. "Look, do you want the fucking thing or not? I don't care about your Indians, and you don't either."

Luther raised a trembling hand to Delray's face, but he kachunked it away with a blow to the wrist.

"Yes, with every fearful thing in me," Luther cried out.

Delray picked him up and slammed him onto the buddy seat and drove him to the notary public so the wedding of machine and man could take place on Delray time.

Luther drove about the streets of Manhattan in a state of fearful ecstasy. He was now Helmet Head, as protective gear had become state law, if not the law of the land. No more with the wind mussing the wild hair of Motorcycle Men. He had a conscience. He was not to psychopathy born, and yet it was of no great concern to him that he had allocated the money Lydia gave him for therapy to the machine his legs now straddled. And there Lydia was, on Riverside Drive, in the company of an older woman, a longtime friend of the family named Molly—Molly of the white hair and one of the little people orbiting around the Van Dines, a single woman with a rent-controlled apartment and a lifetime of secretarial work behind her, a woman who came to them with her small talk and received what love they could give. A woman who lived in the void of singleness, preparing her solitary meals and struggling always to reach the level ground of certainty that her life as it was was all right, that she did not need a flock of kids and a hubby and a 900-acre country place to establish the fact of her self-worth. She saw Luther firing his judgment bullets and understood that he was just young and stupid. She watched as he removed his helmet and cupped his ears to better hear the chorus of the minions that had begun to sing, in voices undetectable to the Van Dines. It was a song of schadenfreude at the ache of the family's loss, for it eased temporarily the ache of their own perceived deprivation, it lessened their pain at the quasi-lives they lived, in figurative proximity to the gas fumes of the Port Authority Bus Terminal, which they were only a missed paycheck or two from living in. They sang with soft intensity, their cells fevered by the drama that had enriched their lives.

Luther stared at Lydia and Molly not with eyes of compassion. He saw histrionics where there was only pain, saying of her, Even with death as her companion she is an actress supreme, taking attention unto herself when it should rightly go to me. He felt his own hardness. *You with your worldly goods, feel what it is to step into the void with nothing.* And yet her unsteady gait revealed the depth of her loss. He saw that he was looking at an inconsolably bereft woman.

Molly called him over only to confide that we were here on the earth to help and love each other, but that he would have to live out his sickness sufficient to see that.

"Is this thing yours?" Lydia asked, with disdain.

"Oh yes. Oh very yes yes," Luther assured her, holding a steadfast gaze into her wounded eyes. Her hair seemed to have grown whiter still. "Your good money has not gone after bad. It has just gone after the realization of the truth."

"Which is?"

"That I'm a stud for all time now."

"You were going to get some help with the money I gave you."

"Help is what you make it. If a man has a powerful thing between his legs, then what more help could he possibly need? I am Mr. Big Thing now, and no one can possibly leave me. I have got my bases covered to the max."

Seeing Peter come along and in need of further monitoring of the developing situation, Luther placed the motorcycle on its stand and sat on a bench facing the Van Dine building. Peter too appeared unsteady.

Driven by desperation Peter approached as a supplicant. "Is there any way that Mona could stay with you? Lydia needs to be alone as much as possible. I know, believe me I know. I have seen her in this state before. You cannot imagine how dangerous a situation this is for her." Peter did not say it was because her baby was gone. This he did not have to say in the full urgency of his request.

Peter was afraid for Lydia, but he was also afraid for himself. Peter, minus his intellectual achievement, was just like Luther's father, a man totally dependent on a woman for his survival. Whatever the death of a child might mean, particularly a suicide, it did not mean stability. But Luther would be in a dangerous situation if he acquiesced. He wanted to. He felt for Peter. He didn't want to see him out in the cold. He did not want Lydia's clobber power to come out of hiding. He did not want him cut from her umbilical cord, not after all the Dutch solidity of structure Peter had shown. He did not want heartlessness to be abounding. But what was he to do? Exposing Mona to his roommates and that ambience of crumminess for even a few days might mean the end of him as far as she was concerned.

"I don't see how I can," he said, feeling shame at his core for not being able to say yes.

Lydia reappeared with her cloak of gentility fully dropped.

"Is the parasite still here? What creature is this that he keeps coming back when no one but no one wants him?"

It was time to exit. That much was clear. Luther put on his helmet and motored off.

Mona gave him a brief course in family history. With the birth of each child Lydia had experienced a trauma, what the doctors called postpartum depression, which in more severe instances had required electroshock therapy. Gone was her positive, giving nature, the one she first displayed to Peter throwing pebbles up at the window in the yellow house in Cambridge where Peter rented a room after his service in the military. Lydia was living nearby in an apartment. A shoe he found in her icebox and rescued her from a life in the bars. He provided the stability she lacked on her own.

"Mother, you will have your delight in Heaven, but I will be a thing of this earth," Luther said, having called her from a pay phone on a street in lower Manhattan. "You would not recognize me because of the strength that I am showing and the powerful steed I am taming."

"Are you being normal, my son? Are you eating normal food?"

"As much as my mind and body will allow. But it is in my strength that I am approximating normalcy, that is, in the energy that my steed is showing me."

"Do you know that we are living in the last days, son?"

"Mother, I know about thieves, and I know about the night, but do not impose your own timetable upon me, not when I am afflicted with the need to cover all the roadways of New York City and beyond that my black beauty bike will take me, and that I want to eat with a knife and fork for having been made in Germany, the very land of brand-name quality."

"Son, I must go now. Call me soon to tell me you are still alive."

Chapter 54

No one could expose the essence of a Garatdjian more adeptly than a physician. Once again that fall medical checkups were being given in Wingate gym on the North Campus. Everywhere Luther heard the word "underweight." His examining doctor, wearing a lab coat over his gray suit, said he was dangerously thin and that his teeth needed immediate attention.

"If you don't take better care of yourself, you won't live to be twenty-five," the doctor said.

Shaken and feeling hopeless, Luther walked downtown along Broadway. The boulevard declined to One Hundred Twenty-fifth Street, then rose. Above, the subway made a racket going over the el. His steed was garaged. "Sally Go Round the Roses" came from someone's apartment but on this day Luther could not thrill to its mystery and sound. Long knives hid in the shadows of old warehouses and tenements on desolate cobblestone streets whispering that impoverished men and women had loved and worked and fornicated and grown old and fat from too much beer here and did he, Luther, know what it was to live with gold teeth in his mouth? He answered back within the confines of his own mind that he had no such knowledge when truth stepped in to tell him that he would. The bells of Riverside Church began to ring, rising high above his subjective current and seeking to flood him free of his darkness with their purifying and uplift sound. Momentarily he surrendered to their insistent pealing.

Tony Pascual was sitting on a milk crate in the middle of the living room. He had a guitar in hand and wore a floppy velour hat. "She's singing one of my songs," he said, in a whisper.

"Who?" Luther asked.

"Janis, baby, Janis," he said, smacking Luther hard on the arm, with the impunity that said Luther was territory he was free to invade.

"Wow," Luther said.

"She's something, isn't she? They're all of them stealing my music." His joyless laughter brought him just this side of violence at the corruptness of the world. "After a bottle of Southern Comfort she likes to do things for me."

Fat Man was not on the scene anymore. He had put his Fat Man weight on Tony in the Porsche, in his Cambridge flat, in hotel rooms. Fat Man got the BSA motorcycle for Tony that he so much wanted but he did not put him into the pages of *Esquire* and was not pulling any strings that Luther could see to get him into Columbia Business School. The mogul track to which Tony's symbolic logic, the logic that did not need words, would take him, was not materializing. Fat Man became nervous when Tony confided his intimacy with Janis Joplin and the plain fact that young women in Brooklyn did not wear panties just as Manhattan women did not wear bras. Logic dictated that Fat Man drop him when he began coming undone because brokenness was a losing proposition for all involved.

"She makes love to me good and tells me I'm her guitar man. She loves the way I play it all over her. She says she can feel it in the tips of her fingers and down into her toes."

Maybe it was acid deterioration that Tony was suffering from and maybe he could get integrated into life no other way. All Luther knew was that he himself was hitting rock bottom with the scene. He could no longer abide the mirror that Tony was holding up to him or his rumination about the computer in the Columbia engineering building down the block working overtime to program him out of his symbolic logic and to leave him completely symbol-less and reliant on words alone.

The institute was on west 81st Street across the street from the Museum of Natural History, the lawns and plane trees offering a touch of nature in juxtaposition with the things of man, the stuffed animals sleeping at night within the museum walls with people of pedigree helping the world to understand what an animal was and an equestrian statue of Teddy Roosevelt to signify what the burden of whiteness was with him on his horse and the Indians walking behind, the building in its recessed position from west 81st Street never apologizing for the space it took up but radiating happiness, the surroundings knowing it was there for more than the commercial purposes of the island. All through the day and night, buses and cars and long distance trucks drove past, but the turrets never blinked nor were the windows ever heard to groan in despair. Equanimity ruled its entire length and width and height, as if it lived outside of time.

Entering the building housing the institute, Luther thought of Dr. Bertram Bernard with sudden longing for the Fifth Avenue prestige of his office and person, but he could not pay what he could not pay to the busy bee doctor with the powerful glasses.

A woman slid an application through an opening in the Plexiglas window behind which she sat. Luther read the form. *What has brought you here?* It asked. Luther knelt so he could speak through the window opening. The woman had a beehive on her head and makeup on her face, no window serving as a shield from such important facts.

"My life has brought me here. Now give me the doctor and give him to me fast."

The woman flew back in her chair but, having the fortitude that came with the experience of dealing with the likes of him, quickly returned. "Can you be more specific?"

Again Luther went to the opening and shouted, "My penis is too small and my motorcycle, of which I am sometimes afraid, is not compensating."

The woman assessed him properly. "Go sit in the chair and don't get up until you're asked to."

"I will do exactly as I am told, because I am here to get well," Luther said. He sat with his hands folded in the waiting area, trying not to look at the woman and not succeeding, for she showed a shine on her pale skin that said she knew the ways of sex. Suddenly he could take it no more. He rushed to the window hole and shouted, "I know who you are. You are right out of *The Pearl.* You are none other than Lady Pokingham in another lifetime, your days spent amidst furious comings and spendings."

The woman slid back, her chair being on rollers. The phone was in her hand. "Your patient is here. Please come get him," he heard her say. Seeking to have contact with the unavailable one, he did the mushy with his face against the glass, willing her to cast off office decorum for lewdness.

A man with thinning hair and wearing scuffed shoes emerged. His face was white and his teeth were yellow but it was the protruding nose hairs that especially grabbed Luther's attention.

"I am Dr. Coslin. Step into my office so we may begin," he said, Luther scanning his face for the signs of fear—the imperceptible something in the eyes—that would let him slay the doctor before the treatment could ever begin.

"Tell me about yourself," Dr. Coslin said, leaning back in his leather chair. A couple of chairs, a desk. A sterile space.

"I am...Wait a minute. Where are your credentials? Where is the Ivy League degree certifying your competence?" He remembered all the framed diplomas on the wall of Dr. Bertram Bernard, whom he had traded in for a motorcycle. "I am reading your thoughts this very minute: 'You've caught me. I do wear cheap suits. I do lack the intelligence to earn anything more than a master's degree in social work. I do buy my suits at Robert Hall and eat my supper at Nedicks.'"

"Go on."

"I need to get out of where I live while the getting is good."

"What is your present living situation?"

"I live with Tony Pascual, who may be bordering on violence. I can deal with the decline of his infrastructure only so much longer."

"His what?"

"He holds me responsible for killing his cat, which I never touched. And then there is my attachment to a superstar named Mona Van Dine, with whom I am only at best in fragile harmony."

"Fragile harmony?"

"She could tell me any minute that I am a stranger in her land."

"Meaning what?"

"I must fuck with abandon just so I can live. It is the only real homework assignment that I have been given."

"Surely you do other things than pursue women."

"Don't surely me. I read to no avail and put the books on the shelf and feel strong in my deployment of them for only a moment."

"We need to establish a regular schedule of sessions. I recommend that you come twice a week."

"I will see what I can do, " Luther said, chagrined over his treatment of Dr. Coslin but resolved never to go back. Central Park was all the therapy he perhaps needed. He headed for Bethesda Fountain, the park giving him a sense of freedom the City College campus denied him, taking away as it did his dream of his own specialness. The park a refuge from the mediocrity of his academic credentials the campus kept him mindful of.

He climbed onto the retaining wall overlooking the fountain below and the lake beyond, the Dakota and the El Dorado and other towers along Central Park West to his left and Fifth Avenue to his right, and began to flap his arms. Below were stoned and stony longhaired kids sailing a yellow Frisbee back and forth.

His mother and father had met in Central Park, way back when, a chance encounter. Luther imagined him in a straw boater on a summer day. "I don't know what would have happened to me if I hadn't met your mother," he had once said to Luther. This dependency on women. It had a lineage, a history. It hadn't come from nowhere. She had been his refuge from the storm of memory that would visit and afflict him: the parched mouths, the severed breasts, the skulls crushed by axes, the gouged eyes, the braids of Armenian girls doused in kerosene and lit as wicks. "I am not love itself but I am from the wounded past. I am one of the bleeding Armenians who does not bleed. I exist here in America as in a dream that has no bearing on the rancor that bubbles forth to give beauty its opposite. Will you take me for your lawful wedded husband and make of your arms my world? Will you give my wandering a port called love? Will you take my complete collapse and give it a shape?" Luther's mother wept. She wept and wept and rushed into his father's arms and took him unto herself in the brilliance of the sunlit day with industry in abeyance.

Luther bent his knees and continued to flap his outstretched arms but soon ceased. "Not a soul has come to me on this day. Not one, not one, not one," Luther called down to the kids milling about the fountain. "Your indifference does not defeat me. Soon I will metamorphose into the very essence of Park-Man and lose myself in the byways of this great park as I continue to try to win the girls who cling so desperately with their pathetic hardness to your attitude of cool." And so he resumed his flapping, using agile footwork to give the park people both a frontal and dorsal viewing of his wretched plumage. Suddenly he nearly slipped, and grasping the hard reality of the pavement below, he began a slower rotation. From this showing of himself good things began to happen. A girl took the trouble to climb the stairs. She had stars on her face and purple on her lips and said the park was her home too. She said emphatically that she chose uncertainty over the curriculum that her school was offering, and was committed to a life of mutilation. They kissed behind a bush and lovemaking followed. Afterward Luther said she had made him so very happy because she had given him insurance against the pain that would surely come should Mona share her treasure with anyone in faraway Boston.

"How can such a place dare to exist?" he asked aloud, and let the wind blow the question where it would. While his new and temporary friend did not directly respond, she offered nothing in the spirit of contradiction.

He signed up for a 8 a.m. biology course but within a week found himself lost in a world of meiosis and mitosis, amoebas and paramecium. The messiness of lab work in general amid the smell of formaldehyde and the dissection of a frog in particular horrified him. Inwardly he heard himself screaming for the security of Mona.

In the basement cafeteria of Shepard Hall, a gloomy North campus building, he called out, "I see all you science and engineering students with your heads full of *formulae.* I see that you don't have room in your big brains for terms like *morbid dependency.* Your comportment divulges every last thing about you."

"Why are you shouting?" A woman he recognized from the class had come to the table, a pretty woman close to the androgynous ideal he had glimpsed in Lenore.

He stared at her with morning stupor. "Are you a heroin addict?"

"A what?" She nearly spit out her coffee.

"You have small bags under your eyes and facial pallor. Please do not take offense. It is just that I am feeling very low."

"Let me turn the question around. Are you on heroin?"

"I rely on other substances, if you must know. And I must also tell you how your unattainable beauty is making me feel."

"Why are you speaking this way?"

"Oh, I just don't know. I just don't know," Luther said, the woman holding his hand, if only briefly, leaving for the lab before he could pose the question whether she was from Brooklyn and had a mother of her own who loved her as a mother should.

Chapter 55

He wondered whether the cold and relentless rain had something to do with the cloak of anger she now wore, her speech now rife with "fucking pricks" terminology and denunciations of her father, saying "He's got such faggy attitudes toward women." Even with an attitude of doubt as to her assertions, he did not dare to question, let alone argue, against her volatility. He quickly came to accept her fiery blasts as part of her nature. He did not tie the change, at first, to the death of her sister. About her father she had always, in fact, been caustic. It was the extension of her critical viewpoint to others that was new. "We've got a bunch of arrogant pricks at the school. They think women are just here for sleeping with and that they can put them down at will. Men think they can fuck over women any time they please."

When he did finally offer a mild dissent, she grabbed him by the hair and said only this: "I'm not talking about you. It's not always *about* you. Get it?" And all he could say was yes very much yes yes, and stand clear of the salvos fired at the pricks, the fucking pricks, and their hegemonist oppressiveness. Because it *was* a yes very yes yes thing that despite his physical assault and the compulsiveness of his attention to her—the campaign of phone calling from all over New York City, the accusations of infidelity, the tormenting interrogations he led her through, the lengthy discussions of her problems and never his—she saw him as on her side and different from the general run of menfolk in the world.

That fall grief and outrage left her no choice but to swing into action, seeing the power filth of men on display from her apartment window. Down below a Boston policeman was in outright harassment of a young woman who had just happened by, compelling Mona to tear out into the street leaving behind turps and paint and easel and the raw sound of Van Morrison on her record player (never Donovan, never "Wear Your Hair Like Heaven," whom Luther so loved), for the apprehension of evil and what she heard as the cries of a woman suffering the omnipresent affliction of man, such being her rage-fed need to support female excellence and the vanquishing of the pricking fuckers.

The full moon was up when she arrived before the museum's obdurately granite face, saying even then that it was the repository of value beyond what the BoSox and "Under My Thumb" Mick Jagger had to offer. She had her dukes up big for the pulverization of the officer's face, the smashing of all his power with a torrent of rage, but suddenly she felt that the evidence was lacking to justify her soaring vigilance, the flower child of a girl telling her through the amiability of her intercourse that she was only playing with the officer, Mona bringing her nose up close to both to sniff for signs of deceit and coercion, and finding none, backing off, but only slowly, with words of warning that she would return if so required.

In the nightly report that Luther elicited from her—and it was nightly, lest he fall down dying from the separation that had been allowed to occur—he heard her say that the mistake had been hers, but then she darkly added, "You don't know the coercive spell of the pricks. You don't know how it can go unseen. It's right there in the big dick nightsticks they all carry."

Luther flew up in the air on hearing her sound. "Trouble could be headed your way if you seek to monitor the movements of the men in blue. Maybe some restraint is needed." He heard what he had just said with some disbelief.

"I dismiss you in a very big way, Mr. Sudden Voice of Moderation. I say let the fucking pricks be restrained. Let's put those patriarchal bastards on the strongest and shortest of leashes," she said right back.

"Oh yes. Oh very yes yes," Luther said, flying once more into the air at the recognition that in the realm of ideas he was entirely hers to shape as she would.

That fall was a season of unraveling, events he could monitor but was helpless to stop in the progression of time that chose unfolding and disintegration over permanent stasis so it could keep its reputation for heartless maturity. Frank, Claire's boyfriend from the suspect appendage called Long Island, packed up his guitar and went off to some arts college in New Hampshire with no sense of order, for the school had dispensed with the cumulative grade-point index as a way of allowing anarchy to reign. It had no use for the cum. The cum was no big thing. It was limiting, inhibiting. Frank was too Irish for Luther to miss him, but his heart was in turmoil and the need was there to closely question Frank as to how he could take his leave without any seeming attention to the fact that he and Claire would be apart, and the only thing that Luther could ascertain was that Frank had no need to appraise situations for their potentially drastic consequences, namely someone coming along to claim Claire for his own. Luther determining only this—Frank had a case-hardened heart, no tug of longing surfacing to leave him weepy and in the fetal position moaning for the softness of Claire but instead going about his frivolously spent days, leaving Luther no choice but to accept that such coldness was a function of *high intelligence.* In the higher mental realms, in big board-score land, comings and goings were no big deal.

"I will hate you forever for introducing me to this truth," he said to them both, but they had no ears to hear him given the clarity of their vision of what had to be.

Oh the rain came pouring down. Oh it struck the earth so very hard. Oh he became quiet as the chastened child, only to revisit the world as it had to be again and again with his eyes tight shut.

And now a further eruption occurred among the mainstays of his existence, Peter retreating to Camp after Lydia banished him from the Riverside Drive apartment. But she was not done with him. It was for all of Manhattan to hear her scream, "Never mind Camp. Get your own place. Get it now." Then she herself fled to her gnome-like therapist, Dr. Glenlivet, a Jungian of great renown who made of his books a bower of bliss in which she could lie for many, many years. He kissed her with the words *animus, anima,* and *collective unconscious,* and she kissed the god of her understanding right back. Oh how she kissed him, he who had been gone forever but was now here.

Lydia did not denounce Peter. She did not charge him with the death of her daughter. She said that she was tired, that mistakes had been made, and that it was time to take a look. Dr. Glenlivet lived inside her, providing her with the words she needed as he busied himself with the rearrangement of her mind. She spoke haltingly of the thing that had come between her and Peter and turned their lives into parallel lines sufficiently spaced so that even with outstretched hands they could not quite touch.

Luther himself communicated his fear. Such a struggle it was to bear up, he noted to the air, Mona being in Boston, Claire being apart from Frank (and vice versa), and now Lydia rising up strong to give Peter the boot. The Van Dine women were clearly moving out from under male control and would find new men to replace the old. He cast Lydia as a heavy. He could hear his mother saying, "What God has made, let no man rend asunder."

Mona as well spoke up. "My father won't make it. He will crumble and die. Mommy is dumping him on me. She expects me to take care of him as retribution for his manifest love for me over her."

And Peter himself had something to say: "I am the voice crying in the wilderness. I am the real president of the United States. Give me back my throne of delight, you impostors."

All through that fall Luther kept his monitoring devices intact. Over and above her face to face with the police officer, over and above her rage at the fucking pricks, the sense that Mona was extremely depressed came strong to him. He heard her despair that her work was awful, that no one liked her at the school, that Mr. Brooks, with the takeout power of his Yale degree, now was showing signs of infatuation with a new female student. And then there was the boy named Lane, whose eyes sparkled in the Boston night and his plutocrat father. Lane brought her to the point of despair with his displayed brilliance and how he made you want to quit painting altogether given the superstar realm that he had achieved. More than anything there was Lenore, whose absence she grieved. She had not been the older sister she should have been to her gone sibling, she saw now, and struggled in an ocean of sorrow that sought to drown her.

Something was stirring in Luther, causing him to lap Manhattan many times on his motorcycle, and when that got tiresome, to run all around the island on his very own and to collapse, of all places, in the hedges around the Van Dine building, its structure having remained the same while the dynamic of the family had changed through the relentless work of time. From there his feet took him to the Van Dines' front door.

"I have come on a mission of mercy that my sensing devices have alerted me to," he announced, when Lydia opened the door.

"Speak English, foolish one," Lydia replied.

"I am going around and around and suddenly the impulse comes over me to connect with you. It just seemed the very yes thing to do, my whole being glowing with good feeling thinking how you would receive the communication I am about to make."

"Is it about that ridiculous motorcycle you purchased with the money I gave you to seek professional help?"

"I believe I am walking more like a man since purchasing my metal steed."

"Your what? Never mind. What is it you want to tell me?"

And so he gave her his status report on Mona, mainly the incident with the Boston cop and her escalating fulminations against men, causing Lydia to journey into the land of pomposity, saying only this, "I will formulate an action through a consultation with Val, who has deep connections throughout the land," Val being the first name of her therapist, Dr. Glenlivet.

So that with the crying sounds of Mona loud in their minds, even in the state of their shaken empire, they could get it going for her to see someone of quality: a few whispered words, a few nods, a few strokes of gentility, and twice a week she was on the train over to Cambridge and then a bus from an underground terminal near Harvard Square taking her to an outlying community and his private home where he sat her down for succinct analysis, teasing out her pain through his long silences in which his inspection of her every word had his full attention and reference books at the ready should they be needed.

Dr. Greene, his name was, with that little "e" at the end to move it into the realm of quality, and the bolstering action of the first name Thayer so there could be no doubt about the New England distinction he was showing and an innate laconism not concealing but signifying the mighty achievement behind the taciturn front.

Degrees from Harvard blanketed one wall. Not only his, but all his forebears, too. A banner was unfurled across the sky:

New England = crisp intelligence = generations of purposeful lives = frightening reserve in an autumnal setting

Because Dr. Greene shone his omnidirectional eye on earthly proceedings, Luther had no choice but to do the dance of goodness for him so that his worthiness of Mona Van Dine could remain no worse than perilously intact.

"Well, look now, why burden yourself with a boyfriend back in New York, especially one who struck you some months before and continues to have an issue with his anger and who hounds you with his incessant calls?" So Dr. Greene was heard to speak to Mona.

Though Luther was not there to plead his own case, he could take to the air. "All I need for you to say is how splendidly, yes splendidly, I am helping her and adding to her life by the endless vanquishing of the patriarchal forces that afflict the earth."

Dr. Greene fell back into his New England silence. After a maddening delay, he wrote his response, using cloud stuff against the otherwise blue sky:

Ariadne to your Theseus, leading you by the thread out of the labyrinth. Thank your lucky stars, unworthy soul.

Chapter 56

Luther continued to visit, drawn by the necessity of witnessing her beauty and the shrine he had built to it in the crispness of Boston's brand of fall and nighttime darkness trying to believe he would ever be able to put the blocks together that would give him a lock on smartness so he could seal in success. Because until then and perhaps forevermore he would have to go the way of the art that Mona was showing him in her dismissal of the life called academia as cars drove by with their tail lights glowing and the trolley behind the Sears building running past any and all feelings that came over him.

She had a two-room apartment now with a pretty parquet floor along something called Park Drive with a view out on the Fenway. Luther brought along a box camera he had borrowed from his brother. Having no relationship to art except to look at and live beside it, he came as a supplicant with an apparatus that would give him what he wanted without creating it in his need to capture time, to have proof that he had been there with this girl who stared coolly into the lens on a Saturday afternoon. He could not fix the present where it was, but he could have a record that included more than Marlboro flip top boxes versus soft packs. He snapped the shutter many times that afternoon, photos of her on a low wall at the border of the park, on the small bridge over the duck pond, and seated on the steps of the museum. He did so with some guilt, as if he were involved in an activity she had some right to be displeased about, namely stealing from her. The photos were not really "decisive moment" stuff. He had her sit or stand in a certain place, and rushed his shots, fearful that some anger would explode from her at having to pose at all.

He did not flap his wings. He did nothing of the kind. It was Boston after all.

She too had him pose, but because there was no equivalence, he understood that anger was not the thing, that she was launched upon the activity that made her what she was, and so there was nothing but to give himself to it. She put his head at the bottom of the canvas, his trunk in the middle, but showed his feet not at all. And yes she dropped her brush in the can of turps, shaking the brush free from its strong-smelling excess, but he minded not at all being in service to her vision in the way that he could be.

The weekend came and went. She did not designate him a desperado and the amity they had found precluded fighting.

Sooner rather than later the time came for him to be on his way, and she clothed him with a coat not of many colors but of substantial length, an army officer's coat that she thought would dress his thinness up fine and lose him further in his ludicrous but ineradicable narcissism, seeking to send him back to the days when her father had been young in the roiled air over World War II Germany. She also gave him culture so he could approximate a human being, packing him off with the current sound of her heart, a three-record set of the *Brandenburg Concertos*.

To save money, he sought to hitchhike back to New York, lying down in the middle of the entrance ramp off Mass. Avenue, where he was run over by the first few cars that would not have their will for the open road thwarted before a fourth one stopped and took him in. He kissed the driver all up and down his face and told him he was going off to war to fight the Vietcong, that they had bushwhacked enough Americans from all fifty states and now the time had come to put a stop to it.

"You will have to get a haircut," the man said.

"Yes, I am very much afraid of that," Luther said, staring into the darkness. "As afraid of that as I am of the tough VC. My hair has been so good in the protection it has given me."

The man told him he was on his way to a bordering state to kill another woman, that this activity gave him a pleasure beyond belief and placed him beyond the contours of his normal life. He said the urge to kill came over him as a craving and had to be satisfied, that there was a huge sexual release in strangling these women and exerting maximum power over them. He said the experience was truly addictive.

"But don't you have a conscience about what you do?" Luther asked.

"It's a gift to them. I am giving them the release that they are seeking. Believe me, they thank me from the grave."

"Suppose someone killed you?" Luther asked.

"No one cares enough to do that," the man said. "People are far too selfish."

Luther tried to think about the matter. It was a hard and concentrated activity that required strength and perseverance. He did not know what to say to the man, whose face was now blank.

"You could be me. You could move up to the next level. You could usurp God's function and be God himself," the man said.

Massachusetts had disappeared into darkness. All the lights in the state had been turned off or were burning low. Luther felt that he was on the ride of a lifetime, that the car had wings and special rules of engagement. He felt in the presence of a great and corrosive power, of someone who had slipped into another dimension of existence that brought intensity and excitement to every second, that this was a man who did not exist in the sunlight but a blue-lit room sharpening his instruments of destruction while laughing at the mundaneness of most people's lives. The man seemed truly a paradigm of nothingness in his stable, four-door car. Luther felt his hand would go right through the man should he try to touch him, and yet he was there nonetheless.

"Yes yes, I believe I understand. You kill with finality and I am just trying to love women so they won't kill me. I feel so turned around in your dreadful company even if your car is a so very fine Lincoln Continental."

The door flew open and Luther was ejected sideways onto the shoulder of the Connecticut Turnpike. If Massachusetts was dark, Connecticut had no play in it. A steady drizzle began to attack him with its insistent coldness as cars sped past showing the savage disdain that the state was known for. He told them all to kiss his Swedish/Armenian ass. He told them to kiss his skinny thing. He pulled down his pants and mooned the mothers of indifference until the rain forced him to cover up, all of Connecticut daring to laugh at him.

Thirty yards down the road an oil truck had pulled over, road flares showing off redness in the dark to signal breakdown, a trooper now on the scene in his Smoky Stover hat and the apparatus of the state—the gun, the handcuffs, the big fat leather belt and black boots and the gray uniform with black piping on the tight-fitting pants. Did he listen to the Grateful Dead? Did he smoke himself some weed when he wasn't apprehending injustice? These were things Luther just couldn't know without a full investigation, he realized, as his mind turned to questions of state. Was it illegal to hitchhike in Connecticut? Again, he did not know, but he felt frozen to the spot and to even think of walking away would cause the trooper to determine he was guilty. If he stayed in place, the trooper would grasp that he was just a hanging string trying to get back home.

The trooper returned to his cruiser after administering to the oil truck driver and threw it into powerful reverse, zooming backward along the shoulder. He then got out and came around to the other side, where he opened the door. "Get in" he said, through teeth so white.

Luther stared at him with numbness abounding. "I have been waiting for you for such a long, long time."

"I said get in the car." He took Luther by the hair in order to bring him lower and shove him in his wetness into the front seat. State trooper Doug Dell then got in the driver's side, as he very well should have, being that he was in full control.

"The name Doug is short for Douglas. That alone makes you all-American, even as a state trooper, although the name is also a strong reminder of egg salad sandwich left too long in the sun." Luther stared long and hard at the trooper, looking for a hopeful sign.

"Your ass is grass."

Luther sought to explain himself. In an earnest voice he told how he had been visiting his girlfriend up in Boston and was now on his way back to New York City so he could resume the study of the great books he could get his hands on. He felt a driving need to please the officer and to be loved to death in the perception of his non-guilt forever.

"What's your name?" the trooper said, having now in hand the paper he would write on and the ball-point pen he would do it with.

Luther sighed. "I will return into my past, but just for you. The name that I was afflicted with is Garatdjian." He spelled it slowly for the officer. "Now do you see the advantage you have, Mr. Doug Dell, you have given your name a shave and a haircut so you do not have to hide your face behind a bunch of consonants?"

"What kind of name is that?" he asked.

"It is a Connecticut name if you would allow it to be. Oh yes. You must not hate me, for I too qualify for this state, even without the blond hair and the egg-shaped head. I too am a WASP, a white Armenian-Swedish Protestant, and have been readying myself for this meeting with your power for a long long time."

"Shut up," the trooper said, seeking to bat away his words as if they were flies, and tore from his pad a piece of paper he had been writing on and handed it to him.

'What can this be?"

"It's a warning ticket, buddy. You wait here now."

Trooper Dell got out of the car and slammed the door with authority, put on his hat so the rain could not violate his head, and relied on his slicker black as night to keep his uniform dry. He walked back up the road straightening his hat for the interaction he was about to have with the driver of the ailing oil truck

Luther sat with his face in the right position for goodness, thinking that Trooper Dell would drive him to the train station or bus station to ensure that he didn't menace the Interstate with his own code of freedom. Whatever was the reason for the trooper keeping him in place, it was for Luther to model his own innocence as he tried to remember if drugs were upon his person or amid his possessions. He had dropped a speed pill before going out on the Mass. Pike. But had he left a roach in the *Brandenburg Concertos* album, and if so, should he open his bag and throw out the offending material? It was only a matter of unbuckling the straps, opening the case, and flicking the roach into the rainy darkness. Or he could even hide it under the seat of the car, simply shred it into particles so Trooper Dell would not suspect he was driving around with bits of marijuana in his cruiser. But no, Trooper Dell would sense what he was up to and see only a pose of goodness. The faith he had built up with the trooper would be jeopardized; he might then be even rougher on him with heavy action of his hands.

What followed was like one of those childhood dreams in which he enjoyed a big lead over his pursuer but his legs turned to jelly and he could not seem to move. The trooper walked slowly back to the car. He took the bag and shook out the contents onto the front seat. An extra shirt, some underwear, a pair of socks, a copy of *Modern Man in Search of a Soul,* by the very great Carl Jung (on the recommendation of Lydia Van Dine). The officer was more methodical than Luther ever would have imagined, going through his notebook page by page and shaking it, as if something was hiding behind the words and blank pages. He showed the same methodical approach with the record album. Luther felt like a young man regressing into childhood as Trooper Dell took over full control of his things. Luther could only watch as the trooper's scrubbed face, impassive to this point, was suddenly transformed.

The roach he held between his fingertips might just as well have been a precious jewel for the euphoria it unleashed in him. "What is it? What is it?" The repetition occurred a few more times. Luther saying that the thing, whatever it was, had a nebulous look to it, and should not involve the apparatus of the state when murderers were zooming down the interstate with tragic consequences for their victims and the victims' families and loved ones. The trooper showed a malign smile, seeming to take savage delight in Luther's feeble words.

"Get out of the car. Now."

Was Trooper Dell letting him go? Luther could only hope, as he reached for his bag.

"Don't touch anything. Out. Now."

Officer Dell exited from the other side and came around. "Hands behind your back," he barked. The cuffs Officer Dell placed on him bit into his wrists.

"Now I am in fear and trembling. You have your supposed freak, and you have me good."

In a short time they arrived at the state police building in the town of Guilford, where Luther was relieved of his belt and placed in a holding cell. The roach, which he heard referred to as a substance, was dropped into a plastic pouch as evidence. Within an hour he was led from the cell to be fingerprinted, a different officer dipping his fingers in black ink and rolling them over a designated spot on a large form and then pressing his thumbs against the paper, too, so Luther could be on file for whatever the state needed. The fingerprints officer saying, "You know what that is you had in your possession? That is narcotics. You've got a class A felony against you. We have drugs laws around here. You're in Connecticut now," then went back to his newspaper and his cup of coffee and his doughnuts.

Trooper Dell had entered a state of ecstasy that put him three feet off the ground and deep into an accelerating rotation that drew his buddies to him for cop talk.

"At first I thought I was looking at some kind of weird mop, with all that shit he has on his head," he said, Luther's compliance unable to close the gap between them.

The cell was cold. He lay down on the thin mattress. The blanket, also thin, covered only a portion of his body, and had the dirt of others upon it. He got up and stared out through the bars toward the area of light where the desk was located and where the munching of the staff was going on. "I am finding the reality of imprisonment hard to grasp. I can hold onto the fact for moments at a time, but then it slips away only to come back and hit me hard as a sledgehammer. The bars are not soft. They do not bend before my gaze, and no amount of wishing can get me from this chill, spare space back onto the very great Interstate or to my girlfriend Mona's warm bed. If she was everything to me before my confinement, my vision of her now swells. She will come for me. Momma will come for me, and very very soon, and with full righteousness as an answer to your falsehoods."

The cops came to the bars. They stood as men will, with legs spread and hands on hips and meat packed solid on their rugged frames, prideful of their procreative ability and holding to silence. They just stared at Luther as he was before resuming their attention to their doughnuts. They were men, after all, and they were strong for their jobs. And so he lay without the sweet breath of Mona, the iron bars running parallel to each other and never touching and the floor itself made of such manly concrete.

"I will wrap myself tight in my own arms," he said to the men with doughnuts, and did just that, lying down in the dark and softly moaning while all of Connecticut was busy sleeping for the day ahead.

In the morning Trooper Dell was no longer present in his life, having been replaced by Trooper Samuel Johnson, who led him away in cuffs to his cruiser. Trooper Johnson was older than Trooper Dell, and he looked down at Luther with a face full of solemnity.

"So they got you for drugs, huh?"

The fall day was clear and bright and the Interstate only lightly traveled on the trip down to New Haven for arraignment. Luther gave his account, stressing first and foremost that the substance for which he had been busted was a roach and beyond that, what right did Trooper Dell have to search his possessions when he was only hitchhiking?

"That's the thing, isn't it?" Trooper Johnson said, as if all Luther's frantic words were simply confirmation of his point of view. "It would be a nice, beautiful world if we could stop there with a little of that marijuana. The stuff would be just great if you could pick it up and put it down when you pleased. But it doesn't work that way. You go from a little of that to a lot, and then you go on to other drugs, and before you know it, you're shooting heroin."

Trooper Johnson stared straight ahead, as if addressing his words to the windshield and points beyond. Luther saw what he should have seen all along, that Trooper Johnson was not seeing him and that Trooper Dell had not been seeing him and that none of them were seeing him as other than the thing he had become for the purchase of their doughnuts.

Trooper Johnson led him into a big municipal building, where he was placed in a detention pen. A white man in a suit and askew tie had preceded him. In a state of exasperation did he profess his innocence of check-forging charges. "I haven't done a thing, not a thing," he said, over and over, in a yammering frenzy. He seemed to be in shock and too middle class to adjust to his new environment. He looked like he had been yanked out of his office.

Soon another man arrived, young and strong and black, with a bruised face and blood-splattered shirt.

"You looking at something, motherfucking white boy?"

"No, no," Luther murmured.

"Cause if you is, you gonna get a taste of black man power. Ain't gonna be none of that white boy sissy shit fighting. You best hear me. You too, motherfucking suit man."

Luther slumped onto the floor, his back against the wall, and with his head down and eyes closed listened to the roar of the young black man and the white man's keening, in that way passing the time until he was led into the courtroom, where Judge Woodruff Pearsonbester was presiding. What Luther saw was a balding man with a blistered, whiskey face and syphilitic nose lost in his black robes. No, there would be no reduction in bail for either of the defendants, Judge Pearsonbester said and scolded their attorneys saying they were lucky that the bail wasn't being raised. Then he descended from the bench and lifted his robes and gave both defendants flying kicks in the ass and said he hoped that they rotted in the hellhole where they were going. Fully invigorated, he flew back to his station and pounded his desk with both hands around his gavel so order would be supreme. A big red sign flashed "Next" and Luther was led forth to be in the center of the judge's obliterating eye.

"You were taken into custody on a narcotics felony. Are you the one bringing all the heroin into our state?"

"Not so, your honor. Trooper Dell apprehended me unjustly."

"Shut up your heinous mouth. I'm setting bail at five hundred dollars."

"I don't have five hundred dollars," Luther wailed. "You are posing an insurmountable obstacle to my freedom."

"'I don't have five hundred dollars,' the sissy says. What's the matter, business on the street dropping off that you can't come up with five hundred clamatos?" The judge was in the full flowering of his good cheer in being able to put the screws to the one he didn't love, at least for now.

"Sir, sir, you have the affliction of your own self-righteousness. You are not my father. You have no right to be mean with me when I could die because of separation from the one I love. And I am never to be called little except in the dimensions of my mind and my apparatus of pleasure and reproduction."

The judge began the music of his gavel once more, pounding it once, twice, thrice, and when he got a rhythm going pounded with the combined power of his two hands until the head was broken off from the handle. A silence of stupefaction had fallen on the courtroom, for everyone's attention had gone to the man in black.

Luther told the judge once more that he didn't have five hundred dollars, but the judge rose up strong upon him.

"Do you have any earthly possessions?"

"I have a motorcycle. It is German and black and so of the very finest quality," Luther offered.

"Well, sell your goddamn motorcycle. It isn't going to do you any good while you're sitting in a cell."

Luther piped up that he was supposed to be in New York later that week for a court appearance stemming from his arrest that past spring in a demonstration.

"You get yourself in trouble wherever you go, don't you? I'm sick of seeing your kind of privileged filth all over the streets and I'm going to do something about it. Now someone get him the hell out of here before I kick his dirty ass," Judge Pearsonbester roared, rousing the sleepy bailiff to call for officers to usher Luther to his new accommodations.

"I've got friends on the street. I've got Johnny Too Tough. He goes into people's chests on my behalf. He's been caving in chests for me for a long time. You know what I'm saying?"

"Yes, I very much do," Luther said, staring at the lit bare bulb dangling from the ceiling. He had the top tier of the bunk and, with his arm extended, could reach up and touch the bulb. How were sleep and forgetfulness to come with it burning through the night?

"Johnny Too Tough. He opened two chests on the same block in the same hour for me. He did some solid work. You got friends like that? You got friends who will open chests when people do you wrong?"

"Frankie Clams and Joey Bag of Doughnuts have knives for fingers and their knees can deliver shotgun blasts and high caliber machine guns fire from their asses so their backs can never be in jeopardy. Flames from their eyes can scorch anyone as far away as China,"Luther replied.

Frankie Bones came up close to the bunk and stood on tiptoes and sniffed. He had small criminal eyes, spaced too close together and shifty, thinning hair, and a narrow head that looked to have been squeezed in a vise.

"What did they get you for?" Frankie asked.

"I killed five people with my bare hands for sounding on my moms. Ain't nobody sounds on my moms, particularly when I'm sitting on my *stoop.*"

"But did you open up their chests? Because I have friends who will do that. A friend is not a friend who doesn't open chests." Frankie had an Adam's apple that bulged when he spoke.

"I excavated their chests with my bare hands. I pulled out their hearts and picked my teeth with their veins."

Frankie Bones backed against the far wall, his hands to his chest.

Through the listening devices of his mind Luther could hear the men and women of nearby Yale pursuing their knowledge quest with vacuum receptors sucking up all the facts and other data necessary for the armor of full information, in their heaven of specialness, with blue blazers and charcoal gray slacks at the ready and *fathers who walked with one hand in their front pockets.*

The bare bulb couldn't cancel out the fact of his fatigue, and he fell off to sleep only to wake in a panic to get back to the sweet scent of Mona, wrapped in the visionary luminousness of Vincent van Gogh and situated in the place of bliss called the Boston Museum School, where she could stand apart from the power centers of learning, having sidestepped all that for the beauty of her art. He smelled the turps and the paints and it set up a calling in his heart.

The next morning the New Haven Detention Center authorities informed the inmates that the phone lines were down, and that loved ones and agents of kindness could only be gotten in touch with through prayer, causing Luther to tremble that his center for love, Mona Van Dine, was now out of reach.

"Will they stay broken forever so that I have to perish?" Luther shouted, but they heard him not.

A black inmate approached him in the bathroom off the recreation room. He smiled as he spoke. "Slim, my friend here wants you to carry him off."

Luther had no trouble with the euphemistic idiom so in line with the false amiability of the smile. And, in fact, to Luther's left stood a denim-dudded soul over a urinal.

"I could not do such a thing in the state that I am in, but are there other ways I could show my love."

The smiling one wore the denim duds of the detention center not as a symbol of oppression by The Man but as a fashion statement, willing his self-proclaimed beauty into the coarse fabric itself and into the eye of the beholder so that Luther, in his whiteness, could only wish the same for the ill-fitting duds he too had received.

"Why you want to be holding out for? Why you not want to give something of yourself? He be wanting to give something to you," the smiling man said, summoning with his words and self-serving logic his grievance profound with the whiteness all around him.

Luther backed out of the bathroom to the common area with his copy of *Modern Man in Search of a Soul*, by the great Carl Jung, who was said by Lydia to be very understanding of what it was to be a human being. She had given Luther the book hoping it would be the beginning of a course correction, this before he had forsaken psychotherapy for a motorcycle. He thought if he read a few pages he could keep the continuity going in the development of his mind so he would not have to slide backward into nothingness and even be perceived as learned among the inmates.

The rebuffed agent for Luther's sexual participation called for his attention once more. The smile had reasserted itself, but Luther better understood the rage that was lurking should the inmate's will again be thwarted. Beyond the disappointment that he should have to lose connection to the spirit of the fatherly Jung washing over him, the inmate's arrival brought with it a renewed threat that raised Luther's anxiety to an even higher level.

"Man, you reading some deep stuff, ain't you, Slim?" The inmate said, appropriating the paperback and glancing at the cover. "I guess you know all about the soul. I guess you investigated it in your college studies, being that you are a Yale man. Isn't that what you call yourself, a Yale man?"

"Oh yes, I am very much a Yale man," Luther said, seeking to be earnest with danger in his midst, "but only in my fantasies." His response did nothing to register cordiality in his interrogator's face.

"What can you tell us that's righteous on the subject of the soul?" By this time other brothers had been drawn to the scene.

"What's going on, bros?" A stringy latecomer asked.

"Shhh. White boy going to tell us some heavy stuff we need to know about the soul," the smiling inmate said.

Luther was at a loss but felt compelled to oblige, though he was sure of the fakery that would show in everything he said.

"Jung says that the soul lives in shadow or has shadows and should never be lost sight of. Though it is invisible to the eye, it can also become invisible to the mind, which has its own agenda rife with willful intent."

'What the fuck you mean, the soul has shadows?" a man with a broken front tooth demanded.

"That is an important question, and if Mr. Jung were alive today in other than his book, I would ask him that very thing. Because the quality of their manufacturing does not mean they should rule the world within as well. Those like me and you should also have a place to go. The thing to understand is that the Swiss are not like you and me. They don't have the time to stand on street corners in an attitudinal pose while feasting on nothing more than beer and Snickers bars."

"What the fuck you be talking about with beer and Snickers bars? What you want to be holding back on us for? You don't be liking us?" His face was fury now. Smoke was seeping from his pores.

"I didn't say that in the way you're expressing yourself," Luther said.

"White boy be calling me a liar?" The hand came hard and fast and to the side of Luther's head, knocking his glasses off. Then he was hit again, a more solid shot to the eye. From somewhere far away but coming closer he heard the rap of nightsticks on the tables and the chairs and all the inanimate things that would resist them and give rise to sound before the sticks had cause to make a thwacking sound on the flesh so soft before them, and in the spaces between the thwacking and at other times right along with it the voice was heard of one of the manly guards.

"We have a commotion here?"

Luther noted, even in his pain, the absence of a fortifying auxiliary verb.

"Ain't got no commotion here. White boy be falling to the floor all by himself trying to get some of that white boy sissy-assed attention."

"Get up," the guard said, and Luther struggled to his feet and collapsed into a chair. "What happened to your face?" the guard further inquired.

"Ain't nothing happened to his face that he don't be doing to himself. He be one of those white boys like I told you who fall down trying to slick the black man out of his natural righteousness and into white boy trouble."

"That's enough out of you, Culver," the guard said, tapping his stick on the floor for the authority the sound could bring. Under the cover of his own authoritative whiteness, he then led Luther back to his cell.

"You must get out of harm's way. You must see life as it is, that people like Culver cannot be denied because they have the power that comes from adaptability and patience and endurance and when the time is right they will finalize their desire."

The guard rose up in paunchy majesty to offer this: "You're not built to last here, son. You don't have what it takes. The thing you must understand is that once a predatory animal marks its prey, that animal owns it, without consideration of time passing or any of the other foolish stuff people try to put between the initial act and inevitability. And you have been marked. You have been marked by an officer of the law and now you have been marked by an inmate. You have been struck by the guardian and the guarded, the virtuous and the corrupt. Can you now exist between these two poles?" "Yes, yes to all of the above," Luther could only say in a state of dejection, the guard having left him where he needed to be before continuing on the rounds to which he had been assigned.

Frankie Bones was no more comforting. "They like you, man. All you got to do for them is pull a little train. You know, the milk train running all through the night." His harsh laughter followed.

When, some days later, the phones were back up, Luther turned to Mona and told her of the fix that Trooper Dell and his own stupidity had delivered him into. He felt none of the pride that had been there in telling her about the Tombs the past spring and his distant acquaintance with the great Mark Rudd.

"Those pigs. Have they hurt you?"

"I'm OK," Luther said.

"You just hold on tight, Luther. You just hold on. I'll call Mommy and Daddy."

Luther was doubtful any kindness was left in Mona's parents for him, given his behavior, and so was amazed days later to be out on bail and to find Peter Van Dine and Lydia waiting for him outside the detention center. He emerged in in a prison-issue pair of jeans the size of clown pants, his corduroy slacks having been swiped.

"It is true I am not as substantial as I could be were my pants touching my legs and making them feel secure. I have such a longing for the weight that may never come to me," Luther said, driven by self-consciousness.

The black Chrysler sped down back streets and up ramps of the city that Luther was a stranger to, as if Peter had an unerring instinct for the path that would lead him to the Interstate. He maintained a steady silence in keeping with his usual way when behind the wheel, but now it seemed more emphatic, as if words were useless to describe the situation he had been called upon to deliver Luther from and the deprivation unspeakable in terms of his schedule for that day. Every deft turn he made was proof of his competence to steer clear of the bog of lostness.

"You have been apart and now you are together, confirming the marriage vow of eternity? Is my heart singing as a result?" Luther asked, in choosing to ignore what he sensed.

"Let me nip that in the bud right now," Lydia said, not turning her head to address Luther in the back seat. "Peter will be returning to the country tonight. We just thought it best to come up here together on your behalf." Her voice had metallic flecks of disapproval in it.

"Is the sun different over the state of Connecticut than the rest of the Union? Does it burn in such a way as to create wealth and blond hair within its borders?"

"Luther, cretin dear, will you finally just shut up?" Lydia said.

"Do I have to die for speaking my mind?"

"Hasn't the fact that you were arrested sobered you up at all? And can you not see that we are human beings? Can you not summon a degree of empathy, notwithstanding whatever wretched circumstances you come from?"

"Well yes, what you say is full of truth, and I will learn my place when I die, that you are symbols of my own making. But the one thing that needs to be said is that Trooper Douglas Dell has big teeth and wears a big hat."

"Yes, of course, Trooper Douglas Dell. Is he the trooper who deposited you in the slammer?"

"Very much so. He is the one who rained down injustice on me on a rainy night on this very road, I-95, that Peter is so expertly negotiating now, with his doctoral mindset."

"Speak English, Luther, English."

"I speak the language of America when I say the words *travesty of justice inflicted* just because I wear my hair as I do to cover my head as I must. I am crying on the inside for you both—such a preserver of dreams would I be—but the fact must always be that I was harassed on the highway of life."

"But are you a drug addict? You must be. Something is wrong with you."

"I am a liver of life on the terms I must have, and take only what aids and abets my impulses. And do not think I am not thanking you from the bottom of my heart for addressing the deprivations that life has inflicted on me."

"Poor unfortunate," Lydia said.

Peter kept on with his driving, showing his intent to get to the destination that sooner or later had to be at hand.

"And you must not think that I was alone in there with my own iniquity," Luther went on. "For there was one fairer than all the rest kept in a special holding cell and she had blondness in her hair that made her more than eligible to be from the great state of Connecticut, her name being Carrie Carruthers. In fact, she was an old girlfriend from a time I do not need to discuss. And yet, in spite of her blondness, she had been incarcerated for a true drug crime. And yes, while inevitability came to pass, while inmates with lewd impulses sought to harass her, I beat them off with all the courage and all the strength my indignation could muster, though what will happen to her now that I am gone is a thought that we must all make perishable lest we die from the pain of abandoning the cause of her inviolability. For she was a straight A student in a premier Connecticut town called Darien, and yet the call of the wild, of those who run and gun and sleep in the streets, was inflicted on her, and now she is behind bars."

Having spent himself with his jabber, he now curled up in the back seat, his head in his hands as a shelter from attack.

"You say you met this girl in a men's house of detention?" That was Lydia, raining down all sorts of doubt upon him.

"Oh yes, and may my conviction override your doubt."

"Astonishing."

"We must be careful how we speak of such institutions, given that Trooper Douglas Dell is still on the loose. Let me simply put it this way. A few lovelies were sprinkled among us so that the words *buttercup* and *marigold* should never be far from our lips."

"How utterly strange," Lydia said.

"And wondrous to behold, shall we add?" Luther went on, as Peter silently kept to the road with his stalwart presence.

Chapter 57

Because he was here on earth and not in heaven, he headed to the Harlem daycare center where he now worked part-time as a tutor with a depressing awareness of the scarcity that needed to be undone. A life marked by a shortage of cash had its limitations. He tried to come out bold and strong in favor of how things were, but it wasn't quite working. No one said he was a bum; it was simply that his own suspicion was mounting. How very much he wanted to be able to devour a book and have it stay in his system. How very much he wanted to brighten the image of CCNY so it could shine forth as a beacon in his mind. And now, how very much he wanted the money he needed to retain a lawyer so justice could be done and Trooper Dell vanquished from his sight for all time.

A black man drinking wine from a green pint bottle sat on the curb outside the center either to thwart the power of the vehicles rampaging past or feeding on their power from his proximity to them. Luther couldn't be sure.

"Don't you be messing with me. I will cut your motherfucking ass to the bone, Jim," the man called out, to a passing bus. Righteous rage, Luther could only think, observing the man.

He dawdled outside the center, postponing his entry through its glass doors to the sterile, institutional interior. A Columbia student in his light blue university sweatshirt and the blondness of the sun upon him headed up the block in his power and glory, the lights of admiration and love and envy turned on in all who saw him as he sailed into the center to declare with emphatic brilliance his presence in the lives of black children seeking an opening into a bigger world but who knew that just as he came in a dazzling shower of sparkle plenty, so would he break their hearts when he left should they not remain immune to all he purported to offer.

On his heels arrived another, a Haitian with a dark cloud maintaining its presence above him, a bomb maker intent on the eradication of all those intent on the ongoing oppression of people who had to live with the weight of judgment imposed on them by virtue of their blackness.

There came one more, Doris, a black girl of teenage slenderness and delight, who said, with a mischievous smile, "So you find out the meaning of the word yawl, and no, I don't mean y'all, like in you all?" Because at the previous tutoring session she had asked what the word meant, having found it in her in her SAT prep book, leading her to say, "Aw, you a college boy and you don't know that?"

"Oh, that and thousands more," Luther confessed.

"What you doing out here? Why you not inside?" And with those words sent shame down into his core.

"I will respond in the way that I can when I can," he said.

"You fucked up today. You fucked up every day," Doris said, and went on her laughing way into the center.

Though the day was gray, the air was invigorating. A sudden gust of wind blew a vision of a new reality into him. He was dumbstruck. A transformational moment had come. "I will leave you now to go into my own life, away from this center that would have me, though I bring nothing to it. Material bounty will be mine. I will hear the call of the Chevrolet billboard in the night and go north past the meatpacking plants down by the river into the mystery of the countryside. And always, always will I have love on my side to forge the new identity that is being created for me," he declared.

Intense excitement fueled his stride as he left behind the failing patch of lawn amid the concrete.

"You going the wrong way, Fool." So Doris called out.

"Right for me," Luther shouted back. Oh, there was the pain of betrayal, of lost love, but so much more ahead if only he could uproot and transplant himself to the more fertile realm toward which he was now streaking.

I must come in from the cold of deprivation to the warmth of bounty. An opportunity has been presented I could not anticipate to right an ancient wrong. Because you do not have to be on the road to Damascus to be blinded by the light. I will take what my father and brother could not. I will claim what they could not.

He came to her on the seventh floor landing, where she was reaching into the laundry cart on castors for clean sheets and pillowcases and towels for the tenants, which the building was obligated to supply.

"Have you come for something, Luther?"

"I am here to pitch in," he replied.

"What?"

"I am here to offer assistance to the enterprise."

"Enterprise? Is this some more of your foolishness, Son?"

"Do not block me from ascension. Do not block me from the wild calling in my heart. Do not block me from my needs in the night that are so very there. Momma, do not block me from the train whistle in the dark and the forlorn tracks that I can sit on waiting for my beloved to arrive. Would you wound me mortally before my new life has even begun?"

The building now stood in full disclosure, the walls and doors to the individual cells removed. He saw Fenton sponge-bathing himself over the sink and Mr. Nordquist peeing in the sink and James Condit hanging by a rope attached to the light fixture with no consideration of the corpse he would leave behind and Mr. Arupal eating peanut butter from a jar with his finger and reading the newspaper alone but not his own tied to the building's fate. That he was not allowed to see.

The doors of the four compartments—A, B, C, and D—flung open and men emerged from their places of solo dwelling, seven altogether, some naked, some clothed, some of the Christian faith, some turbaned and imbued with subcontinental wisdom, one Far Eastern and lewd and with the fire of lust in his eyes in that very moment extinguished. She knew them all. She knew their sins of prurience, having access to their rooms with universal keys designed to unlock every secret. As they formed a ring around her and bowed down, there was nothing for Luther to do but stand back and observe her transfiguration and the robe of white to signify her true purpose and to hear the silent sobbing of the men expressing through their tears gratitude for the victory through surrender that she had brought to them. He could only watch as they prostrated themselves lower and lower, their foreheads touching the tiles. Luther grasped the challenge to his conviction that she must have no dominion over him on the path that he was seeking even as her power was manifesting. For hours—he truly couldn't say—he withstood her presence and kept his intent alive, and when the spell broke and they had dispersed, there he remained.

"I can see into your mind," she said, slipping into her voice of quiet knowingness. "I am in there now looking around, my strange and troublesome son. Is there something that you are hiding from me that you think I will not find?"

"There is nothing that you haven't illuminated that could never not be seen," he replied, lost in the negatives that formed the flimsy wall he had erected against her probing power.

"Tell me again what it is you are seeking, my son?"

"I come with a business plan supreme endorsed by the learned professors of economics from all the great colleges and universities, a plan that seeks to resurrect capital so the diversity of income streams can flow in a macro/micro environment of alternating yet equal durability."

"Talk to me, my son. Just talk to me."

"I will commandeer the renting office for the acquisition of additional revenue by extending the hours of sublime service into the evening, far past the current hours of business, studies having shown that people fork over money more readily as darkness comes to prevail. And of course it is ideas like this that give America its competitive edge in the world."

"Are you coming back to what is already dead, my son?"

'I am coming back to what will give me life. I have nowhere else to turn, and my dreams are driven by a wild fury."

"We will see you then tomorrow, my son."

"Triumphant in my power will I return," he said, but she was not hearing him anymore, lost once again to the dictate of her cart on wheels and the distribution task at hand.

The following evening, at the rear of the lobby, a woman of refinement frail and petite with meticulous ways showed herself. From Maine, U.S.A., via England, the world, had she come. She had a name. It was Mrs. Browne, with that distinguishing "e" at the end. To be in her presence was painful, as a standard he couldn't possibly meet projected from her appraising eye, an eye that set his insides to crying at all that she witnessed working part-time in the renting office. More than once he had wondered what a woman of her caliber, married to a doctor and with an apartment across the street in the doorman building of order, was doing on these premises rife with disarray, for she summered in Maine and gardened in Maine and each winter presented the family with homemade preserves in a jar sealed with wax. Because when you are England you cannot be Armenia, and when you are from one side of the street, you cannot be from the other. And when you have quality, you cannot in the secret recesses of your heart abide non-quality. Because a woman with preserves for distribution does not eat hamburgers from greasy bags. She has only the peace of her own rectitude and a doctor who comes home to her every night. And yet for Luther to get to his destination of plenty he had to pass through the pain of her force field.

Following through on her evening ritual, she placed a folded matchbook cover between the window and the frame to hold the window shut while she went back inside to turn the latch. And it was while engaged in this activity that she noticed him.

"Why Luther, is it you? Are you back from college? I'll bet you are studying very hard. You must be such a busy young man." Mrs. Browne stood her ground in a high collar and wearing wire-rimmed glasses.

"I am studying well in the approximation of my goal, which has not been determined," he said.

She eyed him with circumspection as well but also avian clarity.

"Yes, of course. And what college did you say you were attending?'

"I am in the college of life and I am also taking classes of erudition at the College of the City of New York, where the creme de la creme have been known to gather in cognoscenti circles."

Mrs. Browne held her silence as if in expectation of some more substantial delivery of meaning. She could not reach down to him but had an expectation of him rising to her. Finally, she said, resorting to the hard facts on which her civilization stood, "Greg Chandler is in his second year at Princeton, where he is studying economics. Edward Sisley is up at Harvard majoring in mathematics. Ronald Butterworth will be transferring from Cornell to MIT to study quantum physics."

"Yes yes, I am well aware of and knowledgeable about all these fields and institutions and the three young lads are wondrous examples of the world made what it is through ongoing achievement, but have you ever wanted to sit on a railroad track with some beer and just cry?"

Her stare intensified the impression of being examined by a sharp-eyed bird. "Well, I had better finish closing up," she finally said.

"If I may have a word with you in this atmosphere of reigning shame, Mrs. Browne. A business collaboration has been arranged and I have been called in to assist with revenue building. The skills needed for this task I shall not enumerate, but they will become manifest in the days and weeks to come, as the energizing effect of my presence makes itself known. Now as an expedient to the resurrection of financial well-being, you may leave the office door open when you depart for the evening, for I will be filling the space with my acumen."

Mrs. Browne did not sing to him. She made no bird chirp noises. She simply affixed him with a look of fragile solidity. The rigor of nuanced thought showed through her pale skin.

"I see. Very well," Mrs. Browne said, embracing the fatalism that accepts the turning of youth toward failure. "I will add up the accounts and then be on my way."

"Please do not rush. The trains and beer and the sheer limitlessness of America await me and will not simply vanish now that I have begun the journey toward them. Because meticulousness has, I am sure, been the hallmark of your administration, and once set, a lofty standard must be maintained."

"Well, I, yes, of course," Mrs. Browne said, taking herself away, leaving Luther to reconnoiter the surroundings while managing to stand in one place.

She reemerged in her coat and carrying a small handbag. "I've put away all the money in the envelopes except for a small amount in the tray. I trust that you will find everything in order. Good night, Luther."

He followed with his gaze her path through the lobby, including her startled end run around Fenton, who was being buffeted about by the currents of his power prayer, like the spastic moves of a man in the throes of electrocution. Caution being her inheritance, she looked both ways before crossing the side street and entered the building that had order. Luther felt an old, old longing to be there himself.

The office was a a plywood fabrication with a sliding door and boxy dimensions and a grille so tenant and clerk could keep an eye on each other and be alert to funny business, the whole thing an awkward intrusion on a one-time apartment now subdivided into living units *which you accessed through what once was the front door of the abode, and which he had known in a time gone by, a place for his aunt to live before she took an apartment at the other end of the lobby, once occupied by elderly Miss Swenson, who set the curtains ablaze one fall night. These things were part of Luther's history. They were among his facts and figures, rising into his consciousness for an appearance now and then, remembrance bringing him to that melting pause of love for all that had been his and still was...The coal truck and the black chunks that rattled down the chute, the old Jew with his cart shouting out "I buy old gold" in the middle of the street.*

Fenton was back, his face red with rage and pressed against the grille as he fired off his assassination bullet, saying, "You're not fit to be here," in response to which Luther arranged an expression of innocence and constructive purpose unceasing.

Fenton was quickly displaced by Hannah, his oldest sister, who filled the grille with her largeness and reached through with a chubby hand for a handful of his hair. He attacked her paw with a sharpened pencil and made it beat a quick retreat.

"My son is upstairs. He will pound your bones to powder," she said, holding the wound to her thick lips.

Luther barked like an excitable dog before returning to the calm demeanor his new position required, saying thusly: "May I be of assistance?"

'What are you doing here, you little thief?"

"Have you ever heard the words, 'Lend a helping hand'?"

"Who let you in there?"

"Mother has called upon me for the support only I can provide."

"I will beat down that door and slap your face silly."

Luther held pencil weaponry in both hands, sharpened points forward. Stalled in her desire for further encroachments. Hannah placed a white Hamburger Heaven bag with a big grease spot on the counter.

A small, dusty-skinned Indian man in office attire sought to ask over her for his "post."

"You just wait a goddamn minute, sahib," Hannah bellowed, kachunking him to fuller awareness of her presence. Driven back several feet by her blast, he nevertheless responded to her in the tone and spirit of inquiry of the subcontinent. "Why do you address me in such a way, miss Large Lady? Why should civility be lacking from your manner?"

"I address any goddamn way I please. Now beat it before I hang you by your stringy tie."

But intensity informed his meticulousness and gravity held him steady. "I will have my post or serve you with the police."

Hannah turned back to Luther, so he could have the full volume of her speech intact. "Just remember this, demented brother of mine. Nobody deprives me and my son. Nobody." She pointed an index finger for emphasis, stimulating him to make biting gestures all around the warning digit but never ever touching it. She then stiff-armed the Indian man.

"Get away from me and stay away, you goddamn mutt," she shouted, and directed a glare at Luther as she climbed the steps.

The rattled man presented himself at the window. "That woman is a relation of yours? She is your mother, may I ask?"

"I am not from her originated. That I can truthfully say. Her true relation to me is yet to be determined. All I can say at this point is that the investigation is ongoing."

The man gave his name as Arvin Mehta in room 11A2, and Luther went right to it in seeking his post in the box scheme that bore some resemblance to the thing that had been part of his life at the post office.

"Here you are, sir. Service with an inward if not always an outward smile will forever be my goal."

"You are a good man, a good man."

"Evil can have no affinity for such as I."

"You will tell the large lady from me that I find her behavior rude and objectionable?"

"It has been noted in the ledger of life, good sir," Luther said, tapping the side of his head.

Mr. Mehta backed away cautiously, as one would who was delicate in his interactions with existence, so that now Luther could have standing before him another Indian, a woman with a red dot in the middle of her forehead.

"I am swimming in the rich black pools of your orbs," Luther said. "I am in love with your beauty and can see no reason other than fear that we should stay apart. I can only wonder where I might be led if sexual desire did not rule me."

She asked for her mail in the formal accent of one shy about her physical gift, a sari of many colors adding splendor to his imaginings of all that lay underneath.

"There are ways out of a life of desire, should you choose to follow," she said.

"You will tell me all about it in the dark of night, with only a candle to illuminate your body? You will take me into your personal darkness and spread me out on the vastness of your subcontinent? You will channel all my longing into the one dream of you? You will be raven-haired Lenore to the nth degree?"

"Do not body worship, dear sir. Do not go where the ego leads you. Find the space within and live in that."

He heard without hearing, her lips holding the promise of soft kisses, as if shaped for only that. Drawn by her force field, he witnessed her mouth grow wider than a thousand lakes. Within were towers of knowledge and startling abysses. Canyons with her name on them came into view. Fire scorched the vista clear, followed by an oceanic onslaught of water, as if she would familiarize him with her laughing cycles. And her eyes were on him at all times, so he could see what she was seeing with.

And then she was gone, and not even law enforcement officials could bring her back.

As he administered to the tasks at hand, his mother flashed a message for his mind, explaining not for the first time what it was to receive the Indians and their Muslim Pakistani neighbors, that she had an apparatus in place for detecting levels of violence and saw that it was low in terms of what they were bringing; this she saw even when applying the meter to the bearded, turbaned Sikhs, the endless number of Singhs, sensing that they had left their warrior ways at the shore.

His mother had come from the north and they had come from the South to be elements blending in the mix.

These were the people, living in a dream of fractured unity, who came to the office window: Little Tommy from room 7B3, by way of Altoona, Pennsylvania, who smoked his Pall Mall cigarettes and painted the rooms of the building Auntie Eve green on the instructions she had long ago delivered, a man who oiled his hair real good, slicking it back against his scalp and wearing the sharp shirts and creased slacks reserved for the night in relinquishing his painter's duds to stand in front of the luncheonette waiting for the *Daily News* truck, so strong in the structure of its being and the "yo" of the driver bringing everyone to attention with his arrival as he tossed the bundles from the truck to the sidewalk in the joy of the honest work he did before carrying the bundles into the store and clipping the wires with his pincers so the papers could be set free and the people of that part of Manhattan could be set free too with newspapers of their own and see how the ponies had run and their teams had done. Little Tommy was not a god. He was of the earth and went to the track to be in the open spaces with the needle of his happiness meter in the high zone as he watched the ponies run. He did not now measure Luther's fitness level or accost him for being present. He just said, "Give me five dollars on account. On account of I'm broke." Because laughter was part of his heartbreak sorrow, living in the room so small with tensions so big within him. A man with powerful muscles, he had beaten the woman he loved, beaten her so bad that she had no recourse but to move out of the building to a part of the city where he was not.

"Remember that I knew you when you were small and nothing, and now you are big and nothing, because nothing comes from nothing." Peals and peals of laughter coming from his Little Tommy mouth.

"Oh yes," Luther said. "Oh very yes."

The space now free for Tall Tommy with his harmonica and his gash for a mouth. All he cared to do in the alone and unloved state he lived in was to play "Home on the Range" and tap out tobacco from the little pouch into thin rolling papers to make his smokes. The promise of the day come morning and the non-response to his invisibleness that followed had dimmed the light in his eyes. He did not say anymore, as he once had when Luther was a child, "A secret mission has brought me here to New York. Someday I will be at liberty to say. Meanwhile, tell no one," because he had only the confines of the room he rented and the public bathroom that he shared and the odd jobs that Luther's mother offered him. The childhood walks with the dogs in Riverside Park and the 7-Up Tall Tommy would mix with grape juice saying *This will grow some hair on your balls.*

They were gray ghosts to Luther now. There was guilt that he could not love them more than he did or love them all, these men who had been at the beck and call of his mother and aunt, replacing blown fuses, painting rooms, cleaning out the incinerator and all the rest.

"My name is Mavis Malt , from Abilene, Kansas. I was left at the side of the road. In a city like this they can never find me so long as I remain clean. I am here to pay the rent for room 12A1 in advance, so the street can never loom." She sucked her teeth, a sound that irritated Luther, but she was sly enough to cease her activity with his eyes upon her.

He wrote out a rent receipt and slid it through the grille.

"Now I can live. Now my obligation is met. Now I have paid in advance with my calendar marked for when I must come next so the street will only ever loom."

On into the evening the people came, giving him the money it was their obligation to hand over so they could sit in their rooms with the security they had purchased.

Mr. Patel in 5A7 needed a new fridge.The question was where it was to come from? Was there a housing horn of plenty from which it could be drawn? That didn't seem likely.

Panic overcame Luther; in that moment the building seemed unmanageable. He tore a piece of paper from a legal pad and held it in front of Mr. Patel. "Now tell me, with full and blazing honesty, what it is you see. Hold back nothing, sir, nothing. Simply let the truth come pouring out, without an iota of concern for strategy, for public opinion, for what others might dare to think in their shallowness. Just give it to us good, sir, no holds barred."

"Sir, are you demented? You are showing to me a piece of legal paper in the color canary yellow."

"And what does the word 'legal' mean to you, if I may gently inquire?"

"It means, sir, within the realm of the law."

"And I say to you, sir, it does my heart good that a healing civility is returning to America to ease the fractiousness."

Luther placed the paper flat on the desk and wrote upon it one word and one word only, in letters so big that they took up ten lines. He then held up the paper to the inspecting Mr. Patel.

"Reflect back to me now the miracle of what has just taken place, Mr. Patel."

"Of what miracle do you speak, sir? I see before my eyes the same piece of paper."

"And what is different about the paper, sir?"

"Only that in block letters you have written the word 'fridge,' sir."

"And what kind of paper did you describe it as being, in your very own words, sir?"

"Sir, I believe I called it legal paper, but is the time not over for these questions that do not, in my estimation, bring resolution?"

"Sir, sir, and sir again, that is what you say about a miracle that has arisen before your very eyes?"

"What miracle am I to see, sir, when all I see before me is lunacy?"

"Do the words 'force of law' not mean anything to you, living as we do in America?"

"Sir, I am in need of a fridge, not a piece of paper, legal or otherwise. Is that not clear to you?"

"The realm of action can never be far from the realm of law, sir. Of that you can be solemnly assured."

"Sir, I cannot talk with you anymore. It is a source of distress unending."

'Sir, with the legality of the paper now intact, your nightmare shall come to an end."

Mr. Patel started to refute, protest, or in some way agitate the air, but ceased before the words could give themselves expression.

Others too were soon to arrive in the importuning tyranny of the oppressed.

Mr. Baswani, in 6A6, was in need of a new mattress. The coils had popped through in the night, causing him to sing out his pain and discomfort. He did in fact look haggard in his shiny suit and polyester tie, but did that mean the building had to commit its meager resources to his well-being?

"Behave yourself and your mattress will behave accordingly. But it is you who must take the lead. Which of the two of you has the greater intelligence, you or your mattress?"

"Sir, sir, I am a mathematician, and you would compare my intelligence to that of a mattress?"

"And I am but a clerk, and yet you would ask me to be God?"

"I am in need of a healthy mattress, sir."

"And I am in need of a piece of paper, which shall put us on a path of mutual understanding. And here that very paper is." Luther bent over the paper and when the job was done, he handed the paper to Mr. Baswani. "Read back to me now, not in the language of mathematics, but in pure English."

Mr. Baswani read, "'A mattress under surveillance can bring no peace.' This is hardly useful to me, sir. It is rather peculiar."

"Peculiar it may be, but we have our starting point for dialogue to commence. One thing is of tremendous importance. In the course of your long night, do not ever shake your finger at your mattress. Show no sign of disapproval whatsoever, for it will be watching you with the observational powers of a bright, perceptive child."

"Sir, I have not seen your face before. Have you arrived here from a madhouse?"

"Sir, I have arrived here from Heaven to save the world. It is my sole function in life. For some of us must be very very bad before we can be very very good."

"Sir, you should not speak in this way."

"Sir and sir again, I speak the way my mind drives me. Because there is nothing else to do with words but to allow them to come, to allow them to rise up and sing their song and disappear into the other words that have to have their day as well. But as to where they come from, only the most reckless speculator would say. Let us simply say that they appear through an opening in the mind just as people have to squeeze through an opening to make themselves real to the world. Because the Book of John tells us that in the beginning was the word and the word was with God and the word was God. Who is to say that we are not God himself with the endless supply of words now our very own in syllabic confrontation with the forces of the universe?"

Mr. Baswani was gone. Had he fled into the night? What was the point of such rudeness, to engage in dialogue and then depart the scene without a goodbye?

Oh, a wave of importuning humanity came with its very flesh on fire, saying give me give me give me, and he was not without the ears to hear Mr. Vedant Ray insisting, if his words were to be believed, that roaches had overrun his room. "They incubate their eggs in the grill of my fridge. They eat the glue in the bindings of my books. They run over my face as I try to sleep."

Luther heard Mr. Ray and would have responded if he could. He would have told Mr. Ray to respect all life and to kiss the roaches as if they were his own. Instead he put his head down on the roll-top desk and covered it with his hands, seeking to communicate with the silence he maintained that time worked against everything, being particularly savage in its exposure of this edifice with its weak foundation and the rodent community within its walls and those two killer words *faulty wiring* applying.

The house phone rang, the force of the ring lifting it off the desk. His mother was on the line, saying only this: "I am waiting for you, my son. When you are ready, come to me with what ails you."

He hung up the phone. His thoughts turned to Mona, with her teeth so white and and her turps and the smell of paint that made everything holy, Mona who was his lifeline and because of whom he could be there in the office in the first place, knowing as he did that so long as he had her he could never be trapped in the swamp of family.

He extracted two twenties from the drawer and slipped them, folded, into his right pocket, letting his hand graze against the new sustenance he had found, as a reminder to himself that what was there so potent in his pants was also a secret so deliciously close to exposure by the world, only the fabric of his corduroys serving as a barrier between his dream and destruction.

The tenants punched and slapped him many times as he departed the office but to no avail against the armor of his vision, and now as he mounted the stairs freakishly powerful thunder shook the building, causing it to vibrate in its fragility. He shouted for the walls and ceilings and floors to be still, but more thunder brought more movement, shaking of a more violent nature, so that the premises were as if cast upon a storm-tossed sea.

He lay his head down on the stairs that had been walked by him so many times before. All he had to know was that each floor had its four compartments and that within those compartments were rooms, but that he himself did not live there and that he was not a child running downstairs for the Mission sodas of his past or any of the other flavored waters of America that the stores could sell him to go with the Drakes Cakes and Hostess cupcakes of America so sugar full.

He entered the apartment (yes, it could be called such, having consecutive rooms that led one to the other) to hear the boy Moses say, "Mommy wants me to kill you very dead, so you can't talk or walk no more."

"Stop it, Moses," his mother—yes, her name was Hannah—but not without an unearthly scream of delight.

She sat in her black raincoat, having devoured the contents of her greasy bag of plenty, as there it sat empty at her feet along with wrinkled packets of ketchup.

"Mother, is dinner ready yet? My son and I are waiting." This she screamed out, while holding Luther with the strength of her now victorious eye. Saying to him, "You know my son. His name *is* Moses, and leads me over the hot sands to the still waters. Say hello to your uncle, Moses."

"Die," five-year-old Moses said, pointing a finger at Luther.

"You have already killed me many times. Is that not enough?"

"You talk funny. I don't like you," Moses said.

Moses' birth not a thing of joy but akin to a nuclear explosion in Luther's fearful consciousness; even as an infant Moses felt like an inevitable extension of the wrath Hannah had inflicted on Luther and Luke when they were children. A woman whose dark moods traveled through the walls of the apartment she could not separate from.

Hannah called out once more for food. No one knew her sorrow as she herself did. No one among the siblings had her history, being the firstborn and at one time in her life the object of *all* their father's affections. No one could be saddled with Armenia as she was, even at birth covered with hairs all over her body and bearing the consciousness of historical injustice. Legends could rise and fall, but her wounds would forever remain hidden behind her scowl. She had the ability and the need to bathe in her silence lest God himself kill her dead for her betrayal.

From the street came the sounds of the men (and women) of Columbianess, and all the laughter of the intellect they could muster, the verse from the Gospels on the side of the building now illuminated in the night to wag a finger at the fornicating young 'uns for their lustful merriment.

The screen showing Hannah's life emerged, and on it, in grainy black and white, was a brownstone building and a view of a basement apartment and the man and the infant therein, Hannah demolishing it from sight before things could go any further.

"I never left home. I never went anywhere. I could have gone to Greece and been with dark men if only it had worked out right," she suddenly cried, lost in her tears for the longest time. There had been a man, a sailor. He had come and gone, leaving her with child. Her dream of Greece grew big when she tripped over the cellar grating of a store. A sizable settlement would follow from a lawsuit. It would be her ticket to the Aegean and her own apartment and a color TV. But no, the lawsuit was dismissed.

Moses, still on the floor, made stabbing motions at Luther's legs and crotch with Crayola weaponry, as Mrs. Garatdjian arrived with a plate of chicken and Brussels sprouts and a baked potato, knowing food to be a pacifier for her oldest daughter. As her spirits brightened, Luther saw that Hannah was his sister and so it would always be, as darkness belonged to the dawn.

Others seeped through the walls as a way of emerging from their aloneness, Naomi in a dress too big for her body to give shape to and Rachel maintaining a painful smirk to enhance her ability to be present in her life. They too partook of their mother's chicken, yielding in their standing positions to the law of nature that said they must eat, while their father sat in his wheelchair. He was neither condemnatory nor accepting but simply engrossed in his A. A. Allen evangelical literature and his mind on the divine, a plane free of long knives and the setting of hair and body on fire, the place he called the finishing line where safety and order would reign supreme.

Naomi it was who came on loud, now that she couldn't sing. "Mother's Svenska pojke. Pull up a chair, you hardworking young man. Rumor has it that you have brought your business expertise to the office."

"I am doing more than you could ever know to be on time with my life," Luther replied.

"How is your beautiful girlfriend, your *rich* beautiful girlfriend?"

"Oh, she is a vision higher than the stars from which she reaches down for me," Luther said, seeing the smile of complicity form on Hannah's face as the bond of the women grew tighter in the presence of the recoiling male.

"Mother's handsome Svenska pojke," Naomi said, plunging the knife of intimacy in where it had to go so he could be paralyzed in the shame of incriminating association, all female eyes now stripping him naked.

"You leave my Svenska pojke alone," his mother said, all aglow.

An insane anger rose in him, not directed at his sisters but at his mother for having him turn over the rent receipts in their presence.

"Here it very much is," he said, handing her the rent money in legal-size envelopes in a soiled canvas bag.

"My good little helper," his mother said, sinking the knife in the spot that Naomi had marked.

"Ma, you're trusting Svenska pojke with money? Don't you remember how we all tried to help him when he was a little boy? Don't you remember how I got him to confess that he had gone into your purse? You took him to church and had the members of the congregation pray for him. Don't you remember that? Svenska pojke had something wrong with him. Svenska pojke was a thief," Naomi said, reviving the memory of her winning his confidence only to betray him to his mother.

"All my children are good children. My only prayer is that we all meet in Heaven."

"Amen, Ma, but don't you think we ought to check Svenska's pockets?" the filthy one continued, keeping faith with her own treachery.

"Just remember, no one deprives me and my son," Hannah said.

"You be listening to my mother now," Moses screamed in his ear.

He left the apartment pained that he had not accepted his mother's chicken, that he too had not partaken of his mother's fare, unable to say he could no longer easily touch what came from that roach-overrun kitchen and hating himself for his selective fastidiousness.

He entered a bookstore at One Hundred Fifteenth Street and Broadway. "I am here to explore the twentieth century, if I am not too late. I am here for a devouring. I have come prepared to consume the works of the very best," he announced to the clerk, and headed for the New Directions books of such very fine quality, the essential being *Paterson,* by the very great William Carlos Williams.

That night his mother came to him in a dream. She showed herself in the fullness of her power. She told him how she caused the mountains to move and the seas to foam and gave him notice that she was the meaning of America. She said that she could create buildings and that she could burn them down. She said further that the term "divine intervention" applied exclusively to her. She told him these things as truth that comes only in the dark while sitting on the side of his bed and wearing a robe of white and yes, her glasses were off and her hair was hanging down down to the very ground.

"My power is my power and you must always work within it," she said.

Before he could answer she was gone, and now he stood with a crowd on a stormy night looking up at the building to a place where a window had been smashed out, and where his mother appeared, in that same robe, her smile gone to show her in her genuine purpose, so that he could understand that the smile had been a mask for the thing he was now seeing.

He woke before dawn needing to pee. On the way to the bathroom he could hear Tony Pascual crying for his lost mind while Billy Riley moaned in another room for the head he did not have in the condition that he once did. In that moment he saw his life with a frightening clarity. His involvement with the office was all a mistake. It was a craziness he couldn't begin to fathom. It had nothing to do with goodness or wholeness. It was some strange corruption that would ruin his life beyond all hope of redemption. Along the walls he moved slowly, cautiously, fearing his mother's presence and expecting her to jump out at him. Then sleep came, and after it the morning, and with the morning came activity, and with activity came confidence and the vanquishing of the night, and with that came his hunger once more for the office and the evening, when again he would be there.

Mrs. Browne was present to meet him. She was the self she had to be, with long disappearances into restful silence so she could emerge whole and positive, even if she had the physical pain that came with age. Nothing in her manner that Luther could detect said anything about the missing twenties, so he took it that he would not be arrested, thrashed, humiliated, or ostracized, whatever form the degradation might take. He offered that while it was a great wish of his to go north into restoration territory as she so frequently did, even if he could not see himself ever making quality jam, he must return to the scene of the crime and make things all all right again in a way that would allow him to live. He wouldn't say that she flew up into the air at the sounds that he was making, but she didn't exactly keep her feet on the ground, so that he had to look up at her as she looked down at him through the treasure of her birdlike eyes and with the immensity of her delicate awareness fully showing.

She offered that she hoped he would find everything in order, the key word as she herself returned to the building across the street which constituted order's very essence.

The plan he had in mind would allow him to live alone, and in the doing of that he would have to call on the vision that had been granted him for sustenance, because twenties in his pocket would not do forever. He had to have a plan that would secure the vault he sought to live in for all time. Because no one must ever put him in a race where he could be defeated ever again, the race of time and financial uncertainty. So for that reason he came armed with the necessary something to conceal if not bewilder.

He had seen it in the night, after the visitation of fear and attempted maternal cooptation. He would secure a blank receipt book all his own, with the white tear-off receipts ten to a page and the inky carbon placed between its whiteness and the yellow sheet for copying. Now when Mr. Gupta or Mr. Singh or Mrs. Patel or Mr. Chan came to pay, he would act in accordance with the law in issuing them a proper receipt from the proper receipt book, and their rents would be entered in the logbook as well as in the evening's ledger. But for those two or three whom duplicity chose as instruments for his survival, he would bring out the equalizer for all he had never been given, the second receipt book that he had appropriated for his own personal use, and with it he would make right himself and the world, and only out of jealousy would the heavens not be singing with him. Because while the tenants would always get their due, while the payment would always be entered in the record book, so they could never return with the outrage of the innocent on being told that they had not paid in the first place when they had, their payments would not be listed in the evening's account, so that it would be up to the building staff—his mother, Hannah, Mrs. Browne—to check the evening's totals against the ledger sheets to notice that *something was not on one that was on the other,* and did they have the time for that amidst the things that time could manufacture to distract them?

He reached for the phone to call Mona because without daily contact she would surely be lost to him. There could be no two ways about the consequences of such inaction. But the phone rang with authoritative insistence as he reached for the receiver. On the line was the voice of power, not unknown to him, saying "Mrs. Garatdjian," without so much as a *please*. Luther dropped the receiver on the desk and flew back against the wall and slid into the fetal position, whispering softly no no no so *the caller could not hear him*. He gnashed his teeth and broke his bones, and when his helplessness remained prevalent against the monstrosity on the line, he picked up the third class mail that had been loitering underfoot and piled it on top of the receiver to obscure the thing from his very sight. He ran out of the office and hid in the bathroom, but that gave him no peace either. To kill it dead he had to place the receiver back in its cradle, an action he took with great risk to his life.

On the phone used only for internal communications, he gave three short rings and then three more and then many more but none summoned his mother from her dilatory path. Why would they? Was not stalling him her supreme joy, as when he was a child and she would call him from the baseball game he was watching on TV to *run on his long legs* to the grocery store, only to make him wait as she slowly made out her list? And was it not like her to give him chuckle plenty when he flew into a rage? And now she would be rejoicing that he was up against terrifying Simon Weill, abandoning him when he needed her most and exposing him as a cowering little boy hiding behind his mother's skirt.

But it was not Simon Weill's way to go away. He was not made of going away stuff. And so once again the outside phone rang and rang, in keeping with his intrepid nature. With every insistent ring Luther's rage swelled. He would hunt her down in the hiding place she filled with delirious laughter at having abandoned her son to the father of darkness.

So that Simon Weill had no choice but to enter the scene and witness the young man seeking to balk him with telephone strangeness. He arrived in a black Cadillac with huge fins, a woman with dyed blond hair remaining in the death seat while he stepped into the building. He wore a long coat of black leather. Prayer Master Fenton tried prayer power on him but became dust before his very eyes. Simon Weill came with wetness on his slicked back hair and his rodent eyes and a body of mostly cartilage so he could squeeze through the smallest spaces. In his retinue were men in shades who wore their shirts buttoned at the top to signify their brand of ruthless manliness, for they were men who knew how to hurt and projected their crunching power with legs spread in pants well creased. And while there were many who assailed their boss with knives and other weaponry, his flesh closed quickly over the wounds they inflicted and left no trace.

"Mrs. Garatdjian, I'm here about business," Simon Weill said, standing there in the lobby, and what the ringing of the house phone could not do, his tired voice could, for while there was no noticeable effort put into his delivery, he spoke words that cut through the loudest commotions and traveled through walls and could rouse her from her dawdle dance ways and check her chuckle and flush her from her secrecy space.

Now it was she who was in a state of franticness, pulling Luther from the office so he could stand on the welcome mat she belatedly laid out for Simon Weill and watched as the men in dark glasses toted laundry bags stuffed with rent proceeds to the idling Cadillac.

Luther could only look on as the family as a whole said the following: "You it is who holds all power. You inhabit palaces supreme while our bathrooms are the spaces between parked cars and Chock Full O' Nuts serves as our living room. Even as our hair shirts itch and our stomachs suffer pangs of hunger, let it be entered in the record of life that you are a sinner and a flame everlasting will torch your ass for your worldly ways."

His mother sang for Simon Weill, Luther refusing to join in: "Jesus loves the little children/all the children of the world/red and yellow, black and white/ they are precious in his sight/Jesus loves the little children of the world."

When Luther found his voice, he managed to ask Simon Weill if he had ever worn anything but black, but Simon Weill only belched out bile that smoldered on the lobby floor.

In the wake of Simon Weill Mrs. Garatdjian said it was their job to pray for his troubled soul. She said that Simon Weill could throw them out into the street just like that and snapped her fingers with no sound emerging to show what *that* was. The message was an old one Luther had heard over and over, going back to childhood. He saw a hard pitiless rain pelting his family, soaking his father in his robe and ruining all his A. A. Allen literature, all the rain of the world pouring down on their old, mismatched furniture and washing them toward the seediest streets of New York City while rendering their Hostess Twinkies soggy.

His mother then sang "The Old Rugged Cross," but she couldn't do that forever, for even Calvary had to be returned from. Simon Weill did not care about God, she explained. He cared only about the rent money they took in from the tenants and the store owners along Broadway. "He is not entitled to those store rents. He collects them for us and then we do not see them. It is because the store owners were so mean to me when I came for their monthly rent. You would not believe the things that they said. That is when Simon Weill stepped in with his fine mind to deal with them with an attitude of firmness." Mrs. Garatdjian pinned him to the wall. "Your poor aunt is a saint. She came to this country for only one reason—to do God's will. Are you understanding me?"

Luther nodded his assent.

"To this country she came and struggled to the position of head nurse of the city's finest hospital. From there she bought a tea room. Do you even know what a tea room is, you foolish boy?"

'It's where they sell the tea of all nations," he said.

"You will have to do better to live in this world, my ignorant son. Now tell me the rest, so I can be sure you can understand life as it is and so you can do my bidding."

So he told her the truth as she understood it, that after the famous tea room, Auntie bought the building, with the idea that it should be a way station for missionaries traveling the world so they could have a place to rest up in order to talk more and more about God and the Christ Jesus. "Is that me, Ma? Is it?"

"Is what you?"

"The Christ Jesus."

"Shut up your crazy mouth, you blaspheming boy."

Luther went on. "The vile men of the church were full of filthy jealousy. The jealousy coated their skin with redness and made their breath smell bad. It did not matter how many times they slapped their Bibles. Word of their stench reached all around the world, while the fact that they whacked dear sweet Auntie with their Bibles and called her the whore of Babylon remained a little known fact."

"They called her no such thing."

"They called her Judas Iscariot for her betrayal of them and the Christ Jesus—me...."

"Stop about you and tell the story."

"Auntie Eve was driven into the Garden of Gethsemane, where she asked for the ruination of her enemies...."

"I do not have all night," his mother said calmly.

So he told her that the men of the church—the filthy, filthy men who slapped their big Bibles so well—had accused Auntie Eve in an act of gross injustice of misusing the money, and that later, evil men tried to take the business away from her and that the family had no choice but to allow Simon Weill, with his fine mind, to enter their business life or lose the building owing to the debts they had piled up and which he assumed responsibility for in exchange for the title to the property, and that the family was now running the building on a lease basis.

"Now you're talking, my son, now you're talking." She broke his narrative to refresh his mind about some important ideas. Because God was not in Simon Weill, he could have the money and a fleet of Cadillacs. If God was in you, you rode the subway and spent your Sundays at the tabernacle and ate baked beans in the Automat. "Mr. Weill has a fine mind. Your father has a fine mind but he has a condition in addition to his fine mind."

Luther stared at his mother, and she stared at him. He continued. "Then there arrived the one with the voice crying in the wilderness. For a long long time had Luther wandered in the wilderness…."

"You foolish, foolish boy," his mother said.

Chapter 58

Deeper into the fall, he found a woman who would not run from him, nor he from her. They had nothing to hold them beyond the sex; they could do without each other until the next time they had to have it.

Her name was Laurie Jacek. She had Czech bones in the planes of her face, she attended NYU downtown, and she knew what the word *intaglio* meant.

He met her at a party on Claremont Avenue, a quiet strip west of and parallel to Broadway and famous for its rows of residential buildings that exuded quality. Neither of them belonged at the party. They had simply heard of it, and because it was a Saturday night, they had to have somewhere to be. No door check was in place, so he was allowed to enter and to find her standing awkward and thin amid her own ideas of herself. She said she had an apartment down on Sullivan Street in the West Village, just south of Moogie's Bar, where, she also said, he would not have to feel inhibited by the specter of Columbia intelligence, as he doubtless did at the End Bar nearby. He asked her how she could know such a thing, and she said that it was simply written on his Dexedrine face.

"Are there no secrets for me to conceal?"

Laurie Jacek said that talk was not the thing, that it was important to build on what they had, and that they should go somewhere private for the consummation of it.

"How did your lips get so thin and your face so tense?" he asked.

"Czech out your own," she said, but did not laugh.

"I live just off an avenue that runs parallel to Claremont Avenue but is not so distinguished and I have two roommates who may or may not be dangerous."

"Have they killed you?" Laurie Jacek drank her Scotch fast and had another.

"They have killed no one in my sight, including me," Luther reported.

"Then why don't you take me where they are not in your apartment and be with me?"

"I am starting to feel my power," he whispered, as they entered the dark and depressing apartment.

"Maybe we can both feel your power," she whispered back.

"May I say a word about Claremont Avenue? May I say that argyle socks and penny loafers are part of its residency requirement?"

"Are you howling at your outsider-ness?" Laurie Jacek asked.

"I am just howling," he answered back, to keep the matter simple.

He played *Surrealistic Pillow* on Tony Pascual's stereo so they could be in the embrace of who the Jefferson Airplane were, with all the weight of "Somebody to Love" bearing down on them and then Marty Ballin changing gears with "Today" so that for all time the album had to be tied to One Hundred Eighteenth Street and the age he was when he heard it and the incense and the quality of the light the apartment held on a spring afternoon and the sex that was in the air and always willing to materialize as flesh, and yet starting to cry as they entered smoke heaven on the expert stick she rolled, inserting the thing in her mouth for a touch of wetness. Crying at all he couldn't be, the chasm between what he had wanted and where he was, the high board scores of America having gone one way while he was in his inferiority pursuit of his own death, causing Laurie Jacek to reach down and try to find him as he kept a towel to his face. As he wept, he sensed the steel apparatus in her Czech construction, thinness notwithstanding.

"I'm Catholic and alone and come from Long Island, which remains at an odd angle to your city. I need you tonight." And so they did what was required. And though he passed out on her strong smoke and the party Scotch, and woke in the morning to find her gone, there was her name and phone number, which she had written with a magic marker on his wall.

Her apartment had the smell of dead rats and the spectacle of wet bras and panties hanging in the bathroom. Laurie Jacek didn't dispute him about the rats. She simply stressed that books and the occasional man were all she really needed to live. For his part, he told her that he was on the trail of his own destiny. To be with her in the afternoon light was to have this thought: *It would be hard to make a story out of her white flesh.*

"I heard that," she said, with an air more of toughness than of hurt.

He told her of Moogie's, and the heartbreak and sorrow in the poem on the bar's men's room wall. He quoted the lines, as if they were from Keats:

> Screwed maybe a thousand times/Gone/
> We'll never be together again/It is winter
> in my heart.

"Shouldn't he win the Nobel Prize for pain?"

"They don't give the Nobel Prize for pain," Laurie Jacek said. "He's just another head case pulled along by his dick."

"But don't you feel the ache in your very soul? Don't you see why he shivers at the wintry landscape?"

"He wrote some lines in the bathroom of a bar. He was having a sentimental moment while cruising for another woman."

"I am finding out with every passing second what it means to be a Czech," Luther said. Already, for some minutes now, smoke heaven had been going on.

'Heart of stone in a frame of glass."

"Wow." Now truly zonked, he wrote her words on the air to keep them indelible. A moment of troubling truth came to him. "Let me be clear about the state of my nation. I cannot be fully in love with you. There is one I belong to with all the power. She is now in a far country but one day she will come to make things all all right with me. It is she I am waiting on for my life to begin in an earnest way."

"Si, si," Laurie Jacek said, but it was clear she did not truly hear him, being in the clouds of her own smoke head mind.

"And when she comes, great things will happen. Legendary accomplishments will follow."

"Ja, ja."

She rolled another joint, tight and skinny and unlike the fat things he put together. When it had burned down, she lay him back on the floor and covered his body with her own. "Pay attention to where you are."

"Yes yes," Luther replied.

In this time Mona came down from Boston in the throes of her own development. She wasn't lost. She wasn't found. Her continuing comparison of herself with Lane was a problem. In her own eyes his bold canvases diminished her luster; his bold canvases, she felt, could lead her to feel she was on the level of a Sunday painter.

That weekend they saw a documentary on Bob Dylan, *Don't Look Back,* at the New Yorker theater on Broadway. The world was his because of his brilliance on his tour of England, with beautiful and adoring Joan Baez at his side. Luther left the theater feeling small, a nobody, and evidently so did Mona.

"He's a genius, a genius, absolutely brilliant," Mona said, as they undressed in her bedroom in the family's apartment.

"Not everybody can be," Luther said, feeling somehow her declaration was more than a statement of fact.

"You aren't. That's for sure."

"Did I ever say I was?"

"All you have is your oddness. Intelligence is missing. You have absolutely nothing."

"I guess that's important for me to know," he said, staring down at the gays drawn to the Solder's and Sailor's Monument for nighttime adventure. Life was going on down there and so would he, though he wondered why, as what was the point of it?

That November Richard Milhous Nixon came back from the dead to be elected President of the United States. He hit Hubert Horatio Humphrey very hard. He hit him in the face and the back and he threw powerful punches to his stomach, too, so that Hubert Horatio Humphrey crumpled in the fifteenth round as a foreordained conclusion. Nothing could stop Richard Milhous Nixon from being who he was in the vengeful rise he needed to get even in his life. And nothing could make Luther's mother happier than to know that brand name goods were back in the White House, establishing the law and order that everybody needed. His father too raised a victory flag, and hoped that RMN would enact stoning, like they had in the old country, so the people with the long hair who lay about in the streets could have their heads and bodies hit with big rocks until they couldn't do the disrespectful things they did anymore.

All Luther saw was that time past had now been grafted onto time present in the national landscape that had been wrought, RMN's ascent placing a man in pinstripes amid the hippie horde, but in any case, some connection was being established from top to bottom. From the White House was emanating a national zeitgeist of trickiness and deceit.

"It is time to get back to where we all belong," the president said, in his first national address, "and for this I have brought in a vice president who hits very hard, and hits with both fists," and so, for the first time, Luther could get an eyeful of Spiro Agnew rolling up his sleeves in the gesture of a man preparing for action, for he had the look of peeve and vindictiveness that could get the job done while his slicked-back hair remained in place with the expensive oils that kept it there.

Luther's mother called him to her in this time, seeking to reacquaint him with a past he seemed to have forsaken even if he didn't deny its reality.

"Your father was a walking man. He was seeking the kingdom of the Lord while on these walks. That is what I am saying to you, my foolish son. My, how he could walk, from home to Times Square and back again. Into one movie theater would he go and then right back out again, never finding the thing he was looking for until he came to the Lord."

"Yes yes," Luther said, there at the dining table, cluttered with condiments and his father's toaster and covered with a checkered red and white oilskin cloth that he had never seen it without. In the corner was his father's wicker chair and the A. A. Allen Christ Jesus literature of the Southwest and the Morris Cerullo Christ Jesus literature of the Northeast and the pamphlets of Billy Graham and Oral Roberts as facets of the salvation business the men of the Christ Jesus had found and the flashy ties and expensive suits it had brought them as a result of their hands slapping the pages of their open Bibles so very well as they exhorted their flocks. How had his father come to such a place of understanding, arriving from where he did? How could such a thing be that he would surrender to the likes of them, given their American huckster ways, every month sending them money for their crusades, thinking that this made him worthy of heaven.

A framed photo of his mother and father hung on a far wall, she in a summer dress and he wearing a tie and his suit jacket removed. Both of them smiling, both of them young for the anonymous photographer.

There was a frame but no door through which to pass to the kitchen. As a child, Luther remembered, he would spread his feet against either side of the frame to raise himself to the top of it to draw his mother's attention as she cooked the food that he then would eat.

"Your father will someday be in heaven."

"Yes, yes. He made a reservation. This he told me when he was in the hospital a few years ago for the amputation," Luther said.

"You must get down on your knees and pray for these demons to leave you. Do you not know what your father has been through, my foolish son? Do you not know that the Turkish authorities came for him and his family in Constantinople so they could destroy them as they were destroying all the Armenians in the country? Do you not know that it is only because their Turkish servant risked his life by saying the family was not home that your father is alive today? Do you not know the dark clouds that come over your father to this day from that time in his life and all that it cost him?"

In fact, Luther knew. But were there not enough cares and woes in the family that he didn't need any more?

They sat quietly for a while, his mother adding heavy cream to her coffee and drinking it for her afternoon pick-me-up.

"I'll be going now," he said. He felt a wrenching guilt, seeing her careworn and old, but he had never known her to be young.

He stopped off at the luncheonette around the corner. Moishe, the co-owner, stood behind the cash register. The tattooed numbers on his wrist were a faded but visible reminder of his concentration camp nightmare, not that he needed any reminders.

"So Luther, what do you do with yourself now?"

Luther simply pretended not to hear, while sensing that Moishe was not done with him.

"My son. He has been accepted to NYU Dental School. Is a good school?"

Luther heard immense fatherly love in Moishe's concern, probably forking over half his life's savings for his son's education. Never before had he talked about anything so personal with Luther. Always in previous years it had been the Dodgers and Sandy Koufax, from Lafayette High in Brooklyn, the two of them bonded in the vicarious thrill of Koufax coming over the top, bending that left knee into the dirt in serving up southpaw stuff never seen before, number 32 hurling that bat-breaking inside hard one and the fall off the table curveball.

And Luther? What was he doing? Reading a few paperback novels because he couldn't do the science Moishe's son evidently could.

The store with its treasure of Necco Wafers, Milk Duds, Goldenberg's Peanut Chews, Milky Ways, Mars Bars, Tootsie Rolls and Good 'n Plenty. The racks of comic books and the characters of his childhood: Archie and Jughead, Batman and Robin, Lois Lane, Clark Kent, Jimmy Olsen.

And there were the adult magazines and the pulp fiction novels with illustrations of erotically clad women in garter belts, the cups of their bras bursting, on the covers, books he had now and then filched as a child, slipping them between the centerfold of the *Daily News* and praying that Moishe would not be hooked into his mind on that particular day so he could go behind the bathroom door to read about Eddie and the big thing he had and the furnished room in which he lived, Eddie who put aside whole days looking for the women who would know what to do with his huge apparatus.

Beyond the cash register was the lunch counter where Benny, the tall, lanky counterman, served meals. Luther stared at the metal shelf of drawers in which hot food was stored. He had never been able to sit and eat at that counter. The store's cellar space was accessible from the building's basement. Such proximity could bring rats and roaches into the mix, Luther was certain, as he watched in amazement patrons shovel steaming forkfuls of grease-covered meat into their mouths.

But he put aside this smaller mystery for the larger one, how Moishe could, from his God-forsaken past behind barbed wire, find his way to Broadway and be a loving father to his son. What made a Jew so good, so smart, so prosperous? It had to be that they did not elevate above the earth but lived upon it. They stayed on the ground and took care of business. Did his mother not say, "If you want to see who owns New York, see how quiet it is on a Jewish holiday. Look what they have done. They come to this country with nothing and now they are doctors, lawyers, professors. Your father has a fine mind, but he has no ambition." His father decrepit, disintegrating, at one time a cashier at the great Jack Dempsey's restaurant, while a thick-lipped Jew with a toothy mouth was calling on Luther to offer advice about his son's education.

His presence in the store was becoming too much, the weight of Moishe's expectation of him and his fear of Moishe's hurt and anger if he and America could not deliver. What was this dictate to stand on the sideline and be concerned for others—to feel that they were children in your midst with feelings you must somehow manage?

"A great dental school, from everything I've heard," Luther managed to say. "I will be going now. I hope I have reassured you as to your son's fate. I hope it is understood that America will continue to be bountiful to you so you do not have to see your dream tarnished and explode in anger and everything can stay on the even keel of nonviolence. I hope you will not be disappointed by my offering. Because just as we are the building that takes in all immigrants to these shores and gives them hope so they can be strong in America, so too do I try to be America in the gifts I offer to all those who come to me in the downtrodden state, for magnanimity is my name and magnification must always be the happening thing. But now, with this interaction having taxed my very limit must I run to the open spaces where I can hope to be free of all that you demand of me, as it it is time for me to be alone with my own desires."

Only after leaving did he remember that Moishe had been one of the storeowners who had stiffed his mother when she came to collect the rent money, as had bullfrog faced Harry Frug, the owner of the radio and TV store. From the window of their childhood room Luke and Luther would watch as the store's neon sign would swing wildly on its support, buffeted by hurricane winds, and the frenzy of excitement Luke would be sent into when it crashed to the pavement. And the hosiery store that had a place in his past, owned and operated by the Frenchman Mr. Berg, calling out Luther's name in an accent like silver. Mr. Berg with the nylons that came in the thin little boxes and the chubby daughter who washed Luther's hair, though she was not the older sister of hers who sent him into shock with the slender, dangerous beauty she displayed and if only *she* would wash his hair. And Mr. Berg too a stifferooni, according to Luther's mother. Or the Orange Grove, where he got the Chinese apples that stained his hands purple, or the Robin Dell, with its tomato-shaped ketchup dispensers for the hamburgers so fat and delicious on the seeded buns, or the Drago Shoe Repair where Mr. Delfinico had his eye put out by the outraged black woman from the welfare hotel who struck him with the high heel of her shoe while the Watusi-thin, Watusi-tall Isley brothers, magnetic in their defiance mode and with conks in their marcelled hair, danced wildly, elegantly, in the street outside in the bright colors they flaunted as they continued to live in the ever present now. And all those who owned those stores, they too were stifferoonis.

Free of the building, free of Moishe, free (for the moment) of Mona, he walked in Central Park among the trees and the bronze monuments, unencumbered as a child at play. Tony Pascual, unconnected to anything but his guitar, was there in dark glasses that showed him demented and sinister. Luther did not sing, "Go away from my window. Leave at your own chosen speed," but he thought it and kept going to avoid proximity to Tony . How much he loved the open spaces of the park, for to walk alone with the prospect of pleasure ahead was to live. And if 1968 had a lonely sound with the sunlight of 1967 gone, the speed brought him into the synthetic sunshine that the approaching winter darkness compelled.

Others less metropolitan than cosmopolitan were there to be found, the Fortunatos from Florence and the now Paris-based Plescotts and the Grunattas from the Bahamas, all fresh from their showers at the Plaza Hotel and destined for a nighttime of social event, while on the mall, approaching the bandshell and the Bethesda terrace, a young woman of great beauty approached. Many there were who saw her freeze the Frisbees of the hippie horde in mid-air and dissolve the mask of recalcitrant opaqueness from their faces.

"No, you don't know me and there's no point to pretending that you do," she said, addressing Luther's gaunt presence behind her whispering "Terrible love, terrible love," as the only talisman that came to him.

Many times Luther fell down dying only to resurrect so he would not lose what he had come upon. When he went on his knees to her, she pulled him up by the hair.

"Oh yes, oh very yes yes," Luther replied, now staring into her searchlight green eyes. "Can we be in harmony with the night coming in all around us?" he felt the necessity to ask.

"I am just back from Israel and feel lost. That compels me to overlook the disparities."

"How you talk" was all he could think to say, wanting to touch her face but knowing he couldn't with his hands of Dexedrine coldness. Even the fallen leaves were raised to attention.

"What can you give me that I don't already have?" she asked.

"No resistance to your truth," he said.

She came forward with answers to questions he hadn't asked. She said her name was Bathsheba and that she was the daughter of a rabbi working out of Brooklyn. She said she had lasted less than a year at the great Oberlin College because she could not abide a state whose name had such a preponderance of vowels over consonants, opting instead for the structure born of letter parity of Israel, where she worked the land on a kibbutz, summoning tomatoes out of the desert sand. While there, she fell in love with an Israeli commando who had broken the complex code of fear and made courage all his own, and who talked obsessively of planting his seed in her in Haifa to keep the history and the geography of his origins intact.

"You saw his desire as an invasion of an intolerable territorial imperative," Luther offered.

"Stop with the chatter of your substandard mind," she said.

They were seated on a park bench, the statue of Sir Walter Scott holding strong against the fact of his vastly unread book *Ivanhoe.*

"Do you have any happiness at the thought of him, or is it prevented by the fact of the *Sir* that starts his name?"

"Please, I am thinking of my commando," she said, and so he tried to think along with her, abandoning Sir Walter Scott for the Israeli and the daring he brought to his own life, wondering what it must be to kill a man under the Middle Eastern sun. I have never left Manhattan and I have never killed anyone, he thought, going over his small list of accomplishments. "But I did graduate from high school."

"Are you here to engage me or to talk to yourself?"

"Decidedly the former. Believe me when I say this—you are not Bethesda Fountain material."

"And I will try to believe you are my new commando."

"Tomorrow the very great Cream—of *Fresh Cream* fame—will be performing at Madison Square Garden. Their music will fly right up to us, and they will sing 'I Feel Free' as if from atop a speeding car, with such a strong wind blowing. And so I must require myself to be there."

He cupped his ears and lowered his head to hear her response.

Quickly, she said, "I will match your presence with my own." Unable to restrain himself, he clapped his hands while remaining faithful to the somber mask the Dexedrine had imposed on him.

Madison Square Garden was a bowl of concrete with pastel-colored seating with not a flower showing as Cream made their presence felt. Jack Bruce confessed that he could not sing and Eric Clapton said he was faking it as well, though he did have the right name. Ginger Baker acknowledged that his first name was absurd but said it wasn't the reason he was dying of speed.

Over their tone-deaf sound in the cavernous space he tried to tell her the history of his origins, where his father was alleged to have come from, what it meant to have a building you were responsible for, and what the requirements were for saving a family. He had no assurance that she heard him, but it felt important in the telling, for he had his speed mouth going, and words were a necessary result of the love high it gave him.

Not that he didn't embrace the event, do some dancing in his seat and in the steep aisle when the spirit moved him. Not that he did not relish the extinguishing force of a Ginger Baker drum solo and the momentum it gave him in the world to have a date to go with the concert as a way of bookmarking time, the heavens holy, the earth holy, the speed manufacturing a love that made Madison Square Garden holy, all past and all future falling away into the now of who he was with, if only he could penetrate, not circumnavigate, her solidity and equal her Oberlin worth to the point of touching. And yet it was asking a lot to expect an Israel-experienced woman to get off the ground with Cream and pain struck when he saw in the restroom mirror an image of his frailty and all that he was wanting the drug to compensate for.

Because Cream couldn't sing all night—because they had bars to go to and whiskey to drink and women to see—the agenda with his purpose had to more fully emerge, the matter of nakedness and what to do about it pushing through. Because Bathsheba, given her genetic endowment—melon breasts and skin that tanned without the sun and all the rest—made it a formidable challenge to contemplate what he might have to offer in return. Even with the speed pill running strong throughout him, he could see that Bathsheba was not stringy Laurie Jacek but the real thing, whether she had intaglio in her knowledge store or not.

They hailed a cab at Eighth Avenue and Thirty-third Street, where hidden from the sight of Macy's was the neon cross all lit up in red hanging from the church of the Christ Jesus, while the gray monstrosity of the General Post Office held its ground, work going on within its structure if in a diminished way all through the night, the men of anonymity toiling with their faces to the box scheme and Mr. Ruggiero lashing them with a tongue so active in his Ernie Borgnine face.

"I cannot be a British rock star, and I cannot leave where I am destined to be, not in my current and forevermore stringiness," he said, Eighth Avenue, as it ever was, a strip of sorrow with the darkness of its own depression, the streets lined with solitary men holding their *Daily News* and checking out the ponies while the world changed. He saw them entering the many bars where they went without a woman and beyond the point of even seeking one. Men going to *get their loads on.* As the night gathered its strength and tried to overpower the lights of New York City, Bathsheba moved closer to him in the back seat, Brooklyn being in the other direction and the urban grit that was all around bouncing off her soft and radiant flesh.

She reached for his hand but he pulled back.

"Give it to me," she said. Again he pulled back, lest he die and die. But she was unrelenting, and when he yielded it to her, she said simply, "Where does such coldness come from?"

'I cannot answer when my secret is my life." It was not for him to tell her he was doing the Ginger Baker speed thing so he could be with her.

The apartment was quiet. He was seeing now through her eyes and feeling shame at how he lived. He offered her a joint, which she accepted, and so he had her clouded state on which to move forward. After a while she lay down on the narrow bed.

"Now come," she said, and when he balked, she yawned and began to undress. Only with the light off was he able to shed his clothes and lie on his side beside her and feel her warmth and hot breath.

"Weak, underweight boy with your hands so cold. Drug addict boy with the sad sad eyes so afraid of life. You my such a nobody commando, just give me all of the little you have to give."

By morning the speed demon had ground down sufficient that he could doze while she was awakening from her contamination-free slumber. He had ceded the narrow bed to her and lay on the floor. With his eyes closed he sensed her looking down at him.

"Will my little commando not come to me?" and so he did, kissing her morning mouth and allowing his coldness to be taken in once more by her warmth. Her touch so electric, her flesh so soft. He thinking, this is the flawless teeth of beauty and this the luscious lips of beauty, this the nipple of beauty, this the pubic hair of beauty, this the knee, these the toes of beauty, trying even as he looked with fear to capture it for all time, in the morning light both of them coming alive to their lust.

Over a coffee shop breakfast she told him the truth, that it was hard to be back from Israel and in the matrix of her dominating parents, and he, in his uselessness, had made it easier. A great cry went up from him as she went away. He cried and cried without knowing why, as if some picture of the life he could not fully have had been presented to him.

He called her that evening, his love flag snapping in the breeze but the words *foregone conclusion* flashing in his consciousness and summoning foreboding, as if to tell him that he would experience an execution, not a conversation. And yes, she answered with the pragmatic and savvy strength of Israel, saying, "I have other plans for the night. Life is calling to me at an accelerated pace that you cannot match. It is best to get off the phone. Friends may be trying to reach me. Do not even try to say that you do not understand, my little commando."

So he staggered from the phone booth he had stepped into, a solitary man taking him in through all-seeing eyes, the kind, like him, who walked in the park alone, accompanied only by his shadow.

Chapter 59

It was terrible love, a fire that did not lend itself to suffocation by other women, Bathsheba and Laurie Jacek merely entering his record book as bedmates he had biblically known even as the flame that burned for Mona maintained its staying power.

Witnesses were many to the spectacle he made, his fingers stuck to the rotary dial of the phones he relied on to make her happen and buffeted by waves of anxiety when she refused to answer, he crying out "Mommy, Mommy, Mommy" though it was for the repudiating world in response to strike him on his head and body and order him to be a man. Many many were the times the repudiating world did just this to him. But it was not for Luther to run from that which he needed to be, for hours on end stuck to the phones of New York City, his fingers doomed to dial and dial until she answered.

Mona had made a new friend, Lisa, and gone for dinner at her apartment.

"A very American name," Luther said. "But it must be fully determined that she is not a catalyst for insurrection."

Because she was in the right percentile, Mona's social life could flourish, the women of Boston seeking to have her, and for this he was truly grateful. He did not want her in the place of loneliness and sorrow and rejection, as that would have been cause for him to die. And while he was aware of the cold and drenching rain pouring down on him in the public places that he himself frequented, he could not alter his routines, for "home" and "friend"meant limitation and the voiding of the possibility to *increase the number* that was his purpose as much as life itself.

And though the goal of acquisition was uppermost in his mind (seeing that he could not master the contents of the books he had been assigned to read), he agreed to meet her new friend. As a sign of things to come, he fell down dead on the street once and then again and again, Mona availing herself of her strength by picking him up with a firmness that got him walking each and every time.

Lisa hailed Luther and Mona from the smiling distance she maintained. The bare floors of her apartment and her tortured paintings on the walls offered clues, as did the spaghetti she served with a cared-for sauce. A third woman, Rita, was present to sustain the bright and seamless chatter. They were not in a state of territorial aggrandizement; their words simply flowed from their art, giving them a muscularity and a vigor in scale with the efforts marshaled into realizing their creations.

Luther did not outwardly despair at this plunge into the awareness of what his life was truly like. He accepted that he could not be roaming in Central Park and in the room with them at the same time and sat silent eating his plate of spaghetti and seeking to ignore the word stream he could not seem to enter. The more expansive they grew, the more into himself he receded, seeking the place where he could be invisible in their presence. They were not unaware. They had discerned the sense of angry inferiority that engulfed him.

"He's incredible. He's got two majors," Mona said, her well-meant boast only serving to further his repression. With chattering teeth and knocking knees he spoke from his place of coldness, sufficient to say that yes he was learning the language of English through literature but also through the phenomenon of PoliSci so that he would have the GPA that the world would approve of.

From some depth beyond his reckoning he found his voice. "Listen to me, and listen to me strong. I am erecting a life beyond the strength of your own foundations, even while I sit here in mute and smiling witness of your womanhood, as I have been scripted to do. Someday I will fly above all the things that hold me down right now, and will not have to feel intimidated in your presence. Someday I will motherfuck the integers that would baffle and bind me. Someday I will synthesize my whole life. I don't need to be no motherfucking Bob Dylan for my own greatness."

He fell into sleep and when he awoke he was back in New York with the need to interpret and assimilate all that had happened. Mona would go back to Lisa and Rita and they would share their bodies with each other or lesbianism might not be the thing at all; there might be present the intellectual and artistic men of Boston, Harvard men and Tufts men and Boston Museum School of Fine Arts men, who would take them to bed in the repeated and diverse ways their fine minds could arrange. Images from his personal stash of erotica entered the picture, comings and spendings and gamahuching galore. He was compelled to call her at her domicile, and when the freedom to be had from her forthcomingness was not presented, when she did not answer even once but allowed the phone to ring and ring into the Boston night, he had no choice but to conclude that the party was on, and so what choice did he have but to make the phone the primary instrument of his command center? Dinner was dinner, but now eleven o'clock had come and gone, the time arriving when the women began to shed their clothes and expose the fullness of their breasts and the feature presentation below. The need now for all actions to be directed toward unearthing the truth, he began to dial at five-minute intervals with the same incriminating result, the investigation escalating with the manufacture of Lisa's phone number through stellar research. Though he knew it would be held against him, that all the forces of disapproval were aligned on his border, what was that against the pleasure/pain at the prospect of the orgy scene he would be dialing himself into and that he had been looking for his whole life? It was now after midnight and to sleep alone with the unconfirmed knowledge that she was in the palace of flesh abounding amounted to torture supreme, a deprivation of the ice cream as well as the sprinkles that went along with it *on a glorious summer day in the America he could not reach.* He dialed and dialed his way into the mystery of her Boston life and got a voice husky with sleep that dared to say hello.

"Is the party going on? Do I dare to be naked? Who do I take first with my massive tool? Would you, dear lady, like to ride it into the regions of bliss?" He heard the dial tone reassert itself, seeking to confine him to the hell of non-information. He cleared a space so he could run into all four walls of his room and knock himself out to be spared his own excitation, but thoroughness summoned him back on the line, the wall of truth he collided with being Mona Van Dine, who said, "Was that you who just called? Tell me it wasn't, please."

"Is the party still going on? Please, please wait for me. I will run naked along the old Boston Post Road. I will sleep by campfires. I will eat wild berries. But please let me be there for the plunging action I need to be a part of."

"You are truly insane. You woke Lisa up and scared her half to death."

"Who else did I wake up? Who? Who?"

"Ninny. Imbecile. Dangerous lunatic. There is no one else here. No one. I slept over because it got too late to go home."

"Are you bound together in lesbian nation? Tell me. I won't die."

"You embarrass me. You are ruining my life. I can't take this anymore."

"I have a mandate from the people to search for truth."

Mona Van Dine did not kill him. She was too far away. But she did cry the tears of the bereaved in mourning for sanity and wondering why her vessel had come to flounder in lunatic waters.

Chapter 60

That winter Mona's father called to her, in the voice that fathers use, a voice that no one else can hear, to summon their daughters to them. And because she bore a strong resemblance, with her blond hair shining in the sun and darkness, she had no choice but to vacate the apartment in Boston and the life that had developed in and around her.

Peter told her, without saying a word, that while he had bombed Germany with the bombs of America, he could not bomb away the loneliness, that the spirit that had permeated Camp was gone, that not even standing by the hearth with his back to the roaring fire could bring heat to his bones or his fear-frozen mind. He told her that no one came to him and that he went to no one, and that he had no enthusiasm for the study of American history or the presidents, nor did he relish recording on film the marvelousness of his physique. He said he stared all day at the sound-muffling snow and the vengeance against warmth it inflicted on the earth. He had many things to say under the sedating effect of the sleeping pills he took as a way to administer peace to his mind.

So yes, even though she had already launched her fight against the patriarchal pricks menacing her full existence following the death of Lenore, she nevertheless exited the scene of her development. Initially she did not explain the move in terms of her father.

Nor did she say that there was a special one who wanted her to stay, and that his name was Lane, and that he came in the dark of the Boston night with his hair so black to knock knock knock on her fragile door, importuning her to open to him so he could give her the seed of his youth and genius. She did not say that she was fleeing from him and his soulful eyes anymore than she said to her father, This I cannot do for you. She merely said she needed a break from Boston and from school.

Nor did Luther say, Mona's father has called to her and my mother has called to me. They just went to their respective partners in compliance with the force fields in their lives as they were manifesting.

The snow was something to see and to consider, the crunch of it underfoot and how it covered up its own deceit behind the claim to the purity of its whiteness. Some days the sky sent down wet kisses. Some days the snow was just dry powder that claimed an attachment to nothing but the wind that carried it along. Either way Peter Van Dine was watching it in company with his Tareyton cigarettes and the ashes that he flicked in a house that had no movement without Lydia Van Dine to stir it into the life that she possessed, snow and ice matching neatly with the permafrost he felt inside himself.

Mona set up shop in the guest house to give her a measure of separation from her father and tried to hold off the cold with gas-powered heat. If it seemed unnatural for her to be there with him, nothing was more natural for Peter than to be with a daughter of his own flesh and blood.

"My mother kicks him out of the house and dumps him in my lap? Tell me that hasn't been her lifelong ambition?"

Luther listening with a giant ear from downstate, sensing the power of her anger to melt the snows. She heard him groaning when nightfall came, the thud from upstairs coming through the ceiling as he fell out of his bed time and again. The first time it happened she thought he was having a heart attack, but what she heard was merely the nocturnal groans of a man coming out of a drugged sleep into the pain of his life. Because when he lay on the floor, he lay on her, the responsibility factor kicking in and the bombing of Germany so long ago, when he was young and the crew sat on their helmets as protection from the flak rising from below in its hot metal quest for their inner chambers and would she ever know what it was to get through a day with just a candy bar in the throes of the Great Depression or would she be spiritually deprived by the shrinks of this new world leading her away into their secret chambers for the judgment decrees and the separation of loved ones one from the other that they thrived on?

Peter would try to confront the blank paper, but always now it repudiated him, while she sought to torture the canvas with renderings that would break her from the academic mold into which lethal Lane had placed her. And all the while the Catskills reminding them that it was just a glacial deposit, the earthly remains of a moraine moving south out of the white coldness of its former arctic abode.

Wherever their minds went by day, the restaurants called to them at night, so that they could be seated in public where, by proximity and fact, their resemblance to each other was noticed, to the point where she took to wearing a wool cap even at the table until she saw that it did little to obscure the familial tie. There were the evenings when she cooked, as neither of them wanted the public places to rule. The silences at the dinner table were lengthy. The little conversation she offered was guarded, as there was territory to protect, her own.

Lane began to enter the picture more fully, crowding out her father and the snow and, yes, Luther too. The excellence she had seen and fled from was calling her back. A woman should have the right to access the brilliance she had been exposed to, even if it caused her pain, her most noteworthy fear being not whether Luther would fall down dying should Lane gain entrance but whether in the state of nakedness Lane would find her wanting, given the reality that she had the boyishly narrow hips of her father. And he was the other in his Jewishness, the snow now manifesting as WASP coldness that she had to flee from into Semitic otherness.

All this while Luther was having serious problems with the winter garden to which she had retreated. Yes, it was a people-less environment safe from potential competition that could jeopardize the finish line of her ultimate return to New York so their life could truly begin, but on the other hand he felt unease that she had left her own straight line to greatness, as without an institution to propel her there, what could there be but lostness? Breaking free of the paralysis of his conflicting desires, he cried out to her, and he did so with the timing of the just, as she had wearied of the leafless trees and the deep drifts and the ongoing reality of her father's misery.

Did he not have her mission to achieve greatness to support? Did she not have a timetable for that success to be hers? No no, he had to banish from her midst the prospect of lingering despair and get her life back on track.

Though he could not talk easily about love with his mother in earshot, that didn't mean Luther couldn't feel it, Mona needing to stay on the other side of what his sisters were so he could live in the promise of her America with the Chevrolet sign intact and the sun of childhood summers shining. He didn't come in with his guns blazing. It wasn't that kind of rescue. He just arrived with a rental truck and kissed Peter full on the lips for the happiness he was experiencing at being useful to his loved one #1 in all the universe and all he could bring to the unspoken situations in their lives. Peter pushed him away in a wave of abashment but Luther just came back upon him with affection unbounded for all Peter could be if he just didn't die. He didn't name Peter father of the year but he told him to hang with it while the pain of Lydia's feminine anarchy dissipated, Lydia by this time having unfurled a banner from the apartment window proclaiming love an activity of the male member and not a state of impotence masquerading as harmony.

Because Peter was from a time and place that had had its hardship, and had his own deserts to traverse and mountains to climb and wintry blasts to endure, and had he not been working all this time for the beautification of the land to have it someday as the bed in which he slept, the green grass and the dirt pulled over him, a casket of earthy comfort, for he had bombed Germany and seen poverty and knew the life of his other, a twin living lonely in a rusted trailer in one of America's more dilapidated states. He saw the existence that was looming without the safety net of her, for what could he be without the money of her estate? A lowly teacher? Would he have his suits of white linen? Would he have his cars of power? Or would he be consigned to a slum walkup and Spam and the grinding ambience of the poor? And what would teaching at a university do but milk him of his essence and leave him in soulless conformity with the other drones.

Luther was in full comprehension mode now. Peter was as Luther's father as Luther's father was like Peter, not that Peter sat in the automats of New York City for long hours but without the succor of a woman, there was only the unrelenting harshness of winter. So Luther could kiss Peter on his Dinty Moore beef stew lips and smell his Tareyton breath, but he could not deny what Lydia had wrought in ejecting Peter from her premises and revealing her clobber power.

As they set out for Boston in the moving van, Mona seemed remote from him.

"I'm supposed to live alone. I'm not supposed to have anyone with me, my father or anyone else. It's something I've known since I was a child," she said, when he asked about her seeming distance from him.

"Is it that I am somewhere I do not belong?" he said, feeling unwelcome on the premises of her life. He took his eye off the road to try to look closely into her mind but all he saw was the ball of anger coming out of it.

"Can't you give yourself some answers?"

"After all my hard work, you do nothing but treat me like the dirt beneath your shoes," he said, channeling his mother.

"What hard work?"

"The van. Is that not the hard work of my life, to shepherd you around to the success your life can be, so I can hide behind it?"

"Demented nincompoop. Go find your own life."

He drove in an angry silence that exploded into a verbal lashing when they arrived some hours later in Boston and after moving her things into the apartment she had found, with the help of her mother. He heard himself demand that she come down to New York City the following weekend and could not help but notice her mouth and the calculating intent to provoke him with its redness and so he struck her, as she had no right to present her mouth and tongue in such a way without the blow of retaliatory justice coming down upon her.

"Bastard. Motherfucking bastard," she screamed, and pulled a carving knife so big from one of the boxes and slashed the air to show who truly was the boss and to bring him to the recognition that he was on the brink of his own annihilation. "Skinny prick bastard thinks he's going to kill his girlfriend in Paris? Thinks he's going to maraud without consequence?"

He spread himself against a wall, and slowly slid to the floor as she approached, holding the knife handle with both hands for the extra stabbing power the joint action could bring. Her face had gone livid, he saw. And yet the terror left; he had found a tranquil space within the storm.

"I am love itself, if only you would know it. I am love itself, if only I would know it," he said quietly.

She retreated to an opposite corner.

"I want some peace. I want to be free to have a life without you hanging all over me. You're sick. Don't you understand? You're completely sick. You don't want me. You want what I have. You want my talent because you have none of your own. You have nothing. You have no persona, no psychology, no anything. Your cupboard is bare and you hate yourself because you know that. The only thing for people like you to do is die. You don't have the goods.

You were born that way. It's not your fault, but leave people who do have something alone. I feel sorry for you, but that's not enough. And your pride is so great that you'll never let me go. You'll kill me before that happens, just like that boy in the newspaper article. You thought I would forget about that, but I didn't. I didn't forget at all. You're totally insane with your constant phone calls and your possessiveness."

Luther lay face down on the floor. All the things he had promised himself he wouldn't be when he and Mona first met he had become. How shameful that he had reverted to the ugly aspects of his behavior with Jane Thayer. He had struck a girl. He had struck Mona Van Dine. But did she have the right to exterminate him before he had really lived?

He sat up and opened *Death in Venice*. The pages were laced with coldness. He kept the Vintage paperback in front of his face, but no matter how involved he hoped to appear in trying to understand the dynamic of Aschenbach and young Tadzio in a book wasted on the young, she could see right through the mask to his smoldering wound. And yet he couldn't leave, for where was there to go? To a life he did not have? Without her the shield was taken away and he had only to stare into the death trap of his family.

That evening they walked behind the Sears store toward the trolley. And there it came around the bend, its one car in full faithfulness to the rails. Soon, by stops and starts, it went underground and entered the Park Street station, modern like the subway that took them to Cambridge.

It wasn't like 1967, when he could, without warning, just walk out on her and play "Under My Thumb" in full triumph. Now she wouldn't go looking for him. Now she would just be relieved to have him gone.

Harvard Square showed itself in its unyielding coldness and put its visitor's stamp upon him. The obese newsstand vendor, seeing Luther stare, took the stogie from his mouth and said, "You're not one of them Hahvads. Never could be. Can see it in your eyes.

You're defeated. You're just a bum with long hair." His small fat man's hands had been blackened by printer's ink. The vendor saying, without saying, that the news came and went but he was an enduring presence, acquiring the coins he needed to maintain his bulk as his character came to definition shaped by the repetitive actions of his days.

The Coop across the street, closed for the night, and the nearby Brattle Theater served as a reminder that Boston/Cambridge was now a part of his life through her, and that she defined him more than college, more than family, more than anything. To lose her and the world she had given him was too much,

"Well, do you want me up here or don't you?" The words slipping out. Asinine, pathetic words. He recognized the insanity of remaining with her after all that had gone on back at the apartment, but he couldn't leave.

"You know I don't. You know I couldn't. Want you? You? Woman beater. Potential murderer. Coward. Lunatic. You? You?"

"Look, we're in public," he said, prompting Mona into a burst of hateful laughter.

"Public? Public? When do you ever give a shit about public?" she said, going unladylike on him with her fecal reference. "You act insane in public and now you're cautioning me?"

"I am here," he said, shivering in his pea jacket. "I have not gone to the United Nations."

"Go wherever you want to go, dimwit."

She took off, walking tall on the balls of her feet like the big cheese she now was.

Luther tried to cover his shame by staring without seeing the magazines and newspapers at the stand. The vendor, smelling his feebleness, punished him for it, saying, "You buying or looking?" because he knew where the buck was and where the food was and how to grab the one and eat the other.

Luther backed away, saying with words that only he could hear, "I will be back, and back soon, to wash my face in your newspapers, for they are a definite escape for one who was tired before he was born and who lacks the vigor to *do*. When I will come back, I truly cannot say, but right now my life is escaping from me."

The street traffic was heavy, and seeing the willfulness of the vehicles' goal of ceaseless motion, Luther took on the beasts that would stall him while his love escaped on the other side and compelled them into the pause that gave him new life by running into the midst of their metal reality even as he eyed Mona casting fearful glances so very histrionic behind her as she sought to lengthen the distance between them. Seeing him as the impediment to the honking traffic and his stand against vehicular presumption, she apprehended the safety of Harvard, seeking the very best for her survival in choosing two young men who wore the apparel of the institution, one in a vinyl slicker, the other a more substantial varsity jacket, both crimson and with the necessary white lettering to signify who they were. Beyond that, they were unassuming giants of the earth, basking in the brilliance of the accomplishments that spoke for themselves, for that reason forgoing shrub growth on their heads and outlandish apparel. They were free to go about their days with a quiet sense of purpose fueled by the love they had received by virtue of their admission to a primo institution.

"Help me. Help me, please. He wants to hurt me unto my own death. His only purpose is the demise of all around him," Luther could only imagine her saying, so that when he came upon the scene he could have no doubt about the odds stacked against him.

"I show myself to you as a brother, not as a warrior nation. I throw myself on your court of mercy to absolve me of any intended injustice against the one I profess to love."

How he admired their intelligence, their accomplishments, their capture of the American dream, and most of all their avoidance of hopeless enmeshment with women and the freedom to devote their energy to their studies. They would be the kind who spent their days studying higher mathematics and in their leisure time read chess books.

"Because I go to college too," he said. "I attend the University of Mona Van Dine and the curriculum is called 'Holding onto the Love Which Is America."

"What is this about?" The two of them spoke in unison, having no time for separate words.

"I will go now to the Hayes Bickford across the street. Please note as I walk the innocence suggested by my empty hands and innocuous demeanor. What else do I live for but to be absolved of suspicion, let alone of guilt. I will retreat to the greasy spoons and the men who bet the ponies and who lack the ironical tongue and who have one belt and one pair of shoes and *who have never left the state except in times of war,* yes yes the men with bad teeth and spikes of hair sprouting from their ears and noses. Just watch me now."

He walked backwards with his hands in plain sight and his pockets emptied out so that no one, not the Harvards or the other arbiters of justice, could look askance at his intention to build a life of goodness on a scaffold of pain.

The Hayes Bickford had a counter and a woman in a uniform and the clatter of dishes in a kitchen that went unseen, and if the woman had a wealth of information about the food and drink, she was not sharing it, restricting her truth to the orders she took, Luther's being a coffee and a muffin sure to keep his skinniness intact.

Two officers of the law were seated at one table, and because they gave him the eye, Luther went on high alert. Not that his self-consciousness wasn't already over the moon following the public scene. Once again he would model Norman Bates in *Psycho* as he was under arrest.

Later, he walked along Mass. Avenue, looking up at the stars visible in the sky as they seldom were in New York City. "I too am a star. Even if the light should not be shining on me at the moment does not mean that I do not exist, for darkness is the time for regeneration." And to the passersby he could with conviction announce, "Not one fly. Not one fly am I hurting as I make my rounds."

All around Mona's building guards equipped with fortitude and purpose and intellect stood alert, protecting their treasure from the rampages of evil and depravity. They read standing up and sitting down and even positioned on their heads could do the complex calculations that would enable the world to progress so children could continue to have their fields of play and every American his stick of butter. Because they had bulked up so big he could not get past them to the door of his beloved. They beat him back with Proust and sought to save his soul with Kierkegaard. They even played mournful Mahler in his ear and read to him from *A Thousand and One Arabian Nights* while highlighting the success that was required to have an American life, giving Luther no choice but to retreat from the barrier of rejection set up by these men of vigil with their roadblock ways.

And yet she came back to him. Not that day and not the next and not the one after that. Many times was he rendered unconscious by sleeping pills and in his dreams entered worlds he was sorry to be taken from on his return to wakefulness. When finally, after a week, he began to groggily pull himself together did the phone ring. Mona Van Dine was on the line.

Chapter 61

With the easy money from the renting office Luther could now buy the books and clothing and other goods he thought, in the moment, he needed. Meanwhile, President R. M. Nixon refrained from deploying the language of guns for some and butter for others while trying to create a tidy end to America's involvement in the war far away, even as it was being waged to rock and roll music with the infantry and airborne and seafaring on drugs, Luther trying to convince himself that he had a right to be in New York City among the paperback books of his life.

He went south to the Hell's Kitchen area of Manhattan, where Brooklyn Sid Nizer was in residence in a top-floor apartment of a walkup building and in peripheral relationship to the more trafficked streets of Times Square. The area spoke as one, saying it was for the left-behind Irish who had no education and who sat on the garbage cans outside the buildings when they were not sitting in the bars they had made their second homes. It said it had train tracks running through it in a state of rusted disuse and rats as big as cats and tenements as the norm and a windowless monstrosity called the New York Telephone Building on Tenth Avenue, a strip with a history of wantonness and wickedness as wide as its dimensions that put you on shaky ground in terms of how you thought about your life when you were on it. From somewhere on the tough streets big Jackie O'Neill warned that he wasn't playing, that he was going to kick Dolan's ass should he ever sound on his mother again, even as other young men of the neighborhood were being scooped off stoops and garbage cans and barstools and placed either in Sing Sing or in helicopter gunships.

But Brooklyn Sid Nizer was there now, increasing his marriage vow to the smack that *was* his mother and his bride and operating out of a mouth below his too abundant mustache and a calculator head harboring a desire for freedom from remembered pain, Luther seeing that he had secured an apartment at some minuscule rent.

"Luther's looking for a place. I want him to meet Nikki," Jesse said to Brooklyn Sid, eliciting a sigh from him as he tied a strip of torn T-shirt around his forearm and pulled it tight with his big teeth. Jesse was in his uniform of denim duds and sneakers and a witness to something reckless going on, with Sid Nizer's relationship to the dispensing of drugs as well as using them probably not a well-kept secret in the building, creating the possibility that the police might come to visit.

"I tell her I love her every day and that we just have to get it on, but she won't go that way with me. All she'll do is make curtains for my windows. I guess that's something, right? Hey, Jesse, maybe she'll dig Luther. What do you think, Jesse? You think she'll be digging Luther?"

"Everyone digs Luther," Jesse said, the two of them putting him between the crunch of their simpatico intelligence.

Luther did not go to the dark place of remembering Brooklyn Sid's lascivious intent and possible consummation with Mona the previous summer. For whatever reason, he held his grievance in abeyance, though it remained poised on the fringes of his consciousness.

Sid Nizer opened and closed his fists several times before finding the right vein for his soothing needle and quickly arrived in his pleasure place.

The apartment began filling with men. They brought with them the coldness wrought by their own pleasure-seeking. Young and strong, they did not fit Luther's image of the nodding, corkscrewing junkie on the corner with the Snickers bar or bottle of Coke loosely held. All were seeking victory over circumstances they felt no need to define and to relive the experience of their moms' sweet breath. This they shared while waiting to get noddy on the content of the glassine envelopes Brooklyn Sid was dispensing.

Brooklyn Sid. Scale Master Sid. He was one. He was both.

Luther left the scene of Sid Nizer's sluggish enterprise and walked down the long sloping street toward Tenth Avenue. The smell of manure grew strong as he approached, horses plop-plopping their dung with their dignity intact. Though they had stories to tell of the booted policemen who rode them, they had passed beyond the need for such mundane tales to the place of serene acceptance their eyes spoke of, and Luther could only think that to be so big and strong was to possess all-encompassing wisdom and had to be the reason that even their dung smelled pungent but good.

The building was between Tenth and Eleventh Avenues, across the street from the police horse stables, so safety was assured should he take the apartment. Sitting outside on a metal garbage can in the warm spring air was an old Irishwoman who gave her name as Mrs. Muldooney. She said she had been born on that very block and that she was keeping a vigil so that it would not ever go away and that she was the manager of that very building. She said the people on the next block and the block one over were filthy whores and that, because she was a Catholic, she could tell a good person as well as a bad one from a mile away. She said that spuds were her primary source of nutrition and that with skin as white as hers, she had no choice but to wait for God.

Luther had his own truth to share, a meditation on the word *Catholic* and all it inspired. He said that John F. Kennedy had not installed the Vatican cardinals in the White House, and yet that in itself did not make him a good man. He said that the word *Catholic* itself suggested the coldness within the cathedral on a raw fall day and chasubles and miters and all the regalia of formality in the service of jowly, aging flesh. He said the whole religion stunk of a peculiar kind of incense. He said that the Irish Catholics of his teenage years were now mired in the ongoing futility of fighting the omnipresent now you see them now you don't Vietcong and that Catholicism should know what it was up against when dealing with such a bunch, because Catholicism counted on the thing in place, the edifice without an engine, while the Vietcong rode the wind. He said that the vitality of the church was being vitiated in the course of people winning out over ritual, that fucking in itself was a religion that not even the plain could deny.

Mrs. Muldooney gave no indication that she was considering what he said as she maintained her vigil. She did acknowledge that her grown son shared the apartment with her and that if there were areas of unexplored sorrow and rancor between them, the newspaper and cups of strong tea covered them over. "Because a bridge may be built to last, but feelings come and go," she said, from the wisdom her vantage point provided.

Luther confided that his generation was intent on dying but he himself was intent on living through the scholarship he was inflicting on the paperback books assigned by the great CCNY. He told her further that now that she had revealed her identity as manager of the building, he would do his best to be perfect in her estimation even as he conducted himself according to the needs of his sexualized will, that he had a mother to the north and that he had rebelled against the structures and strictures of her religion and would have to do the same with her, Mrs. Muldooney, even as he tried to please her unto death.

Mrs. Muldooney shared that her Johnny was a fine boy, that yes he had a case of the shyness but overall was doing so much better, that he was down to strangling only one woman a month from his high of two per week. "Polite. You've never seen a politer man. Everybody says the same thing. He drinks his pints in the bar and never bothers nobody. Nobody. Brings the paper home for me every night, so neat and folded." She wore her face very pitted with acne scars and her wire rim glasses very thick and offered a challenge to the sun to make an impact on her skin so white.

Luther applied the warmth of his affection to her rocklike being and passed through a narrow corridor with pebbled walls. Beyond the glass-paned door at the other end a courtyard awaited him and a deuce of tenements in parity with the two that fronted the street. He heard the cooing commotion of the pigeons and saw the lonely trees struggling for their dignity from the New York City earth and saw too the dull and disintegrating boards that made the backyard fence a thing of unreal beauty.

From somewhere in the vicinity he heard the ghosts of families past living as atoms in the air: raging fathers, weary mothers, squalling infants, children running wild, and only the celibate priests to go to with their immigrant commotions, and yet the courtyard was saying he had entered a pocket of peace from all the world had become, a time when milk was delivered in bottles and the men in our dwellings were digging the subway tunnels and off-loading the boats and the bars along Twelfth Avenue were flourishing. Beyond loomed the windowless telephone building, a structure of white brick that spoke of the business of America and the demise of all that did not meet its purpose, saying the future of America was concrete and no one must try to tell it otherwise.

Nikki Ballen was ready for him as he wasn't for her rosy cheeks and cool gaze.

"Are you here for business or to gawk?" she asked, her beauty having momentarily stunned him.

"I will answer you plainly. I will tell you that I am tied to vast resources and am here to do the deal. Now let me ask you how is it that you can leave such a place as this? Do you not want to live and die here?"

"I have a boyfriend who wants to multiply in me. For what else are these hips made? This can only be a chapter in my life."

She told him that she hung on marginally as a student at CCNY, taking a course here and a course there so she could stay registered, but that she had been led beyond the gates of academia to a life of bicycle messenger substance, wearing sneakers on her sock-less feet as she pedaled about the city with packages for the productive.

"Even so, the men of Israel wish to cast their seed into me. The call of Israel is very strong," she also said.

"Yes yes, to all you say, but even as I marvel at your ability to live outside the gates of academia and all the structure, my mind weeps and applies the word 'anarchy' to your posture of indifference to the accumulation of the credits needed to establish one—yes, one—upon the ground of soundness. But I see what it is even as I speak. You are in the realm of the high board score ones. You have elevated above the drudgery of the paperback book curricula, whereas I am bonded to it by my low score status, and fated to struggle for grades that will verify what I can never be, my status having been determined early on."

And so Luther gave her cash on the barrel head and the deal was done, and now he could have a place of his own to love Mona Van Dine and be with himself.

Tony Pascual was dubious, saying "A month, two at most, I give you in this new place. You'll be coming back to me, just like the last time, because you can't stay away."

Luther refrained from saying that Tony Pascual's assertion was untrue. Luther was afraid for him but also afraid of him. (Later he would read a collection of stories, *I Would Save Them If I Could,* and relate to Tony Pascual through the title, long after Tony Pascual was able to be found).

"Just remember that life is about me and my music," Tony Pascual said, as Luther loaded the last box into the rental van, and to show just what he meant he played imaginary chords on the very present air. "I flash on women. I just open my coat and expose myself and one out of every two comes to me. That's not a bad percentage, is it? I have secret hiding places all over Central Park that I take them to so we can be alone together with my music."

Tony Pascual scrutinized Luther's face, sensing that Luther was intent on escaping without arousing the beast behind the mask hiding Tony's accumulated rage. But no such luck. Tony hopped in. "I'm just along for the ride. I have to see what my gargoyle is all about."

Mrs. Muldooney was waiting for them on the garbage can, the sun not yet down. Her only child was with her for the afternoon social, sturdy and pockmarked in his face and wearing the tight black gloves of his alleged avocation and a white T-shirt and jeans to signify it was simply the basics of the world that held his interest. They were not a welcoming committee. They just needed a place for the one to sit and the other to stand, for the son was never seen to place his bottom on the cans his mother so clearly favored as a show of propriety.

In a confluence of event with significance for those involved, Nikki Ballen, in the presence of her coterie of menfolk, evacuated the premises where she had lived and loved, compelling the landlady's son to break his silence with these simple words, "I never snuff close to where I live."

"The little Jewish slut, the little whore of Babylon," Mrs. Muldooney exclaimed, the torque of her words flying her right off the garbage can and onto the pavement.

Tony Pascual could not leave the premises without coming upon Luther with the fold-out knife, pressing the blade against Luther's throat in a way that removed all thought of struggle.

"I could make your thin blood flow into my logic. I could make it into a song for my lady Janis and me," Tony Pascual said, before departing.

That night Luther sat on the bare floor and covered himself with a thin blanket to ensure the full darkness he craved. Outside he could hear the forces of the city and his past gathering, seeking in vain to gain entry and shred him of his safe place.

Birdsong greeted him with the dawn. They were somewhere out there in the trees. This was no flock of cooing pigeons, he imagined, but what did he know of birds or nature's realm? He rose stiff and creaky from the floor, dropped a speed pill, and addressed himself to their unseen presence, saying he respected their avian intelligence but could never be of their kind, not with the cold eyes they cast and their hardness of heart, even if they called it nature's way, eating worms and other living things of the earth. Nor could he ever hope to have their aerial perspective.

Nonetheless he took instruction from them, organizing his new-found nest and applying a fresh coat of paint to the walls. Long after the sparrows had begun their day, Luther toiled, the soft spring air and the wonder drug working overtime to sustain his happy glow.

Many days and many nights passed before the apartment could be brought to a point of order. Sanctuary was a priority, and that meant so be it if even the great William Faulkner, with his many words on paper, had to be put on the shelf to get the job done.

And as the birds flew over the city performing their birdie tasks, the building's earthlings showed themselves. Diane Sunburst, from the top floor, stood outside his door and spoke of the man she loved and how he was corn-fed and from Kansas and with the brain power to be a doctor at Roosevelt Hospital just up the avenue, and how in respite from the arduousness of his medical endeavors he came to Tony's Pasta Heaven for calamari, for linguini, for cannoli, for double espresso, came mostly for the tantalizing thing of her as waitress of the decade with her hair very blond and her legs very long, and that wedding bells were in the not too distant future if she only could hold onto him while admitting that her face showed her to be an aging beauty and she was yet to become the star of stage and screen. She was counting on him feeling these deficits were compensated for by her good loving. But then she began to cry, and through her tears sang a song of fear that she would lose him to a younger version of herself, and Luther cried along with her for many hours before he asked if she wouldn't step into his digs so he could savor the fleshly feast she truly was, but she rebuffed him soundly, saying she would continue to walk proud and with a sense of purpose up and down the building stairs and all throughout the neighborhood that had claimed her with a show tune on her lips and many were those who would continue to lust after her as she did her waitressing thing in Tony's Pasta Heaven right there on Ninth and Fifty-Sixth.

Then it was Olga Nubescu from the floor below Diane Sunburst, and from her affect of sorrow and inhibition and darkness did not speak of the bounty of sun-splashed America but gave her place of origin as a castle-dotted region of Central Europe where feudalism still lingered and vampire bats controlled the nights. She was a thing of beauty without a life within her, a sad woman with tension in her face. She told him that she had been a tenant for several years, that she took dance classes every day and waitressed as a way of paying for them and for her life, and that she felt nothing but nothing when men lay with her. She told him further that her life didn't count, that she was born of Romanian parents who died shortly after her birth. She said she had been adopted and raised in a small Wisconsin town, and that her stepfather ate cheese sandwiches and drank beer all the livelong day and paid drunken visits to her bed in the middle of the night.

Luther interrupted her monologue to inquire about the Romanians and whether they slept in coffins by day and drank blood by night and were lecherous beyond belief in their desire for a carnal eternity.

"You are thinking of Transylvanians, who exist only in the imagination of some writer." Olga Nubescu laughed.

Luther was not to be deterred from his line of inquiry. Were the Romanians related to the dreadful Armenians, and if so, did they grow hair on their teeth and on other unexpected parts? But Olga dismissed his concern with more laughter.

Luther asked if he could visit with her, as he had a need to seek out those to whom damage had been done, and she could only reply that while she never said yes, she also never said no, leaving Luther to understand that he would have to navigate his way to her on his own initiative. He told Olga that he had a girlfriend who would someday be world-famous but that he had every intention of coming up to see her sometime after securing his premises. He said it was important to keep raising the number of women he had been with higher lest Mona Van Dine crush him with further abandonment, and he earnestly asked for her full cooperation in the endeavor.

Another showed his face, that being Billy Billson, a short man with pale skin and thinning hair and a round mound body clothed in jeans and a tired-looking work shirt. He said he didn't like Luther and never would and would reject him no matter what he said or did. He said he had followed his dream from Alabama to New York City, and that he was keeping it alive by practicing energetic singing of Broadway show tunes and that he took jobs as entertainment director on cruise ships while awaiting his big break. He said Luther would be surprised what women would do while on the water and that there was nothing like copulating on the ocean deep, for everything was in motion for lust to have its way. Luther inquired about the bald spot on his head and his small eyes and pasty skin, but Billy Billson just told him to shut his mouth and to go about his useless business. So that they were established in an agenda not of peace but of war, the likes of which they had both seen before.

Jedediah Judd came on the scene, dark and of the Deep South and living in the apartness his ways had wrought, a man who drifted through the old cities of the Northeast in an approximate state of detachment from all that he saw and heard, for while he was willing to go where he was called, he could not stay in any way that he could call the thing his own, the arrangement being for him to be there while Billy Billson was on the oceans of the world, no one any better at determining the bare necessities for perpetuating a life of indolence than Jedediah Judd. Luther was forewarned that if he ever got a call from a woman in the night, he would know by the statements posed as questions that it was Eulanda Briggs from

Mobile, Alabama, seeking to track Jedediah Judd down, alleging as she did that he was the father of her child. Jedediah Judd said Luther was to pay her no mind but to treat her only as another lonely voice in the night.

It seemed all too much for Luther, what with the paint fumes he was smelling and the speed he was experiencing. He had no choice but to shout through the closed door, "I will rescue you from the deep where you have been plunged. I will set you right upon the face of the earth," for Jedediah Judd, given his procreative power, reminded him of his brother Luke, both having the ability to plant the seed that would nourish a woman's eggs and cause her belly to swell.

Jedediah Judd answered that he wandered the earth in a state of childlike bliss, that though he was in a man's body with hair upon it, the years of growing had not impacted the quality of his arrested mind, and so the world would forever remain like the playing fields of yore. He said, in somewhat shaky regard to this, that a villain not profound but of the South, and with violence as a first resort, had partially circumnavigated his face with box cutter deftness, leaving a semicircular scar from forehead to chin as a reminder of how the beast of lust can summon retaliatory wrath, for it was in the context of amorous intentions expressed for one Samantha Spring in a Mobile drugstore, not far from the steamy pulp romance rack and with the cheap suitcases looking down from the shelves above (the Greyhound bus line calling, calling, with the paved roads it took to anyplace but where he was) that the avenger was driven to manifest himself and operate on Jedediah Judd's handsome face. Not that he minded the blemish badge; he simply wore it as the insignia of the damned in fever-pitch hostility to all that had presumed to create him in the first place. All this he shared with Luther so Luther could marvel at the world and the longings of the flesh that made it go.

In this new day time of his life, with the invigorating freshness of spring coming in on him and the money he was accumulating from his renting office employment diminishing the mentality of grayness so he could feel loved by an America now possibly accessible to him and with it the potential eradication of the phrase "nadir of existence," into this state of change Mona returned in the form of a letter from a place called Key West, Florida, in a further sign that the future would work with and not against him.

> I miss you so much, even the pain you cause me with your pathetic dementedness. Daddy dresses all in white to spark appreciation of his tan and offers theories over dinner that the sun is a stimulus to the libido. When he enters my room I know it is to swallow me whole, that he is seeking flesh to make his very own. He says he needs the sun to melt the snows of winter from him and shows himself proudly on the coral beaches. He wants me and Mommy doesn't want him or me and so all is not right in the world.

Peter Van Dine and Lydia were back together in an arrangement that had some strangeness to it. He was to maintain his base on the soil of Camp while Lydia remained in the city pursuing a new direction for her life. Peter was withholding the connubial bliss she was still in need of, and so she was looking elsewhere. To educate Luther free of the Biblical stricture that what God had joined, let no man rend asunder, and all the stonings associated with adultery, Lydia sent him a 16 mm movie of the delights she was experiencing with the men of Manhattan and those who were merely passing through, the documentation of her sexual reality in the bed that once accommodated her and Peter so powerful that it flung him across the room, Lydia having entered a stage of her life where it was not easy for him to look upon her as she would have him do.

Now there were further communications from Mona down in Florida, for Peter, as Mona said, was no longer in wintry climes with the snow placing his sexual apparatus in a deep freeze but in the sunlight of a pagan day drawing on the energy of the equator-bound sun with all the sensual awakenings that heat could engender throughout his body and his mind, Mona providing Luther documentary proof with a movie of her own capturing her father's abiding tendency to make his family his bed by entering her room and lifting her skirt for a lingering inspection of her underwear in an attempt to stimulate his pipeline to her.

> I had this terrible fear that you had been murdered. I would have called, but then I realized you probably don't even have a phone yet.

But Luther did not need no stinking phone to call down his love to her, shouting that he would see her out of the swamp of family, that all she was involved with was a mining expedition just as he was beginning to research the complexity of family life with his renting office venture, and that in any case they were sworn to watch each other's backs, like the lawmen of old slinging lead with the varmints.

"Maybe I'm a little strange in that area, too, like your father," he shouted down to her, being hungry for more good words from her and hoping that now he could be shown to be as good as Norman Bates had wanted to be in that locked room.

> The strangeness of my father is not your strangeness because he has placed his penis all over the house. My father's not the man you think he is. He's not.

Luther turned to RMN. He told him all that he was about in his covert activity on the fiddle and all that he hoped to be as he followed the Republican model for building wealth. The president did not dispute him—in fact, he gave the thumbs up and flashed a malignant smile.

He bought a used Nikon F camera so he would not look too conspicuous on the streets. The camera was an expedient for the entry of time through the lens and onto the film so all that he saw could be preserved. Because even then the world was rushing by, all that was vanishing in need of saving.

On his way to make the acquisition Luther came upon the Hotel Commodore. In a departure from its normal function, it dared to speak the truth of its own memory. A talking hotel was the thing he needed, and it called down to him from above with the perspective that it had, for it had seen the men and women of America and the world and the things they did behind closed doors. "Do you think we do not remember who you were in the year of our Lord 1960? Do you think we did not see you as a twelve-year-old with your Nixon-Lodge reflecting badges as you had once worn the "I Like Ike" buttons?"

An image appeared of him in a crewcut, his box head revealed with the back of his head flat as a board.

Luther answered back. "That was then and this is now. I am America and I am forever young in my own experiment."

More images appeared of him dancing in traffic with the badges of the Republicans pinned to his shirt. It showed the buses of New York City running over him with no success. It showed him filching a twenty-dollar bill from a wallet on a campaign worker's desk in the Nixon-Lodge headquarters in the hotel. It showed him sneaking into the nearby Hotel Roosevelt and knocking on doors, trading badges for coins and dollar bills and urging those who gave to keep America in the governance of the brand-name goods of the Republican Party. Men and women came dripping wet from the showers of New York City. They came from the lying down state. They came from all the different regions of the country.

"Hey, Pardner, are you supposed to be here?" So spoke a man wearing only a ten-gallon hat and with his giant dick exposed.

"We are here for America. We are fighting hard for it in all her glory. Buy our badges. Buy our brand-name goods. Save us from a Democrat death. Keep the Catholic out of the White House and the Pope and his flock of Vatican cardinals from the Oval Office. Keep the country safe for Crosse and Blackwell jam."

For his purchase he went to the great Willoughby's on Lexington Avenue, just across the street from the even greater Grand Central Terminal. Men who were whiter than white and in their forties and fifties stood behind the counter in their paleness, with a lifetime of newspaper reading and coffee drinking behind them and the mustaches that went with it.

"When I was your age, all I wanted to do was screw, too," his salesman said. "The thing you have to understand is that the camera is an extension of it."

Luther stared at the Nikons and Leicas and the Pentaxes, the glass case in which they were displayed separating him from the salesman and the death that he represented. All he cared about now was gaining possession of the object of his desire, and to realize that, he could endure the knowingness of the salesman because the building was being good to him and there could be no consequence, since the money did not belong to Simon Weill in the first place. He could just about do a ha-ha on the earth given all the freedom that he felt.

The camera had a weight and substance to it and a history all its own. He placed it on a table in his apartment so he could study it from different angles, and he could report that its quality remained intact whatever the perspective. He turned the aperture and the distance rings on the 50 mm lens and they truly worked. Then he picked his baby up. It spoke of heft and compactness in his hands and the ways he could triumph over the scenes before him.

He took the camera into the courtyard and announced his intention to the buckling fence of weathered wood. He said that no one was there to take care of it, to restore it to its former quality, that all those who had been a party to its success had died or gone away and that now it simply lived in memory of its former function. He said it spoke to him of neglect and the passage of time and that he was tortured by the idea that things had been nicer when it was new, that mothers made soup for their children who, while staying home with colds, could hear from the warmth of their beds the clip-clopping of the horses outside. He said that things had gotten frightening with cars racing everywhere and with all the new and boxy, soulless structures standing proud in their ugliness. He said he wanted simply to sit there with it and have some peace and respite from the world beyond and not be part of the daily round that even as he spoke was calling to him. Then he did it. He shot the fence, appropriating its space so the earth could have his signature. He didn't apologize. He just went away, whispering that he would be back some day.

"I too am now a Nikon F man," he declared. Mona soon to become the object of the lens's infatuation. He shot her at Camp in the drained pool, the walls and floor of which were calling out in a happy turquoise blue. He shot her naked in the meadow, the apple tree's branches not reaching low enough to cover her breasts. He shot her lying down and standing up in the bathroom of her Boston apartment. He shot and shot and she still stood or lay, so he could have the miracle of the event of her on film for life.

Then he ran with his rolls of film to the Modern Age Studios on West Forty-eighth Street so they could be put through the mysterious process of fixer and developer and stop bath to create the contact sheets that would offer proofs of what he had done.

The contact sheets were remarkable for only one thing, the distance between him and his subject, as if in trying to get everything in, he was getting nothing. The woman behind the counter arched an eyebrow to signal her awareness of his incompetence, and though he fell down dead, he got back up to live and live.

He had the thought, in this time of flaring desire, that the 50 mm lens that came with the camera was not entirely adequate for his purposes. It met him with an iridescent stare when he regarded it in sunlight, and numbers in white upon its barrel to establish the necessities the shooter was seeking. But it also confessed its limitation, to the point that Luther was forced to accept that the lens protruding modestly from the camera's body would not hold its ground in a demanding world. Tormented by his lack, he was propelled outward once again to the great Willoughby's, there to negotiate with the dead and the half-alive for the thing that would bring him back to what he needed in accord with the surging demand of his will, saying to the laughing salesman with the chalk white face, "Give them to me and give them to me now," the salesman instantly intuiting what he meant and lining up the lenses on the countertop, where Luther could lick them and bow down to them in the worship they deserved.

"I will take them all. I will play no favorites here, in my hour of need," he said, gathering them within his arms on the counter—a fisheye lens and a wide angle lens and a telephoto lens and a portrait lens, all with their differentness in length and the chrome now calling tormenting attention to itself and "Nikon" shouting out its name. Thinking now of a camera with the anonymity its darkness could confer so he could be with it on the street without the laughter of those disposed to mockery showered upon him, the money of the building coming through so all that he needed could be provided for.

"I will have the great Nikon F camera in a body entirely black, price not the object but concealment imperative," Luther said, the salesman replying that they had no Nikon F camera with a black body to offer him but there was a Pentax 35 mm camera he could suggest.

"But is it quality? Is it brand name goods?"

"Everything in this store is quality. Everything we sell is brand-name goods. This is Willoughby's."

"But is it Nikon quality?"

"Nikon Shmikon. Nikon is just a name."

"Will it stand the test of time for all eternity?"

"What's eternity? Now is eternity."

"Don't get tough on me, mister. Don't take away my dream."

"What's to take away? I'm here to give."

"Oh very yes yes. Do I kiss you now or do we do it later?" Luther cried with happiness that the man had made things right for him, and minutes later left with the 35 mm Pentax.

Over the weeks and months, he would often retire in the dark to the shame corner of his apartment, driven there by painful awareness of aspirations that exceeded his ability. The apartment now so full of cameras and accessories that he had to wear blinders to ignore what he had wrought. And yet he continued to add to his collection in the vain hope that the next purchase would bring peace, and so his contempt for himself only grew.

Occasionally he did find a way to get outside with some of his equipment, and became one among millions to shoot the ceiling of the Guggenheim Museum and otherwise do the random here a click there a click of the amateur shutterbug while the woman whose face cried out for capture passed in vain, his eye too big or the eyepiece too small for arranging the elements within it, even with the precision manufacturers of Japan and Germany to assist him.

Encompassed in his longing for preservation was the building. Now he could come to it not only for financial sustenance but for the purpose of art, starting with a portrait of Luke, his brother lost to sorrow as he sat up in the early afternoon with a cup of joe, having just awoken. Cups and more cups, first of coffee and then of wine, as they were needed to fill the gaps he could not otherwise fill, the cups neutralizing time by giving him the power to sit in peace without the burn of painful longing. In this pose did he shoot his brother's pockmarked face and his new girlfriend Brenda's face, brimming with a smiling lasciviousness, she being one who lived for the wild nights, the room unventilated and smelling of late sleepers.

Luke himself with his own abundance of camera equipment rendered useless by the workings of his mind, saying, "The subway is not where I can go. There are too many eyes on me, calling me this, calling me that. And there is Mother banging on my door every morning."

Luther not needing to inquire of his brother what it meant to be custodian/janitor of nothingness, sitting in a stuffed chair in the lobby some nights drinking wine and seeing to it that the neighborhood junkies did not steal the furniture while women, their aunt and now their mother, ruled the roost. Luther seeing he was no different, his brother serving as a mirror.

Chapter 62

Despite all the listening devices he had installed and the recent profession of her ardor, Luther continued to fear abandonment by the one he loved. The month of May was said to be merry, and it did have its moments when even the lampposts of New York City could be heard singing, but no such joy was in him the night in the renting office the rotary dial he spun and the ringing that ensued failed to bring Mona Van Dine onto the line.

The Cat Woman watching through the grille as Luther listened to the double rings of the phone, distinct from the single rings in New York City.

"Poor little hanging string. Won't you come to my cat room to have the peace that my cats can bring? They are your friends." Her catlike face so big.

The vicious perversity of life, that those he least wanted to see when he felt most vulnerable should present themselves. But he vanished her from his sight with baleful noises.

And then it was his older sisters Hannah and Naomi and Rachel laughing at his bondage to the phone as he dialed and redialed Mona's number.

"She has gone away and now you have only us, little Flathead, Squarehead, Box Head. You have gone to the nowhere we have gone to. How does it feel?" So they jeered in their hatefulness until he managed to banish them as well.

And there came the Pakistanis and the Ethiopians and the Koreans and all the rest requiring of him real-world solutions for their real-world issues—their post, their rent, the swarming roaches.

"Don't you see I don't have time for you?" he screamed, but they were firm in bending him to their will.

And when they were gone the calling resumed. The new apartment could not save him from this calling, the Nikon F camera in league with the Pentax camera and now the supreme quality of a very German Leica could not stop him from this calling, nor could all the lenses and other accessories he had purchased in his buying spree for freedom. Because sooner or later a woman had to do the clobber thing and his fortifications—the girls he had been with—were inadequate to stop her from being the hurting kind.

Had she been murdered? Was that it? He dialed the Boston police department and promised the officer a box of New York City's finest doughnuts should he be forthcoming with the truth. The officer said he had no time for vagueness and that it was for Luther to emerge from the vapors and into the realm of the factual if a successful conclusion was ever to be reached.

"Mona Van Dine. Hair so blond and curly. Five foot three with legs of thin strength, who has come to this earth trailing clouds of glory with her destination called full renown. Have you seen my lady love? Have you seen her in the dark of night or the brightness of the day? Have you laid her out on a mortuary slab so I too will have to die? And if so, who is it that has wrought such a deed?"

The chief said there was no one of that description laid out on a slab and that Luther should find something useful to do, like join the military and become a man. Then he heard a click, leaving him alone with listening devices that availed him nothing in his fruitless search for the truth.

He turned for his answer to Jesse, who had not let Midwood, Brooklyn, or the City College of New York defeat him. He had been lifted out of the borough of his birth into the Upper West Side apartment of a woman who did not know from Wittgenstein or the great Immanuel Kant or the difference between modern and contemporary but who could show up for work each day so Jesse could have his drug-fueled contemplations. Maude was different from Fran. She did not need to give herself to a professor of philosophy. Jesse was more than enough for her, even if he sat in Buddha-like tranquility induced by downs in front of the TV all night. Post office Jesse did not sing "Born to Lose," but then again, he didn't have to, decorating the mail of the United States of America with the peace symbol so it could go out upon the land with the message that swords needed to be beaten into ploughshares and guns melted into butter and VC Charlie needed to be blessed for the divinity of his soul so oneness could replace the fractiousness of war machines subjecting the planet to ruination. Federales riding hard for justice busted Jesse for defacing the U.S. mail and whisked him from his box-scheme creativity into a federal detention center, Mr. Ruggiero, the foreman, offering saliva-sprinkled venom.

No one can total up the misfortune wrought by opposition to the father or its many blessings. Even so could Luther understand the calamity Jesse had wrought upon himself and understood further why Jesse, out on high bail, had reason to feel stress beneath the Buddha gaze of benevolence his daily fixes gave him seeing the nature of the opposition now in play against his insurrectionist campaign. Maude there as a bulwark against the truth of his own life with her comfortable apartment and her daily ride on the IRT to the nine to five job that she held down, there being no chance that she would ride off with a professor when love, not philosophy, was her specialty.

Nevertheless Jesse gave his full attention when Luther phoned him, saying "Slow down, man, slow down. You're going way too fast." Because Luther was flying at him with words that lacked coherence.

"Why assume the worst?" Jesse said, when Luther was finally able to convey the situation. Luther saw that Jesse was the older brother Luke couldn't be. He didn't fail him in the way that Luke always would.

Temporarily calming as Jesse's words were, they were only words, and had no real life span to them. Quickly Luther was reeled back into his hellish vigil, dialing the 617 area code of Boston, Mona saying into the receiver, way past midnight, "I was over at Lisa's. We had dinner and then sat around talking," her words carrying no hint of defensiveness or guile. Luther was left astonished at the power of her words to liberate him instantly from his pain, and saw in that moment an image of his mother coming to him as a squalling infant and lifting him from his crib. What a woman wrought was what she could take away. Oh the clobber power of a woman. Oh the sweet peace a woman could confer.

But the flame of suspicion flared again, causing him to say, "But you didn't tell me you were going."

"I didn't know until this afternoon. She just invited me over as I was leaving school."

And so restful sleep came to him that night and the next day the renting office called to him once more to continue accumulating funds for his life. And while he was there with Arvin Singh and Raj Patel and the Hanging String woman and Tall Tommy and Little Tommy and all the rest, he was led to pick up the phone once again to receive his nightly Mona briefing but received instead the hideous two-ring sound of hah hah nothingness, and so he called once again, and again received the hideous two-ring sound of nothingness, and so it went through all his repeated dialings, each double ring bringing mockery of him for having been fooled once again, for having failed to expose the insurrection taking place.

Song was now coming to him, delivered in a cracking voice by Naomi, who had situated herself by the office window. "Laura," she sang, only the name was changed to Mona, that she might wound him into death. Luther heard her taunting iniquity, he heard her baseness loud and clear. Gone were the days of his childhood when she would sing "Hard-Hearted Hannah, the vamp of Savannah" and "I'm Going to Wash That Man Right Out of My Hair," with Rachel accompanying her on the piano, bringing heaven to earth or earth to heaven in freeing him for the moment from the prohibition against *all that was worldly* by introducing that world through Broadway show tunes so that even in the night the light could be abundant.

And yet he went on automatic, taking in the rents and checking the post and writing down the complaints in invisible ink on the air before closing down the office, and with a wad of cash in his pocket stood on the corner and shrieked a maliciously inattentive cab driver to an awareness of his waiting presence, boarded the wings of man Eastern shuttle of heartbreaking blue and white out of LaGuardia, this at a time when Eastern could still call itself glorious, drank several whiskies fast on the flight and flogged the pilot free of any machinations to do some airborne dawdling so that earth and sky could be traversed at a speed to fit his timetable for full investigation.

"150 Park Drive. And fly, fly, my man, just fly it on out of here," he said to the hackie outside the Logan Airport terminal building, and waved fistfuls of dollars as an incentive against malevolence. "Because isn't that what money is for, so I can avoid the torture of having to remain in New York and miss finding her out? Isn't that my purpose in life?"

"Pal, pal. Have a ham sandwich. Drink malted milks. Put on weight and take in a ballgame." The advice came from under the man's mustache, the driver talking to him in a filthy, tired voice, mega dollars having to be stuffed into his face before he could dream of being quiet.

From outside the cab Luther grabbed the hackie by his shirt and said, "Now go away and be silent about all my plans, every last one of them." Then he dissolved the taxi from his sight and shouted, "Everyone who thinks Boston is about Yastrzemski and his big dick bat, come out here now," but no one responded, leaving him free to look up at her window from the street, a window dark enough for murder, dark enough for love, and for this he sang a song to the universe in gratitude that the drama had yet to fully unfold. And yet, and yet, he shouted out, suppose she was there and lying with her lover in the bed of sinful delight. He entered a phone booth, illuminated in air customized specially for Boston and dialed her number *with the window in full view* and got that she was not home, not home, *unless too engaged to answer.*

And so he entered the building clutching the key to her apartment in his pocket. A tenant recognized him. She did not call out his name. She did not know it. She was a woman of undeniable beauty. How could she not be with a name like *Rickie?* Yes, he knew her while she knew him not at all. She appraised him in passing with a scalding stare, having seen him with Mona. Her preference was clear in appropriating Mona for her own and making him an outcast forever. It was not for Luther to mind her verdict. No love was worthy of calling itself that without a sizable portion of pain, this as the darkness of Mona's apartment called to him and the key chose to turn in the lock, Luther having put it on notice that subversion would not to be tolerated.

Oh life that cannot be lived without deceit and the squandering of one's youth on the hellbent need for *proof* with the eyes of God upon you. Oh life that sees a copy of her Signet classic *Crime and Punishment* open on the bed. Oh life that smells of turpentine and gesso and oil paints. Oh life that marvels at youth and can't get enough of it. Oh youth that takes you drunk and reeling with your mother's money to a girl of heaven's apartment, knowing that she is closing the door on your existence.

The darkness of the apartment not dark enough. The excitement not enough. The angle of vision from which to view the entranceway below not enough. The bright street lamp took no mercy on the night, setting him up for what he had waited a lifetime to see, every minute that she did not appear terrifying and offering exhilarating proof that she was somewhere else.

As he was about to light a cigarette, a green Corvette double-parked in front of the building. There was no time to call for a posse;

the thing was simply happening. From the passenger side Mona got out wearing a purple sweater and a miniskirt and black tights, as if he needed her outfit to fuel his tortured fantasies. From the driver's side emerged a tall thin black man with a goatee. He leaned down and gave her a big full kiss on the lips before returning to his car and driving off. Luther felt a pain he would not have missed, even if it was too much.

When she opened the door he was sitting naked in the pose of the Buddha that he wasn't. The light was on so he wouldn't startle her beyond the bounds of what a young heart could take, because if he was open about his intrusion, perhaps he could conceal it. Not that he should be denied the right to be informed about his own demise.

"Luther, what are you doing here?"

He did not answer.

"Have you come here to interrogate me? Is that it? I was out with a friend, that's all. I'm allowed to have a life, aren't I? Do you want to create a jail for me? Is that it? A friend, just a friend. I met him in Harvard Square some weeks ago. He calls me up and we go out for sandwiches. Sometimes he drives me around. He's lonely. He needs someone to talk to. He says the other students at Harvard Law School are stuff shirts."

Luther was now up in the air, risen there on his own gases.

"Where are you going, Luther? You're scaring me?" she with her bruised and very kissed lips dared to say.

He was now at the ceiling. Because it was Boston, limits had to come into play.

"All right, once in a while we go to his place and listen to records. He has a great jazz collection and is starting his own record company."

Luther rotating but otherwise holding his position as the minutes passed and the atmosphere thickened with the tension of their interaction until she too began to float on her own gases and came in proximity to the Boston ceiling.

"All right, stalker, you want it, you got it. I've been with him and I like it, I like it a lot."

Luther did not ask what the itty bitty "it" was. He recognized an atom bomb when he saw one.

All through the following day, having been blown back to New York City, he sought the light of forgiveness but could not quite find it. He would enter a phone booth to call her and say that everything was all right, but torment would find him once more, having never left.

Because of which he had to go nationwide, saying: "It's not every day that your girlfriend, who is blondness itself, gets bedded by a black man with a huge endowment. It's not every day that the factor of a zillion magnifies your worst fear into consuming lust. White America, you cannot hold the black man back. His apparatus is too big and his mind too strong. White men of America, come out with your hands in the air. White women of America, come out with your availability revealed and accept that you have been set free by the magic of the black man's power to copulate with an attitude of syncopated cool elevating them above the heartbreak that the white women of America wish to inflict. White men of America, prepare yourself for this: you want to be relieved of the burden of your repression of the black man so you can sit in peace watching their trains of power rumble by. Because once the orientation has been established, there can be no going back. Listen, we have been trying to contain them long enough and now has the time come to accept that they have won. Should you have any questions, please write. If not, simply get the job done."

"How do you spell that?" the receptionist asked.

Outside the building of doorman quality he had seen the brass nameplate that said "Arnold Schwinn, M.D.," and now he was in the doctor's ground-floor office.

"Yes, that is right, my name is Luther, as in 'Lose her,' though not exactly. And now I will spell my last name, for which patience is required. It is good that you have pen in hand." Luther spoke to the receptionist in the crowded waiting area, shifting his weight from one foot to another as his nerves seemed to require.

"What is your problem?" she asked, as he took in her permed gray hair that looked like strands of metal. He had thought the answer would just come with the question, but the words were not there to express the situation neatly.

"If I could just talk to the doctor in private, it would make my circumstance real, for you are woman born of woman and so allied with those who would drive me down, and so I must ask you to exempt yourself, even if you are now in the safety zone of middle age."

"In plain English, please, what is this about?"

"My nation is suffering. Many stab wounds it has received. We are seeking only to stanch the flow of blood and find the center that we have lost. For that reason, it is imperative that I see a doctor of medical degree strength, who in his manly lab coat will order me back to health with the implanting of the backbone that I lack." Luther framed his face with his hands to give the necessary focus to his words.

The receptionist sighed and told him that she was Jewish and from Brooklyn and had been born with the name Marsha, that she lived each day for the gnoshing that was her everything and that her mind was full of the complex equations that she could not bear to chase and that every time she filed her nails she immolated her mind. She said that she had an anger that was built into the fabric of her being. She said that she had a right to slash at men for all they had not given her, and when he asked if she was teamed up in an alliance of the aggrieved with his sisters, she said it was a sisterhood of the many but would release no particulars, and that it took a man with triple strength meanness to overpower her own, and with that she ushered him through a door to the doctor's inner sanctum.

Luther found the doctor scribbling madly with his authentic Mont Blanc pen on watermarked paper specially made to receive the pressure from his strong hand. He sat at a mahogany desk and wore big-frame glasses that would have dominated any face but his own. Minute after minute Luther absorbed the spectacle of the doctor's industry before calling out, "I am bleeding, doctor, I am bleeding. Rush from your desk and give me aid."

The doctor capped his fountain pen and set his gray eyes upon Luther. He had a massive head and wore his tie Windsor-knotted. He had a family that he loved and a car that he drove and a house where they all could live, and his life was surely as excellent as his lawn.

"You don't look like you're bleeding," the doctor said coldly. He had read the newspapers. He had seen the scenes of long-haired disorder. He knew which side of the divide he was on.

"I have been stabbed many times, as I told your assistant. I have been stabbed in the heart and the brain by an assailant living in my girlfriend's pleasure zone. Won't you help me, doctor, won't you, you who pulled me in here with your street-side plaque of brass?"

"Don't be sicker than you are." The doctor hated the fragility that he saw. He hated the hair. He hated the corruption and the lack of vigor in the emaciated frame. All he saw was the blight of the youth of America on drugs, he who had fled the Nazis to learn a new life. That they should have it so easy and yet do what they did.

"I have had this conversation before, in many different guises. Now is the time come to move the conversation forward. Now is the time come to no longer insult the truth. I am asking for the help of your manliness. I have been beaten senseless and the wind rushes through and makes cold all my open places. What life support can I expect from the magic of your regal pen? Can you give it to me good so I never have to feel a thing again and can live in the womb my suffering calls out for?"

"What is it you want?"

"I want Mommy's arms. I want her sweet breath. I want to be a child playing in the field called carefree. I want you to kiss me on the lips without touching me. I want all from you that life can't give me."

"Can you be more specific?"

"I will spell it for you instead. *V* as in victory, *a* as in ailment, *l* as in liberty, *i* as in inner peace, *u* as in unreal, *m* as in more. Because I can't eat, I can't think, I can't sleep."

With resolution in his face the doctor crossed the room to the door with a few mighty strides. He had the nation and the fundamentals of his being to protect in his visceral reaction to the gaunt presence before him.

"Get out," he shouted. Having swung open the door, he now pointed in the direction of the street.

"If I am quiet will you follow my example with the lowering of your voice?" Luther whispered, but the doctor heard him not.

"Out! And don't ever come back," the doctor thundered.

"I am a state of mind that will never leave you," Luther replied, in his full defeat, for the answer had come to him as to the father he could wish to have.

He didn't know if he could live, blown outward as he was on the doctor's exhalation, but he righted himself for the gauntlet of opprobrium formed by the patients in waiting and glaring Marsha. He thought to communicate in any way that he could, and was given a moment of insight. Turning back to the doctor, he said. "You have a son named Harvey. He has gotten in trouble with drugs and wandered from your dictate. Is that the truth and have you chosen to be draconian as the answer to the drug siren call? Are you among the legion who now must mete out this punishing penalty of abandonment?"

The doctor's white hair remained on his head, as did his glasses that had no regard for fashion on his face. All that changed was the bum's rush he put upon startled Luther in eighty-sixing him out the door.

Fifty-Seventh Street west of Carnegie Hall was not known for showing you its love. It had a piano showroom and apartment buildings of doorman prosperity that kept to themselves, leaving you alone on the pavement until you reached the corner newsstand and the smell of the subway maintaining itself beneath the street. It was there that reeling Luther saw the action heating up, a woman-child in a miniskirt heading south with the light under a parasol of bright pink on what was a cloudless day.

"Can you offer me some comfort so I can even up a savagely unbalanced score? Can you take me with you into a place of privacy?"

She had a the face of a young girl but with all traces of innocence gone. The realization came that, young or not, he was with a woman of the night in broad daylight.

"For ten dollars I suck your dick. For fifty you own me for an hour," she said in a voice of the living dead. He thought of the diseases she might carry and the brutal treatment she likely received from a pimp bending her to his will and still he said yes, gone on the power he would have over her and trying to put out of mind her abject condition.

She led him to a seedy hotel some blocks away but seeing a man with a baleful stare and wearing a zebra-striped hat he took to be Mr. Pimp he balked and ran away.

For many days and nights he allowed the railroads of New York City to run over him, and when they did not come frequently enough, he sought out the subways of New York City with their busier schedules, and when that didn't do the trick he called on the rats of all five boroughs to feast upon his outer and inner parts. He experienced drownings and gougings, defenestrations and incinerations, and soiled himself many times through repeated hangings. Many were the cars and other forms of vehicular traffic that flattened him, and yet the condition remained of continuing pain that Mona had done him the way she had.

The rains came, heavy showers all that spring, washing him out to sea and beyond, and when he was returned to land, it was in the middle of Forty-second street, the neon lights glittering and people putting their mouths around the hot dogs that they craved.

When she was finally dying to him, Mona called. She had grown tired of Robert Neal. At all hours of the night the phone would ring and he would be on the line, often with barroom noise in the background.

Luther held his own thoughts to himself, which were really only an image of a quiet landing and dust motes floating in the afternoon light. He could not tell her the aphrodisiacal effect her affair had had on him or that his lust was increased exponentially on hearing that she would be coming to New York that weekend and was further fed by a lingerie shop on Seventh Avenue. He walked past it self-consciously, as if shame shame double shame everyone would know his name awaited him should he show any overt interest in the teddy-clad mannequin and the array of garters and panties displayed in the window.

He stepped inside the door to shelves stocked with thin boxes containing delicate lacy things. "Can I help you?" A woman stared at him across the glass counter. She was middle-aged and thick in her body. Luther had the sense she was discerning with her shrewd eyes his sex fever.

"I have been caught in my nakedness. The question is, Are you regarding me with the eyes of a big sister?"

"This is a store, not a psychiatrist's office. Are you here for something for your lady?"

"Do not speak the language of false elegance. Do not use terms of asininity such as 'lady.' Speak properly or not at all," he said in a whisper, and with his face turned away from the passersby. Even so had they gathered to witness his shame. He saw his sisters. He saw his mother. He saw them and others laughing derisively at his exposed carnality. "I will need all your understanding to make this transaction," he continued to whisper.

"What?"

"You must read my mind to understand my desire."

At this point she did a necessary thing. She cried that men should be ashamed of their own lust. She cried and cried and all he could do to help was to offer a loving and shy reminder that it was 1969 and Richard Milhous Nixon was in the White House and that the tone, like it or not, always got set at the top. She listened to him attentively while staying faithful to her own understanding.

"Are you sick? Are you mad? Do I need to call the police?"

"The fire department. They would do a better job, given the fact that I am inflamed."

"Be basic with me, young man, if that is what you are," she said, placing a shrewd and dubious look of assessment on him.

"Oh, I am very basic, as basic as the earth can ever get, with its polarities of fire and ice and all that is created within those poles." He tried to wink but could only blink and so he gave her the double thumbs up to encourage her understanding.

Just then a man entered the store. He wore rings on each finger and a purple pimp hat with a brim extraordinaire and spoke his desire to the woman.

"Give me a thong for my lady love. Her name be Foxy, so make sure the cut is just right. She a slender thing."

"Are you here to dominate the world or just women?" Luther asked.

"Don't be fucking with me, white boy." The man scorned him with a head to toe look.

"I am not leaving here until I have an answer," Luther said.

"How about I answer you with a fist upside your head?"

"That will not be necessary. I will wait till you have gone so I can have my privacy back."

"You are one *distressed* motherfucker."

"Sounds like Foxy would take a small size. Is that right?" the woman asked.

"Don't be asking no motherfucking questions. No white woman be doing that on a black man," the man said, summoning his firepower.

When the man had finally gone with his purchase, the woman told Luther that he would have to state his desire boldly.

"Red," Luther whispered.

"Red what?"

"What no one sees until you want them to, unless by accident. The thing that delights a man's eyes in a way that nothing else could."

She laid out a pair on the countertop for his inspection. He gave her the thumb's up while covering his face with his free hand.

"Should you not be in a hospital?" she asked.

"Not when my agenda is so full," he replied.

To be with a black man was to be in a life Mona had not known and to live in the power that life could bring, Luther could only imagine, because to be with a black man was to fight the power while being with a power all its own. Luther, for his part, knew in his heart of hearts that he had become a clutching drag, and if he wanted anything it was to live free and be loved by Mona for allowing her to live free, but those times—the spring of 1967, when he would return to the rooming house to find her waiting outside his door—were long past.

To prime his lust, Luther had sheepishly presented Mona with what he thought to be the racy undergarment and, to his surprise she nonchalantly wore it.

"I cried the first night I was with him," she said, as they lay in bed. "I told him that I was seeing you and that you were down here in New York. I told him that I felt like I was betraying you. He said it was important to share the wealth and that sharing the wealth was what reality was all about."

Luther was shaken to his foundations by the Robert Neal reality assertion. He took his fear that Mona's fences were not high enough to keep the future out to the bedroom window. Here and there the lights of New Jersey were still burning and the Hudson River only appeared to have lazy currents and the trees of Riverside Park were not growing to the sky. The year 1969 had iron in the last digit. The decade at its cusp was ushering in an era of coldness.

He tried to apply the words war and peace to what he was seeing and to make an accommodation with her strength. War meant losing her. Peace meant swallowing all his hurt. He made the letter "P" on the air but it didn't hold. The lights on the George Washington Bridge lived within the bounds of constancy. If you turned your back, they were still shining. It was not their way to flicker on and off. Why did other lights have to be in the treachery column? He made no inquiry as to his own.

The weekend came and went. He had her but he didn't. Late in the night a call had come. Sleepless, he had been by the phone when it rang. A firm voice on the line, with music in the background. Robert Neal, seeking Mona. Luther could only tell him the truth, that she was asleep.

"Say I called," Robert Neal said, as if Luther was his messenger, and hung up. He had staked out his claim; Luther was a person of no consequence. All his fears that he would be swept aside by this man were now revived. An implacable force had entered Mona's life.

He walked three steps behind her en route to the East Side terminal struggling to impose on himself a degree of humility that he intuited was needed for a shred of peace. But his emotions were running wild. Why could he not be like the lampposts he saw along the way, with the gentle nature their long and curving frames expressed?

Robert Neal. He could think his name but not say it, if he didn't want to make him more real than he was.

Mona read the anxiety in his face. "Look. You've got to leave me alone from now on. You've got to let me find out what I want."

Words hostile and provocative. Words that served as an attack on civic order and in full support of anarchy. Let her find out what she wanted, which meant, Baby, I'm going to screw anyone and everyone I please, and you can't do crap about it. But did she ever hear him waving the very same banner of anarchy? Did she ever hear him talking about how he needed to find out what he wanted?

He waved dismissively at the departing bus, and soon it was out of sight, as any degree of peace continued to be for him.

Chapter 63

Because he was looking for trouble, he had to find it. That semester he ventured into the world of psychology, which said that formidable obstacles were positioned beyond his face and in his mind. The course was offered in Townsend Harris Hall, near a diner (heartbreaking) where he could order grilled cheese sandwiches and cherry cheese danishes so he could get filled up at the counter where he sat. The diner, living as it did in an area north of Morningside Heights, looked south to Columbia University and Union Theological Seminary and Teacher's College, all of them being institutions of stability in his mind with the brand name quality they possessed. And yet to see vital signs of life in this northern portion of the city that had been unvisited by him, to be away from the center of his life while remaining close to it, to be part of a community beyond the orbit of the stars and yet acceptable, now summoned in him delirious joy.

The course was taught by a young man with a reed-thin neck and a narrow face dominated by horn-rimmed glasses. But if he had boniness abounding in his frame, Luther saw that he had a heavyweight trajectory, having started light with a low-cost B.S. from Yeshiva University in 1962 and an accelerated and blue-chip Ph.D. in psychology from Yale University (New Haven, Connecticut, within driving distance of the train station) three years later. He did not look like anyone Luther could hope to beat in the race that was in his head, judging from the credentials of Professor Katz. He was just one big winning streak, it was very clear, on an express lane to the future.

A light of strangeness was on his life one afternoon in the diner. Standing in the door was a man in the uniform of the New York City Police Department. Luther saw him out of the context of the childhood whence he came, when Bunny was a magical older brother setting off a commotion in Luther's mind one night with his report that a porcupine had attacked him and Clementino there in the Catskill Mountains, where they had been brought to attend the Camp for Those of the Christ Jesus. There in the diner Luther could see him and not see him, know him and not know him, saying to himself Bunny had no right to outgrow the childhood in which Luther framed him, land of the free or not. For to be in the diner with a cherry cheese danish when once he had been elsewhere was a hard thing to reconcile and yet it was Bunny standing there.

Luther saying, "I am presently weightless, but the day your sister spit out a piece of apple that flew into my mouth was the day I fell in love. Did you know that it happened? Do you believe that it ever could have?"

Luther could see that Bunny, in the age that he had come to, had been regimented by his uniform. Luther thought he might cry, seeing what life had brought Bunny to, and half wished he had not bound himself to him through spoken recognition. A wave of embarrassment washed over him that Bunny should see him as he was, the same embarrassment he felt seeing Bunny as he was, defined by a uniform.

"Flathead? Squarehead? Little Boxhead?" Though Bunny suspected he knew who he was talking to, he had to go to the proof, putting on an officer's glove before feeling the back of Luther's head beyond the hair he had grown for his own defense against the words of the world coming in on him.

"Wow. It is you," Bunny said, having found the flatness that was back there. "No one else would have a head like that."

"Yes, but now I have reached the place of normalcy, even if I continue to fear being found out."

Bunny asked Luther if he was sick, to be looking like he did with that mass of hair on his head and the extreme thinness of his body.

"That is why I am here, so I can get filled up on the food of America. It is when I don't eat that I feel like a hanging string."

Bunny pulled away from Luther, his facial expression saying the past could not hold them, that the culture was seeking to fracture their childhood love—Puerto Rican Bunny and uniformed officer of the law Bunny versus the alleged whiteness of Luther and his fragile identity as a student at the city college of the people.

Luther said he agreed with what he read on Bunny's face, but that memory would preserve their shared history in his mind. "Our childhood is in safe keeping, you can be sure. Now I will attend to my grilled cheese sandwich and my danish while you attend to the mission of patrolling your beat and apprehending violators of the law, wherever they may be found."

There was no need to shake hands. There was just the space Bunny had appeared from and the space from whence Luther had arrived and they could nod their heads in simple acknowledgment of that fact and go their own way.

Now Luther quickly ascertained that Professor Katz was stellar not only on paper but in the realm of doing, his demonstration of that being the memorization of the first and last names of each of the 35 students in his Science of the Mind class. Though the student at the desk next to Luther joked that Professor Katz probably lived with his mother and had never been laid, Luther understood that he was seeing a high board score mind in action and had pen and paper at the ready for all the notes that he would need.

The reading list for the class included a book of case studies that followed the lives of three people who had committed no crimes and two of whom were not known to be of ill repute. So far as was known, the two had ruined the lives of not a single human being and the third had ruined only his own. All that was that asked of all three was to reveal their intelligence so that the whole truth could be made manifest, for intelligence was the seed of life, determining not only the bark but the configuration of the leaves and whether one was to grow up stumpy or gnarled or with the magnificent expanse of a mighty oak. Thus, the Stanford-Binet test was administered to them so they could harbor a state of knowledge about their capacities to go forward in life or turn tail and run or just sit in the middle of the road and get smoothed out by a truck. The point was that the choice would have to be determined by the content of their mind as it revealed itself numerically, and for this, the whole world was watching as they gathered before the now-famous blocks by which people were judged in their ability to arrange them in a predetermined pattern.

The woman of the group and one of the two men did very well on the test and were particularly adept at putting together the blocks on the performance part. They did so effortlessly, and with their creativity flourishing. They threw the blocks up in the air and they came down in the pattern that was called for. They bounced them off the walls and made behind the back passes and yet the patterns arranged themselves. Thus, they established themselves on the road to success with their minds working clear of entanglement and with the confidence to know that whatever life handed them, they would be able to put their blocks together. Because now, in addition to the artillery of their words, they had the firepower of performance to organize them into coherent patterns of life-enhancing action.

But the third person, given the fictitious name Brentley de Bisbane, struggled. He did well enough on the verbal part but ran into difficulty with the blocks. A pattern would be shown him and he would try and fail to replicate it with the blocks he had been given. One pattern after another he was unable to recreate with the blocks. In a rage he pummeled the psychologist administering the test for her thwarting ways. His life thereafter reflected his failure: a mediocre college record (in which, quite suspiciously, he hung out in Poli Sci) and years of excessive drinking and picking up women in the bars of America. When all else had failed, he tried politics, but even there the voters read him right and turned him down.

Luther wrote to Professor Katz, Ph.D., what he could not say in class:

> Intelligence means to be strong. It means to have all your ducks in a row. When your blocks are in the right rows, your ducks soon follow. Intelligence means you are a tank whom no one can hurt. It means you can crush your opposition into the ground so that they can never get up again. It means that you are God in the wisdom of your judgment. Without intelligence you are naked in the rain and people pierce you with arrows. The case study shows that the low number of Barkley de Bisbane is a handicap throughout his life. In unison the class is crying out, "God, his IQ is so low." So would you say that an action is required of me to see where I stand vis a vis Barkley de Bisbane? Would you not say that I must get to the bottom of what intelligence is with the blocks all assembled to perfection so that the blocks of my life can come together in the pattern of integration that intelligence needs to call itself by that name, and that someone must establish this for me so I can live? Can I hear from you please beyond the classroom interaction? I will be waiting for you in the stairwell down the hall, and yes, I will be naked for your full inspection of my personality and my mind. Hasten to me, Professor Katz, my Mr. Yeshiva and Yale man all in one.

Luther was good to his word. He showed up in the stairwell. "I am cold. I am hungry. I have not had my grilled cheese sandwich," he cried out. Professor Katz arrived not with understanding but with an officer of the law named Bunny Sanchez.

"He is manifesting a clinically distinct type of narcissistic dementia peculiar to this decade and which is causing a gross infection among the population at this college. A check of his records suggests that he is not intellectually fit—that is, he is lacking in blocks ability—and must be removed from the premises forthwith."

"Forthwith?" Officer Bunny asked.

"With haste," Professor Katz said, from the smallness of his dimensions, Luther reaching out to touch him over the restraining influence of Officer Bunny.

"Take me home, Officer Bunny. Take me home," Luther cried.

"Put on your clothes and we'll see about that," Officer Bunny said.

"I am so hurt and disappointed," he said, to the departing Professor Katz as he dressed.

Officer Bunny walked Luther out of the building and sat down with him on a stone wall.

"Has the Christ left you?" Officer Bunny asked.

"I am the Christ," Luther said. "I am the Christ who was and all the Christs who are to come."

"Look," Officer Bunny said. "I'm not going to arrest you, but you can't be taking off your clothes in public again."

"I wanted him to see the truth so he could work on me in the way that only he could, with the scientific knowledge he has gained."

"All right. You behave yourself now. Because if you act up like that again, you'll be taken to Bellevue. And you don't want to go there."

Luther accepted the truth of what Officer Bunny had said and cried and cried some more. And in the process revelation came to him. There was nothing like a good cry to give him the direction that he needed to go.

Luther called Mona with the news. "My head cannot be made round, but the brain that it houses can be determined to be smart, if only the blocks will go my way. I have made an appointment with the truth. My mind will be ascertained in all its dimensions."

"Tell me what's going on, Luther," she said, over the commotion of her paintbrush swishing in the turps.

"I have only this to offer you: Dolores Gross."

"Dolores Gross?"

"Dolores Gross, Ph.D. Person of quality, with the added virtue of a quality address on Central Park West."

"What about her, Luther? And be brief."

"She is going to test me for the quantity and the quality of my mind. She is going to see if I can put the blocks together."

"What blocks?"

"The intelligence blocks that Barkley de Bisbane failed to master and that led to his downfall so that he could not be a person of substance. So that he had to try to be a politician and live in generalities and not a doctor or a physicist, with all the precision they require. But if I can do the blocks then I can turn the corner on anything and be a part of America."

Continually in the background he heard the cleansing of the brush in the formidable turps, as if it was the sound of her driven soul so ongoing in its quest for more achievement, while he had long interludes of preparation to face the pages of his paperback books, the words disappearing from his mind as fast as they came in. Because how did you build a life on the story line of a novel? But if words didn't have sanctity, at least they had portableness, and who could ever say they needed turps or gesso or *oil-based paints* to be applied?

"You can do any blocks you need to if you just put your mind to it. I have faith in you, Luther."

"May I only say this? May I? You are in the heaven of escape from all that my intelligence can't bring me. You are a Bob Dylan record in defiance of what is, but I have to find my hitching post to the reality of the world, and so I have made my appointment with Dolores Gross so she can fortify me over the top. Is that an understanding that you can work with?"

"Are you telling me that you are taking an intelligence test?"

"I am telling you that the truth is within my reach, and that once I apprehend it, I am free by virtue of the problem-solving ability it gives me."

"Luther, I am busy."

"And I am busy, too, with the future that I am building."

Having said as much, he walked where he would in the latitude in which he lived.

Dolores Gross lived in a building that was very tall and very strong in dealing with the blustery winds coming off the park, having no buildings in front of it to hide from. It had cornices and gargoyles and all the ornamentation that testified to exemplary artisanship. It also had a doorman and an elevator. Dolores Gross was waiting for him. She had a mind finer than most and an apartment she could live in, with dogs and cats and children kept out of sight, if they existed for her at all. She had paintings on the wall and heft on her frame and roundness on her face, the fact being that she was just down the street from the Museum of Natural History. No one had to encourage her to stay where she was. She had built the life she wanted, with listening devices installed for the laughter of children outside the museum and the happy chatter of the checkout clerks in the neighborhood's fine grocery store, all elements in order in her world. She had a desk where she could write out bills with her Mont Blanc pen, like Dr. Eject down on Fifty-seventh Street. What she could not fathom was the man pacing her waiting room wearing a tie-dyed T-shirt and hair out of proportion to his frame and sad yet bedroom eyes.

"Mr. Garatdjian?"

"That is my name standing on its own, despite its deformity. Let me say that I know what walls such as these that seal in peace can do, and I have aspirations in that direction for myself."

His hand was cold when she shook it and she saw the dilation of his pupils and so it occurred to her that he was high. Sensing she knew, he told her that one had always to seek out the higher places by whatever means necessary and that the climb was an effort and how was he or anyone to get to the moon without a booster?

"Do you understand where I am coming from?" he asked, standing close.

"Yes, well come along," she said, leading him to a large table.

"Is this the room where truth is established?"

"Please, sit across from me."

He did fine at first. He had no problem repeating numbers or naming kinds of birds or explaining where rubber came from.

But then came the blocks. Black blocks. White blocks. White and black blocks together. And a card with patterns that he was supposed to replicate with the blocks so he could get the white ones running up the middle or along the edges or holding their own in the patterns that were called for, all of them showing an obstinacy he had not counted on and giving rise to the time that was now a factor pressing in on him and obliterating his ability to think with her watching him, the hateful woman presenting an impossible challenge and sitting back so calm in her chair so that he wanted to throw the blocks in her face. Because she was stalling him stalling him, and now his life was in doubt with the blocks resting there disordered and Dolores Gross, Ph.D., a witness to his shame.

And so he swept the tormenting evidence from the table onto the floor.

"Now they are as chaotic as my life. Are you happy with the result that you have shown me how to have? Are you?"

Surely she was happy that she could now assign him a number and, once he was gone, turn the page and have a new and more presentable number enter her premises. Because numbers were important, the stuff of life, and once they were in place, the person was in place, and that could only be forever. She herself had no problem with the blocks. She had only to command them with a flick of her wrist and they established themselves in their astonishingly correct patterns. And the truth was that sometimes she gave herself over to this activity night and day, arranging the blocks in permutations in the air to confirm her place in the universe, so high above most others. Sometimes too she hugged and kissed the number she assigned herself and even took it to bed and lay with it in her sleep. Sometimes she saw it in the pages of the newspapers and the books and the magazines she read. It was her secret treasure; she kept copies of it in safe deposit boxes all around the city and requested a telephone number with those three integers appearing in sequence. Because when you were number one with the blocks, you were number one with life and could live in quiet contemplation of the gift that had been presented to you.

"You did quite well on the verbal part. It is only that you ran into some difficulty with the organization of the blocks. It is not uncommon for a person to be stronger in one area than the other. The thing that is unusual is that you seemed to show a deep frustration that can only lead me to conclude that you have some underlying emotional issue that it would behoove you to explore."

Behoove. He let the word sit in his mind like some small elongated animal.

"There is a low-cost institute for healing here in the city. I will write out the name and phone number for you."

"Barkley de Bisbane thanks you," he said, as he made payment.

PART II

Chapter 64

I am alone where I can now be found. I am in a doctor's office loud with the sound of its own insistent silence and in seeming harmony with its different parts. Its thick walls offer insurance against nature's eminence. No wild animals have streaked through, and the floors are clear of offal. Outside is the movement of troops in ragtag army formation. They have no truck with discipline. Soon the doctor will come and get large, rip through my fine silk, and access my assets. Wed to the promise of bliss, he will call me irresistible and in turn receive a bullet through each eye for his daring, and only then will he be loved to death for the vigor of his interest as we sing a song for every tomorrow while never forgetting the past. And when he asks me in a moment of tenderness if I am all right, it is only then that I will distend my jaw and swallow him whole. He will come to me, come on me, come for me. His spending will be copious and forever. He will be my minister of truth and I will love him till the bleeding ends.

An incremental spring has arrived, with children of privilege singing out their love of the earth under the branches of the cherry blossom trees of Central Park that would obstruct my sight of them. All of them gay little sunbeams even with the implacableness of their wills.

"What do you hope to get from psychoanalysis?" Doctor Donn says, having come through the wall.

"I want to understand the trouble life has caused me and why, and how I can rise above it and be the Lord."

"The Lord?"

"The Lord Jesus Christ, who stopped all time in its tracks."

"Are you saying that you are the Lord Jesus Christ?"

"I too have multitudes within me."

"Tell me your family background."

"We are mismatched. We are battered furniture out there in the pouring rain. Though we struggle to exist, we are relying on death to give us our bearings."

The man wears a suit and tie, as if such is a requirement for conversing. I want to love him and I don't.

"Have you been active in the demonstrations sweeping the campus?"

"Only my hair is unruly. I love Mark Rudd very much. About Lewis Cole I have nothing to say. They are my superiors but I will nevertheless endeavor to transcend them both. I can tell you this. When I listen to *The White Album,* I know that every march has its end."

Dr. Donn writes for hours and hours. The moon shows itself and goes away. Many people die, never to be seen again. (Hah!) I hold myself close and wait upon his action.

A small, rectangular room. Simple. Spare. A leather sofa with no arms on which I sat, close to the door. A high-backed chair across the room. The kind of space I would want for myself, the niche we are all seeking. Beyond the large curtained window the sounds of traffic, the rush hour congestion that by degrees we become inured to by its daily repetition. It was OK to step out of the bright lights of America and into some interior natural lighted space where quiet reigned. And yet I did hear the call of America.

I did hear it. It was never far away. How could it be?

There was a couch. I was told to lie down on it. So Dr. Zimmer instructed me. A stocky woman with a low center of gravity and a name tag on her red jacket that read, "Agent of power—mine to wield." She had been sent from Germany to do a job; she was here to teach America a lesson that would eliminate the permissiveness that was ruining the nation. She did not sing the "nation" word, she did not put all the Southern feeling there was into it, the second and stressed syllable becoming a sack stretched to the ripping point. Na-shunnnn. Je-susss. She said that life was lived in the minor key and that eating was a necessity.

"What do you mean, minor key?"

"Tell me what you think I mean." Her T-Ball Jotter poised over a wire-bound notepad, as if I had something meaningful to say.

She was a psychoanalyst in training, with a medical degree from Columbia University. The framed certificate on the wall said so, as did the chair she made her throne. I was not fit to be there. If not cathartic, it still felt necessary to enter my emotional reality in the record. I told her that my vileness was legendary. Not only was I a thief and an abuser of my girlfriend, I was also stupid and missing the back of my head.

The doctor's wardrobe was evidently extensive and emblematic of her success and self-regard. From one session to the next, she never wore the same outfit twice in our thrice-weekly sessions and had the pleased look of one who has come in from the cold the narcissistic impulse of her younger years had driven her to.

Though she had my sister Hannah's black hair, she was not that particular sister of mine by reason of the proof she dared set forth—the absence of a correct smacking position for her hands (hands positioned breasts high and hanging down) and the sweetness of her smile and her manifest need to expose me to her healing touch. Though unspoken, yet did I hear her pledge to infiltrate my mind and bring it within reasonable and stable borders by posting sentries at all the way stations that might contribute to my undoing.

Listen, it was very clear from the start that her ambition was to be the taming of America with her knockwurst-eating German heritage.

All I knew at the moment was that a decision was being forced upon me—did I jump out the window, run out the door, or lie down, as she was calling on me to do? My decision, as if fear gave me any choice, was to maintain my upright position in order to confront her hegemonist impulse with a knowing eye.

In spite of my concern that she had the power to confiscate things near and dear to me, my confessional nature began to assert itself. There was the vileness of my behavior with Mona and how I threw women down on the Manhattan streets to make them mine for a brief minute, the fiddle I had going at the renting office in alliance with RMN and his vice president henchman and his personal goon squad, messengers Haldeman and Ehrlichman, with whom I was in subtle contact. Yes, there was much BS, but it was my BS. Like a needle stuck in the groove of a record, I replayed the old song of Hannah rising out of the mists of time with her hand raised to the correct smacking position, of the histrionic madness of Naomi and the real deal madness of Rachel, of the sustained debauchery of my brother Luke, seeking to fornicate his way to freedom, of the menacing shadow of my youngest sister Vera seeking to rule the earth with her anger. Of my father I could not speak, except in the accent of the aggrieved, as he slowly disappeared, limb by limb, from the life he did not embrace. I told her a simple truth, that judgment could not be forestalled, that if I had usurped God's function, so be it, the fact being that I had a stronger claim, that he was my father, not God's, and that the angle of vision from underneath revealed things that would go unnoticed from above. Because she was herself an immigrant, I could see from her dismayed expression that she had an empathy profound for my father that did not exclude me from the circle of her love but at the same time put me on notice that my words might actually have meaning. Nevertheless, I told her that the fatal blow of indifference had been delivered to my father many times over, and now I was free to roam the earth in a spirit of conquest and with no need for a living soul, with the exception of Mona, and clearly no one needed me. As for my mother, I spoke the simple truth that she had swum the ocean deep (the fishes singing to her and she to them) to arrive on this shore and that God was in her and she was in God and that to get between them would be a dangerous thing, given what they could do.

To include her in my attentions, I told the good doctor that I knew a little about Germany, the fertility of its people and its soil, and what it meant to have a Beethovian brow and the prodigious achievement that could mushroom from it, all of this on the greasy fare of a carnivorous people devouring fat-laden meats shaped like feces, the national cuisine no deterrent to artifacts of accomplishment. And that to be a German was also to man a Panzer tank and fire a Luger and to share a desensitized personality with little capacity for introspection. She, I conceded, had been a beauty who had thickened on her own appetites. But just because Germany had all the necessities for superior life owing to its scientific mettle did not mean I had to lie down dying for her. There was such a thing as a stick in the eye reserved for the mightiest. All the same, it was a thing of wonder to be able to manufacture such a tank, with the intrepid action of its treads and the slender barrel of death protruding from its swiveling turret and the helmeted men of Germany crouched behind its industrial strength.

"What can you do for me that God has failed to do?" I asked.

"You are a seriously malnourished young man. I can listen and help you get well in your mind and your body."

"Will you beat me black and blue? Will you adorn me with all the names that I would call myself? Will you promise to exhaust your repertoire of pain and then find new reserves?"

She closed her notebook and capped her pen. "We will see what we can do for you," she said. Her eyes were strong and had the light of life in them, as if she had turned a corner into days of consecutive brightness. Whether that particular manifestation of her disposition had anything to do with Germany, I couldn't be sure. All I knew was that it was important to back out the door slowly so she could not undress me from behind, the women of Germany being very driven and always in need of watching.

I left only to come back, if only for the briefest time. She was still in her chair. "Luger," I said softly, and then, more loudly, "German Luger," and fled for my life.

Chapter 65

I headed west on the downward slope of the long street between Ninth and Tenth Avenue, the sun once again sinking beyond New Jersey. Mrs. Muldooney was waiting for me, sitting on the garbage can in defense of her parochial interests. She knew the localness of her power. Her gaze was clear-eyed, her face pocked and blanched.

Her son appeared, unwilling to leave me alone with her, fearful though he wouldn't say so of the displacement it might cause. He wore the tight black gloves of his serial killer practice. Though she didn't say so for the record, Mrs. Muldooney let it be known through subtle means that a mother will always have an understanding of her child, and place the origins of his wickedness where it cannot come between them.

Neither she nor he was living in the truth; rather, they were exemplifying the bonding technique that co-opts all truth and distorts it for its own foul purpose. Whatever, there was no altering of their connection.

"I too have a mother, and yet do not serve as rogue apprentice to her dark work, should she have any," I said.

The man maintained a level gaze, though beyond it I saw the buzzing rage that only appeared as calm. Perhaps my presence as an outsider served to deepen their simpatico status. And when it became futile to try and force a yielding of their obdurate silence, I walked through the hallway to my new and wonderful home.

Robert Browning was on the shelf dividing the two rooms, while Robert Frost, with his white hair, had been called on to represent America. A fake-tiffany lamp rested on the low-slung night table by my bed, and windows front and back served as a reminder that a world lay beyond, whereas the bathroom was windowless to ensure my utmost privacy. Calls were coming in from all throughout the nation concerning social unrest, but I just had to hold my ground and consolidate my power, captive as I was to my own currents and inhaling fragrant incense.

When night came on, I fell into a sleep that took me beneath the bed and the floor in a vortex with the tight cylindrical confines of a well. There a dust-covered creature unclassifiable and initially unseen awaited me, a tarantula-like thing of magnified size and evil disposition. I woke in terror, dressed, and wandered into the streets to avoid the destruction that the dream was heralding.

My wandering took me down to St. Mark's Place in the East Village, where out of the mist a girl in jeans and a purple T-shirt appeared, full of her youth and her short blond hair a thing of glory. She said her name was Deborah Kramer and when I suggested that the night had brought us together for a specific reason it was for us to together discern and that the fact of spring itself and the promptings of our own blood it stirred would be vital factors in that exploration, she acknowledged the essential truth of what I was saying as I stood transfixed by her entirely kissable mouth and every other riveting feature of her lightly freckled face. Altogether jolts of jubilation rocked me, my task now to steady myself toward an intimacy that could know no bounds.

She had an artist's sex, she said, as we walked, and acknowledged that no one was truly able to care for that sex if she kept it in isolation. When I asked with an interviewer's solicitousness to elaborate on the potent words "artist's sex," she got biographical on me, saying only that she was from the "stupid state" of New Jersey, that she had a younger brother with a straight A average and the ability to throw a football the length of the playing field, and that three hundred colleges had wooed him before he decided on Yale, and while I could have allowed this be a deterrent to my claim of worthiness, she reached out across the divide that was claiming me and said, "I know who you are. It's all right. You can have me in the limited way that I have already set up."

She led me to her apartment in a doorman building on Fourteenth Street just west of Fifth Avenue. It was the kind of nouveau riche white brick high rise the city was seeing a lot of. Yes, she came from wealth, she acknowledged, before we kissed, while keeping the rest of herself off limits, her hands on mine preventing them from roaming.

"You'd better go before my boyfriend Rick arrives. His father is a paper goods magnate and so Rick gets to drive a new Corvette every year, but that doesn't mean because his father is aligned with industry he exists within the law and couldn't have you killed. Believe me, he may already have visited the killing field. This you must understand, as well as my pathetic tie to Mr. Corvette Man, probably on his way over just this minute to nail me to the floor with his thing. I want you so to fill me joy, but you don't know the inspecting powers of this man or what I mean to him. He says I am America itself with the paralyzing beauty of my eyes and merciless twitch of my bottom and so he seeks to enslave me as he is enslaved."

Amid the low ceiling, the sparkling wood floor, the designer furniture, and the modern kitchen—was the corresponding minimalism of her art, dots on a canvas that suggested her own colorful whiteness. A warning was communicated to me not to see the dots as evidence of a dilettante's doodling.

A man came in through the window and took Deborah away from me. Athletic in his build and powerful in his purpose, he lay her on the floor and did all the things I would have done had I the green light. While he pronged her good, I had a chance to study her face fully in lust but also pain; if there was wild abandon, there was also captivity. When he had done his work, when he had filled her to the extent that he could, only then did he remove himself from her corporeal premises.

He showed himself to be utterly frank in his discourse, stating his adopted name as Stingray Man and saying that his father had broken many heads and burned many bodies to get to the position of eminence he now enjoyed, and that while my mind might judge such a driven, ruthless force for acquisition, that was, in the final analysis, my judgment. He said his problem was an out-of-control fear that while he loitered on the premises of the family business in the leather jacket that he had been outfitted with, and with the keys to the very regional family kingdom, she had stepped forward into the world with her lock box open, that while he wandered the localities of New Jersey (yes, a stupid, exceedingly stupid state, he too affirmed), she was roaming free in the megalopolis of New York City. From his place of desperation, he laid it on the table—he was a hang-backer while she was a stepper-outer, and much money and time were having to go into his control-room apparatus for the stifling of her outbound course. He said he had measured the size of his penis and the strength of his brain as a way of keeping the containment fences high, that he had positioned spies on every corner and listening devices on every lamppost, but that here she was involved in a smooch-a-thon with the likes of me.

We did not sing a duet with the theme of fear; it would have been off-key. Nor did he kill me dead. He simply tossed me out the window whence he had come, which required me to land on my feet with shock absorbers at the ready.

For the longest time I sat amid the treasures of the city and reflected on the gift that I had been given, that I had done to Stingray Man what Harvard Man had done to me, that in kissing Deborah and being kissed back, I was Harvard Man feasting on Mona. Women who had men but didn't want the men they had. Women eager to give clobber. Women eager to go off with the first interested man to come along, whether in Harvard Square or in the East Village.

Many people died that day, and new ones were born. The fresh faces were not entirely innocent; they had agendas of their own.

Chapter 66

The institute was housed in a squat building east of the imperious assault by the high rises along Third Avenue. I would arrive early, lest I miss a few precious minutes with Dr. Zimmer. Not that I would tell her how much I needed her. Even a so-called healer was likely to have a dark side and savage you mercilessly should you expose your neediness.

In the waiting area were pastel chairs and a sofa for our sitting pleasure and an office you were separated from by a wall and sliding glass partition. Behind that window sat a young man doing the business of the clinic, including writing a receipt for my cash payment of nine dollars for the three weekly sessions. Like Mona Van Dine, I was experiencing the pleasure and comfort of having money of my own. How far I had come from being the indigent young man languishing in the New Haven House of Detention.

It had long been known to me that all the women of Staten Island had police officers for boyfriends or husbands, men who could hurt you with their mere existence, never mind their fists. There, in the waiting room of the institute, did I meet the lady love of one of these officers of the law. Her name was Mary Jo Flaherty. Irish and with a Catholic school education, she had pale skin and and a downcast manner, and was quick to express to me her concern about being trapped by marriage to her beau, who was pressing her to be his lawful wedded wife that they might multiply abundantly.

The two of us had some strange affinity with each other. Such was clear even from the distance that separated us and without a word being spoken, she in her molded plastic pastel-colored chair and I in mine, there in that waiting room where the man behind the sliding window hummed while continuing with his quiet and annoying efficiency. That affinity was brief and never fully defined itself. Perhaps it was nothing more than the ambivalence we felt in our respective relationships and the vague sense that a crisis of decision was coming. She had a secretarial life and a Staten Island address and the working class in her genes; she also had a religion that would make her burden heavy should she stray from the path of righteousness. Perhaps we recognized in each other our incomplete commitment to our partners. As it was, we sat on a bench in Central Park a few times in uneventful encounters filled with careful words while the tall buildings of Fifth Avenue dared to look on. Evidently, we were not bound for intimacy. Shallow as it will sound, the thickness of her legs and the amplitude of her waist dulled the initiative for such activity.

I returned to Dr. Zimmer and experienced a love supreme for the strength and confidence she exuded; I did not find her bowed down in a veil of tears with "The Old Rugged Cross" as background music for her ways.

I told her how understanding had come to me with the arrival of Stingray Man on the premises of Deborah while we had the smooch thing going, and of the interminable sorrow of the lost and anxious, and how it must be transcended at all cost, and that now I had become Harvard Man doing to other men what filthy filthy Harvard Man had done to me, enjoying sex of the unattached kind with a woman bound to and by another; to know that wherever I walked there was such a woman in the full state of her burden who would undress for me if only I presented my longing for her sex in the right key.

Once again she got German on me, repeating her strong request that I lie down, but I was having none of it.

"I need to look at your face so I can get to the bottom of it," I said, watching as her pen got active with her note taking.

"What is a Stingray Man, please?" she asked, in line with the inquiring nature of her profession. Hers, of course, was an impatient tone used by those who seek to impose themselves on the American experience and capture it through their own skewed understanding. Because she had now the crossness of the insistent German woman, I told her what I could, how a girl eternal in her goldenness emerged form the mists to provide me with the pleasure of connection, how she took me to her princess apartment in the doorman building, how the action of her kissing proceeded with vigor while hand-checking remained a constant thing, with no deaths or injuries reported. I went on with the simple yet frightful truth of Stingray Man's ascension, the suction cups and other paraphernalia with which he came adorned. I told her of the burst-through window and the thousand shards of glass into which his dream had been obliterated, and of the furious energy he would expend on the reconstruction of that dream. I said the fickleness of women left a man in bondage to his fears.

Dr. Zimmer wrote frantically, attacking her pad with her ballpoint pen, and I could see the intensity of her fury infiltrating her flesh-filled face, the black energy summoned by a signal affront eroding her good will.

"Fickleness? What is this fickleness?" she demanded.

"To be armed with an artist's pudenda is to make war on the civilization of normalcy. It is to put the primacy of sex above everything and to make it the lingua franca of all discourse."

"This is vile," she said, stepping more completely out of her analyst's persona.

I allowed silence to dissolve the weight of her oppressiveness. I just sat there in my thoughts while she recomposed herself. I then told her the truth, that Mona had been taken over by Harvard Man and so, measures not retaliatory so much as for my own survival had to be taken, and where else to find them but on an East Village street? Again the flow of the session was interrupted by her inquisitive intervention.

"Harvard Man? What is this of which you speak? I would like to work with you, but for that to be effective, I must understand what you are saying." She had been taking notes with diligence, wanting nothing that could be learned to expire on her.

"And I must gain understanding of you as well as you seek to bridge the cultural divide with pen in hand. At the same time do not think that I do not see the tanks in your armament. Harvard Man is simply a black man existing among the elite with the heightened sexual powers I am somehow disposed to attribute to him."

She seemed to let up on me, simply recording my ramblings while holding to the judgments of her separated self. I began to notice the words emerging, not where they went so much as the force of their own creation and how they were something to hide behind and hang a thing upon and even go for a ride upon the sound of, how you could stay in place and yet send them out to the far reaches of the room to hit a person hard or dispose them to softness, and that Dr. Zimmer had her own words to send my way, and they could meet in the middle or pass in the darkness of their mutual incomprehension, embrace or collide angrily, the important thing being the enterprise that led to their manufacture.

Dr. Zimmer was not happy. She had come from Germany so she could eat every day, and had trained hard so she could have her neo-Freudian lasso to throw around the necks of those who needed to be brought to ground for the purpose of modification. She had a tasteful and colorful wardrobe to demonstrate the suitability of her personality for the high responsibility of her profession. And she had her books arranged for the comprehension of the life that moved outside their pages. But to swing a lasso from your chair was not a feat easily mastered with only textbook knowledge.

"We must talk about this Mona to know who she is," Dr. Zimmer declared.

Oh, I saw the lasso held high. I saw her riding hard for the desperado she would bring to ground and hogtie good.

"Tainted love is not what the world needs. Can you emit a word as big as a beach ball without doing violence to your whole system? Has an apparatus ever been constructed for the delivery of a concept so big as she is to me? She is the breaking dawn and the crepuscular and the darkness blanketing night. She is royalty that requires no crown. She is the lightning detonating my anger so that I cannot breathe with explosions all around. She is America on the move."

"She is young like you?"

"Younger than any god that you could fashion, and immense in the weight of her own preoccupations. She fights the police, she fights the whole white patriarchal system that you embrace by making her sex a tunnel of love."

She went on with her scribbling. God only knew what. All in all, I appreciated the structured environment, the narrow room with its functional furniture and the large curtained window and even the honking cars infected with the impatient energy of the country. I truly savored the specialness of the retreat that I had been given in those fifty-minute hours and the implicit belief that the sessions could only move me forward to whatever my destination might be, so long as Mona was in it.

Mona came in that weekend.To fortify myself for her presence, I sought out Deborah Kramer, who allowed me to unzip her jeans and touch her sex with my hand but nothing more, thus staying technically pure for Stingray Man. I then headed uptown for my encounter with Mona, hoping to arrange my face so that it didn't readily show the wounds she had inflicted.

I took it as a positive sign that the doorman did not impede my progress. In less than a minute I was ringing the Van Dine doorbell and stood my ground as if among the ranks of the normal.

I was introduced to more sexual developments that weekend. Perhaps it was spring and some personal need for renewal, but Lydia too, I learned, had taken on a lover, a middle-aged black man named Milton Du Pre. He was no clandestine amour. Not at all. She spoke of him as her eros and of Peter as her love.

Claire stepped forward to say that she too was expanding her notion of success, that she as well had taken on a black lover, his name being Val Jack. Both revelations caused in me more than a ripple of fear, which I struggled to hide.

Jeffrey told his own truth, that he continued to bop his bologna and laugh out of the side of his mouth.

"How have you been, Luther?" I heard Lydia ask.

"I have been down, but now I am fighting hard for my own freedom with a German on my side."

"What German would that be?" Lydia asked, with amusement in her voice.

"One who has a roadmap of the inner workings of the mind including the express route to mental health. That is who she is."

"Are you saying you have finally sought help?"

"I call on the universe constantly for aid. And now it is coming."

"Well, we can all be glad for that," Lydia said.

I wandered among them in their new family dynamic, and found comfort that Peter had been released from exile and reinstated. With the night came thunderstorms with all their threats of heaven-sent cataclysm, and with the storms came a dream in which more attention to the wholesale abandonment by the Van Dine women of male whiteness and the mysterious synchronicity by which it was achieved. In the dream a procession of virile black men entered the apartment to pleasure the Van Dine women. I did not run away. I did not plummet from the window. Rather did I accept the karmic punishment being inflicted for the fear of blackness I had harbored since childhood and the mindset that their advancement would mean my destruction and even death.

I awoke with Mona in the canopied bed and yet apart from her. The abundant sunlight did not mirror my own mood. I felt tired and grew increasingly out of sorts watching as Mona prepared for the day. It was nothing overt, just sly nonverbal stuff, starting with the overly aggressive way she brushed her teeth and an expression intended to be slyly annoying, even if I could not put words to it, as she examined her face in the mirror. She moved on to outright odiousness with the application of her mascara, opening her eyes wide with the ostentation that befit her in an endeavor to bring her lashes to a darker life. To fully create a universe of rancor, she puffed her lips to facilitate the application of the lipstick coating that she felt required to give them, then severely pursed them, and topped off her hatefulness with a loud popping sound as she threw open her mouth for the air all around. Through all her actions had she established for all concerned that she was deliberately dwelling in the realm of the repellent. Deborah Kramer had offered nothing in the way of a shield from my pain.

The path forward for my own resurrection was now presenting itself. I saw all too clearly that the Van Dines were burying me alive with their hospitality. Had Lydia not called me and my kind parasites following the death of Lenore? And was she not right? Could it be said that Minnie the Moocher had anything on me, eating, as I did, their food and drinking their booze and trying pathetically to forge my own identity by adopting theirs?

Autonomy. Independence. I did not criticize the family dwelling but simply advocated for my own as the territory we, yes *we*, needed to explore. Perhaps she was worn out by the erratic comings and goings of Harvard Man but she acquiesced. The apartment had two rooms but was really built for one, and had no food in the refrigerator lest the rats come and assault me while I was preparing a meal. Nor was there the glow of a TV set for late night warmth. Instead there were only the walls and the silences they held and the awareness of the austerity that those silences bred, the stunning truth that I could now see through her eyes, and that no words were necessary to name.

"You have nothing, not even yourself," she said, confirming the reality anyway.

My single bed converted to a double, which was accomplished with the moving of some furniture, and in that double bed we spent a joyless night.

I fell through the cracks of my own meager life and spent many nights and many days in the pool of shame at the core of my existence. Eye contact was difficult. Conversation was minimal.

In the morning we had breakfast in a coffee shop where waiters in black pants and white shirts showed themselves full of purpose. Mona ordered a hearty breakfast of ham and eggs and a blueberry muffin and a large O.J. Amid the bustle and the kitchen clatter and the industry of the waiters' ways did I hear the song of America joyfully arise in this money-making enterprise.

The coffee shop was on Ninth, not Tenth Avenue, and unlike the latter, did not lie flat for the southbound cars and trucks and buses to roll over but sloped gently downward to speed them on their way to sinkhole Times Square.

Mona dealt with the food of these Greeks. She ate outside the pressures of time, clearing the plate of all its content and providing her body with the fuel needed to maintain her vigor. For my part I did what I could to preserve my health, eating around the edges of the rye toast saturated with butter that came, reassuringly, in wrapped patties. Yes I ate around the edges, but I continued on to the middle till the whole thing was gone. To eat the bread of America and the butter of America was not the same thing as to eat the eggs of America and to be at the mercy of the nasty regions of the chickens they came from. Then to have a Marlboro with black coffee would have been to spend a morning designed in heaven if pain had not been all around.

I did not kill her dead. I did not kill anyone dead. I simply lit another cigarette and filled my lungs with smoke.

"You haven't closed the door on Harvard Man, have you?"

"He has a name, you know. Look. You've got to give me room to hang with people once in a while."

"Hang? Hang? That sounds like Harvard Man in the night."

She grabbed her backpack and headed for Grand Central Terminal and the train back to Boston. I did not follow.

Chapter 67

Professor Kohl knew who Norman Mailer was and had more than a passing understanding of the New England tendencies of Robert Lowell, including his ability to grow inebriated while the glasses remained on his face. He also had the ability to enter Mott Hall, at the south end of the campus, with fortitude. Because he was built low to the ground he never had to stoop, and in his face was all the wisdom and intellectual curiosity of his Jewish race.

He was leading a seminar that semester, and now that spring had arrived, he would teach only with the window open. The seminar's theme was "Truth Throughout the Centuries: The Chimera Lives." What were words *really* signifying? Footnotes might be lowly, and set in smaller type, and yet they were king in the domain we purported to inhabit, for every word to prosper must have a source to call its own if authenticity was to mean a thing. Don Quixote could tilt at windmills and Sancho Panza could bring up his Iberian rear, but methods of research were necessary to surround the text and give it the classification it required. The table around which students and professor sat was the suspicious element, how it brought you near only to fling you far with fear. Only Professor Kohl remained in place, his face smiling while his eyes stayed hard. Through all of it, I kept my pen at the ready, should anything dare to happen.

I fell asleep at the table and dreamt of a single-file procession of young black men in bumblebee black and yellow basketball uniforms. Their expressions were uniformly jovial, as if the sun shining down on them was empowering their radiance. When I awoke I shared my dream, in the hope of weaving it into the fabric of the discussion, but no soap, no cigar, no nothing, Professor Kohl said, conveying with an expression of fortified shrewdness that he knew bushwa when he heard it.

Sancho Panza wore baggy pants and had a friendly name that didn't get serious in a single one of its vowels or consonants. He also had a reputation for friendliness to inanimate objects, while Don Quixote had higher aspirations, checking you hard with the *Don* before breaking you altogether with the demanding Q and with what better motive than to compensate for his lankiness with a demand for respect. This too I offered for consideration, and received the same cold response.

I wandered to other classrooms where many had contracted upward into their own heads to create a universe of their own, spinning the words that had an imagined application to their alleged existence. When I returned to Professor Kohl the horses and the windmill and Spain and all of it was still there as testimony to the staying power of literature that enterprise had found a reason to be stuck upon.

That night I stood in the courtyard of my Hell's Kitchen building—*my building*—with my belt pulled tight should austerity ever need to happen. I saw the white brick building rising above the insistent flatness of the avenue, with the foul river so near patiently waiting, and how the building sought dominion through its height and whiteness. I saw too the stamp of its modernity, the anonymity of its windowless face that shut you in and shut me out, so that only the service rendered could be the fact at hand. I saw the minor apportionment to workers of its profits, and heard in its defense that it was not the obloquy of an org to move the country forward but a cause for rejoicing, that someone had to break new ground where only the old had been. Not with audacity but with a facade of tall and ominous blandness did it put on notice the surrounding tenements, saying they could have their small lives within the rattling windows where the peasants counted their change and *drank their beer*, but something new had arrived and needed bowing down to, as for how long could immigrants be expected to piss and shit and sweat and wash their faces in the newspapers of New York City before their lives got processed into the ways of work that truly mattered and integers could be counted and processed and fees get paid for services delivered? So I took the building's measure and it took mine, and when I said that I'd be watching it, the building answered back right quick (its own words) that it would do the same, for now I saw it had a face among its mammoth dimensions, a face of space rectangular in shape where brick had not been allowed to go, a face high up and dead center on its mastodon size where the cooling and the heating unit could have the air that it so needed for the functioning of the building's life. There was nothing to do but stare it down and try to find a thing of beauty in its numbing and uniform mass. After a time I saw the signals of its change, the laugh lines forming in the wall of brick. I saw it heave and spasm and convulse with merriment. I saw the side-splitting mirth it dared to indulge in and seeing this, knew from where it spoke when it articulated my passion for the things of oldness amid the full-court pressure of all that was new, exposing my need to hold onto the used and dusty while those with ramrod straightness forged ahead with the things of time present that would someday be the paradigm of what still lived from time before. And this it showed me with graphs and charts and the numerology driving its ideological bent, while laughing out its judgment that my only power was in retreat to a yesteryear that never was and boldly affirming that America was predicated on the theme of a modernity as hard as the word itself.

I called on the serial killer man to practice his extinguishing wickedness on the threatening building with its mocking ways but he could summon no interest in things not of the flesh.

Because I had a new community with lines of contact to the one that I had left, I could walk about without heartbreak captive to a fixation on accumulating more assets, which led to the realization of the need for a safer storage space than my apartment for my growing treasure. Chemical Bank was the first to receive the fruits of my enterprise because of the quality of its name. The money could be in your mind if not in your hand and that would be the case whether you passed the bank on foot or on the Broadway bus or chose to splurge and zip past in a New York City taxicab. You could savor the security and confidence money provided and have it show in the health of your nation-self while nobody but the bank had to consciously know the source of your glow.

Along the way Fifty-seventh Street was calling out its love of life under a glorious sun. There was the Holiday Inn, radiating the optimism of America, and the Parc Vendome, a residential building, projecting stability itself. In the leisure that my days afforded me, I bought a *New York Post* for verification that righty Tom Terrific was smashing good from over the top, his right knee grazing the mound as he delivered his smoke, and that lanky Jerry Koosman continued his mastery coming from the left side, while all were free to meditate on the rebellious meaning of the double "n" capping and solidifying Donn Clendenon's first name and what a full name so saturated with skipping n's could mean. On this May day as on many others would I avoid the power sources seeking to place my life on the rack of discipline that sacrifice entailed and that a preoccupation with worldly pleasures can work against. I was twenty-one now, and the clock was ticking. It had occurred to me that a hellish bomb might explode if I didn't do something more than store my assets in my apartment. Now I had a plan.

The bank officer, Ned Nightly, had a thin neck, like me, and wore a tie to support himself. He said that banking might be an industry shunned by those seeking the limelight, but he wore his hair short to maintain his position and learned early on the joy of planning methodically for his future. There was no furtiveness about him; he was level gaze all the way. I asked him where he went on Saturday nights and did he find a way to insert himself into city life when all the forces of loneliness were upon him and he said he stood outside the Plaza Hotel and cried, but that walking gave him a fortitude he hadn't known he possessed.

We settled on a color, canary yellow, for the checking account I had chosen to open.

"The color of light and happiness. I can hardly wait for the joy they will bring," I said, and cried tears of great joy and excitement.

Ned Nightly provided me with a starter kit and assured me my checks would arrive in seven business days. I could count on that, he said.

"Thank you, Ned. I am sure we are both bound to prosper in our own ways."

I left Ned Nightly and walked further east along the avenue in search of another institution of quality that would accept the assets from my enterprise. I had not long to look. There on an avenue of renown was a bank of granite strength with a vaulted ceiling over a marble floor and tellers and bank officers at the ready for any request that you might make, so long as it was about the thing they said made the world go around.

An officer took me in his care. He wiped his brow with tissue he had been hoping to save, he said, for use at home. He had a system in place, he further explained, for the appropriation of toilet paper from the bank's premises in a way that could be construed by his conscience as legitimate. He pointed to his glasses. "You see, fear causes me to rush from the house every workday morning concerned for my very life. If the truth be told, I have to eat my hash browns on the run. Because to be late for work by five minutes means my very death, what with old Mr. Armistead peering from his myriad vantage points to record the tardiness of his employees. Mr. Armistead, you must understand, may sleep on the moon by night, but he is here by day in the most oppressively punctilious way. In any case, my first action at break time is to head for the men's room, where I wash the lenses of my glasses under cold water and then wipe them with a generous supply of the bank's toilet paper. I then carefully fold the only slightly used toilet paper for my personal use at home. By practicing this level of conservation, I give new meaning to the words 'bringing home the bacon,' because just a little less of that bacon has to go to the purchase of this essential bathroom item each month. Because, let me be perfectly clear about this, I apply that wad of toilet paper to my tush after a heavy bombing campaign."

"Bombing campaign?"

"Bombing the bowl with fecal matter, sir?"

"Oh yes, of course," I said, giving a thumb's up for his passion but fearing that I would faint over the image of waste passing through the man's alimentary canal and into the bowl. He went on to share with me about his mountainous breasts and the weeping they caused him before getting back to business, the deposit of a sum of money where it could not be taken away from me by human hands. Mr. Federmanc—that was his name—gave assurance that my money would be stored in the very bowels of the bank and that I had nothing to fear.

I thought to tell Mr. Federmanc of my plan to disperse my money far and wide among the banks of New York City in order to escape the attention of the IRS a mammoth deposit at one locale might bring, but I refrained from concern that he would only magnify my fear.

On the northeast corner of Fifty-seventh Street and Tenth Avenue stood a deli with a slicer sharp enough to cut through bone. It had the quality sandwich stuff that I could take home and eat in the privacy of my apartment. I showed a respectful attitude and ordered a ham and cheese hero with lettuce and tomato, heavy on the mustard. Behind the counter, wearing a white apron, stood the owner, a man possessed of physical strength and unrepentant hardness. I offered girlish niceness to restrain him from any and all impulses for violence he might harbor. He had for assistance and deadly backup young neighborhood men with chops of mustache and knockout fists, men who from their parochial schools of pain had gone on to livelihoods of part-time criminality. Because he had wiry hair and a bull's neck, I told Hank, as the young men called him, my hope that my docility would be as strong as his pugnaciousness, and asked him if owning a store was in some way a compensation for the life of crime he had earlier committed to, because I had the sense that he had done harmful things, driven by the temper he was now trying to control. To his credit, he did not tell me about the father who had chained him to a radiator and whipped him mercilessly or of the mother who had anointed his scalp with boiling water or the maliciousness of life in thwarting his dreams. Instead he took me to the theater of his former bliss and the men specializing in dismemberment covered in blood-splattered plastic smocks as they severed limbs and organs from their conscious, screaming owners, along with the eye gougers and teeth knocker-outers and head drillers. He showed me up close the tools of their craft—electric drills and chainsaws and splicers and dicers and the gimlets called upon for the refined work of ocular reconstruction. He showed me men hanging on hooks with ears stapled to their mouths and cocks jammed into holes in their heads. These things he showed me before Benny Goodman's clarinet temporarily mellowed the bellicosity of his nature. I thanked him for the tour and the directness of his revelation, and promised through my tears to comport myself in a way that would not necessitate the activation of his finalizing equipment.

As I sat eating the hero sandwich, Don Quixote looked down at me reproachfully for my neglect, but drowsiness was a greater force than guilt, and soon sleep took me, the passbook and checkbook held to my chest, this with Tenth Avenue still outside and the trucks in high gear, their lonesome drivers showing off for women who didn't care.

I awoke to my session with Dr. Zimmer pending and rushed out the door. As always, she was there in her chair when I arrived.

Was she my rock for all ages? Was she presenting an image of permanence?

I told her that all I was looking for was a safe place where I could sit away from the whirring blades of the deli owner and his dissection-minded cronies and that because I had been nice enough to him that threat had been neutralized.

"You are not so nice," Dr. Zimmer exclaimed, with surprising vehemence. I indulged her outburst, preferring to focus on the heavy lifting I had done, the transfer of a great percentage of my material assets from my apartment, and how more such actions would follow, but that I had to go slow so as to avoid detection. My money wasn't out there on Fifty-seventh Street for a full public viewing; rather, it had been reduced to passbook size. It was one thing for the government to look in one place, but did it have the energy and the intelligence to look in four or five, especially if the banks were in different parts of town?

"Tell me once more where this money has come from?"

I sighed, but resupplied her with the information that her notebook needed. I told her of the miracle of awareness that had come to me on that Harlem street, how ever since I had been fighting for what was rightfully mine, my feet fully planted in the soil of freedom and release from the ongoing hegemony of women on the one hand—my mother, my aunt, my sisters—and, on the other, the appropriating power of fine-mind Simon Weill, how between the two (and with the zeitgeist provided by RMN, back from the dead) the time had arrived to seize the moment for replacing oppression with empowerment. Where was it written that Simon Weill should forever apply a powerful suctioning hose to the building's money trough just because he had the gall to grow a patch of mustache and the gift of projecting his soft voice around the world? Such a man as this should compel us to use the word *forevermore* and concede legitimacy to his regime of material ruthlessness? Who would dare to say I shouldn't be on the ground in full battle regalia, riding my horse on the perpendicular with honor as the theme of my active tongue, if not my actions?

Oh, she wrote and wrote, the way that Germans do, with sauerkraut and bratwurst on her breath, saying I was but a thief of my own youth in the launching of such a twisted enterprise, prompting my retort that I had plans that surpassed my own capacity, that to be born American was to be born free with a metaphysical dictate to soar into a space beyond form or time and that I must lie and die in my quest for such an exalted space.

"I think you are just afraid to get a job," she scoffed.

"A man must surface through his own history," I replied.

"You will wind up like those other long-haired people selling shoelaces in front of Bloomingdale's Department Store." Once again she showed her laughing ways about America and what she saw as its self-indulgence while holding onto her notion of German steel, saying in effect that the American soul was no bigger than the dinky dimensions that she allotted to it.

So we had a fire fight. She burned me and I burned her right back, for something had to be done about her mocking ways. The stink of burnt flesh was everywhere in the scorched room. Even the normally uncaring commuters below began to cry for us.

Despite the state of physical eradication and sudden blindness, however, we kept up a dialogue, so healing could take place. Whimpering because of the searing pain, I cried out my suddenly realized fear that I could go to jail for my activities. Oh did Frau Zimmer get rank on me with the full measure of her German-ness, standing up from her chair to shout out with her German mouth at full volume, "Jail? What is so bad about jail?" Oh, she was beside herself with her own excess, and yet a measure of progress was being made in discerning her true nature by exposing her repressive cast of mind, as when she said, "Many people have found their higher selves in jail. Look at Malcolm X."

"What do you know about jail?" I screamed, applying another level of fire to her face so even her essence would not remain.

"I go to jails all the time. I even have the keys," she replied with practiced calm, affirming her full alignment with patriarchal rule. In that revealing moment did I see her sucking up to black-robed judges and all those bent on imposing their authority. She had aligned herself with power in contrast with Mona of the paint brush supreme, who had taken a warrior stance against it. Yes, very much had she blown her cover.

A silence of many centuries fell, in which the air had its way as an observer of unending constancy. It showed us its molecules and myriad formations and the pleasure it took in its own unencumbered mobility. With not a word spoken we came to understand it had heard all the arguments and seen all the senses on display but still had no desire to add color to its life-giving essence; rather, it would continue to tend with an invisible hand to the rustling of leaves and the shaping of the earth itself. And it was hard to take issue with this air, which had emptied itself of so much to be in the place that it now could have, free of rock and roll music and the abundance of drugs and the gashes through which the life of the physical continued to emerge with the urgency of its willful need. How nonreactive the air remained as words on fire made claiming sounds on its elusive structure. But really, it was the clearness of the air that struck you, that it could always be there without your attention upon it, and the nonjudgmental quality that was a factor in its rise, its ongoing aplomb unshaken whether you were blowing kisses or breaking wind.

So yes, there was this respite, and while I had no reservations whatsoever about applying the heat that had been required in the course of battle, there was now the chance for contemplative silence to reign amid our fully charred ruins.

And yet a nation can never learn enough caution, for what can Germany by definition be but the implacable will of the strong to impose its thing on those perceived to be weaker, as here she was resurrecting herself with tanks at blitzkrieg speed and legions of helmet heads marching in their heavy boots.

"Join us. Join us," she hissed, her final assault provoking a fire storm unending and the tying of her in unbreakable knots through the binding agency of my endlessly elongating I.

Chapter 68

That summer I flew to the moon, not because of the song, but because the time had come. The astronauts were along for the ride in their clunky space suits and we had much time for dialogue over the staticky directives of mission control back in Houston, whom I gave fits with my aerodynamic displays of maverick brilliance, but that was only in keeping with the spirit of the country that I was blessed to serve. More interesting was how my family's building continued to loom large as a melting pot for all nationalities. Through black holes were we sucked, holes stacked with the souls of the allegedly departed, my mind recalibrated for love, if only temporarily, as the result of for once in my life being on the winning side. Brightly lit cosmic messages abounded declaring the power of detachment and the word *laughingstock* was nowhere to be heard or seen. The world itself resounded with my name, and emissaries of beauty—Brigitte Bardot from France, Gina Lollobrigida from Italia, and the lovely if sometimes severe Faye Dunaway, our nation's own, to name a few—were dispatched to keep me company. A good time was had by all frolicking in the powdery dust of the lunar surface. RMN sent me the nation's highest praise and it was understood that I was to henceforth walk the earth as a man above all men.

Well you might ask what I communicated about with my three able assistants from the space agency. Their names—Aldrin and

Armstrong and Collins—were my focus of attention. I expressed nothing but admiration for their melting pot mentality in bending to the American dictate to streamline their surnames, unless, as I suspected, they derived from cultures that foreswore the burdensome train of consecutive consonants such as I had been born into. At first they tried the cowardly and familiar strategy of ostracism, but I was able to destroy that mission of separation with the agenda I set forth. Thereafter, they shared very candidly, from their point of view, the essential requirements of true manhood: a use for but not a reliance on women, high intelligence, the ability to endure a cold shower, military service, terseness over loquacity, and science and more science applied with force and vigor so that the bacon could continue to be brought home.

Having come to understand and accept the merit of submission to the will of the people that I was now number one in all the universe, we could go on to the more serious matter of the difficulties I had been experiencing—the fire fight with Dr. Zimmer ("Do any of you dare to be German?" I gently asked) and the consequences for my regime for the departure from civility that had occurred. I told them that women continued to arrive in my face as the solution I required, and that the count needed to rise to assure the continuance not of my manhood (a word designed to set off *shudders* in one's very system) but my existence, such was the power of Mona to extinguish me.

The space-helmeted men of American value nodded their heads as a sign that they had been successfully diverted from their mechanical pursuits. Now that I had their full attention, I made it perfectly clear that German-ness in all its manifestations was something that had to be vanquished, lest (*lest!*) we worship it too deeply and all wear Lugers where our penises once had hung. Further, my excavations with Dr. Zimmer would set me free and could lead to an alternative reality with its own constructions. The dialogue, dare I say it, was outstanding.

The return to earth was eventful. The lunar equipped trio chose to reenter the atmosphere in their spacecraft while I showed my face solo and dealt with the terrible friction on my very skin. Once again I was temporarily burned beyond recognition, the elements conspiring to land me in the meadow above the main house back at Camp. Lenore's dead bones were there to greet me along with the ridiculous Fifth Dimension singing a completely disappointing rendition of "Age of Aquarius."

The Van Dines soon arrived to give me the hero's welcome so deserved. Peter, although he had partaken of the higher air as a bombardier, had to concede the excellence of my vision and the superiority of my achievement, and though his admiration was grudging, still could I say that he offered worship in the way that he could. As a final gesture to my newfound worth, Claire stayed on to disrobe so I could enter into her circle of love and ride her home, the space odyssey having made a new man of me in the judgment chambers of her mind, eliminating from the synapses where it hung the association of me with their immigrant maid. She also chose to see my penis in a new light, giving me the status of a stud with whispered words as her nostrils flared—Big Boy and Battering Ram and the like. Her breasts offering a valley so deep and mountains so high and what a world we live in that flesh can come to us on the fly in such proportioned abundance. Deliverer, Plumber of My Deepest Depth, Architect of Joy and countless other sobriquets she moaned from her pleasured space.

I took to the airwaves to address the nation, confessing that it had been my intention to overshadow the boys of America with their shaved names and heads and that the time had arrived for new features to be accepted into the adoration circle wherein they sought and thought to live on the basis of unchallenged assumptions of what an appearance can mean. Oh, the nation, the nation—one can get so tired of its claim to a monolithic nature.

Broken glass now littered the lawn and all pathways at Camp. Agility and vigilance were essential. No one wanted to believe it was

Lenore's legacy, but the unspoken thought was there. The family was Mona's in this time. She had made a window of stained glass, with the image of Lenore upon it for the sun to worship and shine through in its place of installation in the upstairs bedroom. To have such a cozy shrine with the Catskill Mountains looking on was no small feat, with the window there to keep the memory alive that someone beloved had been present for the time that she could be.

Lewdness had its way, and perhaps that could be expected after a lunar landing. Mona opened her work shirt and bared her breasts and positioned a hammer hanging by its claw from the open zipper of her jeans for my Nikon F camera. Away from my lens, she would meet with her brother Jeffrey for love that truly did not speak its name, she saying, "It is all grist for my artistic mill, allowing me to see into the bonds of the familial that would confine me."

Everywhere I went the Nikon F (not Nikkormat) went with me, hanging from my shoulder as the vanquisher of time it was—here a shot, there a shot, everywhere a shot shot in the shooting down of time itself so it could lie there on the print for another time to see, which in itself could be shot to keep the whole thing of it in captivity.

All that summer we received detailed briefings from the world at large concerning the things that were ongoing and the things that were about to happen, some of it signaled by the dancing of the trees, flapping their branches and undulating their trunks in a funked-up rhythm to the beat so loud of Big Janis Joplin, Big Jimi Hendrix, Big Grace Slick and the Jefferson Airplane, Big Crosby Stills Nash and Young, whole villages dancing, all the roadways dancing, all the shops and all the money in them dancing, the beards on woodsmen's faces dancing, the delirium tremens of the drunks dancing, the cancers of the afflicted dancing, the sewers and the cesspools of the counties dancing, the dreams of America and clerical postures dancing, the graves themselves and the dead within them dancing, to the groove to the beat to the made-up thing of what America was, the young of America armed only with face paint for peace, the trees themselves shouting peace now peace now above the whap whap of the helicopter gunships.

So that while the grass and dirt and maneuvering worms that fed within it were dancing to big Carlos Santana, Mona and I set out for Bethel, New York, and Max Yasgur's farm, tearing along on the BMW toward the source of the unhinged sound. We saw the bad acid trips, the full frontal nudity, the bodies coated in mud from the drenched and slippery slopes. We heard the magic of the music go thin upon the open air and sensed the failure of the Benzedrine promise of foreverness. We saw farm boys with cow-shit-covered boots and Texas cowboys with their horse dung boots but mostly we saw America with its asshole and cunt and cock on fire even as the more conservative sought to nail their feet to the floor against the wind that had been blowing.

From music and gaiety and laughter the entire Catskill Mountains went on fire with spontaneous lust, the men with the big guitars strapping their instruments tight for the pelvic action of doing it to the women who wanted it done to them in scenes of grotesque pain and torture. Women posted wanted posters for their own lost innocence on trampled fence posts and nailed them to their own foreheads, while spent men poured bottles of gin into the opening where their heads had been.

The rains came again to lash the guitars from the hands of those musicians who had not tied them to their once private parts, and now they were playing with their fingers only, no one caring to understand how they could continue to make their own sound. The rains remained persistent, dousing the flames and washing us off the slopes and the performers off the stage and sliding us into a pool of mud, the singers trying to sing with slime-clogged mouths and their instruments fled. Blood and broken teeth joined the mix, floating on the phrase "much pain and suffering," while a willful insistence on the freedom of the now continued to win in a landslide over previously existing philosophies.

As the gloop we were immersed in now began to firm up, and rock star feces made their bacterial presence and the lightning took dead aim at what souls remained, we made the decision to evacuate. The BMW, being German, showed its fortitude in dealing with the mud that caked its parts. What a sound is gasoline sloshing about in a half-full tank, and what a smell is gas that has been cooked through the mighty machine's entrails, and what a noise is a machine sputtering and then firing on all cylinders as wetness evaporates off its heating parts. Do not inquire about the mounting discomfort of wet clothes and a cold wind that reduced us to a state of shivering in bed under electric blankets when finally the trip was done. Only know that we were witnesses to what was now no more, with dead men's fingers playing strings upon a turbulent wind.

Now the thing was that after the rock and roll music came and went from the farm where it had tried to grow, the defining essence of the knife appeared, with a select few chosen to affirm its cutting edge authority. He said his name was God, and while this I did not believe, he called me deep into the woodland and I went to him as a child with a flickering candle in the night. Nowhere in the darkness was civilization to be found. Everything was underbrush and thickets and the furtive movements of preying animals. And then his back-lit face made candlelight and moonlight and all the rays that gave one sight superfluous, for there beyond a line of trees that tried to punish with their obstinacy he sat before a fire in a circle clearing on a bed of coniferous duff. His hair was long and Jesus-like and a smile stayed faithful to his face and did not buckle under to the passions behind the mask of beatific calm. He said his pleasure was the pain he could inflict on others but that the karmic thrust of his mission was nothing so shallow, that his purpose was to cause oceans of fear in the heart of America so that the black men of the land, who had fucked him up so very hard in his prison time, would not now be fucking all the white women of America so none were left for him. He said I had been drafted as an agent for fomenting trouble so cataclysm could run its bloody course for the purification of the nation. He noted that we were a country blessed with lakes and streams and rivers and ocean vistas for cleansing action to take effect. He said that to be white was an affirmation of everything, while to be black was pure negation, and that a complex system had been devised by a computer that gave my name a high-ranking number.

"Are you up for it?" His smile grew more intense. His teeth became stabbing implements of the sharpest metal, and all the while his forehead bulged with premonitions of his own American fate.

The details that he offered did not lead me to fall in love. He said that I was to deliver to him all the Van Dine heads, sparing no one, and that my reward would be great in Heaven. He said that in this endeavor I would be ably assisted by his top aides. By this time rivers of numbers had made themselves visible, flowing into the maw of a mammoth computer that munched them good, numbers with fractions and with decimal points and with slashes and the gristle of logarithmic apparel, numbers that flowed and flowed in endless variations without pulling in my own.

When he saw where I stood, he cut me loose with a frown and went elsewhere, to California, for his devil work, slaughtering little piggy rich ones with the mind to unleash more such forces on the world before the year was out.

Senator Edward Kennedy (Democrat of Massachusetts) came calling on me in this time. Yes, he wanted to consult with me about his distress, that a woman so young should be found so drowned in such incriminating proximity to his life. But he also wanted to talk about the sea and aspersions I had made about the Irish in comments I had addressed to the nation regarding little Bobby Kennedy and big Gene McCarthy. He said it was not an easy thing to have been born, ancestrally speaking, on an emerald isle surrounded by a vast body of cold water, that such coldness had a radiating effect into the bones of the country's citizenry, that while it allowed for laughter and gaiety and tears and the eating of fish, it did not necessarily allow for or even countenance warmth. He said Irish words were words of ice and had to suffice. This he said with great conviction. As for the deceased young one, he said I was to concentrate on the name. Certainly Mary Jo passed muster, in its tried and true American cuteness. But Kopechne? Kopechne? Was it a far cry from Officer Krupke? And beyond that, the syllables, once started, rushed you to the last, and wasn't that the point, that a woman born with such a name that rushed you to its very end was herself predestined to rush to her very end? He sighed in wonder at the things he needed to do to shoulder the burdens of his life and his father's wealth, saying of the old man that he had the irresistible urge to sink his big teeth into flesh. He said he was not a patricide or a fratricide, that there was no rejoicing in him that his father was gone and his brothers were gone, only the deep sadness of the bereft. I looked at him in wonder that he could share this way from his position of eminence, and felt his face to verify that flesh was what I was truly seeing, but he pushed my hand away. Then he started to cry. He said fornication and drinking were the only answers he could find to his life, besides legislating for the poor and the needy. He said too that he had called on Plato and Aquinas and all the forces that could be brought to bear to confer legitimacy on the silence he was holding. "The truth is a complex matter," he said. "Sometimes, despicable as it may sound, we must learn to laugh like hyenas outside the cathedral doors if it means the continuance of our pleasure cruise and the forestalling of the obloquy of the nation." He was very honest with me, and I with him, in the mutual sharing that we had established as a model for the nation.

Chapter 69

That summer, having committed myself to gaining admission to law school, I sought to compensate for the dullness of my mind by taking the practice tests in prep books for the LSAT. I didn't wish to repeat the relative debacle of the SAT. The PSAT I had gotten drunk the night before and failed to show up for, having taken to heart the assertion of my ninth grade algebra teacher that one had the capacity to do well on these standardized tests or not, and no amount of preparation would improve one's performance. My arrest was no barrier to admission. The case had been dropped on the grounds of an illegal search and seizure and the arrest itself expunged from the record.

I also purchased cram books that offered pertinent facts about science, history, art, music, and philosophy hoping for an equally decent score on the achievement part of the law school exam. So what if I had dropped high school and college biology courses? A few pages of the synopsizing book would remedy that, telling me all I needed to know about chromosomes and mitosis and meiosis. Did I need my memory refreshed about the War of the Roses or the Bourbon Succession or the paintings of Jan Van Eyck? The books would supply the needed facts. I understood that I knew precious little.

The renting office continued as a theater of operation. Having accumulated funds I could visit the building and my family with relative peace of mind that my fate would not be that of my older siblings. Let me be very plain in saying that persistence had wrought a sense of specialness and being loved and blessed; now, by virtue of my assets, I too could be a Van Dine.

Almost a year had now passed since I came to the office, virtually coincident with the reemergence of RMN. With the keenness of his Republican mind he told me what needed to be done and where my responsibilities lay. And if my presence was required at least three times a week to satisfy the hunger for further accumulation of funds, then so be it.

At the same time, if I had to be there at the building, I could not be on a plane with Mona bound for Europe, as we had planned, given the advent of Harvard Man and the dawning realization that I could not let go of my renting office routine. Do not tell me what I already know, that the acquisition of more money to boost my total savings was becoming an end in itself. And do not ask what is a man who cannot leave home and step out into the world.

My mother had never been young in my eyes, but now she looked old, and my aunt, once such a prime mover, lay bed-bound by weakness and mentally disoriented behind the mirrored door of her lobby apartment. She had been the bright light in the family—leaving the farm in Sweden for America to become a head nurse and then the owner of a tea shop before entering the world of real estate with the purchase of the building. Somehow it did not matter that her vision for the building had not been realized, that instead of a way station for roving evangelical missionaries, the rooms were filled with Hindus and Sikhs and Buddhists and pagans, or that we were now managers of a property she had once owned. It did not matter that a property she had purchased for the glory of God Simon Weill now sucked the proceeds from, as if through a a giant straw.

I sought to behave myself. I did not bark at the tenants or berate prayer master Fenton or ask to view the undergarments of the finer-looking female tenants. Nor did I seek to antagonize my sisters or my brother. I was just there, surrendering to the dollar and my own dream of glory.

Some things didn't change. The family had the momentum of its own failure, Hannah dressing Moses up in the trousers and blazers of the English schoolboy and sending him off to the Episcopalian nuns down the street and startling everyone with sudden eruptions of her anger. Already the boy was showing signs of disturbance, bopping little Billy Baxter with a child's shovel and pail and sending Lousia Hicks down the stairs with a shove and sleeping when he needed to be awake, but Hannah found a way to tend to him in the room they now shared down the hall from the apartment. A part-time legal secretary for a law firm, she continued to man her position in the renting office come Saturday morning just to show everyone who was really boss.

I wouldn't have said in those years that Hannah had married my father and kept my mother hostage with her rage. I wouldn't have had the information. I only had a sense of her darkness and the memory of her hand and the titanic firefights between her and my father as she tried and failed to break free. She declared that she would die with what she knew, omertà being omertà where fathers and their daughters were concerned.

As for Naomi and Rachel, they remained elusive. There was no allure to their downward spiral, only pain. They wandered here and there, seeking out the confines of lonely spaces only to fly against walls with no yield.

Luke had the multiplicity of his short-lived endeavors and he had a woman named Brenda, and he had her son Benjy. Brenda was a match for Luke with the fervor she brought to the sex arena; she did not hold to the exclusivity of him and her alone when she could get undressed for the many and make them sizzle.

Vera was not a nation but she was a power growing more visible in my mind. She had been overlooked by my mother, so she felt; that was the wound she could not easily heal from.

Chapter 70

After my moon odyssey, it was imperative to have my feet on the ground, and with this as my purpose, an orderly succession of days eventually followed with productivity the goal. Armed with such a consciousness, I boarded a Pine Hill Trailways bus and headed for the country, my bag including my Nikon F camera and my newest purchase, a Nikon 8 mm camera, serving as an aid to relieve the pressure I was feeling to get a handle on the things of time.

Mona stood at her easel while Lydia dug with her trowel in fertile flower beds and Peter organized his workday around the wheelbarrow. After working up a sweat, he had clean clothes to wear for dinner, with drinks served beforehand.

Only Claire had it right from her angle of vision to speak the truth. "Bastard," she said, not letting go of the night together when she had shared herself. I activated the movie camera to capture her from top to bottom, but she was not in the displaying mood.

"You're seeing a difference in me. I'm gaining weight in my mind. The bulk of my substance is accumulating."

"The only difference I'll ever notice in you is when you're dead," she said, the camera having no choice but to pay attention to the breasts that demanded it.

"I need you to turn profile now," I said.

'Fuck you," she said, but acquiesced. And when I asked her for posterior perspective, her compliance only soared.

From that point on she took the initiative. She moved us indoors to a secret chamber where only she could live, a room off the attic with a hidden door and a hard-bound copy of *Hudson River Bracketed* heartbreakingly displayed. With the door closed and wantonness as her guide, she tore open her blouse to proudly display the firmness of her breasts, ran her tongue around her lips, and struck a pose with her raised derriere. In a tightly worded statement afterward, she laid bare the truth of who she was, saying a thin permafrost of intellectualism had been melted by the fire of her sexuality. She invited me to revisit the room again, should I be able to find it, and when I did to call her names anathema to feminism.

And yet, the next day, called forward once again by my priapic lens, I coaxed Mona from her easel but hid the movie camera in my knapsack in order to ward off questions about the technology that I was harboring and that enterprise had afforded me, sensing in that moment the investigative power of the Van Dines should they choose, in collective fashion, to see me in an even darker light. So yes, covert action was in order if I was not to be cast once more into the ever-waiting lake of shame should the hard question be asked where the resources for the purchase of such expensive equipment was coming from, given my financial status, and did I, beyond the mystery of procurement, have the tools—*the intelligence*—to master this Nikon technology. A heroic battle was required not to take that shame bath for what was essentially a private affair even with the public element that was attached to it.

And so I led Mona up to the meadow, just a stone's throw from the witnessing shale pile and the Van Dine vegetable garden, the miracle offspring of the fecund earth summoning in Peter pride and joy he was driven to share. And new fertility was showing in his mind as well. Not that he wanted to grow radishes in his head, but he was now at work on a play and earnest in his intention that man communicate with God while reserving the right to punch the deity full in the face or to love him with the conviction that his life depended on it.

Under the gnarled beauty of an old apple tree Mona and I sat. No snakes came to bite us. None even slithered in our direction. Mona undressed and a gentle breeze tightened her nipples. When she took me in her mouth, I began filming. Only afterward did she break the sex silence to say, "Please don't do that again. I'm uncomfortable with that." The "that" needed no elaboration. Pronouns resound where specifics pull back in shyness, having a strategic goal with such a tack, to drive the point deeper still. I did not fly up to the sky, nor did I fall down dead. I lingered somewhere in between.

That night I worked until daylight on a declaration of my intent and a vague acknowledgment of where I had been:

> You have let a stranger into your midst and what must come of that cannot be foretold. This much is certain. Before I die I must walk the earth with a larger penis. Genital enlargement must be on the agenda of every scientist in this land and beyond. Until that day, please be sure that I will try to pretend that my own endowment is sufficient for ongoing interaction in the torture chamber called relationship. I am also working hard to retool my mind so I can come up to the standard set by all of you. Sometime in the New Year I shall venture forth on the LSAT and conquer the demons of my past with a Number 2 pencil. Because the truth is that a low number carries a heavier weight than a high number, and if I am ever to truly soar, my moon odyssey not for discussion here, then the weight of failure must be removed from my back. At the same time, this business of time must be addressed, how to vanquish it while showing up within its mocking tyranny.

In the morning Frank Dolan arrived, Mona having picked him up at the bottom of the road in the family jeep. Claire herself did not drive. She was content to rely on her muscular mind and intact beauty so where she was was where she needed to be and not in the next town beyond, and gas had never to be an issue.

I couldn't be sure if Frank had smooched Mona, or she had smooched him, but something was clearly broken down on this land where once the Indians had roamed.

Now Claire loved Frank Dolan and Frank Dolan loved Claire and they loved each other with a love that could only be called divine. A river of feeling flowed between them with all manner of unspoken correspondences. You could call it a means for ensuring insularity, but that would be to contaminate it with a judgment that did not apply.

All that morning Frank Dolan and I talked, supported by the prosperity and leisure that life had provided us. Yes, the helicopter gunships flew overhead, with the whap whap of their rotating blades and the heartbreak/excitement of uniformed men at war in killing fields that unleashed in them savagery as their primary purpose. And while I saw all the neighborhood boys illuminated under a napalm lit sky, there was no need to obey the dictates of a wild and beating heart and run to the embrace of something that was not there. As worms turn slowly in the earth, that much faster could my desire turn. And yet there was sorrow at having missed not the gore but the glory of war and so I turned for comfort to the instant coffee taken black in a metal cup that held the heat.

Sometimes the choppers flew low, as if to skim the very earth, when their true purpose was to harass us out of the leisure of our ways and plummet us into the gulch of self-reproach, but we had the Dixie cups of our childhood to fall back on, the sweet smell and taste of vanilla ice cream, and the timely sign that simply said no earthly sight that makes itself conspicuous has beauty as its sole intent.

Frank lulled me with his low-level smile designed to break my defensive shield, his Long Island Irish state of being and high intelligence idling in reserve. He had dropped out of an obscure college of questionable status in the state of New Hampshire that dropped grades and threw structure out the window so poetry and other forms of creativity could flourish.

I told him the truth, that Bob Dylan had taken to wearing a hat and a beard and smiling enigmatically while looking down, whether the album cover was above or below you. Whatever possessed him to give it the title *Nashville Skyline,* he was a survivor of all the changes that lay within him and would always capitalize on the momentum of surprise to stay out front, and yet life would never let him escape being from Minnesota and Hebrew to his roots leaving one to wonder if the man's mask revealed more than it hid.

Frank rose up on me with casual rebuttal and yet the cold wind of his ostracizing technique in place. He said the man just wanted to do his art, and that it shouldn't be held against him if he dropped one name for another. "Your problem is that you can't speak without judgment. You drop down into the filth of your own prejudice. That's where you call home."

Claire rewarded him with a strong cup of coffee and as big a smooch as her books and broad daylight would allow.

"All we're doing is growing old in direct sunlight," I said, but they weren't listening, at least for the moment.

Outside Mona's studio I saw Jeffrey looking shifty in the shade, with the tight, jerky movements of the guilt afflicted before entering. Yes, the sight and the implications gave me a hit, a sinkhole into which pain could disappear or masquerade as excitement.

Frank laid it on the line as to what he was doing. He showed the definite ability to come back from Claire's amour with another. He had obtained employment with a sporting goods store in downtown Manhattan that promoted the integrity of the land. He sold fishing rods and hunting knives and backpacks and hiking boots and was at peace, as he had nothing to prove in the world of academia. Beyond all that he had a beautiful bronzed body that made you weep for the perfection that you lacked. I saw in the moment that he stripped down to his black bikini swimsuit that physical attraction had inclined Claire to declare him her man and that it took an artist's eye to find some beauty in someone who dared to look like me. I thought of my mother's tired, sagging flesh, and my father's, too, and how it had collaborated in the making of mine, and what could I expect as the progeny of staggered, weary immigrants? I looked to where the moon had been on the night of my astonishing achievement and the law school effort underway to protect myself against the charge of mediocrity and saw that it was all for naught in the face of what he had to offer without even trying.

While I was praying for the sun to bake me to the point of perfection, Lydia stood up from the flowerbed, the activity of the morning soothing the deep wounds of the night, and brimming with the love that activity could unleash in her—the same joy available to all Americans, whether born to privilege or neglect, the Harvard School of Business or the supermarket checkout register, yes that same joy singing its morning song over the morning coffee and even after it had been drunk. Lydia had this to say, denying any context to its utterance: "Oh Frank, pookum wookums, you are Claire's treasure and our whole family's, if the truth is to be told. No one can light up her day the way that you do. You are a counterweight supreme to her brooding seriousness." This she did not assert to stake her claim to enduring hostility; this she only affirmed as the product of the effusiveness in which she was for now living. I did not batten down her hatches. I just let the matter sit in my mind, where it needed to be.

(Parenthetical observation had its ongoing place, Peter retaining his involved, complex relationship to the land but starting his morning by letting it rip about the American presidents and American history, with Lydia metamorphosing there in the living room into a giant ear. Because Lydia was the booster of all humankind, with the egos she could make to grow like the flowers in their fertile beds. Because you did not miss Peter if he was not in the room. If Peter was there in the room without Lydia, the room was exceeding *cold*, whereas Lydia brought *warmth*. Peter could live on the plane of high achievement, but it was mere compensation for his lack of native ability. Lydia had the native ability, and because she had it, there was no need for her to accomplish this and that. She had nothing to prove. She could just smoke cigarettes and drink coffee and putter about.)

When the sun was past the halfway point to calling it a day, Lydia snoozed on the swinging sofa under the rhododendron-covered trellis. I was by now seated on the lawn with an urgent need to know what I needed to know and so traversed the distance between us to the swish swish of the rotating sprinkler and its arcing emissions. Considerations of my own well-being and place upon the planet had assumed the ruling position within me.

I rattled her everything with my proximate presence, for I had pulled a chair up to her side.

"What?" Having sensed and been startled by my nearness, she reached for her glasses.

"I see only your beauty, if that is your concern," I said.

"That is not my concern. You are my concern. You grow more peculiar with each day."

"You mustn't say that. One of the great minds in psychoanalysis is working on me. And as I said in my note, I am preparing for the realization of my own unfocused dream. I am finding solutions through my own thinking."

She sat up and reached for her cigs and shook one free of the pack. After lighting it she blew a masterful smoke ring.

"What is it you want?" she said.

I heard coldness but pushed ahead. "I am needing to assemble a portfolio of people's intentions toward me so I can carry it about under my arm."

"I said what is it that you want?" Because while she was not shaking from the terrible blow of the year before, her hands and visage showed a slight tremor.

"I want to know if I am good for Mona. Please. I'm not expecting you to protect me."

Having heard my own lie, I went on, "I amend my statement in favor of truth. I *am* expecting you to protect me, but I will understand if you don't." The world fell away. I had closed myself off and was now alone with Lydia and my own deformity. She was, after all, the mother of my dream, and by this time had made her transition from the solace of sleep to me.

"Men are what women are built for. We are ports of storm for your battered ships."

I did a complex computation on the air, and when it didn't add up, there was unilateral understanding that the dialogue had to continue.

"Speak on, woman, speak on," I said.

Lydia sighed, a difficult exhalation on which to get an accurate reading of her intention. "There are some ports with specialized features that can accommodate only one kind of boat. But then there are other ports with add-on features, ports that grow to have multiple docking facilities, ports that grow to have world renown for their ability to accommodate vessels big and small. And because the profit—and shall we say, the thrill—is clearly delivered by the larger craft, they slowly and inevitably win out. Am I making myself clear?"

I adjusted my listening devices to accommodate her sound. Boats and ports. Vessels big and small. To cast my life in such a maritime image did not make it incomprehensible. I simply saw a tall ship and its name was the S.S. *Dread* upon the horizon.

Lydia lit another smoke from the one that was burnt down almost to its filter. "You must understand that bigger, better constructed vessels are on the way."

Many days and nights of pain were endured as the result of her metaphorical assault on my existence. She had confronted me with the mercilessness of time and how it breaks those who hold on to holding on. Expansion. Growth. I heard her articulation on the hideous theme of change and saw the enlargement of her mouth required for such pomposity laden words to emerge. I sank to the flagstone terrace floor and allowed her utterance to crush me, and lay there until a new day could arrive.

I had a mother of my own and was dutiful in reporting my love, spoken or not, to this one who had stood the test of time, and let it please suffice to say that I did what I could for her with my now and then presence (never enough, never ever enough, not with a mother making you a slave to perfection until you had no choice but to rebel and live in the fields of darkness apart from her earthly light of heaven. Oh, who wills himself to have a heart that stinks of its own excess?).

Wherever her mind was going, the building still held her. From one floor to the next she went with her laundry cart, supported by her faith and her rubber stockings, loading towels and linens into the laundry cart so they could be taken out of the laundry cart and placed in the rooms of the men who lived alone and the women who lived alone as well as those who lived together in great numbers so they could sleep and bathe and have the things of America in the new day that they had arrived at, the truth being that she had not seen enough to go just yet, the family unable to reach its final form without the intervention of death.

Because this was 1969, and Hannah had her son, and he had her; and Naomi had not her daughter, who had never had her; and Rachel had no one and nothing but her smirking complicity with apartness; and Luke had his wine and his girlfriend Brenda; and Vera had her dream of scholarship and commitment to excellence, as she defined it. Because we were all of my family's flesh and had to be suspect and yet eligible for memorialization if only for the hammer blows of shame shame double shame raining down upon us.

Still, we had our assigned ways of making our presence felt, and mine was to come to her while the laundry room machinery was running. Never once was there an explosion that caused her to run screaming in pain with her clothes and body afire. And as always the pattern persisted of being protective of her for what she didn't have by playing down my good fortune when standing before her.

"Are they so very wealthy?" she asked, of Mona's parents, as if she had not asked before. She stood amid the piles of dirty sheets and towels, slowly loading them into the cylindrical belly of the giant washing machine. My qualified but affirmative response battered the Jesus door she stood behind with the sharp object of material good fortune, and though she would later, sleepless, sit with her Bible through all the storms of doubt about the efficacy of a rugged cross while women with painted faces strode the streets, fear and doubt could visit, because not to be pulled down into pain and sorrow was to throw a wrench into her machinery of comprehension.

"They have some means, though it is balanced with trouble that binds people to their grief," I assured her, now that she had turned on her scanning meter. "Mona's mother has had nervous breakdowns a couple of times, bouts with postpartum psychosis that required massive and around the clock electric shock treatments. Everywhere you walk on their property there is broken glass underfoot. All the family members have hideous gashes on their feet. Some have severed tendons that have completely immobilized them. Ambulances make daily visits to deal with their afflictions, with the whole upstate medical community on standby alert."

"Mona's mother is so very fragile?"

"Oh, she is punished for the freedom that she claims for herself with blows to her head and to her bowels. Boils cover every conceivable part of her body, inside and out, and she writhes in pain on that broken glass morning to night. In the darkness a creature comes to douse her with gasoline and ignite her flesh, and yet it is her punishment to experience the outer limits of pain and still not die. No one has seen anything like it in all the annals of time, and still does she continue to smoke and drink and watch motion pictures and perform all the acts of the truly worldly. Meanwhile does Mona's father run through the woodland gnashing his teeth and adorned with the barest strip of loin cloth."

My mother began to cry. "What ails you, my son? What ails you?"

She held me in the vise of her tears. It was not long before I joined in with tears of my own. Together we went on for the longest time. Many buses and many, many rampaging trucks flew past on the street above and crimes of violence took their bloody toll. Many thousands of miles we plunged into the deepest hole of sorrow.

In desperation I called out, “Mona’s mother is still recovering from her youngest daughter’s death,” and our free fall was broken.

“Is that right? Her youngest daughter?”

Because if Lenore had emerged into the bright light of day with all her apparatus for living intact, and taken her place among the stars, could anything suchlike be expected from my mother, or would there only be tears of fear that Lenore had not been pulled down as we had, depriving the men and women who wore the hair shirts for the Christ Jesus of their needed validation?

So yes I served it up, how Lenore was distraught over the boy who had left her.

“I see. She was troubled. How sad? And what ailed the boy that he left her? Was she not well mentally?”

Troubled I would give her, but not mentally afflicted. She had to feed on what I had offered.

“And how is her mother now? Is she better?”

“She’s doing all right now,” I said.

“They must all be suffering a lot of pain over the poor girl.”

“Right.”

“Isn’t that sad?”

That evening, after my time in the renting office, I went to the apartment and gave over the bulging envelope to my mother, while hiding in my pocket what I had apportioned for myself.

I did not know then that Jeanne, Naomi’s daughter, was moving on toward her rendezvous with brutality after frolicking with the flower children of Haight-Ashbury. I did not know that she would meet Father Pimp, wholly committed to channeling the evil in the universe to maximize his hardness. I did not know that she would live in the hotels and motels of Seedy Town, that she would develop eyes that saw through you to sex, eyes you had to turn away from because of what they saw.

Nor did I know the ongoing extent of Operation Moses, that he was being prepped for a life of aggression, that his mother was doing all she could to build that career for him by the weight of her upon him in the privacy of the room she took him to with her smack hands hanging down and her grievance profound intact over all that had been done to her, so that in the space afforded by that room she could offer him the slap with her tongue between thick lips and other forms of physicality.

There was much that could not be foreseen with the monitoring devices available, that Naomi would be found drowned in the East River by a police harbor boat, near the Fifty-ninth Street Bridge, that homicidal patients would have access to her body during her mental hospital stay, that they would pound her and then toss her in the rough and feces-full water, and that she would float downriver until she could be found. Nor did I know that some day my sister Rachel would sit on a window ledge scanning the night sky for signs of Jesus or that she would leave faucets running or turn on my mother and try to strangle her, or that she would take an overdose of sleeping pills the day of my mother's burial and die of a heart attack some months later. I did not know any of these things, and yet I did know. I was there getting ready to leave before the ship sank, and so I smiled my smile of diffidence and gave them no words, no anything, to grab onto and keep me there.

Because if you are an investigative reporter, you have to be responsible for the people or things that you are reporting on so that you can care for them with words, seeing as how you have nothing else to give. Because if the meaningless actions you took did not keep them from the ongoing flow of perishing in New York City, then you must find a way to be responsible to their memory as the watchful eye of God, though hidden, is upon you.

Because first there were the words I spoke, that disappeared into the air without hope of retrieval, words spoken blindly, thoughtlessly, in the heat of passion or otherwise. Words spoken from fear without a gravity center to keep them tethered to reality. Words that had no rhyme or reason, as my mother would say, that lacked all sense of normality but only the exhalation of a sound meant to signify something. Words spoken as a weapon of aggression as well as a defense. Words that had their own features in terms of me getting somewhere with someone. Words that said I had the person's number or that she or he had mine. Words meant to structure a thought only to see it collapse. Words that made a claim on reality only to be shown that they had lied. Words that tortured themselves with their own aimlessness.

Because sooner or later you had to make the word behave, you had to capture the word in the time and the place that it had been spoken. Because words shouldn't fly around forever without finding a destination home.

Chapter 71

I bought the typewriter at an office equipment store on West Eleventh Street. The owner treated me with indifference, making a point of turning his back when I walked in. He wasn't just there for show. He had work to do ministering to the damaged goods the imploring brought to him, and wore a smudged apron and had ink-blackened fingers to show for his labor. The store smelled of three-in-one oil and ribbon ink needed to bring the words to life. On the shelves and everywhere were manual and electric typewriters, office models as well as portables; the names—Royal and L.C. Smith and Olympia and IBM and Underwood and Olivetti and the strange combo Smith-Corona—gave testimony to the industry of America and beyond. The keys and platens had been put to much use, but that didn't mean they were spent; it just meant they had character. Some had survived the freezing cold; others had been intimate with their naked masters. And now, for one reason or another, there had been a parting, but their words were not used up, not so long as Mr. Typewriter Man was there to tend to them.

Pencils were to be worn to the nub and scraps of paper covered with words from top to bottom. Otherwise scarcity would reign and punishment would come. An old typewriter meant an old life meant the past, which also could be used. So if you put the old—the past—through the old (the typewriter), then you were likely to get something. You were able to live in the forgotten places with a typewriter of the past, and to build on its very character while practicing your own form of conservation. At the very least, you weren't forsaking the little darlings.

The man would not identify himself beyond the name on his sign—Tango's Typewriters—and I could not seem to sell him on the need. He was simply too strong on the path that life had chosen for him and not inclined to degrade his workday with small talk. In making himself dirty, he was making himself clean. On the dharma path was he, and let it be said that someday America would be crying when his kind was as bygone as the products he was maintaining in too late recognition of what he and his industrious kind had meant in a country of layabouts.

Perhaps it was my insistence—I too was not going away—but finally he put down the rag and the oilcan and the tiny screwdriver and addressed the success I was intent on having in speaking to me from under a mass of gray hair.

"Many become addicted to these machines. Why? Because the machines make them feel good. Because they are broken with despair more than they realize and are turning to the typewriter for relief. And so they hit the keys and words are struck on paper and they get the idea that they are going somewhere with their literary endeavors. They grow excited by the day's output, but then a day later what they did the previous day doesn't seem so good, and they think that the current day will be a better day, and this delusion persists. Even a week of this solitary activity leaves their lives permanently altered. They can't go back to their old life but they can't succeed at the new one either. They buy additional typewriters and install filing cabinets and shelves for their manuscripts, and all they ever do is pile up and the bright light of day is left to others to explore while they continue to literally write for their lives because by now it has become their way of existing."

"I want the big one, so it can't go anywhere on me," I said, pointing to an office model. "And I want it especially if it has that small type that you can fit more of onto the page."

Mr. Tango took me in with a level gaze and with it an assessment of my mentality.

"I don't like you. I truly don't. I don't believe anybody could. For that reason, I respect your need for a typewriter. Maybe it will keep you from killing yourself. We'll see."

"You may not like me, but I like you and your enterprise," I replied. "Now pack her up so the real business of my life can begin and the earth upon which I walk can be but a hallucination of my tilted mind."

I gave him the thumb's up, paid with cash on the barrelhead, and jumped in a cab with my load. Soon thereafter, the typewriter was on the dining table. So happy was I with my love that I kissed its metal strength. It gave me what the birds never could, a clack clack here and a clack clack there, everywhere a clack clack as I sped the words toward their destination on the page, and when my brief workday was done, I had the words I needed—"M. liked to pee in an open field" and "white line continue/white line."

That afternoon I drafted a letter:

Dear Professor Kohl:

You thought you had me with Cervantes. You thought I would have to ride that horse all day, and toil under the hot Spanish sun placing footnotes on the page. But you were wrong, for I have found the peace that passes all understanding, and it requires me only to show my face on the paper that I have amassed to be at the disposal of my purpose. Right this very second I am showering the pages with baby love words that are the essence of my being. And from here it is a journey outward into the stars where you cannot touch me unless I ask you to, and where pain can be testified to and

> recorded for all the days to see and hear. It may be that I have reached my quantum of words for this particular workday. If that is the case, I may soon be stepping out to get me (yes, one should allow oneself to be repulsive in one's syntax) a ham sandwich on hero soaked with slaw, and to wander in the pages of the *New York Post* and to wonder how such a thin lineup can ride such strong arms to a pennant for the New York Mets. Because now I am coming home to myself, Mr. Footnote King, and the century is roaring exhortation for the journey that is now to begin and I am already floating against the pressed tin ceiling thanks to the ecstasy currents that I have been seeking and now have found.

I stopped, hunger having seized me, and put on the garments of fall. I said hello to Mrs. Muldooney on her garbage can and hurried up Tenth Avenue to the deli of Mr. Mancuso, whose name by this time I had learned, and while I felt weak and ineffectual amid the displays of strength, nothing stopped me from contemplating the day when I would not to be controlled by his and his crew's violence. However, Mr. Mancuso seemed not at all attuned to my thought processes in the activity of his day and made the sandwich as I stood in a posture of innocence.

"Don't let me see you in here until tomorrow," he said, giving me a wink as his highest compliment, and yet the elements in place for his violence to show forth.

I ate the sandwich in the privacy of my apartment, and apart from the table where the typewriter sat. I used a big plate, as the sandwich was leaking because of its coleslaw content. I had taken the change out of my pocket so I could eat. I had washed my hands so I could eat. I had even hung up my jacket and taken off my shoes. I was ready to eat and able to do it.

Afterward I sat under the table knowing the typewriter was still there even if unseen, and before drowsiness overtook me attached one end of a long string to the handle of the carriage return and lay down with the other end so I could maintain my connection with the machine even in slumber.

Then I did the things any normal man would do. I reached out for the allies I would need should I be called upon to travel. And it did not concern me that the point size on the portable I purchased was pica while the office machine was elite. Everything could be switched onto the main track once the plan was in place for securing the word blocks in their proper order so the psychologist dare not laugh.

Soon I saw that more would be needed and employed my robust purchasing power to secure for the team a second portable, which featured the elite type of my sturdy office machine. Then I photographed the three typewriters and made every effort to type on all three to keep them happy and faithful to the purpose for which they had been purchased. Only later, in the permanence that I was seeking, did I realize that the portable pica deserved a companion office machine to come home to after a long journey, and so I had to arrange for that as well.

Because there was a need for things to be in alignment. Tracks had to be laid for the smooth run to success and cooperation was also required between the models so oneness and permanence could truly mean forever. Seeing a further lack, I had to call on sources throughout New York City and put them on notice that a crisis was at hand, that I couldn't sleep thinking about the things out of kilter. Mr. Tango offered me what he could, while shaking his head in the sorrow pose of one witnessing what he could only perceive as hopelessness.

Having visited the world of relative antiquity without solving the problem, I thought to turn to the world of newness by arriving at an IBM showroom for the purchase of two new—spanking new—Selectrics. "I need the one for backup, should anything go wrong. And I have come with cash, just so you know I am in honest and serious pursuit of my own peace."

I pressed the salesperson for every golf ball element available. Then I told him the truth, that I had defecated in the holiest of places by placing the hardware ahead of the art and spending colossal sums of money that I would now have to earn, and what could I do to make things right? He told me in a moment of candor to step onto Tenth Avenue and get hit by a truck; in that way would I have the opportunity to start over if I was willing to gamble on reincarnation.

"I came here today with a mighty purpose," I said. "I have stepped out of the past and the ways that have been assigned to me. I have executed the old order of things for newness and boldness. I have plunged into waters that dispose of ancient ties and all that does not align with the present. A bold foray, but do not think it is here that I will stay. Already I am sick with exhaustion at the effort this journey has taken. Have these things shipped to me immediately. Do you understand? Something is rushing me out of here."

The salesman showed tremendous understanding in receiving my money and facilitating my order, this so I could be hurt by the trucks of New York City. They crushed my face. They broke my chest. They put my blood on public display. Through all of this I lived to witness the complications I had wrought, typewriters now arrayed throughout my apartment for the writing strength I would need to maintain the center where I sought to be found. And of course there were further alignments of the objects one with another needed even as the futility of the endeavor I was seeking to perform remained less than apparent.

Chapter 72

In this time I also called upon resources for the mind. I called upon *National Geographic* (so consciousness of flora and fauna could abound in me and my eye could be kept on Borneo). I called upon the *Atlantic Monthly (*for the perseverance of its Boston Brahmin mindset). I called upon the *New Yorker (*to determine for me who the select few were), I called upon the *New York Review of Books* (so I could shower with Heidegger and bathe with the pulse of contemporary America and nothing could be lost that needed to be gained, given the workings of a mind intent on its own tricks).

Also in this time my mother came to me in the renting office with her being on fire. The smoke and stench were unbelievable, but we both held our ground. She said Simon Weill was complaining about a falloff in the building's income. She looked at me but without quite the penetrating stare to which I had become so accustomed, as if she were loitering in a middle ground between complete knowingness and blindness. I told her to have no fear, that she was with me now, that I was now the man of the house—a house where no true man had ever been—and that, in wearing the pants of that house, it would be for me to determine when and where the execution of Simon Weill should take place, and that in the meantime I was in touch with powerful forces in the land and they were on standby alert should it be necessary for their armed might to swing into action against the rat with only seemingly permanent lodging within our walls.

A strategy for progressing with my own life led me to stay on for an extra semester in the hope of raising my cumulative grade point average and improving my chances of going on to law school. A Physics for Poets professor cried over my mind, and another read to us from Chaucer in Japanese, while smoking many cigarettes.

The night before the LSAT, I sought out a hypnotist, who put me in the power of her stare, this in a West End Avenue apartment filled only with quiet. She had me follow her index finger as it moved from my left eye to my right. Instantly I received a real if tentative freedom from the workings of my mind. I was able to walk successfully in my new state, and did not fall down on the subway tracks that called to me.

The year 1969 had come and gone, and now 1970 had showed its face and dirty snow was on the ground. And Joe Namath, from a coal-grit town in Pennsylvania, was drinking scotch with milk and waking up in East Side apartments with the stinky breath that the newspapers never wrote about.

With the prospect of the LSAT looming as a means of attaining respectability and overcoming the devaluation that came with being part of an institution like CCNY, I saw that my life was counting on me. Then too, Dr. Zimmer was telling me constantly to behave and show manly vigor, and any German influence on my being was bound to have an effect, even if we had beaten them.

The downtown law school where I took the test was respectable. I made certain to avoid Columbia University, so I could be free from the inhibiting factor of icy khaki intelligence and the derisive laughter it was prone to. I approached the matter with some simplicity. I wore my own clothes and added no adornments. All I truly needed was February attire and a number 2 pencil.

What happened thereafter was a marvel of relative progress. I tried to stay within the space of my post-hypnotic state so the texts and the charts could appear to me in the strict terms of what they were expressing as their own reality. All the while, wouldn't you just know it, I could hear the waning winter sun singing that it was a new day, for how many times can a man settle for the past when he has a new life ahead of him?

The men and women with whom I shared the space were not noticeable to me except as agents of a collective happiness I could be on the same page with. I was full of sweet surrender to the joy of finally redeeming myself and losing the outcast status of those terminally ill with numerical insufficiency, and that I could do this in an environment of anonymity without the laughing eyes upon me.

The law might have bowels, but bowels are not conspicuous. The law took you into its quiet spaces and allowed you to do research before presenting yourself to the public. It abided with you through your interpretation of its clarifying statutes, and offered a place to come home to apart from the world and yet partake of a goodly portion of that same world. And in the law you did not have to do meiosis or mitosis, or have the rigor of algebra tax your brain. You could simply be yourself, the only requirement being that you imbue your language with a structural sense. Beyond that, you got to appeal to a judge in the courtroom, not the sky, and in these solemn surroundings you could hide your true intent.

My pencil stayed busy filling in the choices with graphite more often than not in the way that they needed to be. The panic that I would not finish in time did not find me. No roar of anxiety propelled me blindly forward. Nor did I ignite in anger against all those who had no more of a primary purpose than to act as the thwarting creatures they were. I was able to section off one element from another, to proceed methodically in the way of one learning patience as a virtue.

Following the aptitude session came a lunch break. The restaurants and the diners were waiting for us. I did not get randy.

I did not get lewd. I simply regarded all those around me with an overflow of enthusiasm for our common purpose, suspending all awareness that we were competing for a place of excellence in the eyes of the world. I gave imaginary kisses to everyone who was part of the scene over their soups and grilled cheese sandwiches and the quantities of cowering egg salad trying to hide out between slices of thin white bread. Don't imagine that they responded in kind, as they were likely mired in calculating strategies for their own forward marches to success (oh you not seeking unity, oh you not aspiring to joy eternal, oh you who have barred the word *abandon* from your personal lexicons, surrender before it is too late and enter the realm of those blessed to sense where we are headed). Acts of kindness were not theirs to make with their cherished belongings clutched so tightly to their chests and fully geared for the more exacting work of performing as only they could with their noses to the grindstone, and so I was isolated by my own foolishness though restraint had been the watchword for the day.

We returned to our desks with the chance to prove in the achievement section that we knew a thing or two about the Albigensian Crusade and Jason and the Argonauts.

Calls came in from foreign capitals wishing me only the very best: Leonid Brezhnev and Ho Chi Minh; Charles de Gaulle, who acted very French; Willy Brandt, who got very German on me in saying that someday I would have to be a man. I handled them all with diplomatic ease and graciousness.

"When will you be getting a job?" Dr. Zimmer asked, pronouncing the word "chob" in her German way.

"You know I am not fit."

"You are just afraid."

"I have a job."

"Stealing money is a job?"

"I am writing. I am reading so I can learn how to do it."

"I think you are hiding."

"How you talk."

"I think it is how you talk."

"I can kill you quickly or slowly. Either way, your life is in my hands," I said.

"Why don't you lie down and tell me what you mean when you say such a thing?"

"I am not your horn of plenty for you to mount me at your leisure. I live outside the brackets of your age range. I am youngness in pursuit of youngness, with a wall of indifference to all those dwelling within my older sisters' realm."

"Tell me about your sisters."

"Only that when you speak, they fly out of your mouth. That they are you and not you at the same time, and that initiatives driven by tenderness can only invite the smack."

We sat in silence for some time, so that the rapport could build. It went on for many centuries, and when the time was up I left.

The hexagonal tiles that paved the sidewalk on the Central Park side of Fifth Avenue sought to hold my attention, and it did not go without notice what the fresh spring air was doing for the vitality of the doormen across the street. And yet my Hell's Kitchen apartment and the force that wished to suction me back to it was an even greater power. A song came to my rescue, "It's a Big Wide Wonderful World," as sung in *Sweet Bird of Youth.* I had seen that movie. I knew who Chance Wayne was and how, despite his beauty and maybe because of it he was beaten into the sorrow space by those who had no beauty, inner or outer, and I began to cry, because Fifth Avenue was the wonderful world and the wonderful world was the world itself and this force was seeking to keep me hidden away. Soon the museum showed itself in its rightful place and with a just-so touch of circumspection, as befit its station in life. The stairs allowed me to walk upon them toward what I could only hope would be a scene of sex and frivolity inside, for this was not art we were talking about, but all the things that went along with it.

A small group had formed near the information booth in the rotunda. We watched as a woman with a purposeful gait approached to lead us into a basement office where we filled out forms and then were photographed and issued ID cards. I told her she was a magnet with her beauty, but she just told me to walk on by, and so I very much did. Then my hand was taken by a processor of records in the museum's Division of High Security and my fingers pressed into black ink so prints could be taken with the understanding that unique impressions were to be obtained from all. I told him of my arrest in the state of Connecticut and that it had been expunged from the records through the stunning work of an on-the-ball lawyer who knew the meaning of the words *illegal search and seizure.* I asked him who exactly he might think I was, that he should take such an action against my fingers? Was I going to walk out with a Rembrandt under my shirt? But he too told me to walk on by, to just walk on by.

If the museum's walls do not fall in and kill you, you will find that sex lies behind all great art, that the men and women who paint and sculpt do not for a moment forsake their libidinous intent, that in fact, this carnality is imposed on the work itself, which explains why studies have shown with complete consistency that the average museum goer is a randy soul who senses that somewhere within the walls of these great cultural resources are the rooms of sex where men and women of the artistic persuasion are doing it and having it done to them, in temporarily abandoning the eternal for fleshly delights.

I was assigned to an audiocassette booth for a Jean-Louis David ("Interpreter of Mankind") exhibit. The tapes were in a number of languages and dollars flowed from those who needed the morsels of facts the tapes could provide to enhance their viewing pleasure. The cassette recorders were bulky—the size of a fat book—and came with a shoulder strap and earphones. On their return, we were to rewind the tapes and stack the cassettes separately from the earphones. I worked hard, believing that someone was watching in appreciation when no one was, and tried not to contemplate the fact that the simple tasks I was performing were not from financial necessity but because I did not know how to structure my own life. To believe that one is a star and loved because he has mastered the art of rewinding a tape is delusional. And yet I became quickly grateful for this place, as I had been for the post office, where I could find temporary refuge from the greater pressures of life.

I shared the booth with a man who had taken the marriage vow, and because Eddie Redondo insisted on the diminutive, my systems were on alert. While he and his wife Alice were fully a team, she worked at a separate booth, for the special exhibition, "The Merovingians and the Art of Darkness." In their mid-twenties, they projected a sad, doomed fate that dominated their features and spoke more than the muted words she, in her shell-shocked goodness, could offer, for she was long-suffering in regard to his ways, Eddie having a nose that ran all the time and bleary eyes.

"I ruined my tear ducts doing too much coke. It also gave me a deviated septum. But boy, was it worth it. You look at one of those still lifes of Cezanne's, and suddenly the fruit, the table, the whole composition is exploding in front of your eyes."

Eddie Redondo majored in art history at Yale University, from which he had graduated summa cum laude. "I've never received less than an A since grade school," Eddie said. By the seventh grade he had committed to memory every painting hanging in the Met, he said.

A customer came by. Although it was a warm spring day, he wore an expensive-looking suit and had Winston Churchill gravitas in his open face.

"I could be here as a curator," Eddie said to the man, who stood unsmiling and with all the weight of his bearing.

"You're a bum," the man said. "Your whole generation is full of bums. You're all about to be flushed down the toilet of time by a new and healthier generation." He had an unlit cigar in his mouth and wore a silk ascot to maintain his neck. He said there was nothing he couldn't buy, and that included art and artists, but all he wanted from us was an audiocassette. "I wouldn't even buy your youth, if you put it up for sale, tainted as it is with effeteness."

I asked him for his name, so I could have him arrested for the crime of gluttony, as he had the wide mouth of a trash compactor.

"Here. Arrest that," the man said, tossing a used tissue onto the counter. At no time did he show a bias toward love and kindness.

"Do you punks know what I live for? Do you?" He had grabbed us both by our shirts and pulled us close so we could study the intention behind his bulging eyes.

'Chardin? Do you live for Chardin, perhaps?" Eddie inquired.

"Chardin I devour every day for the peace that he gives to my system. Everything I see, touch, feel, and eat is food for devouring. But do not believe for a minute that this is the totality of where my pleasure lies. Devouring is only the penultimate pleasure. It is in excretion, the filling of the bowl, and admiration and marvel at the product therein, that true pleasure is to be found. Because that is the true creation. Nothing is more deeply satisfying than a massive bowel movement."

Our tormentor went away, but Eddie remained, at least for a while. He had put himself out to pasture before his journey had really begun. We had in common the back door out of reality.

The museum really was a treasure trove of activity, with a cafeteria to sit in when the art seemed overwhelming. In it, I could contemplate the structure provided by the nine to five world three days a week and be protected from myself in this quiet surrender.

And of course the security guards, both men and women, spoke without speaking, standing in the corners of the galleries with their faces turned to the walls, so visitors would not be distracted from the alleged art on display.

That first day I pocketed five dollars. When I told Dr. Zimmer, she grew impassioned, reminding me of the unforgiving nature of the law. In essence, she was reminding me of the crushing weight of the system she was so much a part of.

"Are you crazy? You could ruin your whole life. Do you think you can practice law with a criminal record?"

I laughed and bared my teeth like a hyena, in the face of her mammoth caring, saying that apprehension forces were more likely to be on guard against swiping an El Greco than a five spot, to which she responded with a snort of cold disdain. Her alarmist tendencies notwithstanding, I was briefly touched by her concern before indulging in more hyena laughter.

Now in this time a woman at the Met called me to her attention. Her name was Debussy and she possessed a model's slender tallness. My senses were active in her vicinity. The song "The Object of My Affection" came very loud to my ears. We do have listening devices for a reason and because she moved in the way that she did and wore the short skirt that she did and sheathed her legs in the black tights that she also did and adorned herself with hoop earrings and had sexily short hair, what could I do but draw near at the booth we shared.

"Why do you dress so fine for a job that pays so little?" I whispered in her ear.

"I will tell you over lunch and an egg salad sandwich," she whispered back.

The cafeteria had her sandwich on the menu, and she devoured the big fat thing.

"I am twenty-nine. I offer you my age so you cannot defile me with your disappointment on finding this out at a later date. I am enrolled at NYU and advancing on an undergraduate degree. If somewhere along the way, I took a wrong turn, I am now trying to get back on track. How deeply my psychiatrist is involved with my development, and how earnestly he has pinned all his hopes on me. And what brings you to this cultural palace?"

I said I couldn't speak to that directly, that I was on a mission of building my own nation, with self-sufficiency as the goal. I said that studies were showing that I was isolated and steadily involved in the manufacture of my own sorrow, and that voices were urging me to verify that people had lives as well as their physical being. I acknowledged too that law school was on the agenda for the reclamation of my soul, but that I did not know how to sit in a library without longing for a woman's touch. I also told her that everything depended on my intelligence being adequate to enter the flow of life and that, if not, I would have to occupy the benches of Central and Riverside Park in all kinds of weather. I told her too that the inexorable force of German power was at my back but also on my back, and where it all would end was an uncertainty.

She removed my glasses. "Your eyes are too close together for you to be intelligent and you don't have the necessary mass of brain power to determine your own fate. You are truly a person of no consequence. My father, on the other hand, is one of the inventors of electroshock therapy. He is responsible for jolting thousands from their funks and destroying the minds of countless others. He has a thriving Park Avenue practice and the most prominent name in the field. He is God and I have spent my twenties defying him in my reckless need for attention. As fast as he gave me Corvettes—all the different colors of the rainbow—I would wrap them around a tree. I was also incredibly precocious. I had only to snap my fingers and the blocks flew together, and even today I can process the lengthiest equation through my mouth and have it come out my ass immaculate and fully solved. And yet I was gone from Princeton University after one semester. My psychiatrist and my art teacher are pinning all their hopes on me. All their hopes. I am that good."

Though the image of anal algebra knocked me back, I held my ground, eyeing the menace of her perfectly white teeth and the aggressive intent of her mouth. She had placed me on notice as to the matrix she was sprung from to manifest such Manhattan intensity, and it was for me to intuit the supply line for the cold gaseousness that sustained her in the illusion that she was the apple of her father's eye.

"Yes, I see your brain power at work right now. I see it bulging against your packed forehead. I see it trying to assign me to the cold place of fear and intimidation. I see the legendary elements of your college career and can only wonder what the ministries of justice were thinking when they gave you so much and me so little."

"My little goy schmuck," she said, the smile of the predator now widening her mouth, her parrot's beak bearing down on me.

The cafeteria had a lightness to it, as if once again we were children but in the school of life. I had no violence in me toward her. I had only this to say.

"I have noted you with my hyena's gaze, and now I will be returning for more. Your high intelligence is not a barrier but a lure; in combination with your physical assets it is what I need for my own torment. I have been reading the very coarse Henry Miller, and although I am not saying that I will take you from behind while we are stationed at the counter with the audiocassettes, I am saying that sex is in the air, given the fact of where we are, and that I shall be arriving soon."

She did not cleave my head. In elegant handwriting, she simply offered her full name and phone number, with the words "Come if you dare."

We met that same night at the Cedar Tavern, down on University Place. Jackson Pollock was gone. He had vacated the premises and his life. The place had a soft amber glow and a jazz combo working in the back. I had two glasses of wine. There was no overt drunkenness.

After the bar we walked through the East Village. Knives flashed in the dark but none came near us. I asked Debussy if she ever cried, but she said the time had not yet come to discuss such things and it was doubtful that it would.

Her apartment was a ground floor thing of beauty on the grimy street where she now lived with her trust fund still robust. Its primary feature was a space-saving loft bed and an array of large plants in designer containers.

It was so wrong, it was so right, it was so inevitable that she would go down on her knees and do the thing she did, as if needing to protect my deluded self-image of sexual stardom in the face of severe bodily deficiencies. When she rose back up and sought compensation with a deep kiss, I balked in horror at the thought of contact with a mouth that smelled of me. A silent communication passed between us; I had injured her.

Debussy showed herself to be profound in her interpretation of dreams. She could even have been Joseph among the pharaohs in another life. I told her that as a child there had been a thing of my dream mind called the er-ra-ra-man lapping the ceiling of the room where I slept, and that this thing of light would coalesce in the center of the ceiling as a luminous white blob. It would then drop down to the floor and announce its presence. In terror I would flee the room with this demon in full pursuit through the dark apartment and everyone else fast asleep. Always I would awaken before he could grab hold of me.

Debussy had one simple question: "Was there a window in your room, and if so, what did it look out on?"

I had no choice but to tell her that the room indeed had a window and that it looked out on the very great Broadway, which had been there since the Indians were vanquished and the white man brought the vehicles that moved so fast.

"It is easily understood if you will allow comprehension to rule. The light circling the rooms was simply from the headlights on the cars as they passed your building. The er-ra-ra man syllables were simply the sound the tires made as they went over the road. Your mind absorbed these sensory impressions and coupled them with a male child's fear of his father for seeking possession of his mother."

I rose up in bed and lay back down again. I then offered thanks while seeking to hide my disappointment that she had so quickly dispatched with the mystery I had attached to my childhood nightmare.

Knowing that the mailbox would one day contain my fate, I would open it cautiously. That day arrived, and I extracted the booklet warily, as if it were a bomb that could blow me into eternity, then sat in my apartment for some minutes before peeling back the label ever so slowly. The numbers would tell me who I was. I was OK on the achievement end of things and to a similar degree on the aptitude portion. For a while I was jubilant but then I recalled glancing at the exam booklet of the young man next to me, and so now I was a cheat as well as a failure.

Boston University accepted me, as did St. John's University and Brooklyn Law School, but Rutgers placed me on its waiting list, the admissions officer giving his assurance that I would be accepted the following year. Pride prevented me from attending St. John's or Brooklyn Law. Only Rutgers seemed acceptable. Then I wavered. Maybe Boston University would be acceptable as well, given that F. Lee Bailey was a well known alumnus. Then too, Brooklyn Law School did have the heartbreaking beauty of its borough's name, so what was a *man*—the key word— to do? Should I surrender my life here in New York City and head for Boston?

"It is only you who holds yourself back," said Dr. Zimmer.

Boston became a torment to my mind, a place so cold and and unwelcoming. Mona would have the warmth of her art while I would have the drudgery of the law and be among men who only wanted to beat me as I wanted to beat them. Where was love to be found in such an environment of gnawing anxiety far from the womb of the renting office? A man was someone who left home, but I was another kind of man who read Samuel Beckett and heard him say, in a revolutionary way, "I am in my mother's house. It is I who live there now," standing firm with his simple declaration against those like Hemingway with their conviction that one need ride a llama over the Andes in a state of drunkenness, for by now I was reading the Viking Portable Writers at Work series to determine where I would stand if only I could put words on paper sufficient to be presentable.

It was not in me to fall down into a state of surrender and say, "Yes, Claire, you have beaten me with your high numbers, and you, Frank Dolan, have beaten me with yours, and you, Lydia van Dine, have certainly beaten me with your Radcliffe numbers, and the world has beaten me with numbers that I cannot match and call my own and be ushered into a high echelon life." Because the necessary ingredient of humility was lacking to endure the coldness of Boston and the forlornness of Brooklyn. And it was not for me to have the elite of the universe looking down and laughing at my failure.

And so I reported to Dr. Zimmer my decision to put off law school for a year, the substantiality of the Rutgers catalog having shown that the wait would be worth it for respectability to present itself. To my surprise she went along with my decision, and in so doing seemed to affirm my concern about the quality of the law schools that had opened their doors to me.

There were others at the museum who were also dawdling, those who had lost their way and were trying to rediscover it or simply living in the spaces where life had delivered them. Isabel Burke was a woman with antecedents of New England renown. Her ancestors had arrived on the *Mayflower* and written on parchment with quill pens. However, she lacked their stalwart quality. A troubled expression ruled her face, as if she were fretting over the answer to a problem that she no longer quite remembered, and dwelt in her mind where healthier souls did not go, having heard the lecture breaths rebuking her for manufacturing her own misery in wanting more than life could give. She spoke a matter of fact truth in the way of those who are rendered honest by their reduced circumstance.

"I couldn't put the blocks together at the hospital when they gave me the intelligence test. My brains have gone south to burn up in the hot sun of the equator. I did well at Smith, but the speed has erased the knowledge and mental ability I once possessed. It has burned big holes in my brain."

Isabel Burke's plain, sad face spoke of the condition that life required her to endure, like the woman I had met at Moogie's Bar some years before. She was in the care of Columbia-Presbyterian Hospital, which sent her out during the day so she could be hard at work on the reintegration of herself into society, even if she returned to her hospital room depleted and defeated to stare at the bare walls. To hear the word "Columbia" was of course to hear the word *excellence*, with a flag of blue and white flapping in a cool breeze and seafaring gents of strength and blondness accumulating their nautical miles between operating room sessions wearing surgeons' gowns and wielding scalpels. I saw the warning signs in her dulled eyes and slow-moving ways that the stars did not come out at night when you advanced too far into the chemical realm, because to fall from high echelon Smith College with its brilliant intellects was to suffer a serious injury, and you did not get back the infrastructure that had produced the high numbers if that infrastructure had been hollowed out and crumbled to a powdery dust in the amphetamine war that had been waged upon it, and yet the bliss of seeming oneness still offered a powerful incentive to do it more.

Now there was another who outshone them all in the compact delivery of her beauty, a woman whom it hurt not to touch given the luster of her short black hair and the smallness of her waist and the expanse of her breasts and the thin strength of the legs that kept her enterprise in motion, the universal declaration being that she had the goods. There were no late arrivals to her altar of worship; they had been there forever, but all I could do was look at her from afar from my hiding place among the El Grecos.

Not that I didn't try to approach her. It was only that her force field drove me away. Finally, when I could take it no more, I put pen to paper:

> I have been assessing you from a far distance to maintain a safety requirement, and can say your demeanor exudes amour propre and suggests you would be loath to indulge in

> shenanigans. And yet, although you do carry yourself with the distinction of a superstar, I am single-mindedly intent on getting next to you. The thing is that you wear your respectability like a shield, and could I ask for a single clue as to how to pierce it? Because my audiocassette days will be as nothing without a love feast with you. I don't want to kiss your feet or sniff your shoes. I just want to be with you. Can we close the gap so magic can do its work? You will find me at the Jean-Louis David audiocassette booth, administering culture where it is needed.

Isabel Burke could not be my envoy to Mara Black. It might overwhelm her fragile mind. And I could not trust Debussy with a confession of my heart when she might have feelings, too. I was left to take action on my own, and so approached the information booth in a crouch, seeking to duck under Beauty's force field and deliver my written truth.

Surfacing before her amused gaze, I blurted, "You will know where to reach me after reading this. Do not dally." And because she snatched the envelope, I had no reason not to hope.

Centuries had to come and go before I could see her next, but the wait was well worth it. She approached my booth with her force field turned off, and as she moved a strand of hair back from her lightly freckled face, she introduced herself and said that the possibility was there to be comfortable with my dementedness. I said that we should go somewhere soon to tell each other our truths and our lies and where fate was taking us and she agreed that the hour was at hand for a protracted face-to-face.

Mara told me right at the start, as part of the service she provided at the information booth, that I would remember her for all time; that she would be for me a prime example of the possibilities that attach to reckless beauty; that the time would come when I would search for her in vain, and call out her name to the universe and plead for her return. She said the sights she would show me with her bra unhooked and her sex fully exposed would be but a prelude to setting a new standard for wantonness, and it was in this context that our dialogue with each other began.

She had dropped out of Bennington College after less than one year, led away, she said, by the call of adventure beyond its tame setting. I asked her did she have a boyfriend who was big in her life and whom she could call her own.

"Boyfriend?" she responded. Her mouth fell open to show her paradise of tongue and teeth beyond reproach. "I had one of those, but he left me. He just flat out left me." She said he had gone off to pursue a Ph.D. in the great field of literature at SUNY Binghamton the previous fall, that he just vacated the premises of their life without a word, and that ever since she had been sipping wine and stewing in her hatefulness.

For my part, I told her that I couldn't wait to see her breasts and anything else she wanted to show me, and that in the meantime I was driving down the pathways of ambivalence and that the potholes, large as they were, had incredible shock value. I told her further, driven by metaphoric abundance, that I was also on the rim of a circle that I couldn't seem to penetrate, that around and around on it I walked. This I said to her in a coffee shop on Eighty-second and Madison while the rains of spring came down and down on the East Side of New York. I told her that I had hitched my star to law school without truly knowing what it was and confessed that I was afraid to go forward for reasons too shameful to explain. But I also told her that I was writing strong on the days of my life, and that doing so gave me a chance to live even if the words had no structure. I said I hesitated to call it fiction since it was just the stuff of my daily round, but that the words gave me a sense of fulfillment and peace that helped me to show up for ham sandwiches with coleslaw at the deli of the dangerous up the way. I started to tell her of the moccasins I had coveted as a child but she cut me short.

"How can you write when you can barely speak? You sound just like him, with his stupid fiction projects. He wrote an unpublishable novel about a man who breaks into gum machines in New York City subway stations." Her laugh was now a cackle of derision.

"He is just trying to keep memory alive because someday the subway gum machines of New York City will cease to be and Doublemint gum and Chiclets will have gone the way of their owners' vanished selves, but the pages will still be around for the readers of his books to explore." I said these things strong to Mara because it did not feel right to be bashing a man in his incipient progress, to make of him a piece of asphalt to drive her scorn-laden car over.

"Right. Move over, Saul Bellow."

"Saul Bellow is of Chicago, and has a last name that proclaims him loud and a first name that speaks to a transition he cannot make until he finds his own personal road to Damascus, while your friend is now of Binghamton, New York, drawing on the strength of the departed Indians who weathered its fearful storms before being vacated from the premises. Meanwhile I look at your breasts as the challenged fabric of your blouse shows them to be and fear that I will faint, now that literature and sex are so close at hand."

She took no detectable note of the interest I was showing, but kept her mind on the evisceration of my life.

"So you think you're an up and coming novelist?"

"I am a thrasher out of the truth as I understand it to be. I do not have any Midwestern linguistic apparatus at my disposal, but I do have the word power to make the typewriters that I have assembled sing a halting song, and in any case the purchase of the machines must be paid for with words on paper. Every day must I be faithful to the production of them or pay the consequence for my negligence."

"Are you ill?" If she thought so, she had made it a laughing matter.

"No, but I am genuinely proud to be an American and itching to record the trouble that my life can bring."

Mara inhaled on her Parliament, daring it to infringe on the whiteness of her teeth.

"What do you want from me?"

"That you be friend and foe until one of the two wins out."

"Offer me some facts. What do you do when you're not at this art joint handing out audiocassettes?"

"I am law school bound, if ever I leave home, as I told you, so I can rise to a level of eminence. At the same time, I seem to have a thing going on with the building of my origin. I'm on a collision course with the landlord oppressor, and if I eat my Wheaties, I should be able to kill him dead."

We were cooking in the coffee shop booth by now. Clearly something was going on, and the waitress did not bum's rush us out the door.

"My father is an oppressor, too. He's a slumlord. He owns a lot of buildings in Harlem. He collects the rents from rat-infested tenements and my family gets to live so well and comfortably out on Long Island."

"Are my services needed in dealing with him?" I placed my hands behind my ears to increase their listening capacity.

"I'll never go to bed with you if you mock me," she replied, anger reddening her face.

"To mock is one thing. To inquire is another. I am very skilled at fighting patriarchs. My résumé abounds with such successes."

"My father would pulverize you," she said.

"I am coming out with my hands up just so I can be with you. Not everyone can or should be Mona Van Dine in the anti-patriarchal wars."

"Mona who?"

"A very famous artist in the making who battled her father so she could live. Someday the story will be told."

As if his words meant nothing, Mara went on her own oral way.

"I go out to visit my parents last weekend. I'm walking along singing 'Honey Pie' from the *White Album*. Nothing more. Nothing less. Just walking along singing 'Honey Pie' and minding my own business. Out of nowhere my father appears and tells me to stop. What right has he to do that?"

Before my eyes did she turn into an incendiary device, smoke rising from her being.

"I am at your service, should the need arise," I said.

Though it was spring and the birds were singing in the soiled air, I felt the weight of my secret life and the fear that something was amiss. The term moral turpitude would visit me concerning activities driven by necessity, such as the launching of full inquiries into the sex life of Mona Van Dine in her Boston realm of art even as I cavorted in the night fantastic with the women of Manhattan. And the money thing of the building could suddenly appear as madness, the appearance of office responsibility belied by the ongoing accumulation of illicit income not leading me to heaven's gate. The awareness afflicted me with knockdown strength, so that I had to lie upon the hard, unyielding sidewalk trying to fathom where my life had gone that my everything would be given to garnering guilt wherever I might. Then I would get back up and do the walking thing all over again just so I could forget, *as my father before me.*

When a girl can rise above the station to which she has been assigned, when she can suffuse the museum rotunda with her presence and rotate her head in a 360 and grow multiples of arms and liquefy her body and her mind and compel the universe to drink her as love potion number nine, then you must bow down to her power. Not that she showed herself in this light her first week on the job, for she was trained in the middle class ways of decorum, but the walls did begin to speak to her of a vitality that was lacking and that she needed to bring into being, the understanding coming to her that the flesh was simply art made real, the bright and dangerous lights of Mara blinking red in the spring of 1970, when I could still be on the earth.

I double-parked the used VW in front of The End, having bought the car as an accessory for my pleasure and to give my motorcycle the companionship it was seeking in the loneliness of its garage space. On the corner I could see my brother Luke hanging out with the boys of trouble, standing apart from the busy flow of life around them. I saw my childhood friend Jerry Jones-Nobleonian thickened to the point of bloat. I saw Lenny Cerone, from Long Beach, Long Island, who at one time could address the issues of any car and have it running in no time but could no longer, now that he was in his twenties and pasty-skinned and strung out on junk. What would I say if they saw me and the car that was now in my life and expressed wonderment that I should be able to make such a purchase given my meager employment?

I saw too in that moment what I had seen many times, that I was more guileful than Luke. He would never be able to take from the renting office the sums of money I had extracted. He could not step outside the confines of the law and justify this infraction in the way that I could. But the price he paid was to stay ensnared. Whatever it took, I could not allow the suctioning force of family to deprive me of the distance I was seeking from which to live in contemplation of all that had gone before.

Mara emerged from the bar, not having given me the time to calculate the odds of her appearing. Hands reached for her from the darkness of its premises, but she found a way to step into the waning light of the spring day and move forward.

I had been on and off about seeing her all day and trying to find a way to live with the consequences of my action if I dared. Because a man could wind up deprived of everything if he took too many chances in the sex realm, but now that she had situated herself in the passenger seat with her glorious gifts apparent, all considerations of heaven and hell were vanished from my sight and there was only the pleasure dome decreed.

"I've been drinking wine all day waiting for this evening," she said, words that reassured me even if they didn't fit my image of her. She was too chunky full with her own beauty to sit around a bar all day.

"Is there some fire you wish to put out or are you seeking to ignite with the wine that you imbibe?"

"Try not to ruin everything by speaking," she said.

With the decision-making apparatus at my disposal, I had come to the conclusion that preparation was necessary before the main event, that however disposed one might be toward the thing of sex, anticipation had its rightful place. To say the Ninth Avenue bar was dark is not to say that we could not see. There were candles burning at every table, and all the rugged boys from the sandwich shop where I got my heroes heavy on the mustard were present, having gathered where their fathers could know to find them in the generational roots of violent love that they had put down here in these Hell's Kitchen parts. They promised me in their manner that on this particular night they were not cooking body parts in the kitchen but simply hanging out before the wars resumed. Like many amateur criminals, they had a passion for Dionne Warwick, and so when she sang 'Walk on By" on the jukebox loud, they just held their Westies tongues so she could have her moment, but this in no way meant that as the darkness increased its hold on the city, they did not return to their thoughts diabolical and the terminating mission that their lives had become. Because ultimately to be one of them, you had to have a talent for the knife and the ability to step out of your hard beauty and into blood.

"You are the kind of girl I could not have approached in high school, a girl with the dimensions of stardom in the brain as well as the body." She seemed to ignore my confession.

"I can't imagine you as a lawyer," she said, over the jukebox noise. "You just don't look like a lawyer."

"I have got to tidy up my life with a professional credential to buttress the anatomy that has been provided for me."

"That's so disappointing. I thought you might want to develop a cosmic consciousness."

"I have been to the moon," I said. "Believe me when I say that it changed me. The perspective of space will cause you to see poetry in lonely places."

The jukebox was now vibrating with the amped up sound of the rock and roll holler heads and the smell was strong of uncleaned toilets. The men with long hair were positioned at the bar in greater numbers for the drinks that would fuel their rage. No one could put some softness in their attitude, not even Three Dog Night.

"Never mind the moon. Sex is at the top and the bottom of everything," she said over the racket, as she ran her hand down the bottle's neck.

"If you mean that God as well as the Devil is sexed, you had better believe it. Otherwise why does Lucifer have such a tail and why do women who align themselves with power have to sex it up with el presidente?"

"You take a simple idea and make a mess of it."

Outside the night was merry with its own intent, people stepping on and off the buses of New York City and arranging their faces in the way that they could. And does the world have to stop that record numbers brushed their teeth that night?

I myself had dressed for Mara in Levi corduroys and a green T-shirt and the denim jacket of my nation, and with Converse sneakers on my feet I walked her down the sloping block toward our destination. From a distance I could see Mrs. Muldooney sitting on her garbage can in full if unspoken expression of her bleak poetry, having moved beyond sorrow into the realm of sheer survival, the sightings of the clip-clopping horses and the number eleven bus offered up as her daily bread. I saluted her as the urban saint of the alone and the repressed and spoke to her thusly: "I am going to taste of earthly delights. I am streaking now for forbidden fruit. Mother, where is your exterminating son? Does he lie in wait for me?"

"Go and have your night, Sonny." She did not take her eye from the street in front of her.

As we walked through the straightaway corridor that led to the rear building, I said, "Mara, she has let us go. She has given us her blessing. We do not have to bow down to her. We do not have to dedicate our lives to her. And yet we do, we do, for Mother is always there, she is there before time and in time and after time."

"That is your mother sitting on a garbage can?"

"Only in a manner of speaking."

As always, in the backyard, I paused before the telephone building to take in how it was that bricks and steel could create a structure of laughing arrogance, its message always the same, to come over to the winning side.

"Oh Mara," I suddenly cried, "we do need a bed in which to lie to relieve us of this excess of spring." And she said yes, she said very yes yes in the way that she could.

So I brought her into the apartment with the typewriters piled high and the cameras hanging by their straps from hooks and she saw the single bed that I had provided for myself, and I asked her did she want to roll a joint before we got down to it. She rolled it big, she rolled it fat, she wet it with the moisture in her mouth, then licked it over all its length.

We were not in smoke heaven very long before the Serial Killer man came through the door without opening it in the special way he had of making himself known. I had never seen him so white, so pale. There he stood clenching and unclenching the fist he made with both gloved hands, neither loving nor hating us but simply examining for his viewing pleasure once again the continuum of life and death, black and white, and whatever it was that encompassed his priest of darkness vision.

"A Jew doesn't have to die because she's in the company of a Christian, and a Christian doesn't have to die because he's in the company of a Jew. Polarities can have their place without the dustbin of history becoming our fate. You don't have to kill us, Mr.

Serial Killer man, because you never left home." I had a good cry in his midst while he stood, seemingly unmoved. The important thing is that he spared us the his trademark finality.

A sexed up Sparkle Plenty Mara showed herself to be.

"Watch me undress. You don't have to pretend you don't want to. You don't have to pretend anything," she whispered, slipping out of her dress and showing herself in her matching beige bra and panties, which she slowly shed. "This bed. It doesn't go with my image of you. I saw you laying me down on a king-size mattress," she whispered. "Such lips. Such hair. I've been dying, dying, to touch you. Didn't you know? I come at the very sight of you. At the very thought. I'm coming now, lying here with you on top of me. Slow, slow. Just go ever so slow, baby. We have all night. We have to make this last. It's all we have. It's all we need. Let me lick you. Let me taste you. I want my tongue in your nose, in your ears, in your mouth, in your ass. I want your cock in my mouth, my pussy, deep in my ass. You didn't know, did you? You didn't know what I was like. I want you to piss on me, to shit on me. I'm bottomless in the things that you can do."

In this brief time she had led me to understand that the bed was her natural element, the only place where she could hope to be fathomed, and I saw with astonishment the gap between my initial perception of her as the queen of fastidiousness and the writhing person beside me.

"I'm a sex maniac. I belong on Forty-second street," she said in my ear, her sharp-nailed finger making inroads up my butt.

Something went wrong. I entered her too quickly and came too soon. Her howl of disappointment shook the windows and caused neighbors to inquire. "You were supposed to make it *last,*" she said.

Having found release, I wanted my space back without the discomfort she was eliciting in me with her all-seeing eye. I wanted her to take all guilt I was feeling with her as well. It was only the way I felt with all women, except for Mona, after being with them. A man had a right to his solitude, just as he had a right to attach himself to the illusions that brought him out of that solitude.

I had bought a piano, an old upright. It sat in the apartment unused. Now and then I would try to practice, but I was too self-conscious to strike more than a single key. Once a week I went uptown to take lessons from a man with a huge belly who often seemed to be nursing a hangover when I arrived. In spite of his bulk he moved gracefully, a gift I associated with musicians. While I struggled with basic chords, he would sip black coffee and smoke sweet-smelling thin cigars, this in an apartment on a street that sloped upward to its summit and downward toward the Museum of Natural History.

"You don't learn to play the piano by studying calculus and solving *pi*," he dared to say. Did he know the soreness of the dull that came over me when I couldn't do what he asked, when flats and sharps and treble clefs were a bafflement generating the same rage that afflicted me in my battle with the blocks so equally black and white? Oh, I wrote a check and tore it from my checkbook and stapled it to his forehead. Many times I did this, before drifting like a tumbling tumbleweed down the corridor of Broadway to my apartment with shame having its day. Tell me if you have ever wanted the world to stop. Write to me with news of this important kind. Say you've reached the point of finality with reckless plunges into spendthrift humiliation—books, cameras, typewriters, pianos, music lessons, the Evelyn Waugh speed-reading course—and so are left with nothing but admiration for Mrs. Muldooney's garbage can-sitting ways and her embrace of idleness. The piano teacher had come out of his room but not out of his dream of playing Chopin etudes with a signature sound to lodge in the hearts and minds and souls of all humanity.

Mara sat at the piano and began to play something familiar but which I could not put a name to. Strands of black hair had trailed down her thin neck. The power of her womanhood was there for me to see in her small waist and ample breasts and the beauty mark on the graceful spread of her back. She could take your heart and make it her own. And yet she had to go.

"What was that?" I said, from the cold place where comparison had taken me.

"A simple Bach fugue," she said. "Couldn't you tell?"

"Stop it. You see that I live in the land of the simpletons."

"But what do you do? Do you do anything? Where are your writings? Your photographs?

"We have got to go out from here. Your eyes have become like sharp glass. They are cutting far too deep. Do you not see I am not prepared for my artistic appearance?"

"We can't just stay here for the night?" Her voice grown plaintive, she sadly retrieved the garments that she had shed, as if the gift of her body was being cruelly dismissed.

And so we drove downtown, drove wherever I would not be up for inspection, to a watering hole in the Greenwich Village night. The patrons who had drunk their poison had fled to fuck or gone home alone to cry. All that remained was a pissed off bartender trying to bring glasses to a shine with soapy water. I asked him for the truth of his existence, if he could summon meaning from the stick he worked and from bringing glasses to a sparkling state. I asked him further if he could make a world from the narrow space he occupied, and if he could expand it into an empire with the concoctions that he had to offer. Then I drilled him harder, asking did the stick he worked behind give him all he power he was seeking, and did his ponytail and the narcissistic posing to jukebox rock and roll gain for him all the attention that he sought and when would he mother-fuck the rock and roll music imprisoning his mind so he could live in the light of a clear and productive day?

"What do you want?" he asked. He had his sleeves rolled up so he wouldn't get them wet.

"I want a bottle of what you have," I said, and he set a bottle of red wine down in front of me.

"He is feeling bad, and he should be," Mara said to the bartender.

The night was turning on her bright and dangerous star, and the bartender had been awakened from the dead to now be in proximity.

And so I drank my wine, in mounting apprehension of the night moves of Mr. Stick Man. And Mara drank, too. We drank the bottle dry and then had another to show that she was right, that sex was at the top and the bottom, because if you didn't discover it at the top of the bottle, it came raging up at you with the dregs to dissolve your fears.

I pulled Mara off the stool and to her feet and raced us back to my place and lay with her as she cried an ocean of tears for the man who had left her for Binghamton. She would see me as I was and I would do the same with her, as the wine and life itself dictated.

All that spring the power of Mara was too much for me, and while I could not do the sex thing fully as she wanted, I did my best to please her in the way that I could.

One afternoon I saw a man in conversation with her at the information booth. He wore a full-length black leather coat. Some days later I saw him there again. That night she had candor in her words and in her face when she said that Leather Coat Man produced porn movies and wanted her for a starring role and that she was considering it, as she was in free fall through the heartless universe and that men could tie her to the railroad tracks and run her over with diesel trains if that was called for.

Now it turned out that Mara loved Debussy with a great love, and if love was questioned by some as what the feeling amounted to, it surely had exceeded the bounds of sheer admiration, and it can safely be reported that nowhere on the screening devices that were being administered did the word envy show its face. It can also be reported that no containment forces could be brought to bear to keep Mara where my studies had shown she needed to be, a fact very much proven by the spectacle of their summit meeting in the cafeteria of the glorious Met, an event I happened to stumble upon.

"Here he is, lover boy himself," Mara said.

"Oh yes I am, even if the shame blitz is hitting me in a way you would not believe," I said, pulling up a chair.

"And what shame blitz are we talking about?" Debussy made a point to inquire.

"I am talking about the shame blitz of women discussing their sex in range of men who are expected to have a share in the subject."

"Did you say that you were in psychoanalysis?" Debussy winked at Mara.

"Oh, I am very much in psychoanalysis insofar as it puts me into a connection with the deep and the distinguished."

"You're a little thin, a little insubstantial, for a man, aren't you?" Debussy pursued.

"I am growing in my substance all the time that I can," I replied. "Now let me turn the tables and tell you thusly—"

"Thusly?" Mara asked.

"Yes, thusly. For it is a man's place to rise to power over the women who have powered him down even as he tries to love them in the approximate way that he can. But you must understand that the fires of lewdness can be unending and a recurring theme, a true life's work."

"Well said." Mara held a finger in the air, and suddenly I sensed Lenore in her laughing way from wherever she had gone.

I let them be and took a table by myself. Isabel, the woman of refinement with the hollowed out head, joined me. She sat nibbling at celery sticks spread with cream cheese.

"Don't worry. I don't see you," she said.

"Yes you do," I said. "You see me."

"I don't see you in a way that makes me want you. That went far away, like my mind."

"Does it feel good not wanting that?" I asked.

"It's like being old when you're supposed to be still young. It's like all I want to do is be in my room at the hospital looking at the clean linoleum and bare walls. Or not looking at anything at all but just knowing objects are there and people are taking care of things for me. All I feel is this constant dullness when once upon a time my mind was on fire and connections were being made."

"Do you want to be on fire again?" I asked.

"No. When it is done it is done."

We sat there quietly for a while. She had stopped eating, as if it was something she couldn't go on with. I looked back. Debussy and Mara were kissing, which I had never seen women do before, either in public or in private. It was no different from what men and women do in its mechanics. I turned back to Isabel. She had not seen or smelled the fire. I felt some responsibility to lift her up from where she had fallen to, but didn't know how, and found her message disturbing.

"I don't know what to say,' I finally said.

"No one does," she replied.

"Debussy has real intelligence. Some people fake it through their manner, their diction, stuff like that. Hers you can't fake. She's great."

The word "great" roared from Mara.

"Greatness abounds. It is all around us on this island," I could only say.

"You're a control freak. You're afraid of everything."

"Have we entered the place of warfare?"

"Always and forever, bastard."

What should we do, now that your oil fields are on fire given the incendiary rage that you are showing?" I asked.

"Do? Do? We should fuck until we don't have to see each other anymore, like everyone else."

"Is it the slumlord father you cannot own? What is it that incites you so?"

"Have you ever been left, bastard? Have you? Have you ever had to live with just the memory of someone's piss and shit and saliva upon you and the remains of his life that you cannot toss, the underwear and socks and pair of boots left behind?"

"Your old record is still playing. For myself, I am preparing for the ether, not with rocket boosters strapped to my person but to achieve through writing the approximation of who I can be. The fire is coming. The earth will burn. Where are the cooling elements that must be in place for us to survive? Only the written word can create the asbestos shield that we should all be seeking, if we are not to be incinerated by the heat of our own tumescence. For this reason I am inextricably tied to the machines I have purchased for the amalgamation of my life, the achievement through keyboard clack-clack of words in single-spaced formation and the centeredness that serves as a precursor to transcendence of the diurnal flow. Because my life is not simply a marriage of heaven and hell but a geometry that demands resolution through the solving of the blocks. While I have not yet lifted off from the basic 'white line continue' and 'Mona liked to pee in an open field,' the promise of new horizons is looming as part of a world to which I am being beckoned. I will not deny the elements of perdition all around me. I must be saved from them at all cost but must also admit I do not know how to factor a law school curriculum into the salvation process."

"Now you're talking," she said, and kissed me generously.

"You are the fire."

"Now you're really talking."

With sex out of the way, I talked to her about my aspirations and of what nation-building on reams of paper could truly mean, how my family could be made real in a manageable way that invited understanding even if we were unloved, some of us standing on street corners with our shirt tails hanging out or sitting on a stool at Chock Full O' Nuts in solitary socialization, not one of us called far and wide by the powers of the universe to create empires in other lands or even other states but just hanging around the building waiting for something to happen and lacking the power the trains possessed, as Gertrude Stein noted. I told her too of the Van Dine clan and how, even as the overwhelming antithesis of my own family, they must be part of the world order I was seeking to create. Was there some way to bring together the unearthliness of my overwhelmed father with the throne of thundering intellect on which Peter Van Dine was perilously perched with his crown half off his head? I told Mara she would also have her place as the perdition path was a well traveled one. I told her further that a resurrection project called Sisters Need to Live would soon be underway. I told her all the elements had to be brought back together even as they needed to be kept separate, and in this way I could have the company I didn't have in life.

Mara struggled to listen amid all her yawning that showed the whiteness of her teeth and the incitement capacity of her so red tongue.

Debussy was reclaiming her life. By humbly starting over, she had taken the pressure off herself, with her therapist's help. The bouts of self-laceration had abated.

"Have you been sleeping with Mara?" Debussy asked, and when I did not respond, she went on. "All I can say is be careful. She brags about not having cleaned her diaphragm in the last year."

A feeling of pride, not shame, came over me at these two connections. I was not a heart of stone Rolling Stone. Women had the power. That they did.They had been running my world for a longer time than I knew, and if this was not heralded on ancient tapestries, then history was a lie. You bowed down to them, you loved them, you mated with them, only to see that they were still in a place beyond your reach.

For whatever reason, I went home with Debussy in mind and called her that night. Mara was not available and I did not want Debussy fully out of reach.

"No, I can't see you. I've got a dear old friend from college staying with me. I've told him about you. We both figure you go out screwing every night. Happy hunting."

A lake of shame I was plunged back into by the ridicule she had dispensed on me, a mental image appearing of Debussy and her friend in the comfort of their own platonic world, while I was a howling wolf in search of victims on the streets of New York City. She showed me the other side of what life could be, and though I could wish to be there, in an alternative world of evenings spent in cozy conversation and with books instead of lust, she had not said how to make that happen.

Some nights later, I called again.

"Sure. Come on down, honey bunch," she said, speaking in an out of character way.

Along the sidewalks were men and women sitting on garbage cans and drinking beer while others did their junkie nod, and the narcotic drone of Yankee baseball was heard along the street. All the buildings housed rats with a long neighborhood lineage.

Debussy came to the door in a faded terrycloth bathrobe and slippers. Her hair was pulled tight in curlers and she held in her hand a plate of cottage cheese and fruit salad.

"Come in. I'll be right with you," she said, her mouth white with food. She turned and headed for the bathroom, and took the plate with her. Shortly, I heard a commotion behind the closed door, the unmistakable sound of a bowel movement, and too late put my hands to my ears in trying to seal off the defecation tumult. The image and audio of her on the can would be a part of me forever. She emerged, bringing the smells of her voiding with her, and plopped onto the sofa, where she resumed her attack on the fruited mound on the plate. Then she crunched the lettuce, stuffing it in her mouth with her hand. When that had gone down her gullet, she gave her fork a sloppy lick with her white tongue.

"Come on over and cozy up," she said, patting the empty space on the sofa.

As I did so, she yawned, a giant hippo yawn that revealed the silver fillings. I turned away.

"I've described you to Dr. Schaff. You know, skinny and not very bright while straining to present the image of intelligence. The kind who thinks life is just one quick fuck with one girl after another. You don't know how women secretly loathe your presumptuous ways. This is a huge step forward for me, showing myself as I am instead of feeling that I have to doll up for some ridiculously inadequate male. Dr. Schaff will surely concur. Men like you make me laugh. You expect women to dig swallowing your come. I've got news for you. It was all an act that first night. I didn't even feel you in there. It was about as thrilling as having a thermometer up my cunt."

I bolted from her lacerating tongue out into the night and slept for many centuries as angels worked to pick her shrapnel from my psyche even as the clock kept ticking.

Chapter 73

Friends took time and effort, and did not seem part of my purpose in life. What I desired was to roam the public spaces and connect with strangers. Because it was still spring and the weather was warm, I wandered into Central Park at the south end and saw the slickness of the sea lions and the sluggish power of the polar bears, with their coats of tarnished white. At some point the trees called attention to themselves. They had a life of their own, a sense of community, and stood as ambassadors for peace; their laughter was quiet and never at the expense of others. All the inanimate objects, I began to see, had a gentle and never caustic wit. They understood what it was to be a spectator, and to watch the daily flow. If anything, they were wishing me well. I knew I could sleep with the benches and the trees and not be a stranger, and was comforted to know that they were there through all their lonely vigils of the night, and though rain and wind and stinging cold could beat upon them, they retained their strength, and the ability in inclement weather to maintain the memory of the sun.

The carousel beckoned, a waltz being piped out of hidden speakers. Around and around the screaming children went on painted ponies.

From there I wandered to the promenade, which gave me the vantage point from which to look down at Bethesda Fountain and the winged angel that topped it. I saw kids hanging out on the terrace fronting the lake and the rough and tumble of their clique and the hierarchy that natural selection brought about. I saw them seeking to shed the status of their families, scrapping prep school duds for T-shirts and jeans and putting it all on the line with the aerodynamic wizardry of the Frisbees they sailed through the soft air.

A man climbed into the fountain and plopped face down in the water. Oh, he wasn't there for centuries, and on emerging pointed in my direction. The hippies gave him a wide berth, seeing he was not one of their own. He made wet tracks with every step as he climbed the stairs. I had no choice but to stand and wait for him, as running would only have revealed my fear.

Tony Pascual showed his face before me, his dirty sneakers still squishing water as he arrived. "Hello, gargoyle," he said, his parted lips revealing teeth yellow and chipped.

"Hello, Tony."

"I had to clean off the filth."

"Good job," I said. He wore a collarless velour top that looked too warm for the sticky day. He was unshaven and his wiry hair resembled a huge ball of steel wool. Finished with his bath, he put on strawberry-colored glasses.

"Let me tell you, my man. I'm free. I have an office with no overhead. All I do is flash for them and they come calling and I close the door and get down to business. After one leaves the next one steps into my office."

"Your office?"

"It's an executive suite, really, with my name and title on the door. Anthony Pascual, CEO. It's back there in the bushes. They want to hang with me afterward. They want to join my firm after they have seen my assets. Most of them I just drop-kick out the door."

I wondered how he had fallen so fast but knew he wouldn't be able to tell me. Bad acid came to mind.

"Still holding onto your capital?" His smile widened, as if he had suddenly entered my mind. Even behind the glasses, his eyes appeared more penetrating.

"What's that mean?"

"Oh, that's right. You were an English major. Economics wasn't your strong suit. What I'm saying is, I hope no one is dipping into your capital. You know, your Boston capital."

"I've got to be going."

"Call me if you ever need a broker. Get it? A broke-her? I'll handle your properties with expertise."

Perhaps language wasn't his problem after all. The message was a clear one, and he delivered it well. Some day, despite all your puny efforts, you'll be just like me, in rags, reduced to unzipping your fly in quest of your American woman. I thought of Fat Man and of Tony Pascual's innocent dream and of my meanness to him and if it in any way had caused him to be as he was. And then I thought of my brother Luke and how it was that the lives of people I knew didn't all turn to gold. I also thought, looking at the buildings all around the perimeter of the park, how, like Tony Pascual, I really didn't have anyplace to go either, and withdrew slowly from his presence in fear of becoming his double.

My museum adventure was winding down, Debussy having removed herself from my prurient fantasy world with her bathroom and cottage cheese performance, and Mara having made the career choice to offer her smoldering sex to the general public for its viewing pleasure. In fact, she articulated a manifesto of sorts, saying "Not every woman has a price. Not every woman wants to show herself before the camera and live in the wanton state. Not every woman wants to be freed from the strictures and structures of the conventional life and relishes the thrill of easy money and endless pleasure. But I do."

What was I to say about the stated impulses of anyone who had been denied the right to sing a song from, of all things, *The White Album?*

"I hope you know what you are getting into."

"Right now you are full. You have been in my kitchen and partaken of my stuff. A fork in the road has come. It has no meaning for you in the way that it will when you are older and hungry and there is no kitchen such as mine to go to, when the flame of loneliness engendered lust is all-consuming and you have no one to call and I am nowhere to be found."

All this she also said, from the place where she was happening, and I had no defense against her truth but no abiding interest in its content either. Assault me with her prophecy though she did, I called on bottom line analysis to determine that her darkness was no match for the lightness of being Mona Van Dine manifested with the steadiness of her labors. Because a fork in the road is not a one-time thing; had I not been there before with Nora the Norwegian of the racy undergarments before my intruding brother Luke stepped in to relieve me of my blunder? Because you never wanted the riptide of your lust to take you far from the one you loved, with drowning as your fate.

At the museum that day Vermeer and El Greco had no need of wide-ranging discourse, their significance resting in the paintings themselves, in one a woman dealing with the male gaze while in the other a garish and preposterous storm raged over Toledo. No one took issue with El Greco over the ridiculous flashiness of his name, which called for velvet pants and a cape and preposterous shoes. Vermeer, on the other hand, offered a name as smooth as butter and he was clearly content to live in the quiet spaces.

In leaving the museum that evening to start out for the renting office, I did notice that the paintings stayed behind so they could be alone and have the respectful silence and restorative darkness that they needed. They weren't exactly wild animals forced into captivity, but the strain was nonetheless there from all the viewing done of them, for even paintings need their time to weep in the privacy of darkness.

It was May, a month more promising than any other of a person's happiness. The cherry blossom trees were in full bloom and the lord of greenness had brought the grasses of Central Park to life. The clip clop of horses tugging hansom cabs and the angel din of children shrieking in their playground adventures could be heard as the park fought off the encroachments of a city gone mad with its own interpretation of necessity. And here I was still busy with the need to circumvent strangeness by staying American to the core.

The thing was to not go extreme north into the park so you could meet your death by gunshot or repetitive stabbing. The thing was to vacate the green at Eighty-sixth Street and say hello to Central Park West with its tall buildings and the doormen in uniform who maintained their stations through shifts that involved an acceptance of the language of stratification in which they had learned to live, for they were physical men able to carry the burden of obsequiousness into the bar for the boilermakers they drank to wash away the reality that they were sideshows in the tenants' lives and that love was not the thing on offer to them. I told them I knew the truth of their hurt and their uniformed sorrow, but they heard me not amid the ham sandwiches they relished so and the newspapers in which they daily stuck their faces.

It did not matter how you came upon the building, whether from north or south, east or west, its griminess remained apparent, as was the threat or promise of complete collapse. For the Columbias on loan to New York City before going on to live their dreams elsewhere, it was just a thing of apprehension to be given a moment's notice and peripheral to their destiny. They did not see the Furies in the form of my sisters upon the facing or hear the rumblings of discontent among the Third World populace housed within its fragile walls,

As I began my shift that evening, old tenants made an appearance, and new ones as well, but if Simon Weill showed his façe, he did so in a disguised manner and set off no earthquakes beneath my very feet. I offered those who came to me the justice they were seeking—security for the money that they forked over—and never thought to tell them they were a long way from home. The truth was that the faces came so fast and so often that they all became one face to me.

An hour into my shift I called Mona Pain. I got the usual two-ring sound, but I did not get Mona. It came to my sudden understanding that Mona had gone far beyond the borders of my security-seeking mind. I dialed again, and once again got the punishing sound of ring ring, and so the time had come to swing into more intense action with saturation dialing. Because I could see now where the mistake had been. In doing the things that I had done with Debussy and Mara, I had allowed my attention to Mona to wander, and now I was being savagely pummeled for this neglect by the rites of attacking spring, because Boston was having its mating season, too.

My escape route had been taken away. With the sudden sense that Mona had strayed I became frantic to leave the premises, for if she was gone then I had to be gone too so I wouldn't have to stay like Hannah and Naomi had stayed and Luke had come back to stay.

The cabs of New York City were vicious that night. First they ignored me with willful and malicious intent, and when one finally deigned to stop, he sought to thwart me with the indolence of his ways. Did he not consider that I might see him missing one light after another accidentally on purpose? Did he not consider that I might see the traffic tie-up he purposely led us into? Did he not consider the consequences for his mind and his heart should he continue to incite me?

I raced to my apartment, where I could be alone to do the repetitive dialing that the situation called for, with incremental happiness spreading through me that each Boston ring ring went unanswered. Yes, there was dread that she had gone and done me the dirt I deserved, but there was also excitement at the possibility that more endowed forces had been summoned to her bed.

She couldn't hide forever in the stalling place she had devised. The phone did get picked up, and the inquisition could begin.

She had been to visit Minerva, a new girlfriend. Minerva had made dinner, and they talked for hours. I asked for the name and address of the alleged Minerva, so my agents could begin the fact-checking process. The effect was immediate and profound. Now she had been with Minerva and Minerva's boyfriend, Lane, the genius artist whose father (yes, *his* father) owned half of Boston. The two of them had asked for the favor of her company.

So the real event of the late spring of 1970 was not Cambodia or the boom of bombs on rice fields or the fatal report of rifles at Kent State breaking the chests of all who dared be in their way. Nor was it Pete "Charlie Hustle" Rose sprinting to first base following a walk or the word "Cincinnati" with its heartbreaking capital C and the double "n" and the vowel that was supposed to close the deal but in fact led it into foreverness. It was the clobber she delivered because of my close questioning and the evasion routes she had been successfully sealed from. It was the clobber she delivered when even when the most artful evasion could not void the logic of my relentless investigative process.

"All right then. So I went to bed with him. It was the best sex I've ever had. At least he was with me."

These were the words she hit me with, so delicious in their force, and though I could quibble with her phrasing (best sex? It had the sound of cheapness upon it), they drove me through the walls of my apartment into the streets of Manhattan. I did not beg for mercy, but took the pain where it was coming from, many, many being the buses and trucks that ran over me before I arrived at a phone booth, from which I called Jesse, rousing him from sleep with the insistent ringing that New York City phones are known for in the hours after darkness has fallen.

"Everything is happening," I said.

"Nothing is happening," Buddha Breath said.

"Oh my heart that is unworthy, that feels nothing of what it should. Hanging string is here. Hanging String is calling out to the Buddha rock of eternity. Can you love a man without a tradition, who has no Torah to call his own? Can you see such a man, Jesse, be a friend to one such as me afflicted with solemnity?"

"I see you, my friend. I see you."

"My girlfriend is being boffed by the prince of Boston. His father is a magnate supreme and she has gone out into the wild nights calling and every cell in my body shrieks with pain and sexual excitation."

"What will you do?"

"Do? I will do what I have to do, but I don't know what that is."

Though the wisdom of the ages and historical perspective on suffering showed in Jesse's face, it failed to offer a buffer from my pain. There it lived in and on me through the night and laughed in my face, saying that my own flimsy ramparts constituted no defense at all.

In the morning my studies showed that no between the sheets action was likely under the sun, given the dictate of art that the call of the canvas came before the call of lust. And so I had a bit of time.

Before my departure for the airport, I had a long talk with Mrs. Muldooney, who assured me I would never be like her son because I lacked the integrity that he was showing in his life. "You're too soft, Sonny," Mrs. Muldooney said. "Whether it's life or art, you have to be able to put people down for good. You have to be able to close in and get the killing done. You also have to be a phony. That's what the world is looking for. People don't want the truth. They can't take the truth. They want lies. All successful people are fundamentally liars. That's why I never got off the garbage can. Because I can't tell a lie."

I thanked Mrs. Muldooney and boarded the airport bus to Port Authority. It felt good to be dealing with the business at hand, as it went without saying that Mona still had my heart in a viselike grip, and while it would have been hypocrisy to say she was playing with my affections, she was doubtless administering the soundest of poundings in the rough-and-tumble of what our life was now about. A sense of blackness came over me when the bus entered Queens, as it must over anyone passing through, let alone living within the blight of such a borough.

A plane was waiting for me on the tarmac. It was not presidential in its markings, but the captain—Bud Budley—promised to get the job done, and spoke from the full aspect of his Americanness. It quickly came to my attention that agents of industry were everywhere on the plane that morning, wearing suits that furthered their purpose and in possession of attaché cases with especially sharp corners, because documents essential to growth and prosperity needed a carrying case to confine them every bit as much as a body headed in the right direction needed the garments to clothe its hard-assed intentions.

I asked the stewardess if she knew that all the businessmen were scoping her butt as she passed down the aisle. Her name was Lucinda and she said she had a secret self that knew everything, that she could even visualize the point of her conception in a cornfield in Kansas. I told her, thinking of Mrs. Muldooney, that I was continually surprised by the things that people knew. Then I asked Lucinda if I could kiss her. I told her that my girlfriend had run off with another man whose father owned all but one block of Boston, and that while I was shattered, it would help me enormously if our lips could meet. Beyond her makeup was an honest woman with the strong Midwestern ability to apply her wares, and so we smooched it up good. Afterward I had a good cry and she offered me her bosom with the maternal care that she had summoned for the situation. At journey's end I thanked her profusely for being part of the bounty of America and for the lightness and efficiency and understanding that were trademarks of the people from the region of her birth.

Boston still had trees and streets with buildings upon them. It had its parks and pedestrians and children captive to their own excitement. It did not seek to match New York but rather to live apart from it in the knowledge that the two were ongoing even as their spaces were thrillingly apart. No one could adequately speak to the stirring quality of what it meant to be a Yaz with the big number 8 on his back and the all-out port-side swing and the rocket blast that followed from it, Yaz showing power to all fields and a pointed need to now and then tattoo the green monster and show it who was boss. Because Boston wasn't a city. Boston was a state of mind, even if it had its flowers and its northwesterly direction and a portion of the ocean to call its own. And though it was past the point of New York City, it too could have the springtime for its own rejuvenation, and the potential for people to fall in love on streets with names all their own, and whatever threats to its existence there might be were purely in the dark corners of time's malignant mind, for no one could say that Boston proper had intentions against itself. And to say it true and to say it loud was to say that all of Boston was calling out my name, from the margins of its own fear, but I was steadfast in the drive for consolidation of what my battered dream could be, just as Mona was struggling with the difficulties of her art, mine remaining the life I had to lead to get to where any semblance of art could begin.

Because all I had asked was that she be reliable, that she answer the phone, that she overrule the guidance of her own wisdom that told her to be vacant from the premises when I called, as if her utmost purpose was to stall me stall me stall me, to become a dawdle dancer when I needed the fullness of her presence, when the very stuff of life was the sounds she made and the corporeal being she offered and the spell she cast. And of course, in the way it had of doing, the earth answered me not when I directed my frustration to it.

The men of business had streaked on ahead for ground transportation. I knew enough not to compete with the ruthless horde in their taxi quest. Instead, I waited like a woman of refinement and soon was rewarded for my patience by a driver who took me down a bewilderment of streets, all of them bringing me closer to my humiliation as the now third party in this triangle. And yet to not appear would mean to be soon forgotten. Yes yes, the fat-lipped one was singing "Love in Vain" only too loud in my ear.

As I opened the big red door and entered the school, the collective resentment of the students and teachers in the hallways and studios struck me like a gale force wind. I heard them calling out my name as the bringer of death to life. Loud and clear did I hear the opprobrium of their bonded mindset. "You don't belong with this girl. Leave her alone. Let her grow in the way that she was intended to grow. Stop trying to deform her through containment." So did their aggrieved faces speak for them and cause me to stagger.

"How did you get on the right side of life? How did you do it?" I could only scream back, in response to their ostracizing efficiency.

There stood Mr. Brooks, Mona's erstwhile teacher, chatting with an almond-eyed girl in paint-splattered chinos. Mona had filed reports with me of the incessant activity of this girl to move Mr. Brooks from Mona's sphere into her own and of the appropriating moves she was employing toward this artful and socially rapacious end, and so I was left to see the paradigm of social failure as the inevitable outcome for all infected by me, even Mona. She had seen his paintings absent the breath of life, paintings now relegated to the attic as the things he could not quite let go of but which he escaped from each morning as he escaped from his wife into the land of distraction and giving called teaching, because if he could not be young, at least he could be among the young, and if he could not have the energy of the young, at least he could be around it. Because many were the days that Mr. Brooks reached the place of despair and the quiet cry that led to surrender to the fact of his dying, and he could, from the abyss, be restored to a measure of gratitude for what he did have—the house, the wife, the children, the intellect. There was no fault-finding of Mr. Brooks for the circumspect attention that he brought to bear on Mona, no fault-finding of the restraint he showed in not making the first move, his policy being to leave it to her, leave it to all of them, to step across that line and engage with him if they dared. Because he did not want the police to come and arrest him. He did not want a life that involved public shame and the ruin that came with it.

I knew there was no reaching out to him, that I was not in the echelon required for his esteem, given the poor features that I carried about. And so I pushed on, the walls lined with bulletin boards covered with for sale signs, apartment shares, art shows, reflecting the transitional nature of the students' lives. (Parents had driven many miles to deposit their children here, some with grave doubts about the income their offspring could earn given that art was to the sidelines of what life truly was. And yet the fact remained that you could be from Ohio or Nebraska and still come to Boston, it was that open and inclusive, and the street on which the museum school stood so quiet and easy to retire into, with the museum itself just down the way to provide granite backup and the ducks upon the water just across the road making their own contribution.)

No one, to my knowledge, has recorded the precise time, but it was in that deeper penetration of the Museum School that I saw him, saw him as the point beyond which I could not go, once the sighting was made, for Lane stood as an immovable impediment, the girls in the adoration circle around him merely filling it out. Oh, it was all there—the richly black hair longer than I had remembered in that first fleeting glance at him near the Brattle Theater those years before and the compact body proportioned for success and the bell-bottom jeans and blue work shirt and low-cut black Converse sneakers that he gave new meaning to by virtue of who he was in his full measure beyond the tanned face and arms and the kissable mouth. Many were those who were now bowing down to him. Many were they who would be compelled to write of him in national magazines. Reports were already flowing in on the lightness of his being, of the Mozart-like quality of play infused in his art, relegating others to the status of Salieri (Mr. Brooks, are you listening?) with his boldness, and if envy squadrons were a potential complicating factor, those who harbored such soreness in their beings kept it behind the admiration pose that all were compelled to adopt. He was to be seen as one who never averted his eye or countenanced intimidation in any form; rather, he would gently inquire what you had in mind when you said such and such a thing as a starting point toward further exploration, for he knew how to penetrate beyond the façade in both his life and his work, and passively had a part to play in the unseen magnets that pulled you toward him. All this was made obvious.

And so, yes, I was one of those who fell down weeping, stricken, by the full shock of recognition of all he was with his vibrant flesh and mind, because to be in his presence was to be in pain over all that America and God had not given me. I was on my knees for many centuries before I could stand. At some point he looked beyond his circle to find me. In an instant he recorded all the data he needed to possess and thanked me with a knowing smile. It was a knowingness I nevertheless surmounted, talking thusly:

"You are a prince of darkness and yet you carry lightness in your being. You fill your jeans so well while my legs are lost in mine. Your every move is the right one while I am a dog in the rain in constant need of a hydrant for my urine stream. You have shown me your glitter and your star-struck retinue as you amalgamate rock legend and art hero. And yet, even so will I slay you with the mediocrity of my persistent being so death cannot be assigned me through your agency. And already I see the fear filming your shining mega eyes as I assault you with this proclamation of my intention." I stopped myself short in pointing a finger at him, and when that didn't do the trick, I called on all my fingers to be pointed in his direction to suggest the firepower at my disposal as I backed out the front door, but not before issuing an all points bulletin for the missing Mona.

In response a girl with a drawing pad under her arm volunteered a clue as to her whereabouts, saying that Mona was still reeling from her bed time with Lane. "It's that way with all of us who have been experienced by Lane. We're never quite the same," she said in a subdued voice. Seeing that I had both ears cupped to maximize my listening devices and as a sign of the deep value I placed on her communication, she went on: "Cambridge. Jean-Luc Godard. Got it?"

I gave her the thumbs up, and then gave her the double thumbs up and a nod of furious comprehension.

The title *Breathless* on a Cambridge movie marquee prompted my heart to race. I knew the name Jean-Luc Godard and could put the two together, having seen the film. I had heard Jean-Paul Belmondo say "As you like it, baby." I had seen the revolutionary short hair of Jean Seberg, and the ideal of the androgynous girl she had forever placed in my mind. And those Gauloises.

Slowly my eyes adjusted to the darkness of the theater. Amid the empty seats I saw scattered about a few solitaries, all of them men. Farther down, seated on the aisle, there she was.

I alerted her to my arrival with a hand upon her shoulder. She only leaped four feet.

"No, no" she gasped. Perplexity and amazement reigned in her face, where none should have been, if only she had maintained a firm grasp of my investigative strength. In any case, now it was for her to appreciate the demented power of my global reach.

"What is wrong with you? I go to a movie and you ruin it by tracking me down like the insane person you are. What are you going to do, kill me?"

The truth being that to see Belmondo on a Paris street with Jean Seberg as his apprentice in folly was to see life itself. And it really was only that for Mona, seeing movies once a week and giving all her energy to her art and her future in that glitter world. No sleepless nights in terror about my whereabouts. No anguish that I might be with someone else. No days dominated by thoughts of me. Not since the spring of 1967, when everything was going my way and Mick Jagger was singing "Under My Thumb" in thrall to his own vanity and men could cling to the fantasy of their personal dominion circle. *He likes you more than you like him.* It was just as Claire had offhandedly observed.

"I am not here for savagery. I am in need of vanquishing the pain in the way that I can. It is a fire with tremendous flames attached to it, and burns unending with the fuel that it has been given. Can you not smell the stink of my flesh? Can you not see that this pain has been crying out for a face-to-face?"

A call came from someone for us to quiet down, and so we went outside, where she looked around. Was she about to summon a posse of the falsely concerned, to shame me further, as she had that time in Harvard Square?

"You have to leave me alone. You're not what I want."

"Yes. Very yes yes." I stared up at the blue sky. Such a gorgeous day. Such a pretty treelined street. And where was I but in the toilet, emotionally speaking.

She hurried off and I didn't pursue. Next door to the theater was a submarine shop. Not a hero shop. Not a hoagie shop. A submarine shop. It was all right for Boston/Cambridge to have its peculiarities. It was all right, I say.

I ordered a ham and provolone with lettuce and tomatoes. I needed to eat. I needed to get filled up so I would not be a total bag of bones on the earth or disappear in plain sight.

I returned to New York that same day. Mrs. Muldooney was waiting for me on the garbage can. "Don't say anything, Sonny. I can see you haven't fixed the problem. When you're ready, just give me the word. My son knows how to get the job done."

From the start you have to reject the counsel of the ungodly and go your separate way if murder of a loved one is not to be a part of your life. Hampered by acute anxiety, I nevertheless sat for many centuries considering the problem. An affair that has been waiting to happen, when it comes to fruition, has consequences that cannot be easily dissolved. Action, not passivity, would have to be a constant.

When the same pattern of willful disobedience showed itself, when the phone rang and rang with not a thought of departing from its ring ring sound, there could be no alternative but further intervention under my own supreme command. Between a person's plan and its execution will always stand the dawdler and outright obstructionist, the malefactor, the one with a perverse allegiance to his or her own thwarting ways. Through all the annals of time this has been recorded, and having dealt with them before, it was for me to explore the treachery of their systems and appropriate their undermining devices so progress with my intention could be made.

Suffice it to say that I performed such confiscation from the person of the LaGuardia Airport-bound hackie, and did the same with the cockpit crew of the Eastern Airlines shuttle. Sound direction and firm instruction are beneficial, but let it not be assumed that travail and fierce resistance were not experienced in the pursuit of discipline in the ranks of those whose single purpose should have been the facilitation of my path. I beamed my contempt at the cockpit crew as they dawdled on the airport runway, thinking they could stay between the blue lights of the tarmac when forward motion must always be the goal of the real world. Over the fuselage I sat with the knowledge that they persisted in stalling me *just quit stalling me,* the iniquity impulses they found it so very hard to lay to rest in full evidence.

'We'll be airborne before midnight, is that right? Or has this become an overnight flight? I just need to know, so I can create new categories for the crimes you are committing." The stewardess pretended to hear me not. She only had ears for the mini-bottles of scotch I ordered to put me in the mood for love.

Unlike the state of mind I had possessed on my daylight trip, I was frantic to witness the nocturnal amour now surely in progress. The taxi driver, however, had his own intention, steering us into a tunnel tie-up. The airline bottles had packed a punch, and gave me the courage to start zzz-ing the cabbie. I sent them streaming into the back of his hairy neck.

"What are you, some kind of human saw?"

"I'll turn off my hardware when you get us out of here."

"Traffic is traffic. What am I supposed to do?"

"Sawing is sawing. What am *I* supposed to do?"

The building was in alignment with the school, taking the same side of the street with it. Yes, it had its students, with their vision of what art could be, as well as older people with their bags of groceries and constant meditations on the word *infirmity*. The older folks did not resent the young. They were merely invigorated by their energy, and it struck them as a marvel of modernity that they could live above them and below them in the same enclosed space.

Lane stood in the lobby, a beautiful sentry anticipating the arrival of the loathsome one. His father was the building owner. Lane did not wear the family's title on his person; he just showed it on his face. Farmer's overalls clothed his frame, the denim duds a fashion statement on his lean, athletic frame. Underneath he was shirtless; only thick straps over his bare shoulders. A hint of who he was without clothes was further given by the bit of chest and shoulders exposed. So tanned. So firm but soft. His eyes took me in. I had no defense against them.

"Are you here to kill her?" He spoke the words softly, as an artist would.

"No," I said.

"I would be more than happy to fight you."

Even in my drunkenness I saw that he was Mr. Out There, the man who had transcended relationships, that life was as open to him as it was closed to me. He was addressing me in the language of my past, the language of the fists that had no place in his civil life.

I climbed the stairs, feeling no anger toward him because my right to it was not there. And even with his gentleness, he would put a beating on me if I dared to accept his challenge. I was in too much pain to feel humiliated.

I remember the lateness of the hour and the key in the lock and my need for possession of her. I remember pushing her back on the mattress and the temporary relief that came with orgasm. I remember the morning when, her face bruised, she said, "You raped me. You raped me."

Chapter 74

Repellent elements of my being were now in sharper focus. Gathered were the brigades of the scornful, including the reviling female nation seeking to pull me into a vortex of endless self-hate. To avoid the fate of a condemning chorus in perpetuity, I flew high over the abysses to mitigate the suctioning power that such mass judgment can exert.

All the while Dr. Zimmer rode my coattails. She was increasingly hard for me to fathom, for underneath her German persona of factual analysis was a woman riding high on the promptings of love. I tried to tell myself that none of this had to matter so long as Three Dog Night kept up its holler singing.

I came to her in my nakedness, and with it brought the power of full disclosure. I told her of the vileness I had shown Mona as a way of reining in her impulses in the direction of the hegemonist genius who went by the name of Lane. I told her I had forcibly invaded Mona's spaces and that nothing could stop my heart of stone. I asked Dr. Zimmer if she could still love me, knowing as she did that I was now a rapist as well as a thief. To my surprise, she lay down her self for me and cried tears of pity over many centuries in downplaying the verdict that Mona had rendered.

The bag of stinky stuff that I had offered Dr. Zimmer was not the bag where my real stuff was truly stored, she seemed to be saying.

I continued on with the assertion that while I still was driven by the American dictate to be number one in the universe, I felt that I was sinking lower than whale poop, but that a study of excrescence had to be ruled out for the simple reason that it could only lead to sustained horror at the stink hole condition of both man and beast.

I continued on, confessing to her that my mission here on earth, lunar landscapes notwithstanding, was to live and die in New York City and stay close to my moms for the warfare that was coming in the showdown with Simon Weill, that it was for me to slay the dragon and show no mercy for his particulars in consolidating what had to be mine. I told her that I could not reside in the far country of Boston, that to do so was to leave my power base, like Antaeus taken from his earth mother Hera. I told her lightning would have to strike me dead before I would be rendered in that forlorn state, that I had been given the necessity of sinking into the reality of my origins even if all I could hope for were glimmers of it.

Apropos the above there was the serendipitous night with the Van Dine clan that we went to the Galli-Curci Theater (America having gone completely wild with the name thing) in the tiny town of Margaretville, and, with the smell of buttered popcorn permeating the space, had seen an austere film of the Orient, a thing called *Woman in the Dunes,* with ramifications profound for a psyche in need of rearrangement, for there I had met my mentor, an amateur entomologist on holiday from his city base to an island where the people lived in dunes to escape the torment of high winds and other imaginable hardships of nature, the island being for him a blessed location for the practice of his meticulous avocation. Nowhere in his itinerary was it written that he had to stay on the beaten path. He simply went where the insects could be found, having traps and other devices set up for their arrival. A turning came when the villagers lowered him into a dune via a ladder. There he found shelter with a widow. Having discovered the next morning that the ladder had been removed, he tried but failed to climb his way to freedom (hah), the friable sand, like the ceaseless wind, insubstantial as a toehold to the firmer ground above, let alone heaven. With the desperation of a captured insect beating its wings against a cage, he tried to claw his way up the dune. Exhausted after a time, he began to survey his surroundings, and slowly was he moved forward to a place of acceptance.

I told Dr. Zimmer of being stunned by this film I had seen the year before, I who was so ruled by anxiety. In that theater in that forlorn town was I introduced to the self I could not yet be, the self that could actually be where his feet were.

It was also for Dr. Zimmer to hear of a dream in which I sat at a table on the patio outside the law school to which I was about to give my life. I was there with Doug Doug and Bruce Bruce and Kent Kent, three who had been given the savage freedom of first names serving as the engine and caboose on their identity trains and who were inclined to leave me on the fringes of their conversation and crunch me in their system of cowardly ostracism. And yet, when my demise was imminent, a goddess emerged from nearby woodland. The blue sky above had been turned into a panoramic screen on which was written *I Can Take You Beyond the Stars*. With the soft touch of her hand on my shoulder, she said only this: "Why are you here, Precious?"

When I informed my goddess that I had to be on the straight and narrow so my life could live, she whispered, with silken femininity, "How common," her warm breath offering me the promise of not so hidden delights before leading me back toward the woodland, leaving Mr. Doug Doug and Mr. Bruce Bruce and Kent Kent to themselves and their own mediocre aspiration.

Dr. Zimmer, as was her way, raised up on me, first firing musket balls and fusillades from other antiquated weaponry before turning to more sophisticated firepower from her vanquished German army. Yes, she fired and fired. An ill-fitting yet riveting Kraut helmet on her head, she shouted over the noise of her explosive weaponry exhortations as profound as they were abysmal: "Stay with your law school Doug and your law school Bruce and your law school Kent. Do not follow a temptress into the jungle of desire."

"Now that you have deceased me and Mona has deceased me, I should go away, far away, to another country, as you did. But where is there to reinvent myself, but in America?"

"You will stay here with me, foolish young man. You will stay here with me."

Hearing those words did I cry and cry before finding my way home.

Chapter 75

Are you surprised to hear that Mona did not take her love away? Are you surprised to hear that she came back to me, rapist and thief and all-around abuser that I was? Are you questioning her sanity? Are you right now running to the phone to call the police on me?

I laugh like the hyena that I am at your self-righteousness and pretense of humanity.

Now can we go on? Can we?

The need to leave America was very strong. If I could not move to Boston, I could at least go elsewhere, in my need for separation from the building and all those it was claiming for its own. No lightning flashes of genius thought were required to recognize that the building itself was granting me my freedom through the money I extracted so I could do the gallivanting thing.

I unstrapped the building from my back. I unstrapped America from my back and took myself and Mona where we needed to go.

Years later, I would express arrogant ideas of what it meant to be an American in Europe. The need to boast would cause me to assert that any American with Americanness in him would emphatically say, on seeing the French Alps, that he could survive a plunge into the deepest crevasse and back-flip down the mountainside with no sweat. I would feel compelled to assert supremacy over all that had come before and throw out Rococo clutter for streamlined purity—the supermarket aisle and the deli delight.

Our progress was measurable. We were doing what I couldn't do when Harvard Man was on her premises and genius Lane walked in through her front door.

The plane was fragile and, to my eye, unusually long, even for a jet. It had noticeable dents in its fuselage and the look of aluminum fragility. An alumni charter, the plane did not go lavender, the school color, but held to its silver coat. Mona and I took our seats equipped with matching red backpacks on lightweight frames that I had purchased as a symbol of our togetherness at an army-navy store.

We arrived at Gatwick Airport in London at dawn, the skies above the clouds becoming light before we dropped below them to see fields of cultivated beauty established on the English soil. We saw no hint of Wordsworth in a green glen, but he was there all the same, and our captain brought us to attention with a crackling voice of authority that our landing was imminent.

The authorities were waiting for us wearing ties and English skin, and though the words they used were the same as ours, they put a sound on them that made them different and above what we were speaking, as if to say they were proprietors of the language. I showed myself as dutiful and compliant with their power so they would know how respectful and loving I could be, and yet even so did they question me roughly about the purpose of my visit.

"I am here to apprehend my own truth and to see the mindless pomp of Buckingham Palace. I assure you that I am not here to kill any Redcoats."

"And might we ask if you have any history of killing Redcoats?"

"In another century I fought hard with the Continental Army. Many times we routed you in preserving the freedom of our fledgling nation. As you can see, I stand before you as an American through and through."

"I believe it says so right here on your passport."

"A certifiable American, and growing more American every day."

"Your name doesn't say you're American. Your name says you're a bloody Armenian."

"That is not a name. That is a weight. My real name is I, as in inviolate."

'Please take your name and move on, and don't make any trouble in our country. We have some lads who will take care of you if you do."

Mona took my arm and shot the men of authority a look, suggesting they had better watch their arses.

We saw the film *Easy Rider* in a London theater, where it was showing as part of a worldwide epidemic. The film clearly had as its purpose to lay the groundwork for American violence to assert itself. It also served as a vehicle for Peter Fonda to show off his big forehead with his hair slicked back and for Dennis Hopper to make fringed suede jackets all the thing. But it was Jack Nicholson who captured us with the intelligence of his face and sound. (Yes, it was very clear, even in the movie, that Peter Fonda was just his father's little boy.) We rode with Captain America—we rode with them all. We saw them in the whorehouse of their dreams and on their acid trip fantastic, and we saw how they aired it out on their choppers divine on roadways forever primed for carnage. And then we saw the meanness of the pinched night as under its cover one was hacked with blades honed for producing martyrdom. Oh we didn't so much see as hear the thud thud thud of the axes impacting with flesh and bone. Where there had been three with the bright drunken ascendance of Jack Nicholson, there were now only two again, Captain America and Mr. Intensity streaking down the hot two-lane road of freedom with faces scarred by the imposition of small-town American peeve imposed upon them. Something about the stretch of road they were on, something about the heat, something about the shimmering currents of air and the coldness of the filmmaker himself in setting them on the road to perdition summoned in us foreboding. Further signs were the pickup truck passing in the opposite direction and its fateful turn let us know that resoluteness was vying with lethal capacity and that men of low character were on the scene. We saw them as they pulled alongside the hogs of Captain America and his loyal sidekick and saw what accompanied them, the shotgun and the blasts from its barrel to send them careering off the road on their journey to kingdom come.

Outside the theater Mona burst into tears, brought to weeping by the axing execution of Jack Nicholson and the feeding of redneck bullets to Dennis Hopper and Peter Fonda and the knowledge that the patriarchs had vicious agents bent on hitting and hitting very hard. She saw me in that moment as the victim that I wasn't and more points were added when a royal guard at Buckingham Palace got rank with me for trying to explore an off-limits area.

Because yes, everywhere we went that summer, we were to see the film *Easy Rider* playing in the great cities of London and Paris and on dusty strips on the plains of Spain, for America was bombing bombing bombing with its planes of war and culture from the right and from the left, it did not matter, the point was only to bomb and bomb and then to bomb some more.

What it meant that she burst into tears on a London street was not that she loved Peter Fonda and Dennis Hopper with any great love; she would have easily seen through them. It was just that she saw the violence at the heart of the America that was coming our way, now that the government had taken off the gloves and was punching very hard at the lawlessness it claimed to be abounding. And she saw too that with 1969 come and gone a darker and crueler ethos had begun.

Skinheads were everywhere, bristle-headed and stomp-booted, serving as eye-catching examples of menace and anger. You saw them in Trafalgar Square, where you shot a scene of kids around a fountain with your Nikon F camera. You used only black and white film because you wanted to be serious about your photography, and understood in a shocking moment that the England of your imagination did not exist, that it was not built on the Magna Carta alone but on aggression and brutality, that you were somehow a prisoner of the images you received. You wanted the tonal values of Eugene Smith and Cartier-Bresson and those of their ilk, not just vacation snapshots. Going into the tube after an excursion to Piccadilly Circus, you heard young voices carrying a tune just behind you, a tune you slowly realized was meant for your ears only. "I'm forever blowing bubbles," they gently yet tauntingly sang. It took some time for the realization that there were razors hidden in their soft voices. You turned and looked into the faces of Kick, Punch, and Gouge, clear-eyed youthful faces with strong, handsome features that not even shaved heads could negate. They bulled past you in their jeans and spiked wristbands and black stomp boots. In a less crowded place they would have hit you, you knew, hit you till you went down, and then they would have had a party on your body. Secretly, you couldn't get enough of them. When, on the tube, you saw one, fifteen or sixteen, a contemporary Teddy Boy in white T-shirt and leather jacket, you wanted to interview him, to know how he had come to be graced with the electric spark of malign divinity. You wanted to know how he had gotten so out there, so defined in his stance toward the world. You wanted to know these things, lanky, flat-headed travel-book-toting American boy/man tied to his immigrant mother's pocketbook.

On the day we were to leave for once mighty France, an incident occurred. It involved the appropriation of Mona's gold locket, a keepsake from her mother she wore to burn her flesh. We had taken lodgings on Belgrave Road near the Pimlico Station, away from the trouble that Piccadilly Circus, in the lulling silliness of its name, was waiting to inflict. Everywhere class warfare was beyond the stage of muted rivalry.

Alerted to this grave international incident, I made a gentle inquiry at the front desk, but only after an exhaustive search. The fact was established that the locket had last been seen on the dresser, and now was out of the owner's sight. An elegant statement of the facts that left no room for implication was gently laid upon the clerk. All we truly sought to convey was that the locket had *vanished.* And with the emphasis that we gave that word came the look of intense focus we dared to offer, causing him to step back in the face of the momentum toward justice that our inquiry had initiated. Because though we were American, we had words as well, and knew how to torture them forward for the occasion. By now the world was watching in wonder as his tie curled up upon his chest. But as England always has, he came back strong, saying he would report the matter to the cleaning man.

Mona swung into a more combative kind of verbal action. "I want my locket back. Got it?" She did not send him into the ocean. She just placed him against the wall. Still, the fact remained that he was English, and no Englishman, regardless of his station, stays against the wall forever. Rather, he came off it in possession of his face and tongue.

"Am I to understand that you are making an accusation?" he said, going high with his tone and his construction.

"Was that an eyebrow that you just raised?" Mona asked.

"Whatever do you mean?"

"Whatever do *you* mean, baby?" She retorted, having the right to call herself a nation, too. She returned to the room, as did I, each of us giving him looks of full significance for so long as he remained in our sight.

With the door locked and our privacy assured, we had a discussion of the nature of truth as it affected English people in particular, Mona being unhappy with the desk clerk's performance in the matter of disclosure. Their passionate consumption of bangers and mash and black pudding and all the rest led us, curiously enough, to focus our attention on the cleaning man. From our window we observed our suspect in his pale blue smock smoking a cigarette in the courtyard below. Was it not the nature of such laborers to explore the intimate apparel of the occupant, particularly should she hold a place of loveliness in their mind? Could the cleaning man be any different, even if there was paleness in his features and reserve in his nature? An edifice of deceit had been constructed, we decided, because reserve was the persona you had to adopt, having received the privilege, through the station of lowness, of access to a lady's delicates. At the same time it saddened me that a man of such potential nobility should be reduced to such a state, even as I identified with the innate curiosity of the male as to the world of the feminine. Where the clerk came in we couldn't be sure, except with the sympathetic vibration he offered in support of the cleaning man's operation.

Soon the cleaning man stood in the doorway in all his features, a middle-aged man with short reddish hair, the neck of a bull, and a sober look on his wide, freckled face. You are too large, too manly, to be a cleaning man, I wanted to say, but instead began my line of inquiry.

"What in your nature makes you a cleaning man? Have you been set out to pasture? Are the more active fields of this earth of no interest to you?"

"Sir?"

"Your nature. Something in your nature has led you to this work?"

"Sir?"

"Sir, we are talking about the nature essential to cleaning, that is, the establishment of order where once there had been chaos and filth. We are talking about the propensity to *tidy up*. Do you understand? There are those whose function in life it is to break new ground, and then there are those whose function it is to see that order obtains in all the places of their lives. So tell me, please, how a man of your manly bulk comes to be in the latter category."

"A man needs a living wage, sir."

"You took my locket. You placed its heart shape in your large hand." This was the voice of Mona, interrupting my inquiry.

"Madam?"

"My locket. You took it for your own."

"Allow me to understand. You are suggesting I stole your locket?"

"I just tell it like it is, baby." Mona glared at the man with hands on her hips.

"And you too, sir? You as well accuse me of taking the young woman's locket?" A troubled look had replaced his placid expression, and a tremor accompanied the anger in his voice.

"Our investigation is ongoing. All we know at this point is that the locket is missing, sir."

Stony-faced, the cleaning man made an abrupt departure. In his absence it began to cry out for acknowledgment that the world had gone one way and he had been able to go another, living apart from the dictates of the ego and the world that he be *somebody,* as if he had never heard Herman's Hermits or the Dave Clark Five or any of the legends of rock calling the drama of his own life to attention. No, the cleaning man had not done that. He had not been galvanized into action by the forces of popular music. The cleaning man had found a way to exist in the afternoon shadows with his pack of fags and had the structure of his tasks to sustain him.

And yet it registered like acid burn that he had stolen the heart-shaped locket from the one and only Mona in the appropriation drive that would allow men to take from her what she would not give them otherwise.

Let me put it this way. Shame engulfed my being when Mona retrieved the heart-shaped locket from the bottom of her knapsack. Both the clerk and the cleaning man had vacated the premises by the time of this discovery, and while Mona did not sing in a particularly remorseful key, I understood that from here unto eternity the cleaning man and I would now be bonded for the injury I had caused him by the look of disgust he had placed upon me.

Having done London town, we took the train to Dover, and it gave my mind some ease to have an appointed destination, for that's what rails were for, to keep you on the straight and narrow. The motion of the train served as a sedative because without the rails to direct me I could easily lose my bearings and fill with anger like a helpless child.

And then a ferry took us. We stood in the prow as the wide-bodied vessel felt its way through the channel fog, the white cliffs of Dover soon gone from view. Now and then a blast of the foghorn would carry on the damp air. The wind was becoming personal, with a downward snap of whiplike harshness, and drove us indoors, where Froggy waiters slashed in tight white jackets between linen-covered tables, their trays held aloft with one hand. No one had schooled them to have such authoritative coldness in their eyes and haughty bearing amid the gastronomic smells saturating the air; it was all au naturel.

"Nous sommes besoin de manger. Nous sommes Americain," I shouted, over the din and despite the looks they shot me for what they assessed as preposterous hair. We were in their element now, the civilized table affair, and if America had overreached itself with its incessant bombing from the air and its Coca-Cola strength, so too had I with my hair too long and my frame too thin for their compact elegance to accept. "Je vous prie," I screamed, but the intensity of their activity only increased, where if once they had been streaking, now they were a complete blur. "Je vous prie encore," I shouted, my words blown out of the dining hall and overboard. "Eats, my man, eats," I was driven to cry out. There were no overturned tables, nor did I trip the waiters to bring them to attention. I simply conceded the ostracizing nature of their Froggy ways and went outside, where prudence directed me to go.

Mona had no choice but to leave as well, and when she did, we dialogued between ourselves. The cold was now in my bones and my hunger was rampant at the sight, through the window, of the Frenchies serving up their boeuf bourguignon and coq au vin with buckets of Beaujolais.

An empty stomach and soreness go together, and not even the fog could blind me to her wandering. "Want to cause some more chaos? Is it time for more of your growth? Have you moved further into the realm of expansion? No one should ever ever keep you from that." Because the weight of Lane was on me and trying to break more than my bones.

"It's my fault that I'm in love with a genius? I love everything about him. I love his talent. I love his clothes. I love his smell. I love the way he is with me and yet detached. I love him, not you. You're nothing. How is it that you don't see that? And now that we're approaching France, the time will be coming for you to murder me, as you promised to do. I haven't forgotten your claim on me. I haven't forgotten that at all."

Her mention of the knife filled me with fear. She was saying that the time was coming for the end. But that was the end she assigned. It was not my own, even if I couldn't help but believe her given the prophecy she unleashed. I did not weep. I had no feelings worthy of discussion. I had only my own earned notoriety and the foghorn blowing and the fog remaining steadfast with the shortsightedness it imposed.

The knife was not in me in Paris. I looked within myself but it did not show. Although she had thrown at me the prowess of the genius in the realm of sex, she did not announce she would be going off to Greece to rendezvous with him as a way of provoking me into losing my head and finding the knife with which to do the fatal deed.

The French left little trails of disdain when they passed you on their wide boulevards and tight streets, rushing by on their way to brilliant salons and dinners for ten. They had social ways they had built up over centuries and seized every minute and made it theirs. There was no American ranginess to be seen in them. They had smaller, finer builds, and minds designed for complicated conversations. Their days were packed and their nights featured nonstop revelry and always concluded in l'amour.

Everywhere I saw people smoking Gauloises and longed to draw the smoke from the coarse-smelling tobacco into my lungs. But I had thrown away my Marlboros before boarding the plane. I didn't know why. It had something to do with wanting to be clean amid the pollution I was feeling.

I became sick the first night in Paris. It was more the pizza than the wine. I made it to a pissoir on the way back to the Hotel d'Etrangeres in the Quartier Latin, and then continued my misery in the w.c., where I puzzled over something that was an approximation of a toilet.

"That's a bidet," Mona said. "The French insist on the cleanliness of their women. It's a national obsession."

The British had bad teeth and went about in dirty clothes, while the French had small eyes and stingy ways and showed a fierce passion for their snails. Still, they were a bastion of normalcy against the hairy and Armenian tendencies of my father's brethren to the east. And then there were the Swedes to the north, who ate sticks of butter so they could have blond hair and that skin that tanned so very well, all of them operating in the beautiful black and white of a Bergman movie and speaking a musical tongue and maintaining a more than respectable gene pool of which I could be proud in the dignity of their isolation. In any case, I was doing my research; that was for sure.

We went each morning to a sidewalk café for café au lait and un croissant, s'il vous plait. I made a point of placing my hands on the table, so Mona could see what they were up to, but otherwise didn't preoccupy myself with appearing more innocent than I was. We had a vantage point from our table to see the outdoor kisses that the Parisians gave, though many had vacated the city's confines, the month being August. The air smelled of Gauloises and the emissions of Citroens and Renaults, with their names that finished strong. Of course, the cobblestones over which they rolled had a song to sing, and no one should tell you different, while the Seine offered a calming influence on frayed French nerves. Altogether the city was operating from a sense of who it was, the citizenry with an unspoken but palpable awareness of what the word *connection* just might mean.

The Eiffel Tower was a surprise, its color the earth brown of a tasteful man's suit and its size immense above the *arrondissement* over which it rose in a sudden declaration of its being. It had no secrets to conceal; from below its concave yearnings you could see right up its metal skirt.

In exploring Paris we discovered it was best to keep to the streets that we could find, and if we came upon the Luxembourg Gardens or Notre Dame or the Champs Elysée, so be it. In this way did we stumble upon the Louvre and a man lying in his own blood. The story was told of a Citroen that had bashed him good and sent him to his cobblestone bed. No, the driver had not stopped or cried remorseful tears, for he had a destination to meet at the other end of town. Other cars had followed in its savage path, and even now were racing within millimeters of the man's bleeding head, nothing able to stop the forward motion they so needed to maintain to their trysting destinations. Only after his demise did the back and forth of the eeh hah eeh hah of the ambulance emerge, over loud discussions regarding Descartes and Sartre.

The boulevards and the leaves on the trees that lined those boulevards, the buildings of the *ancien regime* and the newer additions, the light at night on the cobblestone streets. I wanted to say I had been here before, if only in a dream.

The train took its time along the plain to Madrid. It went in fits and starts and showed itself content to sit in the hot sun. At the border we had made a change. The trains of Spain ran on wider gauge track than the trains of France so the trains of France could not go into Spain and hurt the Spanish where they lived. Nor could the trains of Spain journey into the territory of France and hurt the Frenchies where they lived. Europe was eyes of wariness peeking from behind a curtain and the words *ancient enmity* in everyone's heart. And yet, in the border collaboration that they were effecting, I watched the two nationalities in workers' garb go at it, and saw not a single sign of strife, not even discord of a silent nature, show its face. The two words *French* and *Spanish* screamed for a meditation on how they could be brought closer together beyond their names appearing side by side.

Somewhere I had read that the light in Spain was dazzlingly clear, and so I kept my eyes open to confirm that the phenomenon was true. "Never before have I seen such clarity of light," I said to Mona in rushing to embrace this assertion, even as it was revealed to me that while Spain stood for something in the hot sun, we could truly only understand it in the darkness of her night.

We waited for the motion of the train to resume before dealing with our hunger. Once underway, we entered an elegant dining car with dark-wood paneling and tables set with linen tablecloths and linen napkins and polished silver, all of it laid out in expectation of a different kind of patron, to judge by the look on the dignified face of the waiter who stood with gravitas in his formal wear and who was, like his dining car, from a time gone by, the word *character* intrinsic to his bearing.

I had no Spanish to offer him, beyond *cerveza* and *vente, meda,* and *arriba arriba*, nor did Mona, and so we were reduced to pointing to items on the menu. Yes, it was a humiliation to be seen as just another imperious American imposing English on the citizenry of Spain, but I did not ask him to beat me. I did not ask him a single thing. He brought us back giant plates full of the meats of Spain and sauces that went back centuries, food clearly out of proportion to the way we looked and acted. We ate the serious food of Spain and then were comatose for hours, in which I dreamed that at the end of every train line, no matter how far-flung, the mothers of Spain were waiting for their railroad sons, ready to absorb all the fury they had mustered.

Madrid was not without its modernity, the sight of which left Mona aghast, for she too was threatened by the new, and so we fled to the old city, where we could be protected from the forward trends of life. The sun was a torment, burning us where it could and causing our blood to boil. With such heat no further explanation was needed for the vision of hell that dominated the land.

"All you care about is your own comfort," Mona said, in reply to my ill temper, which did not stop us from finding a place near Plaza Mayor, a square with seventeenth-century buildings serving as a lure for the tourist-minded.

From the slatted window that opened onto the street we watched as young Spanish men announced themselves to the women who passed by. We saw a caballero break off from the pack and pursue his prey in a demonstration of his testosterone fervor. When, face to face with those whom he was seeking, he began to suffer the depletion of his resources, he ran himself back to those who had given him the courage to perform his cock strut in the first place. This we saw thanks to the streetlights compromising the darkness that had overtaken Madrid. Having witnessed the tight street where the assaultive proposition had manifested, Mona hurled her American words, calling upon the aggressive cowardice of the caballeros to surrender itself immediately.

"You sons of bitches wear your dicks outside your pants in this country," Mona screamed down at them, hitting the group in all their sensitive places so that they had no choice but to look up. Their fingers had become knives as a physical expression of their honed anger and made slicing motions across their throats and shouted words that broke the language barrier with their fury. Mona in her American way was not afraid to fly down into their midst and confront their Old World girlie action. I had to hold her tight and love her never more than then for our lives to continue into another day. Lorca, Goya, Velasquez, all of them made their presence felt in the event that action was to commence, though Cervantes was nowhere to be seen. Only the arrival of other female tourists diverted the caballeros from an international incident.

The next day we cowered under the noonday sun; frazzled and fried, we were driven back to our room. Shadows were not permitted in Spain. There was lightness or the dark. Correspondingly, there was only love and hate, the kiss and the stick. When we could we left the room for the corrida and the spectacle of the enraged bull charging the toreador and the question was not to be posed as to why one must die so the other could live. The bull had horns that seemed to twitch with the eagerness to impale, and yet the matador led it on with the swirling majesty of his cape. A bull has weight upon itself, and requires time for slowing down, and yet this one managed to turn in spite of the bulk it had been given. The courage of the matador was not in question as he led the bull around and around. Spanish girls with the beauty to control your life lined the ring, expanding the bounds of his own normal excellence. All this in the blazing sun while the world was trying to live, and before the dark had once more settled in.

At the Museum of Modern Art I had seen a photograph by Walker Evans of sunlight coming through the louvered slats of an American window of weathered wood that gave you cause to cry. I had seen a weathered face that exploded into your consciousness and fleetingly the flight path of angels too fast for any lens. And then I had been returned into the street to see the chasm between the thing upon the wall and the *things* upon the street, and even the very great Walker Evans could not fully narrow the gap for me with his genius. So now I was faced with making an approximation of his art with my own particular stamp. Yes, the sun was burning people witless but we were safe indoors and Mona was napping in the bed that had been provided. I had given myself the money and the equipment, and now relative success was only a shutter snap away. Subtle grays and absolute black and the clarity of whiteness—the tonal values of the great—were within reach. But the film advance lever was balking coincident with her arrival into consciousness. No one could say I didn't see her yawning mouth and the death-dealing indifference she sought to communicate.

"You thwart me at every turn," I said. Nothing more was needed for the fire to begin.

"What is it now, you sick, talentless bastard?"

I slapped her. She hit me back and I threw her on the bed and pinned her arms. I saw madness in her face and felt the strength in her arms. The thought occurred that I had gone too far and would not be able to contain her.

Many centuries passed before I could be myself again. To strike a woman leaves you in the land of the pariahs.The specter of my father was everywhere. It was in the squares and boulevards and in the old stone churches. My hand grew to three feet in length and had hairs so thick they obscured the skin. In the mirror I saw a sloppy mouth and yellow teeth and the glint of metal from my father's bridge that was now my own.

In this time did we wander out in search of food and come to a basement restaurant where the smell of burning fish was strong and took a table by ourselves. Soon a Japanese-American girl sought out our company. We knew she was Japanese because she had the sharp, defined features of her race and raven black hair; there was none of the softness of the Chinese people in that face. She wore a Cornell T-shirt to announce her intelligence and tight jeans that spoke of her wardrobe efficiency. A quiver afflicted her slender frame.

"My girlfriend was raped and her boyfriend beaten unconscious. Some men cut us off with their car. It happened so fast. They just..." She stopped and stared at us as the wounded being that she was. A split occurred, in which I saw myself as perp and victim all in one. The terror stored in her bones radiated with an effect that was palpable. She had seen violence taken to a degree incomprehensible. Wickedness had flared on a halcyon night. The natural coldness in her eyes had temporarily fled. She was going against her normal way in feeling undone. It had taken a seismic event to bring her into the open.

Mona stepped in with the truth she knew. "This is the land of big dicks made of hot steel. The fathers give their sons permission to rape and rampage. It all comes from paterfamilias. Patriarchy is at epidemic proportions in this stark country."

The girl got up slowly from the table with her look of horror intact. She backed away facing us, leaving Mona to polish off her pollo and her flan.

Over a communal dinner the next evening at the pension, we met two women, French-Canadian travelers from Montreal. Denise, short and thickset, had a face blitzed with pimples. Grace, her companion, was tall and slender. Although she came across as nunlike, I did wonder if I could scale the walls of her propriety. For some reason her overbite held the promise of sensuality, and her narrow face compelled you to search it for further clues. Both had a couple of years on me, which should have put them in the realm of older sisters, but it did not, at least in the case of Grace. When I told her in a moment of privacy that the age barrier was surmountable through the forces I was activating, she replied, "Tres etrange," with a wry look for punctuation. Denise was an insurance agent. Grace had the nimbleness of mind to qualify as a schoolteacher and found her love among her grade school students. Both had the stability to be in the world and the freedom that came with paying their own way.

Pride was a barrier to saying things felt out of control without an itinerary and that I was flunking yet another test, just as I couldn't tell Mona that the camera would always defeat me. And so, because hope comes with powerful boosters, I stayed plastered to the dining room ceiling for much of the dinner when Denise and Grace invited us to join them on their journey by car east to the Costa Blanca.

The Spanish took their macho onto the road. They allowed for no flinching of their will, showing their passion with levels of speed and destructive design astonishing for the carnage that such recklessness manufactured. All along the road could be seen the spectacle of the smoldering ruins of crushed cars and the deceased within them as well as the agonized cries of those who had not yet joined them in the netherworld. Every few miles did we have to endure a cape man going mano a mano in matador duds with the fast-moving traffic. For the whole long trip I pleaded with Grace and Denise to yield or die, as the oncoming traffic had no give in it.

"The Espanoles drive with their pricks. They learn it from the caudillo," Mona offered, drawing giggles from the Catholicized Canuck women.

All along the route Denise and Grace bickered, in a way that was within the bounds of civility, and were taking Mona in as a younger sister in molding her to their female intention. I was aware of this orbital pull that threatened to be my ruin from a back seat perspective, for now it was three women and an unmanly man in the country of the manly men.

Several hours into the trip, we pulled into a dusty town with baked white houses. The main street had a store with a Coca-Cola and a Kodak sign. I was desperate for film to keep my record alive, but Mona, without knowing of my need, encouraged Denise and Grace to keep going. By the time we stopped a couple of blocks away, I was once again in a rage and, as I walked off, marked her for my wrath.

A merchant who knew to stay out of the heat was there to serve me. I motioned to the object of my intention and even said the word "pelicula" as a way of gaining access to the goods while clutching a fistful of pesos. I sensed laughter at my urgency in his unhurried gait as he returned with the yellow box, laughter that continued at the salvation possibilities I was placing on the purchase.

"I am battling time in the land of death itself, and I am so angry I can hardly think in my need to get back there and punish her for her crime," I said, and now he was really laughing, having delivered to me not even Tri-X black and white but the color film scorned by the immortals.

By the time I returned they were eating the food that was available. I snapped at Mona for getting cake into her mouth any way she could without a fork.

"Why don't you just push it in his face? That will shut him up," Denise said, her acne growing an ever brighter red. Because she knew how to summon outrage unfettered by guilt so her warfare could be outright and direct.

That evening we stopped at a roadside inn undergoing renovation. The workers were collecting their tools and ready to go home. They knew what it was to live a mile from where they were born and to eat food from their own soil and to seldom read a newspaper. They also measured out their worth in tangible work, and that made them go easy on the words and elevated a grunt to a form of elegance.

Amid the building project—cement floors in need of tiling and constructions of wood that lacked a finishing touch—we placed down our belongings in a room that had a door even if it lacked glass for the window frame.

"The air will be with us tonight," I said.

"The air isn't always with us?" Mona replied.

"You know what I mean," I said, keeping an eye on the window as the portal through which death could visit us in this menacing country.

We took a footpath up a hill on earth that had been spared the commotion of the backhoe.

"I could stay here forever. Don't you feel the same?" she said.

Spanish clouds were scudding across the sky, and in the fading light I realized that the evening had cooled me off. The pressure of destination and the emotional turmoil wrought by the hot sun were gone. Direction had been established and we had a hazardous Citroen to navigate the terror.

"In the land, as you say, of the caudillo and the Espanole pricks?"

"Spanish pricks, not American pricks. Fight the power. Remember?"

Oh, she had a point. No *Newsweek*, no *Time*. No American progress with its interminable balance sheets. But to stay here you had to give up the idea of keeping abreast of history or even making it. You came here if you wanted to die. A cry of protest rose in me. I beat my American drum to ward off the shroud of death as my addiction to the event surfaced, the stream of glossy magazines chronicling the history-making beat of America.

"Let's face it. Europe is a giant old-age home. All its people have been put out to pasture. They are terminally ill with their own fatigue. We are their birth child. To stay here is la muerta."

In a dream that night I raised my fist to the east and blew kisses to the west. All along, I had my eye on Armenia and the giant rats cascading down off Mount Ararat in a direction that could only have been my own. I saw men with armpit hair down to the ground and teeth that had never been white. I called on all the powers of the universe to not impose on me a fate I could not endure. I saw in that moment the illness my father had bequeathed me, and all the repudiating energy that would have to remain in play for me not to be drawn in if I was to stay the course of being truly American. Not one of the rats sank a ratty tooth in my meager flesh in a dream that ended with the innocence of pennant-winning baseball.

I awoke with revolutionary fervor, seeing us for what we were, the sans-culottes sans merci, attacking through the air, on the ground, leaping barriers of protocol and tradition for the prize that had to be. I saw us as Americans burning our flesh brown in the war whoop delirium of number one-ism.

That night we drew to us Spaniards fueled with lust, raucous caballero would-be revelers, five to a car. Stars so bright and within reach above and the palpable energy of testosterone below and the journey now becoming a thing beyond bearing, the fact not so very natural being that twenty-two million tourists had flooded the country, leaving no room at the inn.

"We will find you to a place of lodging," they said, inspecting carefully with stares less than reassuring the women within the car before leading us on.

Fear mounted at the staying power of the tail lights of the cars of the boys of Spain ahead of us, whatever titillation the road courtship seemed to provide Denise and Grace. But one rejection after another for lodging abated their giddiness and they once more began to bicker, with periodic bursts of Gallic fury from Denise. I remained on guard for the moment when the caballero caravan would become the caballero roadblock on some dusty untraveled byway. I saw the knives of coercion for the women and the can of gasoline to douse and then incinerate me from the earth. I saw the armor that had been bequeathed them as a protection from all concern regarding the rape and murder they were committed to performing. All of this I understood and then had to let go of with the vanishing of their red lights down a fork in the road Denise chose not to follow along.

"Do we look so stupid as to not know what the crimes of men can be?" Denise and Grace had done a 180 with their heads to confront me.

"Men are such beasts, and I do not always love them," was all I could reply.

"Si, si," they affirmed, and onward we drove while the caballero cohort dispersed back to the mothers who would have them, having been gone too long.

Weary and hungry, we came to the water's edge in the small city of Gandia, where we parked the car and collapsed onto the sands. The guardia civil was nowhere to be seen but its threat under the stars at night as we lay by the Mediterranean that awaited us was palpable; we had been warned that their punishment was severe for sleeping in the open air and that incarceration in a Spanish jail was like no other hell on earth, with dinner nothing more than the canned farts of the caudillo himself. Heedless of the possible consequence, sleep was calling to the four of us anyway. We rested in our chosen places, Mona next to me as the love supreme I needed her to be. The only cause for apprehension was the breeze that sought to torment our skin with gentle coolness, but the laying on of the extra shirts that we had brought along secured our rest in the challenging air, and not a drop of rain could fall so long as the stars were out so bright.

In the morning we woke to an already blistering sun. With the amenities of a bathroom and breakfast lacking, it was mucho cranky time for Denise especially, and so I maintained myself in a cowed stance to stay free of the red zone of her fire.

The thing is that the heart of Spain opened to us. Chickens scurried across a dirt road before our advancing car. Even from a distance the sea was pervasive as demonstrated by the pacific nature of the family we found shelter with. We were shown to a room in their humble home. All along this painful interior journey my insides were screaming at what domestic arrangements could unleash and my mind bore witness to the apology I offered that we should invade them in this way, payment of cash doing nothing to relieve the distress over putting these poor people out and all systems on high alert for early detection of the anger that was surely to come from the face of the man of the house, when all he was offering was a stolid presence and the restraint necessitated by a language barrier.

We slept real sleep, not beach sleep that lacked the restorative function, and were grateful for the walls that could contain us. The sleep was necessary. Before it came I could feel myself fragmenting, the undernourished, physically and mentally inadequate self emerging for my full viewing displeasure, along with the horror of the life I had committed myself to in bondage to the building and Simon Weill.

On waking from our long and rejuvenating nap, We joined our two companions on the beach. Denise was wearing a tunic for protection while Grace showed off a model's figure in her black swimsuit. Before leaving the house I had put on a pair of cut-off corduroys in a moment of confidence that was quickly eroded as we approached the two. I saw their eyes go to my pencil-thin shanks and read the message they posted on the blue sky: "A man is not a man with an endowment such as this." No longer sleep deprived, I posted my own response. "Defenses are now in place for the warding off of judgments that can kill. My life to live." Those words too came to have their place in the firmament, though I quickly lost any confidence I had summoned.

"Tell your man to be careful with his expensive camera on the beach. It is not a plaything and the sand will ruin it." Denise did not hold back. With these dismissing words did she further reduce me to an incompetent wastrel. A man will always know when he has become an object of a woman's desire; he will experience her disposition toward him in all his senses. He will also know when he has been cast into the pit of inadequacy. The wound that had been there my whole life showed itself plain and prompted her coup de grace.

"Your boyfriend is not Mr. Charles Atlas. You should remember that the next time he tries to terrify you," Denise said.

I heard her voice. I saw the sand. I reconnoitered spaces where I might hide. I walked about the earth with words as hatchets in my fractured scalp praying for both hatchet and head to fall away.

Hotel lodgings were calling to Denise and Grace when we reached Barcelona. No more roughing it for them. They wanted clean sheets and a private bathroom with hot and cold running water. Surely too they wanted a reprieve from us.

Whether we were staying in the city's finest hotel or not, it was an accommodation we could be grateful for, with a front desk and room service and carpeted rooms and hallways that put a hush upon your feet and doors that closed with authority.

That first night I visited the Sagrada Familia alone, Mona having fallen asleep, and found Grace there as well, staring up at the honeycombed spires leaning in on themselves. There was no chance that we would touch, as she had the information on me that she needed to act in accord with her desire to stay apart. Denise had acknowledged that her friend had a first class mind, and my own sense of deprivation in that regard was now too much to overcome. I conceded to her a higher realm of existence. Nevertheless I stood alongside her. Whatever I said, it was insignificant and without the weight to withstand the Spanish wind. And so I walked away crying at what my life had become, that I could not stroke her fine hair or feel her tongue explore my mouth or do any of the things my low state was keeping me from. I cried upon the boulevard called the Ramblas. I cried upon the thing, Parc Güell, with the inverted name and the monstrous, beady-eyed umlaut hovering mercilessly over the poor, defenseless *u*. I cried into every café con leche I could drink. And everywhere I cried I heard the whispered recognition of me by Denise and Grace as strange and unbalanced, *a skinny beater of women* and far less than a man in their French-Canadian eyes.

Behind the locked hotel door the anger returned. Something about the provocations of Mona's mouth action. The way it contorted. Her exposed tongue when she spoke. I caught her with a slap to the face, and she returned fire with a glass that bounced off my head. Our row shook the very foundation of the hotel.

Denise and Grace said goodbye the next morning, the vacated room next door their mode of expression. The silent departure expressed everything they needed to say about me, I could only conclude.

We pushed on. Brussels bore the excessive features of its past in the Baroque churches and on its ornate buildings. A mustached and coiffed city official presented himself to us and said we would be denied hotel rooms wherever we went as a result of our unmarried status. Down some stairs Mona and I went to a dark bar, where I had several brandies, sweet and yet potent, which left me sodden and struggling through the trek to the train station, our departure the only seeming alternative to the extra cost of separate rooms.

At the border with West Germany, a young and slender officer jolted me to attention when he entered our coach car in a bright green uniform and high black boots and requested our passports. An image of Germany's Nazi past was summoned by his presence and his heavily accented English. Would there be any point in denying that I was perversely drawn to the power I associated with his snappy uniform if not his lineage?

Munster's city center had been razed during the war. Everywhere had modernity risen up, including our hotel. We found rest but no life for ourselves in the soul-deprived city and so headed for

Dusseldorf, equally maimed by wartime bombing and Allied ground advances. In a restaurant in this city emerging from ruins, a cockroach surfaced from beneath the string beans I had been eating and no longer could touch.

In Rotterdam, we took to bicycles, keeping pace with the cars around cobblestone curves or wandered along the shoreline, the river exerting a calming effect.

We encountered a Dutch couple on one of these walks. They invited us to their home. They were young and in love and it was clear he did not beat her, given his good genes and good disposition. In a year, perhaps, they would go on to university, but for now they had to support themselves. Through masculine effort, he had exposed the wood beams in the large and previously industrial space and installed new windows and built a kitchen and bathroom. It was everything not to flee out the door in the face of such competency.

And yet they wanted something, or thought they did. They had a yearning for the America beyond their settled world, the one they saw and read about in the glossies—demonstrations, riots, the winds of change. Instead they had their stolid Dutch ways. There were no particulars upon their faces for me to keep in mind other than being Dutch and reflexive hospitality went together. In desperation I mentioned the name *Knickerbocker,* the name *Peter Stuyvesant,* the name Van Dine. They stared at me without comprehension. The conversation was artificial and even arthritic, the words suffering from throbbing pain. Their English being limited and our Dutch nil, we had to rely on them to apply what little of our language was at their command. *Thomas Pynchon, Kurt Vonnegut,* hideous *Richard Brautigan* I threw out. In vain. In vain. (Oh that a period should be left so heartbreakingly alone, only to be stared at through the lens of time, the forlorn book *In Watermelon Sugar* now an object of true treasure resting on a miniskirt Mona then wore.)

We could not stay with them forever. The conversation was too full of pause for longevity to accommodate. The promise of reciprocity being required, we exchanged names and addresses so they too could have the American experience. I staggered out with Mona into the morning light, bleeding from the self-inflicted wound of inanity.

Amsterdam had trolleys with overhead connections adding their weight to the cobblestone streets. It had drizzle and it had sunshine too; in all kinds of weather was its spirit accommodating. We ate patates fritas where the vendors could be found. The gables and the steeples brought some longing for the past, as did the canals and the bridges that arced them, summoning as they did the vaguest of recollections of having been here in the gentleness of a different time. Elm trees stood at attention over all manner of sites, and to bicycle in Vondelpark was to live the dream of what the good life was, the sun kissing your face until you couldn't stand it anymore. A café in the park served beer and cake, and the yellow jackets joined us with the persistence of their ways.

We took shelter in a hostel that lacked an outer wall. All night there was lightning and thunder, the jagged bolts stabbing at the canals and striking the buildings with their flash-filled power. We lay on the third tier, waiting under our one-guilder blankets for the end to come. The economy drive had been on me to live like the rest, but Mona was not having it.

"Not another night like this. I have to be able to take a shower without fifty other women around me. This is inhuman." She took me by the hair for emphasis. "Do you understand?"

I assured her that I did.

We took a room in the gable of a private house along a canal. The room was small and cozy, with a soft bed and a writing desk and a bathroom of our own. We had come to the end of our travel rope and told ourselves we deserved the best. I sat in a chair and read my book, *The Electric Kool-Aid Acid Test.* The author said you were on the bus or off the bus and that hippies with brain power were riding it. The author's prose had a manic power. He never once said he liked the people he was writing about. He didn't have to.

Mona got out her sketch pad. After twenty minutes the struggle to stay with the book became too great because the book had borders over which I saw once again that she was a doer and me a passive soul trying to absorb words that lacked nutritive value and the awareness that within an hour or two she would have put down the pad and picked up a book of her own and read it not to fathom the way of words and why they flew around the page the way they did but what they meant in the totality of what they were saying.

Easy Rider had shown its filthy face again, and America calling us to it, we succumbed. This time Mona did not cry at the offing of Jack Nicholson and the subsequent offing of Peter Fonda and Dennis Hopper with their motorcycles intact. Violence no longer had the element of surprise and grief had no second act within her.

The Dutch were both wary of water and manly upon it. They knew its consequences well. For that reason they built their staircases steep so they could be above its mischief. At least it was that way in the house where we had been led to stay. We returned from the movie, and finding the front door locked, took the appropriate action of ringing the bell. We were not monsters. We knew how to act in accordance with the owner's wishes. And there it was. The door that had stood against us now showed a yielding nature. And there too, at the top of the stairs, stood the owner, Lukas, holding the thick white rope which, for all the distance it had to cover, attached to the door, dispelling my budding notion of its thwarting intent.

Lukas wore the evening apparel of a retired man—slippers and a robe—and a forced smile that we could only interpret as the danger sign that it was. It did not go unnoticed that he kept his eyes sharp upon our presence as we drew close.

"Won't you please come in for a drink?"

He controlled us with the wrath that was to the other side of that smile, and so we did as he requested, stepping into the comfort in which he was living, an apartment with an oriental rug and large stuffed chairs and antiques I had no name for and heavy draperies. The canopied bed was piled high with cushions and to underscore the vitality of its importance in his life, he offered that both he and his wife often awoke as late as two in the afternoon and sometimes wouldn't step outside for days.

"But this is Holland, where the sun has a way of shining," I said.

"What is that you say?" Lukas said.

"I am simply here to listen," I replied.

"Will you have a brandy with me?" Lukas asked.

"I will do you one better. I will have two," I said.

"First you will have one, and then perhaps another," Lukas said. "And the beautiful young woman? Will you also have a brandy?"

"No, but thank you," Mona said.

"You don't drink? It is just as well. Later you will drink," he said, his face threatening to come apart in his effort to maintain his geniality.

The television set was on. The screen showed a phalanx of gray-uniformed policemen holding shields in one hand and truncheons in the other as they advanced on the long hairs in Dam Square. A man atop the tank of a water truck directed a powerful stream in the crowd's direction. Some responded with bottles and rocks. Others held their crotches as an offering of disrespect and youthful power. From the apartment could be heard the weird wail of police car sirens establishing their hee-haw rhythm as they remained mission bound for the delivery of justice or simply trying to freeze the city with the commotion of their loud sound.

Denunciatory impulses took control of Lukas's tongue. "They are not our children. They are rabble. Trash. They arrive from other countries and instead of working lie about like dogs. Bad. Very bad. When I was sixteen my father told me to leave home. He threw me out the door. I worked as a carpenter. I struggled to make myself something. But this, this is unspeakable. They must be beaten, and beaten very severely. That is the only way." His wife, who had jolly features, offered a nodding smile in seeming to agree with him.

Mona kept her words within her mouth so she could have a bed to sleep in.

"A bashing can be a good-time thing," I said, leaning in toward him and smelling his old man scent.

"What is that you say?" Whether in response to my words or simply made irritable by diminished hearing, he pulled back wearing an affronted expression, while for Mona he continued to display the softness his features could deliver.

"Water alone will not get them clean. They need soap and the other accomplices for good hygiene," I said.

"What is this you talk about?" his voice now full of suspicion. He looked at my hair in an appraising way, and seemed to be getting clues from the amount of it. I took strands in each hand to give myself the horns that he was seeking.

He directed his attention to Mona. "You come from a good family."

"Her family is the best. Van Dine. You know, like Van Eyck," I said.

"Your family is Dutch?" Mr. Lukas asked.

"On my father's side," Mona said.

Mr. Lukas seemed to take that in. "And what do you think of those young people who lie about all day in the square."

"I think you have forgotten what it is to be young," she said, quietly.

"But to be young without responsibility."

"What is your responsibility? You have brought us here to die."

"What does that mean, we have brought you here to die?"

"You have brought us to the end. You hold the bomb over our heads. It makes a mockery of our lives."

"And for that young people should lie about in the hot sun all day?"

Mona said no more. She left Lukas with his question, and soon he showed us to the door.

I stared out the window and down at the canal and the elm trees flanking it. The street lamps were on, so people could find their way. The call of nocturnal adventure was alive in me, but what was that without a theater in which it could be satisfied? Mona was already fast asleep, but for me to do the same was to die to all the wild nights calling and the spectacle of women in red-lighted windows with their wares on sad display.

On the table was the *Electric Kool-Aid Acid Test;* it had shrunk to its true size and proved in the moment the assertion that books were a bloodless substitute for life. Something exciting was always waiting for me if I only I could rush outside and make it mine in the darkness.

I left the room and drifted along the cobblestone streets toward the cafés and bars. No more wind and sky and stars in the firmament. Give me the company of strangers and a quick route to pleasure.

The streets were desolate, with the old buildings looking on in tactful silence. Soon an advancing couple appeared, aphrodisiacal by the nature of the sex thing they were showing, he black and strong and wronged in his olive military fatigues and she the fruit of Holland, a blond girl representing the best the country could deliver. He held to her and she to him and both flashed smiles of worldly triumph. I turned and saw her twitching bottom do its twitching thing with his hand resting casually upon it as a neon sign blazed the following in the half moon sky: "I will tell you what you are frightened to hear. The women of wantonness are not yours to possess."

I turned the corner onto a street of bars, a street that ran for an eternity. From the darkened lodgings above the watering holes came moans of pleasure, while down below the drinking places were filled with men in far greater numbers than women to be encouraging. Though the sidewalks had been worn away with overuse, the liquor kept flowing, and an international cast of characters had their dream going on: lonely and disenfranchised men with their dongs outside their pants, flying up and down the street in pursuit of their

Dutch mate. I held to a street sign so the force of my need would not pull me forward, but I was soon within their midst, moving with the flow up and down the strip and joined to their jabber.

Eventually, I crawled away toward the street-level windows where prostitutes sat on stools or stood, eerily isolated in their showcases in a world between the real and the make-believe. From one window to the next I went, trying to penetrate their made-up faces. They licked their lips. They bared their pudenda and ignited the gases from their butts. As they posed in their red-lighted spaces, and looked out through the glass with eyes that derived their knowledge through carnal experience, I heard the click of their heels and smelled their cheap perfume and sensed the hardness of their steel-lined vaginas. In staring at a slender one in a red teddy and black garter belt, a woman whose blond hair had black roots, I saw what I hadn't seen, that a prostitute was a purchase, not a conquest.

As I backed off, she held her thumb and index finger an inch apart, and then gave the thumbs down, suggesting that my apparatus wasn't worthy of her. Nearby could be heard the hubbub of the human hounds. The chill of fall was in the air and brought with it the reminder of responsibility with which I associated it. The twin message of fear and the imperative for consolidation I received, the vast blackness saying there was nothing for me out there but the endlessly lonely streets. Go home. Go home. Point yourself toward the treasure that you have, not the one you cannot find, I heard a voice say.

Looking up, I saw that the light was out in the dormer window of our room. Mona partook of sleep the way she gave herself to art and eating, with full commitment.

I tried the door but it would not yield. Only then did I remember the rope contraption required to get me where I wanted to go. I would simply wait for other restless souls to egress from their rooms into the calling darkness and then slide my stealthy self up the stairs. So began a vigil that went on for an hour, but the house and the streets only got darker and quiet reigned in a more threatening way, even the distant jabber by now having died out. I thought to scale the building but did not see myself thriving on the perpendicular. The wind got snappish, seeking to inflict harm, and the urgency of a full bladder began to press upon me. I rang the bell, which in the quiet sounded like a gong. I rang a second and a third time for my own merriment, and when action was not forthcoming, a fourth and fifth time so the saturation point for the old man's endurance could be reached. After the sixth and before the seventh did my actions bear the result of a compliant door. Nevertheless did I kick it good and promise it a torching should it ever seek to thwart me in such a way again. Lukas was very much there, looking like his censorious self, at the top of the steeply pitched stairs, in the robe that he would wear until his death. As I climbed the steps, he stood his ground, holding in his hand the rope so thick.

"You have been out." It was a statement.

"With my own kind."

"What is that you say?"

"I have been out with my own kind."

"And what kind is that?"

"The kind who howl at the moon while indulging in the mind-expanding matter of the earth."

"And where is your wife?"

"The woman of my life is fast asleep."

'Your wife is asleep and you are out howling at the moon."

"Do you love me?"

"Do I what?"

I drew close to his hairy ear and closed my eyes. "I am here on a secret mission. Tell no one its nature. I have been investigating the insurrection. I can assure you that the outcome will be quite positive if only you maintain your faith in me."

I stood back so he could see me and I could see him. My left hand spoke, giving him the thumbs up. Then my right hand spoke with a thumbs up of its own, the two of them standing as straight as they ever had there in the night where this was happening.

"Your kind I do not need here," Lukas declared.

The next morning we were homeward bound. I was reading something new, by the great Philip Roth. It was called *Portnoy's Complaint, a* novel in paperback about a man who lived his life with his penis leading the way. I sought to share the joy of my discovery with Mona at Schiphol Airport, as here, I thought, was a man of my own kind, but with a bigger brain and bigger apparatus. Our journey was at an end, and we were awaiting our return flight. But she was having none of my offering. After sampling a page, she threw it across the airport floor. I did not hold myself to account for her rejection of a man for telling us who he was.

On the plane, it has to be said, gaseousness was abounding. Farts that registered high on the stink meter came our way with such frequency that Mona was compelled at one point to vacate her seat. Silent emissions these were, their author unknown though he sat beside her. And yet a truth was emerging. A disclosure was being made of genuine foulness in the air.

Chapter 76

Nothing prepared me for what a return to America could mean, given the lickety-split departure Mona's father arranged for her to Beantown along the roads that had been laid down, his car a thing of purpose in running over them. I cried out to her that she was stretching me to the breaking point, but she heard me without hearing. When visiting the place of honesty that even I possessed, I could admit to partial relief that she was gone back into the familiar distance after the intense proximity we had endured.

I had no school to chaperone me. I had no job to afford me the pleasure of integration. I had only myself in my Hell's Kitchen apartment and the renting office and the man on Fifty-seventh street ready to serve me up my ham and cole slaw heroes and the opportunity to fall through the spaces of my own untextured life.

And I had Dr. Zimmer, intact in her listening industry. I gave her a summary of my actions, and never once held her responsible for the cockroach emerging from my string beans in Dusseldorf. I confessed to my criminality, the savage recklessness of the slaps I had administered to Mona's face and the frenzied emotion that had incited it. But she was not in the mood to corroborate the despair that I was manifesting.

"A trip is not an easy thing. People return home not speaking to each other. Believe me in what I say. You have not done such a bad thing."

But I knew different. All I could see was Mona being swallowed up by the legends of Boston as their fall snack, while I was left out in the increasing cold.

"Could you give me the drugs that I am in need of so I can be fashioned more normally in the spaces I have to fill? Could you do that for me? Could you deliver, as a doctor should, the relief that I am seeking?"

Dr. Zimmer looked at me, not unkindly, but as a human being does when experiencing the sense of her own aptitude for miracles. "The clinic does not authorize me to prescribe medications. Try instead the old-fashioned tranquilizer. Try a little wine."

A feeling of promise and of doors opening filled me in the moment of her words' arrival. The room was suffused with a golden light and, feeling the bounty of my own joy expanding me, I rose to my feet and sought to kiss her only to be pushed away, then left the institute with my mind rearranging itself to accommodate the idea that it had just received, and with sentries posted to keep all competitors away. The city sparkled, the lights coming on to illuminate the darkness that had descended, Saks Fifth Avenue shining bright with its display windows of fashion glory and the culture hounds outside Carnegie Hall milling under its black iron awning; even the morose New York Coliseum came to heightened life, and if you looked in the bookstores you saw people ravenous to consume words off pages provided for that purpose.

What I saw more than anything was the green light Dr. Zimmer had provided, whereas the signal had been amber at best before for the train I was conducting. With the caliber of her medical intellect, she had placed me on the express track to my own freedom, removing the proverbial prohibition of my mother that wine was a mocker and strong drink was raging.

I came to a hole-in-the-wall liquor store on forlorn Tenth Avenue, where I said to the clerk behind the counter, "I need wine to power the journey that I will be taking," he wearing a light blue smock and showing a handlebar mustache big on his face. When he heard me not as a way of maintaining his gabfest with his pal, I escalated the level of my request with a note of urgency, placing myself between the two so that their words should have an obstacle en route to their destination.

"Pass me a bottle of wine of the normal kind, and while you are at it, give me two. I have a ticket to ride from my doctor, and she is the real thing, having attended the great medical school of the great Columbia University."

Because I had not allowed his indifference to quell my desire, he was now galvanized into action sufficient to reach into the cooler and extract two bottles.

"The first one you drink real fast, my friend. The second one you *savor.* This wine will assist you, my friend. It will assist you very good."

"I have drunk bathtubs of such wine, and have been assisted very good myself," his friend agreed.

I completed the transaction and hastened to be alone with the bottles in the privacy of my apartment. Lacking a corkscrew, I relied on a screwdriver and then my thumb to push the cork down into the bottle so the contents could be free to flow. The wine was sweet and fortifying. I drank and then I drank some more. I drank to the miracle of release from all pain before passing out, and when I awoke it was to a new world order. I truly was free. An idea of maximum potency had arrived. Whatever its source, it had only this to say:

> I am your friend in a way no one else will ever be. Doors that have been closed will fly open. Your intelligence will be all you need it to be. Creative juices will flow. An answer will be provided for every occasion. I will be with you on the rocky

road of life with all its vicissitudes. When women in their fickleness leave, my presence will remain assured.

On the southeast corner of Fifty-seventh and Tenth, across the street from the deli where the man of hardness made his heroes, stood a saloon with a bartender who combed his hair straight back in the manly style, the scars that had been inflicted on his face testifying to one and all that to the library he had not been bound. He showed a masterful handling of the enamel-covered stick, creating heads of foamy whiteness just so in their proportion to the golden glow of the beer below.

From the TV studio just to the west came a broadcaster, a man of distinction with a gravitas voice and appearance. In his white shirt and emerald green tie signifying his eminence did he arrive. John Jones showed himself not the way he showed it on TV from only the waist up, but with his entire body present for inspection within the Burberry raincoat and silk suit he wore. He had had a hard day, presenting the news of America through the filter of a face as reassuring as granite, a face that projected competence and decency and, above all, earnestness as from his mouth words poured summarizing world events and all the consequences that could come from their transpiring. His heavy eyebrows added to his significance, so you could sit back and listen in comfort to the quality of America being spoken. It was not a bar for Buffalo Springfield or Cream or even the Fifth Dimension, but rather for Tony Bennett, so people could be sad in the middle-aged way they needed to be before the Sixties had ever happened. John Jones had the look that fit the sounds he was hearing. Only later would he drink in the dark with the tie and all the other apparel of civilization off so he could reveal the nakedness of his desperation.

I remained on my stool, observing the bartender to be a man of action. He could see that not everyone was famous like the newscaster John Jones, but everyone was in need of a drink, and he made sure we got them within the limits of his ability. He had projected his own character into the quality of the bar, and so it remained white and sensible and accommodating of the *Daily News.*

I had my beer and then I had another and another. One hand holding the stein, I waved with the other to the buses on their northbound route, they being of New York City, authentically so. I waved to the human traffic wandering past. I told them we were all together now, and if they responded not, ample cause remained for rejoicing.

That fall, with no one knocking at my door, I showed further evidence of my commitment to the written word with my enrollment in a course at the New School for Social Research, a name that did not describe all the activity within. No one legendary was there to guide me, but the catalog revealed that names to which the word *legitimacy* attached had infiltrated themselves into the teaching ranks of the institution.

The class was in the evening, and preliminary to my arrival I gathered my family together and told them of my plan, that although death would sooner or later claim us all I would place them on my pages so they could live and live, and that I would use their lives and the sorrows they endured as fodder for my manuscripts. Hannah said she would break my bones in a thousand places and that her son would do far worse if I slandered either one while my mother emphasized the importance of normal food and my father sat in his wheelchair with his head down in the place where words could not reach him.

The country was in a holding pattern of its own devising, with Jimi Hendrix dead and Janis Joplin dead and the hopelessness of excursions into Cambodia underway and all the faces of the present soon to be the faces of the past and words becoming the only anchor against the driving rains.No examination of Kent State had proven definitive and the Black Panthers were on the scene, and all I was trying to do was find my way out of here.

I said to my family thusly, that when you have lived a life of pain, you turn to paper. When you have lived a life where your flesh does not match up with that of others, you turn to paper. When there are mirrors and proms you have been unable to show up for, you turn to paper. When you are missing half your head, you turn to paper.

"Just remember what I said," Hannah replied, planking me with her words.

The teacher's name was Mag McConley, and she said she had been born in a cornfield in Iowa, far from where she now sat at the head of the conference table in a room where the air did not move. She said her task was to instill in us the flow, the flow, a kind of amniotic fluid of creation in which we were to float. She had a craggy, weathered face, like W. H. Auden, and bangs that hung plastered against the flatness of her forehead. She was old and past the power to write what she had wrought and living with loneliness that prompted her to reach out. It was a face that didn't smile as a statement of who she was, a face of sorrow and sadness that the face police were not authorized to question her about, as it was natural to her constitution and one with her life. She didn't concern herself about the limits of her students' acceptance of her face; she just wore it as it was, while remembering that once she had been young.

"Not to worry. Not to worry. Someday you'll all find yourselves on the front page of the *New York Times Book Review* just so long as you stay with the flow." She spoke from the authority she had earned to her devotees, many of whom had been with her for years. There had been the smashing success of her two thousand page novel, *A Plethora of Summers,* and royalties and speaking gigs untold. She had risen on the time her plainness afforded her to win the love that she had all along been seeking, and while it healed her for the time it could, the reviews had since yellowed and the book faded from sight, so that loneliness sought to claim her for its own once more, requiring her to chain-smoke the cigarettes of America and eat at a table set for one with stained and brittle teeth and the mortuary looming.

As her worshipers read, they made gentle motions on the air to better flow the words, and the listeners did the same. A man of Greece was called upon to share his piece. The prose was seamless. As he read, the only movement in his face came from his lips, which he barely parted to allow the flowing words their freedom. The piece involved his native country and the Aegean Sea and the wines that came from fertile regions. A smile of self-satisfaction took control as he continued.

When he had finished, the room was silent. Everyone sat back, as if they had polished off a sumptuous meal. Belts were loosened, bellies got rubbed. The reader himself was in a trancelike state, his words having delivered him there, though his lips continued to move even after the stillness had come. Minutes or hours passed. A feeling of dread came over me. I saw their delusions. I saw the poverty fueling their intentions. I heard them howling their claims of their own specialness and because it was my howl, too, I had to flee from the mirror that had been presented to me.

But the fall had come, leaving me exposed in my aloneness, and without a place to go other than the renting office and Central Park and yes, Dr. Zimmer, who aggressively exhorted me to stop my hiding. And so I ran back to the New School and found a man named Mr. Tollman, who taught a free-style writing class. He was wheelchair bound as the result of a car accident. Though his legs were incapable of generating mobility, his hands were in a frequent fuss with his pipe, which was a fixture. Intellectual in his appearance, he came at you strong with black frame glasses and tweed jackets with some wear upon them and dark shirts matched up with bright ties. He had been an editor but then he went and wrote a book so he didn't have to be an editor anymore and could teach the things that he happened to know in an atmosphere of classroom informality and with the kindness that his injury had accelerated. It was clear that he was an angel without wings and brave in his intention to tell the truth of his own life.

A middle-aged woman read a poem about a middle-aged woman whose outing on a beach she compared somehow to a Chinese dinner. "She goes in the water and a half hour later she's dirty again," Mr. Tollman said, and the class erupted in laughter. To be honest, it did not sit well with me that he was having his day.

I had been swivel-heading, drawn by several attractive women in the room, but hearing the laughter, I stood up and shouted out all that I had: "The recrudescence of homeopathic dawn."

Mr. Tollman turned and stared, not to menace me, but simply to assess. "Tell us your name, please," he said, in a quiet voice.

"My name is Garatdjian, and I from prison am emerging."

"And what is this offering you have made to us?"

"It is only that I am to posterity bound, that all time might cease when in my presence. I am willing myself to have the face and eyes of a prophet and the voice of the oracle at Delphi, whatever that might be."

"Indeed," Mr. Tollman replied.

I told Mr. Tollman and the class the whole truth of the immaculate conception, that I had been walking up Tenth Avenue away from the Telephone Building and the coldness of its aspect and past the old Chase Manhattan Bank, a site bearing silent witness to the history of Hell's Kitchen, when the words delivered themselves as a truth that made me tremble and that other lines were similarly afflicting me with the possible gibberish of their content and moving me from my law school purpose, and yet without a slide rule and other tools of calibration to work them into the fitness shape the laws of poetry required, what hope could I have of taking refuge in verse? Tears now flowing, I said that Robert Lowell had landed on me hard with the criteria for acceptance and that for many minutes and even hours the sun had stopped shining and I was barely alive.

Then Mr. Tollman spoke, and as he did I cupped both ears.

"You must learn to take shelter from the storm and to watch out for flying objects, particularly those arriving from New England."

I ran from the building out into the street carrying with me the newfound freedom of my words and found a bar, Emilio's, down past the Waverly Theater on Sixth Avenue, where I could drink the beer of Greenwich Village and savor the ecstatic state of my own mind.

The Knicks were on the tube that night. They had Walt "I can steal your jock" Frazier. They had Dick "fall back, baby" Barnett. They had Willis "I don't take no shit from no one" Reed. They had Dave "working man from Detroit" Debusschere, and Dollar Bill "the meager white man" Bradley to make up their starting five in seeking supremacy for the second year in a row.

But for that night I could not live in the vicariousness and was slowly drained of joy by the lack of contact I was experiencing, the people at the tables unto themselves and those at the bar unto themselves in contained conversation. I gave myself the experience of the A train to Columbus Circle and late-night eggs at a hole in the wall just west of Eighth Avenue and Fifty-seventh Street. The store of the ham and cole slaw heroes was now closed for the night and as I stared at the products of America on the shelves and saw the cold cuts in their protective display cases, I promised the owner in his absence that I would continue to be good for him. Jesus, the trucks of Tenth Avenue were savage in their rumblings on that night, nor were the buses shy about their essential nature, while beyond the constant of their mechanized noise all was fairly quiet on the avenue.

I saw the soft lights of the bar upon the corner, and all it promised in the way of vision, and stepped inside and said to the bartender—he had the reality of his own dimensions under a clock that kept the time it could—that something fabulous had happened, that words had lodged in my mind and that when finally I had vocalized them, encouragement was served up by an author of some renown and that now, as a result of my newfound strength, divergence from the straight and narrow was a genuine possibility. I told him of the law school across the river that was waiting for me and how, just possibly, it was my life to live without it. Joe came at me hard—he had served many people in his time and it counted for something—and said only this:

"You ever heard of military service?"

The bar got quiet upon his noise so you could only hear the beer going down. "I've heard of many things," I finally said. "Doesn't mean I have to believe in them. Not even Jesus if I don't want to."

He ran a rag around my stein. "I'm not your friend. Try to remember that," he said.

"Nor are you the helicopter gunships from where I sit."

"When you're done, you're done," he said, pointing to my glass. I left to find a grocery on a lonely block, where I bought a six pack of Miller and a bag of chips. Mrs. Muldooney was waiting as I turned the corner. She had on a fall wrap so her night on the can could be comfortable.

"How is everything in the days of your life, Mrs. Muldooney?" I asked.

"I'm not complaining."

"And your son? Is he doing his job in the way that you would like him to?"

"My son has been coming through for me his whole life."

The last of the mounted police had led their horses back to the stable for the night, and now those horses were deep into their silent knowing of what the world truly was while somewhere in the near-distance a train whistle sounded, signaling the once resolute but now wavering intent of the railroads to keep running against all the impediments that America, in its cruel folly, could erect against them, my mind posting sentries of vigilance along the roadbed. I am coming to you, America, I said. I am coming to you with beer on my breath to taste you, to touch you here in the urban place of inanimate objects that themselves hold so much of life. I said these things that the supercilious might pull down their vanity and enhance America as the ultimate thing of continuing glory and take it to heart that they were as ephemeral as worms even with their foolish posture of ceaseless braggadocio and asked myself if I was listening.

I sat on the steps in the rear courtyard and drank the beer of America and gobbled the salty chips of America and called out to all the nations of the earth to behave themselves before commanding the building where I now lived to come alive in my vision-hungry presence. The facade fell away and Diane Sunburst, on the top floor, revealed herself as a farm girl from Iowa proud of her Marilyn Monroe features and the attention she drew from the men of Manhattan in her miniskirts and cut-off shorts with the American flag bouncing upon her buns. Film clips followed of her former days as a Frederick's of Hollywood catalog model and the blue movies that became a feature of her sideline life and the sustained darkness that followed before she found the light and the true meaning of her last name. I asked if she was a sunbeam for Jesus but she told me that I was just a young punk who had managed to make himself look old and to shut my filthy hippie mouth. Yes, she had hard days when the blues found her that stardom continued to elude her a stone's throw from the Great White Way and that her audience were the patrons at Ralph's Pasta Palace who wanted to nuzzle her slender neck and lose themselves in her large breasts as she lowered the linguini onto the table, leaving them too agitated to speak. Thirty-five-year-old Diane Sunburst too liked the song "Take Me Home, Country Roads," and gave it her best in a nighttime rendition, but always, always reserved "You Gotta Have Heart" for her mornings. I asked her once again if desire could be the bridge I might walk across to her fleshly delight, so overpowered did I feel by the bounty she was showing, and once again did she rain down her fear-filled fire, denigrating me for my unmanly specter. She repeated that her nights were reserved for Dr. Kildare, who just that moment was performing surgery at Roosevelt Hospital a few blocks away. I wasn't aggrieved. I wasn't injured. I was just holy in that fall-filled moment, the leaves turned brown now kissing me, the trees kissing me, the lips of dead immigrants kissing me, all the ceaseless dead as well as the living kissing me, and who was Diane Sunburst to extinguish that?

On the floor below the woman was slow to appear from the dominating darkness, and when she did it was with a subdued aura, a state of repression that had constancy on its side.

"I know you. You will come to me in the night. You will come to me with your wine to cheer yourself up and you will make love to me and I will not feel you. I will not feel anything. You do not have to introduce yourself to me, for we have known each other for a long, long time." More she promised to tell me when finally I arrived.

"I will be there when I can," I said, but the wall was back in place before the words could arrive. Not that she needed them, not from the place where she was coming from.

Chapter 77

Dr. Zimmer did not assassinate me, nor did she hire anyone for the job, but she fired bullets all the same from guns she called scorn and disgust. "You have no talent to speak of, or at best a minimal talent. People like you get nothing. You do years of scribbling and everything you send out comes back."

She was saying that I was not masculine in failing to ride strong upon a llama up the Andes and into battle. It was the same message, if lengthier, as from Lydia, who had it in her mind to say, "Scribble? Scribble? Scribble?" in mocking my endeavors. Because Dr. Zimmer had badgered me and badgered me for my journal, in which I continued my chronicle of the Van Dines and kept a record of my dreams so I could put them together in a mosaic that would deserve the name *understanding.* And now she was passing judgment.

"You think you are so big with your tanks and your weaponry when I have the American military, including the Strategic Air Command, at my disposal?"

"Never mind your armies. This is your life. You are a 24-year-old man. Do you not want to show the maturity your age requires?" She said she had more weaponry of that kind to fire, mainly the sorrowful experience of numerous friends in the arts, destitute dancers with ruined feet and playwrights delivering food to tables in the restaurants of New York City, people without the material sustenance that, although she did not say so, she now possessed.

"You will suffer needlessly if you pursue this life," she said, supporting her familiarity with poverty by acknowledging that yes, in Germany, she had eaten the roach-filled food of Dusseldorf and in this country had survived on a Campbell's three cans of soup per day diet before her stunning elevation above the street to a modern high rise with a doorman by accepting a rite of passage that required sacrifice.

I told her the truth from the angle where I sat. I told her that I did not care for her words, that I was not staying in the straitjacket that was my life.

"I have heard your cannon fire. I have experienced your word blasts. And I will tell you only this, that words are important. Law schools have them in a way that contains people so they cannot be free to get to their real words, which are the things that we need to be after. Because if you find the word that you are looking for and set it on the page, then you can be carried along for the rest of the day in the assurance that you have done right for yourself, but if you only carry the law school words from the textbooks they have given you and the statutes or whatever you have committed to memory, then no real learning can truly follow."

"What are you afraid of, my chickening out friend?"

"I am afraid of law school buildings and the confinement that must result with the narrowing of vistas. I am afraid of those who will find me socially and intellectually lacking and try to contain the fame that must be mine. And it is not even fame but the wild nights calling and all that must attach to it, the forlorn whistle of the train for which my listening devices are attuned. Beyond that, a course of action that allows a man time to think will be required to set me on a truly purposeful course. And then there is Mona. The time will soon arrive when Mona must be in New York so I can secure my dream."

"Dream? You have a social scheme I object to. You are trying to use this girl. I believe in calling a spade a spade."

The snarled traffic outside was trying to honk its way to freedom. I could only wonder if I was doing the same, hearing my mother say, *"Do my words mean nothing?"*

Mr. Tollman was Jewish, a profound fact for me, because to be a Jew was to see your life as the progress of order within a tradition to which you are bound. I told him that to be Armenian was to be invisible and that I was incinerating my own for the crime of hairiness so I myself could live. I told him further that to be Jewish was to be God, and that even Simon Weill, who had the force of his own pragmatic evil upon himself, was to be so considered. I asked that Mr. Tollman give me the orderliness of mind that he was showing, but he simply held his ground and asked me to read what I had brought.

I said that nothing good could come from doing so, for then I would have to own my words. He did not go harsh on me, nor did he show me tender mercies. He simply told me to get on with it.

And so I began:

> Sarah liked to pee in an open field, and always when she was on the phone her father was nearby, but the thing most constant in her life was the white divider line he tried to erode on the country roads he drove in a car so black that he might wear them away and be free of the restriction they would place on him.

It was at that point that I took my leave in passing out so I could meet the floor. Smelling salts were administered that knew how to find me. And when I was once more among the conscious, a woman was kneeling beside me.

"A work of genius. Truly a work of genius. I was so excited I could only hear a fraction of it, but I'm sure it was simply fabulous."

The woman introduced herself as Rowena Blaylock and said I should grant her the favor of extending her night.

Over goblets of red wine at a nearby bar I learned that Rowena Blaylock wrote poetry to rock and roll music. The claim of specialness was in the air, and of my making, because if I was to say anything, and to say it truthfully, then I would need to say that at the previous class I had claimed her before she had claimed me, borrowing from one of my betters those words I had heard him say as he drove the leased car that his mother had offered him for his summer of fun in the year 1967. There had been a torturous road. There had been the Hudson River. There had been World War II destroyers in mothballs. There had been a sign saying 9W south. There had been a town that dared to have the name Haverstraw, and there had been the glamour that was in his face and the respectability and credibility that derived from his Ivy League enrollment. And yes, there had been my ears hearing him say, in relation to the commercials that were airing on the radio between the bursts of rock and roll song, "An epic of American culture," words that captured for all time the brilliance of his wit that I then borrowed in that New School class, borrowed verbatim and without attribution, whispered them, that is, to Rowena Blaylock as a student read her effort entitled "The Moon and One." Because the driver of that car had cemented his fame only the month before with a crushing success, a novel of his college years, a sex-filled chronicle that gave the great Columbia University a solid bashing for the dullness of its academic curriculum, forcing me in that moment to see the pain of who I was in the presence of brains and beauty all in one. And so I had committed word theft and identity theft to win Rowena Blaylock over and yet here was Rowena kissing me with words, saying "You're great, just great," and I thought of the law school dream and the goddess who led me away from the young men with their feet on the ground and I was powerless against the current sweeping me along.

Rowena singled out the song "Maggie," by raspy-voiced Rod Stewart, as her muse. Under its spell galvanization occurred and lines of verse formed themselves on the page. But she spent less time on her rock and roll inspiration than the grievance profound she harbored toward her stepmother, whom she castigated as guilty of an abominable crime against her own stepdaughter by scheming to deprive her of funds from her father's fortune and so denying her the wealth into which she had been born. And this too I recognized, the calling to me of those removed from the material world of daily work and assumed responsibility, beings who could reinforce in me my claim of entitlement to a world outside the nine to five of the many who rode the subways and answered to bosses in favor of days of leisure free of the alarm clock ringing and terror in the jungles of southeast Asia, of bullets to the bowels, the chest, the eye, the brain.

With the wine flowing, Rowena took on a luster she had not previously possessed. In the back seat of the cab, I spoke from a place of arousal. All I remember is her eyes growing bigger.

Rowena was gentle with me the next day, opting for inquiry over accusation, saying "What on earth happened to you last night? You were a different person in that taxi."

I gave her the truth as I saw it to be, that the night had been calling. Any further information would be provided as it came in.

In this time my research turned up a bar farther downtown, The Abilene, on Park Avenue South. A man named Nick Blanco, who wore his brown hair shoulder length, stood inside the door scooping handfuls of chickpeas into his mouth from a bowl atop the cigarette machine. He was not a man given to indolence but the owner of the establishment, and checked a hidden "cool" meter for the assessment of people's worth, and in fact I saw him deny a man thrice for not moving the needle into the acceptable zone. Because he had the terseness that his authority allowed, people understood him even without words being spoken and dared not to query the solemnity of his face. Artists could stop by for drinks and Nick would greet them with a nod, the needle on his gizmo decidedly in the cool zone.

Nick had a second reason for his vigil. In a moment of candor, he acknowledged that he had opened the place so people would come to him, because without it no one would approach him except in passing and he would be left in a lonely space. The dictate of his soul was that he find a mate, and would he not have a better chance to fulfill his heart's desire in New York than in Abilene, Kansas?

Why he should let me enter I cannot say. I was just happy that he did.

That night, after many glasses of wine, I left the bar and saw a woman who had also been at The Abilene hailing a cab. I asked to join her and minutes later was in a loft in a terra cotta building on Prince Street in lower Manhattan. The space had been subdivided into seven sheet-rocked units for each of the female roommates.

I awoke with cottonmouth and the sun pouring through the skylight. It was painful to blink, let alone move my head. My mate, whose name I had never gotten, was gone from the mattress on the floor where we had slept.

In my shirt and pants and barefoot, I wandered about, imagining women still asleep in their prefab spaces. For a while I sat alone in the spacious kitchen over a cup of instant black coffee. Plants hung in the huge window. One in particular, a philodendron in a suspended basket and its leaves like green tresses, was pleasant to stare at against the ubiquitous whiteness.

As footsteps approached, I grew tense. A woman in a cinched terrycloth bathrobe and with her wet hair in a towel entered. I said hello but she ignored me as she passed by and reached into the refrigerator for a quart of milk. She drank from it while keeping an eye upon me. After returning the carton to the refrigerator, she wiped away her white mustache with a provocative backhand swipe before leaving.

The woman I had lain with emerged a short while later, wearing jeans and a sweatshirt.

She had come to New York City from Indiana with only one suitcase. Bleary eyed, she spoke of her artist husband, whom she met in Indianapolis while working as a waitress. He was a firebrand of enthusiasm for the state, dressing in red and painting solely in gradations of red.

She lit a cigarette and blew a cloud of smoke my way. I lit up my own and did the same in her direction. A summit meeting had begun.

"Are you still married? Have I inflicted infidelity on you?"

"It was necessary to divorce him. To be an artist is to be free of everything but your own calling, unless, of course, you wish to be misunderstood," she said.

"Is he not crying his eyes and his heart out for you? Are you yourself not crying out for something more than this multiple roommate life?"

"He's an alcoholic."

"How do you mean?" She had brought the word to horrifying life.

"How do you mean, 'How do you mean?' The man is a lush."

"You must not say that."

"I'm a drunk, too, only I'm not a drunk the way he's a drunk. He's farther down the road with it than I am, that's for sure. Are you all right?"

"I simply do not know if I can live with such an assertion making inroads on my life."

"What inroads are we talking about? The inroads of alcoholism?"

"Do not talk to me in this way. Do not come near me with terminology that would rob me of my joy."

"Yeah, you're a drunk, a starting-out drunk."

The nausea that I had begun to feel on awakening forced me to bolt for the bathroom. I knelt before the toilet bowl, where I heard myself promising God I would never, ever drink like that again before the dry-heaving and then the vomiting commenced. I lay curled on the bathroom floor for a few minutes and ran for the door. No goodbyes seemed needed or expected.

I stumbled home, where sleep found me, and when I awoke, a miracle of new perspective came to me. The night had been full of adventure and the morning hadn't been that bad. The Abilene called to me once more, with the promise not simply of the chick pea breath of Nick at the door but more intoxicating and still prettier delights.

"I have been drinking the wines and beers of America and other regions of the world and they lift the roof off the sky so I can truly see." So I said at my next session with Dr. Zimmer.

"The roof should come off the sky so you can see?"

I ignored her question. "I am afraid."

"Tell me about this fear."

"That I am drinking too much and too often."

"Are you drinking at home?"

"My home is Manhattan, and someday, if the breaks go my way, it will extend to all corners of the globe."

"Do you drink at home alone?"

"I drink where I can."

"Tell me what are you afraid of."

"I am afraid of losing the thing that sends me jolly into the world."

"Again I ask, where is it that you drink?"

She was trying to reach inside me now to take away the thing that had allowed my new life to begin, the very thing that she herself had given me.

"That is the thing of it. I have expanded. At first I went to the bar of the news anchor man on Fifty-seventh Street, but I began to receive body blows sufficient that my ribs were about to crack. Because I noticed after a while that alcohol cannot override all differences, cannot muffle the sound of your own loneliness when you are in the expansive way and yet have no one to talk to who will really listen in the listening way that your soul requires."

"Who were you trying to talk to?"

"The men of stature with their neckties. The men without stature with their blue collars. The women of Manhattan who were not there."

"The women of Manhattan?"

"I must provide my services until those services are no longer needed. I must plumb their depths until I find new depths. I must open their doors only to find new doors. I must allow this adventure to repeat itself, and alcohol is indispensable because it brings those who are so very far away so close in the realm of sexual possibility and allows me to run naked about Manhattan."

I waited fearfully for her verdict. And as the silence continued I was sure she would seek to confiscate the treasure she had bestowed on me. Instead, she offered a warm smile.

"There is nothing wrong with having a drink now and then. You are just worried because your older siblings have so much trouble."

I jumped up to kiss her but as always her restraint was too much for me. No matter. I left with my freedom intact.

Chapter 78

In this time Peter Van Dine reached out to me with an urgent request for a tete a tete, word having come to him of my involvement with the word. And so I hastened to him.

A writer who could produce two pages a day was simply flying, Peter asserted, but day after day the sheet in his typewriter remained blank. Many, many were the impediments that had grown up between him and his desire. Oh, the ideas for projects were there, but he could commit nothing to paper.

Clearly, Peter was in a state of constriction waiting for le mot juste. I wasn't having it.

"They're only words. You make them too important," I said, there in a nutshell expressing my philosophy.

He gave me an appraising look and began to speak but then succumbed to spontaneous and involved chuckling informed by the complexities of his mind in regard to writing and the specific word units that his universe required. I figured he was wanting me to see by this mild eruption the way a pedigreed mentality can work and so had cause to attribute it to unkind dismissal. He was having me understand that my offering to him was akin to coming upon a stymied Beethoven and slapping him on his massive brow and saying, "Loosen up, Ludwig. They're only notes, for Christ's sake." And because shame has to have receptors to receive it, mine swung open to admit their abundant share and it was many centuries that I lived in the place of humiliation that would not allow for my presence on the earth.

But just as sparks fly upward, utterance has the need to rise and find its rightful place so I painted the following manifesto upon strategic sites in New York City itself—the Metropolitan Museum of Art and MoMa and Lincoln Center and the Forty-second Street Library—so that whether it was art or music or the printed word to which you were streaking for refuge, you could be offered the truth as it had been presented to me:

> Words are important insofar as they give a person peace. They have to travel far into the system to achieve that goal. For that reason their journey should be made as happy as circumstances permit. A requirement is that they possess tensile strength and never show themselves as underweight or have the properties of a hanging string. Not to be overlooked is their molecular constitution. The function of a word is to keep the world at bay while at the same time describing it, but the real purpose is to feel good about one's self and live not in the shadow of indecision. By hurling yourself against the word, you have a chance to penetrate the word, to get right into the word and make it your own, so that when you are blown about by experience, you have the word to protect you. And there is no reason to be harsh, to make it a federal case when specific density for greatness is lacking. You can gently stroke the words that are malnourished. Nowhere is the folly of man more evident than in talking when he could be writing, for talking commits nothing to posterity. Always write to the point of depletion so you do not have to do it anymore but now can go and stand in the sun and love the world for what it is and gain the harmony you are seeking because writing is love with the physical property of the word attached to give it the substance of permanence. Of

course, writing is also sorrow and regret and unbelievable anger and dying to all you hold dear so you can live in the space created by the words you have written. It can be a call to the feast of all that you never received.

Not by coincidence had I bought the Viking series of interviews with writers. I had them on my shelf where I could see them and they could see me. In these pages Truman Capote showed his face, and I told him he had the fragile sweetness of youth behind all that middle age pastiness and that he was among my very favorites and that I was not in touch with any feeling of wanting to destroy him for being among the chosen. The indicators of excellence were revealed: his genius IQ; the three stories submitted to and accepted by the *New Yorker* at the same time. The great and generous gift he shared was his ritual of starting each writing day with coffee and then going on to sherry and moving on to bourbon in the afternoon. He assured me that drinking went with writing and that it took you into the wild, fruitful territory you could not reach without it and that a faithful friend was a blessing on your life.

I told Truman my dream of the night before. I had been walking hand in hand with Mona. We were two children in the darkness that had fallen. A storm was raging and claps of thunder shook our bodies as we headed through a mountain pass. Each step seemed difficult with the burden of fear so greatly upon us. Truman assured me that comfort and safety and happiness were only a glassful of wine away.

Chapter 79

As I have said, the building where I was living was known to me now. I had stood in the courtyard taking its measure and from the inside received its smells, as it had received mine. I had slept within its walls and woken to the songs of the sparrows in the tormented trees beyond my windows. The pandemonium of the trucks on Tenth Avenue had made itself known to me and yet I was still there.

Billy Billson lived right above me—not Bill or William but Billy, that easy tipoff to adolescence hung onto. He had legs disproportionately short for his body and a sheen on his pale and aging face and small, mean sliver lips. He had come to New York with a dream of stardom and an imperviousness to relationships with women that could sustain themselves and mature into the mode of marriage and children. He was a child scrounging for the crumbs of recognition that life could bring him. In the low-rent apartment he had lucked into he practiced over and over the song "Take Me Home, Country Roads," the lyrics expressing a yearning for a place he could not go back to and that never was for him to begin with except in the mush of his own mind. And yet the song evoked longing in all who heard it and the desperate desire to do something great so it could be about them and them alone in the emotion that it wrought, the narcissistic component in all the citizenry accessed and activated by those notes. I was not outside the effect of the song; it revved me up as well, but not the abortive version that Billy Billson sang, in the false-start way of practicing the opening but never going beyond to the development, the way he couldn't go on to the development of his own Billy life. I had it in for Billy Billson for being who he was in range of me being who I was. Have you ever wanted to punish your double? Have you? Have you?

My ceiling was of pressed tin, which summoned in me an appreciation of the care with which things used to be made. Above it I could hear his scuffling feet and the squeaking of mattress springs those times he got *lucky*. Billy Billson understood the power of revulsion and why we stayed away from each other except for the meaningless hello.

Then a nomad wind blew Billy Billson's friend Jedediah Judd back into his life and the life of the building. He had come north again to escape the scarcity of the South and perpetuate his itinerant way. Jedediah Judd was countrified. He had grown up with mossy rocks and snakes that bit and hominy grits between his teeth, and as an adult maintained an ability to sleep in the weeds when he wasn't making the YMCAs of different cities his home. He had a mentality that smelled of railroad stations and cheap diners and ravioli out of the can and the slow speech of where he came from. That crescent-shaped scar hadn't gone anywhere. If anything, it had taken on a glow, as if to insinuate more fevered realities of Jedediah Judd's shadow life as he placed his bearish hulk before me. All I can say is that I stood transfixed and in full bondage to my love. Brother of mine, I thought, staring into those eyes like viscous pools and mobilized to do right for him, to bring out the goodness that was surely there if he only had a second chance, the words *reclamation project* flashing on his forehead.

He told me the truth, that he was not afraid of the Automat on Christmas day or the Blarney Stone on Thanksgiving, that he was content to do small freelance jobs and had no big need for people or for things and had the cut to testify to the pain that overreach could bring.

We sat in the quiet of Billy Billson's apartment, where, with Billy off at sea singing "Take Me Home, Country Roads" to cruise ship vacationers, we watched the 1970 World Series—Johnny Bench and Joe Morgan and Tony Perez and Leo Cardenas and all the rest of the Big Red Machine with their home field AstroTurf advantage, and took in rude Pete Rose making faces at pitched balls before punishing them into base hits. In that moment Jedediah Judd had no need of a woman's comfort before she handed you the bill. As for me, I had the opportunity to make of my surrogate brother a walking talking thing outside the context of the building where I was born.

That night I was brought out of sleep by the phone ringing in the darkness. The illuminated alarm clock said 3:11 and because of the hour, I was fearful out of my mind of Mona having being murdered in the Boston blackness. A woman was on the line. She could have been down the block but said she was in another state.

"This is Eulanda? Eulanda Briggs? I'm trying to reach Jedediah Judd? I'm calling from Mobile? Mobile, Alabama? He's a son of the South living on the floor above you? Would you be a dear and go and fetch him?" Those question marks like intimacy hooks at the end of each sentence.

I paused at the door lest it be a ruse and Eulanda from Mobile stood outside with a carving knife held high.

"I'm here, baby, if you are," I shouted, by way of self-exhortation, as I opened the door. The landing being empty, I raced upstairs.

"Jedediah? You've got a call from Eulanda? She wants a word with you and said to bang real hard because you have tricks up your sleeve? Are you there that I can hear from you?"

I was ready to leave when I heard movement inside. The door opened wide and Jedediah Judd stood in his boxer shorts, dark and scowling and looking like Heathcliff.

"She's on the line with the weight of her own urgency? What do I do?"

For a while he just stared at me as an unwelcome messenger.

"Tell her to go away," he finally said.

"Go away?"

"Tell her I'm not here."

"But how does the woman have the investigative reach to get my number in the first place?"

Jedediah Judd allowed himself a yawn and a stretch. "She has her ways. Now do as I tell you," he said, using brevity as a tool of enforcement.

The front door to the building was throwing a fit, banging wildly back and forth, at the instigation of a wind that wouldn't show itself. I saw its berserk motion for what it was, the urgency for evil in the world at large. Suddenly it returned to stillness, but not before the message had been delivered of a world grown pregnant with its own destructive nature, and so I fled behind the door of my own apartment.

"Did he tell you to say he was away? Did he command you with his scowl?" It was as if Eulanda had been present all along.

I answered in the affirmative.

"Honey, I can tell from the sound of your voice that you're a sweet, gentle man? That you want to be on the side of right? That you want to correct historical wrongs? I'll be in touch, baby? I'll be in touch?"

I lay awake for a while. The wind had picked up again and the door was once more banging. The phone held steady on the bedside table maintaining its blackness, as it had through every night I closed my eyes and withdrew from the world. The phone had a sense of its own image and its own strength that it could remain the same from day to day and allow me to place my fingers within the holes in its rotary dial without so much as flinching. I thanked it for its constancy, and told it we should both get some sleep after the night that we had had.

I told Dr. Zimmer that Jedediah Judd really had a hold on me and how Eulanda Briggs had been on the line. I told her about the

Cincinnati Reds and the astonishing contempt Pete Rose showed for pitched balls and the face he made and the missiles he sent into the outfield gaps. But always I came back to Jedediah Judd and how he didn't need to write and didn't need to read, that the men's shelters of the Eastern Seaboard were not repellent to him but had an atmosphere he could endure and of the bus terminal grime that attached to him, no American dream of the big life galvanizing him into materialistic action.

"A bum? You are telling me about a bum?" Dr. Zimmer replied.

Now Diane Sunburst was herself entering into a deeper relationship with "Take Me Home, Country Roads," never mind Billy Billson and his superficial rendition. She proved her development banging open the front door with the song not only in her heart but in the air with savage possessiveness, as if it had a meaning for her life that it couldn't have for any other and as if she alone deserved that meaning, and the smell of her was strong in her passing by.

In spite of her doctor boyfriend, I had an obligation to my own calling nature, enhanced by my wine, which took me out of my retiring pose in an attempt to bring her near when she was settled in her apartment. I dialed her number and I dialed it good.

"It's not going to happen, creep. Not now, not ever," she said, hearing my shaky voice coming from the place of darkness into her brightness, and slammed down the phone.

I stared at the phone and it stared at me, silence prevailing except for the belligerent trucks rampaging along Tenth Avenue. They had their wheels of progress that needed turning along the routes that had been given them, and I needed my own, and the two did not necessarily need a point of intersection; better, frankly, that they never met. And so I sought out the regions of my world that I could find. If Diane Sunburst, in the affiliation with medical technology that she needed, rejected me, if she sought to dream the expiring dream of a thirty-five-year-old beauty queen, if she sought the ring that would save her before her expiration date, it was not for me to judge from the vantage point of my younger years, but simply to move on the wheels of progress that had been given me.

Olga Nubescu had a name that hid itself from American sunlight in the darkness of her Rumanian ancestry. It was simply not for Olga Nubescu to sing "Take Me Home, Country Roads." She showed tenderness as an attribute possibly born of her wounded condition, and her tabby cat, Dolor, was the recipient. No meow or brush against her legs went without a response. But even with Dolor to love, pain was pushing for expression. Olga could not be in harmony with her parts with a memory that kept calling her away.

I came to her nocturnally with all the insistence of my own needs intact. I understand that now, from the vantage point of sorrow not just for her but for myself as I was back then. She was not in the condition for sex, and had dancer's legs almost too strong for it, but with a bottle of wine to provide the cover, I made the attempt on her unresponsive body. This was not the paradise of pleasure that I was seeking.

Afterward, I assailed her with all the things that Mona was doing for me in Boston and gave her the high points of my girlfriend's legend. I mentioned the prospect of law school the following September. She showed neither approval nor disapproval, and perhaps her indifference made the few words she offered impactful before she went on to reconnoitering her own territory.

"You have a lot in you. You should do something with your life," she said quietly, as if my love life and my law school ambition had provided no cachet. Her words were spoken from a solemn, truth-bearing sorrow.

"What are you saying?"

But she had turned to her cat to stroke its fur, as if to say that further access was being denied.

I took her downstairs to show her my life, and yet the only object of her interest was not the typewriters or the cameras or abundance of pencils and pens but a self-portrait by Mona over the piano,

Mona standing with her hands at her side and palms outward, one foot slightly behind the other, present not for the viewer's pleasure but for the viewer's inspection, as if presenting herself in defiant tentativeness of her own womanhood. Even ablaze, her eyes could not hide the sense of a wound.

Olga was struck speechless as she stood for several minutes before the painting. When finally she turned away, it was only to flee the apartment.

(Yes, I hear the hooves of your horses on the trail stirring clouds of dust, you posses of he-men riding hard, savage in your desire to bring me to justice for my insensitivity, as if I was aware of it at the time.)

The next night, when the nexus between wine and sex had established itself, I came calling once again. As if nothing were amiss, we lay together in the dark with only Dolor to keep an eye on us, while upstairs there were the midnight ramblings of Diane Sunburst and from below the dark vibration of Jedediah Judd, Kerouac's dharma bum. Olga started with the present, before summoning the past.

His name was Polesku Nagy, and as I might have suspected, the pianist at her ballet studio. His notes made her come alive in the way that breathing alone could not. He had access to her soul with the chords he struck, and she often fantasized in bed of counting the wiry hairs on his formidable head. She said the sounds of his own sadness were in his music, a music with the will to traverse the distance needed to enter her selective heart. No other man had ever gained such access. No man. But this thing for Polesku Nagy, while it had been going on for a long time, remained unrequited. Did she maybe have to take the initiative so it could be elsewhere than the theater of her mind, I asked, but this she dismissed, saying simply that he knew, he knew, on the basis of the strong thoughts and looks she directed his way.

"So he can make you dance but you can't make him love?" It was doubtful that she heard me. Her mind was active now, but not with direct responses to my words. The past, of which she proceeded to speak, was pressing on her.

"My parents died when I was young. It was snowing hard that day. The accumulation was significant. There was no heat in the house when the authorities came to tell me of the accident that had claimed them. There was, eventually, the foster home in which I was placed. My stepfather was a large man and my stepmother was a small woman."

When the nocturnal visits of the filthy one to her bed became beyond unbearable, she ran away to live with a wealthy family in the attic of their home, where she served her new masters as a domestic. I tried to imagine her in Green Bay, Wisconsin, with slabs of beef piled high on the plate and family members eating dinner in their shoulder pads. The picture seemed a long, cold way from the delicacy of dance slippers and a tutu and Edgar Degas set to music. It wasn't lost on me in the time she needed to tell her tribulation tale that Dolor received it lying down but with ears alert, signifying this was something she too needed to hear. Many hours passed before we released from each other on this particular night, and the only status report I can give is that while my mind and heart remained apart, my memory was operating at a high level.

Chapter 80

Luke had not died yet. That would come later. My brother still had his life going on with his pants out of his shirt as if ready for action. I visioned him in the strategic places he was permitted, sitting in the building lobby at night with the boys of dysfunction from the neighborhood or going for a spot of takeout tea to the luncheonette around the corner, or riding off on that foray into the mountains he so loved with bottles of wine attached to his person and a blueprint for defeat operating within his mentality. The building exerted an enervating effect, sapping him of the rigor that the world required, causing him to turn back rather than step it up a notch.

He still had Brenda to come home to now. He did not have to go cruising the streets of Greenwich Village on his motorcycle. The other women who had been in Luke's life were not factors in his current scene. Maureen had gone away to the Bronx and then Alaska with her son by Luke, enabling Luke to expand himself in the way that he could, and since the son who was born to them was the progeny of someone he had left behind, Luke had to leave him behind too. Maureen had the animal and spiritual tendencies of one who could deliver babies as a primary element for bonding forever, and had it in her mentality to get old before her time. Luke needed something different. He needed the lust engine of Nora from Norway to secure himself to, someone alive and acquiescent and energetic and yes, bold, in the playing fields of sex. But her roving eye left him feeling frightened and angry, the end coming when he crossed the line with his hand.

Maureen worked as a barmaid in some makeshift town that had sprung up along the pipeline. There was, from across the continent, a continual cry from her wounded heart. She was born for the marriage bed, and though she went with the beer and shot men who made love to her with hard hats on their heads and bore the weight of their strong bodies, her circle was incomplete without the father of her child. The hurt was evident in the forced smile she wore in photos she sent my mother of her with her boy, also named Luke. In my mother Maureen had an ally. It was not in God's plan for a marriage to be rendered asunder. My mother was in accord with Maureen that Luke had treated her like dirt, just as my mother had been treated like dirt by her own children. I understood my mother's lock on sorrow and regret and sadness. I saw that they were her domain.

Brenda was another matter. She was not bred for mourning. She too lived in the realm of her senses and danced to the sound of James Brown in the manner of one seeking to get it on with fast removal of her skintight jeans and flimsy top in being true to her own nature.

Before getting it on with Luke, she had gotten it on with Lenny Cerone. Lenny had expertise with cars and at the time of their first meeting had a look with the jeans and T-shirts he filled so well causing women to melt down in desire, Brenda being just out of reform school and back on One Hundred Eleventh Street and in need of social contacts. Lenny had looks and Lenny had sex and a car to do it in. The fabulous features derived from his Italian ancestry riveted Brenda's eye and took her for long distances in her mind. And so they made love to "Needles and Pins" and "Ferry Across the Mersy" and the full-throttle sound of Aretha Franklin, everyone from Percy Sledge to the Fab Four at one time or another a part of their backseat romance. Because the singer had no ownership of the song, it extended beyond the singer to the listener so he could have his dream of love or the sorrow of it being lost never to return.

Lenny Cerone had an assessing mind that read you for what you were worth. He got next to Luke when Luke had no one else to go to, having returned from Europe and still healing from the clobber action of Nancy Becker, his high school girlfriend, on his soul, she having gone on to Vassar College while he hung out on the corner. Luke saw what Lenny Cerone had with Brenda with envy and lust in his heart and took her away. More truthfully, Lenny Cerone took himself away from Brenda with the smack head way that was slowly consuming him, turning his eyes dead in his pasty face. When Brenda gave him a son, he did not know where to go with the destiny he'd been handed. While she gathered herself for motherhood, he got even more of a nod on the junk.

Lenny's father was the engineer for a large apartment building on the Upper West Side. He had long since parted ways with Lenny's mother but maintained an abiding desire to do right by his prodigal son. He saw to it that Lenny was placed on the building's payroll so he could utilize his mechanical skills, but soon noted the disappearance of his tools and noted further track marks on Lenny's arm and, though heartbroken, had no choice but to see him as the absconding addict that he was and banned him forthwith from the premises.

Brenda saw that her man had wronged her. Wrong was wrong, and Lenny in his dilapidated state was all about wrongness. With a newborn in her arms and no chance at a viable life with her mate, she went home to her parents, and it was at this stage that Luke's awareness of her heightened. If it was in the nature of life for some to rise and some to fall, who was he to ignore the pattern established throughout all of human history? Because Lenny had only the street on which to rest his head, Luke took him in, but seeing Lenny's helplessness only boosted Luke's desire to fill the void created by the absence of Lenny in Brenda's life with his own stuff. And let it be said that Brenda responded positively to the overtures being made, her heart not quite fit for love but bent more on revenge. If someone cared to say that Brenda loved Luke and Luke loved Brenda, it would also have to be said that he loved her more than she could ever love him and neither of them in truth loved each other all that much. It was as if they were in the aftermath of love and something else had taken its place; he had his rooftop lodgings and his motorcycle and she had her racy underwear.

The consolidation occurred within a month. Lenny was out and Brenda and her baby were in, though not before Lenny made a loud sound of outrage at Luke's perfidy.

The afternoon that I walked in, she was alone and pulled me close to inspect an ad for lingerie torn from a magazine. Which way did I go, toward the black or the green bra and panties? The ad and her proximity brought the summoning call of sex, but the prospect of drawing near to her was mitigated by her reform school background and the lack of development that showed in her face and my horror at the reality my brother had been cooking in her kitchen before me.

"I can't answer that. The subject of lingerie is for private contemplation," I said, but she waited me out with a smiling, predatory stare. "Black," I continued.. "It's not a color but doesn't need to be to go where others can't in your senses."

"Luke says your girlfriend is very beautiful."

"I think so." Thinking also *Luke should stay away with his words and his hands from what is not his lest a war with lifelong consequence get its start.*

Nothing was said of what was to come: swap clubs and the couples they paired with; pornographic movies for their viewing pleasure; nights of howling pain Luke would endure when she went off with the men that she could find after abuses inflicted by his regime; the poverty of their lust-filled lives that I tried to pretend was not my own.

Later, I turned the camera on myself and found the look that I'd been fleeing: dullness in the eyes and the unyielding reality of my misshapen head.

But then I got lucky on west Fifty-sixth street, with its cobblestone roadway and forlorn warehouses and straight-on view of a Hudson River pier at which ocean-crossing liners had been seen to dock in the long ago, provoking a mood of something lost that you couldn't name while sensing it had something to do with your child's face in your mother's skirt or even the decade before you were born when everything was somehow still all right. The block was flung way over where people wouldn't look to find me and where I could consolidate the apartness in which I was living.

I stood in the middle of the street, with the river behind me and my particulars on display. Mona had come down from Boston, and, being shorter, found the right angle into me. She knew what to do with a camera even while skeptical of its function. I wore a used bomber jacket with the fleece collar turned up and corduroys and leather boots. I had Mona's opinion that I was worthy of the camera but also had her laughter flying up at me that I would consider this immortality.

The garbage trucks were in striking distance, with uniformed workers remaining faithful to them, and the sky above was overcast. Fall had given its own shape and feel to the air; there was the promise of home fires burning and the melancholy of finding them out of reach. Without warning she clicked, and suddenly the trucks erupted into a riot of sound and stench before rumbling past the reach of our senses.

Then it was her turn. I caught myself about to shoot from the height where I was standing, but stooped severely to try the angle that she had shot from. True to form, she stared into the camera with aloof refinement, as if some powerful internal discussion of my personal worth and that of my endeavors was now in progress. A question had formed on her face as to whether she should stay or move on. She wore a brown knee-length coat tightly belted with a black pile collar turned up to ring the back of her head. Her hair had changed; where it used to be long and curly, it was now bowl-cut and straight, as if she were trying to bend without breaking in the direction of an androgynous femininity. Yes, she had stardust on her and the scenario that had been written and was being orchestrated was still in place. Once again I heard it all: she would come to New York and the galleries of Fifty-seventh Street and SoHo would welcome her. And yes, her photo would be on the cover of *Time* magazine, to ignite envy and wonder in one and all. But there was now, for whatever the reason, a sliver of doubt, *a cloud of uncertainty* in my own mind as to her desirability, given that Genius Man did not seem to want her for all time. (I did not know then that the breakdowns would follow, and in their aftermath the pills and the psychiatrists who offered them, that gallery doors would remain closed to her, that there would be low-paying jobs, that she would join Olga and Diane Sunburst in the slash brigade and cower indoors, her ears stuffed with tissue paper to shut out the taunts of people on the street she knew to be talking about her. These were things I did not foresee, even if I was no longer in the full grip of fear and admiration of her powerful, glittering American express.)

Chapter 81

Failure waited for spring to come calling, not for the first or last time, of course, as that is the way of failure, to be adamant as to its purpose and sequestering in its result. Failure requires you to retire to the quiet corners of life. It requires you to shroud yourself in its staying power and to say you are its own. It tells you the justice you are seeking is the justice you have found. It says the repositioning of a used tissue in a dilapidated room will have to count as a successful day.

My mailbox had a place of neutrality in the life of the city. It had housed many letters over the years, and now it was giving shelter to mine. No study yet has shown that it had a predisposition toward evil. In fact, the mailbox was stuffed with magazines required for the adornment of my mentality. Still, it didn't take an excavation to find the letter. Though I had great apprehension, I did not carry it into my apartment as if it were a rotting fish.

The letter told me things I didn't want to hear. The green light to success had turned to yellow. A giant thwack rose out of the letter and knocked me silly, robbing me of all feeling save pain. It said that I remained unchosen, and said it in the way that it could:

Because of the unusually high number of applications for admission to the class of 1974, the selection process has been extremely difficult. We regret to inform you that we cannot offer you a place in the entering class at this time. We have, however, placed you on our waiting list. There is, of course, no guarantee that an opening will occur, and so we will understand if you explore other options.

I took my rage to Dr. Zimmer. No one needed to hear what I had to say more than she, and mannequins were seen leaving their storefront windows that they might hear as well.

"He promised. He promised. He gave me his word," I said, over and over, referring to the blond, buttoned-down man in the rep tie and gray suit who had interviewed me the previous year. I carefully reconstructed our conversation from that fateful interview and the image of his short, thinning hair despite his relative youth so as to give her detail against which she could contemplate the words *betrayal profound,* and yet, even with a virtually verbatim recital, there rose in me the frightening suspicion that she was believing I had simply heard what I wanted to hear.

A slave to my need for validation, that same day I rushed out to Newark and entered the pristine law school building amid the ruins of the city, certain that defeat here would sideline me forever.

The dean's secretary sat with her spine ramrod straight typing on a pale green IBM Selectric.

"I am here to see Mr. Bennett Foxhall Grant."

"Do you have an appointment?" Her fingers had lifted from the keyboard.

"A sense of urgency requires that I see him."

"What is your name, please?"

I gave it to her.

"And the purpose of your visit?"

"Justice in its full dimension."

Though she looked at me askance, she reached for the receiver. "Dean Grant, I have a young man who says he has an urgent need to speak with you. HIs name is Luther Garatdjian… Yes, well, all he will tell me is that it is about justice in its full dimension."

She hung up the phone. "You may go in now," she said coldly.

Dean Grant was sitting back with his feet on his desk, the worn soles of his loafers there for my inspection and his chin resting on his joined hands.

"What can I do for you, Mr. Garatdjian?"

"I was here to see you last year. At the time I had been wait-listed for admission and you assured me at the time that I would surely get in this year if I reapplied. But once again I have been placed on the waiting list. I would ask you to meditate on the word *promise* and hear the legions of children worldwide saying over and over, in the repetitive fashion of those deeply wounded, 'But you promised. You promised.'"

"Promised what?"

"I was promised entry to a world of recognition so I could be properly dressed and properly function in the world. This I was promised, Mr. Bennett Foxhall Grant. And do not tell me not to use your full name, since you have gone public with it for the intimidation of mankind."

He went to his file cabinet and pulled out a folder. "Oh yes, I see. You are on the waiting list."

"And as I said, that is the problem. I return to the fact that I have not been apprehended by the facility and made secure on its premises. That is a giant problem."

"Mr. Garatdjian…"

"Mr. Luther Norair Johan Hatchidor Garatdjian, for two can play the name game…"

"If you will forgive me, I am running out of patience. Your application is entirely reasonable. In most years it would get you in. But the fact is that we have had two exceptional years in a row. Who could predict such a thing? We have a large number of successful applicants who in other years would breeze into Harvard or Yale." He resumed resting his chin on the interlaced fingers of his hands.

"Yes, I can imagine them in their attitudes and postures of excellence. And I hear your assertion that one must be crushed by the evidence of their assaultive high numbers and so I take my leave."

I stood up to go about my business. As I did so, I sensed that I had pushed against the limits of decency in asking America to give me more than it should, that in fact I had entered into a state of loathsomeness that would require an outward sign of recognition. And so I exited in the posture of a doofus, with my shoulders hunched and my arms hanging down and my knees bent in a way that would convey to him that my understanding was keen as to what had just happened, that once more I had disgraced myself before the royalty of America.

I continued to live with my mentality for days on end. People were kind. They came and poured gasoline on my body and anointed my head as well and danced around my crushed stature before striking the ignition match. Oh, what a stench I made as I shared my burning flesh with the environs, but finally the fire won out as a purifying element and I could rise from ash and be whoever I now was.

The flight path to sanctimoniousness had been taken away from me. Vileness should not be met with success. And yet, following the maelstrom of my ill nature angels flew from the law school building and the coldness heart of Mr. Bennett Foxhall Grant was seen to be melted in a letter that began, "We are happy to inform you..."

Was it this positive response arising from my unlovely aria that inevitably ruined me, that sunk me deeper in my lake of shame for having forced the hand of the administration through guilt of my inducing? Was I now set up to go where I truly was not wanted and truly did not deserve to be? Were the flaws multiple in my own peculiar system of justice that had led me to such a place?

At first I was radiant as a star can be at my newfound success, and reveled in the joy my inebriated senses could bring at the knowledge that I had achieved the status of the lovely, and I felt the sweet harmony of my public and private parts in a world gone mad for the promotion of my own pleasure. Gone was the blackness of my previous days, as Dr. Zimmer was quick to see.

"You are a different person. Astonishing."

As if operating on some internal clock the time came for a hard-eyed appraisal of the failure stations that my siblings were intent on manning. I saw them at their posts of impoverishment and saw further that they showed no signs of flagging fidelity to them, the sole exception being Vera, who had no sanctions in place against success, no need to brutalize her nation should such a thing occur. She was now at CCNY, and rather than ridicule its academic standards, was lapping up evening school credits and developing a taste for steaming As upon her plate to buttress her assertion that she was Phi Beta Kappa material. All told, when her parts were gathered together, she stood six feet tall with added inches on the horizon, this with a look of confidence and even triumph on her smiling face to further unsettle all provinces of my mind.

And it was in this context that I tried to adapt myself to the new reality and have a human contact with her in a coffee shop where we sat with our Cokes and cherry cheese danishes, for which the nation is deservedly famous.

"I feel the weight of law school upon me. I feel it as a muzzle on the language I would dare to speak."

"You shouldn't do anything you don't want to do," she said, a smile of satisfaction appearing that had less to do with her pleasure at devouring her cherry cheese danish than the verbal evidence of my attempt to disguise weakness as uncertainty. I saw her rising high above my crumbling structure; she communicated a stance of inevitable triumph, an unspoken message that she had the stuff to move ahead with her life regardless of the developmental flaw in my own. It was a smile that told me we could only be friends on the surface with the agenda that had been set.

It was in this context that I made my fateful inquiry, and set in motion all the forces that could and would destroy me, so that I would have to rearrange my face in all the public and private places where I was present so no one but no one could see the envy and hurt and *defeat* my sensitive mug was being conditioned to express.

"What are your plans?" I asked, sensing I did not know what, only that it was something ominous.

Her smile seemed to widen and her words did nothing to comfort me.

"You'll find out shortly," she said.

I didn't know what to say. My mind had left my body and sat outside for her full and easy inspection. Powerful trains driven by powerful women crossed over onto the main track, the boxcars adorned with a quote from D. H. Lawrence about men in their vanity sucking at the bitter weed of failure. In that moment one such train ran over me at a clip that left me shredded, then put together, only to be shredded once again by the repetitive action of unending wheels and at a volume that shattered all mechanisms for hearing. Many were the trains that ran over me. Many were they that deserved to. You could say that a new world order had established itself, only it was one that had always been there.

I was an artist without an art. Because words can only mean something if they have some pedigree and images from a worthless source can never stand on their own. Nevertheless Vera was drafted for a photo project that brought us to a place of unhealthy proximity. I had assigned her face to the multiple lenses of my multiple cameras, less to move it from a place of obscurity to a shining presence among the uninformed masses but to utilize her photogenic quality for the building of my portfolio.

There were others as well I sought as subjects:

I shot Olga Nubescu in the natural light of her apartment and appropriated her nakedness for my own purpose.

I shot Auntie Eve, in the addled state that age had brought her to.

I shot Naomi and Chuck on their bed with pills and bottles all about. I shot the sound of his gravel-voiced meanness. I shot his lies. I shot his distortions. I shot and shot until he was not there anymore. I shot Naomi in the face but I also shot her in her body. I shot her out on the ledge and within the barred windows of the city and state institutions that second-homed her. I shot her droning on with her monologue of misery. I shot her in anticipation of the sorrows that were to come. Believe me, I shot her so her life and death could live in my memory.

I shot Luke. I shot him in a stupor holding a coffee mug as he sat on the side of his bed with the afternoon air smelling of his sleep.I shot the leash the building had assigned him. I shot his rage at my mother knocking upon his door. I shot his sadness and his tissue of lies that passed as understanding and every last concoction of his pleasure-seeking mind.

I found Rachel and shot her too and shot the smirk I did not then know was in the last stages of its reign, or that her caustic wit would merge with the deeper currents of her spiritual track, and that it would never again be her intention or her act to run naked down Broadway for the eyes of the young president who was no more. I only know that I shot her good in the confines of the escape hatches she fled through to a further state of her own aloneness. I shot the memory of her brokenhearted over the boyfriend she couldn't keep. I shot her tears and the surrender to her loss that they evoked. I shot my mother holding her and providing the comfort she could give for the loveliness lack her daughter had that caused the man who held her heart to say no more, no more. And yes, I shot the Chock Full O' Nuts restaurants and the hope they provided with the daily presentation of soups and sandwiches and coffee and cream pies on their menu board and one in particular that it should be across from the Columbia University campus and from which she could keep an eye on what the Ivy league was doing. Trust me when I say I shot her in all the meadows of madness she wandered in her afflicted mind.

I shot Hannah with her tongue between her lips and her hand raised to its correct smacking position. Then I shot the violence of her nature and the sorrow of her wound, seeking to get within the center of her turmoil and finding only havoc where I went. I shot her at the refrigerator at night, when, in an act of supreme revenge, she tore open my father's brown bag and devoured his stinky blue cheese. I shot her leaving Hamburger Heaven with a greasy bag intent on devouring the contents therein. I shot the secrets she wouldn't tell and the guards on around the clock duty outside the storage site where they were kept. But I could not shoot her from the point of view of understanding where she had been before I was born in the world of my father when he was larger upon the earth. This I could not do with the cameras that I owned.

I tried to shoot my mother but was turned back by barriers of love, beyond which I could not go. I tried to see the fragments that made up her constitution but found them not, and had to flee the scene of the crime I would commit in the presence of the light she sent to blind me.

Nor did I shoot my father. His smile had more parts than my film could quite contain, and when I was not looking, the tide of his own history washed over my cameras, dousing them into uselessness.

But when I shot Vera she shot me back. I could not shoot her adequately to have her mine *when I told myself I didn't even want to have her mine.* She was my sister and that went back a long long time. Because it is something to have a sister and a trick of nature to have four when you only wanted none, knowing you cannot see around them but only into them. The shooting took place indoors, on a street where she dared to live. In the confines of that apartment I exploded the flash in her face so she could be brighter than the natural light would permit. Then I set the camera down tight on the tripod so I could have the luxury of a slow shutter release that would give the natural light the time that it needed. Oh, the camera did its work, and Vera's face got truly involved. But then I made a faux pas. I presumed to see a peace where none had been. I asked her for a follow-up session, and when she balked, words got spoken from a friction place that heated our emotions. "You have serious problems. Get some help," she said, and took the effective action of slamming down the phone to seal her triumph, leaving me no choice but to be found some days later in the bushes with the stamp so very permanent of defeat upon my face.

Chapter 82

In all this time tenants from far-flung countries and wherever remained a sea of faceless sustenance as they appeared at the renting office window with their American money, and I could be of the mind that nothing touched me so long as distance was ensured with a sign that read:

I have zilch to do with you but you have everything to do with me.

Now fork it over.

The thing was that Vera also committed herself to make an appearance and you can count upon the fact that she wore a face of malign radiance with scanning devices fully operational for an examination of my thought stream.

"I got in. I got in," she said, in a voice of exaltation.

"Got in where?" I said, sending out words so very packed with fear.

"It starts with a *C* and ends with an *a.*"

"Tell me what you are about, so the torment to my pride can truly begin. I am on the verge of expiration," I said.

"Columbia, gem of the ocean," she began to sing, but got no further, for she was not the kind to have a mind retentive of lyrics. "Well, aren't you going to congratulate me?"

As I struggled to respond I heard her from my place of pain turn her voice of victory elsewhere.

"Mother, mother. I got in. I got in to Columbia. They're going to give me a full scholarship."

"Oh, that makes my heart so happy," I heard my mother say. Not knowing where to go, not knowing what to think while trying to rearrange my face so my happiness too could show.

Some months later, on a warm September day, I boarded a bus at Port Authority for Newark, New Jersey. I took with me some fear, as if the bus was taking me far from Mona and into a land where the cruelty of competition and masculine hardness reigned supreme and love had no possibility for existence. And yet, after leaving behind the tangle of ramps and passing through the Lincoln Tunnel, the bus emerged into the light of day once again, and with that light came inner light, a surge of astonishing joy that banished my disturbance in a flash. *I would be the son my mother wanted and star-bright in Mona's eye. I would shed my thievery—call it what it was—and be a man of the world with the capacity to provide for those I professed to love.*

Charred ruins remained from the riots of four years earlier, but rage did not show its face; young blacks were not seen fighting the power with fury fists. At Broad and Market stood a Chock Full O' Nuts holding to its standard of quality in a city not my own and there I stopped and ordered a nutted cheese sandwich and an orange drink and made a full meal of it with two doughnuts so I could be filled up and deal with what was to come.

Some blocks away I came to the law school building, but a force field of phobic fear rose to meet me at the sight of incoming students chatting outside. It went through my mind that they were there on their merits; they had not pleaded their way in. Further, I saw them in the full flower of their socializing power and capacity for integration into law school life. And so it was essential that I stay on my side of the street and not indicate by facial expression or body language that I had any association with their purpose.

An orientation had been scheduled. Soon the sidewalk was empty. Everyone had moved inside. The feeling of pain and loneliness that overcame me was insufficient as a prod to join them. I knew my place; I was not fit to be among them.

On the bus ride home, a truck passed with the name "Hemingway"in large letters. I had not been an ambulance driver in World War I. I had not run with the bulls in Pamplona. And yet, maybe in defeat I could fall back on words to comfort and console me as well. Soon thoughts of future greatness drove out the shame that I was not suitable for the company of the budding lawyers of America who would go out upon the land with righteous anger as a corrective to all that was wrong. I would find my place in a world apart from the confines of that law school building and the apparatus for justice it instilled in all those who passed through it. The important thing was to continue my own personal narrative in order to remain in sync with the zeitgeist of the nation and not be a law-bound cripple living in the circumscribing jailhouse that the law school building would only turn out to be. I had freed myself to magnify and distort and be all things in order to live at a fuller size here upon the planet. Fidelity to words and all that they can bring was not fidelity to a curriculum.

That evening I rode a city bus crosstown for my appointment with Dr. Zimmer. The riot at Attica, a prison in upstate New York, was on the front page of the *New York Post* and all the dailies. I thought not only of the prisoners rebelling against the cruel conditions of their confinement but of those bicycle caravans of tough young blacks back in my childhood coming from Harlem to the two welfare hotels on my block and the brutal, terrifying, and unprompted displays of violence against white kids, including my brother, that followed. Fear was still my primary lens for viewing race relations, fear that because I was white they would come for me should their uprising collapse the prison walls. If I had other, more rational and compassionate feelings, and I did, they followed after that. Oh you who stand in judgment, understand what a place of origin means.

Dr. Zimmer sat on her throne of judgment ready to continue taming America of its unbridled instincts. To duck the anticipated savagery of her blows, I crawled into the office and sat on the floor in an opposing corner by the door. Then I lay down on my side, with my hands covering my face. Then I lay face down with my arms at my side.

"What is it today? Tell me."

Her words came softly, but harshness was sure to follow, and so I made no reply. Because that is what it means to be German and of a forward motion makeup and to have no truck with American aimlessness.

"So what is it that you are trying to say with your strange behavior?"

"Who are you, even stranger woman from a demented land now wearing a cloak of normalcy who would render a verdict regarding the ambition whose fruits I have yet to place on the table? Who are you to say that from the sounds all about me I cannot put my worth into a form for reading in the pages of a book? Who are you to sequester me from the national noises of the developing decade by wedding me to a law school building situated in the ruins of a city of the dead? Who are you to torment me with your own aspiration so you can present me as your finished product? How can I get back to a childhood I have never left if I have to prosecute to the full extent of the law those more innocent than myself? Why can I not be left in a room to rearrange the Kleenexes until the words I need come forth? Who are you to make a man of me in the way I cannot be, and to separate me from the life force my vital organs are promoting?"

Her fire burning now as hot as ever, she offered up some of her word scorch. "You chickened out, as you Americans say. I believe in calling a spade a spade."

"I chickened out? What constitutes chickening out? And what does it mean to call a spade a spade when a man is running for his life toward the words that can free him and that can be found more in boxcar banter than in the writs and torts of America?"

"Do you not want to be a man?"

"Man? Man? Abolish the word from your vocabulary. You are in America now."

"You are…." She stopped there, the impasse having arrived.

Chapter 83

It was a typical summer night, with the city living in its filth and yet in working order—Picasso's Blue Period resting peacefully within the confines of the darkened Museum of Modern Art and Circle Lines heading up the Hudson River and elevators maintaining their up and down operation and the subways with their steel wheels turning and Park Avenue men in tuxedos and their mates in evening gowns more than holding their own at lavish affairs.

I took my thirst to the local bar and noticed something neither strange nor sinister and yet eventful. The deli across the street was closed, meaning that the man who hit so very hard had gone elsewhere with his night, and I wondered at the victories large and small he had won over the bodies in his way. The anchorman arrived in his Aquascutum trench coat and with the celebrity assigned to him, having presented all the marvels of the American economy and other news that he made worthy with his meaty face so bushy browed. Because he had given the news, he could drink his martinis down. He drank them hard and he drank them fast, and when he was done the bartender gave him the words of respect that he was due. He didn't bum's rush the news anchor out the door by the seat of his pants and stomp his face. Because the news was the news and the anchorman made it more than the news with the face that he had that could tell the news in the way that he did with a voice of earnest authority that made it American and credible. Because the anchorman's news was Aquascutum news, news of the very top-shelf variety. And for that he was rewarded with a tie with a thick knot and other clothes in working order.

The Mets were all over the Reds on the TV. They were beating them with infield singles and passed balls and the three-run long ball, and Jerry Koosman hurt them all night long with southpaw aesthetics, the mechanics of his elegant delivery. He threw sliders that darted and sinkers with the heavy weight of the gravity he impelled and fastballs on the corners and curveballs imbued with drop off the table action. He made George Foster look like a fool. He made Charlie Hustle wave his hand in disgust. He made Johnny Bench push down the helmet on his head even harder before fanning him with his express. He even made Leo Cardenas write his mother in Venezuela that he wanted to come home. Only Tony Perez with his face of patience could solve his mystery, and that was only once.

At the same time let it be clear that New York did not hang proud behind Jerry Koosman all night long, baseball being a forlorn activity in a city that heats up as the night progresses with the urgency of sex and other passions calling. And it was not clear that Shea Stadium should ever have been built, or that the city could forgive itself for such an act, for baseball was known to belong in the Flatbush section of Brooklyn with its double-voweled power and its consonants aligned and the formidable staying power of its historic bridge, whereas the borough of Queens, while it too had double-action vowels to see it through, lacked the ache of memory that only Brooklyn could induce. Because what is a borough that starts its name with a "Q" and ends with an "s" and would have us believe it is royalty in the plural? The name itself bestows an obsolescence in the losing battle that regimes of hauteur fight with the rising tide of democratic impulse that would sweep their privilege into the sea, the borough stinking from the ruler's unclean britches as she sits atop it in the frivolity of aristocratic ritual. All this while airplanes fly in and out, lauding it over the decimated railroads that they conspired to ruin.

It does not matter. All that should concern us is that he was throwing hard and throwing well, and if you would not wish to kiss him deeply and cherish his face or sleep with his uniform jersey on your back or even know that it was his, you can still get on with the business of recollecting that he was there on the TV in the bar that is no more in the time that is no more when the thing that was called to your attention did happen.

I left after the third beer, sensing once more that the manly man bartender wanted no more of my silent niceness, so I picked up a bottle of Burgundy at the neighborhood liquor store. The clerk exposed his bluish gums so I could better see the gold in his teeth. He was obese and unshaven and as I left with my purchase heard him laughing like a hyena, possibly at the jackass ways of the world.

The phone was ringing as I entered my apartment. Vera was on the line.

"Daddy's dead. Daddy's dead. Do you even care?" she said, and in that moment did I hear Van Morrison singing "All right, all right, all right," as I did to this sister who sought to get the jump on me, first with jubilation and now with grief, for I had a remembering mind for the things I held important. Histrionics are not to be encouraged at any time or place, my cruel thought went, seeing the personal drama she was attaching to the life she said was there no more, that life having expired in the washed-out lighting of the hospital emergency room where he was taken by ambulance following his diabetes-induced stroke.

"Mommy wants to be sure that you will come to the funeral. You will come, won't you?"

She still did not know to say *father.* She still did not know to say *mother.* She still did not know not to dwell in the land of the diminutives so she might be released from the idea that something would come to her from them when the time for that something had long since passed.

On Tenth Avenue I flagged a cab, but not before the Serial Murderer Man could say this: "He's sleeping. That's all it is. He's sleeping with his father, and now you have your moms all to yourself. Rejoice in the victory that you have won," while Mrs. Muldooney banged garbage cans together as clashing cymbals in the night.

The driver put the Checker in gear with no seeming acknowledgment of the address I had given her. When she wasn't sucking on her eyeteeth she would erupt in fits of laughter. Altogether she seemed in a world of her own, but then, so was I.

Mercedes Pellagra was the driver's name; so I learned from the hackie's license displayed on the dashboard. At Broadway and Seventy-eighth Street we slowed for an accident. A gray sedan had smashed through a railing and onto the the traffic island. The front end of it was mashed against a tree. The driver was slumped over the wheel. A wailing ambulance could be heard in the distance.

The wreckage lit her up. She laughed with delight, showing a hyena's nature. She was OK with feasting on the torn flesh and shattered bones of half dead men. She had seen death of one kind or another. It was part of her world. I recognized, for all her ugliness, a kindred soul.

"One gone driver," she said, which brought another peal of laughter proclaiming herself to be a new world order existing outside the bounds of empathetic reaction. Only when she had feasted to a state of fullness did she cease her rubbernecking.

I had the gauntlet of my older sisters to run when I entered.

"Svenska has been drinking," Rachel stated. Her smirk was gone.

"Svenska steals and now he drinks," Naomi further stated.

"Do whatever you do, but nobody deprives me and my son," said Hannah.

I went deeper into the apartment—the dining room, the kitchen, down the hallway past the bathroom where Garatdjian ablutions and eliminations had been going on for decades. It was not a long journey, shorter than it had been as a child, to the room where I had had my chance at growing up. And yes, it was the same room, with not the toys of childhood but boxes piled high and stuffed with unsorted content to signify the chaos of who we were. At the end of a narrow but navigable space lay my mother in the bottom tier of the bunkbed Luke and I had once called our own.

I stood in the doorway, at a distance from her. She had taken off her glasses and let down her hair and was in her nightgown. This was my mother. She had been laid low with the building resting on top of her.

"I'm sorry," I said. And I was. Sorry for something. Sorry for the fact that I couldn't feel sorry. Sorry for the fact that I was wrapped up in my own world. Sorry for the detachment that showed on my hideous face.

Without her glasses I was surely just a blur, but she had no need of seeing me, appraising me. She knew who I wasn't and who I was, that I was stone cold with the winds of fury at my back in regard to my father and quite useless in spite of my guise as mother's little helper. There was no softening my lifelong dismissal of him with any words of solace or regret.

She sat up and reached for the amber prescription bottle of sleeping pills on the nightstand. "Lie still so it can take effect," she would say to me on those high school nights when I would go to her for a pill to ease the pain of yet another breakup with Jane Thayer. She had taken off her rubber stockings, and the sight of her blue-veined legs set off waves of horror that caused me to visibly shudder.

"He was taken from me before I could say goodbye." Weeping, she turned off the night lamp and lay back down. She had loved my father. Frightening as he could sometimes be to his children, I had never heard him so much as raise his voice to my mother. She had been his rock.

Only Hannah remained when I returned to the living room.

"Isn't it awful? Don't you think there's something wrong that he should die right under the doctor's nose in the emergency room? Don't you think they should have saved him?"

No one can save the Armenians. Their history has rendered it so, I thought but did not say.

"I mean, don't you think there might be some negligence there that we should see a lawyer about?"

Are you wanting to take flight, Hannah, on the weak wings of whatever case that you can build? Are you seeking once again to journey to Greece and the dark men who will love you good under a blazing Aegean sun? Are you seeking to rise above your own circumstance on the death of the one who has kept you down? Or was it simply that in order to be free he would have to leave because she couldn't, wedded to the scene of the crime as she was with all the horrors of her history intact in her repository of personal secrets. This too I thought but did not say.

She joined me in my silence. And yet the adversarial force field remained impermeable to the love that wished to enter.

That night I called Boston. Because he was of no consequence to Mona and in her memory simply an ancient and infirm creature, she offered only a grunt of acknowledgment, an implicit warning attaching to her sound that I was to go no further than I had lest I be perceived as seeking to mitigate her ongoing assault on patriarchy.

My face contorted by the pain of her brusqueness, I sought out warmth where I thought to find it. I turned to Lydia Van Dine, who had gained sufficient recognition working with learning challenged children that she was being offered free tuition to Teacher's College and a permanent position with the New York City school system. This emergence into the world was in contrast to Peter's commitment to apartness from all systems that sought to impose governance over him.

So once again it was Lydia time. To her I had to go in a state of openness before the wall of estrangement could once more rise. I presented to her the demise that had occurred, presenting only him, my father, and not the particulars of the rest of my family. She in turn spoke to me from the world where she had dwelt, the land of a father deceased by his own hand.

"I have heard it said by our family doctor, who also knows your family, that a great divide exists between the two sets of children, a divide engendered not merely by age but the fact of parentage. He tells me that you have the same mother but two distinct fathers, and assures me that this truth has come from highly informed sources."

A cloud of cigarette smoke came from her mouth as if to belie the clarity she was claiming as her own. But this signal alerting me to obfuscation I could not see. I drank her insanity potion and went in a fevered state to Dr. Zimmer demanding a profound and sweeping inquiry of national proportions as to why a lifelong hoax had been perpetrated on me, with a subpoena out for my mother as the star witness.

Dr. Zimmer met me with savage and predictable resistance.

"I know you are sadistic, but if you should say such a thing to your mother at a time like this, it would be lower than even you have ever gone." She could not continue.

Let me just say that it is not every day that the force and reach of patriarchy so clearly manifests, that a woman of German birth should be animated to such ire, and I could only answer with the smile that my face happened to summon.

I took refuge in Central Park and stared at the rowboats on a lake the city would do well to keep its eye on. I walked in shoes too small for my feet along the pathways that had been laid out for me. The day was cloudless, the sky a cover of blue, and there were only soft breezes to caress my face. The band shell spoke from the point of view of desolation and neglect. Sighted were men and women from the real world, among them nannies pushing strollers with their infant charges. There were dogs with instructions not to bark and riot police hiding in the trees. If the gamut of emotion was being run, people were keeping it to themselves so the day could live in peace.

As always, I was led back to the retaining wall and the Bethesda Fountain below, and the clusters of kids and those older than kids except in their minds. Yes, reefer Mary and hashish Harry were down for the action of the flying Frisbees, but so were dealers wearing opaque shades with harder stuff to peddle and harder dispositions for the harder time that had come.

Death had been presenting itself to me since my father's passing. It had done so before, with the departure of Lenore and the unfolding nature of the event, and now it was back in a similar way, my mind struggling to contemplate its domain, and then moving away, the thing being that once death was there, all rushing was over. It had you in its spell. You could sit down at the breakfast table and read a newspaper. Because death was relief from something, from chaos, and the assertion of a binding order with finality to it.

I left the park and strolled west along Seventy-second Street. The grimy darkness of the Dakota could not fool me as to the opulence within. On Columbus Avenue a bar with plants in the window and a lively Friday evening crowd drew me in. Their workweek done with, the patrons could relax and unwind over drinks and dinner and whatever else the night would bring. I had a beer and then two more. They went down like water.

On leaving the bar, I saw a girl in faded jeans and a T-shirt half a block ahead of me. Her leisurely pace suggested she had no place to be and was just out for a stroll. Her slender figure sped me forward. Under the awning of the funeral home where my father lay, I pulled even with her and introduced myself.

"I have a viewing to attend here. Please meet with me afterward."

"What? Who died?"

"A relative."

"Are you trying to pick me up?"

"I want to see you. We'll have fun." I was in a zone where I felt I could do no wrong, and so it came as no surprise when she wrote out her name and number on a piece of paper and handed it to me.

"I am staying with my grandmother before I return to school."

"Now that I have your address effective action will surely follow."

"Are you as crazy as you sound?"

"I have my bearings in normalcy," I replied.

In the confines of the funeral home my father's name was there in white plastic letters in the vestibule directory. A new arrangement of letters would soon disappear him just as Ross Delmonico and Abednego Suarez and Hermione Schlementhaler, on the third and fourth and fifth floors respectively, would be disappeared when the letters became restless for change, having allegiance to no one and nothing apart from their fickle nature.

I stood in the tight space of the small elevator that took me to the second floor, where floral arrangements surrounded the open casket. As I stared down at my father's waxy face, the girl's number went through my mind like a ticker tape.

Suddenly he raised up from the dead and bats flew from the ceiling, and though no one seemed to notice, pandemonium reigned. "You have aggravated me in life. Will you now do the same to me in death, my worthless son? Remember this. I will be waiting for you here to give you all that you deserve for the slanders you have heaped on me and the others you are planning."

Though I was taken back, I stood my ground and told him to lie back down and show some respect for where he was.

These are the people who were present at the funeral home on that Friday evening to engage with their sorrow:

My mother, who through the mediation of prayer, continued to live in the surrendered place of wanting nothing the world had to offer.

Hannah, alive in her shame and grievance as to the life she had had with our father, and Moses, her son.

Naomi, who came to sing so her gift could be cherished and she might maintain the narcissistic insanity that was her refuge. Jeanne, her runaway daughter, was still missing. She had yet to break free from her captor, the administrator of broomstick love for whom she performed on the streets and in hotel rooms and in the vehicles of the Johns she serviced.

Rachel, for whom the death of her father would have the profound implication of switching her onto the piety track in a time soon to come.

Luke, who wore the full complement of bruises, psychic and physical, as the insignia he had been gifted with as a result of our father's blows, and who now could inaugurate additional pathways to freedom through debauchery set to rock and roll music.

Vera too was there, in the glory of her grief, for having won she could weep and have in tow a man of Columbia quality she called her own and needed now as a witness to her pain. It was not for me to know how she had arrived at the normalcy of her emotional state or seek to expose it as an artifice of the first degree.

Fenton, in his piety pose, saying "Two good men, make that three good men, now that your father is gone." Like Casper the ghost he was in his paleness, his head bowed and his lips moving as he went into indoor prayer.

Miss Beck, who with my mother fed the washed and dried sheets to the mangle so the tenants could have clean and pressed bedding. She was there in her native understanding of what the Lord had given her.

Sister Hanasian and Sister Henry, who lived in the Lord and the Lord in them and who worshiped at the tabernacle where my mother and they and everyone under that roof were on knowing terms with the Christ Jesus.

The unfilled chairs. They were there, too.

A gaunt older woman played "In the Garden" on a piano elevated above the carpeted floor so that my childhood could rise up before me and I could see back to the tabernacle mural of the Garden of Gethsemane and the Christ Jesus in his aloneness. The softening effect of the hymn made me want it to go on forever but the funeral director, a silver-haired man with the paleness of middle age and overindulgence in the *New York Post* upon his face used hand motions to bring the piano woman to a stop, such being the power of the funeral home director within his own domain. Not that it mattered to the woman, seemingly detached from the hymn she had been playing.

A blond man of about forty with chipmunk teeth stood at the front of the room in a shiny black suit and loud yellow tie.

"Who is he? He looks like he is gearing up for some serious flapdoodle," I said, seeing his self-satisfied smile.

"Shush with your foolishness. Pastor Nyborg couldn't be here. He's ill, so his son has come in his absence." Pastor Nyborg being the owner of the garage where the men living in and through the Christ Jesus in Astoria, Queens, came to worship, as my father had done before the amputation.

"He's going to crank it up and bust a big one on us. They're all the same. They live to do the yak yak."

"Ushtah."

PastorNyborg, Jr., did not know my father, and so he could not stand on the ground of fact in his eulogy.

"Dear ones, we are here to celebrate a man made great through the love of the Christ Jesus, a soldier for the Christ Jesus who wanted only to spread His light through the world....And what of Sister Garatdjian, his dear wife? Does she too not deserve our prayers and loving thoughts in this time of grief and sorrow?"

The pastor called on Naomi to come forward. Brother Garatdjian's beloved daughter, he called her, not remembering her name. Unsteady in her gait, she soon stood before the gathered. "And He Walks with Me" she sang, or began to sing. Her voice cracked and there was the added problem of forgotten lyrics. Abashed, she lowered her head and returned to her seat.

All throughout the service, my focus had been on Vera's boyfriend and the audacity Vera showed in allowing an outsider with an Ivy League pedigree to witness our family. Once again was I forced to see my shame was an involuntary reflex reaction. Why it should grip me and seemingly not her I couldn't say.

Like the others, I approached the casket before leaving. When I touched my father's hand, my own hand recoiled at the feel of his cold embalmed flesh.

Sheila Moran was the girl's name. Desperate for refuge from myself, I ran to her that night in the doorman building on Central Park West where she was staying. I wanted nothing more than to stretch the night beyond the limits of what some would see as the realm of propriety.

And there I was being allowed by the doorman into an art deco palace. Sheila Moran stood before me in the same jeans and T-shirt as when we had met. Behind her were two steps leading down into a sunken living room and beyond that a view into Central Park.

From another room a voice called out. "Who is he, Sheila? Have you let a murderer in the door?"

A gaunt, elderly woman emerged. With the cane she relied on she moved Sheila out of the way. Her narrow face had a quiver, I could see as she approached.

"He hasn't got it, Sheila. He's nobody you want to be with."

The woman frightened me beyond recall, and if not for Sheila, I would have been gone.

"Grandma, please. You're being unbelievably rude." Sheila said her words with the affection needed to handle the old woman, suggesting with her intonation that her grandma was not so much on the warpath as into her shtick.

"I know what I see," she countered.

"Well, see what you want. We're going out. I'll be back in a short while."

"If you're not, I'm calling the police. You can count on that."

I started to say something, but the woman pointed with her cane so the rubber tip was in my face. "Zip it. I know disaster when I see it."

"How about we head downtown to my place and get into the thick of it?" I said when we were out of range of her fire dragon granny.

"The thick of it?"

"Smoke heaven."

She was OK with that, and so we headed off, stopping for a bottle of wine on the way.

Mrs. Muldooney and her son the serial murderer man were present in their poses outside the building. The son was gone into a meditative state of gratitude for all the gifts he had received through the administration of death and Mrs. Muldooney was simply grateful to have her seat. A simple wave of greeting sufficed.

The building towering over the courtyard had not changed its black and white stripes or the laughter from its obscene maw. I pointed out the problem to Sheila and asked her for an assessment of what it was we were confronting, but she was from the Midwest and her roots were in health and she could only say that no nightmare was encroaching.

Inside we had smooch heaven to go with smoke heaven and the wine but her hand served as a brake when my own began to roam. Even Bob Dylan crooning his lay, lady lay stuff could not make her yield, as she had a boyfriend back in Michigan.

"So who was this relative?"

"My father."

I saw with my own eyes and heard with my own ears her grandmother reappear and speak through Sheila, saying, with the certitude of age, "How can you be so cavalier about the death of your father?"

"Have I not slain him many times over the years?"

Her decrepit and channeled grandmother rained down some more of her judgment on me. "God, you are sick," I now heard Sheila say, before she fled the apartment.

When morning came, I went to the bar on Fifty-seventh and Tenth for fortification. The bartender did not greet me, but that was his issue, not mine. When he put more emphasis on polishing the bar and serving the few sots in business attire also present, I extended my understanding, as there are those with dinky dimensions whose life's work is to ostracize. Eventually, he came out of his peeve sufficient to serve me, a beer and a Scotch and then a second round a while later. I then headed uptown, but at one point had to stop and steady myself, the drinks having left me feeling sodden.

In the morning light my siblings looked shabby and vulnerable, all except for Vera, who, to my dismay, again had her boyfriend in tow. Luke had bulked up since high school; the old blazer he wore with his jeans and Frye boots was clearly too small and his tie didn't reach his navel. Both Hannah and Naomi were drably dressed, Hannah seeking to hide her obesity in the black trench coat that had become her signature garb. When I approached Rachel, she said "Do I know you? I don't speak with strangers," and moved away before I could respond. An expression of fixed purpose had claimed her, as if she were bent on solving an insoluble problem; on her feet were oversized and floppy black Converse sneakers out of the Goodwill bag.

The two chauffeurs leaning against the limousines were in appearance Mafia types quite blasé about the matter of death and equally dismissive of the entourage they would be driving to the burial site, as if we were riffraff unworthy of their vehicles.

Boston Latin. Columbia. Juilliard. Vera gave us her beau Joshua's step by step progress on the cushioned ride that took us through the Lincoln Tunnel and onto the New Jersey Turnpike en route to the cemetery. Her assassin's bullets found their target in my brain.

I stared out the window. I didn't know New Jersey. I didn't know anything but Manhattan. Was my father to be dumped in some industrial wasteland by petrochemical plants belching clouds of toxic smoke from their stacks? It didn't seem right that he should be taken so far from our orbit.

My mother remained silent. She did not have a wayward tongue. But was her silence now generated by grievance? Was she attributing his death in part to me? Only once before had she hit me, when I was twelve, during a time when my father was away in France visiting his sisters. He had wandered from her, so Naomi said, for a period of years, and so I could only believe she was taking out her hurt on me and that now, once again, she was in the place of a cold anger that her spirituality could not overcome at my dismissal of my father as irrelevant to my life.

When it was not my mother or Vera's beau Joshua with the huge head housing the huge brain as the focus of my attention, I found myself captive to our chauffeur, Salvatore Guido Ponzarelli, and the poisonously supercilious thoughts his mind might be harboring about us. How was it that my mother felt no similar need to monitor his mentality for scorn but instead remained within her own internal enterprise was beyond me, but she had always been a soul in transit and now her system was on full alert to the possibility that she might be next to hear the call up yonder.

Salvatore knew what was what in keeping the windows up and the air conditioning going. He understood the dynamics of New Jersey and the stench it created that made seclusion from its heated air so very necessary, and yet it was a knowledge he was able to contain within his face while accomplishing his mission of getting us to the burial ground intact. Because New Jersey had roads that led somewhere, the limo eased through a wrought-iron gate that featured an enclosed checkpoint for a guard to sit in should the dead get out of hand, and a sign that read, "Pay Now, Bury Later."

We all of us exited the car and put ourselves upright upon the earth, and as we entered the burial ground saw endless rows of tombstones risen from the grass. Tall trees flanked the driveway, and bulldozers, to the observant eye, were also present behind them. They could not be accused of hiding, for though compact, they had bright yellow paint jobs that shouted out their presence. The machines were slow in their nature but steadfast in their resolve and able to do what they wanted with mounds of dirt in terms of filling the excavated holes in which tiers of American coffins lay in what was called the final resting place.

The names on the tombstones called out for attention, Italian names seeking the respect they could expect, given the state they were in, New Jersey otherwise overriding all attempts at dignity with its Drake's Cakes and Wonder Bread mentality and strip-mall population, the whole state a burial ground of the living dead.

The names on the gravestones neither broke your heart nor prompted laughter. There were names of stiletto stiffness, like Capone, and names that bogged down in the middle like Antuofermo, and others like Ferrari with sleekness upon them.

I stood back from my family. The word and their presence made for a mirror I did not want to face. We were not meant for a natural light setting, not with our tainted flesh, our stained teeth and bad breath and unlovely knees, our big feet and protuberant noses and depressive, hapless personalities. I did not call in the firing squad. I did not commandeer a bulldozer and schnell schnell order them into the hole and disappear them under mounds of earth, but yes, I saw it as my life's mission to make it so I could stand apart in a state of non-affiliation. All this I thought in the thought stream that was allowed me in the false triumph of my separatist nation. Because to be in the United States was to be one with yourself with the picket fence around you so you weren't obliged to let them in if you didn't want to.

Only my mother and Vera and her boyfriend could hold their own in the light without the taint of decay. The glow was apparent from his sunbeam mind. Nor did I accost him with my jaundiced view that he was there less as emotional support for my sister Vera but to *witness her performance of the thing called grief.* I did not want to start a ruckus on these acres of the dead, lest they be awakened. I did not want to aggravate my father into rising up in righteous fury with his hand in the correct smacking position. No, no. I didn't have to do any of that.

The shiny black coffin, now sealed, came with handles for easy transport by the cemetery workers. We watched as it was placed on boards laid out across the hole. The boards were then removed and workers on either side of the burial plot strained to lower the coffin into it on canvas straps, which they then slid free.

Pastor Nyborg, Jr., who had arrived in his own car, read the Twenty-Third Psalm. We then stood staring down into the hole, none of us knowing what to say. This was our father, after all, the father I had never really known, the father who was absent more than present, even when physically there. The polished coffin situated far down in rich brown earth was jarring to witness, as if a brutal abandonment was taking place. We tossed flowers into the hole. Hannah threw hers and Vera threw hers and Luke had his to throw and Rachel and Naomi, too.

We moved away, but when I turned, I saw that my mother had remained, still holding tight to her single rose, as if in holding it she was holding him. Her father had died when she was still a child, giving her a stunned acquaintance with death. But she had her Christ Jesus so she didn't have to feel so alone and to see her through the pain that my father's abrupt departure had brought, or so I could only hope.

My father's history tried to rise up out of the hole but his Old World baggage had no legs with which to travel and no strong voice to speak with. It was a history that involved men and women and children herded together to be demised with axes; women whose heads were doused with kerosene and set on fire, their braids serving as wicks; mass deportations into the desert and wholesale drownings in rivers; gougings and other forms of mutilation so the other could live without a trace of them; and then it was the adamancy of governmental silence. It was my uprooted father reeling in exile.

By now the bulldozer was approaching and workers with shovels had gathered. Salvatore, our chauffeur, was also on the scene; even at a respectable distance I could discern his eyes narrowing to slits and smoke streaming from his ears and a film of peeve covering his meaty face, all of this suggesting that Salvatore had had enough, that the allotted time for emotion had been spent and the hour was at hand to dispose of us as well.

Given the charged emotional climate, I appointed myself to act, and did so with the resolve of a man determined to keep the peace when warring elements were massed at the border. In remaining faithful to my mission, I approached my mother and placed my hand on her arm, which prompted her to awkwardly toss the single rose into the hole, the way a toddler might throw a ball. She moved her arm free of my touch and turned to me with an expression of coldness I had not seen before, as if to convey that she would rather walk alone than with the likes of me.

A woman not of the family had made her presence felt at the funeral as well. Tall and erect and without the Garatdjian features, she maintained the severity of her Scandinavian face, as if her life was spent climbing out of the trauma gulch into which the affliction of some demented one had dropped her. But Birgitta Nilsson was in fact flourishing, receiving men in their imaginary glory before giving them the forearm shiv so she could explore the love that dared not speak its name in claiming an identity of her own, her independence requiring short hair and a lean figure and a sparely furnished and tidy apartment and the knowledge that in a man's world it was her necessity to perform and rise to the level of her own excellence. She too was now plugged into the power of the great Columbia University in her pursuit of a master's degree. I could not value her before the achievement of that acceptance, and then it was not even esteem so much as fear of those who had dared, dared to cross over that line into the world that I too so much wanted with the screaming thing within me but which had turned me away.

So that yes she was there with Vera, and Vera was there with her in her attractive apartment just one door down from the building where commotion reigned and she had started over a century ago, arriving with her infant daughter with no place to stay because of the collapse and institutionalization of her husband (hah), a man who could dance on one leg and make it look like trouble and thought a bottle of ink could save his life. I did not accost Birgitta Nilsson. I did not tell her that the apartment she had graciously offered us for a reception was a reproach to our existence because the apartment where I was born and raised was unfit for such an event. No, I opened myself to the fear that had massed within me.

Hannah dispatched me to the liquor store for bottles of wine, saying, in her amplified voice, "You'll have something to drink, won't you?"

"What do you mean, will he have something to drink? Stand within five feet of him and you can smell the alcohol." Vera said. "My doctor says I can't drink," she went on. "He said my severe headaches are because of it, though I do have fantasies about the great things I could do when drinking."

"You drink, my son? You drink?" My mother had been drifting away until this point.

"Smell his breath, Mother. Smell it." Vera's voice was like a lash upon me.

"None of my children should drink. None of you. 'Wine is a mocker. Strong drink is raging.' You know that's what the Bible says," I heard my mother say, as I headed out the door for the liquor store and minutes later returned with two bottles of Burgundy.

"Oh come on, Mother. Break down. Stop being a saint," Hannah bellowed. "Have a little drink, for crying out loud. It won't kill you."

Hannah poured the wine into the glass and placed it in front of my mother. I watched in the belief that I was a witness to evil in my older sister's attempt to degrade her so she could not exist anymore on the plane her religious faith had elevated her to, as I had believed in witnessing, since childhood, Hannah's previous attempts to do the same, as if she had never heard my mother say, with traumatic and repetitive recall, that she had never touched so much as a drop of wine, having trekked as a child through the snows of Sweden to find her inebriated father before he died, while passed out, of frostbite and of her mortal fear of developing the same craving for alcohol.

I took the glass from in front of my mother and drained it and poured and downed another and saw the face of Vera in her continuing triumph and heard the words she spoke. Like bullets they sped from her mouth seeking to shatter their intended target. "I feel it's for me and me alone to carry on Daddy's name."

And then I heard the alcohol say the thing I couldn't otherwise say. "Why don't you just drop dead?"

"Mother, did you hear? Did you hear? He threatened my life. My life, Mother. Kick him out, and kick him out now," Vera ordered.

But she didn't have to kick me out. I ran among the trees and over the grass of Riverside Park and into the railroad tunnel that would have me, and there I sat until the centuries could pass and I could walk upon the earth once more.

Chapter 84

It is not often that one father leaves the scene and another arrives soon thereafter, but the following week, as I resumed my duties in the renting office, diligently tending to the growth of a personal trust to ensure my own renown in keeping with my covenant to be like America itself, an America that took pains to live in the hearts and minds of millions, such a man appeared. With my own eyes did I see darkness personified that had beset me my whole life.

Short and wiry and leather-jacketed, with a rodent's face, he beckoned me through the grille to kneel before him. Quickly reassured as to my subservience, he said, "Mrs. Garatdjian. Pronto."

I rang three powerful signals on the house phone, but my mother had gone and gotten vicious, done the dilly dally so she could do the chuckle chuckle while relishing my distress. I followed with three more rings and three more and three more after that and still she continued to stall me. Having no choice, I took refuge in the kneehole under the desk and, with eyes closed, held my head.

Only after an eternity did my mother relent and deign to appear. "Is that you, Mr. Weill?"

"We need to talk." Each word was memorable, and delivered with only the bare minimum of energy required, this so all ears could strain to hear what the oracle of doom had spoken.

She came toward him. He did not go toward her. By now I had come out of hiding and was back in my chair. Seeing me, she said, "Mr. Weill, do you know my son Luther?" She did not know to be embarrassed by the people she loved.

Mr. Weill looked at me and I looked at him with the eyes that I could bring to bear. When I could stand the tension no more, I blurted, "Father of all evil who rules the earth, where have you come from?" but silence was his only answer.

They went off for some time and when my mother showed her face once more, I asked only this: "Did he come to kill me, and why were you not here for my protection?"

"Ushtah, son. Who would want to kill you? Who?"

"Mr. Bad Man Weill, who took all your money so you could die."

"Why do you talk such foolishness, my son?"

"Why does he have the same eyes as you, eyes that see right through me to where my intention lives?"

"Ushtah," she said once more.

"Was his visit fraught with significance that you need to tell me something?" I had become a trembling thing, with my lifeline in the balance, as by now there was no place in the universe for me but where I was.

My mother put her face up against the grille. "Mr. Weill says there is money missing. He says the income is not what it once was." She did not put her knowing eye on me but held it in check.

"Should we be full of fear and trembling? Is that it? Will the roof come down on where we stand?"

My mother looked at me and I looked at her. "Love the Lord, my son. Love the Lord and know that we are living in the last days and that the Lord will come like a thief in the night. More than that you need not concern yourself with."

And so yes, the understanding was there. The green light was flashing.

A wheel will come around and things will run to ground and still the earth keeps turning. Peter Van Dine wrote a play about a president and God's will and became almost famous when it reached Broadway for a week before fatality struck. At the same time I pushed the limits of my own capacity for exploration in seeking to penetrate New York State on my own, and stayed the night with a man and woman who broke wind loudly, the couple made flatulent by the organic vegetables they grew and ate on the land they farmed. I felt in their presence the destitution of my own ways but then found the bars so necessary in the parts of New York City that signified they were aligned with art and rose up on the wings that alcohol gave me. In those bars I drank with women some of whom had the moxie to mix it up with strangers in carnal delight. And I had the words that called to me and then abandoned me or came to me and made me large with excitement even if the following day they lost their luster, words which by now had become the organizing principle of my life. Remote and invisible by day I would crash the party of life by night in the alcoholic theater that I had found, and without which no reason for living could be found.

It was some kind of competition year for Mona, a vague and unstructured year that was supposed to result in fame if she won the award that would be presented. A review board made up of people she didn't necessarily know were setting the standard for her worth. In the spring work would be submitted for appraisal and a prize given out to the student whose images conformed with their reality, and then respectability and hope would be his or hers with which to initiate contact with the world. Because fame was everywhere to be had if only one could vie for it and meet the requirements for it to be conferred.

The Genius had entered the competition as well, as he had entered her heart and mind, overrunning her flimsy defenses against him. His internalized presence brought with it a tide of self-doubt pulling her farther and farther from the work she clung to as the source of her stability. But Genius Man was a plunderer. He had taken her assets not because he needed to make them his but because he was only curious as to what they were. And then he had gone off to Europe with contacts provided so he could remain on the path of success assured to him.

Apathy seemed to overcome her, the grayness of her mood a match for the granite of the museum just down the street from her school. From the island of Naxos in the sun-splashed Aegean his paintings arrived for display in the school, furthering her destruction as she compared herself with the wild boy who romped far beyond the bounds of mundane confinement and moon-danced as the god of excellence he was, with his lustrous black hair and athletic young body. Her paintings so lifeless by comparison, or so she now judged them to be; the monoprints she ran off on her little press equally stillborn.

Though I saw the shallowness, a reappraisal was going on within me. What did it mean if Mona was never to appear on the cover of *Time* magazine? What were the prospects for my own respectability if she were not wedded to renown? I had no choice but to wear her depression and her gloom as my own and to be as alarmed at the prospect of her failure as I was threatened by projected implications of her success.

As the reality took hold that school life was ending and a new phase was soon to begin without the same cushion of money, fear entered. How would she make her way, she who harbored her father's resistance to employment? For myself, a question mark was now attached to my plan for us to live together in New York City. Had she not sworn that at all costs she must live alone in a space unviolated by a man. And while I had been a battering ram of just resolve against the adamancy of her stance, I now had to ask whether I was perversely pursuing a situation I no longer wanted.

Mona was nuclear in the explosion she rained down on me for the demolition of my life. She called not as the spring itself on which I was feasting but as a dark intrusion on that season of light. The phone rang and in truth jumped at her anger and the urgent need to express it.

"Well, bastard, do you still want me? Do you?"

"I am here on my own property and speaking."

"Shut up with your crap and tell me."

Lacking all courage in the face of her rage, I replied, "Sure, sure," and so betrayed the promptings of my own heart.

Her inner turmoil had reached a new level with the continued ascendancy of The Genius following the announcement of his award-winning ways. He returned home triumphant, having won the competition with paintings of museum level quality and now, in the apartment on the floor below her own, was immersed in the premium grade social activity his success had earned him—the society of elite men and women of the art school milieu as well as reigning dignitaries from the world at large. He dominated these soirees, which Mona had no power to resist. After each visit she sat more desolate, no longer stirring the turps with the vigor of her glory days. For chunks of time she would remain in a passive daze, as if black-haired Lenore had come back as black-haired Lane to triumph over her. She tried to accommodate herself to his new and enhanced social life but there was a sad visibility to her disorientation among the gathered and a scent of fear they could smell that whetted their appetite for the kill. Without social graces she had to fortify herself with wine and, with her senses reeling and judgment suspended, began to remove the clothes of a girl with more womanly features. Exiled from any belief in her own beauty, she placed her mouth between the legs of the girl, who had opened to her in a state of passive acquiescence. Once she had appropriated the girl's sex for her own oral manipulation she didn't quite know how to progress, because sex had happened without emotional connection. Having run its aborted course, she found herself in a state of extreme abashment at what alcoholic impulse could lead her into, her exit coming on the heels of getting sick on the wine that she had so desperately imbibed.

Now a search went out upon the land for a lodging where we could live within spatial dimensions conducive to harmony and infinite ambition. The sky had opened up sufficient for an extraordinary light to shine and make the search a radiant inquisition of those who possibly held the keys so necessary to our new beginning. The suspects were narrowed to a precious few in the time-honored area of Chinatown where bok choy brigades in quilted jackets enlivened the streets with their *chi* and glazed, golden ducks hung in meat store windows as reminders of the magic that the East possessed. Everywhere the old and infirm hacked and spit while the young and spry showed off their cartwheeling locomotion as the favored mode of local transportation.

The street we chose had a quality of loveliness over and above its routine features. It had active shops bursting with commerce where bags of rice could share a space beside coolers jammed with beer. It had a public library for the acquisition of knowledge to be found on printed pages. It had the stellar presence of a fire station ready to draw on its hard and masculine strength. It had the Golden Dragon Lounge, where bang bang boys with backgammon skills and menacing smiles shot you dead, for they were Hong Kong-born and fueled on Johnny Walker Black and had the nerve born of their own uncompromising apartness. A coffee shop stood on the corner as the last American holdout with the men from Greece manning their positions behind the counter in a state of ecstasy over their newfound enterprise bringing home the bacon so they could prosper in the land of eggs over easy and hash browns and jelly doughnuts and coffee with a touch of Sweet and Low. They had urns full to overflowing and grills that stayed hot and the grizzle of working men on their cheeks and American words flying from their mouths as a reminder of what country they were in.

All the while Third Avenue was flowing down to the Bowery, curving its way to its rightful destination past Delancey Street and the Williamsburg Bridge and the dangerous crossings at Canal Street onto the Manhattan Bridge and into the thing called Chatham

Square and the memorial arch that stood at its center. Third Avenue and the Bowery could go whichever way they chose—the road could style itself as a major artery past the flophouses and the restaurant supply stores and the Salvation Army. It could be conspicuous and continuous, but the angle of intersection East Broadway had as an esoteric tributary made it a land apart, far-flung from the center of New York City while toiling in its midst, and it was there that Mona Van Dine and I set our hearts on living in a community of Chinese, some with *lo fan* attitude.

The loft was in a walkup building with steep stairs. Lighting fixtures had been installed to keep the stairway bright. The loft offered 2,500 square feet, the space divided into a work and living area by a loft bed with shelves and closet space below. There was a tiny bathroom with a shower but no tub. A garden hose ran from the water heater to the connection. Duct tape had been used as a seal and so the place smelled of gas, and was cause for wonder whether the time for an explosion was coming nigh.

A painter named Kadar held the lease but he was too busy to be there. That did not keep Kadar's wife from serving as an agent for the change that was imminent. She met me at the top of the stairs with a manifest overbite and a Hungarian accent and the recognizable pose of affability of those frightened and insecure at their core. As a consequence she offered me a truth born of desperation.

"Every day he builds and builds. Every day he makes love to a different woman. Every day I'm having a nervous breakdown. There is no place for my books in the new place that he is constructing. There is no place for me," she shrieked, giving voice to the honesty she would need to set herself free.

Something was made quickly clear about Kadar and his wife. While she sought to throw the net of understanding over the untamed substance of world art through the lens of factoid study and critical evaluation, being a doctoral student at the legendary Columbia University, Kadar himself was the wild child from Eastern

Europe, seeking an exploration of his life through doing rather than living in the confining localities of her printed pages.

Kadar's wife sat me down in a wicker chair and served me tea on a scuffed wooden table, having boiled the water on a hot plate and with no stove in sight. I gave her the lines that I thought worthy of repetition, words that would eventually tire me of myself, but which I could not go beyond in the fear that I might otherwise be found empty of content: My girlfriend was an artist and needed the space; Spain had a population of 31 million in the year we visited it, and there were 22 million tourists in the country that summer.

Kadar's wife gave me all the directions she said I would need for finding Kadar. She said the site was high up in a building of remarkable solidity on a street named Wooster that intersected with Houston Street, this in a part of the city undergoing continuing development on the basis of artists who had to have their way. She said I was to visit him with Mona present, as I was not and should not aspire to be a man who took unilateral action, a position which, if I were to understand the situation, Kadar had staked out for himself. I more or less grasped the direction Kadar's wife was coming from, and in any case did not leave before we both had the chance to finish our tea.

A person can start out fearful or he can start out strong in the country he comes to call his own, and Kadar was showing himself to be strength itself with the project he had underway. Things being what they were, Mona rooted to Boston by her despair and the acquisitive impulse of The Genius in regard to her soul, I was charged by her with visiting Kadar on my own, with no requirement attached to fess up to Kadar's wife concerning my solo mission.

The elevator took me eight floors above Wooster Street to a huge expanse of open floor space covered with plaster dust where I witnessed the single-minded enterprise of a stick-thin man utilizing applied physics as part of the Hungarian ingenuity allowed to flower on American soil. Kadar's hair did not lie flat. It stood straight up in line with the aspirational spirit infusing his own industry. Everywhere the signs of mammoth construction—two by fours, tubes of piping, toilet fixtures, new flooring. On the walls were blueprints and diagrams rife with complication and integers for the mathematically gifted.

"What do you want?" Kadar said. He was laying a mosaic of tile on the freshly cemented surface of what was to be a bathroom where none had been.

"I want to enter the bastion of art but from a place where I can hide within it," I said.

"Are you some kind of deranged woman that you talk this way?" How sharp and birdlike his features were and mathematically proportioned to deliver beauty.

"You are so very right. Do you want me to lie down before your power?"

Kadar lit a smoke so he could see me better through his Hungarian eyes. "You Americans. One is weaker than the next."

"Yes. But we have the strength of our metaphysical dictate and the roadmap for our own happiness. And that is why you have come, so we can wrap you in our softness."

"So what is it? I have no time for such as you."

"I am here to create my own new beginning, not at where you are but where you have come from. For that to happen, I must move forward from the place of aloneness to the joining of forces with one I truly shouldn't be with. We are venturing forth onto a larger stage, but even so I will need a place to hide and I remain hopeful that in the shadow of her complexity I can continue my own concealment."

"Do you have a dick?" Kadar asked.

"Dick is not a word I answer to. It seeks to confuse itself with a man's name that stands as an unattractive diminutive."

"How about a pussy? Do you have a pussy?"

"Why do you talk to me in this way? I could call the language police on you."

"You are a pussy. All you American girl men with your long hair and your sensitive ways. You think you are being so nice to women but you are being their slaves. You are like my wife. You look around here and you see chaos. You don't see the plan. All you want is some little corner where you can sit and read your paperback books and perform for your monkey shit teachers. You're like a woman who can't give birth because she cannot alter the mold of her own body. All you can do is sit there in your corner with your books and your tea. You live in the straitjacket of your conscience except when you get drunk. Otherwise you behave like the little pussy that you are, making everything about your girlfriend and nothing about yourself."

"Are you leaving your wife? Is that what you are doing?"

Kadar ignored my words and in the seconds that passed I put up the white flag of defeat but that did not satisfy him. He delivered me a royal kick in the ass, dragged me into the elevator, and barked out the address where I would need to be the next day to consummate the deal.

All that night the mental machinery was in place and operating for the contemplation of Kadar and his wife, not only the kick he had administered and the overbite she had shown but the charts and diagrams with integers of grave complexity attached that he enabled himself to master in a language not his first far from Jan Masaryk and the violins of Budapest and the rough hegemony of Soviet occupation, Kadar revealing himself as sun and moon with his own brand of gnarly incandescence and possessed of a heroic grasp of what needed to be done, not in the context of Lenin's monstrous agenda and the misery it wrought but in the land of art in which he danced to his own drum apart from the books that people read for distraction from the quotidian afflicting their lives, Kadar's secret until stated weapon being his immigrant scorn for the effeteness of the land in which it had been given him to make the art he had to make with his task-oriented mentality and driven nature wrapped in a childhood vision all his own because the things of the oligarchs did not attach to him, the language of the Soviet apparatchiks did not adhere. No institutional goon squad could make him conform to that which wasn't his native essence.

I woke from my night of mental commotion and went to Kadar in broad daylight, without the anesthesia of alcohol the wrecking ball of doubt and misgiving on me, a voice telling me to stay in place with the smallness of what I had so the visibility quotient would not be increased causing me to be seen. A fist came down from Heaven on Forty-ninth street. It sent me hard to the pavement. On Thirty-fourth street a second fist from Heaven put me through a plate-glass window and left me bleeding. The sky parted and a voice thundered, "Thief, thief, lunatic thief of all the ages, running with the loot of your momma to buy a loft and pursue your dream of decadent folly." God shat on my face and pissed in both my eyes and nowhere could I get my bearings and move beyond pain, the buses and trucks of New York City repeatedly running me over with the vigor they could muster. Even Kadar, with his Warsaw Pact toughness, had to brace himself seeing the wreckage before him prior to the signing and cash on the barrel head with the lawyer in our midst.

Listen! The moon was up and muscular folks were in the ascendant on the night my consolidation effort of the loft began. Kadar's wife had vacated the premises, hoping to take the texts of the learned where she could peruse them in an orderly fashion to the sound of a teacup rattling far from the racket of Kadar's insistent activity informed by the egg-breaking vision that he had. A box spring and mattress and tired wicker sofa that squeaked when you sat on it were all that remained of them.

Directly across the street, smack dab in my field of vision, was the fire department that had risen out of the soil as a nonorganic thing to show what man could do and stake its claim to a sliver of Manhattan. Men with masculinity bred into their bones enabling them to bond were standing in the night air with their blazing red fire engine behind them. Some wore only blue FDNY T-shirts to display their beefcake status. I looked down at them and at one point they looked up at me and I felt the pain developing that I could not reach them further with a loving heart owing to the fact that they were the kind of men Mona would go up against with words for the articulated appraisal that they offered to the women of beauty who passed before them in the Chinatown night alive with the crackling report of firecrackers, some skewed sense of what the Orient truly was overlaying the whole scene. I fell to the floor at the fact of my good fortune to be in a world not my own and rose up to the ceiling with my heart singing that I should have a slanting avenue at a wishbone angle to the Bowery from which to explore my nights and survive my days with the call of sexual adventuring at maximum strength.

A party was in progress in the building next to the firehouse and the Golden Dragon Lounge. Kadar's wife had suggested I come, and in preparation I was drinking down a six-pack of Bud. The beer was made of the finest hops and barley and Clydesdale horses pulled wagon loads of it to your local store so you could savor its deep foaming action. If you turned elsewhere, Schlitz drew blood with its sound and Miller did not greet you with a friendly taste, whereas Heineken, in the green bottle, had the body and the smell to provide an experience profound that you wanted to stay with, its tormenting red star on the green and white label suggesting wanton passion beneath Holland's placid facade as well as highest quality intoxication.

The party was already in session. The gathered were mingling, one with another. I found the wine that was a requirement for my participation and had a glass. Then I had another as it spoke to me in its I am your friend forever language. Even with the beer and the fortification of the wine I saw a playing field of distinction a cut above anything that I could enter. Seeing my plight, Kadar's wife provided a woman's touch in introducing me to a man named Bill as my downstairs neighbor. And although I liked the entrenched sadness I saw in his face, he drove me down with the pedigree of Princeton University that he had abandoned after a year for military service in Vietnam, and now he was on East Broadway trying to build a film business in which his excellence would remain intact, if I'm not simply to record his words but interpret them. Hearing of his academic stardom and the army in which he proved his mettle as a man and the word *business* with its connotation of individual endeavor, my heart went to the frozen place where it could only be when in the midst of danger. I said my girlfriend—"SHE ATTENDS THE MUSEUM SCHOOL OF FINE ARTS IN BOSTON"—would be arriving the next day and when he merely stared at me, *seeing* but not responding, I bowed at his feet and told him he was the stuff the real America was made of, and that I had to go away from him, for there was no room in me for simple admiration.

"But what is it that you do? Everyone does something."

"He doesn't do. He is a little girl." I recognized the voice as Kadar's, and when I turned it was for sure that he was behind me in bowler hat and trademark short shorts. I thought to tell Kadar, for Bill was love itself, that he shouldn't anger me to the point of violence and that I had wine in me that could make me stronger than he thought, but the two of them went off with each other, bonded by their excellence.

I was also introduced to a man named Vjt, which he pronounced *vit*. In a whisper voice he pointed to his wife, Halina. She was beginning to make a name for herself with her sculptures and so was the dominant figure in the household. He said he wrote poems in a tiny scrawl so no one could read them as an act of self-preservation, and I saw the fire of self-hatred in his searching eyes for not being able to play big on the stage of art, as his wife was doing. I saw further in that moment that hiding behind Mommy and hiding behind Mona were one and the same and all that portended for me in a world too masculine for its own good peopled with muscular men with chops of mustache.

"I am not in hell. I am only in a movie," I said, but he had his own concerns and showed no indication that he had heard me. I then called out "Rescue me," and a woman standing in the stillness of her own self-acceptance appeared in my line of vision. She did not so much as flinch in the aloneness she was experiencing. She just drank her drink until she had drunk it all and went and got some more. I followed after for a refill of my own and engaged her at the place where the bottles stood. There was beauty in her face and I told her she was the refuge I was seeking and that I would even kiss her sandaled feet.

"Though you are a woman, you remind me what the word *girl* can mean."

"I have been living in Africa and am not used to the likes of you," she replied.

She had rented a place on East Fourth Street, a storefront outside of which men with knives danced in the spring air, with only a fragile door between us and their mayhem. Once the storefront might have been the scene of mom and pop industry, but now the premises were committed to her artistic intention.

She had been stationed in Kenya as a member of the Peace Corps, and while she had never been threatened by lions or stalked by hyenas, she had sensed their presence and survived by not opposing the earth but only caring to exist within it. She said the quiet spaces were where she lived. She said all this was a consequence of having been born in Modesto, California, where the people were mild and the sun shone, and now she was here in New York City to begin a life for herself as an artist.

"I'm an alcoholic," she added, as she removed the cork from a bottle of red wine.

"You are what?"

"An alcoholic."

"Why do you create terror where there was none. The Bowery is where such a person is to be found, passed out on the sidewalk."

"Because when I open a bottle, I have to finish it."

We drained the bottle and then we drained another.

"I should take a shower first," she said, but I was too eager, and so she removed her clothes, pulling T-shirt over her head and shedding her pants.

The gift of herself to me was shortened by my premature climax. She freed herself to take her postponed shower, likely assuming this was the beginning of a nightlong exploration. I watched her walk naked up a small set of steps and when I heard the water running, I quickly dressed and bolted for the door, underwear and socks in hand, only the door wouldn't open. Guilt and remorse over my betrayal of Mona had prompted my attempt to flee, but now I was faced with being caught in the act of such cruel abandonment. Clothes or no clothes, I would stand far more naked than she as the thief and bastard that I was for betraying the trust she had showed in me to share her bed and extend the night. Any moment she would reappear and catch me in my cowardice and I would have to witness her shock, her hurt, her disgust. What was I to say, that my flight was prompted by the need for order and consolidation, a loft only in its beginning stages and a woman I was emotionally tied to coming down from Boston? Did I murder the woman? Did I kill her dead with her own pain? Did she sit and cry until the morning light?

The lock stayed within its dead-bolt certainty. There was no hope. She would nail me to the door. She would pound me to the floor. I thought to shed my clothes once more but saw I could not change my internal gear, saw, that is, that she would know, she would sense the exit mentality that I had embraced. The lock just had to open, and it did, it did, and I ran, I ran past the knives of the mayhem men of violence, I ran past Delancey and Eldridge and Rivington, ran past Broome and Grand and Spring, ran in my Converse sneakers, ran from Modesto, California, and the horror that my lust could inflict. I ran into walls. I ran into trees. I lay me down on third rails strong enough to shock the Devil. I took all the actions required to obliterate consciousness and yet it was still there, telling me I had betrayed the one so I needn't betray the other and in fact had betrayed both.

Dawn was breaking out all over now. It was radiating through the Manhattan clouds and kissing tenements on their faces while sending rats into the cover they could find. I had drunk the stuff of the night and drunk it good and saw that I was not operational for the daylight hours, while noticing that nothing stopped the trucks of New York City from their rampaging purpose. The pathways had been laid out for them in a monopolizing grid so you had to stay to the side as they passed on by and show them the deference they required, standing like a cowering thing at the light waiting for permission to avoid their death. I saw all that had been lost so they could have their way, and so I took the action they were happy to give me—garbage trucks and trailer trucks and trucks of all descriptions, for me the luminosity of the night having yielded to the darkness of the day and depression billboarding itself for display: THERE IS SHIT UPON THE STREET AND GRAYNESS IN THE SUN. FIND YOUR COVER AND STAY THERE, it said to one and all.

I caught a man rolling back a protective grate to reveal his store and went inside. I bought a Miller six-pack this time for the clarity and the fortification it could bring and added a bag of chips and Hostess cupcakes and a loaf of bread with gratitude that in a Chinese grocery you could find the products of America still shining.

The Chinese landlord was a marvel of constancy in the light he shone on the stairway all through the day and night with long fluorescent bulbs. As I began my climb up those stairs, my neighbor Bill, the Princeton eminence, was descending, and stripped me naked with his sober Southern eyes.

"Have you seen me? Is that it? Have you seen me clearly and all at once, so you know just who I am?" I asked.

"Long night?"

"Endless and yet not enough," I replied.

Back in the loft with a beer in hand I stared across to where the party had been. Below the fire department was still there, a few of the daylight crew standing outside. My day was over before it had hardly begun. I took off my clothes and lay down on the box spring that had been left to us when the phone began to ring.

"I'm on my way this afternoon," Mona said.

"Where would that be from?" I asked.

"How about from Boston? Ever hear of Boston?"

"Stay inside the plane as it's flying. You will have a problem if you don't."

"Don't talk crap to me. This is an important day."

The beers were a comfort. They kept me strong. A good friend able to go where love was not supposed to reach. If there were those who traveled on the highway of life, with toll booths and potholes and traffic snarls, I had my own roadway with no such annoyances to frustrate my ambition and the bonus feature of garter-belted women on the roadside holding up signs announcing pleasure pits ahead. The word *growth* had come into vogue.Such a filthy, filthy word when others dared to apply it to themselves. *I'm into growth,* I would hear the viciously pretentious cretins say, when there was no personal growth to be had. All one had to do was shut up and drink, and then drink some more, for the magic to unfold. Modesto, California, needed to be careful about her words as well. *Alcoholic.* Such an unpleasant sound upon the air it made.

I entered into dreamland. A young man in a three-piece suit balanced himself effortlessly on a guy wire high on a bridge. Down below cars and trucks sped along a two lane roadway. So why, when he had it all his way, did he go down down where the cars and trucks could mash him in the repetitive fashion of steers trampling a fallen cowpoke, their hooves smashing his eye socket and ensuring that his nose was broken flat upon his face? Why did he have to muss his hair so fine and shatter his bones so strong and shed his blood for all to see?

I woke with sweat upon my face, the cans in random order on the floor, defying me to individuate their contributions to my state. Practicing the art of concealment, I deposited them on the street so, out of sight, a new day could begin in this new home.

Some hours passed before there was a ringing of the downstairs bell, signaling that the time had come for no more partings of the way. I ran to the window and looked down just to be sure it was not a felon seeking to do his felonious thing. No adoration council of lustful rabbis and priests drawn from their houses of worship had formed. Nor did I see long lines of enchanted businessmen clogging the street. No banners were hung, no fireworks were on display, neither did the gallery owners of SoHo form a welcoming committee at our door. Instead I heard a few loud whistles from across the street, whistles of admiration from the macho firemen speaking from the constitutions that they had, and a "Fuck you, pricks" response as Mona went against them with her angry words, and so it was that I knew the woman of my dreams was on the scene and our new and exciting life had now begun.

CPSIA information can be obtained
at www.ICGtesting.com
Printed in the USA
BVHW051109090323
660080BV00016B/726/J

9 798218 096267